THE MANTLE OF THE PAST

A Scattering of Leaves Book One

Lewis A. D'Ambra

The World of Kolgennon

Copyright © 2024 Lewis A. D'Ambra

All rights reserved

The characters and events portrayed in this book are fictitious. Any similarity to real persons, living or dead, is coincidental and not intended by the author.

No part of this book may be reproduced, or stored in a retrieval system, or transmitted in any form or by any means, electronic, mechanical, photocopying, recording, or otherwise, without express written permission of the publisher.

ISBN-13: 9798326461285

Cover design by: David Leahy

AUTHORS NOTE

Thank you for giving your time to read my work. It is much appreciated as it is you, the reader, that really makes the world of Kolgennon come to life. If I could ask for a couple of minutes more of your time once you finish this book to leave a star rating or review, I would be very grateful.

If you would like to find out more about the world of Kolgennon and be kept up to date with upcoming projects, please visit my website.

www.theworldofkolgennon.com

On my website you will also find an extended appendix for this book outlining all the characters and important places you will encounter in the following pages.

A NOTE ON CHRONOLOGY

Although the chapters occur in broadly chronological order, some do overlap in time with one another, and each chapter does not cover a standard set of time. Some may take place over a few hours, some a few days and some even a couple of weeks.

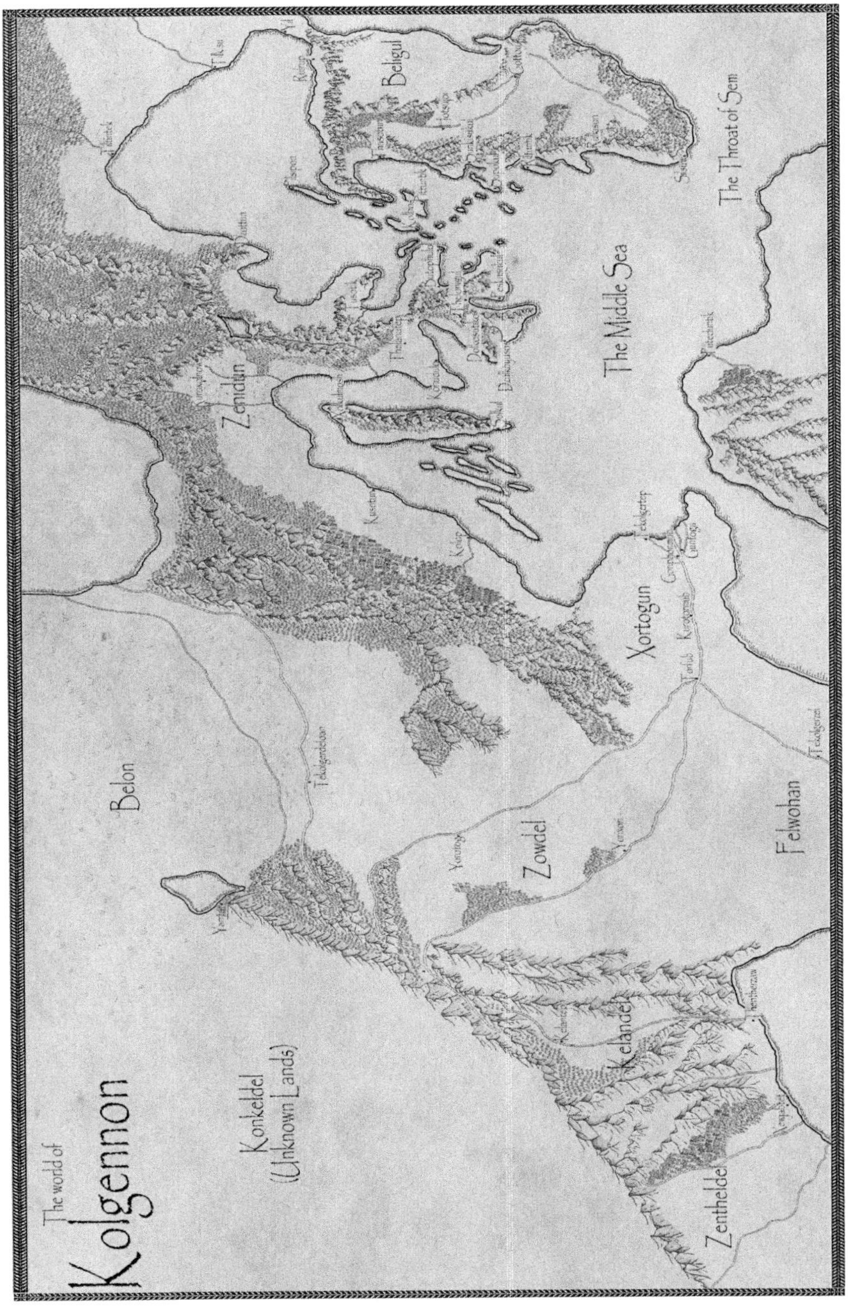
The world of
Kolgennon
Konkeldel
(Unknown Lands)
Belon
Zowdel
Felwohan
Kelandel
Zenthelde
Xortogun
The Middle Sea
Zenidun
Beligul
The Throat of Sem

An arrow drawn to bring a bright new dawn,
a flame to light the red tree,

A cleansing fire, pure and free, release to sail the green sea

The bow loosed brusque over creeping dusk,
lifting sky red, white, and gold

Xosu rise to mantle old, which the light bringer held bold

Riso of the Tilxosu on the coming dawn

PROLOGUE

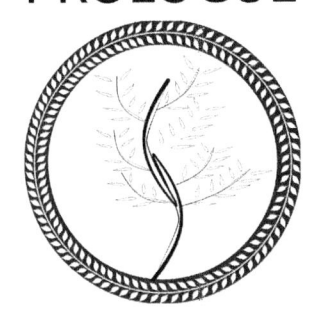

"Rage!" the voice echoed down the ship, "Your howling rage has transformed you. How many need to be slaughtered before you close the gate to this world of violence? How many good men would you see go to their deaths to satisfy your anger?" His words danced along the deck of the ship only to be scattered by the wind.

The sun dipped under the horizon, the bright light of the day turning to twilight. This argument had gone back and fore all day, and no resolution was in sight. None of this felt right. Pitae Kinsol wanted to do nothing else but turn and run back to Pittuntik. The rolling of the ship upon the water was making the feeling of dread in his stomach overwhelming, as if the sea were swallowing them whole. His head was spinning, as if floating on a dreamscape, the void between worlds, through which he could see only more death to come.

"We should go back." he said, forlorn, "Return after we have had time to stop and think." He was met by silence, none of his brothers in arms even looked at him. A hard voice, forged in anger, came from the prow of the ship,

"He murdered Kolmosoi, what else is there to think about?" There was iron in those words, the sound of a hardened attitude bent on a single purpose. Kunae was not a man to be deterred from his path.

"Kolmosoi was his captain too, and you don't know that he killed him Kunae. If he did, it was almost certainly an accident." Pitae replied, tired of this duel.

Kunae Rososthup turned to face him, blocking out what was left of the sun's light. An intimidating armour-clad, shadow fell over Pitae. Despite having the typical black, almost navy, hair of the Salxosu, with the pale skin and sea blue eyes to match, Kunae was not slight like many of his people. Instead, he was thickset and well-muscled across his shoulders, like an archer grown accustomed to years bending a bow. Those eyes of his now had flaming arrows in them. Kunae had not taken Kolmosoi's bronze cuirass off since they boarded the ship. Pitae could swear that the heads of each hydra embossed on the front, picked out in white gold, had become enraged ever since Kunae had put the harness on.

"He was never really one of us." Kunae said. But before he could continue, Thil Kolkisuasu spoke up,

"And what of that consort they say he has taken? Hulsen the mad prophetess come again she is. Sol was not in this alone, and his actions since speak of guilt." Thil's argument had more art to it, but the point remained the same. Thil's eyes were always sharp enough to see the truth of things.

Pitae had no answer. It was true, Sol's actions since Kolmosoi's death only seemed to confirm their suspicions. Disappearing looked like guilt. But poisoning Kolmosoi, if that is indeed what happened, it did not feel right. *What motive did Sol have?*

"We should still go back, nothing good will come of this." The only answer which Pitae could muster. The words barely had the energy to leap from his mouth. He felt like a shadow as he said it. A wraith of what he had once been.

Silence fell again, the waves breaking against the hull of the ship, the only thing to cut through the tension. They had a calming affect which Pitae found comforting, and the smell of the salt was soothing. He longed to dive in and find the tranquil world below the waves, the sea a void where he could forget about the troubles of his own world, about the turmoil that had engulfed them.

The chaos unleashed in the White Islands in the wake of Kolmosoi's death had drained the spirits from all of them and left them mere shadows, trapped wandering the open sea. The shockwave of his murder had scattered the groups of sellswords he had been gathering, and they had gone wild. Turning to hunting and scavenging what they could. Each becoming a tribe unto themselves, gathering for protection in an untamed land. It was a wildness of which their small band were not entirely blameless.

The journey from Pittuntik was long. Pitae had hoped that two days aboard the trireme with nothing to do but think would allow calmer heads to prevail. If anything, the others had moved towards Kunae's way of thinking. Sol had to die, a sacrifice to this new world.

A soaring wave crashed against the prow, the ship rolled over the crest and dipped back down, land came into view. Usually, land would be a welcoming sight having spent so long aboard ship. This time was different though, land meant that the reckoning was getting closer. It felt apt then that the lands that came into their vision were the ruins of old Kolbos. That wonderous city of a time before the Dusk, destroyed by its own hubris, and a family tearing itself apart. The haven loomed large in the minds of all the Xosu, but especially the Salxosu as it was where their spirits still lay.

"Kolbos." Thil muttered under his breath in an almost reverent way.

"A reminder of what once was, and the tragedy that folly can bring." Pitae answered him, eyes transfixed on the ruins.

"Debris is all that is left of that world. The gateway to the old kingdoms was slammed shut when the city fell." Kunae replied with an almost complete disinterest.

Their craft drew ever closer to the ruins, as if they could sail across the sea back to the time of the city's heyday. But more of the destruction came into sight each time the prow of the ship descended, slowly eroding that thought. Instead, an eerie feeling danced its way into Pitae's mind. The sea around old Kolbos always felt rougher than everywhere else, raging like an angry leviathan, furious with all who crossed it. The air smelt acrid, tinged with iron, and a storm always raged like a canopy over the ruins. The result of some dark actions which brought about its fall.

A distant rumble greeted their approach, like the hooves of a thousand thousand horses rampaging across the sky, released from the storm above the ruined city.

Dusk was falling quickly now. The fires of the sunset erupting from the horizon, and the light of the evening star was all that was left to illuminate the world. Even so the half-submerged ruins came much sharper into focus. He could see down the arrow straight channel known as the Funnel into the great circular harbour of the city of smiths. It was said that fire had spewed from the forges of Buto, below Mount Zilgulon, which loomed over the port, and down the Funnel, when the city fell, like the death throes of a monstrous hydra.

The ruined port curled around the broken land that had been shaken by the god's fury. At the head of the ancient metropolis, he could make out the temple of Buto, resting on the island of the Eye of Sem within the Thelonbet. The white gold zilthum wall of the Thelonbet coiled around the abode of the god and rose straight as a trunk to meet the branching arms of the raging storm above. Inside the temple the oracle of Buto still lingered, the last vestiges of life left in this place and the only remaining connection to the world that was lost when old Kolbos fell. Pitae suddenly felt as though he had to try one more time.

"It was the word of the oracle which set us on this path, Kunae." He tried to speak in a commanding tone. "The people of Butophulo ignored her warnings, and as a result we were thrown down in defeat by the King of the Doldun. Twenty years of bloody stalemate and then the mantle held by the Salxosu when old Kolbos reigned supreme, so close to our grip again, was cruelly snatched away."

Kunae looked at him with a renewed fury,

"What is your point Pitae?"

"Those of us cast into exile by the victorious Doldun have been determined not to make those mistakes again. How many years have we listened intently to the utterings of the oracle, searching for a way home? Why be so reckless and single minded now? How does this help us achieve that noble goal?" Pitae answered with a passion he had been struggling to find. Kunae merely allowed a sinister smile to be drawn over his lips.

"It was those whispers that led us here, Pitae. Sol stands in the way of those plans; his corpse is a stepping stone for us to recapture Butophulo. Enough of this! Sol dies today." With that he turned his back and paced to the prow of the ship.

Pitae sighed, forlorn. He turned back to face the ruins that were quickly passing by and letting himself get lost in the white haven's wonder. *How many people once lived here?* He thought. Hundreds of thousands, at a time when Butophulo was little more than a village. The stories his father used to tell of the city came flooding back. Site of the Xosu's greatest triumph, and their downfall.

Pitae imagined the old heroes assembled on the plain in front of the city. Men greater in stature, strength, and greed than those of today, dancing their deadly dance. The losers condemned to insignificance, the winners, fame and immortality. Their lot decided by the single thrust of a spear. He could almost hear the clash of arms as the wild, fiery king, Tildun, duelled with the calm and scholarly Semontek in front of the Gate of the Hydra. He imagined the twins, Kilposh and Koltik, attempting to scale the great, god-built walls and bring death into the city. Every single glorious act all turned to dust and ruin now, but immortalised in poems that granted a window onto that wonderous past. The crumbling moon pale ruins passed slowly by as the ship made its way along the coast.

Another few hours slipped by before a small, ruined watchtower rose into view. Perched on a rocky outcrop which in the twilight loomed over the ship like a mountain scraping the sky. They had arrived.

The tower had been built by the League of Butophulo, at the height of its power, to control the trade passing by. It lay in ruins now, the island overgrown and dense with trees and shrubbery. Only twelve years since the fall of the League and nature had already reclaimed the place, returning the land back to its natural splendour before the rise of man. Sol was rumoured to be using the island as a base from which to raid the passing shipping.

The pilot of their trireme steered the craft as close as he could without running aground, the ruined jetty no longer fit for purpose. They would have to wade to the shore. Kunae spoke. His voice hard, with a purpose as true as an arrow loosed from a magnificent bow, brooking no dissent,

"Put your armour on."

Pitae wanted to answer, but he could see the fight was lost. He stood and picked up his horsehair crested helm. Brushing the sea blue crest lightly, letting his fingers dance across it, before sighing and slowly putting his panoply on. His brothers in arms, Thil, Kivuun and Puso followed suit, as did the company of spearmen on board. All that remained of The Daemons of the Deep.

The rest of the company had gone east to fight under the banner of the King of Gelodun in another vainglorious war. There was little to no glory in the life of a mercenary, but it was all that was left to them since the Doldun had smashed the League of Butophulo on the field of the Bulodon's Wail.

The water was surprisingly warm and calm, the expected cold shock as he hit the sea did not come. Kunae was already well ahead of him. Pitae began to wade forward, pushing against the current in a strange dance. His armour felt heavy in the water. The layered cotton of his lamellar cuirass soaked up the sea and felt like it doubled in weight. Pitae found himself envious of Kunae wearing Kolmosoi's bronze cuirass now. He gripped the ashen shaft of his spear tighter, the splash of the others following them sounding behind.

The slow paddle to the shore gave Pitae time to think. Sol was once their brother in arms it was true, but, even if he wasn't the murderer, Kunae did have one point in his favour. Sol's actions had poisoned the peace that Kolmosoi had managed to forge.

"What next?" he called to Kunae, "After Sol dies. What do you see us doing next?"

Kunae continued walking forward, silent for a moment, but eventually Pitae heard a reply,

"We continue with Kolmosoi's plan. Build our strength in Pittuntik, return order to the White Islands, and then we sail to Thasotun and overthrow the Red and White Council and kick out the Doldun's puppets. It is the purpose that The Daemons of the Deep were forged by Kolmosoi to fulfil. Maybe then, the door to Butophulo itself will be open to us."

Pitae had expected that answer,

"Kolmosoi tried that once though. Years we spent feigning loyalty, building a power base in Pittuntik. Coiling ourselves around its hoard of mineral wealth. But the plan failed."

"The plan did not fail! Kolmosoi was betrayed!" Kunae shot back.

"One break in the plan and the whole edifice we built collapsed, just as we were about to break from Thasotun. What do you think would have happened if we had taken that step and our coalition was proved to be so fragile when the stakes were so much higher?" Pitae retorted. Kolmosoi's death had changed everything. No one was sure what had happened, poison probably. Kolmosoi had lingered in a coma for days, his skin pale and scaly, the only signs of life the occasional writhing in agony.

"These are all ifs and buts. The truth is that Sol murdered Kolmosoi and for that he must pay." Kunae seemed to increase his pace as he spoke. Sol was the last person to have seen Kolmosoi conscious and his disappearance immediately afterward would seem to confirm his guilt. That he had then taken to piracy was even more suspicious.

"Then we rebuild our weak alliance and try again. Will the same sacrifices be required Kunae? Betraying others like we were forced to turn on Zolmos the Conjuror?" Pitae shouted, now the forlorn feeling was returning. Kunae did not answer. *Maybe he is right*, Pitae thought. Perhaps it is the only way to fix this mess and bring justice for Kolmosoi, Sol must die.

The beach was quiet as they approached, no sign of life and the dark of the night had descended. Kunae was the first on shore and eager to forge ahead to the tower. Pitae called out to him,

"Kunae, wait! If we are to do it this way, we will do it together. You don't know what kind of force Sol has waiting for us and I would rather meet that with twenty spears than two."

Kunae faced him, clearly pained to wait, but nodded in agreement.

* * *

With the full complement of men assembled on the beach, they began to make their way up the wooded hill to the watch tower in close order, wary of what waited beyond. The trees seemed to close in as they began their ascent. An eerie silence fell that felt deafening, and the air smelt of deceit.

No sooner than when they had entered the dense foliage in front of the tower Pitae's fears were confirmed. A shout echoed and something breezed past the side of his helmet. A scream, and blood splattered across Pitae's shield, painting the hydra emblazoned on it red. The man next to him dropped, death spiralling down on him as he held the shaft of a javelin buried deep in his shoulder. No time to stop, Pitae pivoted, elegant as any performer. He turned to face the danger and shouted,

"Close ranks on me!"

The well drilled men moved as one, locking their shields together just as the wild charge of the enemy smashed into their ranks. Brave but foolish, the lightly armed foes had underestimated them,

"Push!" He yelled and the Salxosu spearmen drove forward with their shields as one, throwing back their assailants. Then the slaughter began.

Pitae thrust his spear, plunging it deep into the gut of the man opposite him who wore a helm of boar tusks and antlers, and a greenish brown leather jerkin which could not stand the blow. Death swirled across the young man's eyes. He stepped forward over the body, eyes scanning, looking for his next opponent. The slaughter was wild, but over almost as soon as it started. The men who attacked them were savage, but ill-disciplined and ill equipped for an open battle, like the Wildmen in the old stories. Those who were not cut down soon melted back into the woods.

The company quickly reformed and continued to press up the hill, eager to not waste their advantage.

They emerged into a small clearing, an empty circle of ground in the centre of which loomed the tower. It was strange, the whole island had been reclaimed by nature, but this small circle around the ruin was untouched. Within the empty island of land, the tower sprouted from the earth, reaching toward the heavens. Though nature had left the area around untouched, the same could not be said for the ruin. Vines had tangled themselves around the moss-covered rock and the spindly branches of new trees were thrusting their way through gaps in the stone. Where a tiled roof once stood, the canopy of a young sapling now burst forth. The feeling of unease returned to Pitae,

"Night is on us!" he shouted to Kunae, "We have defeated most of his force, let us retreat to our ship and return with the dawn."

His cries fell on deaf ears. Kunae was already surveying the ruined fortification. His hands, strong as any hunter, gripped the shaft of his spear tightly, turning his knuckles white. Ruined though it was, the small redoubt was still formidable, it would be a challenge to get inside. The men surrounded the structure and Kunae, his blood up and eager for battle, shouted,

"Sol! Come out and face me!"

No answer came.

Pitae thought about intervening, but it seemed pointless. *Let him vent his anger,* he thought. Kunae had come to the same conclusion, he stopped shouting and began pacing up and down outside the tower. Pitae set about organising the men and setting sentries, not knowing how many foes still lurked in the woods. Then he stood back and watched. *This needs to be resolved quickly.*

"Kivvun, give me a leg up and I'll climb the wall" Puso Sisosi shouted with the surety of a philosopher, which matched his scholarly demeanour. Kivvun Polriso started to make his way to the wall, no doubt already imagining the boastful story he could make of it, but Thil intervened,

"The walls are high and steep; you will never get in."

"It's a good thought Puso, but you will never make it up. The wall is too steep and sheer, besides what will you do once you are inside and stuck at the top? Far better we find a way to draw Sol out." Pitae counselled.

Kunae spoke, the fury clear in his voice,

"Fire! Gather all the wood we can, pile it against the side of the tower and light it."

*　*　*

The dawn came, following the morning star. Dunsun ascended to his throne, and the sun rose above the horizon. A new day and a new beginning.

With wood piled high against the tower, all was set. Kunae, impatient to put an end to Sol, would not wait or rest. He ordered the pyre lit.

One of the men approached the pile with a torch to set the fire. The wood crackled and sparked, and a flash of bright light met the dawn's warm red glow. As it did, the door to the tower creaked and swung open. A figure emerged.

The warrior was shorter than Kunae, but broad and thick in the chest as you would expect from the son of a blacksmith. Dressed in the full panoply of war, he was a formidable sight. He wore a white-gold helmet in the Rinuxosu style, all one piece, but not simple as the Rinuxosu would make it. Instead, elaborate carvings of serpents twisted their way around the helmet and onto the cheek pieces, as the Salxosu of the islands would have forged it to invoke the protection of the Great God. A moon white horsehair crest ran horizontal across the top and two great bull's horns protruded from it. A white-gold muscled cuirass, embellished with lapis and emerald, which shimmered like blue and green shadows in the morning light, protected his chest. An impressive piece, it could have even been zilthum forged if Pitae did not know any better. He held a huge round shield, familiar to any Xosu, with the image of a writhing white serpent painted boldly on the front. A leather kilt and shining bronze grieves completed his garb, with an ashen shafted, iron tipped spear gripped tightly in his right hand. Finally, Sol had answered Kunae's call.

A flash of delight crossed Kunae's sea blue eyes. The fire of the torches the men held bathed him in a warm red glow which matched the crest on his head. In the dawn light, he shone like the star that rises before the sun.

"Nobody touches him!" he growled in a fiery fury, "We will settle this in the old way Sol, the way men have done since before the Dawn. A duel."

Sol nodded his approval and approached. The men instinctively forming a circle around the two warriors, torches held aloft to light up the area. Kunae prowled in front of Pitae, blocking his view of Sol. The two men stood silent, eyeing each other, trying to get the measure of their opponent before the inevitable clash of arms.

"Before we do this," Sol's voice boomed like a hammer on an anvil, "you should understand, there is more going on than you know. Kolmosoi showed me…"

Kunae cut him off,

"I don't care what tricks you have lined up for us Sol! You killed him you will die for that."

With that Kunae darted forward like a cat, quick as Pitae had ever seen him move. The red of his crest streaked forward like an arrow, like Xosu's arrow that had been seen in the sky all that time ago during the year of the dark spring. He caught Sol off guard. Sol just managed to raise his shield to deflect the spear blow, almost knocking him off his feet, and so the dance began. The clash of arms, shield on shield, spear grazing armour, echoed throughout, drowning out the waves gently lapping the shore below them.

At first Kunae landed blow after blow, driving Sol back and keeping him off balance. The hammer emblazoned on Kunae's shield bashing relentlessly against the retreating foe. An easy victory looked assured as Sol struggled to keep his footing, barely managing to deflect the rain of arrow-like blows falling on him.

Then there was an almighty crash in the sky. A roar that showed the anger of the gods and a flash so bright that it seemed to speed the day into being. The heavens opened as a flooding torrent swept on to the earth. Lightning crashed into the tower as Dunsun raged in the heavens. The tree at the top of the structure burst into flame, flames which leapt into the air. For a moment Pitae thought they would all be engulfed as the fire roared like an unchained daemon towards them.

Kunae was undisturbed by the blaze. Another flurry of blows fell on Sol. Kunae's shield thumped into Sols', knocking him to one knee, sending his helmet plummeting to the ground and leaving Sol's round, pale face bloody and bruised.

Another crash across the face of the sky and the fire roared higher as somehow Sol regained his footing and set about an assault of his own. Kunae was forced on to the back foot. The skill of the mercenary showed as his expert footwork kept him as steady as a cat on his feet, calmly blocking each spear thrust as it came.

Kunae was forced back, right to the edge of the circle. The men backed off and Pitae had to move. He found his feet shifting and shuffling quickly. A crash in the sky seemed to echo the clash of shields. Kunae thrust with his spear, the iron heart of the weapon darting toward Sol's face with a burning fury. A swift move of his dome of a shield and Sol brought the rim down hard on the shaft of the spear. A loud crack echoed, and the weapon broke.

Thinking quickly, Kunae barged his opponent with his own shield, buying time to draw his leaf shaped blade. Sol charged, Kunae met him head on. An almighty crash occurred as the two shields smacked into each other. But Kunae had the better of the clash, his feet planted.

Sol stumbled and, in an instant, it was over. Kunae's shield had concealed his blade. As Sol stumbled back, Kunae raised his shield and thrust his sword, plunging the razor-sharp blade deep into Sol's unprotected throat.

Sol let out a hiss of pain, or delight, like a mother in the last bout of labour, as the breath of life left his body. Death came whirling down upon him and his lifeless corpse crashed to the floor.

Kunae turned to the men and raised his arms in triumph, panting, exhausted, but the victor. Sol's blood began to pool on the ground around his helmet. The rain hammering down quickly turned a red-black colour as it mixed with the blood and seeped into the earth. The men sprung up and joined their cheers with Kunae's roar of victory.

But Pitae's gaze was elsewhere. The flames had leapt to the trees, and, despite the rain, the fire was spreading. Then there was a cry, it was a sound like no other, nothing that would pass the lips of man. It was like the cracking of branches and rush of air through the leaves. Primal, like nature itself was calling out.

Pitae froze to the spot, time slowed down, the flashing flames illuminating the small open area and making it seem like an obscure and twisted otherworld. The cry came again, and then the trees seemed to come alive.

"Wildmen?" Pitae whispered to himself incredulously. But then he was brought to his senses as the dawn light fell on the men emerging from the trees. Only a small band of sellswords, the remnants of their foe from the night before. Kunae shouted,

"Form up on me, lock your shields!"

The well drilled men's training and years of experience kicked in and they moved together to form a wall with their shields. But the wild men barrelled past them, seeming to pay them no mind. A terror etched across their faces as they melted into the trees behind the Salxosu in a panicked flight.

Then there was another flash, brighter than the first, the rain hammered down harder, like the sea was trying to overwhelm them, a watery portal to another realm opening to swallow them whole. It tasted acrid on the tongue. Through the torrent, Pitae could just make out wraith like figures wandering towards them, dancing almost, so elegantly did they move.

As the rain eased, the wraiths became obscured no more, but shifted, transformed. They were not men, their presence seemed more mirage than material. Graceful, though they were, they had a sinister air. Their skin honeycombed and alive with the arsenic blue and green shadows of the sea, lit as if by pale moonlight. Their long flowing hair, coloured like the deep ocean and writhing like the waves, striking like serpents. Their faces covered with honey pale, white-gold masks with impassive expressions which spoke of death. They wore no armour, or even any clothes of which to speak, but in their hands they carried blades not forged by the sweat of man. White gold they shone with the light of sorcery upon them.

"The Kinsolsun." He mouthed in disbelief. The words felt like poison on his lips. No one would believe this tale if he survived to tell it. Kunae yelled again, urging the men to step forward and turn their attention away from the woods.

One of the creatures stood over the horned helmet of Sol, its white crest soiled with blood. The creature picked it up as if an artist inspecting its work, or a teacher about to instruct its acolytes. Then its spectral gaze fixed upon the Salxosu.

It took several guarded steps forward, cautiously eyeing Kunae. The mercenary raised his bloody sword and cried out, as if in protection of the men who stood in worried ranks behind him. The creature's gaze swept from head to toe, eyes to blade. Then in words Pitae did not know, it spoke in a way that sounded like a prayer.

Although he did not understand the language, it was tipped with dark magics and wicked poison, the sound of them burnt upon the breath. Like wraiths the Kinsolsun darted across the blood-soaked field. The wizards moved like shadows, like spectres, cutting a bloody swathe through the men.

Pitae was not sure what happened next. The flashes of lightning, the scorching fire and the light of the dawn sun transformed his world. None of it seemed real, but the fear, the pain, and the exhaustion were real enough. With each crash of lightning, more men fell. A flash brighter than the last and with it Thil was struck down,

"Run!" a cry went out. Pitae did not know who from, but the men responded, bolting in all directions. Pitae's legs seemed to carry him off into the woods.

* * *

He was brought to his senses chest deep in the raging, cold sea, struggling towards the ship. The slosh of the waves and the ringing in his ears felt like a dream. A couple of men struggled either side of him. Pitae felt a sting in his arm and reached towards it, his hand came away covered in blood. He did not remember being struck.

Next to him, sodden with blood and barely staying above the ripple of the wine dark sea Kunae was battling the waves, a shadow of a man. Gripped tightly in his hand was Sol's helmet. The ship was close enough to touch.

Pitae used his good arm to pull himself close and cling on but was unable to climb on board, his spirit had left him. Resigned to his fate, he waited for the sea to take him. But Sem was not to have his body yet, nor his shade. Kunae managed to grasp the bronze of the ram, but the exertion seemed too much.

"Hold on!" Pitae struggled to shout, but his voice was hoarse, and the words barely echoed above the din of the storm that raged all around them. He could only watch as Kunae's eyes glazed over and with the crash of a final wave he slipped below the surface, into the void to dream before his shade was taken to the halls of the dead.

Pitae felt a hand take hold of his injured shoulder, hard. He yelled out in pain, a sweet, unbearable pain that washed over him as he was hauled on board.

The pilot pulled him upright, panicked and confused,

"What is going on? Where is Kunae? Kivuun? Puso? This storm came from nowhere, but the sea still looks calm a few stades out. We need to leave; I can't wait much longer for them."

"Just go!" Pitae replied, "They're all dead, those things killed them."

The pilot stared at him for a long moment, but did not question him, instead ordering the crew to the oars.

The ship creaked as it turned towards the dawn sun, the sky still red before the blue of the day was swept over by Bul's breath. The ship creaked again as it gathered speed, the oarsmen began to get into a rhythm, fighting with the raging, wine-dark sea as they went.

A surreal feeling washed over Pitae. For some reason he felt hope. He would return to Pittuntik, finish what Kolmosoi started, rebuild the League, retake Butophulo even. Soon the Salxosu would turn once more to Butophulo, bringing riches, wealth, and tribute to the city, like they did Kolbos of old. The pain, exhaustion and loss of blood was overtaking him, and his vision went blurry.

The ship crashed through a final wave and into the calmer waters beyond and Pitae again began to find comfort in the softer waves splashing against the ship. A final crack came, louder than the others. He felt it through the soaking timbers as the ship made it completely clear of the storm. Pitae watched the sun appear over the horizon, he knew they should have turned back when they had the chance, none of this felt right.

KALASYAR

1

"Gather round!"

Her aging grandfather shouted as the sunlight streaked through the window and illuminated him in the centre of the room, as if he were being taken to another realm. The vigour of youth in his voice and the glint in his sea blue eyes gave away to Kalasyar Sisosi the topic of today's lesson.

The children surrounded their mentor, eyes gleaming and eager to learn. Her grandfather had a rare gift for inspiring people and planting the seeds of action in their minds. Koseun Sisosi revelled in the role he had carved for himself as a teacher to the children of Butophulo's rich and noble families. After all, who would not want their child learning from one of the most famous orators and statesmen the city had ever produced.

Every family of the old blood sent their children to learn from the great man. Even the tyrant's kin sent their sons in a tacit admission of Koseun's knowledge and learning. Even if they were only the younger sons, those not taken by the Nine to be educated by Kunpit Posuasthison, as the new guardians and rulers of the city.

Looking around the room she could see several Polriso, a Rososthup and a Kinsol, a number from the Kisurusosi, and one or two of the Kolkisuasu, and of course her own kin from the Sisosi. The tyrant's progeny in the shape of one or two Kosua, Posuausthison and a Rusos were there as well. There was also a scattering of children from rich merchant families who did not possess such a great lineage as the blood of old Kolbos.

Kalasyar smiled warmly and turned to find Tilmosh, her grandfather's secretary, standing just inside the entrance. He had been with the Sisosi since before Kalasyar was born. Captured as a youth far to the east, beyond the Throat of Sem. Her grandfather had bought him from some passing Putedun traders when he noticed the boy's quick wits. She looked back towards Koseun, but spoke to Tilmosh,

"It pleases me to see grandfather find a new vocation. I have worried for years that he would never adapt to the loss of the League and the citizen's assemblies. He may like to claim that he only spoke in front of the people for the good of the city, but he loved that life, the joy it brought him to have his words heard and admired. When the Nine banned public oratory and expelled poets and artists from the city, it almost broke him. I know it did."

She was not looking at him, but she knew Tilmosh was smiling just as warmly as she was,

"Yes, losing his position and his prominence was hard. He is a stubborn old snake, but who wouldn't have found it a challenge to adapt? To have been the foremost orator, statesman, and philosopher in the city, and to have all that taken from you overnight. Especially after he had negotiated the surrender of Butophulo. It was a task he carried out with no satisfaction, but he deserved some respect for it." Tilmosh answered her with his guttural accent that marked him out as a man from the furthest reaches of the east. He had never lost that quality in his voice; despite the decades he had spent among the Xosu.

"Tekolger disrespected him." Kalasyar replied, allowing a little bitterness into her voice, "My grandfather was his guest-friend. But what could we expect from the Doldun? They are half savages themselves. Grandfather was wrong to place so much admiration in Tekolger."

"No child, the Nine tyrants disrespected him and those in the city who went along with them. Koseun may have known Tekolger when he was the young heir to the throne of the Doldun and a restless victor of the games. And he may have held a fools hope that the qualities he respected would stay with the boy when he became a king. But that is rarely the way in politics, Koseun knew that deep down. Besides, Tekolger did show a kind of respect to your grandfather, he would not have been so merciful without it. It is the tyrants who haven't. They fear him and what his words can rouse in the people. We are just fortunate that they fear Tekolger more. That is why they have never acted against Koseun openly." Tilmosh spoke again, ever eager to defend his master. "And don't think Koseun blameless. He loves to be contrary. A follower of the teachings of Rolmit of Rulkison finding so much to admire in a boy raised by the school of Kunpit of Thelonigul. It made for great conversation at the symposium."

Kalasyar scoffed,

"Tekolger still saw to it that the followers of Kunpit gained much from Butophulo's fall though. He knew that would mean grandfather losing everything. Where was the respect in that? And yet grandfather still speaks admirably of what Tekolger has gone on to achieve."

"You were young then. Politics is a fickle game, Tekolger and Koseun both knew it. Koseun could never have kept his position in the city once the Doldun had defeated and destroyed the League. He said as much to me the morning he left the city to negotiate with the king. His only goal was to see Butophulo spared a brutal sack. But the Nine still could have shown him the respect he deserved. He was no threat to their power with the Doldun ensconced upon Polriso's Hill. I suspect they fear his name as much as the man. The last time there was a revolution in the city it was led by a Sisosi." Tilmosh retorted.

She sighed, "Yes, I was young when that all happened. In truth I remember little of it." She paused and pondered, "Perhaps you are right. And as I have grown older, I have feared that things are as you say. It is only the well-known friendship between grandfather and Tekolger which has prevented the Nine from arresting him. Even if Tekolger did disrespect him. Every time one of the patriarchs of the old families is swept off the street by the Nine's enforcers, or a show trial held in the old theatre, that fear has grown in me, maddened me. So now I am pleased he has found something that will keep him quiet and out of the minds of the tyrants. Especially if the rumours of the king's death are true."

Kalasyar could feel the anxiety rising in her as she spoke. She felt Tilmosh squeeze her shoulder in a way a father might. It was almost comforting.

"I will be in my chambers if I am needed." He said as he turned to leave. Tilmosh could always be found in his chambers. He looked and acted as much the scholar as her grandfather, but he still had some of the wildness of the east about him. He had taught Kalasyar her letters and her numbers and much more besides at the long table that stretched across his hall. She viewed him almost as another father.

With his class assembled, Koseun, seated on his chair close to the open window, began to speak in his way that flowed so effortlessly,

"Which of you can tell me who the master of the Cosmos is?"

A child sat right at the front raised his hand and Koseun picked him out. One of the Posuausthison clan Kalasyar guessed,

"Dunsun, Lord of the Cosmos is. That is why he sits on his shining throne and lights the world from the realm of the gods in Dzottgelon."

A smile uncoiled on Koseun's face. Her grandfather had a bright quality and a wit as quick as a snake when he spoke. It was what had made him so loved in the city. Through his smile he replied,

"Correct, and can you tell me why?"

The child paused and puzzled over the question for a moment, before answering confidently,

"Because he is the strongest of all the light and fair gods. He wields the thunderbolt, which the other gods fear."

Koseun smiled again,

"A good try, but no. Dunsun is master of the Cosmos because he knows how power works and how to use it. Who here knows the story of how Dunsun became the master of the Cosmos?"

The puzzled faces spread throughout his audience. No doubt the children were reluctant to answer after that first rebuttal. Koseun, in full flow, carried on,

"No one? Then I shall tell you. Thousands of years ago, when the Cosmos was still a young and vibrant place, alive with the energy which had burst forth from the egg of creation, there was only chaos."

Another child plucked up the courage to speak,

"What about Bul and Phenmoph?"

"And Sem!" A second child shouted.

"And Geli and Gelon!" another said. Confidence building again,

"And Gennon!" shouted a fourth. Koseun's laugh crashed like a wave against a cliff,

"It is true that the Belithelon, the gods of the second generation, had entered our realm from their own world of light and lorded over Gennon's creation, the world we now inhabit. For this was a time when the gateways between the worlds were much easier to cross than they have been since the Dusk.

Geli took the deep woods and forests as her home and Gelon the rolling hills and plains. From his realm of the sky Bul ruled. But you must remember that some of the gods, the ones who are dark and shadowy, came from that dun, hidden realm below. Indeed, Phenmoph still rules from that realm, and, of course, Sem emerged to take the oceans for his home. At this time there was no order in the world, chaos reigned. This would all change."

The children looked on fascinated. Koseun had their undivided attention now. He continued,

"When the last and greatest of Gennon's creations was finished, so proud she was of her finest work that she named the world on which we now live Kolgennon, the great conception of Gennon. On the final day, once all her labour was complete, from the remaining foaming blood of her twin, the giant Gingel, unused in the creation of the world, emerged the shining goddess Yulthelon. With her birth she uttered this prophecy to the Belithelon.

> *Gennon, kind mother earth, her wayward*
> *children roam free on her great tree,*
>
> *Bul, your cry branches over sky, Sem your*
> *tails take root under sea,*
>
> *The wheel will turn, from your loins you'll sire*
> *your demise, worlds shocked by your duel,*
>
> *Fruit from high, a golden jewel, seed of soil to end your rule.*

This prophecy drove great fear into the gods because, powerful though they are, even they cannot outrun fate." Koseun paused, as if to catch his breath, but Kalasyar knew he was revelling in the role of storyteller and merely stopping to build some tension as he supped from his cup of wine as dark as the sea drawing upon the wisdom deep within,

"This was a barbarous time, before the laws of marriage and the correct relations between man and woman had been established. Both Bul and Sem had lusted after their sister Geli, and she had not refused them. This unruly and barbarous act would come to haunt them. Geli became pregnant, giving birth to twins soon after, a boy and a girl."

"Red faced Dunsun and white armed Tholo!" One of the children shouted out, pleased with their foreknowledge. A smile slithered its way across Koseun's lips, and he carried on the tale,

"Wary of the prophecy and fearing the male child, who Bul and Sem thought threatened their power, they resolved to act. However, their mother, Geli, stole the children away, hiding them far to the west, in the shadow of mount Betgennon in the care of the Wildmen. Here the young gods were raised to maturity and in turn began to lust after one another. They gave in to these urges. Tholo, the white armed goddess, birthed the next generation of gods in the shadow of the mountain, the Kolithelon.

Sem and Bul had not been idle in this time, raging across the world searching high and low for the children of Geli. But it was the birth of the Kolithelon which would bring war, the rise of Dunsun to the mastery of the Cosmos, and a new dawn for the world."

The children had gathered closer now as if to hear every syllable clearly.

"Curious of the world and resolving to see more of Gennon's creation, Dunsun led the Kolithelon east into the full light of Kolgennon.

The movement of the gods revealed their existence to Bul and Sem, and quickly the two mighty deities began to plot and scheme to destroy those that they saw as a threat to their lordship of the world. But Sem, the great serpent, cunning and duplicitous as the sea he made his home, saw the chance to overthrow his brother Bul as well. He proposed to Bul that he would lure Tholo away and destroy her, allowing Bul the mighty cloud gatherer to bring destruction to her brother and consort, Dunsun."

The children nodded knowingly.

"Seizing his chance when Tholo left the group to explore the white land to the north, Sem revealed himself to her and told her the tale of her birth and how he had searched for her all this time, and then he planted the seeds of his trap. Spinning a tale of how he wished to protect her from his brother and allow the Kolithelon to rule the lands of Kolgennon as he did the depths. He explained that Bul intended to destroy fiery Dunsun, feeling threatened by Tholo's twin, and lusting for dominion over the skies and Kolgennon. But Sem told her he had a plan. With his skills of craft and metallurgy, he could show Tholo how to forge a weapon for Dunsun to contain the power of Bul's thunder and turn the force of his fury against Bul.

In this time, Bul released his children from his cloud, the Bulodon, to harass the new gods unused to such menacing behaviour. Bul then revealed himself to the Kolithelon and demonstrated to them his power over the skies by taming his children. Overawed by the might of the cloud gatherer and open to his suggestion that Dunsun unfairly dominated their small band, hoarding all the power and respect for himself, the Kolithelon sided with Bul when he openly challenged Dunsun.

Against such odds, even the red Lord of the Cosmos could not stand, he was defeated. But Bul could not destroy Dunsun entirely, for even a god cannot destroy the flame of life once the spark is lit. Instead, he would destroy the body of Dunsun and drive his shade into the arms of his brother Phenmoph, Lord of the Hidden Realm, who had no interest in the world above.

Bul, using the power of the divine flame, burnt away the flesh of Dunsun that he found so threatening, releasing his shade to the dwelling and embrace of the rich lord. Some say that from the blood of Dunsun, spilled on the fertile earth, the first men sprung forth and this is why men revere Dunsun more than any other god."

The children looked on in fascinated horror as Koseun described the death and transformation of Dunsun,

"Geli was distraught when she learnt of the death of her son from Tholo. The pair determined to travel to the underworld to plead with Phenmoph to release Dunsun's shade.

Upon arriving in the halls of the dark realm, they made their case to the rich lord. Phenmoph had been expecting them, for he also lusted after his sister Geli. He made her an offer, in return for her agreeing to stay with him in his realm, he would release the shade of Dunsun.

In her grief, Geli agreed on the condition that she could spend a part of the year with her children and the life she loved so well.

Phenmoph, pleased that his strategy had paid off, agreed to this indulgence. The first marriage was conducted then and there. We always know when Geli is fulfilling her bargain with Phenmoph. Without Geli here to tend to the fertility of the soil, no crops can grow, and all plants begin to die; winter descends."

That fact filled some of the children with wonder and glee, fascinated by the explanation for the seasons.

"With Dunsun's form recovered, Tholo forged the thunderbolt as Sem had shown her and the twins returned to Kolgennon. With the power of the fire of the heavens in his grasp, Dunsun would be able to bring down the mighty Bul.

Dunsun, red with fury, tracked down Bul and the rest of the Kolithelon, who rejoiced to see him return as they chafed under the rule of the overbearing lord of the skies. With the thunderbolt in hand, Dunsun savaged Bul, relieving him of his manhood which he cast into the sea. Some people claim it was this act, not the shedding of Dunsun's blood, from which the first men were born. Bul was defeated and broken, but the Lord of the Cosmos was magnanimous in his victory. He banished Bul to the realm above never to return to Kolgennon.

However, Dunsun was not finished. For he saw through the schemes of Sem who had contrived to seize the land of Kolgennon whilst conflict raged between Dunsun and Bul. In a final confrontation, more savage than that with Bul, Dunsun faced Sem who rose from the depths to meet the challenge. The battle of the gods raged across the world, reshaping the land. For a time, it looked as though Sem and his acolytes might best the Lord of the Cosmos and the Kolithelon. But with thunderbolt in hand and the cunning of cat, Dunsun would eventually prevail. The great serpent was banished to the depths as his bloody defeat saw peace and renewal brought to the world.

The tradition of marriage was still young then, and the gods are not bound by the same rules as mortals, and so the twins, Dunsun and Tholo, married. Dunsun completed his quest and in a location high above the centre of the world he built the great palace of the gods. Dzottgelon, the golden gateway. From there he rules, sitting on his golden throne by day to watch the world go by, just as Tholo sits on her pale white throne at night.

After his victory and marriage, Dunsun was able to take up his title as Lord of the Cosmos. It was now that Dunsun demonstrated his divine insight into how power works. Knowing that as master of the Cosmos he had no need to prove his power any further, and if he controlled everything his children would become restless and conspire against him, chafing under his rule as they had under Bul before him.

Dunsun took inspiration from the bee. The queen bee of a hive rules over all, but needs others to ensure her hive survives and functions. She achieves this by allowing others to have dominion over certain roles within the cosmos of the beehive. Dunsun resolved to hand out responsibility.

Buto, Sem's crippled son, he allowed to keep his father's bounty of the oceans and all those who travel and trade. To Kol the realm of thought and ideas, to Palo that of freedom and liberty. Dolkoli would preside over war and statecraft, Sunkeli the arts and the written word, Tulo farming and agriculture. Bosguli would attend to justice and fairness, Kelimoph the skills of building and construction and of course many more aspects besides these. Dunmosh oversees many aspects of what we would call culture and Yulthelon herself prophecy and the threads of time.

This is how our city worked as well. The tyrant kings who ruled Butophulo before the League brought order and stability, but they could not fulfil the needs and desires of the people to control their own fate. So, we banished them and spread their powers to rule among the people. Creating the citizen assemblies to administer the city and then founding the League of Butophulo for the other Salxosu to be brought under the benevolence of the new mother city." Koseun paused and watched, his viper sharp eyes carefully gauging the reaction of the children.

"But the League is gone now, isn't it? Because it became bad? That is what my father says." one of the children pondered.

"The League is gone now. The tyrants are back and are trying to keep their order. The League may have seemed sometimes chaotic, but it kept our freedom and protected us from the worst excesses of the tyrants." Koseun carefully replied.

The children sat pondering further,

"Then the Council is bad?" Another asked. The kin of those same tyrants had gone noticeably quiet.

"Some may say that, but you must be careful who you ask questions like that of. This is an open space for you to ponder these bigger questions, you must be more cautious on the street." Her grandfather was almost teasing them now.

"Because the Nine will take us if we are not careful and send you to be imprisoned with the Doldun, just like the Kinsolsun used to do." A child said with some misplaced glee in his voice. One of the tyrant's own kin, Kalasyar noted. *Strange how children can make such statements and misunderstand things with such enthusiasm*, she thought.

Koseun's liquid smile returned,

"Perhaps. Just be careful you do not give them a reason to take you." Koseun paused, this time with a sad look on his face as he glanced beyond the children and out of the window toward the sea,

"That is all the time for your lesson today. I want you to go away and think about why Dunsun handed power away when he could have kept it all to himself."

The children darted out of the room in all directions. Koseun got up to leave.

"I wish you wouldn't do that." Kalasyar said to her grandfather as he approached.

"You don't want me to teach the children?" Koseun enquired, his white hair a contrast to his dark, sea blue eyes, knowing very well that is not what Kalasyar meant.

"No, talk about the League like that. What happens if they start talking in the street about it or to their families? Next thing you know you will have a few dozen sellswords barging down our door. Some of your audience are kin to the men who you are denouncing. They will not think twice about sacrificing you for their own advancement." She replied showing her anger with a viper's tongue, concerned for his safety. "You know, the Posuausthison, Rusos and Kosua yearned for centuries for the power they now hold. No doubt they would relish the chance to remove you as a threat to their status. It is only a fear of Tekolger that has stopped them acting, and it seems Tekolger is gone now."

"The children need to learn about our past, and hopefully our future." There was a serious tone to his voice this time, matched by the look in his eye.

"It is our present I am most worried about grandfather." She shot back at him in a friendly but scornful way, with less of the venom she showed before. Kalasyar knew what it was like to lose parents. The war with the Rinuxosu and the plague which had gripped the city at its height had taken her mother and father, one to battle the other to the disease. She would not lose her grandfather as well. Her concern gushed forth as it did so often these days, "The Nine feel fragile about their power as it is, and the news of the king's death is making them more so. They are crushing anything they consider dissent. Unsanctioned public gatherings have now been completely banned."

She knew none of this would deter her grandfather, but always thought it was worth trying. Koseun looked pensively into the distance for a second and said,

"You will be pleased that I don't intend on any public assembly then, just a private one. I wonder if you might head to the market and order some supplies for tonight's symposium? It is a special one as your cousin is due to return to us, his education in Rulkison complete. What could be better than a symposium to see what he has learnt? I would send Tilmosh, but he has other duties to attend to and Pito has yet to return from his latest venture. He promised to bring me the finest wine from Thelizum."

She could not help but smile at that. Her grandfather never seemed deterred in the slightest,

"Tell me what you need?" She replied,

"Wine mostly." he answered, "Something to get the conversation flowing. Speak to Tilmosh, he knows what I require."

***

The heart of the city was as bustling and busy as ever, the meeting point of peoples from many different realms. Kalasyar covered her long dark hair and pulled her veil over her face as she headed into the throng. Of noble birth or not, everyone walked in Butophulo, a relic of the League that the tyrants and their Doldun masters were yet to quash. Her handmaids struggled to pull their own veils over their hair which had caught in a gust of wind and sent their long braids writhing around like a cluster of snakes.

Tharoroz and Ralxuloz had been with her since she was a small child. Like Tilmosh, they too had been taken as slaves by the Putedun far to the east. They claimed that they had been virgin priestesses of a goddess called Lollon, chosen for their beauty, before the Putedun slavers flooded into their village and seized them, despoiling the sacred grounds, seizing the precious metals, and dragging the girls off to the be sold.

It was a tale Kalasyar could scarcely begin to imagine as a young girl, but she could see her handmaids being chosen for their beauty, their visages much sought after by heroes, kings, and gods alike. They were a few years older than Kalasyar and she had looked up to them as a girl as they had always seemed like immortal goddesses to that young child who would hang off their every word. Now though they were more like older sisters.

Kalasyar stumbled as if her leg were crippled in the strong gust of wind as they emerged into the Kobon, the district of the city which coiled protectively around the bottom of the towering trunk of Polriso's Hill. It was where all the families of the old blood still lived. The first area beyond the walls of the Sanctuary on top of the Hill to be built on when the survivors of old Kolbos fled to the safety of the land that would become Butophulo.

At first simple dwellings, over the centuries as the city grew rich and powerful, the old families built increasingly extravagant abodes from marble, gold, and even zilthum where it could be found. But many of the lavish villas lay empty now as the scions of the old blood fled from the regime of the Nine or were arrested in the first days of their rule. Some were sent to Doldun as hostages, others just disappeared.

At this time in the morning most of the Kobon still sat in the branching shadow of the walls of the Sanctuary on top of Polriso's Hill. The morning mist gave the Kobon a tranquil feel, leaving a sweet damp smell in the air. The Sanctuary had been the spiritual heart of the League of Butophulo as well as its treasury, storing the wealth that the other members brought to Butophulo to pay for the great fleet. But now it served as the garrison fortress of the Doldun.

Ralxuloz slipped a hand through Kalasyar's arm and said softly,

"Come, the ships arrived with the morning sun. If we do not hurry then the best wares will be snapped up, no time to dawdle and daydream."

Tharoroz had already begun the long walk towards the agora. Kalasyar, under Ralxuloz' guidance, followed on toward the Hunpil district which wrapped around the Kobon and branched out in all directions. The Hunpil district was a contrast to the Kobon. The homes of the poor scattered behind the great market where the wares of the world were sold, and one could sight men from a hundred different nations. The echo from the market reverberated around the city and the smell, a mix of wine, bread, and perfume, drifted and covered for the less pleasant odour of the hovels of the poor.

Past the slums, obscured by Tholo's Tear, a hill on which had been carved out the great theatre, sitting almost as high as Polriso's Hill, was the Pusoan district and the old military port, amongst the dwellings of rowers, shipwrights, and blacksmiths. Abandoned now after Tekolger forbade Butophulo any ships capable of making war, and those few captains who could, had fled. Beyond the circular military harbour, open like a gaping mouth, was the largest merchant port to be found in the Xosu world, thankfully still a hive of activity even after the fall of the League.

Tharoroz turned as if to beckon Kalasyar and Ralxuloz to quicken their pace,

"Why does she hurry so this morning?" Kalasyar whispered to her companion. Ralxuloz smiled.

"She would not admit to it, but there is a ship's boy that she is sweet on. She rushes to see if he has returned with the latest wave of ships." Kalasyar joined Ralxuloz in smiling and they hurried to catch up with Tharoroz.

Despite its defeat and occupation by the Doldun, Butophulo was still the largest metropolis of the Xosu. A sprawling city branching off from Polriso's Hill, filled with countless people from all over the world, even many from beyond the horizons of Xosudun. Its riches a tempting fruit to any who could seize it, as the Nine had shown when they took the opportunity afforded to them by the victory of the Doldun.

"What troubles you today? I can see the worry in your brow." Ralxuloz asked as they walked.

"My grandfather. He is so uncaring, risking everything. He has found a role teaching the children, and yet he still tries to goad the Nine. They are nervous about maintaining their grip on power and the news of the death of their patron has started to turn that to paranoia. But my grandfather seems to want to provoke them."

"Is this not the game that the great families have always played in the city? I thought they relished the competition?" Ralxuloz answered. "I do not understand you Xosu, even after I have lived among you for so long."

"Yes, the contest between the families of the old blood for political power has always been ruthless. But the way the Nine seized control… That was beyond acceptable competition. Not since the days of the last king of the city have the Salxosu experienced such tyranny. The families may be placid now, but the Nine know how vulnerable they are. It makes them dangerous. The news of Tekolger's death has brought a wave of restlessness to Butophulo. Have you not noticed the tension hanging in the air, Ralxuloz? It cannot be attributed solely to the turn towards autumn and the storms that will bring. Yet my grandfather seems to insist on standing in the way of the coming storm, and it will be on the minds of the Nine that the last king was overthrown by a Sisosi, Yunsunos my most illustrious ancestor - they will fear my grandfather wishes to repeat his actions."

"He is a wise man though. Surely, he knows what he is doing?"

"Wise he is, but he has always been reckless too."

Kalasyar and her companions snaked their way through the Kobon, moving out of the Sanctuary's shadow and heading toward the south side of Polriso's rocky hill. Here the path opened. She turned on to the main thoroughfare of the city. A wide and open road, known as Xosu's Arrow for its straight and true path to the heart of the metropolis. From the southeastern side of the hill, it unfolded like a tree root directly to the sea, the real lifeline of a city too large to feed itself from its hinterland alone.

The route was lined with market stalls selling wares from all corners of the world, hauled up every morning from the port. Basic staples like grain from Zenbel and Gelmophon sat alongside wine from Gelodun, crocodile skins from Xortogun, and precious metals brought from the far east, beyond the Throat of Sem, by Putedun traders.

At the foot of Polriso's Hill, where Xosu's Arrow began, sat the Kolmob, the stage where the citizen body of the city used to gather to listen to fiery debates on the important issues of the day and vote on the course of action they wished to take. Benches had been carved into the trunk of the hill for citizens to sit and listen. Below them the stage where the politicians spoke and debated. Behind that a row of podiums upon which used to stand statues of the great orators of the past, placed to look up to the assembled citizens, as if appealing to a higher authority. All the major decisions of the old League were taken here. Citizens would vote by raising their hands to be counted in full view of the gods.

Kalasyar had been just a girl when the city was occupied by the Doldun, but she vividly remembered the statues being taken away by the Nine in another of their decrees. She had cried when her grandfather's statue was removed. An honour he had won saving the city by his actions when Pittuntik had rebelled against the League and the Rinuxosu laid siege to Butophulo itself. The beginning of a twenty-year struggle which ultimately led to the city's present state. Looking at the half-abandoned site of the Kolmob even now filled her with a sadness and melancholy.

"You are daydreaming again aren't you." Ralxuloz' soft, matronly voice whispered in her ear. "Always here I catch you with that look in your eye."

Kalasyar smiled, sadly.

"Where do you think they took the statue?" She asked. Ralxuloz matched her smile,

"How many times have you asked me that? I do not know, but do not worry, you have the man himself to talk to, you don't need a statue."

"I know, but it should be there. One day I will put it back." Kalasyar answered.

They turned away from the Kolmob and made off down Xosu's Arrow heading southeast toward the sea. In the far distance the water glistened in the morning light and against this backdrop the port appeared, a hive of activity. Ships sliding into the harbour and men rushing to unload their varied cargo. This abundant trade was what had made Butophulo rich and powerful and the envy of all the Xosu.

Further down the road, the walls seemed to grow as the great fortifications which protected the city loomed over her. The walls spread outward from the Kobon to encompass the whole city. Butophulo was shaped almost like the canopy of a tree.

Her grandfather had told her that the walls had been built just before Yoruxoruni of Xortogun had invaded Xosupil. The first time the city felt the need for an impregnable defence to keep them connected to the port. That was over two hundred years ago now, six hundred and thirty-five years after the fall of old Kolbos by most counts. Before that, only the

Sanctuary itself on Polriso's Hill had been fortified.

Yoruxoruni had been stopped by the combined might of all the Xosu on both land and sea before he even came close to Butophulo and his empire fell apart shortly afterwards. It was a story all Xosu knew well, recorded by the historian Kisonkenril of Supokul who spoke to the Rilrpitu and the Xortogun themselves whilst he was a guest of the Rilrpitu king of Xortogun less than fifty years after the events. His account of Yoruxoruni's reign was one of her grandfather's favourite examinations of rulership and the hubris of absolute power.

Her grandfather claimed that it was that war which had allowed Butophulo to rise so far, even though it happened far away from the city. The invasion had crippled the Rinuxosu. Their king had died, their Sacred Band was slaughtered, and their lands ravaged. Butophulo was finally able to break completely free of their influence and that of the followers of Kunpit of Thelonigul.

It was from that point on, her grandfather liked to say, that the League of Butophulo had become the pre-eminent Xosu power by looking to the sea for strength and the other Salxosu for support, just like Kolbos of old. Thankfully Butophulo had avoided the fate of that ancient city though.

The sun was halfway through its journey across the sky when Kalasyar arrived at the docks. She could have found what she was looking for at the market, but it would cost her twice as much coin, as the traders passed on the cost of bribing the mercenaries in the employ of the Nine, and the best products would have been already taken by those same mercenaries. With the Butosunril, the festival of Buto, fast approaching, the celebration of the crippled god to mark the change of the season, good wine would soon be hard to come by.

She was in luck. Tharoroz, though disappointed that the ship she sought was not in the harbour, pointed out a vessel that had just docked and was beginning to unload amphorae filled with wine. Kalasyar pulled her veil aside and approached the merchant as he checked his wares off the ship,

"Where does your wine come from?" She inquired,

"All over the middle sea. We have fine whites from Thelizum and a red from Gelodun so rich you will think you have transformed into a god." he said in a nonchalant manner, scratching his salt-stained hair. "The whites will cost you. You are not like to see much more of it for a long while I fear. The King of Gelodun has swept down the valley and even now marches on the gates of Gottoy."

He turned to face her. As he looked up his face portrayed his surprise, taken aback that an unveiled woman of the old blood had approached him so boldly. Kalasyar always enjoyed that shocked expression,

"I would try the red." She replied. The man nodded and opened an amphora, pouring a drop of the wine into a bowl. She took a sip. The wine had a rich taste which matched its deep red colour. *A fine example of Gelodun red,* she thought, *rich enough for the gods themselves to find wisdom in, Xosu could not have made a better wine himself.* She passed the cup to her handmaids, who each took a sip and nodded their heads in agreement,

"I will take four amphorae; my attendant will tell you where to send them and pay you." She said to him with the surety of a smith testing the metal of a new blade.

The man nodded again and shouted to one of the slaves unloading the ship to set four aside. She pulled her moon-pale veil back over her face and twisted on her standing leg, her sea blue dress striking like a hydra in the wind behind her.

* * *

Kalasyar spent the rest of the day acquiring items for the running of the household. Much and more needed to be bought in the city to keep the family in the conditions expected of them, like the many raw materials needed to keep a forge hot and functional. The list Tilmosh had given her was extensive. Even during the time of the League and the tyrants, some of the expectations of being of the old blood of Kolbos did not die.

Her final stop was at the temple of Buto and the sanctuary below. As she always did when she visited the market, Kalasyar had bought tribute for the temple and the priestesses of Sem, her sacred duty. The sanctuary of Sem felt like a second home to her, a place of solace ever since her mother was taken from her during the great plague.

Her brief stop at the temple meant that the sun was well into its descent before she began to head back home. Sipenkiso, the High Priestess of Sem, had urged her to head straight back as the Nine's enforcers, mercenary companies hired from all over Xosupil, were once again out in force. Best not be caught on the streets as a woman alone. Sipenkiso had taken a motherly affection to her since her own mother had passed.

Kalasyar took a glance back at the temple as she left. It had always been one of her favourite buildings in the city, even more so than the temple of Buto on Polriso's Hill. The sun now setting behind the dome of the building gave it a divinely inspired outline which highlighted its beauty. The marble from Thelonigul, brought by the old kings to show their power, seemed to glow. The red of the sun, just visible behind, made it look as though the marble was alight with the fire of the gods giving the white stone a ruddy hue. Atop the structure sat the bronze statue of Buto. Red, gold, and resplendent, his eyes captivating, illuminated in the evening light as if being raised to the heavens, or perhaps falling, crashing to earth in a blaze as Dunsun cast him out from his golden palace of Dzottgelon. The sight always reminded her of her visit to the oracle of Buto in the ruins of old Kolbos. The temple there was even more grand and magnificent despite its dilapidated state.

The distraction of the temple meant that she did not see the horsemen approaching, but the rumble of hooves alerted her to their advance and a touch on the arm from Ralxuloz warned her. Whirling round, she saw a squadron or more ahorse heading into the city, from the Gate of the God toward Polriso's Hill.

Fearing for a moment that the tyrant's men were upon her, she soon came to her senses. The enforcers of the regime never rode around the city, and none wore such splendid armour as the men at the front of the column. One was carrying a standard, a deep navy blue, almost black, with a dazzling silver white eight-pointed star in its centre. The star of Tholophos she knew immediately, the standard used by the kings of the Doldun and by Tholophos himself when he was the High King of all the Xosu, his own version of the star of Xosu still used by the god's cult.

Her grandfather had told her much about the Doldun when they took over the city and why they carried the banner of the controversial Tholophos. A king who had saved the Xosu and united them once more, but then brought the ire of the gods upon them and, many said, caused the Dusk that fell on the old kingdoms. The Doldun saw things differently, her grandfather had claimed. They say that Tholophos was a great king who united the Xosu and took their civilisation to heights it had not seen before or since. Koseun told her that the Doldun say it was Tholophos' son, Tildun who brought that mighty civilisation low, through his hubris and folly.

The horsemen came to a halt next to Kalasyar and her attendants. The beast at the head of the column approached, covering her with its shadow the way gathered clouds would cover the sun. A man in ornate armour dismounted in front of Kalasyar, his purple cloak, the mark of his station, slipped over his shoulder as he did. Doltopez of the Deltathelon, the general of the Doldun garrison in Butophulo. He had a look which could almost pass as Xosu, but his reddish-brown, cropped beard and long tan hair showed his origins in the kingdom of the Doldun.

Kalasyar had come to know him a little over the last few years. He was always courteous and respectful, helpful even at a time when she was a stranger to him. Although she was sure this was a front. Maintaining civility whilst allowing the Nine to do the ugly work of maintaining control of the city. The young commander smiled at her and said,

"Kalasyar Sisosi. Even under that veil I recognise those pale grey eyes." His voice was deep and low, like thunder rolling in the distance. "It is pleasant to see you, especially after a long ride back from Doldun. But you should not be out on the streets at this time, the Council of the city have made that clear."

"I think we all know that you are the real governor of the city General. I don't think the Nine would dare to arrest me whilst you are with me." Kalasyar replied quick as a snake, a hint of sarcasm in her voice.

Doltopez's laugh rolled like thunder,

"Very well, then allow me to escort you and your attendants back home."

Kalasyar nodded her agreement.

Doltopez liked to talk and so the journey back to the house passed quickly despite Doltopez dismounting to walk alongside her. Kalasyar even found him pleasant company. Outside the large city mansion of the Sisosi, Doltopez stopped to bid her farewell, with the parting shot of,

"As always it has been a pleasure. Give your grandfather my regards and remind him to keep his head down. The city finds itself in a delicate state politically and the Council is worried. You wouldn't want him to be accused of stirring up trouble in this difficult time."

The remark hit her like a lightning strike, and though Kalasyar smiled, keeping her face calm as the sea on a clear day, underneath she felt anger flow like the currents beneath the water.

"Thank you for the escort home. I will be sure to send my grandfather your regards." She dipped her head in acknowledgement to the general and turned to enter the house, unsure whether that last remark from Doltopez was a threat or a warning.

KALU

2

The column of mounted men thundered over the rough-cut road. Kalu of the Zelrsaloz could sense that the horses were grateful to be off the mountain paths and were finally able to stretch their legs again. It was a relief that Kalu could relate to. Crossing the towering, moon pale mountains from the Vale of Kelandel had taken quite a toll on his squadron. The snow had come from nowhere and fallen thick and fast, slowing their progress to a crawl. Now emerging from the white and obscure realm onto the plain beyond the pass, a new world seemed to open before them and the effect on the horses and men was invigorating. Slipping down from the mountains with the dawn sun not quite visible far to the east, the first light streaked over the horizon like an arrow, showering the mountains in a blood red glow. Everywhere else there was darkness.

Kalu had known that crossing this late in the year would be a risk, with autumn close and winter just behind it, but the army could not afford to be cut off from the rest of the empire until the spring, not with the changes that were to come. He had not remembered the mountain passes being quite so hostile when they crossed three years past though. Then again that crossing had been in the summer, still at the dawn of their great adventure, the next step in the Doldun's glorious march across the world to the unknown and mysterious west. It was a time full of optimism and hope. This return trip was a more sorrowful affair, a duty rather than in the pursuit of the vision of their all-conquering king.

'Protect my legacy' were the last words the king had said to him in Kelantep. The role of the panther had been passed on to Tekolger's Companions now, to rule over the world that he had transformed.

The mist which had washed over the mountains giving them an

otherworldly feel, like a shimmer of moonlight sitting on a lake, and had obscured their path for the whole crossing, now it slowly cleared. The shadowy silhouette of the fortress he had been hunting began to come into view. The sheer stone of its walls blocking the light on the horizon and casting its own shadow onto the pale mountains. Once they had made a little further progress down the rocky road, the glow from the sunrise draped a plethora of colour over the plain, the shadowy citadel becoming a brown earthy colour with the flame of the dawn light touching the peak of its towers.

"Never thought I'd be pleased to see that place again." Zonhol of the Zelrsaloz called out. Clan membership had come to mean little during the years on campaign, but it did feel comforting to have one of his own as his captain of the White Shields. Zonhol had the classic ruddy olive skin, dark eyed and tan haired look of the clans of the Doldun, it was a welcome reminder of home. Zonhol's shout had shaken Kalu from his thoughts. Replying to his kinsman, he said,

"Nor I. Though the last time we were here, we were still eager. Whose idea was it to volunteer to lead the vanguard of the assault?"

Zonhol laughed,

"Yours if I remember right. You fought off some fierce competition for the honour of being the first man over the walls. And dragged the rest of the men with you." Zonhol was smiling as he answered, a cheerful, nostalgic look in his eye.

Kulanzow, the great gateway to the mountains, towered before them, scraping the sky. Three years past he had approached the citadel from the east. A trusted commander in an army buoyed by conquest, continuing its glorious progress spreading peace and civilisation. The sun, the Lord of the Cosmos, red Dunsun's great eye, watching his back.

"How could I turn down the challenge? Impregnable Kulanzow, a man-made mountain of stone and earth impossible to overcome." Kalo said. "Tekolger wasn't going to let the place slow him down, and the others would have taken the glory meant for us if I hadn't been so bold."

"True, we are the bite to Tekolger's growl after all." Zonhol answered cheerfully, a hint of nostalgia creeping into his voice too. "I am grateful we won't have to build another tower here though, gods that was harder work than the assault. Tekolger could have led us to storm the very halls of Dzottgelon itself it was so big."

Kalu answered him with a laugh, but he couldn't help but feel a strange longing for that time. Looking back from all that had happened since then. Already he missed the close quarters battle in service to the vision of his king. He had had purpose and the chance to prove himself in the eyes of gods and men, the chance to display his quality and fulfil his potential, forging a reputation to be remembered. It was Tekolger who had given him that opportunity.

Lost in his thoughts, he found himself hoping that in the future such opportunity would dawn again. Tekolger had brought Kalu a long way from his birthplace in the hills of Doldun amongst the clans so derided by the men of the coast. The Deltathelon, as his own people called those who dwelt near the sea, looked down on the clans of the hill country as backward semi-barbarians, seeing themselves the only true descendants of the people of the bright god, Xosu.

Tekolger was different though. Unlike his father who had warred against the clans, he had reached out to them and forged their unruly horsemen into a formidable and disciplined cavalry with which he would conquer the world. The king's patronage had seen Kalu rise to be a trusted general and Companion, a member of the king of the Doldun's most valued inner circle. Indeed, Tekolger had ensured that all the clans of the Doldun were represented amongst his Companions, as was the office's original intention.

It was this legacy that Kalu had come through the mountains determined to protect. Any dreams he had for himself, of lordship or even something humbler, paled into insignificance. Kalu sighed at those thoughts, the smile dropped from his lips, and he answered Zonhol,

"Let us hope the welcome we get there is warmer this time." He urged his horse onward. The column followed on, a tail of men and horse trailing behind Kalu, steam rising off rider and beast alike, hot from the ride despite the cool, crisp air of the silvery mountains.

The great size of the edifice blocked the view of the plain beyond, the sweeping lands of Zenian lay on the other side. Through the heart of Zenian flowed the rushing torrents of the Kelonzow river. Following its path would lead them to the city of Yorixori, the old capital of Zowdel before its fall, then the towering city of Torfub, once the seat of god-kings, and finally the great valley of Xortogun, shining and golden in the light of the sun. All lay behind and beyond the massive, thick, earth-coloured walls of Kulanzow.

The fortress seemed much more imposing now than it had when he had led the king's White Shields, with their pale white, zilthum lined armour, over the barricade. Now it struck Kalu as a permanent block to any progress one would hope to make. A blot on the landscape, trapping all who approached against its mighty facade and dividing the realms of east and west.

Kalu could not decide whether it was his previous naivety, the enthusiasm to impress his king or the melancholic mood that these memories now brought him, but Kulanzow certainly struck him differently this time. A block on the road to progress rather than a challenge to be overcome. Whatever the reason, he could appreciate the foresight of its builders, occupying a perfect position to impose order on a fractured and chaotic countryside.

The sky was beginning to glow red, crimson with a certain murderous beauty. The crowing of a flight of birds caught Kalu's eye. A maroon eagle, crowned with the light of the morning sun, and a white winged hawk rushed overhead, a huge snake caught in their talons, the creature writhing, struggling to break free and close to succeeding. The two birds appeared to be working together to carry the beast, but even so the serpent was on the verge of escaping their grasp. The two birds were followed by almost a dozen others, each desperate to catch up and share in the bounty.

A cry echoed overhead as another eagle, much larger and older than the first, burst from the clouds and descended on the group. A fight in the heavens followed as each of the birds tussled for the possession of the now limp snake. The hawk, which moments before had the beast in its grasp, suddenly fell away from the group and plunged toward the ground as the bigger eagle burst away, snake clutched in its talons. But the hawk was not done yet. Composing itself, it soared above the melee, before descending on the larger eagle in a fury. So ferocious was its assault, the other birds backed away, and the large eagle dropped the snake as it now began to fall. The hawk swooped in and took the snake once more in its grasp, joined again by the red eagle, the two birds flapped their wings and ascended to the heavens.

Kalu did not know what to make of such a spectacle, regretting that he had not brought one of the army's seers along for the crossing. But the birds flew off to his right and then toward the sun rising in the east. He decided to take this as an auspicious omen.

The column had come right under the shadow of the fortresses' earthy walls, the light of the sun still not quite bathing the world, just the pale mountains glimmering red to light the way. The rough-cut road they had been following ever since they left the peaks of Kelandel led the men directly to the western gate of Kulanzow. A bronze barrier now blocked their path, Kalu raised his hand to signal a halt. The rumble of the huge, old, reddish gates opening finally shook Kalu out of the last vestiges of the daydream he had been having ever since the citadel had come into sight. He had not realised how long he had let his mind wander for, but his column had covered the distance to the fortress in what seemed like an instant.

Kalu raised his hand again as the gates clanged open. Kicking his horse, he rode inside. The black hole of the entrance felt like descending through the missing eye of some god. His column trailed behind him like a long tail. He could feel the heat off the horses in the confined space of the entrance, and the men themselves seemed to glow in the darkness. They emerged into the central courtyard of the fortress. People scattered in front of them in all directions. From the skins they wore and their bearing, they looked to be the men of the mountains, wild and ferocious. They dispersed in a wave, and soon the courtyard was transformed, only a small group of officers was left there to meet Kalu's squadron.

The sun must have risen by now. Kalu was sure of it, but the smoke-dark inner walls of Kulanzow, rising high, were blocking it out, casting a shadow across the yard. Kalu leapt, agile as a deer, from his horse. His white cloak swished behind him as he did, like a serpent striking wildly at the air. It was now that he noticed the cold and felt his face flush as the cool air touched his hot skin.

Standing in the courtyard awaiting him, Kalu recognised an old comrade. No, more than that, he was almost a father to them all, Tekolger and his Companions. Zenukola of the Deltathelon. Zenu *Silver Eye* as many called him. He was held in much esteem and renown. Like many of the Deltathelon, he had the paler look of the Xosu about him rather than the clans.

One of the old guard, he had served both Tekolger and his father before him. Firmly committed to tradition. Hard, and unbending as he was, the old man was nevertheless reliable, loyal, and experienced. These qualities were why Tekolger had left him as his Hegemon of the west and Governor of Zowdel, the Togworwoh. Tekolger had revived the ancient Xortogun title. He was the perfect man to keep order in the newly conquered provinces and ensure the supply lines of the army remained open as Tekolger led his conquerors across the Vale of Kelandel and into Zentheldel, the twilight land.

Kalu smiled when he saw Zenukola, though his tongue felt thick in the cold, and a cloud of air sprung forth from behind his teeth. The one-eyed, one-armed veteran had a shaggy grey beard, longer than Kalu remembered it, and a cloak pulled over his head, no doubt to keep off the cold. Despite this disguised look, the one raven like eye and the shard of silver which glinted in the morning sun where his other eye used to be, gave Zenu away. He had lost his eye fighting for Tekolger's father and his arm on the field where the old king fell.

The grey governor held a stern visage like there was a troubled cloud lingering over him, and Kalu could not tell whether this was due to the circumstances of their meeting. The wily aged veteran had always been a difficult man to read, you did not survive long among the Doldun without being so. Despite the sternness of his look, Zenukola greeted Kalu as warmly as could be expected, but the gruff almost furious quality he always had in his voice was still there.

"Kalu of the Zelrsaloz! It is good see you. I trust your trip through the mountains was easier than the last time you made the crossing?"

The crescent of a smile crept over Kalu's face as he replied,

"There was only snow, ice, and the occasional rock fall. Only the gods trying to kill us this time."

Zenukola laughed like thunder and signalled to his guards to tend to Kalu's men and horses,

"Come inside Kalu, I have had quarters prepared for you next to my own. Rest if you will, tonight I have laid on a feast and I have even acquired a bard from back home. It may be cold and isolated up here, but a warm fire and a bard and you'd think we were back in Doldun."

Kalu smiled again, a full smile. Zenukola had not changed at all, still clinging to the old ways. Getting a bard to come this far could not have been an easy feat. The mention of home stirred up a longing to see the rolling hills of Doldun once more, or even the city of Konudulo which clung to the rough, windswept coast, but most of all the palace of the king at Thelanutep. Tired of the long years of war, the last few months had made Kalu realise just how much he missed Doldun.

"I see you are yet to go native Zenu? The exotic food and women not enough of a temptation for you?" Kalu said. The old man laughed his thunderous laugh again. As keen on tradition as he was, Zenukola could always laugh at himself. Answering he said,

"Our traditions were given to us by the gods for a reason Kalu. They won us an empire greater than any that has come before. Even at the height of the old kingdoms when god-kings ruled these lands, none could claim to rule as vast a kingdom as the Doldun do now. It would be foolish to abandon that which has given us so much." he paused, "No matter how exotic the women."

Kalu laughed, the crescent of his smile getting wider,

"Tekolger changed many things to win his empire and never lost the favour of the gods. You should at least give the food a try Zenu."

Still smiling, the old man replied,

"Maybe one day you'll convince me Kalu." He paused, a pensive look emerged from his wolf like mouth, "On a more serious topic, you need to tell me what happened in Zentheldel. Take your rest now. Later I will hear the whole tale from you."

Zenukola gestured to a man of the garrison to show Kalu to his quarters. Kalu thanked Zenukola and followed the soldier into the fortress.

* * *

The evening came quickly. The sun disappeared over the horizon as the haloed lord Dunsun descended from his throne into the underworld to seek out his lover, Betithelon, the rich king of the hidden realm's daughter. The moon crept over the horizon, the white goddess's watchful eye. Tholo, Queen of shining Dzottgelon and Dunsun's jealous consort was searching for her straying husband as Kalu looked out from the window of his quarters.

He was high up over the Kelonzow river as it snaked away into the distance. He felt a melancholy as the light drained from the world, the pale white moon was all that was left. There was a red tinge to its hue as the last vestiges of the daylight dripped away like the blood of a sacrifice on a priest's knife. The days always seemed shorter than anywhere else in the Kelandel mountains.

He changed into the pallid, silver-white tunic which Zenukola had left for him, warmed himself by the fire and left to make his way down into the fortress's great hall. Leaving his quarters, the heat from the fire trailed after him as he descended into the cold darkness of the stairs, down into the throat of the citadel.

The great hall of Kulanzow was dark when he entered, night had taken grip outside and the fire at the end of the hall was yet to be lit. A huge dolthilwood table stretched down the centre of the room, food had been laid across its entire length covering the blood-red wood beneath.

Zenukola had ordered a white bull to be sacrificed to the bright god, Xosu, specially for the occasion. Its blood had flowed like water when the priest cut its throat, cascading across the altar like a flood. The skin, pale as moonlight, now hung above the table. The bull itself, transformed over the open fire, lay at the centre of the table, the bounty of the earth strewn all around it, as if growing because of the sacrifice.

Eager guests hovered nearby, ready to devour the prize at the dawn of the feast. One man, a gruff man of the mountains, with wild dishevelled hair and a snow-white beard to match, had already taken his share of the bounty. He sat slumped at the table, head against the wood so that it was hard to tell where his hair ended and the snow cat fur which trimmed his blood-red cloak began. In his hand was clasped a drinking horn full to the brim with a deep red wine as dark as the sea. His bright red face and deep rouge tongue showed that he had already had more than his fill of the liquid though.

As Kalu moved further into the room the man stirred, a low rumble *Oh* echoed from him and the horn teetered precariously about to flood the table with its contents. The other guests paid him no mind, enjoying the fruits of the earth. Twice more the man stirred, before the horn tumbled over sending the wine cascading over the table and the men fleeing in all directions to escape the deluge.

A flash at the far end of the hall signalled the lighting of the fire and the return of light and warmth to the room. The men fleeing the deluge of wine found seats scattered around the central table. Zenu's guards, distinctive in their sky-blue cloaks and the white cloaks of Kalu's horsemen, were most prominent in the room. Interspersed amongst them were members of the local nobility, the furs of mountain cats and their long, greased hair and beards making them easy to see. Elsewhere one or two men of Zowdel could also be spotted, wearing the robes of the nobility of Xortogun, betraying their heritage.

Soon the whole room was indulging in the wine and food and the decadence which the bounty of empire had brought to this far-flung corner of the world.

Kalu hunted down a cup of unmixed wine from the huge bronze cauldron near the fire, a custom he had picked up on campaign, and took his place next to Zenukola on the raised platform at one end of the hall, feeling the warmth of the fire.

Zenu looked more relaxed now, wearing a white chiton in the Xosu style, trimmed with sky-blue and gold. Kalu sat silent, sipped his wine, and watched. Truth be told he was not in the mood for such a gathering.

At the height of the feast, a hush swept over the hall as Zenukola stood to speak. The light of the fire seemed at is brightest now, the darkness completely banished from the room. From the dais, Zenu loomed over everyone, the guests gathering round him in the same way that a storm gathers clouds, keen to hear his words. His voice was surprisingly booming and loud given his advanced years, echoing off the walls like a furious, uncontrolled thunder rumbling over the sky,

"Honoured guests, I hope everyone has had their fill of wine and food, because now is the time for the entertainment you have all been anticipating."

With a sweeping gesture from his one good hand, Zenukola drew everyone's attention to the door as it was swung open by two of his guardsmen. The open door ushered in a breeze from the darkness which lay beyond, blasting the fire and dimming the light of the room. The blasted fire answered by sending a surge of hot air into the face of everyone assembled, even reaching as far as the dais.

A blind man with a hooded cloak, clutching a staff, was led in by one of the guardsmen. The bard looked like he came from a story himself, gods knew how Zenu managed to get him out this far from home. Kalu whispered to his host,

"Where did you find him Zenu?"

The old general smiled, as if he had some hidden knowledge,

"He comes from Supokul, but was found roaming the countryside of Doldun, telling stories to survive. Two fishermen brought him to the king's court, puzzled about what to do with him. They claimed that he was a riddle but that his voice flowed as if he was born of a river. One of my men took him into my service and brought him out west to me."

The great hall quieted as the bard stepped in front of the fire. Invoking the gods in a rasping but melodic voice, he began to tell the tale of the Sinasa, the life and legacy of Tholophos and the fall of old Kolbos,

"Goddess, I speak of the tumult amongst the gods and roaring Tholophos, greatest hero of the Xosu, and his sons, inheritors of his legacy and the woe and strife that burden brought upon the Xosu. I speak of old Kolbos and the terrible destruction wrought on that haven by Tholophos' heirs and the Dusk which followed in its wake."

Kalu could not help but reflect on the last years and months. Strife seemed to be the legacy of all the Xosu and the Doldun, a thought which made him fear for the future and what dawn or dusk would fall upon them. Bards had a way of sewing the threads of time together so that no one knew when the present began or where the past ended, a cycle that made them seem prophetic.

"Dunsun's great son, Tholophos, lived through a time of growing darkness. As Dusk fell on the old kingdoms, their golden age came crashing down, the god-kings were cast from their thrones and man's connection with the realm of the gods was severed. The hubris and the decadence of the god-king's realms was their downfall. As disaster erupted from the earth, daemons emerged from their hidden worlds to overrun each kingdom in turn. But Tholophos was a bright light in the darkness, the light that rose even as Dusk fell. Xosu come again, he reunited the bright god's people. A saviour, as prophecy foretold."

Kalu was immediately thrown back to his childhood as the bard began to get into his stride. The tales of the past had always fascinated him and the roaming rhapsodes captivated him, so much so that he had dabbled in the arts of storytelling himself as a child, although he was always more skilled with the lyre than the spoken word. That was before he had met Kelbal of the Deltathelon and Tekolger, who brought him to the court of the old king.

The story the bard was singing rung true to him though. The meddling of the gods in the affairs of men was often the source of chaos in the world. A family dispute, turning the world of men to strife and war. The weight of such a burden was not lost on Kalu, such a load now awaited the leaders of the Doldun.

He took a long gulp from his cup of wine and looked around the room, everyone's gaze was transfixed on the blind bard as he recanted the tale of

Tholophos' legacy. All but those who were already too drunk to stand or who had taken the opportunity to raid the table for the choicest pieces of meat remaining.

"As a child Tholophos was cast out from his royal home through the manipulation of the jealous white armed goddess. He was found and raised by Wildmen, those horned lords of the woods, and he became a fine huntsman."

With the recital in full swing, Zenukola, in a hushed tone, said,

"Kalu, you must tell me what happened in Zentheldel. The reports I received were intermittent at best. I was only able to piece together your movements; it gave an impression of chaos and slaughter but no coherence. How did it happen?"

The question brought Kalu back to the present, away from his dreams of the past,

"I'm not really sure what happened Zenu. Everything moved very quickly, decisions had to be made fast and I don't think any of us was certain what to do."

Zenukola's black, inquisitive eye narrowed, but there was a comforting look to him,

"I understand that Kalu and you made the right choice to bring the army back. Difficult decisions will need to be made in the coming months and the empire is still new and fragile. Tekolger was the glue holding it all together, without him there will be strife. Already I hear rumour of rebellion here in Zowdel and the Rilrpitu are gaining in confidence and daring. Tales whispered on the wind talk of a new great Saradi gathering men to him on the steppe."

Kalu nodded his head in agreement. The bard continued in the background,

"In the grip of madness, Tholophos raged, slaughtering and driving back the cruel Bulodon, the children of Bul, whose wail reverberated around the world."

Kalu continued,

"It was Kelbal who made the decisions, the only one with a clear enough head to step forward and act. Without the king everything spiralled out of control very quickly, we found ourselves having to fight rebellions and then the veterans we settled attempted to march back home. Zentheldel is an alien and strange realm, most of them were demanding to be given land back in Xosupil instead."

The stern look from before returned to Zenukola's face,

"What arrangements were left in the new provinces? Will they hold?"

Kalu turned to face the old general,

"The garrisons and colonists were sent back to the fortified settlements we had constructed and the kings who had submitted were made to reaffirm their oaths of loyalty. It will hold for now, but who knows what future Yulthelon has in store for us. Thentherzaw, tragic as it was, will serve as an example and go some way to deter further rebellions. The shock of it seemed to stem the worst of the chaos, although the lands are now broken and much diminished."

Zenukola nodded in approval. The mention of Thentherzaw did not seem to register with him, but then he asked,

"What happened at Thentherzaw?"

"Dolzalo happened." Kalu replied, "He blamed Talehalden for what happened to the king, although I could see little evidence of his guilt. Talehalden had left the army to return to his city. Whilst I led the White Shields to put down the rebellions, Dolzalo turned the bulk of the army on the city. The sack was total, that haven was completely destroyed. He hammered it into the ground. Burnt and bleached bones and the corpse of a city was all that remained when I arrived."

Zenukola nodded again and said,

"Dolzalo always was a slave to his emotions, give the man an army and chaos was always sure to follow."

"His mind restored to him by the sorcerers of old Kolbos, Tholophos was proclaimed High King of all the Xosu. But when the Salxosu refused to submit, he defeated their king in single combat, Dzotthisoni, and placed his own son, pale faced Semontek on the throne of white-gold Kolbos. Uniting all the Xosu once more under his rule, a feat not achieved by any save Xosu himself." The bard's voice sang in the background.

Looking Kalu directly in the eye, Zenukola said,

"Tekolger was more than just a man, he was the best and brightest of us all, he was half a god the way he forged this empire and spread his message. Without him there is no one to hold the army together, a return to the fratricide of our past is almost inevitable if we do not find a strong ruler. But I fear no man can replace Tekolger's bright presence at the top. We need to appoint a successor quickly and all gather round behind them, a show of unity. Otherwise, I think our new empire will not be the most welcoming place for us. For now, our new subjects are in awe of Tekolger still, unable to comprehend how a man achieved what he did. They look upon him and us as demi-gods, we need to use that and act quickly to stave off chaos."

Kalu listened carefully. No man knew better than Zenukola of the fratricidal nature of the Doldun's past. He had lived through it after all;

the invasions of wandering Rilrpitu, the raids by the Zummosh and the civil war the bards called 'The Defiance of the Clans' which Tekolger's father had bloodily ended. But such things are easily forgotten and, with the great prize of empire in sight, no doubt the Doldun would not remember their history. And none of them could hope to fill the void left by Tekolger.

The bard raised his voice,

"The unity of Tholophos would be fleeting, a bright shining light amongst the darkness of the Dusk. War, turmoil, and destruction would follow his poisonous death at the wraith-like shadowy hands of the Kinsolsun. The children of Sem, those tale telling, wandering wizards of the sea.

In the years to come fires would gut old Kolbos, and the gods indulged in the orgy of destruction. Tildun, Tholophos' eldest son and successor, would be struck down as his men burned old Kolbos. To this day no one knows who struck those blows. Some claim it was his jealous brothers, some that it was the art of the Kinsolsun before they danced back into the depths, maybe it was even the gods themselves in revenge for the sacrilege committed the day that old Kolbos was destroyed. But it was on the point of those blades that the glory of the Xosu fell.

The years following would see the Dusk of the old kingdoms. A time of darkness would rise in their place, a broken world where chaos and disorder swept civilised life before it. The heroes would disappear, the connection once shared to the realms of the gods was lost, and man became much diminished in stature and achievement."

The bard had finished the recital for the night. The rhapsode would need many more evenings to tell the rest of the tale of Tholophos reign and the Dusk of days, for now he sat and let his words sink in.

ZENUKOLA

The quarters he had found waiting for him at Kulanzow were not what he had come to expect in his old age. As the elder statesman of the king's inner circle and his effective regent whilst Tekolger was campaigning in the west, Zenukola of the Deltathelon had grown used to a royal level of luxury. The governor's residence in Yorixori had once been a king's palace and the standard of living it had afforded him as Governor of Zowdel, the Togworwoh in the Xortogun tongue that Tekolger had insisted on using, and Hegemon of the West, matched that pedigree.

The realisation made him shudder and a sense of shame slowly crept over him. His younger self would have laughed to see him. How he had changed from a young man schooled in the crucible of battle and the rigours of war. Now he was an aged veteran annoyed that the quarters provided to him in a frontier fortress were not luxurious enough. Wallowing in the shame for a moment, indulging in the feeling of guilt, he almost let the notion overcome him. It was a fleeting moment that felt like a lifetime, but Zenukola soon shook himself out of the remorseful emotion, reminding himself what an arrogant fool he had been in his youth.

It was true that his younger self would not have needed such luxury, but he had worked hard enough to secure some comfort in his old age. It was not like he shirked from battle and avoided a glorious death on the field. He had merely been unable to find the right man to give it to him. He had sacrificed an eye to gain the knowledge that death in battle was perhaps not as glorious as the bards would make out and lost an arm to punish his hubris.

The feeling of shame dissipated completely as Zenu stood quickly, reacting to the sound of footsteps coming down the corridor. The hurried pace of the steps let Zenukola know their reason for coming was urgent.

Scratching his missing eye and placing the silver shard he always wore in the socket when in public back in its place, the aged governor moved toward the door. He was greeted there by Pelu of the Deltathelon, his trusted aide, breathless and wind swept, mud strewn over his legs and stinking of sweat and horse. Pelu had been with him since he was appointed to the governorship of Zowdel. With the ruddy hue of his skin, dark eyes, and bronze hair, Pelu was the image of what one imagined when conjuring up a portrait of a man of the Deltathelon. Zenukola had come to seem him almost like a son.

"Hegemon, I came directly from Yorixori with a message for you. I thought it best to seek you out immediately on arrival."

"Well, you had better come into my quarters, Pelu."

Taking a stepping back and allowing Pelu to enter the room, Zenukola gestured to for the young man to deliver his message,

"These words come direct from the mouth of Dotmazo. His messenger told it to me in person having spoken to no one else beforehand.

Dotmazo says that he will mourn the death of the king and will sacrifice in his honour. He assures you that all is well in Doldun and Xosupil and that the empire needs stability now. The new king must be crowned quickly and brought to Xortogun to be introduced to the army with all haste. He also wants you to know that Dotmazo is ready to welcome Tekolger's closest Companions back to Doldun."

Dotmazo was always cryptic and cautious in his messages, trying to keep his own hands clean and his intentions hidden. But Zenu had known him long enough to read between the lines. He replied,

"And what of the army?"

Without hesitation, Pelu answered,

"All is in place, Supo arrived in Yorixori before my departure. He has marched his northern garrison south and the men are encamped a few days north of Torfub. They have been informed of the doubling of their salary for the year to see in the new king's reign. Supo will meet us with his personal guard in Yorixori. I even heard rumours that clouds of Rilrpitu horse lords have been spotted blowing south."

A smile rippled over Zenukola's lips,

"Thank you, Pelu. What news of the rest of the empire, of Tekolger's wives and son? The babe?"

Pelu was ever a source of all the goings on in the empire and beyond. Zenu had come to rely on the whisperings he heard from across the empire. Pelu continued,

"The rumours of rebellion continue and there has been some sporadic violence, but nothing serious. The preparation for the coming winter is what concerns many.

Tekolger's Xortogun bride is well, though her birthing bed has sapped much of her strength. The babe is strong and healthy, he has the look of his father I am told. She will await the arrival of the army and the king's body in Torfub to accompany him to his final resting place.

His other wives are in Doldun, Dotmazo is keeping them close. Especially Keluunsen and Koliathelanu, her son." the young man paused to gather his thoughts to him. "I also hear that the temple of Xosu in Tekolgertep has finally been completed and the Putedun have appointed a new emissary to the king. Konguz the man names himself. They are pushing for trading rights in the city again.

Beyond our borders, the Red and White Council of Thasotun are still struggling to control the White Islands. Piracy is rife there, the rumours of ships disappearing increases daily, some completely without trace. But the King of Gelodun's campaign into the lands of Thelizum goes well. The last report I received he was marching on Gottoy. Not a bad outcome for us, a powerful republic on our border would have created all sorts of problems in the future."

Zenu would be blind and deaf without Pelu he reflected. Satisfied he said,

"Take your rest, tomorrow morning you are to return to Yorixori and have Supo send this message on to Dotmazo:

Zenukola agrees with his assessment that the empire needs first and foremost stability with a new king to continue to rule the empire in the manner in which the Doldun have always ruled themselves. I will make the arrangements in the west if he sees to the situation in the east."

Zenu paused for a second and considered the cloud of darkness that suddenly came upon him, then continued,

"And let Dotmazo know that the shades of Tekolger's comrades must indeed be shattered. A return to Doldun would be most welcome for them."

Pelu nodded his head and left the room at a pace.

Dotmazo's message and Supo's actions meant everything was ready. Zenu followed in Pelu's footsteps. He may be an old man, but he still had something to give the new world whose dawn Tekolger had overseen. An ordered transition of power to ensure a dusk did not fall on the great king's legacy. Tekolger may have been wise and formidable, but he had not lived through the years of civil war like Zenukola had. Zenu had seen how men, kin even, could tear themselves apart in strife. It had taken a strong and capable king to end that war and it would take a strong and capable ruler to keep Tekolger's empire from suffering the same fate. *The oath I gave your father, Tekolger, to watch over you has tested me in ways I could not have imagined, but I will see it fulfilled.*

It was well known that Tekolger wished that a son by the Xortogun woman Surson Tora Ya Kuria would succeed him, but the long regency that would ensue would only bring back the days of endless infighting. Besides, she was not of the Doldun, and Zenu did not care that she was a descendent of Yoruxoruni. Making her child king would mean handing over the empire that the Doldun had fought so hard to win to the Xortogun. Zenu would not see that happen and the suspicion of a wider conspiracy around the death of the king was one he could not shake.

Heading down into the bowels of the fortress, he found a new spring of energy as the evening set in. All was in order in the empire, now he would check to ensure all was in order for the following morning when he expected the main body of the army to arrive. Kalu of the Zelrsaloz had given him a good idea of what to expect. The young Companion had been a great help in the last few days of preparation and Zenu hoped he would be an ally in the future as well, so long as Kalu's innocence could be proved beyond doubt. His closeness to Kelbal was a mark of concern. It would be a shame to lose such a talented Companion, but Zenukola would do whatever was necessary to preserve the empire, even if it pained him to see it done.

The fortress was alive with activity as the garrison busied themselves preparing for the arrival of thirty thousand veterans. The citadel was too small to keep such a host inside its walls, but quarters had been prepared inside for the generals and officers. The rest of the army would sleep in a camp Zenukola's men had constructed on the plain below the walls.

He knew the whole force would not arrive at the same time. Kalu had informed him that the army had set off from beyond the Vale of Kelandel in three marching columns a few days apart. They planned to regroup at the stronghold of Kulanzow on the other side of the mountains before departing for the heart of the empire. The supplies at Kulanzow would not last long, however, and it may suit Zenu's own purposes to see the army continue the march into Zowdel divided. That all depended on Kelbal and his fickle red moods.

Unpredictable things, mountains, Zenu thought. Old and solid as they were, seemingly unchanging, but hidden within their depths the unexpected always lurked. The plan may have been as such, but it would not play out like that. The columns would have become drawn out, or delayed or even lost, or all three. The best Zenu could do was assume the entire army would arrive sometime over the next few days and prepare as best he could.

He reached the inner courtyard of Kulanzow. The space inside the towering walls of the fortress was surprisingly large, big enough for a whole squadron of horse to mount and form into a marching column, but the yard was still overshadowed by the towering black walls. Zenu stopped the duty officer to ensure that all was ready for the army's arrival,

"Captain!"

"Yes, Hegemon." the captain answered confidently, clearly taking pride in his work. This pleased Zenukola. Koloathutalaz of the Deltathelon was the man's name, another of Zenu's own clan, the only men that could be trusted in such positions.

"How are the preparations progressing? Is all in order?" he boomed.

"Yes, Hegemon. The officer's quarters are all ready and the marching camp is finished. The carts behind you are filled with supplies ready to be taken to the army once they are settled in the camp." The captain said assuredly, lifting an arm from under the blue and white cloak he wore over his bronze cuirass to point to the carts filled with food and firewood.

He looked around at the meticulous preparations. The clans may have helped in the conquest, but it was only with the firm hand of the Deltathelon that the world would be steered toward civilisation,

"Very good", the old general rumbled with satisfaction. A well-ordered world brought Zenu great joy. A simple pleasure he found increasingly pleasing the older he got, less chance of a need for impulse and recklessness. He felt his phantom fingers flex at the thought of impulse, it was such things that had cost him his arm.

Satisfied he had done all he could to ensure the fortress was ready to receive its guests, Zenu finished his inspection of the preparations and returned to his quarters.

The door squeaked as he pushed the heavy wood open. The walls were a contrast to his quarters in Yorixori. Those were constructed from a sandstone imported from Xortogun with friezes of the gods of the great valley and its distinctive hieroglyphs. Zenu's quarters in Kulanzow were simple, functional, plain and a grey black colour carved from a stone quarried from the mountains themselves. Well-made and solid but lacking something. The room may not have been up to the standard of luxury to which Zenu was becoming accustomed, but he could still feel the call of his bed creeping up on him and decided that he would succumb to its cries.

* * *

The blast of the trumpets echoed off the sides of the mountains as the gleaming snake wound its way into view from the ice-covered peaks, emerging from the eye of the cataclysm to a world transformed. Just as Zenukola predicted, the first of the columns of the army slipped out of the mountains as Dunsun took his seat on his throne, the sun surfacing over the horizon to warm them. He wondered if the experience would have changed the Companions, and which of them was most suspect. For it surely must have been one of the Companions who dealt the king his death blow. He was almost certain that Kelbal was involved.

Zenu stood on the walls of Kulanzow and observed the column of men slide its way slowly down the rough mountain track. He had been on the walls watching since before the dawn. Zenu found himself rising earlier and earlier the older he got, the relentless march of time did have some benefits.

Just specks in the distance at first, but slowly, even his old eye could make out individual shapes. The pearly serpent, with glinting spears like sharp teeth, disintegrating into a mass of humanity. *That is the future marching towards me*, he reflected. The fate of the empire would be decided in the coming weeks and months and Zenukola could do nothing but react when the inevitable confronted him. Whether the result be a dawn or a dusk for the Doldun was the only question that haunted him.

Turning to the guardsman on sentry duty stood next to him, Zenu sought the power of his young eyes,

"How many do you think there are?"

The young man leant on his spear and squinted at the column, as if he were trying to count every man and horse.

"A few thousand Hegemon, maybe ten thousand. But I cannot yet see the end of the column."

Zenu nodded, as he had expected, this was only a part of the force. Thirty thousand men had set out from Kelantep, but Kelbal had sensibly divided them. Standing abruptly as the sun streamed into the valley beyond, Zenu shouted thunderously down to the captain of his guard,

"Make ready to receive our guests, you will have at least ten thousand tired and hungry men to feed."

Already halfway to the courtyard as his bodyguards fell in behind him, Zenu shouted to the men in the stables,

"Bring my horse, I will ride out to meet them."

The courtyard erupted with activity, the silence of the morning shattered by the shouts of guardsmen and stable boys. In an instant ten horses were brought forward. Zenu mounted his horse with his one good hand. Refusing the assistance offered by the stable boy with the distinctive long greased black hair of the native mountain men. Without waiting for his bodyguards to mount their rides, he set off like lightning.

Despite enjoying comfort in his old age, Zenu missed the life on campaign. The hardship and the comradery, but most of all the ability to charge off astride a horse and challenge body and spirit to their limits. Those feelings flooded back to Zenukola as the gate opened and the tips of the pikes of Tekolger's legendary phalanx glistened like the teeth of some great leviathan in the distance.

He rode hard, harder than he should have on this mountain track, the breeze of the fresh mountain air breathed the vigour of youth back into the veteran general. Even his one-handed grip did not slow him down. Eventually, Zenu's guard caught up and the men formed up behind their general as they covered the few stades distance to the column.

At the head of the formation rode a man in an imposing antlered helm, crested with long eagle feathers dyed red, that blazed bright in the morning sun, mirroring Dunsun on his throne. He wore the fire red cloak of the King's Companions and white gold, zilthum lined armour, that near indestructible ore which the Kinsolsun had used for their craft. There was little of the metal left in the world, but Tekolger had acquired the sets of armour and swords that were held in the treasury of the League of Butophulo after he conquered the city.

It was said that the League had painstakingly gathered what zilthum items remained from old Kolbos at huge expense, scattered as they had been after the city's sack. Three hundred sets of zilthum lined armour, forged by the smiths and sorcerers of old Kolbos, were given to the Companions and the White Shields, indeed it was how his elite soldiers had gained their name. Tekolger had also gifted his Companions with a pure zilthum blade, each one named and storied with a history dating back to before the founding of old Kolbos. Not even the smiths of that great city could work with pure zilthum. Only the Kinsolsun themselves possessed that skill and they had not been seen since the bright god, Xosu, cast them from the Thelonbet.

It had been three long years, and Kelbal of the Deltathelon had been transformed in the crucible of red hot Zentheldel, even so Zenukola recognised him instantly. Despite having the look of the Deltathelon about him, paler than the other clans, a ruddy hue to his skin more than olive, he wore his red streaked, bronze beard braided in the style of the Xortogun kings, jutting out from his chin like a tongue, but it was his eyes which gave him away. One as green as the forest and the other amber like the sun. Both of which flashed like thunder when Kelbal's ire was roused.

Zenu, Dotmazo and Supo were the king's most experienced and trusted generals, but Kelbal had grown up with the king and was as close a confidant as Tekolger ever had. Too close perhaps, they had picked up some strange habits and customs from their Xosu cousins.

Kelbal had been there since the beginning, at the point of every cavalry charge and in the vanguard of every lightning advance. It was a natural choice for the army to turn to him when the king was taken from them. But, like Tekolger, he had the naivety and the arrogance of youth and a head full of philosophies and prophecies. The challenges ahead would need the experience and wiser heads of older men to keep this ragged band of survivors from destroying the empire Tekolger had forged from so many disparate worlds.

The feeling of suspicion overshadowed everything for Zenukola though, despite the dawn light. Kelbal was the king's closest Companion, but that also gave him the greatest opportunity to poison Tekolger, and Kelbal had become worryingly close to the Xortogun.

To Kelbal's side was the unmistakable gigantic figure of Pelapakal of the Keluazi, on foot but still almost as tall as Kelbal riding beside him. The figure to the other side of Kelbal must have been Doluzelru. Pelapakal and his twin brother were almost inseparable. *Gods, I barely recognise Doluzelru, he has become lean and wiry*, Zenu thought, *the scorching heat of the twilight lands has transformed him as if by some arcane trickery.*

Behind them rumbled a gold-plated carriage. Simple, but clearly a work of devotion by men on campaign far from home. It was pulled by Thaludaban, Tekolger's wild but loyal horse. The stallion wore the raiment of the king and the red feathered headdress which made them both seem a fiery menace as they streaked across the field. The pelt of the panther Tekolger had brought down on his first hunt, for which the horse was named, was strewn across his saddle. Tekolger's preserved body no doubt lay inside the carriage.

Kelbal raised his hand and a trumpet blast rank out, the column coming to a halt as one. Zenu, impressed with the discipline the men still maintained, rode forward to greet them and boomed,

"Kelbal, it is good to see you return safe from Zentheldel. I would have wished it to be under better circumstances however."

Kelbal answered in the solemn way he sometimes had,

"It is good to see you too Zenu. Right now, I think we need some of your wisdom."

He brought his horse alongside Kelbal,

"The way Kalu told it, you showed flashes of Tekolger himself. It can't have been easy to keep the army in line given the situation you found yourself in."

Kelbal looked straight at him, a hint of a tear lurked in the depths of the young man's mismatched eyes. He replied,

"I couldn't keep everyone in line. It took Tekolger raising himself from his death bed to rein Dolzalo in. I fear that last exertion may have been what killed him." Kelbal stopped before his voice cracked, but the emotion in the thought was plain to see on his face. His pain was further revealed as he abruptly changed the subject. *But is it with grief or guilt?* Zenu wondered,

"Kalu arrived here safe then? That is welcome news. I feared for him in these mountains, but there was no one else I dared trust with the vanguard."

Nodding his head, Zenukola replied,

"Yes, he has been here for several days now, his aid with the preparations have been invaluable. Zentheldel must have had a positive effect on him, in some ways at least." Zenu dropped his voice so the men could not hear,

"You did all you could for the army in the twilight land Kelbal, Yulthelon had already decided the king's fate. It is our path now to ensure the king's legacy is secure. Where is Dolzalo?"

"He is bringing forward the rear column. I let him have a command to keep him busy for the march back. We won't see him for at least a week yet." Kelbal answered, not acknowledging Zenu's attempt at consoling him. This Kelbal seemed different from the one who Zenu had known, there was a melancholy to everything he did. Raising his voice to a boom again, Zenu continued,

"Very good, I see you have learnt more than just the art of war after the years of campaigning. Come let us head to Kulanzow. Quarters are prepared for you, and a camp for the men that they will not have to build themselves. We will talk more of what happens next there."

Kelbal nodded and gave the signal to continue. Zenu's mounted guard falling in behind him as the column set off again.

After a moment of reflection, Kelbal spoke in answer to Zenu,

"First, we make sure the empire is secure, we fought hard and sacrificed much for the lordship of Zenian. It is Tekolger's legacy and must be held. Once that is settled, we can decide how that legacy will be passed on."

Zenukola could hear the resolve in Kelbal's voice, but he pressed his point anyway,

"We may only be able to secure that legacy by passing it on quickly. Give the peoples of the empire a stable succession and a quick and smooth transition of power before the seed of rebellion plants itself."

Kelbal looked at Zenu pensively,

"You are much more experienced with these matters than any of us Zenu, but the king's heir is yet to be born. Tekolger's wishes for the succession are clear, but the conditions of it are not. Who knows whether the gods will grant Surson a boy or a girl. Either way a long regency is sure to follow."

Zenu could see the steadfastness on the Companion's face,

"You are right, but the Doldun need a strong king. With the past as our guide, the nobility has always selected a successor from the king's family if no clear heir is present at the time of his death. Stability and strength are needed now more than ever, else I fear a return to our past strife is inevitable."

He did not reveal the news of the child's birth. An underhand trick unbecoming of a man of his rank, but sacrifices needed to be made for the good of the Doldun. Kelbal's expression turned to one of suspicion with a wildness behind his eyes that stabbed deep into Zenu's gut,

"A clear heir to the king will be present imminently, Zenu, and Doldun's power lays in the arms of its men. These will give us the stability and strength you talk of."

Zenu smiled, laughed like thunder, and replied,

"And a strong arm you will be indeed for the new king. These are questions which I am sure we can find an answer to in time. But you must be tired and fed up with marching, go to your quarters and rest for a while."

Kelbal nodded as the column came under the shadow of the fortress.

* * *

The snaking column dispersed, and the army soaked into their temporary quarters sprawling over the plain. The officers made their way through the heavy bronze gates and into the imposing citadel, disappearing into their respective accommodation. Zenu retreated to his own.

Kelbal had proved more resolute than he hoped for, which only made him more suspicious. If he was set on holding the kingship open for Tekolger's Xortogun child, then a lengthy and difficult regency was inevitable. Far better to appoint the son of one of the king's other wives. Koliathelanu, Keluunsen's son, was almost a man grown and his mother was of the Deltathelon. Besides Surson was not of the Doldun and so the child was not a full-blooded king, an heir to the line of Tholophos. The army and the leading men of the Doldun would surely not accept that now that the king was gone.

Zenu ordered his guard to summon Pelu before he left for Yorixori and headed to his quarters. Moments later there was a knock at the door and in stepped the slight figure of Pelu, in the riding leathers of the Doldun clansmen. A short cloak to keep off the autumn wind and the fur lined leather cap prevalent among the hill clans. The riding gear was probably the best contribution the clans had made to life in their homeland.

"Pelu, our well-ordered transition looks to be in jeopardy. I sounded out Kelbal on the road into the fortress. He seems intent on following through with Tekolger's absurd wish for his heir to be Surson's child. We both know the danger that will bring with it. I swear Tekolger's obsession with Yoruxoruni was something more than natural, almost like that Xortogun witch cast a spell on him. It is a trick to have a man of Xortogun once more sat upon the Amber Throne and I fear Kelbal has been taken in by the conspiracy. I have seen enough of the woman to know that she is that Salxosu women come again. You were not in my employ at the time, but in his eighteenth year Tekolger attended the games at Thelonigul, he even won prizes in the sprint and the javelin. He should have been pleased with the glory he had brought to the Doldun. Instead, he returned with an entourage of philosophers, scholars, mystics, and courtesans, not least a sultry Salxosu woman who spoke with earthy tones, Kisuunsinu she called herself. She left Tekolger restless and ranting about kings and prophecy, she had even taken him to see the Oracle of Xosu. It was all a trick of course, I had hoped the king had learnt his lesson, but then Surson found him. It will be the death of us all if her and her kin were to succeed."

Pelu pulled the same pensive face he always did as his mind raced to tackle a problem, and Surson had been a problem ever since she put the notion of marriage and an heir with the blood of Yoruxoruni into Tekolger's head. The last attempt to remove the witch had gone sourly and Zenu had lost several dear friends and comrades, barely escaping suspicion himself. The blood moon conspiracy men had taken to calling it, due to the hue of the moon on the night his comrade's blood was spilled. The superstitious side of Zenu suspected that the Xortogun woman had used some ancient magics to spy on them through the moon. How else could she have known their intentions? Pelu continued,

"That would be inconvenient Hegemon. Kelbal almost certainly will have Tekolger's army at his back. The White Shields for sure and the others will likely follow their lead. The memory of the dead king will do much of his work for him. They would give Kelbal teeth and from those teeth who knows what may spring."

"What is the but, Pelu? I know that look on your face" Zenu said impatiently,

"That is only one army. This is an eventuality we planned for. You have another army, as do Dotmazo and Supo, none of which serveed directly under the king. All of you have long years of experience behind you going back to before Tekolger. Everything is in place, stick to what we planned. The army must pass through your territory now, and with

Rilrpitu warbands heading south, Kelbal will be forced to dispatch men to deal with them. With Supo's forces at Torfub, we gain in strength and Kelbal weakens every step the men take closer to Xortogun. As well as this, Dotmazo holds Doldun itself for us, and the king's other wives, his son and mother. And if our suspicion is correct, Kelbal will fall."

The words brought back some hope to Zenu. Kelbal's utterances had made him fear the future for the first time for years, worrying that Tekolger's reign would prove a false dawn. The civil war of his youth and the invasions of Zummosh and Rilrpitu which had plagued the Doldun seemed like a bad memory now, but a long regency would only make them more likely to return. He had spent his youth fighting to keep the kingdom intact, putting down the pretensions of the clans, sacrificing an eye, an arm, and a king in the process. He would not spend his twilight years doing the same.

"We will need to act quickly. Those advantages will only diminish with time, and I don't want any bloodshed."

Pausing to think for a moment. His old age had made him more cautious than he used to be, and the realisation that he would need to put his plans into action had made Zenu nervous for the first time in many years,

"Very well, we continue the path we have started. Move to force Kelbal into a position he cannot escape and compel him to listen. I fear we will not be able to prove his guilt, if there is any, and it may be that he is just a pawn of the Xortogun anyhow. Besides, if we spill blood, civil war will surely follow, and our actions will all be for nothing."

Pelu nodded in agreement and said,

"You need to act as quickly as possible. It would be best to force the issue before we reach Torfub. Whilst the Companions are still divided and in shock, and in Zowdel where we are strongest."

Zenu acknowledged this fact and Pelu left to ride for Yorixori.

KALU

4

He hit the ground with a thud, so hard that he thought his head would leave a crater in the earth. The wind was knocked right out of him, the dawn sky spinning above him and his heart pounding in his ears. *I should have known better than to accept his challenge,* he thought.

Pelapakal of the Keluazi stood over him and laughed, as Kalu desperately sucked in air and tried to catch his breath. Boxing with a man known as Bronze Fist because he hits as fiercely as the ram of a ship was a bad idea. Pelapakal was as tall as a horse with the broad chest of a builder and had won the boxing and wrestling competitions in every single games Kalu could remember. It was a shame that he was not allowed to compete at the games in Thelonigul. He could have been the greatest champion in their history, the crowds would have followed him to the ends of the earth. His enormous opponent smiled through his thick beard and said,

"Is Pale Arm ready to give in yet, or is there still more fight in you?"

His jaw ached where Pelapakal had landed the blow. It felt like the man had cracked him open as easily as he would an egg, but Kalu stumbled to his feet, pain washing over him,

"You will have to do better than that if you want me to back down." He said defiantly, hiding his discomfort. Pelapakal laughed deeply and smiled again, the sweat on his brow had begun to steam in the cold mountain air. Pushing his sweat soaked, tan hair from his face he raised his fists into a boxer's stance and sailed forward like a hunter who had acquired a new quarry. Pelapakal may not have been the most subtle or calculating of the King's Companions, but he had the instincts of a warrior. He loosed a fist, straight and fast as an arrow, at Kalu, who ducked and weaved to avoid another blow. The fist flew past him, so close it felt as though it may scorch his cheek.

Quicker than Kalu imagined the big man could move, he was poised to strike again. Kalu was not so fast. The second jolt caught him in the gut and burned through him as if he had been struck by some god idly tossing thunderbolts from the sky. But this time he managed to keep his feet, stumbling backwards.

"You are too focused on the obvious threat my friend. Be aware of the fist that is poised to strike. This is how I learnt to prowl the arena like a panther." Pelapakal said, clearly enjoying himself.

The giant is right, he thought as he tried to compose himself. Kalu had been focusing on tackling the enormous challenge in front of him head on, grappling with a man twice his size. It was a battle he could not hope to win, yet the greatest danger was where he least expected it to appear. Strength against strength was a fight that Kalu was destined to lose, but there were other ways to overcome an opponent. Especially as Pelapakal became more confident in his superiority in the fight.

Kalu started to circle around his spirited adversary. The patch of earth they had cleared to become the arena was imperfect at best. There was no flat land around Kulanzow and so the fighting circle was on a slight hill. Kalu had been sticking to the higher ground, figuring that he could negate Pelapakal's height advantage that way, but that strategy was clearly flawed. It had put him eye level with the giant Companion, but that only made Kalu an easy target forced to try and play Pelapakal at his own game. A far better approach was to sacrifice the height advantage to force Pelapakal to play by his rules. He slid to the bottom of the hill. His opponent looked to be three times the size now, looming over him like some giant from the old stories with a catlike grin. But now Kalu had placed himself between the sun and his adversary, enlisting Dunsun as his ally.

Pelapakal advanced on him swiftly, the hunter in him sensing the time to strike. In that moment, the clouds cleared, and the dawn sun dazzled the giant if only for a second. That was the chance. Kalu bounded forward, getting inside Pelapakal's reach for the first time that morning. He threw all his weight behind his strike and buried his clenched fist in the Companion's belly. Pelapakal heaved as the breath was knocked from him. Not wanting to waste his advantage, Kalu threw another punch and another, like a cobra recoiling and launching itself at its prey. The giant stumbled backwards, stunned from the blows. Then the warrior spirit in him took over and he lunged forward, catching Kalu off guard once again.

The two men tumbled down the hill, landing in a pile at the bottom. They lay there in a dazed silence, only broken when Pelapakal roared with laughter. Kalu was taken aback for a second, but soon found the laughter flooding over him.

"You learn quickly my friend, but I don't think boxing is the sport for you." Pelapakal said as the pair struggled to their feet. Kalu clasped him on the shoulder and answered,

"I think you are right; the gods did not see fit to grant me your size and strength. I will stick to hunting and the sprint from now on."

Still laughing, they made their way back up the hill, to the wagon where Doluzelru of the Keluazi was sat. Doluzelru could not have been more of a contrast to his twin brother. Where Pelapakal was giant, Doluzelru was slight. Whilst Bronze Fist was impetuous his brother was calculating and considered, one had the strength of a builder the other the mind of an architect. The only ways in which they were alike was the tan-coloured hair and olive skin that they shared. But the same could have been said for all the men of the clans, Kalu included, even if Kalu's lighter eyes marked him out.

Despite their difference the twins were inseparable. They had come to the court of the king together, or in truth they had been chosen to be wards when Tekolger's father, Kenkathoaz, chose to build a new royal palace in the lands of the Keluazi. Along with Kalu and Kelbal, they had been the first wards of the king and the group had been raised and educated together with Tekolger. Kalu saw them almost as brothers.

Exhausted and aching all over, Kalu took a seat next to Doluzelru and began to unwind the wrappings on his hands, enjoying the cool breeze and the midday sun.

"I trust my brother wasn't too rough. He does get carried away and forgets his own strength." Doluzelru said in his measured way without looking up from the scroll he had in front of him. Kalu laughed again,

"No damage done. Thankfully Yulthelon looked on me sympathetically." He said as he felt the quickly forming bruise around his eye and a second on his jaw. He knew he must already look flush, and his face felt like it may swell into a large round moon. He touched his lip, as it burned, and felt blood on his fingers. He wondered if he had left any teeth planted in the soil watered by his blood.

"What are these scrolls? You have not taken your head out of them since you arrived." He asked Doluzelru to distract himself from the pain.

"A new horizon for the Doldun I hope. It is something which has troubled me for many years now. We have conquered the world but have done very little to organise our gains into a cohesive whole. Our empire remains one of many realms, some with little knowledge or contact with others. It is only with unity at the top that the empire can hope to survive." he paused and looked up pensively, "Tekolger's passing makes this even more true. Now we must be the panther, protecting our territory like a predator."

It was a question which had troubled Kalu too. He had many sleepless nights as he crossed the mountains from Kelandel thinking on Tekolger's last words to him. *'Protect my legacy',* he could still see Tekolger's face as he said it, red and troubled by fever, every time he shut his eyes.

"You have written plans on these scrolls to see this happen?" Kalu asked.

"Some, others require more thought. To control both the east and west, properly control them, we need to dominate the sea. It is the key to not only holding onto the west, but also linking it with the east. Without it our territories will remain a disparate collection of lands. These scrolls contain my plans for a royal fleet."

There was sense in what Doluzelru said, communication over land between Xosupil, Zenidun and Doldun with Xortogun and Zowdel was long and difficult. Dotmazo of the Deltathelon had been left as Hegemon of the east by Tekolger, but communication had been so hard that Dotmazo and the homeland had almost been forgotten.

"We have all been caught up in the emotion of Tekolger's passing that none of us have thought long on the future. The Putedun will not take kindly to a new fleet though."

"For too long the Putedun have controlled the main sea lanes without challenge. But they lack the strength to pose a military threat to us. No, they will have to accept the new reality. Besides how can they complain if we allow them to keep plying their trade and take on the expense of policing the seas. Their trading routes are the only real links between east and west, but they are thin and fragile. My plans will strengthen the bonds, as they were said to be before the Dusk came to the world." Doluzelru said with a confidence Kalu could only pray for.

"The Doldun have never been great seafarers though. Ever since our ancestors burned the ships which carried them from old Kolbos, we have viewed the sea with suspicion. Other than your heroics at the siege of Kolop, none of the Companions have ever sailed either. It may be best not to upset the Putedun too much, they can be jealous and vengeful as Tholo herself when slighted. You know their reputation. Besides their expertise may well be needed to build and maintain your fleet Doluzelru."

Doluzelru mulled the thought over for a moment,

"We will need the Putedun, we will need the Xortogun as well. A fleet is just the start. The institutions of the Doldun were only imagined for the rule of a small domain of fractious and blood thirsty clans. If we are truly to dominate our territory like a predator, we need to learn from others who have done the same. The Xortogun kings had a royal council to administer their domains as well as governors to keep order in the provinces. Our Companions may not be up to the task of a royal council. They are warriors and generals not statesmen, but they could be governors. I have many ideas I wish to propose, but I would talk them over with Kelbal first."

"What you propose may not be welcomed by the others Doluzelru and with Tekolger gone it will be hard to attain some agreement from them. Each of the Companions will see their chance to step out from Tekolger's shadow and grab some glory for their own. Speaking of Kelbal, where is he?" Kalu answered cautiously. He knew Tekolger would have liked to hear what Doluzelru said, but the other Companions were not so bold or imaginative. Without Tekolger's drive and will, it would be hard to make them abandon their traditions. Maybe Zenukola would listen.

"Kelbal is where he has been since we arrived. He only leaves the king's side when forced to do so, ever since we passed back through the Vale."

* * *

The great hall of Kulanzow seemed completely changed from the first night he had arrived, when the blind bard had sung of the war which brought the Dusk. Now it seemed as if the dawn light had been brought within.

The long table had been removed and the dais dismantled. In their place, surrounded by candles, sat the golden carriage which contained the body of the fallen king, preserved in honey. The man who had conquered the world, and some whispered the son of Dunsun, come to fulfil ancient prophecy. To Kalu though, he was a friend, a mentor, and his king. A formidable man worthy of praise and poem, but a man, nonetheless. His untimely death had proved that if nothing else. In some ways his passing made Tekolger all the greater than if those claims of divinity were true.

Kalu forgot the ache in his jaw when he saw the carriage. The emotion of Tekolger's loss was still raw and he felt a tear come to his eye as he approached. He wiped the tear away and continued into the room, his footsteps echoing eerily.

At the foot of the carriage was sat a man who looked more Xortogun than Doldun. The light of the candles and the golden carriage thrown over him, gave him an otherworldly glow. He wore a fine fire red robe of the Xortogun style with a long oiled and braided beard in the Xortogun way, dressed with the flamboyance of a man of emotion prone to eccentricities which had earned him the moniker Two Shades. His long hair was left dishevelled, as if a wife in mourning. His ruddy brown locks streaked with cerulean gave Kelbal of the Deltathelon away, the mark of the royal blood in him. His bronze skin shone like the sun, lighter than the olive hue that dominated amongst the clans, it was closer to that of the Xosu, showing his Deltathelon heritage.

Kelbal had been closer than anyone to Tekolger. The two had been raised together since they were babes, going through every trial, every victory and even some defeats together. The conquests were as much Kelbal's as they were Tekolgers'. The vision to create the empire was one they had shared.

If Tekolger was a mentor, then Kelbal was an older brother to Kalu. Taking him under his wing when Kalu was warded by the old king. With his friend now the logical choice as regent of the empire and with Tekolger's final words to him ringing in his ears, Kalu was determined to repay his debt to both men.

He moved alongside Kelbal quietly. His friend was silent and deep in thought. He looked as though the entire weight of the world was on his back, like the wild giant Rilsoro who was condemned to bear the cosmos on his shoulders, to hold it above the swirling chaos of the primordial abyss.

He took up a cup of unmixed wine and drunk long and deep of the fiery liquid as if trying to find the knowledge he would need for the trials to come. Then he turned his round disc of a face towards Kalu and smiled. There was a sadness in that smile and a fear behind his mismatched eyes, but even so he still glowed fiercely. Kalu could not blame him for his melancholy. At the time of his greatest loss, when the man he was closest to in the world was taken from him, the greatest challenge he could ever face had been thrust upon him. No one had ever been asked to rule so great a realm, even Tekolger had not been tested in this way.

"You must excuse me Kalu." Kelbal said in a sombre hush, "I have not been myself recently. I have not seen you for a moon's cycle and yet I have paid you no mind."

"Do not worry yourself about such things. The burdens which have been placed on you more than excuse it." Kalu replied, taking a seat next to his old friend. Kelbal looked back to the golden plated carriage. The craftsmanship was crude, it was obvious this close. Even something that small had pained them, but it was the best they could find in Kelantep which had plenty of gold but few craftsmen of which to speak. Kelbal ran his fingers like talons along the gilded surface,

"Yes, the pain of his loss is still very raw, and yet it is for the future which I fear most. It was not supposed to end this way, it was not what we had foreseen, a new dawn was to come, not a dusk. A new golden age to rival that of the old kingdoms themselves. Tekolger was supposed to see it, not just lay the foundations. A king for the dawn and the day that followed, not a messenger."

"You cannot blame yourself for that Kelbal. We cannot know the minds of the gods, they took Tekolger from us for some reason. Maybe he flew too high and too fast, his star rising to trouble the gods in their golden palace. But there is still a chance for a new dawn, you can lead us to the fulfilment of Tekolger's vision." Kalu answered trying to sound sympathetic.

"If it was the gods who took him, I doubt they acted alone." Kelbal said distantly.

"What do you mean?" Kalu replied, although the thought had occurred to him as well.

"Tekolger was stronger than any of us. This was foul play. The diseases we were struck by in Zentheldel could not have done this." Kelbal said, some strength returning to his voice.

"I believe we all feared as much, but there was not time to stop and think." Kalu replied, he felt a dread in his stomach as he did so. Hearing the accusation out loud was difficult. "Once we are back in Xortogun, with the new king crowned and secure, then we can root out any traitors amongst us." He found himself saying.

"I fear that will be easier said than done. I have not been back in Zowdel for a moon's cycle and already I have Zenukola pushing to crown the boy in Doldun and not Surson's child. He is the first of many. Once the others arrive, they will want their own slice of the spoils. To have their riches, and the chance to win their own glory without Tekolger to overshadow them. But we cannot let that tear us apart. Tekolger may be gone, but his vision survives, incomplete though it is. That task falls to us now Kalu." Kelbal grabbed Kalu's arm firmly as he said it, and thrust Kalu's hand towards his heart,

"Will you help me?"

'Protect my legacy' Kalu heard the words again and saw the face of his king. He nodded. A horn blew outside, a long and drawn-out call, haunting in its simplicity. The noise sent fissures through their thoughts and brought them back to the realm of the living. It could only mean one thing. The two of them silently got to their feet and left.

* * *

The encampment beyond the gates of Kulanzow was already sprawling, filling the small plain beyond the fortress. Now a new column snaked its way out of the mountains and into the camp. The standards showed the white star of the Doldun leading the way with Tekolger's pikemen marching behind, followed by Rilrpitu horsemen and Xosu spears. At the head of the column rode six more Companions and the famed Doldun cavalry that had conquered the world. The horsemen of the Doldun were easily recognisable in their distinctive felt lined, moulded leather caps and short wrap around capes, which had become invaluable in the cold mountains. All Tekolger's Companions were here now, except Dolzalo and Palmash, but they had grown distant from the others in Zentheldel.

Zenukola Silver Eye had already arrived by the time Kalu and Kelbal reached the camp and was greeting the new arrivals. He stopped when he saw Kelbal and instead made his way over to him. Scratching his shaggy grey beard with his one hand and adjusting his chiton, he shouted in his deep booming voice,

"Kelbal, it is good to see you amongst the men. Might we speak in private; I fear the arrival of so many more of Tekolger's veterans will push this camp to its limits."

Kalu heard Kelbal sigh softly,

"Very well Zenu, you are probably right. We cannot linger here too long."

The other Companions had already begun to settle. Zonpeluthas of the Kelawath had his lyre in hand and was beginning to pluck a tune. As always, he was attempting to outshine Zela of the Zelkalkel who was quoting some old poetry about the wanderings of the gods before they settled in Dzottgelon and talked of how blind he had been to the beauty of the land.

The twins had come to greet their comrades too. Pelapakal sized up Deluan of the Balkakel, who was not so tall as the giant man but broader in the chest. Thazan of the Kolabon thanked the gods for their safe arrival and greeted Doluzelru in his solemn, priestly way.

Sharp eyed and cunning as ever, Zalmetaz of the Kalupelbon picked out Kalu, despite him lingering away from the group. Zalmetaz made his way over to Kalu, accompanied by Polazul of the Kolbun and his hunting hound, Hurricane, who had crossed the world with the army.

Zalmetaz was one of the quieter Companions, not so bold as Zela and not so devious as Palmash, in fact he tended to avoid confrontation, to the point where he almost seemed passive. *A strange trait for one who had conquered the world*, Kalu reflected. Despite that impression, he was quick and cunning when needed, a man made for the subtly of an ambush rather than the headlong charge on the field of battle. A subtly which suited the learned red-haired man. He was easy to recognise too, even if he was the quietest man in the room, due to the fox pelt cloak he always wore, with the head of a fox peering over his shoulder almost seeming to merge with his red beard and giving him another set of sharp eyes.

"Kalu, it gladdens me to see you well." Zalmetaz said as he approached in his softly spoken way. "How fair things in Zowdel?"

Kalu let the crescent of a smile grow on his lips, "It is good to see you all as well, we will need the support of each other in the coming months, I fear. Zowdel fairs as well as could be expected. Some rumblings amongst the local magnates I am told, but nothing serious yet. Zenukola is just as he always was, thank the gods. His experience and wisdom may mean the difference between stability and chaos."

Zalmetaz nodded knowingly, his long red hair falling across his eyes,

"Yes, I should think that Zenu knows exactly what is about to come. I would be most interested to hear what he has to say."

Polazul was kneeling next to Hurricane, feeding the hound from his hand. But his hunter's eyes were fixed on Zalmetaz. The two men were close and competed in everything they did, although Polazul always failed to keep up with Zalmetaz's quick wits. Whereas Zalmetaz was considered and calculating to an infuriating degree, Polazul was loud, boastful, and impetuous, a man of impulse usually found hunting. He liked to boast that there was no prey which could outrun Hurricane, a claim that always brought a mocking smile to Zalmetaz's lips.

"Do not put so much stock in the old man. He is the same as he was and that is reason for concern. His time is done, and his world is gone. It is to the future now that we should be looking." Polazul boldly proclaimed.

"The future is as of yet uncertain Polazul." Zalmetaz answered him swiftly, "Where the surety of past events may be our guide. I would not be so quick to dismiss the old eagle. He may only have one eye, but he sees more than you ever will."

Suitably chastised, Polazul ignored the slight, scratching his newly grown beard of beaten bronze, "The future will bring what it will bring. We are all hungry and Hurricane brought down some choice game in the foothills. A hoary old boar the like of which you would have never seen. Its piercing tusks came close to making an end of me and Hurricane, but we saw to it together, soaked the earth with its blood. I will have it served up in the great hall to celebrate our safe return once we have settled the men in, come join us Kalu."

* * *

The evening rolled around quickly, and as Dunsun got off his throne to journey to the dread realm once more, so Kalu descended from his quarters to the great hall of Kulanzow. The second column had been settled into the camp; a thousand thousand campfires now bathed the plain below the walls in flame, as if the fires of the earth were erupting with the dusk. The Companions had seen this done and then made their way to the great hall. It was as if nothing had changed on their last campaign, as if Tekolger was still with them. The aftershock of his death was still there though, deep in Kalu's gut.

The great hall felt different than it had done on the previous nights.

The dais was gone, and in its place Tekolger's golden carriage lay in state. The royal regalia now placed on top, watching them.

None of the mountain men had joined them this evening, there even seemed to be less of Zenu's men about, although the nobles of Zowdel still lurked. A recognisable setting for Kalu, but it somehow felt different. The music was very familiar though. Zonpeluthas sat alone but for the serving girls who surrounded him, lingering to listen to the melody of his lyre and the sweet song which accompanied it. Zela, blind to the others, had corralled another band of serving girls and was regaling them with the tragic poems he so loved. This time tales he had learnt in Zentheldel. Both men acknowledged him with a nod as he passed.

Under a burning lamp, Thazan sat straight as a tower and hard as oak, distant from the rest. A single cup of unmixed wine in front of him. He was the only Companion who was clean shaven. He looked ever more the priest in the fine robe which Zenu had provided for him. He watched on from his high table, his gaze as unyielding as a sword, grinding his teeth as was his habit, watching Deluan wrestle with one of Zenu's men.

Deluan's long braided hair which fell all the way to his backside, whipped through the air as he bowled Zenu's guardsman over and laughed. He was a bull of a man, thick across the chest and well-muscled. It was for this, and his pale skin which looked more Xosu than clansman, that men called him the Silver Bull. It was good to see him again, Kalu reflected. Deluan's earnest nature and sense of adventure was always refreshing and lifted the spirits at the most difficult of times.

Kalu reached the table which had been placed below the king's carriage and took a seat next to Kelbal. His friend was already into his cups, he could smell it on Kelbal's breath and see the purple stain on his tongue when he smiled. The regent poured Kalu a cup of the unmixed wine and, without taking his eyes from the room, said,

"Zenu thinks we should begin the march to Yorixori as soon as possible. Kulanzow cannot hold this many men for long, supplies will run short quickly."

Kalu nodded,

"Zenu is right, this place was not designed for it. Besides the quicker we return to Xortogun the more secure the empire will be. We need to protect Surson and the king's heir."

Kelbal sighed again,

"I know, you are right. It is just…" he paused, "I am concerned. Zenu has already suggested that crowning the other boy would be better and I see many cracks between our comrades here. Many do not even realise the seriousness of our situation. Look how they carry on as if nothing has changed."

"I have heard the same argument from Zenu myself. His heart is in the right place, and he means well. He does not wish to see the Doldun fall back into civil war, the last one cost him too much." Kalu replied.

"It is a dangerous thought to discuss, nevertheless. The slightest hint of division amongst us and all may be lost, especially this far west. Who knows what our new subjects may do if they see weakness in us? Besides, Tekolger's wishes were clear. I will not have it any other way, even if old friendships must be sacrificed."

'Protect my legacy', Kalu could see the king's face even clearer here in the dark room.

As Zenu and his men entered the hall, the silence was broken by a flame erupting from the firepit and a shout from Polazul loud enough to shake the earth.

"The beast is ready, and this daemon of a boar will not eat itself! Where is this bard of Zenu's I have heard so much about? Some entertainment whilst we eat, and I am tired of hearing Zela's musings and Zonpeluthas' endless plucking."

"I am afraid you missed his performance Polazul." Zenukola answered in his booming voice. "He is an old man and the strain on his voice is great, today he rests." Zenu turned to Kalu, "I heard you were quite the storyteller in your childhood."

Kalu smiled thinly, feeling the cut on his lip reopen as he did, and his face grow flush.

"I was fond of the old stories and used to tell the tales in front of my clan, but I was never as skilled as your blind bard, or even Zela and Zonpeluthas here."

Zenukola replied,

"True as that may be, a story has been asked for. Might you tell us the tale of what happened in Zentheldel? The great king Tekolger's final heroic campaign bringing light into the twilight lands. I am sure that is tale all here would wish to hear. The last of the heroes striking out into the mysterious lands of the dying flame, spreading the message of order and civilisation in his wake. It is surely a tale worthy of a bard."

Kalu shifted uncomfortably in his chair, but he had to admit the chance to be the storyteller once more did call to him. *'Protect my legacy'* the words seemed to be whispered to him.

"Very well", he said, "I will tell you the tale, and do my best to do it justice. Perhaps this way the legacy of Tekolger will not be remembered so tragically as that of Tholophos. But I would wish to tell a story of light, like that which came before the fall of the old kingdoms as I fear that dusk hangs over us right now. Although I will not pretend to be a match for the others when it comes to weaving tales."

He stood in front of the fire, in a spot where the moonlight streaked in an illuminated the hall. Through it he felt he could channel Tholo, the white armed goddess herself, and the words would come to him from her like a torrent giving life to the tale.

"Glory. The pursuit of glory drove far famed Tekolger, swift as an arrow, bold as a panther, and fierce as a hydra, to the edge of the world, to the land of the evening sun. The king's desire to go beyond the limits of those which came before him and glimpse the encircling ocean pushed him onward to unite the fractured realms of men. It was a pursuit which cost the Doldun dear but brought with it countless riches and tales of great deeds which would echo down the ages. For it was clear that light bringing Tekolger was a man like no other. The son of Dunsun, king of gods and men, it was whispered, for who else but the son of a god could be capable of such things, the last of the heroes of the glorious past long prophesised to return.

The cities of the Xosu had fallen easily to his spear, the Zummosh of Zenidun and the land of Gulonbel followed soon after. Even the great valley of Xortogun, ruled over by the Rilrpitu horse lords, could not stand before him. Twelve years of conquest and the world now lay at thrice blessed Tekolger's feet, all added to his glory. Zentheldel, far to the west, could not escape his ambition, but the judgement of impassive Yulthelon was soon to catch up with Tekolger. Even the son of the Lord of the Cosmos, the bright shining sun, cannot outrun fate…"

ZENUKOLA

Trumpets blared and men bellowed out orders, slowly the long snaking column groaned into life, shuffling its way out of the shadow of Kulanzow. The arrival of the second column had pushed the temporary encampment to its limits, almost twenty thousand men quartered under its walls. Together with the garrison and Zenu's personal guard, the fortress was almost ready to burst. Within days the stockpiled supplies would start to run low, and another ten thousand strong column was expected to arrive at any moment. This reality allowed Zenukola to act, insisting that the army begin the march to Yorixori, the capital of the province of Zowdel.

Yorixori was once the seat of kings, before the Dusk of the old kingdoms when high kings still ruled the Xosu from golden Thelonigul and god-kings dominated the great valley of Xortogun from their Amber Throne. Zowdel had its own god-kings then. In more recent centuries, the city had been re-established by Yoruxoruni during his own conquest of Zenian. He rebuilt it in the image of Xortogun and planted his veterans there. He even gave the city its current name, Yorixori the city of gardens. There were few who remained that still spoke the old tongue of Zowdel, and it was doubtful any of them remembered what name the god-kings gave their garden city, the only hint a blind whisper of poets who once filled those gardens. For the last three years Yorixori had been Zenukola's own seat, from which he had ruled over the western half of Tekolger's vast realm.

Kelbal had not taken much persuasion to march, agreeing with Zenu as soon as he heard about the supply situation. Although Zenu thought his eagerness to leave came more from a desire to avoid having to reunite with Dolzalo of the Zowo, who was commanding the third column. A sentiment the other Companions seemed to share, *or perhaps they were feeling their guilt*. Whatever the reason, the men were now on the march. The godlike conquerors of the west returning from the unknown to take their place as rulers of the world, or so they thought.

Following the path of the Kelonzow river as it weaved its way over the rolling hills of Zenian, their route was long but relatively easy. With open plains to march over and no armies to fight, the only threat this time were the wild cats that roamed the country. The course of the river would take them eventually to Torfub, the extraordinary city of towers sitting at the point where three rivers, the Kelonzow, Thelkelonzow and Zolkelonzow, met and the gateway to Xortogun. From there they would enter the great valley itself, marching through the lush fertile land which made the valley so rich, to Kurotormub, the old capital of Yoruxoruni, last native king of the valley and the only man to rule the whole of Zenian, before Tekolger. *At least Tekolger's end was better than Yoruxoruni's*, Zenu thought, *humiliated by the Xosu, and then betrayed.*

The army would not stop in Kurotormub however, it was the old city of kings, but a new city awaited. Passed the iron black ruins of Gonphonmub, ancient seat of the god-kings of Xortogun, waited Tekolgertep, built on golden sands at the mouth of the Kelonzow river. The new seat of the King of Kings. It was Tekolger's metropolis looking out across the sea to connect Xortogun, Zenian and the other lands of the empire together, and it was the place in which Tekolger would be laid to rest. But first they would arrive in Yorixori. *It will be good to return,* he thought, Zenu had grown fond of the place.

The wind swept along the unfolding plains of Zenian and Zenukola breathed in the crisp morning air. Marching at the head of an army again had reinvigorated him, he felt like a man half his age and ready to take on the world once more. The march back to Xortogun may not be as glorious as the march to the west was, but it still had the feeling of a grand military procession about it. Zenu was in his element here, away from the politics and intrigue of governorship.

The gilded carriage carrying the king's body rumbled along the rough track behind Zenu. A crash as it bounced over the broken ground shook him out of his daydream. Riding beside him at the head of the column was Kelbal, both his green and amber eyes still taken by a solemn melancholy. Next to him rode Kalu, his round moon of a face covered under dark hair, pale eyes, and olive skin a contrast to the zilthum lined armour and white cloak he wore. Behind them the twins flanked the king's carriage.

The carriage may have been gilded, but it was still clearly a rushed construction. No fine adornments or freezes depicting the marching gods and the events of the king's glorious reign, just the crimson hue of the dolthil wood beneath. Even the cart itself looked as though it had been hammered together in a hurry. Up close the rough edges and loose fittings were obvious. The glint of the gold would be enough of a distraction from afar, but if anyone came within touching distance, the carriage did not seem like the transport for the body of a king who had conquered the world. It would only remind them of the black death which lay within.

The thought of Tekolger filled Zenu with a mix of admiration and jealousy. How could a man not be envious of another who had achieved so much that he rivalled the gods? Especially when his success was built on the back of the hard work of Kenkathoaz, his father, and the men of Zenu's generation who had ended the civil wars and finally bent the clans to the will of the king. Tekolger had been formidable though, even as a young king his vision, and bold, decisive action had been impressive.

Zenu turned to Kelbal,

"I have sent word ahead to Torfub. A carriage fit to bear the king back to Tekolgertep will be waiting for us on arrival. More spectacular than anything we will have seen before I have been told."

Kelbal nodded but stayed silent. A silence which Kalu must have found uncomfortable as he was the first to speak, a hint of his clan origins in his voice,

"I am glad to hear that Zenu. We did the best we could in Kelantep, but the very least we need to do is see that Tekolger receives the veneration he deserves."

Zenu nodded and replied,

"Yes, Tekolger blazed across the world like no other and the people of the empire see him as such. We need to ensure that is the last impression they have of him."

Kelbal now spoke,

"Any word from Surson?"

It was unsurprising that Kelbal shifted the conversation. He still had not gotten over the king's death, rarely even speaking his name, but Zenu could not decide if that was out of grief or guilt,

"I have sent word north to Supo he will meet us in Yorixori. The king's Xortogun bride will meet the army at Torfub and accompany the procession into Xortogun itself." Zenu answered. Kelbal nodded again, slowly,

"And what of the child? She must be close to giving birth now. The last time we saw her was in Kelantep before the campaign in Zentheldel, that was eight moons ago."

Zenu responded,

"I have not received word yet. Though you are right, she will be very close now."

A delicate sleight of hand was needed, much as Zenu found it distasteful. Kelbal seemed happy with that, a smile lit his copper face as bright as the morning sun. Another clue of the man's true intentions perhaps,

"Good, then we can begin to plan for the birth and the coronation of the new king. It was one of Tekolger's final wishes to name the child his heir, a descendant of himself and Yoruxoruni to unite all the lands under his rule. Tekolger deserves to have that wish honoured as well."

When Kelbal spoke the king's name, his voice almost broke, but he swallowed the heart in his mouth and composed himself, looking stronger for it. Zenu nodded, wary not to upset Kelbal,

"We don't know it will be a boy yet and Tekolger has another son of good Doldun stock, almost a man grown. The aura of Tekolger will only last so long, but a quick transition to a new ruler will be a good thing. Strong leadership will be needed over the next few years, I am already hearing rumblings of rebellion, wild and scattered though they are, and the Rilrpitu always cast a troubling cloud in the north. As soon as news of the king's death began to spread the whispers of our weakness started and attacks on our patrols have steadily increased. A child king with a weak regency could do a lot of damage to the empire."

Kelbal became much more animated, and visibly annoyed, his fury cutting through the crisp autumn air. From one extreme to another in an instant,

"We have already discussed this Zenu! The boy may be Tekolger's son and of good and noble birth, but he is not the man to unite the empire. Only a child of both realms, east and west can do that. It was Tekolger's vision and the legacy which he left us to complete. We will crown Tekolger's heir, and a regency council will be appointed. Any rebellion will be crushed with force. I will make sure Tekolger's legacy is passed to the right person, that is what he deserves."

Seeing that he had gone too far, Zenu backed off,

"I wasn't suggesting we went against the wishes of the king, Kelbal. I am merely making you aware of the challenges we now face."

Kelbal, still unhappy with this line of thought, spat back a reply with a burning fury to his voice,

"We faced worse challenges in Zentheldel, and we are here now to tell you of it."

Taking the opportunity to blow the conversation a different way and gather more insight on what threats the empire may yet face, Zenukola said,

"You have told me little of what happened in Zentheldel Kelbal. Kalu's account of the battle at the Talwab river is all you have given me and not to be disrespectful, but Kalu told that tale in the style of a bard. It is hard to separate the truth from the story in such things. Beyond that I know almost nothing of what befell the king." Continuing bluntly, Zenu said "What happened to Tekolger?"

Zenu expected Kelbal to explode in rage, instead he became visibly smaller, shrinking in stature,

"Fine, I will tell you." Kelbal finally replied after a long pause, a black tone to his words. "Tekolger became sick after a banquet was held to celebrate the victory and Herethalthawe's agreement to swear fealty to the king.

It was late into the night, the feasting and the drinking had been going on since dusk, but nothing unusual. Tekolger was handed a large drinking cup, golden in colour with two vast handles, one either side, around the edge were depicted scenes from the siege of old Kolbos, like Kuso's cup in the Sinasa. He was told to drink deep to find the wisdom at the bottom of the cup, as in Kuso's cup where it gave the knowledge of the gods to those who drank from it, but that knowledge would drive the drinker mad. The cup had a trick to it though, it had a strange mechanism in it so that it would refill itself from a hidden reservoir inside. Meaning that you would have to drink long and deep to find the knowledge which hid at the bottom. We were all in our cups by that point and all the others encouraged him.

Tekolger stood and drunk the whole thing. It was unmixed wine, but on campaign we had grown used to that. It was excessive, but not much more than usual." Kelbal paused and looked off into the distance, across the wide-open plain toward where the star which rises before the sun should be. He continued after a moment of silence,

"Not long after Tekolger passed out drunk. We thought nothing unusual of it, some of the guards took him to his bed. The next morning the king didn't get up, and when checked on, he was found to be caught in a deep fever and barely conscious."

Zenu listened intently, replying,

"And you don't know what happened? Was it poison? Who handed him the cup?"

"I don't know what happened Zenu. It could have been poison, Palmash claimed it was, but none of us had seen a poison work like that before. He lingered for weeks, and even rose from his bed on several occasions before it took him. All I know is that it was Talehalden, King of

Thentherzaw, who handed him the cup." Kelbal replied.

"So that is why Dolzalo blamed Talehalden." Zenu said thoughtfully.

"Yes, Dolzalo immediately blamed him, especially after Talehalden left to return to Thentherzaw." Kelbal paused again, a look of regret and melancholy in his eyes, "But that he did with my permission. The news of the king's illness sent a shockwave through the land. We were already hearing reports of rebellions stirring and I allowed him to return to his city to ensure it stayed loyal." Kelbal answered, with the fire returning to his voice.

"And then Dolzalo descended on the city?" Zenu asked,

"I blame myself for that." Kelbal replied, "There were rebellions appearing everywhere, and the colonists we had settled began marching home refusing to dwell in Zentheldel. The whole situation was wild. I sent Kalu with the White Shields to deal with the rebels whilst I took the cavalry to intercept the colonists, and left Dolzalo in charge of the rest of the army. He took the chance and marched on the city; the men only too eager to participate once Dolzalo publicly accused Talehalden."

Zenu paused for a moment,

"That was not your fault. Dolzalo is responsible for his own actions."

Kelbal nodded but did not seem to hear. Zenu continued after thinking on what he had been told. Nothing he had heard had alleviated his suspicions, but how far did the conspiracy spread? Was it just Kelbal, or were other Companions involved?

"If Talehalden did poison Tekolger, how did he know to use Kuso's cup like that? Surely it is not a story they tell in Zentheldel?"

Kalu replied before Kelbal could speak,

"He didn't, or at least I don't think he did. That's why we did not suspect his guilt, it made no sense. Talehalden handed the cup to Tekolger, but it does not mean that it was his cup. The great hall was busy, filled with Doldun and Xosu as well as the men from Zentheldel and even the Putedun traders who had followed the army. In fact, it was their wine that we were drinking. The room was noisy, cups were being passed around all night, it would have been easy to give the cup to Talehalden and tell him to hand it to the king. The story on the cup was a convenient way to ensure that only Tekolger would drink from it. Although I cannot say any of this for certain. It was easy to then make Talehalden look guilty. That is if it were poison, it could just have been a fever, there were many diseases in Zentheldel that ravaged the army."

Zenu thought further on it before replying. A plausible story, difficult to argue with, but it failed to pin the blame anywhere. He spoke again as the swaying of his horse brought him back to the moment,

"That would make sense, although it is all speculation as you don't know if it was poison."

Kalu nodded,

"If it was poison, it is not like any I have heard of before, and why not give him something that would have worked quickly, and then do nothing after the king died?"

"They don't need to do anything else yet Kalu. Just wait for the chaos to unfold and take advantage. It would make whoever it was look like the hero coming in to save the empire." Zenu replied assuredly.

"You think it was one of us then? One of the Companions?" Kalu said defensively, some irritation in his voice.

"I don't know anything yet Kalu." Zenu replied calmly, "But that would seem the case if Tekolger was poisoned, and if so, we have a traitor in our midst."

The trio rode on in silence. Zenu contemplated what he had learned from Tekolger's closest Companions. No doubt the others were all thinking through the consequences of Tekolger's death, if by their hand or not. The whole situation did not sit with him well at all.

* * *

The first few days of the march Zenu had spent at the head of the column alongside Kelbal, Kalu and the twins. Pressing the case for swift action in the succession, but to no avail. The nights had brought wild drinking sessions led by Kelbal. Not the best place to engage in delicate politics. There was still time though, the army was a day's march from Yorixori, where Zenu hoped to be greeted by Supo of the Dolozolaz. He knew the support and strength of his old ally would be needed.

Having failed to push an increasingly difficult Kelbal into swifter action or allay his own suspicions, Zenu knew he may also need to find allies amongst the king's erstwhile Companions, to ensure the stability of the empire. Or if he could not find allies, then he could question them to discover their guilt. It was these needs that had led Zenukola to ride at the rear of the column on the final stretch of the journey. Leaving Koloathutalaz to lead his guardsmen, Zenu dropped back to the rear.

Commanding here were Deluan of the Balkakel, Thazan of the Kolabon, Zonpeluthas of the Kelawath and Zela of the Zelkalkel. Deluan and Zela were amongst Tekolger's closest friends. They had been taken as wards by Kenkathoaz, a notion of the old king to keep the clans inline by fostering the sons of their most prominent members at the royal court. The children served as useful hostages, and they were educated like their more civilised cousins on the coast. In time Kenkathoaz had hoped that this teaching would spread to the clans themselves. Deluan and Zela had therefore grown up together at the court with Tekolger and received the same education from the wandering philosopher Yusukol Kosua. It had made them men carved very much in the mould of Tekolger and the journey they set out on, a boyhood dream to see the world and the encircling ocean beyond, was as much theirs as it was Tekolger's.

Surely, they will see the sense in ensuring the stability of their king's legacy, Zenu thought, *but how can I trust them? They are close to Kelbal as well.*

As for the other two, he was less certain. Thazan's Kolabon had been the last clan to submit to Kenkathoaz and he had not been warded by the king. Zonpeluthas was younger than the others with no memory of the civil war at all. *Did that make them more or less likely to be involved in a conspiracy?*

Deciding to try and take a more tactful approach, Zenu had spent the morning of the march staying quiet, merely observing and listening to the Companions.

"This land is not how I remember it." Deluan was saying to Zela in his ponderous way. His voice almost dying off as it was lost in the towering labyrinth of his thoughts. "War has that effect I find, distorts everything. But the day's seemed brighter and filled with life those short years ago. A sweet scent followed the king wherever he went, it's why we followed so eagerly."

Zela nodded and replied,

"Even Zentheldel, wet, humid and disease ridden as it was, seemed that way."

Deluan answered, throwing his long, braided hair over his shoulder, and looking off into the distance as if remembering another life. His hair reminded Zenu of a bull's tail wiping at flies, or a striking serpent,

"Before the king was taken by one of those diseases. The days got shorter and darker after that."

Zela was not quite so dower, then again, he never had been. The man always had a smile behind his eyes and a laugh came quick to his lips. He responded to the ponderous Companion,

"Even after the king was taken, the campaign still had purpose, we were still fighting for a vision. It was hard and more dangerous than any of our other ventures, but it was still of value. It felt as though we were panthers defending our territory. And now we march out of duty, a long funeral procession rather than an advance, but still with a clear purpose.", Zonpeluthas voiced agreement, but Thazan stayed silent and Deluan clearly did not agree,

"The king was the panther, a sweet voice but a driving force behind everything we did, without him there is no purpose. I am sure the gods had their reasons for taking him away from us, but to do so in such a manner, disease rather than death in battle, I will never understand."

Zela looked at him curiously with his deep-set laughing eyes which never failed to blind others to his true thoughts,

"You still think it was just an illness?"

"Dolzalo is a hothead and wrong about most things. It didn't look like poison to me. One of those awful diseases that the twilight land was filled with seems more likely." Deluan replied earnestly. "Besides, the gods always seem to take the greatest heroes in the most mundane ways, just look at Tholophos. Even Xosu, a god and one of the Kolithelon. His time amongst men ended without the glory it deserved, even if he did choose the path he took and promised he would return."

Zela laughed and scratched as his beard. Both the hair on his head and his thick braided beard were darker than was typical amongst the clans, more teak than bronze,

"That is the fleeting nature of glory I suppose. The fall is always disappointing, and the higher the climb the more mundane the fall and the end of the story may seem, especially for mortal men."

Deluan, more melancholic than Zela, said,

"And Tekolger had climbed higher than everyone, rivalling Tholophos and even the bright one, Xosu himself. He was like a hero from a by gone age, before the Dusk brought an end to the old kingdoms. That is what people will remember him for."

Zela, always sceptical, replied,

"The king will be remembered. If his legacy is protected, he may even be held up alongside Tholophos. A difficult act for us to follow."

Taking his cue from the men, Zenu took an opportunity to intervene. Although he would hold off on asking them about Tekolger's death. One of the Companions surely knew something, but it would be best to speak to them individually to discover the truth of what had happened,

"You are right Deluan," The rumbling sound of Zenu's voice caused the two Companions to pause. Conquerors of the world or not, they still showed deference to their elders, "if there is one thing I have learnt in my long years it is that men remember great deeds and impossible feats. Why do you think Tholophos is so revered throughout Xosupil, and he is almost a god to many of the Doldun?"

Deluan nodded with approval, but Zela replied, blind to the suggestion,

"What you say is true Zenu, and the king will be remembered down the ages, but what is left for us now? We must walk in his shadow and never eclipse his achievements."

Zenu smiled,

"But Tholophos' achievements collapsed after his death. Dusk fell, the Xosu went back to fighting each other and the high kingship faded into memory once more. Go and see the ruins of Thelonigul. The bards describe it as golden and shining, a place to rival Dzottgelon itself, but very little glory remains there. Only the zilthum walls survive to remind us of a long dead civilisation. Nothing but folk memories left and an oracle that lingers deep in the caves behind as the only connection to a world that has passed beyond our reach."

Deluan now spoke as if compelled to by Zela's defiance,

"What are you saying Zenu? All this was for nothing?"

"What I am saying is that we should learn the lessons of these memories and not just revere them. No, you cannot eclipse Tekolger's achievements. The man subjugated the whole world, but the threads placed before him by Yulthelon took him on that journey. You each have your own threads in front of you. The shining goddess places them there at your birth and it is up to you to reach the prize at the end. I assume you know the tale of Kolgophoas."

The Companions nodded, but Zela answered again,

"How is that relevant Zenu?"

"The man who thought he could redraw his fate and defy the gods. He strived for too much, burning too bright and rising too high. Tricking his way to the kingship of the Silxosu, for that he was murdered. Then he tricked the gods by not drinking from the waters of the river Rinukol. When he was born again, a different body but his shade remembered his previous life, he grew up to take his revenge." Zenu explained.

Zela interrupted,

"Apologies Zenu, but what is the point you are getting at here. We all know the story."

"How does it end, Zela?" Zenu replied,

"Kolgophoas tried to trick his way into Dzottgelon to become a god. Dunsun let him think he had succeeded. In reality he was cast into the underworld where he is punished to this day by having to climb a mountain to reach what he thinks is Dzottgelon. When he reaches the top, he drinks from the cup of the gods, which contains the waters of the Rinukol and immediately he forgets his purpose and is sent to start again." Zela answered, it was a well told story in Xosupil and among the Doldun.

"Kolgophoas thought he could ignore the will of the gods and it brought upon him nothing but eternal punishment and wrought destruction on the city he once ruled." Zenu said, as if revealing an obvious truth. The Companions stopped and reflected on Zenu's statement. Predictably Zela came back,

"What path are you suggesting we follow Zenu?"

Zenukola laughed. Zela was ripe for the suggestion but very sharp. He was one to watch, a friend one day an enemy the next. He had the simple look of the clans, but there was nothing simple about him. *If there is a conspiracy, this one is at the heart of it*, Zenu thought,

"Tekolger has left us all a great legacy, as Tholophos left his sons and even the bright god Xosu did way back at the Dawn. Yulthelon has clearly laid tangled threads before us, we must choose which to follow. Protect that legacy, as Xosu's sons did despite the division of their people, or leave it to fall to ruin, as Tholophos' sons did after the war for old Kolbos and the ruin of that metropolis. Think of how you will be remembered if you did not allow the patterns of history to continue, but protected Tekolger's legacy and kept us all united."

Zela now smiled,

"What are you getting at Zenu?"

"I am pointing out that a difficult path may lay ahead of all of us and that it would be wise to bear in mind that the stability of the empire is now the most important undertaking for us to commit to."

Deluan answered,

"We are doing that as we speak. The provinces in the west were subdued and secured. Now we are returning the army home to lay the king to rest and keep the peace in the empire."

As he said it, the rear of the column crested a hill, and the silhouette of a city came into view just as the red light of the evening began to descend. Yorixori, the city of poets and gardens, sprawled out over the plain. The shadows of its pyramids and ziggurats, the summits of which were lit by the setting sun, a contrast to the flat alluvial plain filled with farms that surrounded it. Bisected by the mighty Kelonzow river, the old capital of Zowdel had seen better days, but it was beginning to grow and thrive again under the rule of the Doldun.

Zenu retorted,

"Yes, and it was a wise thing to do. Soon we will arrive in the first city on the long road home. Things have changed since you left. The shock of the conquest has gone and those who do not like the idea of an empire ruled by the Doldun will begin to gather their strength, seeing weakness in our loss. Not everyone will weep for Tekolger's death. The road will not be easy, stability and unity are key now."

***

Twilight had descended as trumpets blasted to collapse the silence and announce their arrival at Yorixori. Passing through the small farms encircling the city, Zenu took care to note the reaction of the farmers slaving away in the fields to bring in the last of the harvest before winter set in. It was a habit he had picked up since becoming governor of this vast realm.

The king had left him as Hegemon of the western half of his new conquests, and the unruliest parts at that. Although the Rilrpitu tribes had been defeated and driven back over the Thazzow river to the open steppe of Belon, where they had originally come from, they were always a constant threat. Some of the newly liberated lords of the land had felt themselves emboldened to use that threat as leverage. It had not been an easy three years, but the most important lesson Zenu had felt he had learnt was the reaction of the people to events. Their feelings were often an indication of whether a rebellion of some high lord would gain momentum or just burn itself out. Now Zenu felt himself watching the people once more, anxious to see their reaction to the returning army without the king. Many stopped to bow their head as the king's body rumbled passed. Some even appeared to cry openly. How much of this was show for the army it was hard to say. The people of Yorixori were of Xortogun stock, ever since Yoruxoruni rebuilt the city two centuries ago. The Xortogun had a long tradition of open displays of grief for dead kings, who they viewed as gods. Some farmers paid the column no mind at all, which Zenu found even more disconcerting. He felt his phantom fingers flexing as he watched.

The gates of the city rumbled open. The army, barely breaking its stride, entered the wall ringing the lower town. The first time he had entered this place it had felt strange and alien. The sound of the Xortogun tongue otherworldly, and the smell of incense making his stomach churn as it lingered in the still air. Now he found it welcoming, after his brief sojourn at the dank fortress in the mountains. Zenu spurred his horse and headed for the front of the column. At the column's head Kelbal and Kalu rode. Zenu pulled his horse alongside them and said,

"Welcome back to Yorixori. The city has treated me well these last few years."

Kalu laughed. A crescent smile rising over his round face,

"I hope it will treat us just as well. The entrance has already been more welcoming, the last time I had to climb over those walls and the locals were less than pleased to see me. Although the priests were very pleased to see Tekolger I recall. But ancient prophecies will make you happy to greet many a conqueror."

Kelbal replied in a more sombre tone,

"It will make good place to rest and wait for Dolzalo to reach us."

Zenu interjected perhaps too quickly,

"Would it not be best to push on to Torfub? The quicker we can get back to Xortogun the better."

Kelbal shook his head,

"I think that we need to be at our full strength when we enter Xortogun. You are right that our enemies will be looking for any sign of weakness now. It will be best to present the full force of the army as we enter the heart of the empire. A show of strength."

Zenu replied not wanting the opportunity he had been presented with to go to waste,

"A show of strength will be needed, but speed is also of the essence. The quicker the army is back in Xortogun the more secure the empire will be. Supo has marched to meet you here. This column, my forces and his guard will be more than enough strength to cow any challenger. With the other column arriving later to sure up that position."

"Disagreement is rife within our ranks now, Zenu. Isn't it best for us all to come together to make these decisions collectively? As you say we need unity. Decisions will have to be made on behalf of the new king. We can't do that unless we come together quickly."

Kelbal's mind was clearly made up, a man used to making decisions on the march and sticking to them. Zenu could see he was not going to be able to persuade him otherwise. Supo would be needed, and Zela at least seemed open to persuasion.

"I can see you are decided on this matter, Kelbal, but you are not the regent yet as there is no new king. Let us see what the Companions think before deciding. It is the reason for the existence of the institution after all." Zenu answered, the irritation with the obstinate general clear in his voice. Kelbal was no Tekolger, the king would have had made the decision and had everyone behind him in an instant. Kelbal nodded in agreement as the column was ordered to halt, but the rouge creeping over his face showed he was not happy with Zenu's opposition.

Leaving the White Shields to be billeted in the city by their officers, and the rest of the army to construct a camp outside the city gates. Zenu led the Companions toward the governor's residence, passed the encircling gardens of dolthil trees, with their thin red branches always reaching for the sky and fragrant golden leaves rustling in the evening wind.

The garden's seemed to hang from the tiered gold walls of the palace, as if suspended in the sky in some supreme paradise realm. If the stories of its past could be believed, the whole of the city which once served the god-kings of Zowdel had a similar look in its heyday. As if a city suspended in the air by the slim branches of the dolthil trees. But none still lived to confirm the tales and now only the palace remained of that time.

Awaiting them at the ornate building was Supo of the Dolozolaz, Zenu's old comrade in arms. Supo was a strong, well-built man in his middle years, his tan hair shot through with waves of grey and the lines around his eyes hardening into tridents. He had the olive skin of the clans, but ocean blue eyes which spoke of another heritage. He wore a sea green Xosu style toga, the material bunched and clutched in one hand to stop it falling to the floor.

The sight pleased Zenu. Supo was a man of the clans but had learnt the civilised arts from Zenu. He was like a younger brother to him. Along with Dotmazo back in Doldun, they were the only survivors from the days of the old king, Kenkathoaz. Grizzled veterans of those difficult days when the Doldun were more likely to be fighting each other than anyone else. Now they were experienced governors of a vast and diverse empire, but they still remembered the dark days of civil war and understood better than any the need for stability now.

He greeted his old comrade warmly, the first time he had seen him in many months, he was eager to catch up with his old friend. Supo gripped Zenu's arm vice like by way of greeting, the taller man casting a dark shadow over him. Supo had been entrusted with the difficult role of controlling the northern border. A thankless task with no glory in it, but he had taken to the assignment with dedication and skill as he did with everything the king had asked of him. In fact, Zenu could not have held the west so tightly without Supo's aid for the last three years.

He wished to discuss the future with him, as his comrade was crucial to what needed to happen. He would also be instrumental in any deliberations with the Companions, especially given Kelbal's obstinance and hold over the others. Zenu ushered his guests into his palace.

**

The evening came swiftly, and with it the opportunity to speak with Supo in private. He poured a cup of mixed wine for Supo and himself as the younger man entered his chambers. Zenu signalled to the guards to summon Pelu and informed them that no one else should be allowed entry and he was to be alerted if anyone attempted to. Turning to the grizzled veteran, he felt he could finally speak his mind,

"It is good to see you again, but I fear the pleasantries and reminiscing must wait. Kelbal has been sensible up until now to bring the army back from the west intact, but he believes that we should crown Tekolger's child with his Xortogun consort. I need not tell you that a long regency is a great risk to this newly won empire, and the half barbarian child will not be a fit ruler for this kingdom. The Doldun have won an empire for themselves, I for one am not about to hand it over to a foreign queen. Besides, Kelbal has done nothing to allay my suspicions of his and the Xortogun's involvement in the king's death. Fortunately, he does not yet know that the child has been born and that it is male. That information would mean an end to any chance we have of steering toward a better course. I swore an oath to Kenkathoaz to watch over his son. Tekolger may be dead, but I will not break that oath and hand the realm to these people."

Zenu looked to Supo for any sign of approval or agreement. A worrying pause which seemed to last a lifetime was finally broken by Supo,

"Very well, then it seems that we must act as we planned. We all must have our say as equals. My army waits just north of Torfub, but the Xortogun men Tekolger ordered trained I marched here with me. You remember how much trouble Tekolger's decision to train them caused? If we need to sow division amongst the Companions, we could not ask for a better tool. All is set in Xosupil too. Dotmazo has Tekolger's wives and son close by. He awaits your signal to bring the child and the mother to Xortogun. What were Tekolger's instructions to Kelbal before he died?"

Zenu came back quickly as Pelu entered the room,

"I don't believe Tekolger was in his right mind or realised he was about to pass. Kelbal tells me when asked about the succession that he muttered something about his empire would see a new dawn after much strife. But he had previously said that he wished the child of his Xortogun bride to succeed as he would be the descendent of Yoruxoruni and Tekolger. That is what Kelbal intends, taken by the Xortogun as he is. The black ring Tekolger did hand to Kelbal, who now wields it as if he were the anointed heir, although he would deny it."

Pelu replied pensively, taking a cup of wine for himself,

"Then it is as we thought. Kelbal holds the key to the succession and with the army at his back he is a force to be reckoned with. A break with him would cause civil war. Supo is right, we will need to divide the Companions to weaken him."

Zenu agreed, although the prospect of such intrigue did not please him,

"Surely a king almost of age and of good Doldun stock, ready to put a firm hand on the wheel of the ship is better than an unknown child with a family and a people of doubtful loyalty. That will only cause years of infighting and instability when we can least afford it. The army and the other Companions will see that, even if we cannot prove Kelbal's guilt, or a conspiracy. Besides Surson, is not of the Doldun, without Tekolger the army will not warm to the child."

A smile washed itself over Supo's face,

"Then as we thought we will need to create distance between Kelbal and the other Companions. He will fall into line once he realises he cannot command their loyalty, and then we can start to make decisions collectively as we are supposed to. As for the army, we already have a plan to weaken its position. It is not the only armed force in the empire and without leadership any resistance will melt away."

Pelu interjected,

"We need to be sure that we have not overlooked that those forces loyal to us are spread across the empire, keeping peace and stability. This army is concentrating on Xortogun, Kelbal will have that to his advantage. If the whole host combines, then our forces near Torfub will not be enough to overcome them. If it comes to that."

Zenu replied,

"This is why we need to move quickly, get the other Companions on our side. It appears that a force of Rilrpitu has crossed the northern border as we hoped. We will need to persuade Kelbal to dispatch some regiments to deal with them. You can then ride north with them Supo, an excuse to break away and take command of your forces at Torfub. With the royal army spread over the northern provinces, and our forces concentrated at Torfub, we can force Kelbal to comply and have everything in place before we arrive in Xortogun. The army united or not will have to accept the situation, and it can be then divided up and sent to garrison the provinces of the empire. I want no bloodshed if it can be avoided, the last thing we need is war amongst ourselves."

Supo responded,

"Very well Zenu, we are of one mind on this. The empire must stand strong, although I do not like the thought of going against one of our own. But we must be careful Zenu. Only show Kelbal that he cannot rule as an absolute monarch but as one of many equals until the new king is ready. Which of the Companions do you think is most likely to split from Kelbal?"

"The only ones we need worry about are those twins and Kalu. I have sounded out Thazan, Deluan, Zonpeluthas and Zela. I believe they are open to suggestion and are persuadable, and I see no evidence yet of a wider conspiracy amongst them. We just must persuade them that it is in their interest to not let Kelbal have all the power. With those four on side the others will begin to fall into line. Dolzalo will do anything to humiliate Kelbal, we all know what he is like. And Palmash will follow Dolzalo. If we can ensure that this force keeps moving before Dolzalo's column catches up that will be a third of their strength gone anyway."

Zenu, satisfied that they all were of one mind and that the plan was the most sensible course of action for them to take, poured another cup of wine and signalled the guard that all three would take their food in his chamber.

THUSON

Thuson Kosua was growing used to the monotony of the march home. The years of campaigning had made him accustomed to the constant rigours of war, the need to be always alert. Even if he was only the king's secretary, it was a skill they had all needed. The time on the march was a welcome relief to be allowed to put his guard down, if only for a moment,

"Are we finally on the move?!" Dolzalo of the Zowo, the man they called Mountain Strider, bellowed as he approached mounted on his favourite black stallion. Palmash of the Tholmash, as always not far behind, played a short tune on his pan pipe to signal his coming. Thuson's guard was back up. The campaigning may have been over, but Dolzalo was as lively and unpredictable as ever.

He cursed Kelbal under his breath for leaving him with Dolzalo. Thuson was increasingly feeling like he had been abandoned to look after the unpredictable Companion with the rear column. Although the opportunity to prove himself useful to those who would undoubtedly be the new rulers of the empire was something Thuson had jumped at, Dolzalo was becoming increasingly difficult to control, and there was a reason the others called Palmash Weaver, and it was not just because of the spider web shaped scar on his neck. It was times like this he questioned what sorcery it was that had convinced him to leave Butophulo with his cousin Yusukol,

"All moving and in good order. Another few days' march, and we will be at Yorixori." Thuson replied assuredly, hoping that would mean catching up with the forward columns and escaping from Dolzalo. The red bearded Companion looked out across the well-ordered column snaking its way along the plain following the line of the Kelonzow river,

"There is a magnificence about the sight of a disciplined army on the march. Stirs something in the spirit I find."

The look of thunderous delight in Dolzalo's eyes made him feel uneasy. The same look he had had at Thentherzaw, but Thuson had been blind to it then, until it was too late. He still remembered the fires reflecting from the hot-headed Companion's eyes and crowning him in flame, as he stood over the body of the giant king of the port that he had left a smouldering ruin.

Dolzalo had always been bold and quick to temper, but those tendencies had only increased with Tekolger's passing. It was after Thentherzaw that the other Companions had started to distance themselves from Dolzalo and began using Thuson to control him. As if the philosopher and scholar from Butophulo had some mystical powers to tame the unruly Companion.

As the king's secretary, he was only there because Tekolger had trusted him. The other Companions, especially those his cousin Yusukol had educated, treated him well, but most Doldun always held him at a distance and his motives were viewed with scepticism. Thuson did not blame them for that, it must have seemed strange for a man from Butophulo to have become the King of the Doldun's trusted secretary, but the path he was put on was not one of Thuson's choosing. Tekolger had offered an opportunity to him, but more than that, the Xosu needed the king, begrudged though they would be to admit it. Tekolger was the living embodiment of all the teachings of Kunpit of Thelonigul, as Yusukol had intended to raise him to be. But there was also something otherworldly about the King of the Doldun too. Xosu's oracle had seen it, blessing him with the word of the god and hailing him *'the arrow of the light bringer, the shaft that would fly and bring a new dawn.'* Then the wise women of the Zummosh and the oracle of Kurotor had discerned something in Tekolger as well. Yusukol had asked Thuson to go with the king on his great expedition, to guide him in his destiny. How could he have refused?

With Tekolger gone, Thuson knew the mistrust and suspicion some of the Doldun had of him would only grow. For the first time he had become very conscious of his obvious Salxosu looks. Dark, almost navy, hair, blue eyes, and paler skin than even the other Xosu. He could not have been more of a contrast to the dusty brown hair, olive skin and dark eyes of most of the men of the clans. It would be best to play along and prove he could be trusted and relied on he had decided, even if it meant being used as Dolzalo's muzzle. He needed to ensure that Tekolger's vision was seen to its fruition, he owed the king that much.

Dolzalo spurred his horse and bolted to the head of the column. Palmash smiled in his menacing way with poison on his lips and followed swift as an arrow. Thuson and the small cavalry squadron accompanying them did the same.

At the head of what he had taken to calling his army, Dolzalo seemed in his element. He had always felt stuck in the shadow of a greater man Thuson knew. The death of the king had been like taking the leash off a rabid dog. Dolzalo no doubt saw it as the chance to finally step into the light which had crowned Tekolger for so long. With Palmash always close on hand to encourage Dolzalo in his actions, the hot-headed Companion had become very unpredictable. To Palmash it was all a game, something to entertain himself on the road, but to Dolzalo it was personal.

It was Palmash who needed to be watched closely rather than Dolzalo though, Thuson had slowly come to realise, but the others could not see through his jester-like grin. He was as slippery as a fish that one. Always lurking in the shadows like a wraith, with poison on his tongue for any who would listen. Thuson would have chained Palmash to a rock in the mountains if he could, if only for a moment's peace. Dolzalo turned to Thuson as he caught up with him, and in a booming voice proclaimed,

"To Yorixori. The fate of the empire will be decided over the next few weeks, I need to be there."

Thuson decided to probe him. It was best to know Dolzalo's intentions. Any spark of conflict was likely to emanate from him,

"What do you suppose will happen?" A simple question, but the well-built Companion usually lacked the tact to hide his intent.

"No doubt Kelbal will want to wait for the child to be born to Tekolger's barbarian consort. Kelbal will have his eye on a long regency with himself as regent. Maybe he even has his eye on Surson, he shared everything else with the king." Dolzalo's laugh rumbled in the way only he could at his own insight.

Thuson ignored the inconvenient fact of Dolzalo's own mother being a barbarian. His sky-blue eyes and shocking red beard gave that fact away, despite looking in every other way like a man of the clans of the Doldun. Indeed, Dolzalo's whole clan, the Zowo, were closer to the Zummosh than the Xosu, both in proximity and culture. Polrinu Sisosi's *The People of the Twins*, A study on the two peoples of the Doldun, gave a fine account of all the clans of the Doldun. Thuson had found it most helpful when he first came to the court of Kenkathoaz. He pressed further,

"No matter what Kelbal thinks, surely a regency is correct. Even though the king had other wives and children, Tekolger named no other heir."

Dolzalo replied,

"An answer I would expect from a man of the great city of Butophulo.

It is centuries since your city had a king, isn't it? The line of succession is never that straight, especially among the Doldun. Yes, the child is Tekolger's chosen heir, but its mother is a barbarian and who knows if it will be a boy or a girl, only the gods."

Palmash played a tune on his pan pipe again, before transforming the melody into words,

"The clans will have their say. Through words or deed." He finished the sentence with a grin. Dolzalo scratched his shock of a beard and continued,

"Yes, the clans will not be silent. A chance to stamp their authority and choose a new king. One cut from their own mould. And Tekolger had wives of good Doldun stock, a son who will almost be a man grown now, and other children, I am sure. Tekolger was not exactly lacking in charm or boldness. There was a reason his father sent him into exile." Dolzalo paused and laughed like rolling thunder, "Everything is up for grabs now. When Doldun was one small patch of land we would fight tooth and nail for whatever scrap of it we could get. Whole worlds are now on offer, don't expect anything to be easy." It was a true enough statement. When Thuson had first moved with his cousin to the court of Kenkathoaz, the Doldun could scarcely call their land a kingdom. The clans were fighting the king and each other in what seemed an endless cycle of violence.

"But surely none of the King's Companions would allow anyone but his flesh and blood and chosen heir to inherit? The blood of Tholophos, and through him Xosu, needs to run in the veins of the King of the Doldun." Thuson replied.

"There are plenty of people who could claim to be Tekolger's flesh and blood." Palmash's words flew into the conversation.

"I am myself a descendent of the royal line." Dolzalo bellowed in response.

Thuson smiled. He knew full well that Dolzalo was of royal blood, a distant and minor branch of the royal family. A fact that Dolzalo liked to remind everyone of. Thuson pressed him further,

"I don't think any of Tekolger's Companions would jeopardise the empire they all put so much into forging."

"Tekolger's closest Companions maybe not, but there are others. Zenukola is an old man, but still a schemer, he did not stay alive so long among the Doldun without being one. No doubt he will be up to something. And Dotmazo, he was not given the command of Xosupil for nothing. He will want something out of this. Remember the blood moon conspiracy, I knew then as I do now, Zenu and Dotmazo had their hands in that. I told Tekolger as much, but he would not listen. They've tried once and failed; they may not fail this time." Dolzalo was clearly pleased with his ability to discern his countrymen's intentions, but it was a disturbing thought. The blood moon conspiracy had almost cost the king his life. Dolzalo seemed to think that Zenu had survived to succeed at the second attempt, a troubling notion if true. Sensing that he would offer more, Thuson inquired,

"And what about you?"

Dolzalo laughed,

"I have earned a reward for my service. Recognition of that would be a start."

* * *

The march continued dull and eventless until Dunsun had almost completed his journey across the sky. A few more days marching, and they would arrive in Yorixori and Thuson could finally escape from Dolzalo and Palmash. Dull and eventless would suit him fine until then.

The evening rolled around and nothing of note occurred. Until, on the north side of the river, a small column of smoke began creeping over the horizon, behind a block of trees. Like a fire bursting from the green earth.

From the woods emerged a horse galloping towards them, a man slumped over on its back. The horse cantered into the shallow but fast following water and the rider slid from the saddle and disappeared under the murky depths.

One of the men from the cavalry squadron rode forward, splashing into the swift flowing but shallow river, and brought the horse under control. A second man dragged the rider onto the bank. The wounded rider was in the dress of a Xosu spearman. He spluttered out the river water, suddenly coming back to life as Dolzalo demanded to know what was going on,

"What happened?" The Companion impatiently snapped,

"Rebels." the man forced it out, "At least a hundred, been struggling with them for a few weeks now, came out of nowhere, like they burst out of a cloud or something. Only warning we had was the shaking ground from their rumbling hooves, but it was too late. They jumped us in the village beyond those trees. Slaughtered my comrades and started to plunder the place. I was fortunate that the gods saw fit to let me live."

Dolzalo's eyes flashed into life,

"Finally, something to liven this march up. We will swing in quickly and take them by surprise. We can't allow an attack on the king's men to go unanswered." Turning to Thuson, he said, "A chance for you to prove yourself secretary. Take the Thulchwal and advance through the woods. I will sweep around with the cavalry and catch any who try to run. The Xosu spears will follow up behind you." With that he turned and rode off toward the river, the cavalry close behind.

Thuson could not help but feel this was hasty. It was a village within the empire, they were not campaigning in enemy territory now and had no real information on the foe they faced or the terrain which lay beyond the boundary of the river. But an opportunity of command, a chance to prove himself to the Doldun as more than just a secretary to the king. He would need to prove himself a warrior if he were to hope to retain any influence at the royal court. It was worth the risk.

Thuson took a deep breath and signalled to Llalon, the ferocious chieftain of the thousand strong force of Thulchwal marching behind him. Then he whispered a prayer to Xosu and spurred his horse, splashing across the river.

The woods were a lot denser than they first appeared, thick with foliage despite the fast-settling autumn. Thuson dismounted from his horse. A wave of exhilaration overtook him, he could feel his heart pounding in his ears. He had been near plenty of engagements before over the years of campaigning, but he lacked the skill and training of his Doldun comrades, and this was the first time he had been given the command of soldiers on campaign. He was a scholar and a philosopher not a warrior. Nerves overtook him in his eagerness to get this right, small as the undertaking he was set may have seemed.

What are you doing? he thought. Suddenly he felt ridiculous and uncomfortable in the panoply of a Xosu warrior. The bronze greaves felt heavy on his legs. His cast bronze Rinuxosu style helmet a black hole, and the panther picked out in lapis, rubies and jade on his cuirass, a gift from Tekolger, seemed absurd. He had barely taken two steps on the crunching carpet of leaves before he could smell the sweet stench of sweat on himself.

Without a word from Thuson, Llalon barked out some orders from behind his long, oiled moustache and the Thulchwal men spread out into loose order and began their march through the woods. The men drew their curved falx, the savage swords favoured by these warriors, as they entered the dense trees.

The Thulchwal were a Zummosh tribe that lived in their own secluded valley north of Doldun. Tekolger had forged a unique bond with them after marrying a woman of the tribe. Where most Doldun kings would have sort to defeat and dominate them by force, Tekolger had seen a different path, even spending a year living amongst them whilst in exile from the court. Llalon, the chieftain who commanded the king's forces, was a close and loyal friend to the king, having fought by his side in every battle. Thuson was thankful for their years of experience. Wild as they may be in conflict, they were experts in their craft. He drew his own leaf shaped blade and followed them into the trees.

The walk through the woods was long enough for Thuson to regain his composure. As the village on the other side came into view, nestled amongst a clutch of dolthil trees whose golden leaves were stretching across the sky, the bottom of the smoking column could be seen.

What was left of a tower-like structure was still ablaze and the silhouettes of several figures could be seen against the twilight sun as the chill of the autumn evening began to set in. They looked more beast than man in the flickering light. But short and stocky silhouettes emerged as the light from the flames flickered and changed the shadows to more man-like shapes. Swords slung on their waists and the distinctive curved shape of the recurved bows used only by the Rilrpitu of the northern steppe were in their hands.

Thuson had seen them up close when Tekolger recruited a few of the tribes which had not fled Zenian to serve under him. He had tried to learn as much as he could of the tribes from those men. Xosu scholars who had written about the Rilrpitu had always had little to say, and what they could say was based on myth and rumour. One day he would like to write his own tract on the people of the steppe himself, with information gathered from talking to the Rilrpitu, maybe even live among them for time to better understand their ways.

It was clear that the wounded rider had the truth of it. They seemed to be ransacking a cart filled with military supplies. The bodies of its owners lay strewn on the ground, the distinctive panoplies of the Xosu clear even in the dimming light, and the corpse of what must have been the owner of the cart was hung limply from a tree, peppered with arrows. But these were not rebels, rather they were raiders from the north. How they had managed to slip passed the garrison at Tekolgerdeloan and ride this far south without being stopped was a question that would need to be answered.

Sending a small detachment to follow the line of trees around to the top of the village, Thuson intended to draw the men into the open ground between the hamlet and the tree line.

A tense wait followed as the Thulchwal snuck around to their position. The tension was broken as the men, following Thuson orders, stepped out of the tree line and began to make their way down the road into the village. Making enough noise to alert the raiders. The setting sun glinted off the golden armbands the warriors of the Zummosh wore. Most also wore mail like a second skin, but a few went into battle with their armbands, tattoos and light trousers, nothing more.

Thuson stayed still and silent, observing. The feeling of excitement and a nervous, impatient energy returned to him once more as he watched the Rilrpitu take note of the men entering the village and slowly begin to move towards them. Some drew swords and others raised their bows.

Waiting for as long as he dared to, Thuson, blood pounding in his ears, stood, raised his sword in the air, allowing the setting sun to flash off it as if it were the last star in the sky. He bellowed a war cry as he began his charge, praying to Xosu that the men would follow, and luck would be with him. Rushing forward he could hear the Thulchwal answer his call. The Rilrpitu to his front, no more than twenty strong, turned and watched on, frozen to the spot.

As he rapidly approached the settlement, his heart pounding, several of the men turned to run. One dropped his sword, but two stood their ground. The first man came upon Thuson, his eyes feral behind a long flowing beard, with hair bellowing in the wind. The warrior swung wildly at him. Thuson parried his blow and slashed the man across his face. He screamed, and blood splattered. Thuson could feel the warm, wet splash across his cheek and the smell of iron filled the air and finally drowned out his own sweet sweat. Death came spiralling down on his foe, but all Thuson could hear was the blood pounding in his ears.

Turning to his right. Another man was coming towards him, the bright colours of his pattern trousers flashing and the scales of his bronze armour glinting. The warrior raised his spear, but before Thuson could react, the man's skull burst open as the point of a vicious, two-handed, curved sword came crashing down on him.

He continued his advance, the rest of the Thulchwal had already spread into the village. The corpses of several more armed men were in front of him. Two of the men attempting to flee had been taken prisoner.

Pushing on into the centre of the village, Thuson could see a few dozen more men fleeing toward the open country on horseback. As they left the boundary of the village, war horns blared and the thunder of hooves signalled the arrival of Dolzalo, cutting off their escape.

Satisfied that he had done his job well, a calm once again rushed over Thuson. He called over the towering warrior Llalon, whose spiked hair made him seem a savage giant.

"Search the village, see if you can find any more of them. The villagers must be somewhere as well."

As the Llalon turned to go, Thuson grabbed his arm,

"No more killing, especially the villagers. We don't know if they were involved or not."

He let the chieftain go just as Dolzalo's men thundered into the village, carrying torches. Shouting from horseback, a cavalryman bellowed,

"Burn it all down, show them that rebellion will not be tolerated!"

Before Thuson could step in, torches were being thrown into every building and fires were spreading to the whole village.

Thuson's blood was immediately pumping again, his ears pounding, he shouted to his men,

"Get the villagers out!" as he rushed into the nearest building, finding a group huddled in the corner he ushered them out of the building and ordered two of his men to see them safely to edge of the village.

Chaos and flames were all around him, but the calm fell over Thuson again. A calm and a fury.

***

As the sun rose over the horizon, the smouldering embers of what was once a village crackled and popped. Thuson had spent a long night dragging as many people as he could from the burning buildings. Dolzalo and the cavalry had disappeared into the night to track down any other raiders.

With rosy fingers creeping over the horizon, a squadron of horse came galloping back into the village. Thuson found himself getting to his feet and approaching the column of horse,

"Where is your commander?" He demanded. A young man mounted on a great charger, the formidable horses bred on the hills of Doldun, trotted forward. The boy was a typical product of the nobility of the hill country of Doldun. Wiry and tall, taller than the Xosu, and with an air of arrogance only youth could give. He wore the distinctive felt and moulded leather cap of the Doldun clans, instead of the beaten bronze Tilxosu helmet usually preferred for battle, with a short linen cape wrapped around him and pinned at the right shoulder. Under the cloak he wore a moulded bronze cuirass, silver-lined, a gift from Tekolger to all his cavalry men, below that a leather kilt and the calf height, open toed, leather strapped boots of all the soldiery.

"Who gave the order to burn the village?" Thuson demanded.

The young man looked him up and down, the condescension dripping off him. Tekolger had always treated everyone by their own merits, not so much could be said for the other Doldun when it came to the Xosu,

"Rebels need to be crushed; examples need to be made." The boy replied.

"I asked who gave the order." Thuson replied, his tone getting sharper.

The boy turned his head and looked to the horizon as another column of cavalry rumbled into the burning husk of the village.

Dolzalo and Palmash, who was wearing a sun hat which looked to have been looted from one of the local farmers, came thundering into what was the centre of the village. Lively as ever, Dolzalo leapt from his mount shouting Thuson's name,

"Thuson! Where were you? I needed the support of your infantry."

Thuson wearily turned to face the conquering spearman,

"We stayed here, helping the people whose village you set on fire."

Dolzalo laughed,

"We set an example to any other rebels. It will not be tolerated, and we will stamp on any insurrection. It would have been far better for you to have supported my men."

Thuson rolled over one of the corpses of the fallen men and said,

"Look at him Dolzalo. He is not a rebel, he is a Rilrpitu tribesman, and look at the headdress and the pointed skull. One from the north, from beyond the Thazzow river. We have a lot more on our hands than a few rebels if a Rilrpitu raiding party has managed to get this far south."

Dolzalo took a few moments to study the man, before replying,

"So, he is. Well, we had better get after the rest of them then, no time to lose."

Dolzalo paused for a moment and looked around at the embers of the settlement, pleased with his work he turned back to Thuson,

"You did well last night, next time follow it through, and we will make a general of you yet."

Feeling the fury of the last night rising in him once more, Thuson replied,

"There was no need to burn the village. These were simple farmers who were the target of raiders. If we burn their villages and kill their families, we will only create actual rebels. Tekolger was trying to create an empire of all the peoples of this land remember. One whole, united under the crown of Xosu."

Dolzalo simply laughed again,

"And we will crush those rebels as well. The one thing that unites people all over the world is an understanding of the power of force. We did not conquer this empire by being timid and we will not keep it that way. It is how Kenkathoaz united the Doldun as well, or have you not heard The Broken Spear?"

It was clear to Thuson that Dolzalo could not be reasoned with. The same look in his eye as he had at Thentherzaw was there once again. He said with force in his voice,

"Did that work in Zentheldel Dolzalo? The fighting only got worse after you put Thentherzaw to the sword, the whole country rose against us."

"There would have been more rebels if we did not act quickly. Who knows what else Talehalden was planning." The answer came from Palmash. Dolzalo continued,

"And we crushed that rebellion. Besides that, duplicitous king needed to be made an example of, he poisoned Tekolger, or had you forgotten?"

"You have no proof of that Dolzalo. the king died of an illness. Maybe it was poison, but we had no reason to suspect Talehalden, no authority to sack the city." Thuson sighed. Tekolger's death haunted them all, but he was sure it was not Talehalden who had poisoned the king. It had been Thuson who handed Talehalden the cup after all and it was already filled to the brim with a deep red wine that the Putdeun had brought. With all the fatigue of the last few months returning, he continued,

"We were almost lost in the fighting. What if the whole of Zenian rose like that?" Thuson answered, tired of this argument. Dolzalo, with the same enthusiasm for violence he always showed, replied,

"Zenian won't rise. They are terrified of us, godlike men who won the whole world with our spears. All we need do is keep those spears at their throats."

"Only if we want to spend the rest of lives looking over our shoulders. Tekolger's vision was an empire that united the peoples of east and west, not pitting them against each other." Thuson answered again.

"Tekolger is gone." With that, Dolzalo left, clearly unwilling to engage any further. Palmash flew off after him.

Thuson took another look at the burning ruin that used to be a village. *The sooner Dolzalo is brought under control the better,* he thought. Reuniting with the rest of the army could not come soon enough.

He called over a rider and said,

"Ride to Yorixori and let Kelbal know that we have encountered a Rilrpitu warband who we believe have crossed into the empire from beyond the Thazzow and are raiding south. We are pursuing them north and that we request reinforcements, cavalry if he can spare it."

SONOSPHOSKUL

7

The sun had begun its descent from its peak before he saw them. Dunsun's Throne drifting past its pinnacle as the glint on the horizon became blocks of soldiers. *Finally, a battle*, he thought. Sonosphoskul Polriso was a veteran of dozens of battles, enough to know that the blood, sweat and death about to erupt on this dusty plain was nothing to long for, but it was the tension before the turmoil that he had never gotten used to. *Better to just get it over with*, he thought, especially when the army's seers had proclaimed this to be a good day to fight.

This brief reflection on the reality of war did not distract Sonosphoskul from his duty for long, a lifetime of conflict had honed the demands it made into instinct. As soon as the blocks of soldiers became clear on the horizon, he began assessing the enemy's disposition.

A small force of horsemen on their right, dressed in white cuirasses, were covering the gap between the enemy's flank and the mountains, the chain which cut through the heart of this eastern land. Expensively dressed though they were, Sonos did not think they looked like a threat. Soft sons of nobility rather than true horsemen.

To the cavalry's left and out to the front of the main force was a formation of skirmishers. Lightly armoured javelin men screening the approach of several blocks of heavy infantry, armed with a tall shield and a short sword. These swordsmen were the core of the enemy force, and the real threat to Sonosphoskul's men. The few encounters they had had with these warriors during the campaign had been enough to realise how dangerous they could be. The men from the League of the Twelve Brothers, who he had fought beside for half a year, used the same equipment. Hozfotou Hotthuzishoz Kuthozuz, one of the captains of the

Legion from the League, had allowed him to try the sword and shield for himself once. The sword was short but well balanced, good for slashing, but the men who wielded them were mostly trained to thrust. The shield was no heavier than his own round shield and equally cumbersome, but it did allow more protection for an individual. Xosu shields were better suited to be used in a formation, to protect one's neighbour as much as oneself. *Those swords will be even more dangerous now that the war had reached the walls of Gottoy and the men wielding them become more desperate*, he thought.

He looked further down the line of the army of the Republic of Gottoy. The men from the city that had overwhelmed the League of the Twelve Brothers had anchored their left flank to the Thelizum river. A wise move and showing the opposing general had some sense. Toyoroz Hozhoz Dozthozfiz this general was called. A politician from a rich and ancient family raised by Gottoy in the wake of their defeats at the hands of the Gelodun and Xosu to be their salvation. *At least this battle may make for a good tale*, he supposed.

Still making his assessments as some stragglers fell into his line, Sonosphoskul could not help but reflect on how he had become entangled in this war. More than ten years since Sonos and his comrades, were exiled from their home. Left to wander as shadows and wraiths of what they had once been. They had forged a life as sellswords, praying for the day they could free Butophulo from the grip of the King of the Doldun. Although they had spent most of that time fighting their fellow Salxosu in the White Islands in service to the city of Thasotun which had tried to rise to take Butophulo's place.

Pirates, Thasotun's rulers had labelled their enemies, it was not entirely a lie. No doubt some of those slain were marauders taking advantage of the chaos that followed the fall of the League. But many more were the remnants of those still loyal to Butophulo with nothing left to do but fight for the few islands that remained to them. Names like Kolmosoi the Hydra, Zolmos the Conjurer and Dinon the Wanderer had still commanded a fierce loyalty even after Butophulo itself fell.

Sonos couldn't help but sympathise with the men he had fought against for so long. His own desire to reclaim his home had only grown in intensity as the years dragged on. But now he found himself further from that dream than ever. Instead, he was marching with the army of Hunthisonu, King of Gelodun, far to the east. Fighting a war for another man's glory against the armies of Gottoy. Worse than that, the King of Gelodun was close kin of the King of the Doldun who had driven the men of Butophulo into exile in the first place. The glory sought was in imitation of Tekolger.

Gripping his spear tightly as a twang of anger coursed through him,

Sonosphoskul was pulled back to the impending battle as he heard a noise ripple through the ranks. The men were passing the watchword through the lines,

"Buto the saviour and victory"

The words echoed down the line as each man passed it on. Sonosphoskul repeated them, touching the amulet which he always wore around his neck as he did,

"Buto the saviour and victory"

The tranquillity the captain of Butophulo found in this moment was shattered by the approach of hammering hooves and the cheers of the men following them down the line. Looking up, Sonosphoskul saw his commander, Runukolkil Rusosthup. They were of an age, raised together, educated together at the Academy of Rolmit of Rulkison and they had fought together in the closing years of the War for the Forge against the Rinuxosu, under the command of Kolmosoi Kisurisosi. Runu was a quiet man, but practical and competent, if a little melancholic at times. The men had grown to trust him though, and his classic Salxosu looks helped with that. Runu had the jet-black hair, light blue eyes and pale skin which made him seem more like a man of old Kolbos than Butophulo.

Forming a mercenary company, to keep all the exiles from Butophulo together and to offer those yet to flee a home when they did, had been Kolmosoi's notion. After his murder, when the men were asked to select a new commander, they had unanimously chosen Runukolkil. With that vote the Daemons of the Deep had been saved from themselves as Runu forged them back into a cohesive force.

"What news of the king?" Sonos asked with a smile,

The general replied in his considered way,

"Don't be sarcastic Sonos. The king is in good spirits, finally getting to fight a proper battle. He will be launching the main assault along the river trying to push them away from its bank and roll them up from there. Our job will be to hold the left flank. We are not just going to take it though, push them back if you can. I want an active defence and be prepared for anything; I have little confidence in this hubristic king."

The general galloped off to brief the other captains. No doubt Kusuasu Kinsol and Pusokol Kolkisuasu, would also see the recklessness in the king's plan. They had all pursued a heedless glory in their youth, as many Xosu were want to do, to bring fame and repute to themselves and their families. It had been easy to recognise that lust and desire for fame and glory behind Hunthisonu's eyes the moment they had met the King of Gelodun. Not a bad trait for a young man to display provided it was properly checked by his elders. But the young King of Gelodun also showed a naivety which had the potential to endanger the entire army.

The king can have his glory, Sonos thought, *but it is not a tale I will tell happily.*

He glanced down the line. In the centre of the army of Gelodun he could see the king's infantry, men from Gelodun itself. Armed with small shields, conical Tilxosu style helmets, and long pikes, in the fashion of the Doldun. The aping of Tekolger's new way of war said a lot about the King of Gelodun and his desire to emulate his illustrious cousin.

Sonos knew what it was like to encounter the wall of pikes slowly and methodically coming towards you, he had faced Tekolger's men on the field. A helplessness had gripped his heart that day as his shorter thrusting spear could not find a way through the forest of pikes. And then cavalry thundered over him and the League of Butophulo died. But the men of Gelodun lacked the iron discipline and training of their Doldun counterparts, their wall of spears less formidable and more prone to panic as a result.

Beyond the pikemen, the king's cavalry was forming by the river. Left of centre had been placed the legion from the League of the Twelve Brothers. Good men, eager to avenge their previous defeats at the hands of Gottoy. Further left still were the companies of Xosu mercenaries, famed throughout the world.

The Exiles were next in the line. Rinuxosu whose commanders had abandoned the Sacred Band of their king when the Grand Assembly of the Rinuxosu had invited the Doldun to invade Xosupil. The men of the Sacred Band of the Rinuxosu had been the most fearsome foes Sonos ever faced. Selected from birth and sent to the nine gated fortress of Dolkosutiko to be raised as warriors. They claimed that they were Xosu's famed band who sprung from the white hydra's teeth come again. It was said they would be paired with an older man from a young age, who would teach the boys to fight, to march, to survive and to love. The men of the Sacred Band spoke little of their training themselves. Whatever the methods, it was a harsh regimen that scarcely three boys in every ten apparently survived. But at the end of it, the man who emerged was a deadly weapon. It was strange to think of them as allies now, but Thusokosa, their commander, was the type of warrior you wanted at your side in battle.

Further down the line was a company of Silxosu, The White Hydra's Teeth. Holding the far-left flank were the Daemons of the Deep. Exiles from Butophulo mostly, with a few other Salxosu from the White Islands amongst their number as well.

Protecting the exposed wing of this phalanx was a company of Tilxosu called The Bulodon. All mounted on the famous steeds of the northern country of Xosupil.

Turning back to his own men, Sonos looked around with satisfaction as he observed the discipline in the ranks. The left flank was their responsibility, he could have confidence in that part of the line at least.

He lifted his own helmet. Solid bronze in the Rinuxosu style, all one piece, with two cheek plates and a nose guard which closed off his ears and left only a small part of his face exposed. Many of his comrades preferred the Salxosu style of open-faced helm, but Sonos had always opted for the heavier garb. Brushing the royal blue horsehair crest that ran horizontally, left to right, which matched his own eyes and marked him out as a captain. He placed the helmet over his head. The world seemed to shrink when he did, and the pounding of his heart and heaviness of his breath became overwhelming.

The trumpets of the enemy blasted in the distance signalling the beginning of their advance. In reply came the trumpets of the King of Gelodun.

Off to his right, Sonos could perceive movement. A glinting light rising like the star which comes before the dawn as the blocks of pikemen, the men of Gelodun, began their approach on the enemy line. A great swirl of dust came over them as what Sonos presumed was the king's horse thundered forward, streaking across the open plain like an arrow. The king himself would be at the point of the wedge leading the charge like Tekolger always did, with a burning desire for glory, striking the writhing lines of the enemy like a thunderbolt. Behind him would be the Companions he had raised in further imitation of the Doldun.

Not now, Sonos thought, *its surely too soon for a charge.*

The Xosu mercenaries, numbering almost five thousand, and the men from the League of the Twelve Brothers, also numbering five thousand, half of the army's strength, did nothing. They waited for the enemy to close the distance before they began the dance of the day. The commotion to their right as the army flooded forward, men clashed with men, iron, and bronze, sweat and blood, the noise and horror of war, did not even draw a curious glance, fixed as they were on the foe to their front. Holding their nerve in complete silence until the enemy force was only three or four stades from their phalanx, the Xosu struck up their paean and advanced as one.

Moving swiftly into the dust cloud that was beginning to blow over them, changing their sight of the world, the men of Butophulo clashed the shafts of their spears against their shields, letting out a din that would have shaken the gods in their golden palace and cracked the world. Breaking into a run they let out their war cry,

"Buto!"

The speed of their advance and the dust limiting visibility must have taken the javelin men by surprise. As Sonos led the Xosu on, a few javelins landed amongst them, but most of the light infantry turned and fled before releasing their volley. The cowards clashed into their own advancing infantry, causing chaos in their ranks. Then Sonos crashed into the morass of men gripped in discord and panic. With a thump, the surreal world of the dust that had engulfed them, dimming the senses, broke as Sonos collided with the front line.

Easily overpowering the first man, his spear found the belly of the second, spraying blood over Sonos' helmet, his horsehair crest turning a crimson red.

Stepping over the corpses of the men, Sonos encountered his first resistance. A shield thrust into his own. The round, moon shaped, dome of his shield rang as they clashed. *Some courage at last,* he thought, a crescent of a smile gracing his lips. A swift strike of his spear and Sonos brought death whirling down on his opponent. His spear cracked and the head lay buried in the gut of his foe who lay motionless on the ground as his blood soaked into the earth.

Leaving the broken shaft in the man, Sonos drew his leaf shaped blade and looked to his sides. Smiling as he saw his men driving fear and death into the ranks of the enemy. *Sem will be pleased with the Salxosu on this day, sending the shades of countless men down to his dark halls.*

Urging the Xosu forward, he continued the advance. Two more soldiers, two more lethal strikes and the hands of death coiled around them. The infantry to his front turned to run. Maintaining the discipline learnt from a lifetime of war, Sonos resisted the urge to follow and reassessed his position. *Where is the cavalry?* he thought. Instinctively he bellowed out orders,

"Back into line, prepare for the cavalry!"

In an instant the phalanx reformed, bristling with spears, just as the cavalry burst into view. Sonos was pleased as they drew near. Inexperienced youths they were after all, showing no sign of slowing down, he shouted again,

"Tighter, keep it tight!"

The Xosu bunched together as close as possible. *The men may be foolish,* Sonos thought, *but the horses are not.* They continued to thunder closer,

"Hold!" Sonos shouted. The men raised their spears as one, as they did the horses reared. Sonos bellowed his battle cry and charged, tearing into the now chaotic melee of horse and men. Death came red and bloody to the white cuirassed cavalry, their pale armour-soaked wine dark as they crashed to the ground.

Those riders who could not flee were cut down. The rest of the young horsemen turned and scattered. Sonos was careful to pull his men back into line. The horsemen may be inexperienced, but they would make short work of any of his men caught in the open.

Pacing the line ensuring the men were back in order and ready to receive another assault, Sonos looked back and fore scanning the field for the next threat. His breath was heavy, his muscles ached, and the iron smell of blood hung on the air. In the distance, the cloud of dust surrounding the melee obscured his view. All he could discern from the noise, the sight and even the smell was that a fierce battle was raging in the centre and on the right flank.

Through the dust, he could make out the standards of the king charging headlong into the enemy line. The Gelodun may be Xosu, but they fought with the wild ferocity more worthy of the Zummosh. Admirable, but foolish, nonetheless.

The increasing commotion and chaos, and the ever-growing swirling cloud of dust made discerning what else might be going on impossible. The lack of knowledge did not faze Sonosphoskul though. The battlefield was always a confusing place, all you could do was focus on the task in front of you and hope everyone else carried out their role as well. On this field, he would defeat the enemy to his front and sack Gottoy for this foolish king. A task he did not relish, but the plunder may be enough to allow him the chance to return and free the Salxosu from the grip of the Doldun. He would march into the halls of the dead itself if it were necessary to allow him to return home.

A mournful wailing grown seemed to ripple down the line in that moment. Movement closer to his position caught Sonos' eye. The two other contingents from Butophulo were moving toward them at pace, Runukolkil at their head, the other Xosu mercenaries close behind. The men streamed by in a rush, clearly shaken but maintaining their discipline. Runu, riding alongside them barking out orders and maintaining their cohesion, drew up next to Sonos,

"What is happening?" Sonos asked, but already confident that he knew what the tale would be.

"The king has fallen. Withdraw your men to the top of that hill and prepare a defence. Sonos, I want your company to form the rear guard." Runu replied pointing to a tall, flat-topped hill in the foothills of the mountains without even a hint of panic or emotion in his voice. Sonos was impressed with his composure, but the Xosu had never found the King of Gelodun a very inspiring figure, there was no reason why his death would have caused Runu any real anguish. If anything, the death of the king brought Sonos a pang of relief. The obligation he felt to serve Hunthisonu, through the swearing of a sacred oath, had now gone. He was free to return and liberate his home. But first they would have to survive, stranded deep in the territory of the Republic of Gottoy.

Sonos felt the rush of adrenaline flow through his veins again, as at the start of the battle. The field had just become a whole lot more dangerous. The world he had woken too that morning transformed when the king fell, the men would be changed with it. Keeping his composure, he bellowed out a command for the company to form up on the rear of the retreating Xosu and prepare for a fighting retreat.

SANAE

8

A dull ache was coursing through her legs. *How much longer must I stand here?* Sanae thought. What seemed like an age had passed. She looked to the sky for the third time, and it had gone completely dark, whilst twilight still held when she came to stand. The sky now had a canopy of stars to cover it, the towering dolthil tree, which sat in the grounds of the temple, had stretched out its thin, flame red branches across that canopy. The light of the stars shining through its broad, golden, and fragrant leaves made it look as though each star was a ripe fruit ready to be plucked whilst the tree blazed, alive with light. A sound came from behind her, the creaking of a door, the bellowing of a bull and the chanting of a priest. *Finally, they are here,* she thought.

Slowly the procession made its way from the new temple down the steps towards the altar. Konthelae opened the door and drifted out of the chamber, the first of the priestesses of the procession leading the way for the light of the sacred flame, her face covered in pigment, half red, half white, resembling a sunrise. The High Priest, Helupelan, followed Konthelae. The light of his lantern, which carried the sacred flame brought from golden Thelonigul itself, gave the bearded old man an otherworldly glow and crowned him with the glory of the sun. It made his grey, almost white, hair seem golden, despite the darkness all around him. The image accentuated by the red paint that covered his face.

The flame had been gifted by the priestesses who keep the sacred books and spoke the words of the bright god himself, his oracle. The smell of the incense he carried filled her nose as he passed close by.

Behind Helupelan came Zenthelae, the light emanating from the lantern dimming as it reached her, to cast her in a warm glow like the fading light of the twilight. Her face was made up in the inverse of Konthelaes'. Behind them trailed the High Priestess, Kolae. Only a hint of the light reached her, giving her round face a pale shimmering glow which complemented the pure white pigment she wore. Her long dark hair looked almost a deep, rich blue.

Two more of Xosu's priestesses followed on, a battling moon white bull between them. They struggled to keep up as the bull wrestled with them. Its long sharp horns swinging left and right like the vicious fangs of some great monster, its tail darting back and fore as a serpent would to strike its prey. As they passed, the assembled priesthood took up the ululating chanting and Sanae joined them. The bacchic rhythm filled her, an ecstasy overtook her, and she no longer felt the dull ache in her body, only the fury, the delight, and the frenzy.

The procession filed onto the altar as the gathered worshippers looked on. Helupelan turned to the statue behind him draped in a covering sky blue in colour and featuring the golden star of Xosu. The High Priest whipped the cloth away in one swift movement.

Sanae immediately forgot about everything else, the sight of the statue taking her breath away, feeling like she had died and be born anew. Surely it was more than the work of a master craftsman, it must be truly imbued with the spirit of the god. A beautiful milk white marble, quarried from the hills around Thelonigul, had been crafted, chiselled, and shaped to reveal the bright, all knowing, benevolent figure of Xosu. The paint which had then been applied showed the god in all his shining glory, adding a brightness and a scarlet glow to the marble. A long flowing beard of amber lined with lapis lazuli and hair to match, the goat-like horns, covered by a robe made of jade and glistening red gemstone eyes, glowing like fire. In his right hand he carried his famous white-gold bow, made from the curved hydra's horn with serpents carved to curl around its length. In his left hand a bunch of grapes, purple and glistening as if they were about to burst.

Helupelan raised his arms and began to speak, as Kolae took the flame and placed it at the foot of the statue. Small and dim in comparison to the shining god,

"Xosu, Bright One, Giver of Knowledge and Bringer of Light, just as you gave life to the Xosu, leading them to a dawn from the darkness, sharing the knowledge of the gods, so we now give you this life." His voiced echoed as if it came from every direction.

The High Priestess drew a razor-sharp sickle shaped knife from her robes and in one swift movement, slit the bull's throat. The white light of the moon glinted off the dripping blade as she lifted her hands. The braying stopped and red blood sprayed out, violently lashing the High Priestess across the face, and careening into the fire as if a rock dropped into a lake from a great height. As the bull let out its dying groan, the crowd came to life and cried out in anguish and relish. The flames drank the creature's lifeblood and danced up in delight, licking toward the heavens and illuminating the whole temple in so bright a light that Sanae could have believed that dawn had come. The heat of the flame flooded over her, intense as a furnace, but Sanae was captivated, transformed. She watched the flames which dared to dance the highest, almost reaching up to the heavens and touching the dolthil tree which loomed overhead. For half a heartbeat it seemed as though the great tree would catch flame, but the fires danced back down, and the world seemed smaller again.

Sanae's eyes now fell back to the scene before her as wine dark blood spilled onto the altar. Sculpted from a giant black stone found abundantly in Xortogun but nowhere else. It looked like iron but gleamed like precious jet when polished. The blood oozed through the well-cut channels and fed into the bowl-shaped stone at the end of the altar table. The bowl drunk the liquid eagerly, absorbing the life and essence of the beast. Helupelan continued,

"Bright one, we give you this life, and bring your fire into this new city and your new temple. We pray you offer Tekolgertep your protection for as long as your flame burns within the city's heart."

A strong wind blew from across the bay, creating a ripple along the reflecting pool at the foot of the statue. It made the god's reflected image grow and seemingly reach out towards Sanae from the realm of the gods, his grasp maddeningly close. The flames licked up toward the sky again to signal Xosu's approval. The worshippers and the priesthood once again took up the ululating chant.

The worshippers were led by Keluaz of the Keluazi, one of the four great governors of the valley of Xortogun. A tall and skinny man in a pale white Xosu style toga, lined with silver, who walked with a cane and spoke with a long-drawn-out slur due to a childhood accident which shattered half his body. His slurring speech and his style of talking had led many to name the governor the Meanderer. Though some of the crueller Doldun said it was because he could not walk in a straight line due to his shattered leg. Keluaz seemed not to care about those jibes though, he had a jovial attitude and beaming smile even with the burden assigned to him of building king Tekolger's city as his clan were famous for their skill in the craft.

Next to the governor knelt Rososmosh Kolkisuasu, a wandering philosopher who the governor had taken into his service as an advisor. A bald and plump Salxosu man, who dressed as flamboyantly as his master did plainly, wearing a Xortogun robe of many bright colours and cloth of silver. It was said that nothing happened in the city without his knowledge or say so.

Keluaz and his advisor struggled to their feet at the signal of the High Priest, one due to his ailment the other to his overindulgence. The others followed suit, queuing at the altar to be anointed with the blood of the sacrifice. But Sanae stayed still, caught up in the spectacle, her gaze straight as an arrow onto the statue. The image of the god filled her with wonder and hope for the future of the city. She had first arrived in Tekolgertep a young child after Tekolger had conquered Xortogun. He had decreed a city to be built in that ancient land to serve as the capital of his new empire. Helupelan, Xosu's High Priest at the king's court, had been summoned from Doldun to tend the sacred flame. Sanae had arrived with the High Priest as she had been taken into his protection as a babe. She had grown up watching the city appear from the swampy land at the mouth of the Kelonzow river. The inauguration of the temple of Xosu, felt like the culmination of those events, the closing of that chapter of her life. The thought occurred to her as she stared at the statue of the god who wandered the world, maybe she would cast out now, find something new.

* * *

The temple grounds had emptied quickly after the ceremony ended. Only the uninitiated, those who hoped one day to learn the mysteries of the bright god, and the acolytes, the god's loyal servants, remained in the presence of Xosu. The acolytes began filtering into the temple behind the towering statue.

Sanae was the first of the uninitiated to move, taking the initiative after shaking herself out of the trance of being in Xosu's presence. The mysteries of Xosu may still be unknown to her, but she was closer to the High Priest than anyone as his ward. Helupelan had made a promise to the old king, Kenkathoaz, Tekolger's father, to look after Sanae and raise her. With her closeness to the High Priest, she liked to think of herself as the high priestess of the uninitiated.

Standing over the carcass of the sacrifice to the god, she lifted the head, motioning to the others to lift the corpse. Even with Sanae and nine others carrying the body, it was still heavy. It seemed to her that she was lifting the beast by herself despite her small size, the others like mere wraiths, blue shadows in the evening light. Sanae could feel the slowly congealing blood oozing between her fingers which made her grip all the harder to maintain.

The ten of them struggled with the corpse through to a separate enclave of the temple to prepare the body. A set of razor-sharp sickle knives had been laid out for them, the tools to carve up the sacrifice. Sanae had been taking the lead on this important task for years. Despite her youth, her expert hands made quick work of the animal, stripping the flesh, and separating out the sinews and bones. She had aid from her fellow uninitiated, but none worked as quickly or neatly as she did. Sanae prided herself on this skill. If the bull was to give up its life for the god and his adherents, then its body should be treated in a manner deserving respect, as if a part of one's own body.

The separated remains were placed into two neat piles. The sinews and bone to nourish the god in one and cuts of meat for his followers in another. The uninitiated cooked the meat as it was handed to them. The head was separated out for special reverence, placed to one side, its eyes watching them as they worked. Each pile was placed on its own silver platter. The uninitiated, carrying these platters, formed a procession of their own. Sanae stood at the front carrying the head of the beast on a platter with the lantern and incense hanging from her wrists. This time she would be the light to lead the way, the others trailing behind her like a tail.

They made their way into great hall of the temple, walking behind the statue circuitously, passing up the stairs to the temple entrance and under the shadow of the statue which engulfed her as she walked by. The sacred flame still burned bright, lighting their way, and bathing them in a warm red glow.

They entered the great hall, in which roared the mother flame unseen to the worshippers earlier in the night. The smaller flame in front of the statue was drawn from this larger one, hidden in the depths of the temple. The rest of the uninitiated sat on benches lining the sides of the room, the god's acolytes near the centre. In the middle a dais had been raised on which the High Priest, Priestess and their attendants sat.

Sanae walked around the room, her tail following her every move as she slowly headed toward the raised platform. Finally, she stopped beside the High Priestess. Kolae's eyes had followed Sanae around the room from when they entered. Jealous eyes, deep set in her moon shaped face which flickered in the red glow of the sacred fire in.

The platters were placed either side of the god's chief servants and the uninitiated stepped away. With the solemn process complete, Kolae slowly got to her feet. Picking up the sinews and bone from the platter and approaching the golden fire, her attendant following with the platter of charred meat. The High Priestess faced the assembly and announced,

"We thank Xosu for this gift and give to him the sinews and bone of the offering as sustenance for a god."

Turning to face the fire, she threw the offering into the flames. The dark room suddenly lit up as fire licked toward the ceiling, turning Kolae's white armed robes, which marked her office, red for just a moment. The intensity of the heat became unbearable, but Sanae forced herself to face the roaring flame to feel its power of life and the promise of death.

Kolae made her way back to her seat circuitously, dropping a portion of the blackened meat lined with glistening white fat to each of the uninitiated and then the acolytes as she went. Finally arriving back where she started, she placed a portion in front of Sanae and gestured for her to sit down. Rich, wine dark juices rushed from the meat in front of her, flooding the dish on which it sat.

Wiping a bead of sweat which trickled down her forehead, Sanae took her seat next to Helupelan as his attendant. Before he sat himself, Helupelan raised his cup of wine and poured a libation to Tholophos as protector of the city and one to Tekolger, the founder. The gathered priesthood copied, and the High Priest sat down. The room waited for Helupelan to take the first bite, the succulent juices dripping down his chin as he tasted the god's gift. With the High Priest's approval shown, the feast began.

The atmosphere was wild and euphoric, the wine flowing freely. Sanae watched the flames as three arrows of light danced upwards, reflecting on the night's events. Finally, as if only just noticing her, Helupelan spoke,

"Why are you not eating child?"

Sanae was shaken out of her daydream just as she found herself wondering what her own future would be and if Xosu would offer guidance, courage, and protection. Perhaps she would come to serve a great hero, or a king.

"No reason father, the sacred flame had grabbed my attention."

Helupelan smiled approvingly, a warm smile, his face glowing red in the presence of the flame which matched the hue of the arms of his robes,

"It has that effect on many of us. The essence of the god calls out through the flame. But you must eat, for your sake and not to disrespect the sacrifice to the god."

She found herself speaking without thinking,

"When will I be initiated father? I am almost a woman now, the longest serving of the uninitiated. My life has been dedicated to Xosu. I would learn the mysteries of the god if I could, I know the time of testing is fast approaching."

Most would not dare to speak so out of turn, especially in the presence of the High Priestess, but Helupelan only smiled, warmer than before,

"Commitment to the god is not an easy thing. You must dedicate your whole life to him, body and mind. You have served well, but you were a child when I brought you here, it will be a big change to join the ranks of those acolytes who know the secrets of the bright god."

Sanae replied,

"But I am ready, and I wish to dedicate myself to Xosu. Let me prove myself."

Kolae interjected,

"Helupelan knows what is best for you child. Your time will come soon enough."

She gave the High Priestess a searing look. Kolae always took a condescending tone with the young girl. She was jealous of the attention the High Priest had always given her ever since Helupelan had taken her in as a child among the Doldun and raised her like his own. There was a reason why many of the uninitiated referred to her as the white armed witch.

Ignoring the High Priestess, Sanae continued,

"Give me the chance father, I will not let you or the god down."

Helupelan pulled the same sympathetic face he always pulled when torn between her desires and the High Priestesses condemnation, fatherly but pitying,

"Ok child, we will put you through the tasks and see if the god deems you worthy. I will not promise you anything though and you must think hard on this yourself. It is a big step to take and one you might not be so willing to do if you knew more of your world. May the bright one light your way."

"Thank you, father. I will not let you down, his light will guide me."

Sanae shot Kolae a cutting, triumphant look and began to eat.

* * *

That night, although her mind was alive with the thought of her coming trials and the burning intensity of the sacred flame, sleep came quickly to Sanae. She dreamed like she so often did when the god had received an offering.

In an instant she was lifted from her dark bed chamber to a green, lush and fertile plain. An abundant paradise unfolded before her. Water trickled through gentle streams, trees both tall and short, brightly coloured and flourishing, stood alongside animals of all kinds that frolicked in the pastures and under the sun, which provided a warm but pleasant temperature. Amongst the animals, tall men roamed, stranger than she had ever seen before, they wore antlers on their heads, *or had they grown them themselves?* Their lower parts were more of beast than man, like horses or goats or cattle.

For what seemed like an age Sanae enjoyed this garden of plenty. But slowly the sky began to blacken until a veil of night fell. A red light flashed across Bul's vast canvass, a screaming, raging serpent streaking white hot across the sky. Then there was a rumble in the distance, so loud it seemed as though giants were moving the very earth. Then the fire and the flood rushed down upon her, ripping open the very fabric of the world. The once wonderous paradise burst to flame, the trees crying out in anguish as they burned. The flames were unbearable, but she could not look away. Then water streamed in from all directions, wine dark waves so high they blocked out the sun crashed through the paradise, driving all before them. Sanae tried to run, but to no avail, the deluge swept her away.

She came to her senses, a new dawn unfolding before her. Looking around she saw a wooded valley fed by a rushing river with mountains either side. The trees were reaching to the heavens, tall and strong and glowing crimson as if illuminated by some power, and atop they seemed aflame. Then she turned as a sense of trepidation overwhelmed her. Antlered men, half human, half stag, part goat, it was hard to tell, skin now green, now golden with auburn flowing manes, lay scattered dead and dying all around her, their blood soaking into the dark earth which sprung with new abundance. This world was different somehow, changed from the gentle paradise she had first seen.

Her attention was drawn to the river's rushing torrent, the survivors of the sea were gathering. Sanae followed stepping around the discarded antlers strewn on the floor. The people were following a shining light. As she got closer, she realised the survivors were drawn by the sweet smell of a man, some willingly, some coerced, all harassed by a menacing cloud that had burst upon them from an unseen realm.

The man was like none she had ever seen. Red of skin and a brilliant three-tiered aureate crown of red and white and black upon his head, topped with red feathers, light radiating out north, south, east, and west. His long flowing beard glistened like the rays of the sun, his eyes were afire, as if they had swallowed the conflagration of the heavens and thundered as he blinked. He seemed more than mortal to Sanae, a god come to the world of men. In his hand he carried a staff made of dolthil wood with an iron black pommel on top.

This red king led his people, prowling toward a throne sheltered by a giant dolthil tree. Its branches alive with celestial light, its roots drinking the blood of the broken men laying scattered on the ground and its amber, tear shaped, fruit getting fat as its broad leaves grasped for the sky. The throne was golden and glowing like the disc of the sun, with amber coloured wings of some thunderous, deadly bird spreading from it.

The red king took his seat and she approached. The crimson god locked his gaze upon her. Sanae froze and could not move. Slowly standing and raising his glowing long arms, he opened his mouth to speak, as if to declare that from him a new people would arise, but only his tongue appeared. Black as if scorched by fire, and the noise seemed to echo all around her, *Blood* It said or shouted or whispered.

The light disappeared and she fell to the ground. A hand gripped her and pulled her to her feet. The wild antlered man looked at her with a ferocious glare and thrust a wine skin into her hand. She was thirsty and drank long and deep. The dark rich wine sent grasping fingers down her throat.

She turned to face the red king, but two others had taken his place. One held an iron sceptre, the other a spear with a dark black head. The first led a band of survivors away from the river towards the mountains, the second took his followers towards the river's source. Then the red king re-emerged from the dark earth, holding a child aloft. The child held a magnificent white gold bow. Now a man grown, he came towards her. *Xosu?* she thought. Her legs took her, *or was it the god that ran towards a distant forest?* Half mad in their pursuit, no matter how hard she or the god ran, the trees came no closer. She would cover half the distance, and then the next quarter, and the next, but the trees always seemed so far away.

Exhausted and despondent, caught in a maddening fury, she collapsed to the ground and choked on her blood, *or his*, soaking the ground. For a moment all was darkness, until a single star appeared in the heavens, the one which rises before the dawn, but the face of the bright god was clear to see, *or was it her own?* Then she saw the others, the people lost in terror, rising from the earth where she just lay, and she knew what she must do.

Blood the voice echoed. The face of the first red king looming large, tongue blackened and bruised.

The world faded to black again. *Blood*

Sanae woke with a shudder, bolt upright, her heart pounding in her chest and cold beads of sweat rolling down her face.

KALU

9

"Pretty aren't they."

The voice came from over Kalu's shoulder. He turned quickly, recognising the firm tone of Thazan of the Kolabon. The Companion stood tall as a tower, his olive-skinned clan looks hidden behind his solemn and stern face,

"They can show off on the parade ground, that much I will admit. Would you trust them on the battlefield though?" the grim man they called the Priest for his piety continued.

The new regiments had arrived in Yorixori from Xortogun, ready for their final inspection, led by a man named Xurtoga Poroa Yo Gorturuf. He had been personally chosen by Tekolger to command the levies he raised in Xortogun. Effeminate and slight, he was not a man to inspire fear or vigour on the field, despite the fearsome looking white falcon headdress he wore. Even the gilded scaled armour, sculpted to look like feathers, made him seem more foolish than fearsome. But he was a prominent man of Xortogun's old warrior caste, of the House of the Falcon, one of the three great warrior houses of the valley, the others being the Ibis and the Owl. Surson had assured Tekolger that his service would bring the loyalty of the fighting men of the great valley.

In the absence of a king, Kelbal, acting as regent, was conducting the ceremony. In the full regalia of a member of the King's Companions. He wore a white gold zilthum lined cuirass and grieves to match, forged in old Kolbos before the Dusk by smiths whose skill was now lost. At his side was slung the zilthum blade Tholo's Curse. Even with the falcon headdresses that adorned the Xortogun's elaborate armour, the flashing terror of the red eagle feathers of the crest on Kelbal's golden helm, open faced in the Salxosu style, made him tower over the green boys from Xortogun.

With his scarlet cloak thrown over his shoulder, Kelbal was pacing up and down the lines, inspecting the green boys and watching them perform elaborate manoeuvres. He seemed distracted though, his face a ruddy shade as he suffered under his armour in the surprising heat of the autumn day. He was shadowed by two of Kalu's White Shields, in their zilthum lined cuirasses and wearing their ceremonial masks which made them seemed transformed as if by some artful sorcery, their shapes shifted into impassive moon white protectors.

The men from Xortogun marched up and down the square, raising and lowering their pikes, swinging them back and fore to make a terrifying, otherworldly swishing noise that haunted the dreams of the foes of the Doldun. Kalu watched on, answering Thazan,

"They have passed the training, same as our Doldun did."

"But they are not Doldun though. They aren't even Xosu. They are men who have been downtrodden by the Rilrpitu for centuries. Hardly the sort you can rely on in the field." Thazan, in his solemn and serious way, replied.

"True, the people of the great valley have lost some of their martial vigour after so long under the hooves of the Rilrpitu. But they were great empire builders once, and training can put iron into the back of any man." Kalu found himself arguing back, "The Doldun know that fact better than any. Before Kenkathoaz implemented his reforms we could hardly have been described as formidable on the field. Xosu, Zummosh, Rilrpitu and even Xortogun armies rolled over the land with little to fear." Thazan merely scoffed in reply. Kalu, still watching the display, continued, "They will need to be tested on the field of battle, but Tekolger wished for the empire to be more than just the realm of the Doldun. This is how we win the conquered people over in the long run."

The Priest did not seem convinced,

"We fought too hard for this empire to merely hand it over to these men. Tekolger was a great man, but sometimes his visions went too far."

Kalu recalled the opposition to Tekolger's decision to train the men of Xortogun when he first conceived of the idea. Protestations that they were not worthy seemed more a fear that Tekolger would no longer have to rely on his Companions and the Doldun for support, Kalu had thought back then. Or in Zenu's case, opposition came from a deeply held conservatism. But it seemed those protests had not lessened with the passage of time. This continued objection seemed even more hypocritical coming from Thazan. His own clan, the Kolabon, had been the heart of the defiance which had caused the last civil war. Kenkathoaz had spent most of his rule fighting in the hills and woods against the Kolabon and their leader Dolzolaz the Nomad. Thazan's kin had put their skills as huntsmen to use fighting a fierce guerrilla war after the other clans had been beaten in battle. *'It seems as though the Kolabon has swords hidden under every rock.'* he remembered Kenkathoaz saying, *'ready to be seized by every man of them when they come of age.'* Not letting his thoughts show, Kalu replied,

"Let us face it, we will need the extra manpower. Come on, there is a council meeting to attend. Kelbal will be done here soon."

Kalu turned on his heel and marched off toward the palace. Thazan did not reply but followed on behind.

* * *

The chamber which they had been using for meetings of the regency council was grand enough to fit the occasion, perched atop the great pyramid structure that was the old royal palace of Yorixori. Kalu had been told that it was once the throne room of the god-kings of Zowdel, before the Dusk of the old kingdoms, when men sat close to the gods themselves and heroes roamed the world.

The palace and the gardens were the only parts of the city which were still said to hail from that time though. The rest had been sacked and destroyed too many times to count in the centuries since. The latest iteration of the city emerged from Yoruxoruni's conquest, when he settled men from Xortogun to rebuild the metropolis. That more recent history was obvious just by looking at Yorixori. The style of the buildings, the look and attitudes of the people, even the gods they worshiped, all came from the great valley, the legacy of another empire.

The throne room was a long hall, stretching far off into the distance. Along the walls were painted friezes in the Xortogun style, side on views of their strange animal headed gods. Underneath the friezes ran pictograms which Kalu remembered Thuson Kosua had excitedly proclaimed to tell the history of Yoruxoruni's conquest of the west. *'I Yoruxoruni, Thoruri of the Great Valley, King of Zowdel, Master of Zenian, King of the World built this city after smiting those who opposed me. Ten thousand men I slew in a single day.'* Were all the lines Kalu could remember from Thuson's translation. It all seemed arrogant and hubristic to him. Yoruxoruni's eventual defeat and death at the hands of traitors proved that he supposed.

At the top end of the hall a carving into the black walls, which could have been a spear or a sword or the haft of an axe, was set up high. It was too worn to make any sense of. That fact had seemed to excite Thuson even more than the pictograms he remembered with a smile.

Tekolger's coffin had been brought into the chamber to sit below the carving. That sight gave Kalu more pause for thought then the rest.

Waiting inside for Kelbal to finish entertaining the new regiments were Deluan and the twins, Doluzelru and Pelapakal. Sat to the twin's side were Zonpeluthas, Zela, Polazul and Zalmetaz. All Tekolger's Companions were here except Palmash, Kelbal and, of course, Dolzalo. Stood huddled in the corner was Zenukola and overshadowing the old man was Supo of the Dolozolaz. *The gods have treated him well, he barely looks to have aged a day.*

A huge table had been placed in the centre of the room. Too long for the makeshift regency council to fill on their own, even if all twelve of the Companions were there to join Zenu Silver Eye and Supo, the man Tekolger had left to govern the northern frontier. That must have been *a thankless task*, Kalu reflected.

At the head of the table, a large and ornate chair was situated. Perhaps the throne of the god-kings of Zowdel, Kalu pondered as he paced his way into the room. Placed on the seat were Tekolger's crown and sceptre. The crown of the Kings of the Doldun was iron black and polished to such a shine it looked almost wet. Inside the black circlet sat a white one, smaller than the black, that shone like moonstone. It was said to have been the crown of Xosu himself, worn when he ruled over his people from Thelonigul at the dawning of the old kingdoms.

On the table in front of the crown lay Dusk, the sword of Tholophos, the zilthum blade of Tekolger's illustrious forbear. The white-gold weapon shone with a different hue to the other swords of that mythic ore. Somehow blood red, dark and menacing as if it was the last light of the day and pulsating with an unknown power. The elaborately carved hilt showed vines coiled around the grip in silver. The blade thrust out from the handgrip like a budding flower, widening at the top into the shape of a vicious serpent's tooth. It was a sword which moved through the air like a poem and had slain man, beast, and daemon alike, if the stories could be believed.

Near the sword, had Tekolger's wine cup had also been placed. The king may be gone, but his shade still presided over his council and his empire. It gave Kalu an eerie feeling, like he was being watched from another realm, like Dunsun's great shining eye was in the room with them. He sensed the others felt the same, they were almost scared of the royal regalia.

Zenukola saw Kalu and Thazan enter the room and broke away from his conversation. Striding towards Kalu to greet him, with Supo racing up behind,

"Pale Arm, what do you think of the new men? Do they pass the test of your keen eye?"

Kalu laughed with the crescent of a smile,

"They look good on a parade ground. We will have to wait to see how they perform on the field, but I am quietly confident. They can manoeuvre as well as any Doldun."

Zenu smiled in his fatherly way,

"They will be fine with some Doldun at their side."

"How goes things in the north Supo?" Kalu asked, eager to learn more of the goings on in the empire since they had departed for the west.

Supo sighed, "As well as we can hope for now. The Rilrpitu may have been driven back to the steppe of Belon, but that is a land they dominate, and we could never hope to tame. They are kingless and scattered, and they have not recovered their strength from their defeat in Xortogun and the campaigns ranging across the north. And we have finished the rebuilding the fortress of Yoruxoruni to guard against raiders from the steppe. But I am not complacent, we regularly strike out against them to keep them divided. As soon as a new king rises to take the place of the old, a Saradi in their tongue, the tribes will unite again, and they will become a formidable foe once more. It requires constant vigilance, so I welcome the chance to see you all again, even in circumstances such as these. But I am eager to return to Tekolgerdeloan as soon as possible." Supo replied earnestly.

"Tekolger couldn't have picked a better man for those duties Supo." Kalu answered him, not envious of Supo's position in the slightest. "It is quite the accolade to have had such trust from both Kenkathoaz and Tekolger."

"Indeed, it is. Supo is one of the most loyal and trustworthy men among us, the gods have been kind to send him to us. We had best take our places, no doubt Kelbal will not be far behind." Zenukola interjected.

Silver Eye gestured toward the table, and the group went to take their seats next to the other Companions. A space had been reserved to the right hand of the royal regalia for Kelbal. Kalu took his place on the next seat down. Opposite him sat Thazan. Zenu took a seat with Supo at the end of the table with the others in between.

Not long after everyone had settled, the doors swung open again and in stepped Kelbal. He had changed out of his ceremonial armour and was now wearing a Xortogun style robe. Red and flowing, trimmed with gold thread. It was a custom Tekolger had adopted soon after the conquest of Xortogun to be more appealing to the people as a legitimate king. A true descendent of the god-kings of old and a liberator from the hated Rilrpitu. Kelbal, and a few others, had imitated the king soon after, but many of the Doldun had resented Tekolger's westernising ways. They did not understand what it took to build an empire that lasted, fixated as they were on the clan rivalries of the past. Kalu had understood the motives of the king, but he had always been more comfortable in riding gear or armour.

The others watched in silence as Kelbal strode over to his seat next to the royal regalia. He sat down and gestured to Yare, the servant he had acquired in Zentheldel, to bring him a cup of wine. Unconsciously he toyed with the black ring of the Doldun whilst he waited, the symbol of the power he held in trust. The ring was an heirloom of Xosu himself. Like the crown of the Doldun it was made of a smooth black substance almost like iron, but with a shining wet look. Zenu cut short the silence,

"Whilst it is fresh in your mind Kelbal, shall we discuss what we intend to do with the new regiments?"

Kelbal took his first sip of wine and then answered from behind red lips,

"Is there anything to discuss? Tekolger made it clear what he wished to happen. The infantry will be integrated into our brigades, each squad of ten Xortogun will have a leadership of three Doldun officers. Eventually a new regiment of royal guards will be raised to stand alongside the White Shields. Tekolger wished to revive the famed guard of Yoruxoruni, The Tears of Xura they were called, I see no reason why we cannot do that ourselves. The new king will be of Yoruxoruni's blood as well as Tekolger's after all. A new royal squadron will also be created from the best of the Xortogun."

Silence broke out again. The others were not as comfortable with the succession of Surson's child. Kalu knew it even though many did not wish to say the words out loud. The more traditional among them had never come to accept Surson as the woman who would bear the king's heir. The custom was an alien one to the Doldun, even Kalu had found it strange. Declaring an heir in a land like Doldun came with a high risk when the chances of making it to maturity were low. The custom of the Doldun had always been for the king to take multiple wives, the heir being chosen from amongst their progeny by the clan leaders when the time came. Thazan was the first to speak,

"The men won't accept that. They have laboured together with us for longer than a decade, some even fought under Tekolger's father, and now you want to break them up. They will see this as betrayal." Thazan had always been vocal in his thoughts. Sturdy and reliable as an oak though he was, the Priest had never understood Tekolger's drive to integrate the Xortogun and unite them with the Doldun. *Not surprising*, Kalu reflected, Thazan's own clan had barely united with the other Doldun themselves.

Kelbal's face changed from the smile which he always had rising across his lips, to a visage of anger, from calm and serene to wild in an instant, his green eye flashing as he did. But before he could speak, Zenu intervened,

"I think what Thazan means is why would we break up veteran formations now? With Tekolger gone, there may be instability in the empire, and we will need those veterans fighting together to ensure order." A murmur of approval went around the table before Kelbal replied,

"I don't mean to break up the veteran formations, merely integrate new and fresher men who can learn from our most experienced. It is the plan Tekolger himself put in place. Or have you forgotten that?" Thazan spoke up again, his pride pricked,

"Nobody has forgotten that Kelbal, but the men have gone through much since then and the loss of Tekolger is still raw. They will feel that replacing them with men from Xortogun is an attempt to get rid of them. They won't like it."

"The empire must continue to move forward. These soldiers are trained and ready for battle, and we need to replace our losses. It is Tekolger's vision and as regent I will see it fulfilled." Kelbal answered. Thazan went to speak again, but Zenu Silver Eye interrupted,

"Kelbal, we understand why you wish to see this carried through, but now may not be the right time. Send the Xortogun to the garrisons or blood them on the northern frontier. Let them gain some experience and we can revisit this issue in a year or two." Kelbal took another, longer, sip of wine before answering. The wild look returning, as if he would have happily devoured Thazan whole,

"Tekolger wished to see this happen, and the issue will still be the same in a year or two. Best we integrate now so everyone can adapt. I will not move on this Zenu." For a moment silence fell once more. Several Companions looked as though they would speak up, but Zenu raised his hand slightly as if to calm them, speaking himself instead. Kalu felt relieved at that. Zenukola could be relied upon to be a calming influence on the hot-headed Companions,

"Very well Kelbal. We will carry out Tekolger's wishes. The new manpower will be welcome." The rest of the table nodded in agreement, although Kalu suspected it was done so begrudgingly. The Companions were conquerors of the world, but they were still mostly traditional men of the clans and would defer to their elders, as they took their lead from Zenukola here. Kelbal gestured to his servant to refill his cup and continued,

"What of the Togworwoh? I believe there were some appointments that must be made. I fear you will need to enlighten us on the goings on in the east Zenu, three years is a long time to be away." Zenukola nodded and replied,

"The arrangements in the west will need to be settled properly. As for the east, Hunthisonu, the King of Gelodun has marched an army into Thelizum. It seems he wishes to emulate Tekolger. Thasotun still struggles to control the White Islands, but Dotmazo holds Xosupil and Zenidun firmly in his control. The news of Tekolger's death may have given some of the Xosu ideas of revolt, but none is yet to stir. Xortogun is quiet as well. The people there worshipped Tekolger like a god and his death is not like to change that. My only concerns would be about the more worldly pursuits of some of the governors Tekolger appointed, and the Putedun. They persist in pursuing access to the markets of Tekolgertep. The city has grown much in the last three years. For my own hegemony, there have been some stirrings amongst the nobles of Zowdel, but I have seen to it. The Rilrpitu are becoming bold once more though. Supo tells me that the number of raids is on the increase and that the tribes seem to be gathering on the steppe. Nothing we need worry too much about though. However, there is the matter of Dalzenu."

"I am happy with the arrangements in the west. Herethalthawe is experienced and capable. Bala, Talehalden's son, will make a good and loyal vassal and the colonists a useful garrison in Zentheldel. We saw on our way back that the Vale of Kelandel is in safe hands. It seems from your report that Dotmazo can be left to deal with the east until we are settled back in Xortogun. As for the Putedun, Tekolger's wish was clear. The city must be given the chance to grow and Doldun and Xosu merchants establish themselves before the Putedun are allowed access. I do not see why that should change now. The Rilrpitu should always be a concern, but Tekolger saw to the garrisoning of the northern frontier. This is not something the royal court need concern itself with, is it Supo?" Kelbal inquired.

Supo shook his head as he replied,

"The northern army is strong, and the old wall is being rebuilt. A few raiders may get through, but they will be hunted down. My men range across the country regularly to deter rebels and raiders alike."

"Good. What is this business with Dalzenu?" Kelbal said.

"He has been accused by his men of stealing from the king. They say he has been taking a portion of the tax revenue and their salaries for himself." Zenu told Kelbal. With some surprise, Kelbal replied,

"Dalzenu? I refuse to believe that of him. I have known Dalzenu of the Balkakel for as long as I have known Kalu and Deluan here. All came as wards of the royal court after the Balkakel placed themselves under Kenkathoaz, we grew up almost as brothers. He has always been an upright and honest man. Too honest for his own good in many ways. It is a shame he did not become one of Tekolger's Companions like the rest of us, but he was never of a marshal nature. Tekolger placed Dalzenu as the Togworwoh of Torfub because he trusted him so, who better to hold such a vital strategic point. So, stealing from the men and the king? No, I cannot believe it."

"Nevertheless, that is the accusation that has been levelled against him." Zenukola answered. Kelbal sighed,

"Very well, it will have to be investigated, if nothing else to keep the garrison happy. In the meantime, have Gota Tora Ya Kuria take over his duties as Togworwoh." Thazan once again was displeased with the decision,

"You don't mean to have a Doldun general take over as governor? Torfub is an important strategic point, it should be held by a Doldun not this Xortogun of dubious loyalty. Or do you forget that he also served the Rilrpitu kings before us?"

"Gota was a loyal servant to Tekolger and is a native of the city. He understands how it works and will be a competent Togworwoh. This empire is more than just the Doldun now, any loyal servant to the king should be trusted with high positions, it is what Tekolger would have wanted." Kelbal calmly replied, his composure and sunny disposition returning as he sipped once more from his cup of wine, his tongue had turned purple from the rich liquid. Zenu once again signalled to the others, imparting a calm in the room like a cool morning breeze, and replied,

"Gota is not a military man though. An experienced general should at least be there to command the garrison and win back their trust." Kelbal nodded,

"That is true. Who do you suggest Zenu?"

"One of the Companions. Thazan is correct Torfub is a key strategic point, it will need someone reliable." Silver Eye answered.

"The Companions will be needed with the army; they can't be spared." Kelbal fired back, barely pausing after his latest sip of wine.

"Thelupalkel has done a good job in Kelandel as you say." Zenu replied again.

"And I wish him to carry on there. Kelandel is a difficult province, and no one could replace him." Kelbal answered.

"Then we are left with Pelu, my aide. He has always served well and faithfully. He would make a reliable general in the region, reluctant as I would be to forego his advice." Zenu said.

"Very well, send Pelu with a contingent of soldiers and orders to bring Dalzenu to us and for Gota to take over the duties of Togworwoh. Is there anything else?"

All around the table shook their heads, and so Kelbal supped his wine and continued,

"In that case, Zenu I want you to begin making preparations to lead the oldest veterans back to Doldun."

The doors opened once again and a soldier rushed in, covered in dust, clearly eager to speak to Kelbal. Kelbal carried on talking, barely noticing the man entering the room,

"Many are close to retirement now, some even served under Tekolger's father. They will be paid a handsome sum from the royal treasury and allowed to retire in Doldun. You will take them home; I am sure you wish to see the old country again."

Zenu tried to answer, but Kelbal had already stood and was enquiring as to what the soldier wanted. Kalu gave Zenu a look as if to say that he would talk to Kelbal. The old general should at least have been given the courtesy of knowing about his retirement before it was announced in front of the council. He stood and approached the regent, as he did, he could hear the soldier saying,

"An attack on a village to the north of the Kelonzow river between here and Kulanzow. Dolzalo is pursuing a Rilrpitu warband, maybe a thousand strong. I have been sent to request cavalry reinforcements as they do not have enough horse to pursue and destroy them."

ZENUKOLA

10

A clatter of arms rang out and the noise of flutes and trumpets filled the still autumnal air, and then a shout and the row of warriors nearest to Zenukola fell to the ground like the petals of a dying flower. The Doldun men in the front line immediately got to their feet and an almighty row broke out, the officers jumping in to pull their men away from the novices of Xortogun. The other Xortogun men stood watching the chaos, frozen to the spot. Their commander, an effeminate man called Xurtoga Poroa Yo Goturuf, tried in vain to restore order. He came from the caste of warriors that once built an empire, but now were a sorry shadow of those ferocious ancestors. *That white falcon headdress makes him look ridiculous*, Zenu thought as his phantom fingers flexed at the sight. Thazan looked on silently too. The man the others called the Priest was shaking his head with one hand on the gilded hilt of his zilthum blade, Discord. Deluan of the Balkakel stood opposite him, more vocal with the men, encouraging the novices.

As expected, and as Kelbal had been told, the order to begin integrating the new regiments into the ranks of the army had not been received well by the Doldun. They had spent years training and fighting together and as such these basic battlefield manoeuvres had become second nature. But the men of Xortogun were struggling to adjust to the speed and skill of Tekolger's veterans. Zenu had sent his own men to mix with the returning army, to measure the mood and stoke the fires of discontent, the task was proving an easy one.

He had spent the days since the order watching the training efforts taking place on the open plain outside of Yorixori. Looking at the new soldiers with the critical eye of an experienced general, Zenu had to admit that the light infantry and cavalry raised in Xortogun would add something to the army. A different approach which would provide a new outlet through which to engage the enemy. However, the integration of the men into the infantry phalanx was a mistake. There was a reason that only the Doldun fought like this. Even the Xosu phalanx was smaller and used thrusting spears. Years of training had led the Doldun to adopt and perfect the pike square. Zenu had been intimately involved in the process of reforming the army of the Doldun as the closest adviser to Tekolger's father, Kenkathoaz. He felt his phantom fingers flexing as he watched his legacy being picked apart. The memories of those times were seared into him for good reason. The previous king may not have been an all-conquering hero like Tekolger, but without Kenkathoaz' efforts Tekolger would have been nothing. He was a new Phalazkon uniting the kingdom once more.

When Kenkathoaz came to the throne, Doldun was a broken husk, the king's authority barely stretching beyond the coast. Kenkathoaz' father, Dazuphalaz, had been affable and gregarious, but weak willed. A king for a time of concord and plenty, and sons he had had aplenty. Kenkathoaz was the seventh boy, with little possibility it seemed of inheriting the throne. But his brothers one by one had died in battle, with the clans or the Zummosh, as the kingdom had steadily spiralled out of control. Kenkathoaz only escaped that fate through being sent as a hostage to be raised with the Rinuxosu as his feeble father had tried to placate his neighbours. *The gods were smiling on Kenkathoaz, even as a child. He was the real hero of Doldun's rise.* Zenu reflected. In Zenu's youth the clans, backed by gold from the League of Butophulo, had run riot. Dazuphalaz had eventually tried to control them, but he blundered and was slain with two sons in a cowardly ambush. The perpetrators had evens stolen the white heart from the crown of Xosu. With Kenkathoaz' brothers having fallen by other means, fair or foul, the young man was all who was left to take the throne. The last of the line of Xosu and Tholophos. *A heavy burden to place on any young boy, even heavier than that which fell to Tekolger.*

The looming succession had brought those memories flooding back to Zenukola these last few weeks. Only three clans had sent representatives to Kenkathoaz coronation after he was returned by the Rinuxosu to take the throne, and the king could only be crowned with the black circlet. His commands went unheeded, and his tax collectors were driven off or killed. Kenkathoaz was determined and undeterred despite this. He resolved to rescue the kingdom at any cost. Zenu's missing eye itched as he allowed himself to remember those days of trial and hardships.

They spent the first three years of the king's reign reinforcing the foundations of the crown, finding new sources of money, from mines and trade, building an alliance with the Rinuxosu and the clans which remained loyal. They even built a new royal palace in the lands of the Keluazi so that the king could be closer to his more unruly subjects. But most importantly they trained an army. They built a new army and a new way of making war, a system which one day would see Tekolger conquer the world. But first Kenkathoaz and his Companions would use the new army to subdue the clans and restore the kingdom. *And what a magnificent sight they were, the ranks of trained men marching out to restore unity to the realm.* His phantom fingers flexed less intensely as the memories of the restoration of the kingdom came to him.

He found himself reflecting on how Kenkathoaz had gone to the Koloabon, the spear people, at that time the largest and strongest of the clans, and demanded their fealty. Zelrdetzal, the clan chieftain, known by his friends and foes as the Bloody Spear for his violent rage and habit of taking women who caught his eye by force, was a stubborn and foolish man. Zelrdetzal refused and mocked the king for holding *'half a crown and even less of a kingdom'*. So, in the year of the dark spring, when the sun was covered by a twilight hue, the king's new army was put to the test.

What was left of the Koloabon now was barely worth a thought, a clan in name only. One of the roaming rhapsodes had even foolishly turned the tale into a poem praising the defiance of the clan and lamenting their fall, The Broken Spear. But the ode had soon come to be seen as a warning to those who crossed the Kenkathoaz. The king had enjoyed that, as had Zenu. *What better way to keep the clans controlled than the rhapsodes reminding them of their defeat.*

The war had only started with that battle. The ravaging of the Koloabon sparked the other clans into action. Although the Keluazi, Zelrsaloz and the Dolozolaz remained loyal to Kenkathoaz, the Zowo, Kolbun, Kelawath, Tholmash, Kolabon, Zelkalkel, Kalupelbon, Balkakel and what was left of the Koloabon all united against him. Tested and blooded, Kenkathoaz' army met the combined might of the clans in a battle beneath the peak of Phalazkon's Crown on the day of the spring equinox in the dim light of the year of the dark spring, when only Xosu's Arrow lit up the sky. A day that came to be known as Kenkathoaz second coronation, where all the clans attended, and all were forced to kneel in submission as the white heart was returned to its proper place. The gods even signalled their approval by lifting the veil which had covered the sun for many weeks that spring, an event the seers had said showed that the gods had turned their back on the kingdom until it was restored. *That was a glorious day, but I hope this time that battle will not decide the fate of the Doldun.*

Zenukola had lost an eye at his king's second coronation, the lesson taught him to be wary of the clans and cherish the stability of a strong monarch. He was determined to preserve that, whatever the cost. The shard of silver he had taken from a fallen foe to replace his eye reminded him of that lesson every day. His phantom fingers flexed again, an overwhelming urge to scratch his lost eye with his missing hand.

With the men separated by their officers, calm descended once more over the field,

"Again!" Thazan shouted firmly, grinding his teeth in frustration as Deluan reorganised their ranks. The stalwart Companion was still not happy with the decision to integrate the Xortogun, but he would whip his new charges into shape, nonetheless.

Thazan was of an age with Tekolger, but he had been raised in a more traditional manner and had always shown a suspicion of Tekolger's westernising tendencies. It was an instinct which could make him a natural ally in the events to come. The only man Zenu was sure was not a part of a wider conspiracy amongst the Companions, his dislike of the Xortogun was too well know. But Thazan was sharp and ambitious in his own right, it would make any alliance with the man a double-edged sword. The Companion was also of the Kolabon, Zenu had spent more time battling that clan of hunters than fighting alongside them. They had been the toughest opponents of the Defiance, having to be subdued several times before they finally gave in. Even then, they had secured a marriage into the royal family as a concession for the precarious peace. Zenukola had never been able to trust any of their scions, but the Deltathelon had always had to make compromises to succeed. He felt his phantom fingers flex.

"The men aren't happy about this." Thazan said to him.

"Many of the Companions aren't either Thazan, but it was Tekolger's wish, and we do need the manpower." Zenu replied. He might have said he was unhappy with the decision himself, but it was a battle with Kelbal that he did not need to have. Besides, the discontent it generated could be used to his advantage.

"Tekolger is not here to see it." Thazan answered,

"The phalanx does bother me, I will admit. The cavalry and the light troops will be an asset, but it would be best to keep the infantry separate." Zenu said, prodding Thazan for more information.

"Yes, skill and language are the problem. Our Doldun are much too fast and skilled for the manoeuvres of the training ground and, although the Xortogun have been taught Common Xosu only our officers speak it regularly. My Doldun speak their own tongue on the field, it is creating confusion. I told Tekolger this when he first conceived the notion, but he would not listen." Thazan said, standing tall as a tower, his eyes fixed on the men as they reformed to practice their drills once more. The Doldun dialect was a bastard cousin of Common Xosu, perhaps only one word in ten was mutually intelligible, especially the way the men of the clans spoke it, half barbarian as they were themselves.

Zenu nodded as he watched one of the officers admonishing a man from Xortogun who barely seemed aware of what was going on,

"And it is just the practicalities of integrating that is an issue for you?" Zenu inquired.

"Why? What are you implying Zenu?" Thazan asked, the suspicion clear in his voice. His solemn and stern face made him look a little less clan like, despite his olive skin and dark bronze hair.

"None of the others seem happy with the order either. I am trying to find out what the problem is, nothing more." Zenu came back.

"What are the others saying?" Thazan replied, his eyes fixed on Zenu with a hunter's glare. Zenu knew now that he had the Companions attention,

"Some are concerned with the practical problems and how it will affect the army." Zenu paused, before continuing, "There is some rumbling about diluting the Doldun in the army. There is a small fear that Kelbal wants to be less reliant on the homeland for replacements so that he has more control over the empire. I am sure it is nothing though, there was always going to be some difficulties with integrating, its natural."

"The practicalities are the main problem Zenu." Thazan said, the suspicion in his voice still clear to hear. "It will be difficult to find the efficiency we built up over the years with green men who don't share the language or culture of our own."

"I intend to raise these issues with Kelbal. When he forces the veterans to retire, this problem will only get worse." Zenu replied. Kelbal's presumption that he could compel Zenu to retire had cut deep and hardened the old general's resolve to see his plans through to the end. Especially as it may well be an attempt by Kelbal to remove Zenu as a threat, more evidence of his guilt perhaps.

"He is forcing you to retire as well Zenu, is that what this is really about?" Thazan probed back. Zenu felt his phantom fingers clench.

"I will admit I was not happy with the decision, but a quiet life in Doldun may not be all bad. I am old and my day is done." Zenu said hoping to kill off any further questions.

"Your wisdom will be a loss to the army though. We could use your experience now." Thazan replied, eyes back on his soldiers drilling to their front. Zenu almost told him that he had no intention of going anywhere, but it was best to be discreet for the moment. He held his tongue.

***

The morning spent watching the soldiers drilling on the open plains in front of the city had been an entertaining and useful distraction, but Zenukola was still governor of Zowdel, and the responsibilities of governorship could not be ignored forever.

As Kelbal had turned the governor's residence into the capital of the empire itself, dealing with the running of the entire realm from Zenu's old quarters, Zenukola had been forced to move to the other side of the palace. Though he had secured the old royal chambers for his blind bard, a courtesy to the rhapsode that even Kelbal could not refuse.

It was in his new quarters that he found himself stuck for the rest of the afternoon, sifting through piles of scrolls, issuing orders to ensure the region stayed well governed and fit for the coming winter. A task made more difficult given the number of tongues he needed to communicate in. A small team of scribes and translators had to shadow him everywhere for that purpose. His new quarters barely had enough space for them all and the smell of the incense the Xortogun habitually burnt clouded the air and sickened his stomach.

He put to one side a petition from the priest Thorniub to build a temple to honour Tekolger in Yorixori. Such a thing may be useful in the future, but it could wait. Tekolger's conquests had not been quite as total as Zenukola would have liked, especially this far to the west. The king had left many of the minor lords and petty kings in place so long as they feigned loyalty and paid him homage.

Huryur, the Black Spear as he called himself, was a nuisance in the south, but he could be cowed. Thorniub Kurotor Ya Kuria, the High Priest of Kurotor in Yorixori of the priestly cast of Xortogun, the same as Tekolger's witch queen, had pretensions of authority over the city and talked too much. But Yorotog was his biggest worry. Its king, Thorgon Oathmaker, had a weak claim to descent from both Yoruxoruni and the old kings of Zowdel. If a rebellion were to be sparked anywhere, that is where it would be. Up until now the city had been subdued, but it was too quiet. The threat of the army on the northern frontier and Zenu's own forces in Yorixori was enough to cow Thorgon. But he would surely know by now that the northern army had moved. With Rilrpitu warbands reportedly striking towards his own lands, rebellion may begin to seem an enticing prospect. Especially as the forces left for Zenu in Zowdel were spread amongst small garrisons.

The Silxosu colonies Tekolger had planted to the south were too far away to offer much support if Yorotog rose. The Salxosu, who had been left to build a new city down river from Yorixori, were of dubious loyalty. They had been placed there to keep them away from Xosupil more than anything else. A Tilxosu colony along the southern bank of the Zolkelonzow was close enough to Yorotog to offer support but lacked any real fighting strength. Besides Zenu had trouble putting his faith in so many Xosu. A few Doldun regiments in Yorixori was all that he could really rely on. Thorgon may have been cautious, but he was restless, ambitious and a schemer at heart.

Zenu took a scroll of papyrus and wrote to the King of Yorotog informing him of the safe return of the royal host and its position in Zowdel. *The threat between the lines should be plain enough*, he thought.

He spent what seemed like hours at the tedious work governing could sometimes be. The Putedun in particular, were causing a lot of headaches for Zenu, determined as they were to increase their trading rights within the empire. As was their way, the Putedun wished to establish trading posts deep into Zenian and eventually even Zentheldel but needed Zenu's permission to do so. Not a warlike or threatening people, sweet words and generous gifts were their chosen weapons. Although poisoned gifts were rumoured to be sent if provoked. On this occasion a long letter requesting permission for a permanent trading station to be established in Yorixori was accompanied by a gift of a metal bird whose wings would flap when water was poured through it. The Putedun were fond of such toys. It was from a man naming himself Prince Konguz, emissary of the confederacy to the court of the Doldun. Zenu put the letter aside. He found the politics of empire tiring, more so than the clan rivalries of the Doldun.

Well into the evening, Supo came to his quarters. The wily general appearing as if from nowhere.

"We need to talk." He said, once Zenu raised his head and noticed he was there. Zenu gestured for his old comrade to sit,

"About what?" he enquired. Supo washed a wary eye over the scribes and translators,

"Out!" Zenu boomed, "I will summon you should I have need." They frantically scrambled for the door, mercifully blowing out the incense as they breezed past.

"Once we have wrested power back from Kelbal and returned it to the Companions, what are your intentions?" Supo spoke once the room had fallen dark and silent, a pensive look on his face.

"These Companions have shown that they cannot lead this empire without a powerful figure to guide them. I would expect to take up that position for a while. I swore my oath to Kenkathoaz to watch over his son, I failed there, but I can see that his legacy is protected." Zenu answered his comrade honestly, there could be no other way.

"So, you will be regent? Wielding the power of a king?" Supo answered, the words flowing slowly and considered.

"I am afraid that is the only way, until the new king comes of age. He will need someone to guide him in his rule. You saw what happened when that Salxosu woman, Kisuunsinu, got her claws into Tekolger. A rift between Kenkathoaz and his son, another civil war loomed before we had recovered from the last one. To this day I do not know exactly what happened, or what passed between them, or even where Kisuunsinu went. We cannot let a situation like that unfold again and I do not trust the others to keep this empire together. I will not see us descend into civil war again. The Deltathelon have always guided the rest of the Doldun in times of need." Zenukola answered him straight. Supo nodded, his eyes fixed on Zenu's, the trident shaped lines around them narrowing,

"You are sure of Kelbal's guilt? A conspiracy to place the Xortogun child on throne?"

Zenu paused,

"I have no firm proof this it is true. But who else could have done it? Especially with poison? Kelbal was close to the king, true, but he seems to have given himself over to the Xortogun, just look at the way he dresses now. The seduction of power and the wiles of the Xortogun witch no doubt whispering in his ear. The chance to rule as regent an empire the like of which has never been seen. It is the only explanation which fits. Why else would the murderer seem to have done nothing else? As for the other Companions, I am not convinced. Maybe Kalu was involved in some way, but the boy is loyal and earnest, so I doubt it." he paused, "But I fear we may need to remove him anyway. He will follow Kelbal's lead without proof to convince him otherwise."

After a moment of reflection, Supo said,

"Very well. Then we must act quickly. We have the perfect opportunity to isolate Kelbal and show him to be unsuited to rule the Doldun. His determination to press forward with integrating the Xortogun will be his undoing." Supo continued.

"Kelbal is doing a fine job of that on his own. The army is disgruntled, and the Companions feel left out of power. Their faith in Kelbal is being questioned." Zenu answered, but he knew that his old comrade was right. The gods may not see fit to present them with another opportunity.

"It is happening too slowly. Once we reach Torfub, closer to the heart of the empire, and with Surson, and her young child in his hands, it will be much harder to accomplish. Kelbal will be stronger, and the Companions more settled under his rule.

Kalu is the immediate obstacle, I fear. Whilst he is around it will be much harder to isolate Kelbal. Those two are too close, like brothers, and the other Companions have too much respect for Kalu to go against him and Kelbal." Supo paused, he was clearly picking his words carefully, "It seems that some Rilrpitu warbands have come south as expected. You need to ensure Kelbal sends reinforcements to Dolzalo and have him name Kalu the commander. It would weaken the army and remove

Kelbal's greatest ally in one move. That would be the opportunity we need to act."

Zenu put down the scroll he was still half reading and looked at Supo's dark eyes,

"Once Kelbal realises the scale of the issue in the north, he will have no choice but to send reinforcements, as we planned. Using the opportunity to remove Kalu would be helpful though. Kelbal is already in a self-destructive cycle we just need the others to see it." Zenu said, speaking his inner thoughts aloud.

Supo spoke again, his words cascading out now,

"Kelbal trusts you and Kalu is the only one he will trust to give an independent command like that to, you just need to plant the thought in his mind. We can use it to put a further wedge between Kelbal and the rest. They will be jealous not to be given the task themselves, then you will just need to stoke that tension. Have Kelbal send Kalu and myself out and include some of your guard and my men in the reinforcements. I will see to it that Kalu is removed as a threat, and you can deal with Kelbal."

Things are moving too slowly, and the Companions have proved more loyal to Kelbal than anticipated, especially given Kelbal's unstable state. He thought. Supo always had a snake like cunning, much more adept at the intrigue of politics than Zenu had ever been, a skill that would be useful in the coming years. Zenu nodded his agreement.

KALASYAR

11

Her grandfather's symposiums were becoming more and more frequent, this was the third one in as many days. Koseun had never really replaced the hole his forced retreat from the public arena had left. The symposium was all that remained to him from his life before the fall of the city to the Doldun. She knew it reminded him of the time he spent as the head of the Academy of Rolmit, The Apiary as the common people called it, and so could not begrudge him these nights, no matter how frequent.

Kalasyar stood in the centre of the room and poured water into a huge bowl filled with a deep red wine and mixed it, filling a cup for each of the guests. Wine to ease the conversation, the water to hold off the madness which comes when one seeks the knowledge of the gods. Around the sides of the cups were scenes wrought in red against black depicting the events of The Sinasa and the siege of old Kolbos. It was usually a job for the household slaves, but she wanted to keep an eye on her grandfather and Kalasyar enjoyed the discussions herself. Persuading Tilmosh to let her attend was never hard.

A smaller group of regular attendees tonight, the others could not handle the pace it would seem. Even those in attendance had made a vow at the start of the night to limit their drinking to one or two cups. Koseun had also honoured the Nine's ban on music for once, sending away the pipe players who usually provided the night's entertainment. But the vows had done nothing to dissuade her cousin Rolmit, named for the philosopher, to hold back. Nervous at the presence of the seasoned older men, he had drunk himself into a stupor. Still, welcoming her cousin back to the family villa and been a happy moment. The Sisosi clan had dwindled somewhat in recent years. First with the death of her father,

Kildol, in battle with the Rinuxosu and her mother to the plague at the height of the war. Then the departure of Rolmit for his education in Rulkison, the city famed for its honeycomb cliffs, whose own father had also perished some years before.

The three older men were reclining on couches deep in conversation. Her grandfather at the centre taking his usual pose as something of questioner and mediator, with Dunobos Rososthup and Kolkobuas Kisrurososi either side of him locked deep in a dispute. The two men were of an age with Koseun and patriarchs of their own families. The three had become fast friends as students at the Academy of Rolmit.

Two younger men, who Kalasyar had not met before, sat opposite, looking on with interest. They seemed a little uncomfortable in their white togas and in the presence of the older patriarchs. Polrinu Kinsol, kin of Pito the richest man in the city, patriarch of the Kinsol and Koseun's great friend, and Buso Kolkisuasu, the two boys were called. Dunobos and Kolkobuas new favourites no doubt.

"Civilisation is the first step to freedom. No man is free to pursue the good in this world without the freedoms that civilised society offers. Rolmit of Rulkison had the right of it when he compared it to a beehive." Dunobos said as she handed out the cups of wine. Concealed beneath the dark liquid at the bottom of the wide cups were images. The death of Xosu was on her grandfather's cup. To Dunobos she gave the one which showed the folly of the hero Kusukirtil when he tried to best Bul and Sem, and to Kolkobuas an image of the sons of Tholophos sharing Kuso's cup during the siege of old Kolbos as each agonised over a plan to take the city, all of which would fail.

"And what do you mean by civilisation Dunobos?" Koseun asked.

"It is what we share with others. The Xosu share many things together, language, art, theatre, rituals, but also farming, trade, and government, through these things we have learnt to work together." Dunobos replied.

"The Wildmen shared many rituals and, some would say, art and certainly language with each other and were able to communicate with humans. Their rituals were like theatre, and they certainly worked together and traded. Did they have a civilisation? And did they not live a good and free life?" Koseun posed the next question, the way he always enjoyed doing. It flowed off his tongue like a river.

"No, the Wildmen lived in the woods and the wilderness, before the Dawn of the old kingdoms, and civilisation only came with the Dawn. They had no society, no institutions, no organisation, no farming, and created little. They had culture yes, but not civilisation. And so, they were bound by the constraints that come with lacking those things. Relying on the goodwill of the gods to survive day to day. Therefore, they may have lived what they thought was a happy life, but it was never truly free." Dunobos said forcefully.

Kalasyar smiled, she knew how much her grandfather relished these conversations. He would say he knew nothing and so must question everyone and everything. She found herself lingering after the wine had been handed out.

"The Bulodon then, the galloping men of the plains. They had culture and chieftains and a tribal society and made plenty, weapons, and jewellery for a start. On occasion they traded, and they certainly knew what farming was. They must have been a civilisation and therefore living a free life. Indeed, they had the freedom to roam the plains going where they would and taking what they needed, and they lived alongside the Dawn of the old kingdoms like the Wildmen. You seem to be forgetting the old stories Dunobos." Koseun put to his old friend with a grin snaking over his face.

"If such tales can be believed. I think you are taunting me now Koseun. You know as well as any that the stories of Wildmen, Bulodon and other such creatures are just confused accounts of man before the Dawn and those that were not bathed in its light. But even if you believe such fanciful tales, the Bulodon did not farm, and they gained their wealth through the raiding and exploitation of other groups. Demanding tribute from the Xosu for a start. The absolute and brutal rule of their chieftains was a poor substitute for actual political institutions. They may have been free to roam, but they relied on raiding others to survive, that did not give them freedom."

"The Kinsolsun then. Surely you cannot argue that they were not bathed in the light of the Dawn. Indeed, the old tales talk of how they brought order and progress to the people of the islands after the paradise that the first men dwelt in was destroyed by the warring gods and the shattering of the heavens. If anything, the world they built was a mirror of the beehive you so admire. They created sophisticated art and their skill in metallurgy was beyond anyone. They had a proper political structure and their society produced without resorting to plunder." Koseun answered with a viper's speed.

"True, but they relied on humans for much of their labour. They merely exploited human civilisation which they ruled over in a cruel and oppressive manner. The cruelty shows that they had no freedom as they knew they needed to oppress those who did have it to survive. They were sophisticated in many ways, but they did not have civilisation." Dunobos replied.

"So, it would appear then that only humans are capable of producing true civilisations in your eyes then Dunobos." Koseun proposed.

"I think you speak again in jest, but I will indulge you. After all what better test is there of a credible civilisation than that of endurance. I do not see any Wildmen or Bulodon around and the Kinsolsun were driven to destruction by Xosu himself. None have survived the test of time. Yet humans still flourish. Indeed, human society flourished after the Dawn of the old kingdoms, after men had driven the monsters to destruction on the fringes of the world, or back into the realms from whence they came. Dusk only fell on those civilisations when those beasts returned. Although perhaps those creatures that brought the Dusk wore the skins of men." Dunobos said triumphantly.

"What do you think Kolkobuas?" Koseun said, turning to his other guest.

"Dunobos makes a compelling case, and I think he is right that we must give some autonomy up for us to be able to be truly free. However, Dunobos, what do you mean by civilisation? There are many different human societies, are they all civilisations?" Kolkobuas replied.

"Well, Dunobos, can all human societies be considered civilisations?" Koseun fired back to Dunobos.

"Perhaps, but some civilisations are superior to others, achieving higher levels of freedom for their people." Came the reply.

Kalasyar knew she should not be there, but the guests were too caught up in the conversation to notice her.

"Well lets us consider some examples. The Zummosh, fierce warriors to our north. They are great metal smiths, even with gold and silver. Their bards are famous wordsmiths, and they conduct many collective rituals, if sometimes a little brutal. They farm and trade and have a political structure, with tribes, chieftains, and collective assemblies. All this would seem to qualify them as a civilisation in your eyes." Koseun pitched to Dunobos.

The other man sat and pondered the question for a moment, and then replied,

"What you say is true, the Zummosh have civilisation, but it is one with many flaws. You are right they produce great art, poems and songs and they farm, but the flaws in their civilisation are found in their brutal relationship with their gods, which is oppressive, as it needs to be because their political institutions are lacking. The tribal chiefs are said to gather at a place called Ruroxolnow to make decisions for all the Zummosh, but the chiefs themselves rule over the individual tribes as absolute tyrant kings. An oppressive relationship with the gods, overseen by a priestly class, which makes the people fearful, is therefore necessary to keep the people in line. But this denies the Zummosh a large amount of their freedom and so it is a deeply flawed civilisation."

Dunobos drained his cup and turned to Kalasyar, pausing for a moment, and viewing her with a suspicious, fiery eye. His disc of a face red from too much wine. She took the bowl from him and refilled it as Koseun spoke again,

"So, it is your proposition that all the elements of a civilisation must work in balance with each other for people to experience freedom. The Rilrpitu chiefs rule by the consent of the other warriors of the tribes, being selected for their courage and skill in battle. Where does their civilisation rank?"

Kalasyar finally felt comfortable enough to take a bowl and fill it with wine for herself. The image on the bottom was of Kusosu slaying the man-eating eagle of Tusotik with her trident and presenting the Kinsolsun and Buto with the bounty of her labour. It was one of her favourite tales, the maiden huntress. Hubris was eventually her undoing as her father cast her out, disgusted by the changes the reward of the Kinsolsun wrought upon her, it was a sad story. The dark liquid splashed into the bowl and the fragrance bounced back to her nose, filling her for a moment with a sense of the divine. Her movement caught the watchful eyes of the two younger men. But Dunobos paid her no mind as he delivered his verdict on the Rilrpitu,

"The Rilrpitu are a diverse people and in many ways successful. Not least a Rilrpitu tribe manged to conquer and rule Xortogun as its kings for almost two hundred years. But I would rank their civilisation below the Zummosh. The Zummosh use the fear of the gods and the absolute rule of their chiefs to uphold a sort of stability. This allows the other important elements of civilisation to flourish, farming most of all. The Rilrpitu on the other hand do not farm, they raise animals yes, but they rely on raiding and tribute for their own survival and so are parasites on other civilisations. Just look at the way they exploited Xortogun."

"You would argue that some elements of civilisations are more important than others, farming for example?" Kolkobuas asked.

"There are certainly elements which are more important than others. Without a proper tradition of farming, a society must resort to raiding, like the Rilrpitu. So, it must be a fundamental part of the whole." Dunobos answered.

"The old kingdom of Xortogun was the first great human society and we draw many things from its example still. But the great valley was for centuries ruled over by god-kings. All powerful absolute monarchs who would brook no opposition to their rule. Few would argue that it was a not the pinnacle of civilisation though." Koseun interjected.

"And I would not argue with them. That great kingdom grew from almost nothing, but it had all the important elements of civilisations. The most fertile lands in the world, and sophisticated farming methods to go with it. Great architecture, the tombs of the god-kings are something we could not match today, and a relationship with the gods which was effective and reciprocal, rather than cruel and oppressive benefitting only a small elite. The only element that the great civilisation of the valley did not have was a political institution that was balanced and not oppressive. The god-kings were tyrants, using the allure of their apparent divinity and their command of sorcery to make the valley so fertile and the sun shine all year round. If you believe those tales as well Koseun." he paused, basking in his own wit, before continuing "By nature of ruling as an absolute monarch, the god-kings had to be oppressive to maintain control. It is this oppression which over the course of time eventually brought them low, and some day even saw the Dusk fall on the world."

Kalasyar by now was sat listening to proceedings. Dunobos had clearly thought about his proposition long and hard, but she felt that it was too neat and linear.

"It seems we will only have the Xosu left for you to consider a true civilisation before long Dunobos." Koseun said only half serious. Dunobos was quick to reply,

"Well, we must remember that before the war for old Kolbos the Xosu were ruled by a High King who had more in common with the god-kings of Xortogun than even the kings who remain in Xosupil today. But you are correct. I think that the societies of the Xosu now are the closest humans have come to realising a true civilisation. All Xosu have the essential elements, sophisticated farming chief among them. We have art, architecture, poetry and music and a good relationship with the gods. Most important of all, the cities of the Xosu govern themselves in a collective way without oppressive tyrant rulers." he paused, "For the most part."

Kalasyar took the moment of silence to make her own contribution, feeling comfortable in the room and accepted into the discussion,

"Maybe you could say that, although the elements you propose for civilisation are correct, different societies have their own interpretation of each. For example, the people of Xortogun were content with the rule of their god-kings for centuries. Maybe they did not consider themselves oppressed. Here in Xosupil, Butophulo had its League and did not focus so much on farming as trade. Whereas the Rinuxosu have their king and are a much more agricultural people. It seems to me each civilisation's focus is determined by their geography as well as the temperament of its people."

Her words echoed off the walls like the ring of a hammer on an anvil. Koseun looked to his granddaughter, some surprise on his face, but Kalasyar could see the pride hidden in his ophidian eyes. Dunobos, however, looked displeased and said with a fire in his voice,

"Koseun, I don't believe your granddaughter was invited to take part in this discussion. It hardly seems proper that she is here."

Kolkobuas went pale and just stared like a beaten housewife. Koseun looked at him, and then back to Kalasyar. Silent for a moment, he said with some reticence,

"Kalasyar, although your intellect clearly surpasses most, Dunobos is right. A symposium is not the proper place for a woman. Especially an unmarried woman such as yourself. I think it would be best if you left us to our discussion."

She felt a crippling emotion well up inside her. Upset, disappointed or angry, she was not sure which one, maybe all. She kept her face calm as placid water as the current of anger washed through her and fixed them all with a stare which could turn men to stone. Kalasyar had come to expect such attitudes from most, but her grandfather had always encouraged her to engage in intellectual pursuits.

She was unsure what to do, argue? Refuse to go? Instead, she just dropped her bowl of wine. It clattered to the floor as she stood and walked swiftly toward the door. She could not bear to look her grandfather in the eye. Feeling like an outcast, her head spinning like she was falling, she left the room, and fled down the staircase towards her bed. Faintly behind her she could hear one of the younger men, it mattered little or less who, say,

"I hear that Gottoy has a constitution which mixes monarchy, aristocracy, and democracy. A balance of many elements."

***

The next morning came quickly, dawn's rosy fingers crept into Kalasyar's bedchamber to rouse her gently from her sleep. Despite the night before, she found herself excited and eager for the day to begin, washing and dressing quickly but methodically, aware she should look her best. She applied the pale white pigment that the old blood always wore on such occasions to her face. Then she painted waves, like writhing serpents radiating from her eyes in blood red and a thick red line around her throat. Finally, she coiled a light blue veil around her head, took the morning's freshly butchered meat, still a deep blood crimson, and stepped out the door into the warming sunlight and the crisp autumn air.

Tharoroz and Ralxuloz slid out the door behind her similarly snaking their veils around their heads. Her handmaids looked alike, aside from Tharoroz' golden hair and Ralxuloz flaming red locks, they both were tall with fair skin and light blue eyes, but they couldn't be more different. Where Tharoroz was forceful, strong, and wise beyond her years, Kalasyar would have taken her for an old, enlightened crone if not for her beauty, Ralxuloz was quiet and maternal. Ralxuloz was younger than

Tharoroz, but more widely travelled, having served a Putedun merchant as a slave before the Sisosi acquired her. Their presence was a comfort to Kalasyar, still hurting from the events of the symposium.

The gilded dome upon which the statue of the bold young smith sat was an awe-inspiring sight. The statue of Buto, bronze of skin and gold of hair, perched atop the temple and gazing out to sea was a most welcome sight. The god's hammer poised to strike the world and shatter it into a thousand pieces was a feeling she could relate to. Kalasyar was still flooded with emotion from the previous night, the wave of anger had subsided, but the slight by her grandfather cut deep. She knew how Buto must have felt as he was cast out of Dzottgelon by Dunsun and came crashing down to Kolgennon after he had dared to challenge the Lord of the Cosmos. The temple of Buto had always been a place which brought her comfort though. The bronze figure, with its red gold adornments and cobalt lined hair was a triumph, but it was the crippled god's great father which had always offered her solace. Him and his attendants. He would protect her now in the same way in which he had protected Buto. His servants rushing to aid the crippled god, raising the Thelonbet, watched over by the wise white goddess, at the heart of old Kolbos to shield him in the forge where he was bound. She found herself incredibly grateful that a meeting of the Great God's worshippers was on this day.

As always, the heavy bronze doors to the temple were swung wide open. Merchants and sailors, some of Buto's chief worshipers, were thronging in and out, making offerings and short prayers to bless their voyage, to keep the sea calm and trip rewarding. Some were even quietly asking the god to curse their rivals. Hiding themselves under the ink blue leaves of the hulthul tree which sat squat and thick below the dome, its pale white trunk bursting from the ground. She left her handmaids to pray to Buto as they were sometimes want to do.

Kalasyar pulled her veil forward to cover her eyes completely. She knew how to make herself an inconspicuous figure. A useful skill when her grandfather was one of the most recognisable people in the city. She quickly moved toward the back of the temple; confident no one would pay her any attention as the High Priest of Buto read the augers to a group of city magnates.

She slipped behind the altar and the wall it rested against. Behind the wall, she pulled back a finely weaved drape and opened the door which it covered, a dark staircase led down underground. *Grandfather and his friends can keep their philosophies* she thought, *there are old powers beyond the comprehension of man to which I must attend.*

She descended with her veil and robe flowing behind her, the heat of her body a contrast against the chill underground. Kalasyar could hear voices and the faint flicker of light around the corner at the bottom of the stairs. The others were already there, all servants of the Great God a duty which had been performed for countless millennia from the great flood which brought with it the riches of the sea down to Kalasyar's own day. Of course, in the time of the flood, Sem's servants were his own children, his daughters, the wizards of the deep, the Kinsolsun. Those times were gone now though, and the women of old Kolbos and then Butophulo had taken up the sacred duty. This was her calling.

The descent into the Semtekmoph, the sanctuary beneath the city, always brought the memories of her visit to the ruins of old Kolbos flooding back. All the children of the noble families of Butophulo, those descended from the old blood of Kolbos, made the journey to be initiated at the great temple of Buto, and the sanctuary of Sem below, in the ruined heart of the old metropolis. The temple was spectacular even now and must have seemed a wonder beyond the abilities of men in the days before its ruin. But Sem was not worshipped widely throughout Xosudun anymore. Even in the colonies beyond Xosupil the people had largely turned their back on him. Although Kalasyar had heard it said that he was still worshipped widely by the Putedun, but they called him by a different name. The trader who told her that also claimed it was the reason why the Putedun were so rich from trade and why Butophulo's wealth, despite its powerful fleet, had never rivalled the merchant princes of the Putedun Confederacy.

It was her mother who had taken her to old Kolbos, it was probably the most vivid memory Kalasyar had of her. The crescent of a smile which grew over her mother's round pale face as they approached the city was the happiest Kalasyar had ever seen her. Her mother had always been melancholy, her father had said it was because of her past. She was of the old blood of the islands, blood as ancient as that of the nobility of Butophulo. But that lineage always came with a price. For her mother's family that price was Hulsen the mad prophetess. Kalasyar's father had rescued her mother along with so many others when the League brought about the fall of the daemon witch and her acolytes. But the experience had left her mother's light faded. A warm moon's glow her father always said, friendly but distant. Only the gods knew what she suffered at the hands of Hulsen, but all agreed that Kalasyar's birth had been an unexpected gift from the gods. Achieved only with help from the oracle herself. A fact that always made Kalasyar feel uniquely connected to the Great God, as if she had some purpose. All that was before the war took them both, like it had so many others.

At old Kolbos, Kalasyar had drunk of the blood of her ancestors and been washed by the salt rich sea before the oracle of Buto had blessed her herself. The Semtekmoph was not only special to her for this reason though. It was also a place where she could be herself, where women ruled. Yes, men were initiated, but they served Sem out on the open sea, it was the women of the city who tended to the Great God.

Kalasyar rounded the corner at the bottom of the stairs and was greeted by a welcome sight. Gathered around the table which sat at the heart of the sanctuary were all the noble women of the city. She felt a sudden sense of relief, like she had been saved from the domination of men in the world above.

At the far end a statue of the Great God stood. Imposing and watching over his faithful servants, a pool of water surrounding him with his alabaster white serpent's tail coiled around and poised as if about to strike. His long blue-black hair flowing like a river, grasping his seashell horn in one bleached hand, a blast of which could shake the earth, and his fisherman's spear in the other's pearly grip. Surrounding the god were smaller arsenic white figures under blue shadows. Long headed wraiths bringing offerings to their master, ministering to the god, the Kinsolsun. Kalasyar entered the room and carried her own offering to the Great God to the foot of the statue. Then she took her place at the table, as close as she could get to the priestesses who served the Great God, the place where she felt most secure.

With everyone seated the ritual could begin. Sipenkiso, the High Priestess of Sem, entered the room from behind the Great God's statue, through a doorway surrounded by the coiled roots of the hulthul tree above. She was of the oldest and noblest blood of old Kolbos, but from which of the great families she hailed Kalasyar did not know. The priestesses of the Great God gave up their families and names when they came to serve Sem.

Sipenkiso had a mystical quality to her. Despite her advancing years, the god had not taken her beauty. She still looked like a maiden, despite her motherly disposition. Behind it all she hid the wisdom of a crone. Her long dark, almost navy, hair flowed behind her as she entered, her teal-coloured robes doing the same, a crescent of a smile over her round face. Two other priestesses brought in a garlanded bull, with a gleaming white pelt and gilded horns. The bull was led into the empty stone basin in front of the statue of the Great God. It entered calmly and stood facing the congregation. Sipenkiso turned towards her gathered audience and said,

"Great God Sem, we thank we for the bounty of the seas and all the good it brings to our people, accept this offering as a symbol of our thanks."

The two priestess who had accompanied her into the room, lifted out a part of the statue which was holding the water in place around its base. The water flooded into the lower bath, quickly filling it to the brim. Soon the bull began to struggle as it gasped for air, the two priestesses just managing to hold it in place, their hands pressed against the back of its head. When it seemed they could hold on no longer, that, with the last of its strength, the bull would struggle free, a white gold blade flashed in Sipenkiso's hand. With one smooth motion, a contrast to the panic and struggle in the bath, she cut the bull's throat. Black blood flowed, pouring over the white-gold marble at the foot of the statue. The marble seemed to glow and shine as it soaked up the wine dark liquid. The blood ran back into the bath and mixed with the crystal-clear water which glistened like moonlight. The bull continued to struggle, but each time it lifted its head a little less, until there was no fight left in it.

The priestesses moved quickly, like fish in the open sea, releasing the bull, they took up the bowls which had been laid out next to the statue. Filling each with the gory liquid and passing them out to the worshippers. Kalasyar took her bowl and sloshed the blood and water around, making sure the contents were mixed as well as they could be.

Sipenkiso stepped to the fore again, raising her own cup above her head,

"Today we share in the bounty of the Great God." She proclaimed, before draining the cup, her voice reverberating as if animated by sorcery. The others followed suit, pouring a libation on the floor to Sem beforehand. The gory liquid tasted acrid and salty, even so it filled Kalasyar hope, a sense of renewal. The last gulps tasted like honey.

With the ritual complete, the body of the bull was taken to be stripped and cleaned, re-emerging from behind the statue ready to be offered up to the god. First the bone, fat and sinew were placed in the middle of room and burned and then the meat was thrown into the raging flames. The worshippers were brought out platters of every kind of sea food, shellfish, lobsters, fish, and encouraged to eat. The bounty of the enriched sea.

With the meal progressing, the conversation turned to more human affairs. The nine priestesses sat at the front, including Sipenkiso. Alongside them was Hisukol Posuausthison, the wife of Puskison, the patriarch of the Posuausthison and the head of the Nine tyrants. Posukison, the wife of Foson Rusos, another of the Nine, was also sat near the head of the table. Runthilae Kosua, the daughter of their patriarch Kera was present as well.

The three families each held three seats on the Council of the Nine Philosophers as each had worked to see the League overthrown. Her grandfather had always said it was no coincidence that those three families had also kept themselves distant from the others, raising their sons with the teachings of Kunpit of Thelonigul instead of Rolmit of Rulkison. In the three hundred years since the end of the rule of the kings of Butophulo, their decision to follow Kunpit seemed to have cost them status and power as each of the families became less and less influential. That changed with the coming of Tekolger.

Kalasyar knew they were talking of important affairs concerning the future of the city, but they were too far away from Kalasyar for her to hear every word of the conversation. The most she could pick out was talk of what the Doldun would do now that their king was dead and where that left the city. She heard the Rinuxosu mentioned and the Tilxosu and Silxosu, the city of Thasotun and the Putedun.

The women closest to her were mostly the wives, sisters, and daughters of rich merchants. One or two even looked to be the wives of Putedun merchants. Kisonae Kisurusosi, Kolkobuas' wife, and Yulsonos, the sister of Dunobos, were the only ones Kalasyar had more than a passing acquaintance with, however. These women seemed more concerned with the strange activities of pirates around the White Islands, taking the crews of ships but leaving the cargoes to float pilotless. There were apparently even rumours of isolated farms being seized and stripped. Some insisted that the Red and White Council of Thasotun would supress them once again, others saying that Butophulo was the only city which could keep the peace.

Pusae Polriso, the wife of Rinukiso, the patriarch of that family, sat right at the far end of the table. Haughty as ever due to their royal blood, the Polriso always sat apart even from the other old blood, despite their own fall from prominence and standing.

The woman next to Kalasyar, who she did not recognise, got up, so Kalasyar moved closer to the end of the table. She could hear a little better now.

"We still have no sway over the Doldun." Runthilae Kosua was saying.

"Best to get rid of them." She heard Posukison say firmly,

"No, we should invite them to join us" Runthilae replied, "Many of the officers have their wives here with them in the city. The Putedun can help." Both were looking toward Hisukol for support.

Sipenkiso did not seem interested in any of this. She looked off into the distance as the women argued their point. Kalasyar wanted to intervene herself, but still upset from the night before, could not find the confidence to do so. *No, I will wait until the end* she thought, *best to talk to Sipenkiso alone.* The debate between the women went back and fore with no real conclusion being reached.

As the meal ended, the Great God's worshippers began to leave, until only Kalasyar and Sipenkiso were left in the sanctuary. The High Priestess was leaning over the trough of water at the feet of the statue of Sem. Kalasyar went over and did the same. The High Priestess glanced at her as she did, smiled and looked back to the water with intent. After a few moments of silence, Kalasyar spoke and found the words flowing out of her like a waterfall,

"I listened to the conversation over the meal. What is the point of arguing about such things if we, as women, will never be able to have power as men do?"

Sipenkiso looked up, as if shaken from some trance. Her eyes took a second to adjust, her wide pupils narrowing in on Kalasyar, and then she said with a liquid smile,

"We will never be in same position that men are, you are right. Things are not made that way. But that does not mean we do not have power."

"What do you mean?" Kalasyar replied.

"Each of the women who came today are loyal initiates to the Great God's mysteries. Each of their husbands, sons, brothers, and fathers are important men. Who do you think they share their deepest secrets with? With whom do they share their darkest fears? Who do they trust and listen to? This is where our power lies. These men may be on different sides of politics or war, but they all listen to the women they trust the most, and those women are all on the same side.

Think of the sea. It is unpredictable, dangerous, and destructive, but it also offers great opportunity, an abundance of food and limitless wealth, if we use it in the right way. Power is like this too. Why would we wish to be at its mercy when we can instead be its guide?"

Kalasyar looked at her intently, the way a smith may inspect a newly forged blade,

"I am not sure I understand your meaning?"

Sipenkiso continued,

"The sea on its surface may appear calm, but below its waves strong currents push and pull those on the surface. Helping ships sail and fish to find their way. Much like this we can use our connections and influences to push events in a direction we wish them to go. The mighty warships which sail on the oceans may look impressive and indeed be powerful, but they are at the mercy of the sea below them. Do not trouble yourself with the appearance of power, like the warship, be more like the current below."

Kalasyar nodded,

"But how can I do that?"

"There are many ways child. First you must discover what is the best course to take, and then you can plot your path." Sipenkiso said, a crescent of a smile grew on her pale round face, "Come here and I will show you." The sound echoed like the words of a spell.

She gestured to Kalasyar to stand over the bath of water. The blood still sloshed and mixed with the murky water inside.

"Do not be scared." Sipenkiso said. She then uttered something in a foreign tongue. Kalasyar could not understand the words, but they sounded like the crash of the waves against a cliff, and they felt as though they had power in them. The blood began to swirl and twist, separating out from the water.

Soon the blood circled around the outside of the bowl, twisting, and turning, like the flames of a forge, but forming a perfect circle. Inside the blood circle, the now crystal-clear water settled so still that it seemed as though it was a mirror. Kalasyar could see her reflection in it. She looked scared,

"Find out what your path is." Sipenkiso said.

Do not be scared, be calm like the sea, she thought, and she plunged her head into the water, shattering the clear mirror and entering the realm below.

She held her breath at first and shut her eyes tight, but the water still found its way in. It tasted of salt, as sweet and sickly as the sea and it burned against her eyes.

The world blackened and when she opened her eyes, she was in a different chamber, not the one under the temple of Buto but it was somehow familiar. The walls of the circular room seemed to shimmer and move as if made of water and lit by moonlight. It was only looking closer that she saw it. A great serpent, snaking its away around the walls, slithering twisting as if to keep the world itself moving. Around the edge of the room sat nine shapes, shadows and wraiths flashing arsenic pale, blue and green, enthroned as if holding court. She could not make out faces or get a sense of them, the images shifted like the sea, everchanging yet always remaining the same. Kalasyar could feel their burning eyes on her though, judging her.

One of the figures stood and began to walk towards her. In its hand it carried a white gold cup. It stopped in the centre of the room and knelt next to a circular pit. It was only when she stared closely that she could see a small white gold rock nestled in the centre. The rock sucked the light in, giving off a power so palpable she could feel it reverberate around her body. The wraith dipped the cup into the pit, filling it with a dark liquid.

Kalasyar was on the ground unable to move, as if she had lost the use of her legs, feeling like she had been discarded by some cruel god. The pale blue shadow approached; even up close it held no shape, just a mass of writhing serpents.

It pulled her to her feet and poured the rich dark wine down her throat. The liquid was sweet and rich and sour at the same time. It tasted bitter, metallic and of the salt of the sea. She drank eagerly as the rich fiery tentacles crept through her throat and into her stomach. In the end it tasted like honey, and she remembered the bees kept at the Academy of Rolmit from her childhood.

Then there was an almighty crash. One of the other wraiths was stood near the white gold rock, striking it with a hammer. Each blow sent a shockwave which felt as though it would rip a hole in the very fabric of Kolgennon and it reverberated through her, flooding into Kalasyar as if she would be torn in two. A storm seemed to rage around her, but she felt somehow safe here, like a power was surging inside her, forging her anew. A fire being kindled deep inside her, like those that burned at the core of a smith's forge. The wraith before her looked deep into her eyes. She could not tell, but its look was perhaps approving. Then the world went black again and the sanctuary of Sem emerged once more, the High Priestess stood over her smiling.

"What does it mean?" Kalasyar demanded, spluttering as she did.

"That wheel is for you to turn, to wander and find your way home. But what I can tell you is that the Great God wants us to be able to guide society for the better. Right now, there is an imbalance in our knowledge." Sipenkiso explained, wiping the water from Kalasyar's cheeks and forehead.

"The Doldun?" she posed, already knowing the answer.

Sipenkiso smiled, there was something of the sea in that smile,

"You know more than you let on. The Doldun are very guarded and keep themselves closed off, but you are on good terms with their general I understand."

She answered quickly, spluttering the words out,

"Doltopez? Yes, he has come to know my grandfather well and has been kind to me when our paths have crossed."

"More than kind so I hear. You think it is just your grandfather that he would like to know well or is it the maiden too? And you are not yet wed."

The bluntness of Sipenkiso surprised Kalasyar. She stuttered,

"Oh…he has always been courteous towards me, but he is just keen to ensure that my grandfather does not stir any trouble."

Kalasyar was panicking now, maybe she had said too much.

"Staying close to the Doltopez may be a good idea for you then. He would be more likely to consider your grandfather a friend with you at his side. He may even begin to listen to what you had to say." Sipenkiso suggested.

"I am betrothed though." She did know where those words came from. She had not thought of her potential husband in many a year. Zolmos, named for a famous scion of the Kisurusosi. They were matched when she was but a child. Her grandfather had never insisted on the match being fulfilled though. Zolmos had been taken west by Tekolger, over a decade ago. The last she had heard he had been forced to settle in a colony in far off Zowdel by the king, she did not even know if he still lived. And in truth, his removal had felt like a burden being lifted.

Sipenkiso merely smiled,

"Go home now child. Rest and think on your vision and what we have talked about. The way will become clear to you when the Great God deems it right."

Kalasyar headed back up the dimly lit staircase toward the bright light of the temple above.

* * *

The sun was at its height as she made her way back out on to the street. Dunsun's great eye illuminating the frantic activity of the city. Kalasyar's eyes took some time to adjust to the light, the saltwater still stinging against them. But it was the words of the priestess which really pained her. There was no hope of her achieving anything in the world of men, if Sipenkiso was to be believed. But she could make an impact in other ways. The suggestion did not sit well with her. Tharoroz found her as she left,

"Your eyes are red and sore, what happened?"

"The Great God showed me something, as of yet I don't know what." Kalasyar answered, she kept no secrets from her maids. Ralxuloz took the end of her veil and dabbed it against her eyes to dry off the water,

"Visions of the gods are a blessing; its meaning will come in time." she said softly.

A large crowd had gathered near the foot of Polriso's Hill as they headed home. Kalasyar made her way towards it, rubbing at her eyes still under her veil. The garment finally felt useful, covering the sore redness which seemed to have engulfed her eyes.

As she got closer, she could tell the crowd was gathering to hear a man speak. From the back it was hard to see, but a man was stood on one of the empty plinths where the statues celebrating the great men of the city once resided. From his position it seemed he was stood where Tikolkir Polriso's image once rested. The thirteenth man to win that most honoured place, if only for a short while, as his rhetoric and action held the city together when Tekolger, invaded Xosupil. His statue was erected and pulled down in the space of a year as the League collapsed and the city began to forget its past. It stood just long enough to be included in one of her grandfather's lessons though. A star which rose fast, burnt bright and died just as quick.

The crowd grew silent as the man began to speak,

"My name is Dorthil Rusos. Some of you know me, others will come to know me better as I take my father, Foson Rusos, place on the Council of the Nine Philosophers. My father is ill and has decided to retire, leaving it for me to take his seat on the ruling council."

Kalasyar knew the name, but not the man. He was young, with windswept hair and the face of a man who had spent a long time at sea. He must have been one of the graduates of the Nine's attempt to train the next rulers of the city as philosopher kings. The city's new rulers had taken over the old Academy of Kunpit on the northern edge of the city to use to educate the children of the elite and cement their rule. It was in the old philosopher's school, known to many as the Panther's Den, where the Nine themselves had been educated. *'The city will remain one whole through the wisdom and skill of the multitude of children taught here'*, the decree which began the teaching had read. Dorthil continued,

"I have recently returned from the west, where I ventured with the great king himself and bore witness to the mysteries of those lands and the fantastical deeds of the king. The stories you hear of him may seem like those of a hero from an age long since passed and only encountered in the realms of the gods, but I was there, I saw them. At Kulanzow I saw the king ascend the fortress like a god. In Zowdel I witnessed him drive the Rilrpitu away with a single roaring cry. In Xortogun he bested the savage warlord of the horse lords like Tholophos made the Bulodon wail. I also observed the sweet odour which drew men to his cause like no other. I wish now to give the city the wisdom of my experience.

I know that many in this haven are worried. More sellswords on the streets and the passing of the King of the Doldun, the Hegemon of our precious League of all the Xosu. Not to mention the tales of pirates at sea and the war between the King of Gelodun and the Republic of Gottoy. These are uncertain times. I have come here today to reassure you that I will do everything I can to keep the city safe and you and your families secure. This is the purpose of the council, the safety and good governance of the state in the name of its people.

The uncertainty and risk are why the council needs to be hard right now and impose stricter rules and curfews. It will not last forever, you have my word on that. As a gesture of good will, I have ordered that the guards to withdraw from the market during business hours, to allow you to go about your trades without fear of interference. As well as this, every free man and woman of the city will now be entitled to one measure of grain every day, at my expense."

The announcement seemed to go down well with the crowd. A cheer rang up as Dorthil made his gestures. Another ambitious man making a grab for the attention of the people to see his star rise. *I wonder which of our noble women is pulling his strings*, Kalasyar thought. As she did, a darkness fell over the city as clouds blocked the sun. *A storm is coming*, she could smell it on the air, autumn was upon them.

Dorthil stepped forward into the crowd to receive their thanks a smile on his face beaming like the sun. His guards advanced with him, but he gestured for them to stay back. A man emerged from the crowd, a pale hood covered his head so she could not see any of his features, but when he slowly raised his face to meet Dorthil a flash of recognition blazed across the young politician's face.

The man moved quickly then. His arm raised, a flash of light and a blow to the gut. It was all over in an instant. The brilliant white of Dorthil's robe was stained red, another blow and then the man turned to run, pushing through the crowd and barging Kalasyar out the way. He was covered head to toe in blood. He burst through the rest of the crowd blocking his way and made for the open streets, pursued by Dorthil's guards. Tharoroz and Ralxuloz caught Kalasyar before she fell.

The assassin only made it a few steps before Yulthelon caught up with him. His feet tangled and he fell, his head thumping hard into one of the columns which lined the road. He lay on his back dazed but looking almost relaxed, his round face smiling in a crescent with no care in the world. He was soon proved wrong as the guards descended on him and took their swift revenge. Blow after blow, cuts and thrusts tore the life from the assassin and sent his shade whirling down to the lord of the dead.

SONOSPHOSKUL

12

"I come before you with a message from Toyoroz Hozhoz Dozthozfiz, General and Consul of the Republic, who has been empowered to act on behalf of the people and the senate of the Gottoy."

The army of Gottoy sat encamped on the plain before the walls of their city, where they had defeated the King of Gelodun, under the canopy of a thousand stars. The emissary, Thizusqut Fozkutfoz Juszot he named himself, had come to treat with the survivors. Without any recognised leader, the men insisted that the envoy be allowed to address all the survivors, the collectivist instincts of the Xosu coming forth in the jaws of defeat.

"The general wishes you to know that he recognises that you fought well and valiantly. The battle today under the walls of the great city was a close-run thing and fortune a fickle mistress. Another day and your king's reckless assault would have yielded a great victory."

Thizusqut spoke Common Xosu well, only a trace of an accent sang from his lips, but there was a wild delight in his voice that unnerved Sonos,

"But now you sit here, defeat haunting you, the gods forsaking you and casting you down in this foreign land. Be of no doubt it was the god's fury which saw to the cataclysm that engulfed your army and changed your world. No doubt you are unsure of what to do next. Toyoroz wishes to help you in that decision. The people and senate of Gottoy have no quarrel with you. It was the King of Gelodun who led you against us and wrought destruction in his wake. For you and for us. But his shade has been thrown down to the halls of the dead. The Consul has no wish for further conflict, and so, as a gesture of goodwill, he will give you supplies, and provisions and you will be escorted back to your own lands in peace. Provided you give up your weapons and agree to pass under the yoke in supplication. As a show of friendship, he would extend an invitation to your leaders to dine and treat with him tonight and you will be provisioned tomorrow."

Hunthisonu fell on the field at the head of a reckless charge into the massed ranks of the men of Gottoy. His desperate grasping for a name and reputation to rival his cousin and the gods themselves, cost him his life and placed his people in mortal danger. The effect of his death had sent a wave of despair flooding through the army, like Dunsun had struck them with his thunderbolt. Runukolkil's swift action led the Daemons of the Deep and the other Xosu companies to craft a defensible position in the foothills of the mountains which enclosed the valley of the Thelizum river. Before the day was out, they had been joined by the remains of the Legion of the League of the Twelve Brothers and those Gelodun regiments who had managed to cut their way free. Almost ten thousand in total, but perhaps a third of them were camp followers and only around fifty horsemen.

A murmur rippled through the assembled ranks of soldiers when they heard the offer made to them by the emissary from Gottoy.

Discipline had remained steady to this point, the men's instincts had kicked in and they had quickly fortified their position on the hill, ready to meet any assault by the victors of the day. But when no attack came, the pause allowed their predicament to dawn on the men, creeping into their minds. Fear had spread throughout the camp. Directionless, lost and surrounded by an enemy bent on their destruction. Inevitably amongst so many Xosu, debate and division broke out about what options were left. Survival now the only objective. The tale they would tell if they made it home would be very different from the one they imagined when the campaign began.

Sonos had not escaped the creep of fear, a fear that could transform a man. Surveying the field of battle, strewn with corpses and the cries of those near death, had brought back memories of the fateful day when Tekolger's army had streaked into Xosupil and destroyed the might of the League. Sonos' own uncle had led the army of the League on that day. Tikolkir Polriso had spoken eloquently in the assembly and convinced the people of the city to meet the Doldun in the open. It was a chance for his family to rise once more and shake off the miasma which hung over them. Buoyed by recent victories over the far-famed Sacred Band of the Rinuxosu which had brought the foe to their knees, the people of the city threw out their past caution. They had even refused to heed the utterings of the oracle of Buto, who had warned them of their folly,

> 'The arrow is loosed, its landing upon the field will start the flood.

From plain of weeping wind flows an empire of wine dark blood.'

She had said it clear as any oracle ever was. The whole city knew the uttering by heart, but too many believed that the oracle had prophesied their own victory against the Doldun and the Rinuxosu to see the warning. Even Sonos was guilty of that foolish belief. He had voted, like so many others, for Tikolkir to have command of the largest army yet assembled by the League to swarm and overwhelm the upstart king. Sonos had allowed himself to be taken with the mood, dreaming of glory as all young men did. That was until the armies clashed on the field of the Bulodon's Wail. It was said that Tholophos himself had won a great victory on that flat plain, the victory which allowed him to seize the high kingship of the Xosu, it proved the same for Tekolger. Sonos knew the truth now. The truth of false promises and hubris. He would not fall for such folly again. He had felt the sharp thrust of Doldun pikes on that field and fled from the rumble of hooves. He saw his uncle fall to a thousand cuts and tasted sweet victory turn to a bitter defeat. No one ever thought about the vanquished in the old stories, but in those moments of defeat he knew how they must have all felt. The same hollow feeling had returned to him that evening. On the field of the Bulodon's Wail he had lost his home, today the prospect of returning had shattered before his eyes as the fickle favour of the gods had brought the world of the Xosu crashing down in an instant. Then the emissary from Gottoy had arrived.

Sonos looked around the crowd of warriors now with the worrying realisation that Thizusqut's words seemed to be finding favour as they drifted through the cool evening air. The men were eager to believe that the world had not changed and suddenly become a lot wilder and more dangerous. His offer made things seem easy and simple. The feeling of bitter defeat sat in his stomach like a bottomless hole as he watched the Rinuxosu, Tilxosu, Silxosu and the men of Gelodun all begin to believe what they were hearing. It was only natural for men to hope when struck with such disaster.

The men of Butophulo were used to hearing such poisoned words from demagogues addressing the assembly, rarely were they proved correct. Runukolkil stepped forward to address the men. Like Sonos he also sensed a trap, and attempted to hammer home the danger the men faced,

"Do not be taken in by such sweet words. This Toyoroz is a politician and a victory over the famed Xosu will no doubt propel him to great power in Gottoy. Why would he pass up such an opportunity for power? No, this offer is not what it seems. Toyoroz knows that he cannot defeat us outright if we stay united, despite his superior numbers. He saw how we cut through his ranks even in defeat. He has seen what the Xosu can do as we came hurtling down the valley of the Thelizum to the walls of Gottoy. He fears you and he means to find a way to disarm you and make you vulnerable. This course of action will only result in slavery and death."

Some in the crowd shouted out at the words, but the gods only knew whether they were in agreement,

"Comrades, brothers in arms, I speak to you now not as a general or a warrior but a fellow man. We marched here as an army of disparate elements, like so many bees without a hive. Some were promised plunder, some glory, some land, the only thing uniting us was the king. That king was bold and brash and foolish, and now he lies dead on the field, the armies of Gottoy triumphant and we are all that is left. But the death of the king and the defeat of his army need not mean our surrender. Broken that we are, we are more united now than ever. No longer an army of different elements motivated by many different goals. Now, like a smith re-forging a broken blade, whether we are Xosu, Gelodun or Hotizoz does not matter. We are all men motivated by one goal, the goal that has united all men since the dawn of days. Survival!"

A murmur rippled through the assembled ranks. Agreement or fear it was hard to tell what it meant. Reading a crowd's mood was a fine art, as many an aspiring leader found addressing the assembly of Butophulo. Crowds were difficult, fickle, and hard to predict. Runukolkil continued,

"That gives us a single unified goal. Escaping the land of Thelizum. To the west, east and south lie the lands of Gottoy and their allies. Those routes are closed to us, too many enemies will lay underfoot. The way we came is closed as well, I fear. Those cities of the League of the Twelve Brothers who continued to resist Gottoy lost their freedom today. The Hotizoz are a proud and fierce people, but they no longer have the strength left to fight and instead will hide under ground to wait out the coming storm. To the north, mountains, the plain of Beligul and yet more mountains. But beyond that the sea, the city of Rulrup, lands inhabited by fellow Xosu. A haven of safety and freedom. A hard task to march that far over that terrain to be sure, but it is the only solution to escape our current crisis."

Runukolkil spoke powerfully, his voice booming, his points hitting home like a smith striking the anvil again and again. Years of training for the assembly of Butophulo made sure of that. A silence took over the assembled Xosu. Surely they knew Runukolkil was correct in his assessment, but many did not want to admit the truth of it, did not want to admit the dawn of their new world.

The men from the League of the Twelve Brothers had sent only their commanders and a seer to hear the emissary. Hotizoz culture was much more deferential than the Xosu it would seem, and the Hotizoz had dealt with Gottoy for long enough to put much stock in their words. One of their own had been the king of the city until he was thrown out in a bloody coup and the new republic had then turned its greedy eyes on the twelve cities of their former rulers.

Dzotdoz Hotthuzishoz Fotisoz, the supreme commander of the armies of the League and Hozfotou Hotthuzishoz Kuthozuz, the commander of the sole remaining legion, rose in support of Runukolkil, along with Sonos and the other Salxosu in the crowd. But the arguments of the emissary were in the ascendancy as the crowd looked for the easy solution.

The two Gelodun nobles who had managed to cut their way free having rallied two thousand men from the reserve, were also in attendance, along with many of the men they had led to safety. Rilrpitrol and Yilthuso, both claimed descent from the House of Gelo, and as such the royal blood. The noblemen of Gelodun had yet to shake the sense of superiority that came with such lineage, a trait they shared with the Doldun. Yilthuso, the elder of the two, weak and weary, still in his blood-spattered ornate armour of the Rinuxosu style, rose to speak,

"And the solution you offer means death for us all!" he spat the accusation at Runukolkil, "You men of Butophulo are too used to the open sea. What do you know of marching through mountains, caves, and arid plains? You may has well march us straight to the gates of Phenmoph's rich halls. Your suggestion is only true if the men of Gottoy are bent on sending us to the realm of the dead. Why would they do that now? We are much reduced and leaderless. We should accept their offer and make a deal to recover the body of the king, then retreat to the coast. You men of Butophulo are so fond of voting, let us put this decision to a vote of the assembled men here and now."

Thusokusoa, the Rinuxosu commander of The Exiles, then rose to speak. The gruff and grizzled veteran was thick set but had a typical Rinuxosu look hidden behind numerous scars and a flame red cloak. He had light brown skin and hazel-coloured eyes with a dense beard and long oiled, brown hair which was lined with grey. The Rinuxosu were not exactly renowned for their eloquence and his speech was typically short and brisk,

"I may have fled my brothers in the Sacred Band, but I did so out of duty to my king and the Rinuxosu. My dispute is with the Grand Assembly, and I intend to live to see that through. My ancestor may have fought to the death in the Jaws of Zilthil, but that was in defence of the Sacred Land, death here would be foolish. I say let us have this vote and accept the Consul's magnanimous offer."

In that moment Sonosphoskul knew the argument was lost. Looking at the scared and vulnerable faces of the assembled men, a vote now would only lead one way. But how could they refuse to allow a vote? None had the strength to enforce their view and division now would mean death for certain. *This is the folly which demagogues can bring to a free people.* The distant dream of returning to the islands, which had seemed so real only that morning, now shattered before him, fading into an old tale to be told at a feast. All he could see now was death in this foreign land, or slavery or worse. The fall of the king had stripped away any notion of a civilised end to this war, but the men would cling to the possibility.

He found himself toying with the amulet he always wore around his neck. The Polriso clan had carried it all the way from old Kolbos. His father had claimed that it was an automaton forged by the Kinsolsun themselves, but the sorcery used to animate it was gone now. For Sonos none of that mattered, it was just a memory of home.

Despite the Salxosu, the Hotizoz and a few of the other Xosu voting for Runukolkil's plan, a clear majority voted to accept the invitation of the envoy from Gottoy. The Rinuxosu shouted their approval, as was their way. Every man from Gelodun and most of the other Xosu also signalled their approval. A second vote confirmed the Gelodun noblemen and some of the other company commanders as the army's representatives. Those men promptly left with Thizusqut to treat with Toyoroz. The Hotizoz refused to participate after the first vote and returned to their men.

* * *

It was deep into the night, the moon hanging high in the sky, Tholo's great eye observing the darkened land, before sleep welcomed Sonos. But his respite was short. No sooner had he shut his eyes, he felt a hand on his shoulder shaking him awake.

"Captain? Come quick." The face before him was a mask of bronze that startled him. Alert and awake once more he replied,

"Why do you wear your helmet? What is it, does Gottoy come already?"

The sentry replied,

"No, at least we do not think so. There was shouting from the camp, and Pitae swears he heard a clash of arms. Someone is riding towards us. Come quick."

Sonosphoskul jumped up and grasped his spear after he pulled a tunic over his head. He sent a man to wake Runukolkil and rushed to the sentry position by the crudely constructed gateway. A commotion on the plain below, near where the army of Gottoy had encamped, had caught the sentry's attention. Torches flashed amid the distant echoes of shouting. A rider emerged from the darkness, thundering toward the Xosu encampment. The charger ground to halt at the hastily built entrance and its rider slumped forward. The sentries crept out of the gates to aid the man, still wary of the world beyond the camp.

The man they dragged inside the palisade was bloodied but still recognisable. Rilrpitrol, the Gelodun nobleman. After water was handed to him in the up turned helmet of one of the sentries, he found the breath to speak,

"You were right, it was a trap. They tried to seize us as we entered Toyoroz' tent. We fought back. The others were killed or taken; I am not sure. Toyoroz, tried to take me himself. I managed to reach a horse and escape. They planned to hold us captive and wait until you handed your weapons over, then seize the men as they attempted to march off."

By then Sonos' men had roused Runukolkil. He answered Rilrpitrol softly and not unkindly, but Sonos could hear the melancholy in his voice,

"Don't blame yourself, it was a difficult choice and a tempting offer." Turning to the sentries he said, "Take him to have his wounds seen to and tell no one what has happened." They nodded and disappeared into the camp. Then he looked to Sonos, "We don't want to spread panic. Quietly wake the remaining commanders and bring them to my tent. I want you to go to the Hotizoz yourself, we need them." Sonos nodded and quickly headed into the camp.

The remnants of the Legion sent by the League of the Twelve Brothers were encamped separately from the Xosu on an adjoining hill. A well-ordered construction considering the desperation of the situation. Sonos knew all too well the danger of a descent into chaos after the gods visited a disaster on an army.

He had donned his own armour before approaching the camp and the sentries recognised the hammer of Buto painted on his shield as he approached. The Hotizoz had also noticed the commotion in the plain and their commanders were already awake and gathered. The sentries led Sonos to their ornate command tent in the centre of the camp. The Legion was well ordered, but the men were all awake clearly preparing to leave. A sight which did not surprise Sonos.

Inside the tent he found a fire blazing and a large bronze cauldron of wine being mixed by a slave. Dzotdoz, the captain-general, appointed by the Senate of the League of the Twelve Brothers, was stood in the shadows of the corner of the tent. He was a stubborn and suspicious man and pious to a fault, seeming more of a minister to the gods than a general.

The Legionary commander, Hozfotou, a man who Sonos had come to know well, was close to the fire warming his hands. A contrast to his commander, Hozfotou was an open and friendly man. A traveller who seemed to have spent more time exploring than amongst his own people. The amber necklace from Xortogun and the golden armbands from the lands far to the east he wore were a testament to his travels. A third man, a gruff senior soldier, stood over the cauldron as if inspecting the mixing of the wine.

"You coming here now can only mean one thing. Have the men of Gottoy proven themselves not to be trusted?" the captain-general said, brooding over his cup of wine.

Sonos nodded,

"It was a trap. Only Rilrpitrol escaped and his wounds are grievous."

"I warned your Xosu. Gottoy is greedy, like a hydra with a lust for plunder. Sooner or later, they will turn on you. Your general at least saw through them I will give you that."

"You are leaving us?" Sonos asked already knowing the answer.

"Nothing for it. Your Xosu are lost without your king. You will abandon us, so we will march home and make a fight of it. You know this feeling yourself. The Doldun's king drove you from your land. You fled because you knew the folly of fighting a man who the stories would have you believe is the son of a god. Yet you still yearn to return and fight." Dzotdoz said nonchalantly.

"You will die if you do. Your cities will burn." Sonos said.

"They will. But at least our memory may linger for those who resist tyranny to aspire to or for the children of Gottoy to fear perhaps." he replied, with a morbid grin on his lips. "Our people were only ever visitors to this land. Our ancestors settled here in a time of need. We always knew that someday we would leave again, why not in a blaze of glory?"

"It does not need to be this way. The men voted the way they did because they were scared. They will see the folly of that action now. Runukolkil has called all the captains together for a council, he will put his plan to them again, with your support we are sure to sway them. We can find safety in the White Islands. You can rebuild your strength and live to fight another day."

The captain-general chewed on the thought for a moment, but it was the young Legionary commander Hozfotou who responded,

"Runukolkil spoke in our interests before, and I trust Sonos. Besides, what do we lose by attending this council? The men will still be ready to leave when we return and if successful, we will have allies to march alongside us."

"We will not be marching home though. Runukolkil wishes to head north." Dzotdoz replied.

"For now, that may be true. But surely it is better to survive this and return home with our strength regained. That way we may at least stand a chance of making a fight of it." Hozfotou answered.

The captain-general only nodded, but Hozfotou looked to Sonos and said,

"Go back to your general, we will be there."

Despite everything, during the walk back to the Xosu camp Sonos felt a little less disheartened. Maybe they would be able to escape this mess, maybe he would have his chance to return to home, or to the White Islands at least. His thoughts turned to Kolmosoi then and those that had remained behind. Maybe Pitae and Kunae had found some way to hold off Thasotun. Maybe they had put Kolmosoi's schemes into effect.

What remained of the company commanders had been quietly and calmly roused and a council of war organised in the dead of the night in Runukolkil's tent. Thusokusoa and Dzulkoten were there from The Exiles, in the scarlet cloaks of the Sacred Band they still wore proudly. Possosous spoke for the Tilxosu company named The Bulodon, raised up by their men as their commander lay dead on the field. The Tilxosu were famous as horse breeders, and it seemed they all walked as if they were more comfortable a horse. Possosous was no different as he swaggered into the tent in his leather kilt and sweat stained tunic. He carried the look of the Xosu and his gait and posture revealed which of their tribes he belonged to.

Bospitu, the commander of The White Hydra's Teeth, a Silxosu company, was also in attendance. Rilrpitrol was there to represent the Gelodun, although he was too grievously wounded to offer much council. Last of all Dzotdoz and Hozfotou strode into the tent.

Speaking to the assembled commanders, Runukolkil said,

"We have been betrayed. The men chose to trust in the oaths of Gottoy and they have been found wanting. But recriminations would be pointless now, we are still stuck in the same predicament, but now lacking many of the company commanders. We have but one course of action left to us. Break camp as soon as we can and march north before dawn and the enemy are upon us."

Runukolkil was met by silence until Possosous raised an objection,

"That is not the only option left to us, Runukolkil, and who put you in charge? Gottoy will still negotiate with us. You said it yourself. They lack the strength or conviction to overrun us. Why else would they try this treachery?" He insisted as he drained a cup of unmixed wine. The men of The Bulodon all had a cruel and self-interested streak in them, more barbarian than Xosu in attitude despite their typical Xosu look. Kildol, the fallen commander, had been the same. But the shining goddess Yulthelon favoured Runukolkil. The suggestion raised nothing but derision from the other commanders. Sonos knew that fight was won when Dzotdoz stood and spoke,

"Even we no longer see that as an option Possosous, and it is our land we will be abandoning. Survival now, then we can think what comes next. Our ancestors did the same when they fled from famine and war in Gulonbel. Runukolkil speaks sense here even if it is a difficult thing to hear." His words calmed the room again and within the hour a plan was made to escape the clutches of Gottoy.

This is why the Xosu are renowned throughout the world and valued so highly as mercenaries, Sonos thought as the camp quietly and efficiently organised itself. Transformed by the god sent disasters which had befallen them, they turned with quiet determination to survival. New commanders were elected by the men to replace those that had been lost and each of the companies, even the Gelodun, now voted in favour of Runukolkil's plan.

Whilst the bulk of the soldiers and camp followers set about preparing to march, destroying anything that was not essential and gathering everything else onto wagons or marching packs, Sonos was sent with a small force of twenty men from the Daemons of the Deep toward the enemy camp.

They removed their armour and covered their faces and weapons in the blue-green mud to be like shadows. Then they began a slow crawl into the plain between the Xosu and the army of Gottoy, like the snakes that were numerous in this land, towards the epicentre of the cataclysm of the battle and the camp of the enemy.

Near the river, Sonos found one of the irrigation ditches that honeycombed the hinterland of the city, deep but only half filled with water. He slipped down into it and slid along as close to the camp as he dared. His men followed and took position alongside him.

The wait was long, the night was at its darkest now with only a few hours left before dawn. The noise from the Xosu camp floated across the plain, but from Gottoy, nothing, which worried him even more. Sonos could just make out the sentries left to guard their defensive ditch and beyond that the looming walls of the city itself on the other side of the encampment. He settled down and waited.

A fear crept over him again. If they failed here, then all was lost. The army of Gottoy would surely catch them in the open and that would mean only death. He found himself touching his amulet and saying a prayer to Buto, asking himself how he had arrived here and thinking back on his actions.

The League of the Twelve Brothers had called to Thasotun for aid and Thasotun had appealed to the King of Gelodun. The Red and White Council of Thasotun was keen to get rid of the Daemons of the Deep he did not doubt. The Council was unsure of its own position and must have known, or guessed, what Kolmosoi was planning. He was sure it was them who ordered his death, *it had to be.* Although the method of the killing was too professional, no doubt they had hired an assassin, *from Puteduntik perhaps.* The White Islands had been secured. The mercenaries had become an inconvenient burden, a hangover from the past, and Pittuntik under Kolmosoi's control was starting to look like a rival to Thasotun rather than an ally. Its famed forges working to arm the Salxosu, and the colonists planted there after the sack of the city when it rose against Butophulo at the beginning of the war with the Rinuxosu, were still loyal to the memory of the League. But it was the oracle that had persuaded them to sign up to fight with the King of Gelodun.

'From the funeral pyres beneath the walls of Gottoy a new power will rise to challenge the old.'

It all seemed like folly now. *Pitae and Kunae were right to stay in Pittuntik.* They all should have stayed, maybe they could have broken Thasotun and restored the League.

A light flickered on the hill behind them, then a hundred more. That was the signal. Sonos looked to the camp of the enemy, alert now, but all attention was fixed on the Xosu camp. Sonos tapped the shoulder of the man next to him then climbed out of the ditch, emerging on to the land above. In the dark he moved like a wraith, sliding up by the sentries whose gaze were fixed on the burning pyre of the camp on the hill. The only noise he made was the soft padding of his feet. His men bundled the sentries over, gagged them and bound their hands.

The horse lines were easy to find. His men quickly fanned out amongst the lines and cut the horses loose. Each man mounted a horse, the prisoners were pulled on to the lead horses. Then they lit the torches that they carried with them. As one they burst forth, driving the now loose beasts of war into the enemy camp.

Panicked as they were by the sudden appearance of men emerging from below with torches, the horses thundered into the army. As they galloped through the unsuspecting men of Gottoy, they tossed their burning torches into the nearest tents, causing madness and desperation amongst the ranks. With chaos sewn amongst their foe, Sonos and his men galloped off into the darkness to catch up with the Xosu already on the march. Leaving the shouting and the screaming of men and horses in their wake.

* * *

As Dunsun's shining gaze cleared the horizon, the light of the day helping the events of the night, and day before it, seem like an old story. Sonos had even started feeling a little more secure and confident.

A hard night march guided by the light of the stars, without stopping, had seen the survivors put good leagues between themselves and Gottoy. The daylight now revealed the sense in the decision to march. The mountains were beginning to loom all around them, a small river lay ahead, one of the Thelizum's many tributaries. Beyond it a sheer mountain pass which would take them through to the plain of Beligul. Not an easy path to take, the wild tribesmen who lived in the mountains were notoriously hostile. But the Hotizoz were certain the men of Gottoy would not venture into the mountains, and their prisoners would make passable guides and hostages if necessary.

They had marched in a hollow square rather than a column. It was slower going, but the camp followers and baggage train that would be vital for survival could be kept safe inside. The Exiles had taken the vanguard, the remains of the Hotizoz Legion were protecting the flanks and the Salxosu took the rear. What horses they had, had been turned into an improvised scouting force. The twenty stolen horses had been handed over to the Tilxosu, better horsemen by half than the Salxosu, taking their numbers up to seventy. Sonos was grateful to have his feet planted on the ground again, he always felt uneasy a horse.

The Rinuxosu called the column to a halt as they reached the edge of the river. The Tilxosu scouts crossed the fast-flowing water to make sure the way was clear. Sonos set his men to watch the rear whilst the army settled down for a brief respite. But the scouting force had only just crossed when a dust cloud appeared on the horizon, Toyoroz' army could not be far behind. They must have marched through the night when they realised the Xosu were gone.

In most circumstances this fact would have heaped pressure and panic into the situation, but the immense danger had sharpened the minds of the Xosu. A calm seemed to descend on the army, and without orders being given, preparations to cross were swiftly completed. Thusokusoa bellowed out orders and The Exiles and The White Hydra's Teeth crossed in force to secure the far bank of the river as the Hotizoz Legion saw to the crossing of the camp followers. Runukolkil organised the Daemons of the Deep into a rear guard and they waited.

Within the hour enemy cavalry loomed into view, as the last of the camp followers splashed on to the far bank. Runukolkil shouted out his orders and the Salxosu company began a slow withdrawal over the ford, the men chanting out a beat to keep formation. The Rinuxosu were leading the way into the pass, but the rear of the column would need to be protected as they found their way into the mountains. Sonos splashed over the river, the last man to reach the far bank. He shouted out orders,

"Form phalanx on me!"

As one his men turned to face their opponents, locking their shields together to form a phalanx, their spears a bristling wall shining in the morning sun. The horsemen trotted up to the riverbank eyeing the Xosu warily, but none dared to cross. A few bolder men splashed into the river and threw their javelins. But they fell harmlessly in front or sailed overhead and eventually the horsemen drew back to wait for their infantry to catch up. The cavalry would stand little chance of forcing the river on their own. Sonos ordered a slow retreat toward the mountain pass, melting away into the depths of the peaks as another cloud of dust signalled the arrival of the legions of Gottoy.

SANAE

13

She had had to wait almost a full moon's cycle for this moment, since the night of the inauguration of the temple, but Helupelan had insisted that the trial must be conducted when the moon was at its height. The tests of Xosu's acolytes had to be conducted in the proper way he had said. Over the next few nights, as the moon sat bright and full, several of Xosu's faithful would begin their trials.

No matter she had thought, she had waited all her fourteen summers for this moment to dawn, a little longer should not have been too much of a sacrifice. But the last few weeks had been maddening. It was all over now though; the first of her seven initiation rituals were to begin, although she knew little of what to expect. The rites of initiation and Xosu's mysteries were a secret to all but those who went through them. Even so, Sanae was overwhelmed by excitement. So much so she had forgotten her nerves and was bullish about the coming test.

Helupelan had guided her out of the temple, down the steps and onto the street. He now turned her around and they basked in the light of the full moon. He paused and stroked his beard, as he always did before delivering his teachings,

"The steps you are about to follow echo that of the bright god himself. By walking down his path you will learn what he learnt and strive to achieve what he achieved."

Sanae nodded, searching eagerly for any clues as to what she would have to endure. Helupelan continued,

"In the dawn of days, before the rise of the old kingdoms and the war between the gods that changed the world, Xosu was birthed from the blessed union between two domains. The chthonic world below and the heavens above us.

Dunsun, king of the gods and lord of the Cosmos, and Bosithelon, daughter of the lord of the dead and his reluctant wife Geli, queen of that dread realm were all men must go and mistress of the earth. Dunsun saw the child Xosu as his natural heir, a way to prevent the strife which can come when a son comes of age to challenge his father, and the child showed the inclination his father wanted. Even as a babe he was able to ascend his father's fearsome throne, burning bright in all its glory."

Sanae nodded along intently. It was a story she had heard a thousand times before, but there must be a clue in it that she was missing.

"You must emulate the god now. Go inside and seat yourself on the throne. See the world as the child saw it and think on what it means to rule the Cosmos." Helupelan finished.

"Is that all I must do?" Sanae asked, confused. It seemed such a simple task.

Helupelan nodded,

"That is all. May the Bright One light your way."

Not quite believing what she was told, Sanae began her ascent back into the temple which looked like another world to the buildings and streets below it. One of brick and marble compared to the wood and mud. The stairs to the great edifice were steep, but it was hardly a difficult task like she had expected. Xosu famously suffered much and learnt from it, bringing the fire of that learning to the Xosu people. The trials of his followers were renowned for their difficulty too. The initiate was tested through the same rigours that Xosu endured. It was true, Sanae pondered, that the child Xosu was given every privilege. His mother gave birth in secret, away from the eyes of her father, Phenmoph, and the jealous queen of the heavens, Tholo. But Dunsun was so pleased with his son and heir that he brought him to his palace at the centre of glittering Dzottgelon to be raised as the future master of the Cosmos, striding bright and true through the heavens for all to see. Perhaps this was a test to show how easy things were for the god before the fall. A simple walk up the stairs to a throne was how his journey seemed at first.

She reached the doors of the temple; the huge bronze entrance was shut. She pushed one side and heaved, it ground open. The temple shined as bright as the sun when she entered. Candles littered the main hall, around its edge and towards the centre. The reflecting pool shone brightest of all, the ring of candles around it mirrored in the waters. The whole room appeared golden. In that moment, Sanae could believe it to be like Dunsun's palace in Dzottgelon.

The flickering light danced across the statue of mighty Xosu, moved inside above the altar after the temple was inaugurated. The image still took Sanae's breath away even though she saw it every day. At the foot of the statue there was an amber gold coloured throne, bright like the sun. Sanae made her way towards it, burning with excitement and watching her image catch the light in the reflecting pool. It looked as though Xosu's own reflection was watching over her. She took her seat at Xosu's feet, her first task complete.

A gust of wind swept through the temple and as one the candles went out. The veil of night descended, only the moonlight shining in through the open roof allowed sight of anything at all. A voice echoed off the walls,

"The path seemed clear for the bright god. But Dunsun's wife, white armed Tholo, Queen of the Heavens, would not have the child of another succeed and deprive her of her throne. One night, when Dunsun had slipped away down to the underworld to visit his mistress, the Queen of the Cosmos acted to protect her throne."

Something flashed across the front of Sanae, she sensed movement. Then, out of nowhere, a liquid was splashed over her. She desperately wiped at her face; her heart was pounding in her chest. *What is it?* It was too thick to be water, too sticky. Her robe was sodden and clung to her chest. She smelt it, tasted it. *Blood,* she thought, *am I hurt?* No time to check, her arms and legs were seized, bound by ropes and she was lifted off the floor. Three shapes in robes and masks lit only by the moonlight, the round full face of the goddess jealously staring at her. Instinctively, Sanae grabbed out, striking one of her assailants. She felt the mask come free in her hand and she gripped it tight as she was lifted by her binds, pulling her limbs in all four directions. Pain shot up her arms and legs. They began to carry her, stretched out as she was, the voice echoed again,

"The child was seized upon by the queen. Brutally attacked, torn limb from limb and cast out of the heavens."

It was at this point that Sanae realised where they were heading. She desperately tried to struggle free, but it was no use, they held her too firmly. The opening at the rear of the temple came on quickly, she had given up the struggle.

With a heave they cast her out and she was taken by the air. As she fell, she tumbled, over and over until the world became a blur. Her robes trailed behind her like a tail as she felt the rush of the air go passed her head. Her ears were filled with a burning sensation, her face scorched by the air. She fell, straight as an arrow loosed from a bow. The mask still in her hand, she gripped it tightly and tucked it in to her chest, desperately seeking some comfort from her own embrace. The water came on with a thud. A wave of pain rippled through her body and her ears rung like the drums and trumpets and other instruments of war. She was in the river she knew. Despite the ringing in her ears, she heard the waves crash against the riverbank before she slipped below the water.

Struggling to tell which way was up, three times she spun around until she pushed her head above the surface. In the darkness, the water looked thick and black as a rich wine. *There are crocodiles nearby*, she thought, *and I am covered in blood.*

She kicked her legs and made for the bank, grasping the thin, red trunk of a sapling dolthil tree not yet grown to reach the heavens. She pulled herself onto the sodden ground. A wave had clearly hit the shoreline when she plummeted into the river causing a flood to wash over the low bank of the river. She let go of the tree, leaving a sticky, wet handprint to soak into its trunk, as she struggled to pull herself away from the water and its potential danger. A hand gripped her under the arm and pulled her to her feet. A feeling of relief like the bright light of dawn swept over her. Helupelan was stood there with a beaming smile on his face. Her heart was still pounding in her ears, but she felt safe now with the High Priest there. He said nothing, but just took her arm and led her back to the temple.

Helupelan sat her down at the entrance to Xosu's temple near a burning torch. He wrapped a cloak around her. The heat from the flame felt like a hot sword cutting through to her wet skin, but it was welcome. Kolae approached them, wearing her white armed robe, and carrying a round mask of a waxen hue, splattered with red blood, which betrayed her involvement in Sanae's ordeal. No doubt Zenthelae and Konthelae of the Zelrsaloz were the others. Where the High Priestess went, the twins were always close by. The other uninitiated called them Sunset and Sunrise, due to their respective roles in ensuring that the temple was opened in the morning and closed in the evening. Zenthelae, with her dark demeanour and sinister smile, would always appear to signal the coming of the High Priestess, and Konthelae, with her bright eyes, would be following close behind their mistress.

As expected, the twins appeared. Ignoring Sanae, they danced past like blue shadows in the night and retrieved the pale mask which had transformed her attackers and she had abandoned in the water. Without a word, they slipped away, carrying the pale mask toward the temple. The red earth had half covered the mask, its smiling face seemed to be mocking her, its piercing teeth coiled into a menacing grin.

"Did I pass the test?" Sanae asked breathlessly. She did not know the answer, but in her heart she felt different somehow, transformed.

"Don't be so foolish child." Kolae said, "No one passes or fails. It is not a test, but a process to make you reflect." The moonlight glinted off one side of her face and the torch the other, pale, and red all at once. Kolae turned to Helupelan, "I told you she was not ready. The Bright One shines a light on the path and yet she is still blind to it."

Helupelan smiled warmly and touched the High Priestess' white robed arm,

"Kolae is correct. This is not a test, but you are right to think of how things went. Dig a little deeper into that thought. What can you learn from the experience? What did Xosu himself experience? At the end of this process, you will know if you have passed or failed in yourself, if you reflect on it wisely."

Before Sanae could think, or answer the High Priest, Kolae interrupted,

"You are not an acolyte of the god yet. So, whilst you think on it, I have supplies I need you to acquire tomorrow. Come to me in the morning and I will tell you what I need."

Sanae would have given the priestess a sarcastic reply, but she was still in shock from the fall and her fire had been doused by the water. Before she could think of anything, the High Priestess spun around and disappeared into the temple, the moonlight illuminating her path.

"Will I dream again tonight?" Sanae found herself asking the High Priest. She had never told him about her dreams before, but now seemed like the right moment.

"Dream child? About what?" Helupelan answered. A perplexed look on his face.

"Sometimes I dream when we sacrifice to the god, about red kings on their thrones. I thought I would dream tonight as I have completed Xosu's first trial." She replied. Suddenly feeling foolish for asking. Helupelan pulled a pain expression as he considered her words, as if the thought of it troubled him. Finally, he said,

"I wasn't sure before, but I know now you are ready to take the trials."

The answer took her by surprise, "What do you mean? Because of my dreams?"

"Some say that those with the blood of the gods have dreams sent to them by Xosu. As if their blood was made from supping of the wine of Gelithul, a fanciful notion no doubt. Others say that they have visions when the rituals of the god are carried out. This I can believe. There is little of the power of the old kingdoms left to us, the link to the worlds of the gods shattered with the Dusk, but some residual memory may reside in these practices. A glimpse to another realm of what once was. A time when gods and heroes, taller than mortal men, red and white of skin and bronze and azure of hair, the marks of the blood of the gods, still walked amongst us." He paused and stared off into the distance, then looked her in the eye as if remembering himself, "but no, I am pleased because you have shown the right instincts. To question and take nothing for granted. You are following the light of the bright god."

***

Sanae hardly slept at all the rest of that night. But she found herself rising with the star which comes before the sun and watching dawn's fingers appear on the horizon, grasping toward the heavens. Kolae was already awake and quickly set her off to purchase incense, oil, wine, and cloth, all were important in the running of the temple. The way in which Kolae ordered her to collect the supplies always made her feel it was a punishment though.

Helupelan found her before she left and gave her a letter to be delivered to the High Priest of Xosu at Thelonigul. He trusted her with a bag of silver Tributes to pay a merchant to see it done.

She stepped out of the temple and made her way down the stairs, taking a moment to admire the city she had come to call home as it stirred in the early morning sun. The city was built on a series of twelve marshy islands named after the gods, at the mouth of the Kelonzow river, but the delicate light of the dawn sun reflecting from the water, which permeated the city, made it appear as if it was floating on a cloud, shining brightly and not tied to the toil and tumult of the world. It was a sight which calmed Sanae, made her feel tranquil.

She had been very young when she arrived in the valley of the god-kings and so barely remembered what Tekolgertep had looked like in those early days of its construction. The only memory she could recall with any clarity was sitting in a small boat as it was rowed up the river and into a small cluster of wooden huts, the dawn light following them, but the sun not yet risen. When they landed on the swampy islands that would become the city, they were greeted by king Tekolger. He was younger than she had thought a king would be and he wore a hat to keep off the sun which made him look more of a farmer than a conqueror. But still he gave off a paternal aura, with wise crimson eyes and the bearing of a hero, like Tholophos come again. Helupelan had tried to make her stay in the boat, out of the way of the king, but she remembered how she had snuck out behind the High Priest's trailing robes and surprised both men as they spoke. The king had laughed and roughed up her hair in a kindly manner. It was a memory of her childhood she held fondly.

Helupelan had told her that all that was there before Tekolger was a small fishing village. But when the king liberated Xortogun from the cruel domination of the Rilrpitu, he saw the opportunity of such a place. The king ordered a city to be built, one which would unite his empire, being a meeting place of the worlds of high mountains in the east and the seas and coasts of the west, the greatest centre of trade and knowledge in all Kolgennon. Tekolger had even mapped out the limits of the city and planned the main buildings himself, the temples to all the Xosu gods and those of the Xortogun as well. The royal palace sat on the central island, named for Dunsun, and Xosu's temple, as the king's patron god, sat alongside it. Helupelan always said it was a miracle to see the city rise from the fractured and broken countryside. The king's vision had proved correct, people from all over the empire had flooded into the new city. Not just Xosu and the Doldun, but Xortogun and other peoples of Zenian. Even many Rilrpitu and Zummosh had given up their old ways and settled in the city. Most came to work as labourers, and the city was in large part still a vast building site. A few grand public buildings had been completed in the centre. The palace was nearing its finish and the great lighthouse in the harbour, standing many cubits tall, topped with a golden statue of Tekolger holding a flame to guide the ships, loomed over the entire city. But many more still lived in hastily constructed wooden shacks surrounding the monumental central islands. But even half built the city was still vast. Sanae was sure it must be bigger than any Xosu city, even Butophulo.

Each community had also brought with them their own skills and expertise. Sanae knew which of the peoples produced the best products for the temple and would visit each in turn. First, she would head to the Xortogun for the incense, their gods demanded so much that the people had become renown for it. Their district was found in the centre of the city, where the islands ran into the mainland. It was not hard to tell when you left the Xosu district behind and entered the realm of the Xortogun. The architecture changed from gleaming marble to dusty sandstone, the people's skin grew darker, almost maroon in colour, and their hair greasy and bronze. The priests twisted theirs into fanciful shapes in reverence to their gods. Gods who dominated their entire lives, as the temples of their chief gods, Kurotor, Xura and Tora loomed over the entire district. The temples of lesser gods also nestled amongst them, but Sanae did not know their names. She liked to wander amongst the Xortogun district, and she found that if she covered her cobalt streaked hair of beaten gold, the bronze hue of her skin just about allowed her to blend in with the people. Although her amber eyes would give her away, especially when the red shone through. But that was a gift from the bright god himself Helupelan had said, it was the reason he knew even as a babe that she was destined to serve him.

The wine and oil could be found at the bustling harbour where traders from Xosupil and beyond would bring in the best the world could offer. The people from Torfub produced famous cloth, Helupelan would be pleased if she could acquire it, the traders could usually be found at the lively river port.

She had reached the bottom of the steps by now and was about to head into the heart of the city. Although Kolae thought this a chore, in truth Sanae enjoyed exploring the city, meeting the new settlers, and learning about the different practices of the people of the empire. If it meant that she could spend most of the day away from the demands of the white armed witch, then it was a most welcome chore.

She passed by the shrine of Tholophos at the entrance to the temple and began to cross one of the many bridges that linked the city together, heading towards the sea front and the immense curved harbour that sat between three of the islands. On the central island stood the great lighthouse. A core of pure white marble reached for the sky, supported by four trunks of the iron black, smooth rock of the valley, a pillar on each corner. On the sides of the tower, carvings as tall as mountains depicted Tekolger's liberation of Xortogun. Some in the Xosu style, others in that of the Xortogun, even giving the king an eagle's head. At the top a golden statue of Tekolger carrying a flaming touch stood on a dome which at night housed a larger fire which shone like the branches of a burning tree, whilst by day the smoke blew elegantly like leaves in the wind. The towering building cast a long shadow like a canopy over the whole city, often a welcome shelter from the heat. Many of the merchants claimed they could tell the hour just by observing the shadow.

The sun had barely risen, but already it was beginning to give out a tremendous heat, though that was not unusual even in the autumn, and it was something that Sanae had become well accustomed to. The furnace beating down now made the freshly caught fish in the harbour smell as if they were being roasted. Her homeland, as she remembered it, was hot and dry in summer, but nothing like Xortogun. The great valley would be a barren desert if not for the nourishing waters of the river which made it some of the most fertile land in the world. The valley of Xortogun was extensive and secluded, allowing a prosperous and large population to flourish, producing as many as two or three harvests a year. Now the harbour of Tekolgertep gave the valley a gateway to the east that was quickly seeing that produce turn into riches.

Despite the early hour, she found the port to be overrun with people. She heard at least five languages she did not know as she passed through, as well as the Doldun dialect and the Common Xosu tongue. She stopped to watch a dishevelled looking Xortogun augur, not often seen this close to the docks, who was gathering a crowd,

"Beware!" he bellowed in broken Common Xosu, "A new age beckons! The king lies dead. The solar barge which brought him to this world heralded the return of the gods, and the reopening of the gateway to their realms. Prophecy foresaw his coming, an outcast from the land of the sun's rise, born of blood young and old as fissures opened the realms. A golden age is coming to rival that of the old kingdoms. Famine blighted the land, the wrath of vengeful gods struck at every turn, people fled as the great kingdom of Yoruxoruni fell. Tekolger swept it all away, he was the Herald of the Dawn as prophecy foretold, sweeping away the night which fell when the old kingdoms crumbled, and the god-kings were cast from their thrones. The blood of the sun is now present once more, the dawning of a new age, but its birth will be troubled as the god-kings return to claim their thrones."

The sailors watching on, many laughed and jeered, a few of the more superstitious offered up a prayer, most people walked on by. The news of the king's death had shaken the whole of the empire and caused some strange reactions. Wisemen and fools alike were claiming that the king himself was divine and his death signalled some sort of doom. Most people just seemed concerned for the future of the empire and the stability and peace which the Doldun had brought.

Traders from Xosupil were unloading ships in the harbour. Alongside them were priests and acolytes of Dunsun and Tholo and others of Sunkeli strumming their lyres. There was even a group of wandering philosophers, followers of Kunpit of Thelonigul debating calmly with an animated and flamboyant adherent of the school of Rolmit of Rulkison. Sanae knew that wandering philosophers were common in Xosupil, but they were still a rare sight in Xortogun.

It was clear that there would be plenty of wine and oil to choose from, but first she wanted to head to the Xortogun district of the city. She knew that the priests of Xura, the name the people of Xortogun gave Tholo, would be conducting their morning ceremony as they always did to give thanks to the goddess for holding the demons of night at bay once again. Sanae had been to the temple of Xura several times. She had heard talk amongst the Xosu of the strange rituals of the Xortogun, the most pious people in world, and had wanted to see this famous devotion to the gods first-hand. The ceremonies were mesmerising, if a little odd, as they paraded the statues of their strange animal headed gods around. Watching them when she had the chance had become a custom of hers.

She arrived at the extravagant temple just before the morning ceremony was beginning. Xura was said to be the protector goddess of the great valley and the protector of the god-kings of Xortogun's past. When Tekolger had conquered the valley, he had become one of those kings. Helupelan had told her that the king had provided the coin to build this ostentatious temple dedicated to Xura as his patron and protector, in his role as king of the Xortogun, the Thoruri of the Great Valley as the old kings were called in the Xortogun tongue. Here the people of Xortogun worshipped the bird headed protector of their land and Tekolger, the son of Kurotor and his representative, or at least that is how they saw it.

She went inside the temple, still dark, with just the morning light shining through the open doorway. The cult statue stood at the far end of the great hall into which she emerged, surrounded by already burning candles, the air thick with the smell of the incense she was after. The figure of the goddess was shaped like a woman, but with the head of a strange bird-like creature with a long and thin beak. The statue was made from the cream and brown coloured stone found out in the desert, but its head was a strange jet-black colour, and shined almost unnaturally. It had been cast rather than carved, from the black iron like metal that the valley of Xortogun had deep rich veins of. It made the moonstone eyes glimmer in a sinister way that unnerved her. She was not sure whether this is how the Xortogun believed the goddess herself actually looked. Helupelan had claimed it was so, but a Xortogun man had told her it was because the birds were powerful protectors of the valley and its great river, watching over everything. Xura's loyal servants and so she was depicted in this way to show her power and protective role. The menacing bird head certainly looked like a fearsome protector to her, but the disk which surrounded it, gave the otherwise intimidating creature a warm glow. Like the moon offering light in the darkness to those who needed protection.

A voice echoed to her from the shadows. The mysterious, ancient, and elegant language of Xortogun bounced off the walls. The language was lyrical, but Sanae did not understand a word. A moon-like face appeared in the darkness which draped the inside of temple, it was a face she recognised. Kurmush Xura Ya Kuria, a priest of the temple, she had spoken to him before. The only one of the priests who seemed to speak any Common Xosu. Sanae, despite not understanding, replied to the voice,

"I was hoping to buy incense for the temple."

The man smiled, and replied in a broken Common Xosu,

"If the lady has coin, this servant can spare the goddess some of her fragrance."

She took out a silver Tribute, named for the coinage used in Butophulo and old Kolbos before it, but these coins had the head of Tekolger depicted on one side, the horned Xosu on the other. She handed it to the priest. He inspected it carefully and then disappeared behind the statue. Just as she was getting worried, he returned, stepping fully into the light. She could see that he was wearing a red robe, blood red, no doubt to cover the staining of the garment from the sacrifice of animals to the god. His bronze hair was greased and shaped like a crescent perched upon his head with an elaborately decorated beard, plaited into a point which jutted from his chin. In one hand he carried the incense, in the other an iron-coloured mask with a red face, covered in blood.

He smiled again and handed over the incense,

"Thank you." she said. Kurmush replied, in his broken Common Xosu which still had the lyrical sound of Xortogun to it,

"We all must serve the gods. This incense will go to the same purpose, but the coin will also serve."

She nodded just as the sun reached a point high enough to illuminate the whole room,

"Kurotor arrives once again, Xura's work is done." Kurmush said, "You know that the moon used to shine just as bright as the sun?" It was phrased as a question, but Kurmush carried on before she could answer, "When the world was still young, not this sun, this sun is the third, but the first sun. Xura, once shined as bright as her husband, but the feathered demon serpent Yob was jealous and attacked the gods. The serpent king murdered the first sun, Xur, and left Xura bloodied and weak, dimming her light forever. It is a tale this servant will tell you one day child." He said with a crescent smile. Sanae nodded again, intrigued. But as Kurotor arrived, she left, taking the steps in threes, and darting off toward the harbour. She had no time to listen to tales right now.

* * *

Sanae arrived at the harbour just as a large merchant ship was arriving in the port bearing the banner of Butophulo, no doubt full of the city's famous olive oil. It cut its way across the calm waters, like a god riding their chariot across the sky.

The harbour itself was awash with people and with merchants loudly calling out to their customers, selling wares from all over the empire and beyond. Sanae headed straight to the largest wharf in the centre of the island, the part of the harbour in which the Xosu merchants gathered.

Although the city was full of people and traders from all over the world, the Xosu and Doldun merchants had the blessing of the king and every advantage to trade freely. Tekolger had even gone so far as to exclude the merchants of the Putedun confederacy from his city to prevent their domination of trade as they did in so many other cities and kingdoms.

Sanae was quickly able to find and buy oil from Butophulo and wine from Gelodun and have it sent to the temple. The ship out of Butophulo would stop near Thelonigul on its return to Xosupil. She paid the captain with the bag of silver Tributes and trusted him with Helupelan's letter for the High Priest, promising him more silver if he returned with a reply.

She found herself thinking on Helupelan's words as she headed away from the main harbour and following the river's course to the west. She had always felt her dreams were special in some way as if the god had singled her out, but the High Priest must be right, they were probably just the residue of a bygone age.

She crossed several more bridges with the shallow river racing beneath and came to the river port. This roughly made stopping point just inside the city was where the barges which floated down the river finished their journey. Starting at Torfub, where the three rivers of the Zolkelonzow, the Thelkelonzow and the Kelonzow itself met to form one mighty torrent, the people of that famous city moved through the great valley selling their finely woven cloth. At Tekolgertep the cloth could make its way out to the east. Helupelan loved the soft touch and vibrant colour of the material.

Usually almost as busy as the harbour itself, the river port seemed quiet today, none of the familiar traders were out. It was strange as the traders should have been due to arrive in the city the day before, on the night of the full moon. Sanae approached a woman sat on the side of the river, hoping she spoke the Common Xosu,

"Where are all the traders from Torfub?"

In a very broken Common Xosu the women replied,

"None come, the queen goes to them."

The Common Xosu was bad, but the point was obvious. By the queen she no doubt meant Tekolger's Xortogun bride. The Doldun kings always took many wives, but the others had remained among the Doldun and the people of Xortogun had taken to calling Surson Tora Ya Kuria, the wife Tekolger had taken of old Xortogun nobility, the queen. She had taken up residence in Torfub to await the return of the army, the body of the king and to give birth. Why would the traders make the journey to Tekolgertep when Surson's court was in their own city and willing to spend lavishly?

"Where can I buy cloth?" she asked the woman absurdly, not expecting a helpful reply.

The woman smiled and said,

"Zummosh." Pointing to the south. The direction of the Zummosh who had settled on the southern bank of the river, outside of the city. Sanae had never been amongst the Zummosh before, the south bank of the river was not a part of the city and Kolae and many of the others at the temple had warned her to stay away. The Zummosh are savages they all agreed. *'If you go there, you will not return',* the High Priestess had told her. *'They may serve as fierce and loyal warriors for the king, but they can't be trusted in civilised society.'*

Sanae did not really believe the scare stories. After all, Kolae's own view of the Zummosh was coloured by her experience as a child having to flee to a temple of Xosu to escape a marauding tribe crossing into the lands of her Zowo clan. It was a tale which Kolae told often. She could not imagine the trauma of such an event, but those were different times, before Tekolger and the empire, surely not all the Zummosh could be so vicious. But something had made her cautious about going into their district alone. The south bank of the river was wild and untamed, nature still ruled there, it was like another world with the river the border in between. Kolae would not approve, but Kolae would also punish her if she did not get the cloth, and she did not want to disappoint Helupelan before her next test. She set off south.

* * *

The southern bank of the river appeared as less a city and more a collection of villages hidden amongst dense vegetation. Wooden buildings with thatched rooves surrounded small muddy squares, Helupelan had told her that the Zummosh were not civilised enough to understand life in cities. It was ironic then that many of the Zummosh who lived here had come to the city to work as labourers, building the magnificent buildings of the city's centre, under the guidance of the best Xosu architects. There was no bridge to get there, so she paid a man a silver coin to ferry her across on his small barge, whispering a prayer to Xosu to calm her nerves.

She made her way to the largest of the villages which the Zummosh tribes called home. She headed toward a huge dolthil tree which grew wild, its canopy of golden leaves covered the sky over the village. Even though she was only on the south bank of the river from the city, the area felt like a different place altogether. The people were tall and pale, many with blond or red hair. The men had beards and long moustaches, and they wore trousers and cloaks patterned with a series of squares, clasped with finely worked broaches.

She had hoped to find the main market square of the Zummosh on this bank, but there seemed to be no point which she could call a market. Instead, everyone was sat in the shadow of the tree, blacksmiths working a forge, women weaving and others grinding corn.

As she spun around searching for a trader selling cloth, she heard a loud guttural tongue call out. She could not understand a word, but she understood that it was directed at her.

"Zan!" was the only word that Sanae thought she could make out. Three thickset, bearded men were stood staring at her. One pointed at her and barked the word again, "Zan!"

They approached and carried on talking in their guttural tongue which sounded like it came more from their throat than their mouth, like the growling of a hound. Sanae imagined it must be almost painful to speak their language.

She had no idea what they wanted, but they seemed agitated. She knew they were questioning her about something. She could not answer, they must surely have known that, but her silence seemed to make them angry, so franticly she tried to speak,

"I'm sorry…"

One of the men with a long drooping red moustache howled. Sanae did not know whether it was words or just a cry of fury, either way for the first time since she had come to the city she was scared for her own safety. The men continued their furious questioning. She did not know whether to run or try and calm them down, in her fear she did nothing.

A voice echoed from behind her, angry like the others, but it was female,

"Xuloz!" was what Sanae thought she heard; it sounded like a command. The three men stopped and looked at each other, muttering something between themselves they turned and left. A voice in broken Common Xosu then said,

"Sorry for them child. These young men, this place they think they own. But raven-feeders they are not, just boys pretending to be men."

It was the same maiden's voice which had shouted, the guttural tone was still there in the Xosu she spoke. Sanae turned to see a woman of middle years, but spritely, red haired, with a kind smile and a youthful energy in her eyes. She wore a plaid robe of red and blue and green, cut to reveal a strong thigh and tied with a hempen belt. Around her wrists glistened golden torcs with a thick one twisted around her neck to match. There was something formidable about her. A girl about Sanae's age, but with a much fiercer and wild look in her piercing green eyes, which seemed as though they contained the wisdom of a woman in her twilight years, and thick red hair like the older woman's, was stood next to her, dressed in a similar manner. They had stopped grinding their grain to come and see what was happening,

"That they still know to listen to their elders and those blessed by the god, you are fortunate. Child, come with us, I will bring you the guest friendship those boys should have, then tell us why you have come. Not many clansmen visit us, unless from the palace looking for workers."

She followed the woman who now seemed ever more the maiden, to a nearby building. A long wooden hall with carved idols at either end, completely alien to anything she had seen built by the Xosu or even the Xortogun. She was led inside.

Sanae sat down on a wooden bench, and the kindly women insisted on making her a warm, bitter, but not unpleasant drink.

"Those boys, I must apologise." she continued, "They believe they rule over some great tribe rather than this land of black earth. Their fathers are not here but serving the king or dead. Palon is my name, and this daughter is mine, Lulpo. I am the Powouzo of the Zummosh here, the guide and conduit to the thrice knowing god. Without leadership, judging and arbitrating the disputes of the tribes falls to me. The mistress of these unruly boys if you will, so the Powouzo remember." Palon smiled as if they all understood.

Sanae did not understand much of what she said, but the lyrical rhythm of her voice was comforting. The woman continued, "With any kind of manners lacking from the young men, it falls to me to extend friendship to the guests we have. Child, what brings you here?"

"I have come from the temple of Xosu. The High Priestess sent me to gather supplies for the god, but the traders from Torfub have not come to the city. Instead, they await Surson Tora Ya Kuria in their towers. I was told that I could buy cloth here instead." Sanae told her, she felt comfortable again and the drink was growing on her.

A smile sprouted on Palon's lips, like the first shoots of spring,

"Not many clansmen come here looking to trade, but Zummosh cloth is the finest in the world. Much better than that from Torfub."

"So, the Powouzo remember." Her daughter said with an aged wisdom in contrast to her years. Palon turned to the young girl, "Lulpo, fetch the cloth."

The wild girl left the room and soon returned with a bundle of colourful material. Lulpo beckoned Sanae over to her and began to show her the different textiles. All sorts of patterns and varieties were on display. She was impressed with the craftsmanship; this was not the work of uncivilised barbarians.

"Child, how much would you like?" Palon asked.

Sanae produced another few silver tributes, "All of this." she said. Palon smiled like a maiden on her wedding day,

"Then you shall have it and a gift to seal our new friendship." The kind woman handed a woollen cloak patterned with a forest green and a rich red the colour of pomegranate to Sanae. On top of the cloak rested a bronze broach shaped in the image of a man sat cross legged in front of a tree. The man had three heads, one looked left, the other right and the third straight ahead. The central head had small antlers, like a stag, with rings hanging off them. In its right hand the figure held a wheel and in its left hand a sword. Sanae took it and inspected the broach.

"What does it mean?" she asked.

"It is the symbol of The Paron, the giver of life and his three aspects. The Chwur, who rules the skies, The Pare as he appears in this world and The Shaf who rules the otherworld. His servant I have the pleasure to be and the emissary of the tribes to the god, trained since I was young. This is why it is my job to oversee the disputes between the tribes and act as judge if they cannot be settled, the Powouzo remember the old tales."

She threw the cloak over her shoulders pinned it with the broach.

"Perfect, I hope that now we are acquainted you will come and visit us more often. This is, after all, a city for all the people of the empire." Palon said.

"Thank you, and I will be sure to maintain our newfound friendship. I am eager to learn all about the peoples of the city and of course the temple of Xosu is open to you all. May the Bright One light your way." Sanae replied, pleased she had decided to make the trip to the south and forgetting all about her earlier encounter. With cloth in hand, she headed back toward the temple.

* * *

Xosu's temple was filled with people as she arrived back. The wine and oil she had ordered was being dragged into the temple's grounds, so Sanae followed it inside to find Kolae and let her know the supplies had arrived.

She passed by a line of supplicants looking to gain the bright god's blessing and protection. Helupelan was stood over the altar reading auguries. She found Kolae behind the altar in the enclave closed to the public.

Placing down the cloth and handing over the incense, Sanae said,

"All the supplies have arrived. The wine and oil are being brought in now."

The High Priestess gave her a piercing look. Her round, pale face red with anger,

"Where have you been? Helupelan has been worried sick."

"I had to go to the Zummosh district to get the cloth. The traders from Torfub have not come." Sanae protested.

"You went alone to the Zummosh? I knew you could not be trusted with a simple task. Heavens know why the High Priest thinks you are ready to be initiated." Kolae said dismissively.

"The Zummosh were very helpful and the cloth they provided is of excellent quality." she replied, showing one of the pieces of cloth to the High Priestess.

Kolae ignored that,

"I suppose they gave you that cloak as well, or did you use the temple's money for your own gain?"

"This was a gift from a friend." Sanae exclaimed, allowing the anger to bubble up.

"And that broach, what barbarous symbol is that?" Kolae said, "Some abominable deity who the barbarians perform ghastly rights for. Maybe we should just cast you out to live amongst those barbarians."

Kolae whipped the broach off Sanae and with it her bright mood, her cloak fell to the ground,

"You cannot wear such things in here. The High Priest will hear about your behaviour. We have had a new delivery of cattle, many very young. It will be your role to see that they are cared for, are we clear?"

Kolae left before she could answer her, but Sanae could feel the anger building inside her and felt tears swelling in her eyes. She gathered up her cloak and left.

THUSON

14

Since their first encounter with the Rilrpitu, the pace of the march had increased from a crawl to a sprint. Dolzalo and Palmash had taken the cavalry and led a hard pursuit of the raiders. A bold move as they still did not know how many or exactly where the horse lords were. The devastated villages he had encountered on the march worried Thuson, but he could not know if they were the Rilrpitu's doing or more of Dolzalo's reprisals.

He had found himself left in command of the infantry, almost ten thousand of them, to follow on behind Dolzalo and Palmash and cover their rear. A daunting task for an inexperienced general. Zowdel consisted of wide-open plains and rolling hills, especially so north of the Kelonzow river. Covering the rear over such a large area had stretched the infantry very thin. Concerned about his men being overrun and feeling blind in this vast terrain, he had been sending reports and requests for reinforcements to Kelbal, but he was yet to receive a reply.

Dawn's rosy fingers were creeping over the horizon, but Thuson had already been on the march for some time, burning to keep pace with Dolzalo. As Dunsun finally raised the sun over the horizon, sending light cascading over the land and changing it before their eyes, a column of smoke ascended the edge of the skyline. *Dolzalo has been busy in the night, or the Rilrpitu are still getting the better of him*, Thuson thought uneasily. But at least it gave him a target to march toward. He ordered the small unit of horsemen he had been left with to scout ahead and get a clearer picture of what was happening. Thuson was determined he would not allow himself to be ambushed.

He had spent the days of the march wondering if the task he had been given was a reward, a test, or a punishment. The chance at a large command like this was the opportunity he had been waiting for to prove himself to the Companions. Some of the Doldun had always struggled to accept Thuson as an important member of the king's court. But Thuson had endured this suspicion as he had seen in Tekolger the chance to bring unity to the Xosu, a unity not seen since the time of Xosu himself. It was a vision in line with the teachings of Kunpit of Thelonigul, everything spread from one unity. Tekolger was the philosopher king to bring about a new golden age. But now with Tekolger gone, his position at the court was vulnerable. It seemed the only way to protect the king's legacy was to ingratiate himself with the Companions. The only way to truly do that was to win renown on the field. But when Dolzalo handed him the leadership of the infantry it felt more like he was shedding himself of a burden to pursue his own glory.

Dolzalo was one of the Companions who had always been ambivalent towards Thuson. Friendly but he treated him as of lesser importance. Dolzalo had spent some of his youth being educated by Yusukol Kosua with the other wards of the king, but only after Kenkathoaz had subdued the Zowo for a final time late in his reign. Dolzalo had not taken to the teachings like the others, there was too much of the clans in him. Then there was Palmash. Palmash had never been a ward of the king, the Tholmash were too seclusive for that, keeping to their forests. Even more so after Kenkathoaz had ravaged their lands. *Left with the two who trust me the least. If the gods are real, then it seems they have a sense of humour.*

Dolzalo had quipped as he left to pursue the Rilrpitu *'You will command the rear like a good Xosu general'*, it was a crude stereotype. Xosu generals always served in the infantry line or had the sense to stay to the rear to better assess the situation, and most of the Xosu were not great cavalry men, excepting the Tilxosu. The Doldun clansmen all seemed to believe this was out of cowardice and any general worthy of the title would be at the point of a cavalry charge. Still Thuson was determined to make the best of the opportunity, he needed to show his usefulness now that Tekolger was gone.

The approach of a rider shook him out of his thoughts. They had made good progress towards the smoke on the horizon, but the rider approaching in a rush from the left flank gave him pause. He had been forced to leave his left flank exposed to the northeast, with only a small tributary of the Zolkelanzow as protection. With his forces spread across the country to sweep it clear of Rilrpitu, Thuson had felt dangerously over extended. It seemed his worst fears were about to be confirmed.

"General!" the word was still new to him, and it took him some time to answer, "General!" came the cry again. Thuson turned and responded,

"Yes, what is it?" He knew the answer that was coming.

"The left, they must have slipped passed us in the night. We need reinforcements." The rider replied with panic in his voice.

Doing all he could to maintain his veneer of calm, he turned to the Thulchwal marching behind them as his reserve forces. Looking to Llalon and waving his hand in the air to signal for the ferocious warrior to follow him. He had known his flank was vulnerable, but the smoke surely meant the Rilrpitu were still ahead of them, unless there was another band out there that they had not yet encountered.

He turned his horse and made off at a trot. He would lead the counterattack himself, as Tekolger would have done. Nerves gripped him when he realised what he was about to do. He was desperately trying to remember all he knew of military tactics, but observation and theory would only help him so much. He nervously searched his mind for some clue about what to do next. He knew every word of Polrinu Rososthup's *The Machine of war*, but that treatise was a masterpiece on the supply, resourcing, and administration of an army. Runukolkil Kolkisuasu's *The Canvass of Conflict*, was a work with much more flair and elan on tactics and strategy, but the text seemed to scatter before him like leaves on the wind. He had not fought in the war between the League and the Rinuxosu, his cousin had taken him north before he was called to fight, and his family had never really believed in the cause. But now he would have to prove he was not just any other Xosu general.

* * *

Thuson pushed the pace hard, eager to arrive on the scene before his left flank was overwhelmed. Despite being on foot, the Thulchwal kept pace with him showing their impressive levels of endurance that Tekolger had used and valued so much.

The full light of the day was washing over the plains as he arrived at a small ridge that the men on the left flank had withdrawn to. Ordering his reserves to hide behind the ridge, Thuson went forward to survey the situation. Suddenly feeling vulnerable in his open faced Salxosu style helm despite his bronze cuirass with the panther picked out in lapis. Immediately he regretted not opting to adopt the closed helm of the Rinuxosu.

Out on the sweeping plains, a swirling cloud of dust had brought horses and screaming riders to flood the area. The riders seemed so as one with their mounts that they could have been a single creature, terrible and magnificent, bellowing like the wind. Their hooves pounded the earth and rumbled like the thunder of an angry god. It was like a sight straight out of the Sinasa, the hordes of amazons who came to the defence of Semontek, swirling under the walls of old Kolbos. Like those amazons, these Rilrpitu had appeared like a mist out of the night. Unexpectedly, bursting over the small river which the men on the flank had used as an anchor, assuming that no force would be able to cross and turn its flank. The tributary of the Zolkelonzow was small but deep. However, a small depression in the plain gave away a ford where the Rilrpitu must have crossed.

As the last of the flank guards scrambled over the ridge, the first shoots of a plan sprouted in Thuson's mind. Calling to him the captain he had left holding the flank. A fellow Xosu, the panoply of finely worked bronze and the conical Tilxosu style helmet gave that away. The sight of another Xosu commander was very welcome, someone who would perhaps understand him a little better. The flank had been driven back from the river under his command though, some harsh words and swift action to prevent a collapse would be needed. He called out to the Xosu captain,

"What is your name?"

"Riso." The man replied, clearly shaken.

"Riso, named for the poet?" The man nodded.

"Well, Riso, you and your men lost our footing on the plain, you will go and retake it. Get your men in tight order and advance them out into the centre of the plain. Then form your spearmen up at the fording point of the river. Make sure none of the Rilrpitu can get back across." he said firmly, pointing to the ford, "The Rilrpitu all fight as light cavalry. They will harass you, but if you stay tightly packed, they will not engage. Keep marching and don't stop until you are at that ford, then hold your ground."

"General that will be suicide." The captain replied. The thought gave Thuson pause for a moment. He was still not sure of himself in command and the reality of ordering men potentially to their deaths suddenly struck him. He took a deep breath and gathered himself. There was no other way, a sacrifice would need to be made to win back the fortune lost at the river crossing.

"Not if you stay tightly packed and trust in my men. We will not leave you abandoned." He snapped back trying to sound stern and in command. Riso uneasily nodded and set about assembling his men.

Thuson turned to the Thulchwal, dividing them into three columns, he placed one on each flank and one in reserve ordering them to stay in tight formation and ready their javelins. A company of slingers from Xokulmosh who had accompanied him, reputedly the finest in the world, he placed behind the ridge and ordered to wait.

The discipline of Tekolger's veterans shone through as order and organisation was restored quickly. On Thuson's signal they began their advance, cresting the ridge before the swirling mass of enemy horse had managed to reorganise themselves. The flank guards, armed in the traditional Xosu way as heavily armoured spearmen in flashing bronze, tightly packed, shuffled forward, slowly but inevitably making their way toward the river.

This new threat prompted the cloud of riders to their front into action. With lightning speed, they wheeled around, kicking up all the dust and debris of the plain. A whistling filled the air, and a rain of arrows began to fall on the Xosu spearmen as they moved forward. But with discipline and courage, the advance continued. With shields locked, the rear ranks holding theirs overhead, few casualties were taken. It would remain this way so long as they kept their formation and discipline. Thuson watched on, nervous, impatient. Uncharacteristically he found himself muttering a call to Xosu to guide them straight and true.

Waiting for the dust to build until it was almost blinding, he gave the order to his flanking columns to begin their advance. They made good progress at first, covered by the cloak of dust, but soon the Rilrpitu spied the Thulchwal, and small groups of howling horse riders broke away to harass them as well. *No matter,* he thought, *less to slow the centre.*

He was fortunate that the Rilrpitu lacked discipline. It was a weakness he could readily exploit, acting as the Xosu general and taking a position with the reserves to direct the battle. Dolzalo probably would have charged headlong into the midst of the foe and died fighting. A glorious death no doubt, but pointless as well.

A long agonising wait followed, as the Xosu in the centre slowly but inevitably made their way to the ford in the river, the one place in the small but fast and deep flowing rush that could be crossed easily.

As he had ordered, and despite the growing pressure and gradually mounting casualties, the men formed a spear wall, anchoring themselves to the riverbank. A few of the Rilrpitu noticed what was happening and began to panic. Some desperately assailed the spears, but the boundary was now closed to them, others turned to flee. A wiz and whoosh filled the air as the slingers brought them down.

Thuson turned to the enormous, flame haired Thulchwal next to him, who had a stag tattooed across his face. The other Zummosh called him Puro the Horn Blower. Thuson nodded his head. The man blew on the towering carnyx he held. The sound rumbled up the bronze pipe of the instrument and through the mouth of the antlered Wildman cast at the top. The Wildman let out an ear shattering roar and the wild Thulchwal all around echoed it back and charged.

***

The blood, sweat and adrenaline seemed to last and age. In reality it was over in moments. With their advantage of mobility gone, what Rilrpitu did not try to flee were slaughtered. Those who did run were cut down by a shower of stones and javelins.

Thuson knelt to look closer at the corpse of a warrior brave enough to have stood and fought. Despite the malformed skull, the results of the binding the Rilrpitu carried out as ritual from birth, he could tell the warrior was a woman. Not unusual for the Rilrpitu, there were legends of whole tribes of women roaming on the steppe of Belon. Looking around at the corpse strew field, he realised all the warriors were women. This was not the same group which Dolzalo was pursuing. Different feathered headdresses and patterns painted on the warriors and horses alike. They were from some other tribe.

He had taken time to get to know the Rilrpitu and understand their society as best he could when Tekolger invaded Xortogun and in the subsequent campaigns to drive them off the plains of Zenian. Tekolger had asked him to learn their ways to better understand them as an enemy and as potential subjects under his rule. He had learnt all he could, but in no way could he claim to understand them completely. What scholarly works he had found were few and he had only a passing knowledge of their guttural language, but any knowledge would be useful right now.

Some of the Xosu spearmen approached Thuson, bundling amazons down on the ground in front of him. Most did not raise their heads to meet his eye, some were too wounded to notice him. One sat defiant. He looked the woman up and down. She stared back. The fierceness of her glare gave him pause for a moment. Tearing himself away from her intense, captivating eyes, he turned to one of the Xosu spearmen,

"Have a rider take a message to Dolzalo. Let him know what happened here and that the group he is pursuing is not the only war band in the area." Turning to the other man, he continued, "I want you to ride for Yorixori and tell Kelbal that we were lucky this time, but we need more cavalry and there are more than just one band of Rilrpitu. They may be spread across the whole country by now."

SONOSPHOSKUL

15

Dawn came and with it a new battle.

The cool of the night still lingered as they broke into a run. They had marched before the light bathed the world. One column had pushed east beyond their target and now, as Dunsun's great eye rose over the horizon, they moved into the attack, the blinding light of the sun keeping them obscured from the enemy's sight. Once engaged, the second column would attack from the west and sweep in on an unsuspecting enemy. The objective was small but well-fortified, no more than a village and couldn't have been held by more than a few hundred fighting men. Sonos reached the walls at a run, his men keeping pace with him. *No sign of the enemy.*

Despite the imminence of the coming fight, Sonosphoskul's thoughts couldn't help but linger on their journey to this spot. They had struggled their way through the mountains after slipping passed the army of Gottoy and the cataclysm on the field outside the city. The army had spilled out on to the plain of Beligul tired, hungry, and close to breaking. A trail of corpses of those who could not keep up were left along the mountain pass. The commanders had decided to make camp then and there on the plain, the men were exhausted and needed to rest. *We could so easily have broken in that moment. Accepting this task is what saved us.* He told himself. Fortunately, discipline had held long enough for a sturdy camp to be built from what material could be found. Each company had then nominated their strongest men and sent them out in groups to forage. *The thought of food kept us moving, but also threatened to overwhelm us.* The Bulodon, those still mounted at least, had set off to explore the countryside. Although that looked more like ravaging from Sonos' point of view. The Bulodon had become increasingly violent as the march went on.

He placed his hand against the daube wall, it was dry and crisp to the touch. He took a moment to gather himself then, to prepare for the coming struggle. But he could not pull his thoughts away from the previous days. They had had no indication as to how the local people would react to an army of Xosu suddenly appearing from the mountains, but they were more concerned about the host of Gottoy. Toyoroz' legions would have had an easier, if longer, march going around the mountains through friendly territory. No doubt they had also sent messages out to their allies to warn them of the approach of the survivors of the battle.

It had been almost dark before the scouts and foragers returned on that first day on the plain. Some supplies had been found, but not enough to sustain the army for long. The horsemen returned having burned a village but found little of use there. Its people seemed to have vanished. *Despair, it was in everyone's eyes, though none of us said it aloud.* His thoughts still clawed at him. Beligul was shaped like a crater in the mountains, like some vengeful god had punched the ground in fury. It seemed like that scorn had destroyed the fertility of the earth as well and infested it with snakes and lizards. But the goddess had smiled upon the Xosu. The final foraging party returned with some of the natives and one who could speak Common Xosu as he traded with the Xosu cities to the north. The trader informed them of a fortified village that was filled to the brim with supplies for the winter, built on top of a rocky hill to the east of their position. It would be more than enough to see them cross the mountains safely and reach Rulrup on the coast. The merchant had proposed that they ally with his tribe in taking the village and in return they could keep the supplies. *But was that a gift from the gods? Or a trap set by those divinities whose displeasure we seem to have invoked?*

They had been wary of getting involved in local disputes, not wanting to bring the wrath of the local rulers down upon them. Especially with an army from Gottoy likely to appear at any moment. They would have preferred to slip across the plain like wraiths unseen. But the supply situation was dire. An assembly of the army was called for, the situation explained and put to a vote. Desperation had won the day and the men voted to join in the attack. The cheers of the Rinuxosu to signal their consent, as was their custom, had felt like hubris. *With that vote I found myself once again risking my life in another man's war in the hope of finding enough favour to survive for another day.* His hope of returning home seemed to be becoming more and more distant and the guilt of abandoning the White Islands was only growing. He could not even say they had much plunder to show for it. It was a sorry tale barely worthy of note.

The men brought up the crude ram they had constructed from trees felled on the mountain slopes. Without a word they positioned it before the gates and shattered the silence of the crisp autumn morning with an almighty crash. They burst through the poorly constructed gates as others threw grappling irons to scale the walls. Sonos was one of the first through the breach to be greeted by surprised defenders clad in crude bronze plates which barely covered their chests, wicker shields and rough-hewn spears.

Sonos pushed forward quickly as his men poured through the gates. Despite their surprise and poor weapons, the defenders organised fast, forming a wall of shields in the central square, but they were few in number. Sonos bellowed his war cry and charged, clattering through a flimsy wicker shield, and driving the point of his spear into the guts of the man behind it. Blood flowed like a red tide and the spark of life fled from the man's eyes. The rest of the men then plunged into the fight.

A bloody slaughter followed as the Xosu went street by street, building by building, the ground was slick with blood. It was all over before the blast of horns signalled the arrival of The Exiles in the second column.

The fight was easy, and few men were lost, but there were few to resist them anyway. Then the search began, his men went house to house looking for the promised supplies. The hunger and desperation had driven the men into a bloodlust beyond their usual discipline. Many of the others succumbed to their base instincts like The Bulodon already had. Even a hardened man of war like Sonos was uncomfortable with the vision of the village as he searched. The fighting men lay strewn all over, in some places there were no bodies, just body parts. No prisoners had been taken and some of the bodies had clearly been executed rather than dying in battle. He was disgusted at the sight but could not bring himself to blame the sudden change in the men, they were fighting for survival. *At least there are no women and children amongst their number*, he thought. The crossing of the mountains had been hard with death hanging over them at every turn, those pent-up feelings were bound to emerge in battle. *We should not have agreed to this folly.* Folly it may have been but accepting the trader's offer and putting their arms at the tribe's service was the only option left to them. Sonos reflected on it all helplessly as he paced through the village, watching an increasingly frantic search unfold as the men broke into each building one by one.

A noticeable anger soon started to sweep through the ranks as the village was searched. The men began to shout of betrayal and deceit. Their apparent allies had lied to them, there were some supplies in the village, discovered hidden in a pit under one of the buildings, but barely enough to sustain the army for more than a couple of days. It left a bitter taste in the mouth, agreeing to fight for another man's cause again with a promised reward that turned to nothing.

The commanders were gathering in the large brick structure in the centre of the village which might have been a temple. Next to it another building had collapsed in on itself and been swallowed by the ground below. Sonos entered more dejected than angry, feeling his body change with the emotion. The same could not be said of some of the others.

"We've been played for fools!" The shout came from Thusokusoa, but the fury was clear on Dzulkoten's face as well, after all he had learnt his code of honour and ethics from the older man. The Rinuxosu were always prickly where they thought their honour had been slighted. Many a man in the army had learnt that lesson when they suggested that the commanders of The Exiles had foresworn any claim to honour when they abandoned the Sacred Band of their king. In Thusokuosa's eyes the opposite was true, he was the one who maintained his honour when he refused to submit to the Doldun. The men still called him the Spurned Lover anyway, but not to his face.

"You can't be sure of that." Runukolkil was trying to forge words to calm the situation but having no luck. The Hotizoz commanders were brooding, like dark blue shadows in the corner. Something which might have been an altar had been smashed on the floor, two men lay on top of it, their hands had been bound and their throats cut, their blood still dripping over the pale gold of the broken altar. Even the usually pious Silxosu did not seem to care. In the far corner another man lay, sprawled over a drape against a wall, left in a position as if he were shielding the tapestry from those who would remove it.

"I shall not have us slighted in this way. I say we turn our fury on the men who tricked us so. No doubt they have plenty of food hidden behind their walls." Thusokuosa continued.

It was Bospitu of The White Hydra's Teeth who answered. Typically for a Silxosu he was a very pious man, pursuing the mercenary life was almost an act of devotion to them. He could not have looked more Xosu if he were the bright god himself, with a shock of earth brown hair, nut-brown skin, and hazel eyes.

"Thusokuosa is right. Tricked or not we can't be seen to be played so easily. Not when we are left wandering and starving in this foreign land. Strength and respect are the only way we keep the natives from turning on us."

Runu tried to calm the room,

"And what now? We turn on those we gave our word to? Show ourselves to be untrustworthy? Break our oaths? How long before there is an alliance formed against us? How long before the army of Gottoy arrives and finds willing allies amongst the people here? A beehive cannot survive by attacking everything around it, this is why the gods saw fit to make the sting deadly to both the bee and its opponent. We must choose carefully who feels our sting."

The faces on the assembled men told Sonos that there was little point arguing.

"We need the food." The blunt voice was Kusoasu Kinsol's, a voice that poisoned Runu's words. Kuso was chewing a hulthul leaf, a roll of the leaves was the only thing of any value they had found in the village. Its leaves were highly prized, although they tasted of bitter earth, they were said to give a man a glimpse of the knowledge of the gods. They had stained Kuso's lips black.

In that moment Sonos knew the argument was lost. Runukolkil knew as well, "If we don't come across supplies soon, we will begin to starve. Already the camp followers suffer, how long before the strength of our fighting men dwindles? And when Gottoy arrives, it will be a simple task to sweep us all up." Kuso's green eyes shone in the dark room. Agreement came from the other captains. Pusokol spoke in favour too, crafting his words carefully, like a sculptor, "We never meant to linger here long. Let us seize what supplies we can and head over the mountains toward Rulrup before the army of Gottoy arrives." Puso's brightly coloured armour made him stand out in the darkness, a contrast against his pale skin.

Runukolkil reluctantly replied,

"I can see your minds are set on this. Very well, I will not stand in your way, but we must put it to a vote with the men before we set off on such a task."

All agreed and runners were sent to assemble the men.

The thought of betrayal left a sour taste in Sonos' mouth as he made his way to the central square of the village. They had thought of betrayal once before and planned so meticulously. Having secured the White Islands for Thasotun from their base in Pittuntik, they had schemed to overthrow the rule of the Red and White Council and restore the League. Kolmosoi's planning was prudent and seemed likely to succeed, a many headed hydra rising against the Council all at once, although the thought of betrayal was difficult to swallow even then. But the oracle of Buto seemed to have given the god's blessing for their endeavour. Then it all fell apart. Kolmosoi slid off to the hidden realm and the White Islands spiralled into chaos again. *At least this time the betrayal will be done for necessity.* It was a choice between sacrificing their allies or starving, Kusoasu unfortunately had the right of it.

The men assembled quickly in the blood-soaked streets of the village. Despite the best efforts of calmer heads to suggest that perhaps their allies were mistaken, anger and the bloodlust of an easy victory took hold and the men soon voted to turn on their allies. The cheers of the Rinuxosu echoing in Sonos' ears.

***

They wasted little time; the village was put to the torch and the army was on the march within the hour back the way it had trekked that morning. The Rinuxosu insisted on taking the van this time. Little could hold back Thusokosoa from avenging his perceived slight. The rear guard fell to The Daemons of the Deep. It was a task Sonos was happy to take. Justified or not, the gods would surely not look favourably on the breaking of their oath.

The afternoon was bloodier than the morning. The Xosu descended on their unsuspecting allies like a flood. Their pleasant and unprotected land was turned into a sea of blood and death. Those who could flee scattered in all directions to a hard and short existence on the barren plain. Taken unprepared as they were, few defenders managed to rally in the tribe's only fortified village. The Rinuxosu swarmed over the walls and through the gate without much resistance, putting man, woman, and child to the sword.

The fighting was done before the main body of their force arrived. The remains of the Hotizoz legion, their camp followers and the Salxosu bringing up the rear. Sonos was glad for that as well, no need to bloody his spear in this betrayal, his oath not entirely broken.

The army's bloodlust was sated and plenty of supplies were found in the village when a prisoner led them to a hidden cavern beneath the fortifications filled to the brim with food for the winter. They lingered there one night to gather their strength for another march through a harsh mountain pass. The herds and cattle of the tribe were slaughtered, a grand sacrifice to appease the gods in the hope that they would forgive the breaking of the oaths they had sworn, as the army's seers suggested. Fighting men and camp followers alike feasted that night and plenty of supplies were still left to fill their captured wagons to bursting. They even found a store of rich wine from Gelodun buried in the cellars of one of the buildings. The wine and meat went someway to sooth Sonos' feelings of guilt, and that night a deep sleep took him quickly, in a way it had not since he fled Pittuntik. When dawn broke the next morning, the village was put to the torch and the march north, toward the sea, began in earnest.

The fight seemed to give new vigour to the army they made good progress, and their violent actions had an unintended consequence, news of the slaughter must have spread quickly throughout Beligul. The column encountered few natives as they marched north, those that they did meet brought them supplies as tribute to ward off their fury. The army crossed the plain quickly and soon a second chain of mountains were in sight.

KALU

16

The horse brayed as he brushed its neck. Kalu found the simplicity of caring for his charger calming and a welcome distraction from the complications of life. The routine of tending to a horse always brought him back memories of childhood in the rolling hill country of Doldun, in the lands of the Zelrsaloz. Amongst his own clan, horsemanship was a way of life, everyone could ride almost before they could walk. As a young child, he would ride across the plains, raiding the other clans, stealing their horses and cattle. The rule of law was weak in those days, the reach of the king barely extending beyond the walls of his palace as the fiercely independent clans asserted their freedom. But the clan rivalries and the civil war that the bards called The Defiance that came with Kenkathoaz rule had made the hill country a dangerous and fractured place in his youth. Open to raids from other clans or Zummosh warbands and even the odd marauding tribe of Rilrpitu who had ventured that far north and east.

Tekolger changed all of that. Finishing the work of his father, he had united the clans firmly under the banner of the king. Not by crushing them in the field like his father, but by inviting them to join him in his vision for the future and leading them on a blazing path of glory. It was an act Kalu would forever be grateful for. His clan, the Zelrsaloz, had found themselves torn between the warring factions and it had ripped Kalu's world apart. If the king had not finally united the clans, all his kin would surely have all been slaughtered. Even then many did not escape that fate. It was why all that Tekolger had built needed to be protected, from the Doldun as much as from anyone else.

Tekolger had shown the clans another path, taking the skilled but fractured horsemen and forging them into the greatest cavalry force the world had ever seen, the hooves and lances of which had streaked across the world leaving an empire in their wake. All that started with as simple a task as caring for a horse. *'Looking after the small things will bring you the big rewards.'* his father had once told him, wise words.

Kalu finished brushing down his steed as the door to the stables creaked open. He carried on, not paying much attention to who came in, filling the trough of water back up to the brim. A voice called out to him over the sloshing of the liquid,

"The horses need exercise; they don't like being stuck in here."

Zonpeluthas of the Kelawath, The Stray Singer. The Kelawath were famous for their music, living secluded in the foothills of the mountains on Doldun's eastern border. They had not always been loyal to the king, and had incurred the wrath of Kenkathoaz, since then they had been trying to regain their lost favour.

Zonpeluthas was a little way down the row of horses, beginning to brush his own braying steed. Kalu replied absent minded, focusing his attention on the horse's glossy coat,

"I was thinking the same. They are too used to the open plains, even a few days in here depresses them."

Zonpeluthas smiled. With his long hair and small, lean figure, he had a femininity to him that the other Companions did not. His liking for fine clothes only emphasised that difference,

"I think we all are too used to being on campaign. Tensions are running high and Kelbal doesn't help himself sometimes."

His horse snorted, Kalu brushed his fingers across its mane and replied,

"He is anxious to see that the empire has a firm hand to steer it, and that Tekolger's legacy is kept intact. The death of the king has changed us all, it will take an almost divine effort to keep the disparate realms of the empire together, but he will get used to the role."

"I am sure he will, but some of the others aren't happy with him at the moment." The young Companion paused and stopped brushing his braying horse, "Why hasn't he sent Dolzalo reinforcements?" Zonpeluthas asked. Kalu knew he was after something. The young man was competent, but had a fierce ambition in him, a drive to prove himself. The Kelawath had always been somewhat isolated from the rest of the Doldun and were often perceived as weak by the other clans, it was why the men had dubbed him The Stray Singer. Zonpeluthas himself was younger than the other Companions having only been elevated to the position before the army crossed the mountains into Kelandel. After Benan of the Kelawath was slain at Kulanzow. Such pressures had made the man and drove him. Kalu liked him well enough, but sometimes his naivety got the better of him. One day it would see him torn to shreds, caught between others more forceful than himself, Kalu had no doubt of that.

"Dolzalo has a small army at his back. I'm sure he can deal with a raiding party." Kalu said cautiously.

"Come on Kalu, we both know that Tekolger would have led the cavalry out himself, thundering off to meet them immediately." Zonpeluthas replied.

"It is not the same. Tekolger was conquering an empire not ruling one. The politics of empire are a different beast to those of the clans back home, our priority now is to protect all that Tekolger won for us. The same way a panther protects its own territory." Kalu shot back.

Zonpeluthas stopped brushing his horse and replied,

"You are right, Dolzalo probably has the men to deal with it, but it would be a good way for Kelbal to keep everyone happy. If he just sent a small contingent out, with a couple of the Companions. It will placate them somewhat. We all know he listens to you, talk to him." Even now his voice had a musical quality to it. Kalu stopped brushing his horse as well, and, turning to face Zonpeluthas, said,

"I suppose you would like to lead the contingent out, would you?" He paused abruptly. Such a venomous retort was out of character for Kalu, the tension was getting to him as well. He composed himself and in a more reconciliatory tone he continued, "Ok I will speak to Kelbal and see what he is thinking."

***

Another evening came around quickly. What was planned as a short stay in Yorixori had turned into a moon's cycle as the army waited for Dolzalo to arrive. The journey to the heart of the empire delayed by the Rilrpitu. Kelbal seemed to have taken to the life of a ruler quickly enough, but the other Companions, and the army, were becoming agitated with the slow pace of ruling. There were only so many games, competitions, and hunting expeditions that could be mounted to keep them entertained. The change from conquest to rule was too much for some, a different world requiring different men.

Although a sizable city, there was not room in Yorixori to billet all the men inside. Kalu had taken to ensuring the army was well kept and discipline was maintained in their marching camp just beyond the walls. His own way of dealing with the humdrum of administering the empire and necessary given the indiscipline that was seeping into the ranks. He had just finished his nightly inspection of the army. Having spent the last decade of his life constantly tearing through enemy territory, vigilance had become second nature, a survival mechanism. With that task completed he paced his way back to the city.

Yorixori dominated the land for leagues around. Its recent Xortogun heritage was clear in its construction and the culture of the people. The colonists Yoruxoruni had planted here when he conquered the city had built what they knew, constructing a city of pyramids, ziggurats, and obelisks which rung to the sound of hymns and chanting to the strange animalistic gods of the people of Xortogun. They had even tamed and civilised the dolthil trees which otherwise grew wild in Zowdel, and the city was littered with stray cats, like any in Xortogun. Little trace remained of the great kingdom of Zowdel which had once been ruled from the city. Even in Yoruxoruni's day the kingdom had been gone for six hundred years and one hundred petty kingdoms had taken its place.

Walking through the empty streets Kalu found himself reflecting on the day the city fell to a swift assault. He had walked down this same street that day, though then it was ablaze and the sounds of weapons clashing and men screaming had echoed through the air. Tekolger had been deeply moved when he captured Yorixori, he remembered. A short but bloody assault had seen the Xortogun potentate who had ruled with pretensions of kingship overthrown. Such petty claims had held little interest for Tekolger though, it was the message of Yoruxoruni's foresight in planting his own people here that had drawn the king's attention. Tekolger had expressed a desire to see such success emulated with his own city of Tekolgertep and the colonies of Xosu and Doldun he had established throughout his new domains. But Yorixori's fall was more important than just that. With the taking of the city, Tekolger had come to rule all the lands of what had once been the old kingdoms. Just as the oracle of Xosu had predicted he would.

That fact was not lost on the priests of the city either. A vivid memory struck him as he traced the path they had followed as they entered Yorixori for the first time. The priests were patiently waiting in all their finery for the king while their city fell around them. They paraded Tekolger to the temple of Kurotor, the king of the Xortogun gods, while flames and the screams of the dying reverberated. In the shadow of the temple, the holy men had declared Tekolger the fulfilment of an ancient prophecy and proclaimed him to be the Herald of the Dawn.

Kalu had never put too much stock in prophecy himself. The philosopher Kunpit of Thelonigul had taught that man could be perfected to rise to be a philosopher king with the right education. Kalu could see the logic in that and Tekolger was proof if it were needed, but prophecy seemed a step too far. Tekolger though had had a quixotic and mystical side to his character and had always been sure to keep the gods of any land he conquered happy. That trait was down to the influence of the king's mother, a devotee of the bright god said to practice many of his secret arts. It was even rumoured that Kenkathoaz had taken her to wife at the instigation of Xosu himself through his oracle. Some of the more imaginative men in the army even liked to claim that Tekolger was driven by visions sent to him by the gods to build an empire that would save the world. Others said that his mother had lain with Dunsun himself in one of her rituals and that the Lord of the Cosmos was Tekolger's real father. Fanciful notions, but Tekolger had never discouraged such things. Being a living god and a fulfiller of prophecy was after all a useful way to keep his subjects in line.

Zonhol, his reliable captain, strode alongside him. Clearing his throat as they paced through the empty streets he said,

"The army grows more frustrated. The news of Dolzalo's hunt in the north is making them even more restless and…well they still complain about the Xortogun. That is the thing that worries me. I fear for what will happen if they are ordered to take the field."

Kalu sighed,

"They have grown too used to being on campaign, they find a return to civilised life a difficult adaption. I think the complaints about the Xortogun is just a symptom of that." He paused, "There is a part of me that is glad for our lengthened stay in Yorixori. The plains of Zenian are wild, open, overrun by wildcats, only peopled by what was left of the once proud men of Zowdel and dominated for so long by Rilrpitu raiders. Staying within the city means that the men will have to quickly adapt to the civilised life of the great valley again." …and their return to Xortogun would not come so fast. Once back in the heart of the empire he would have to confront the reality of the loss of the king and all that came with it. He did not say the last part out loud.

Zonhol did not look convinced,

"With all the waiting, the frustration coursing through the army has only grown. There has been more fighting in the city between the different contingents. They are especially hard to control in the overcrowded inns and brothels, hidden as they are down the winding backstreets. Twice more I have had to send companies of White Shields into the streets to restore order. The second time Polazul and Hurricane were the cause of the trouble."

Kalu let out a bigger sigh and replied,

"No doubt driven to it by Zalmetaz. I will speak with them."

The behaviour of the men was troubling him, but Kelbal was an even bigger worry. The fate of all of them, the entire empire even, rested on Kelbal's shoulders right now and the strain was beginning to show. Although Kelbal was adapting to his new position, the wine had begun to flow more freely than usual and he was spending too much time locked up with Yare, the man he had captured in far flung Zentheldel. His wilder shade was straining to get out. That was the immediate problem Kalu would have to confront this evening. They stopped at the base of the palace pyramid at the heart of the city.

"Go back to the men Zonhol. Do what you can to placate them, we will need our White Shields to stay disciplined if we are to keep the rest of the army in line. For now, I must attend to Kelbal."

Zonhol nodded and marched off toward the barracks on the reverse of the pyramid. Kalu began to climb the steps of the towering structure.

From the lowly military camp to ascending the steps of the mountain of a pyramid that was the old palace at the centre of the city was quite a contrast. Up into the garden that seemed to float in the sky. He now found himself tending to his second task of the night. Kelbal had taken to long nights and late mornings, and Kalu felt compelled to attend him at his nightly drinking sessions even though the others had long since stopped coming. He hoped that was just because they could not take the pace rather than due to frustration with Kelbal.

The doors of the palace were wide open, two White Shields stood guard either side of the entrance flanked by time worn statues of old Zowdel. The ravages of the ages meant that it was no longer possible to tell what the statues once depicted, but even with the stern unmoving faces of the pale bronze masks the White Shields wore, Kalu knew his men by sight. Tepo of the Dolozolaz and Dazkeltel of the Zelkalkel, good men. He made a point of learning the names and origins of all the men under his command. Being given command of the White Shields by the king had been Kalu's proudest moment. Winning the honour for the valour he showed on the field of the Bulodon's Wail, when he had personally led the assault which broke the League of Butophulo. In the process he had cut down a man who was about to deliver a mortal blow to Tekolger. Kalu acknowledged the guards as he entered the gilded hall.

He found Kelbal in his usual spot, reclined on a couch in the old throne room, attended by serving girls and eunuchs, and Yare. Kelbal was dressed in a flamboyant red and green robe of the Xortogun style. He looked ever more like the western potentate, the absolute rulers which had dominated in the west for so long, poor imitations of the god-kings of old. Only his Deltathelon looks shattered the image, but his cerulean streaked, dishevelled, bronze hair had a hint of royalty to it, set off more so by the rouge tint to his face, a gift from the wine.

Tyrants the Xosu would call the god-kings, Kalu thought, unsure if Tekolger would be pleased or uneasy. His eyes glanced over to the gold coffin that still loomed over the room.

Kalu strode to Kelbal's couch as the new regent finished off a cup of wine and signalled a close by eunuch to refill his cup. He appeared to be sifting through a selection of messages on papyrus scrolls. Without raising his eyes from the scroll in front of him, he signalled Kalu to sit on a couch opposite.

Kelbal was like an older brother to Kalu and had always found time for him, even when the pressures of rulership were becoming intense. Without Kelbal, Kalu would never have risen as high as he had, and with the demands of the regency weighing heavy on his old friend, Kalu would do everything he could to aide him, to help him protect Tekolger's legacy.

He sat down, uncomfortable laying on the couch in the style of kings of the great valley. Instead, he sat upright, awkwardly, and poured himself a cup of wine.

Kelbal put aside his papers and looked up, saying with a wild, shining smirk,

"Kalu, it seems you are the only one who has not abandoned me."

Kalu smiled,

"The others haven't abandoned you. They do not have the stomach for administering an empire, it is a hard adjustment to make. As far away from Doldun as we are, they are still men of the clans at heart."

Kelbal nodded in agreement, taking another sip. The wine had made his lips purple,

"They knew this was the way of things to come though. Those of us who learnt with Yusukol at least. We are no longer the predator carving out his territory, rather the panther patrolling its lands. And you? How are you finding our new role?"

"I'm more at home with the army I have to say. It is a simpler life." Kalu answered.

"Well, that is understandable, Kalu. The army is where you made your name and grew your fame. Kalu Pale Arm, covered in blood but for your sword arm as you slew foes to left and right and made the Bulodon Wail once again." Kelbal recalled the tale with some elan, "Commander of the king's White Shields. Men who chose exile among the Thulchwal with Tekolger when Kenkathoaz cast him out and were rewarded for their loyalty with a set of enamel white, zilthum lined armour and weapons. Held in the sanctuary of Butophulo but forged by the formidable smiths of old Kolbos with skills and sorcery now lost to the world. It is a story the poets will tell for centuries yet to come."

Kalu smiled,

"I am afraid it is a tale that will pale in comparison to that of Tekolger and his Companions. The men who conquered the world wielding the pure zilthum blades of old, which shone like moonlight, forged by the Kinsolsun themselves when only the Thelonbet stood at the site of old Kolbos."

"That is but one tale of many that will be told of our deeds. Who knows maybe one day the story men will tell of your blade will be those of your exploits and not of its original carrier…you see I have forgotten his name already…and the sword if I am honest." Kelbal laughed at himself in a way only he could.

"Vigilance the blade is called, a storied weapon carried by the hero Thilsol, the grandson of the sea." Kalu answered, enjoying the distraction, if not the reminder of the weight of history, "I have been aware of its legacy ever since Tekolger handed it to me. Thilsol was sent on an impossible task to slay the pearl hydra. Zilthil's monstrous marauding child, who had destroyed the watery haven of Solpulo and settled in its ruins. The test had been devised by Kusoi the thrice dead, the ruthless King of Supokul, as the price of freeing Thilsol's mother from bondage. The king expected Thilsol to perish, but he underestimated the hero. Thilsol tricked the wizards at the Thelonbet into forging for him the zilthum blade. Wielding the god given weapon and with the unexpected aid from Kusoi's wayward son, Thilsol cut his way through the hydra's children. The blood of each victory soaked his blade and grew his strength before he finally confronted the pearl hydra. The son of the king sacrificed himself to allow Thilsol to deliver the blow which finally slew the fiery daemon. Thilsol returned to Supokul to free his mother, mourn the loss of the king's son, and dethrone the tyrant.

It seems to me that I need to achieve much to overshadow that story. My own exploits pale in significance. It is quite the burden to bear if I am honest, which is why I worry for you. The regency is an even formidable weight. You seem to be fitting into the mould well though. A vision Tekolger would have approved of." Kalu replied.

Kelbal laughed madly, his forest green eye lively,

"You have been spending too much time with Thuson. That man is obsessed with those old legends. You are right though, I could get used to the comfort afforded to a western potentate, and the robe fits me well. It is a good reminder of what we are trying to do, the legacy of empire and the mark we can make. Here we are leagues away from Xortogun and yet we find the court practices of the great kings of that valley. You could put this city at the mouth of the Kelonzow and it would not look out of place, but here it is near the source of that great river, closer to Zentheldel and Kelandel than Xortogun. By contrast, what memory is there of the kingdom of Zowdel before its fall? Very little, and what there is, are just a few stories and some ruins."

Kelbal was prone to tangents and whimsy. Kalu replied defensively,

"But it is a legacy which could overthrow us if we embrace it too much."

Kelbal still smiling warmly, answered,

"This is the legacy of king Yoruxoruni, the last flash of brilliance from the valley, a throwback to the god-kings of old. He remade this city in his own image and conquered most of Zenian. His rule ended two hundred years ago and yet we still talk about him. That is the challenge for us now. Ensure that one thousand years from now people still talk of how Tekolger and his Companions conquered the world. To build a legacy that men remember and aspire to or else we will fall into dust, ruin and half remembered tales. That is the measure of failure and victory. It is something I fear our brave Companions do not understand."

Kalu was impressed, it was a lofty ambition, and echoed the message of Tekolger. But it would be hard to sell it to the others. He replied,

"As long as we don't lose ourselves and our history in the process. Do not forget that Yoruxoruni is seen as a tyrant by the Xosu and was betrayed and murdered. There are more lessons to be learnt from his life than empire building."

Kelbal smiled again and drained his cup,

"We won't lose our history; we will enhance it. One thousand years from now, men will talk of the Doldun in the way they talk about the kingdom of Xortogun and its god-kings at their height. Think of how you remember and seek to outdo the story of your own blade's wielder." he sighed and glanced over to Tekolger laying in rest, "We won't fail him." he whispered with melancholy. Kalu nodded and drained his own cup. Yare stepped forward to refill Kelbal's cup and one of the eunuchs did the same for Kalu, but he put out his hand to stop him. Turning back to Kelbal, he said,

"Those goals are all well and good, and I share them, but it is the detail that has the others concerned. The integration of the Xortogun into the army did not go down well, but they will swallow it. It is not sending reinforcements to Dolzalo which has them really riled."

Kelbal carefully sipped from his cup, a pensive look on his reddened face, responding,

"Dolzalo has ten thousand men, five hundred of which are a horse and one thousand are the Thulchwal. Palmash and even Thuson are with him as well. He has more than enough force to deal with some marauding Rilrpitu."

"But the Rilrpitu will be all a horse. An extra couple of cavalry squadrons would make the task easier. Besides, I think the real agitation comes from boredom. The men are used to acting swiftly, you know

Tekolger would have been on their trail as soon as heard about it." Kalu replied.

"I know, but the politics of empire require more control than the conquering of one. This is not Doldun and the Rilrpitu aren't just another clan to raid or subdue." Kelbal answered, a hint of annoyance in his voice.

"And this has nothing to do with not sending aid because it is for Dolzalo?" Kalu pressed, unsure if he had gone too far. Kelbal looked hurt by that suggestion. Kalu poured another cup of wine as Kelbal answered,

"Of course not. We would not know about this situation if Dolzalo was on his own, he isn't even asking for aid. It is Thuson who has been keeping me informed and requesting reinforcements. I am aware of the Companions frustration, Zenu has been pressing me to send aid for similar reasons. I will look to send a couple of squadrons out once everyone has settled down and I have selected a commander. Supo will need to go too, the north is his responsibility. But a few raiders are not my main concern right now. An empire demands its ruler's attention on every front and so I must trust in subordinates to deal with smaller problems."

Kalu was pleased with that answer. Kelbal was a man of principal, and cared deeply about Tekolger's legacy, he would keep his word,

"You need to let the Companions know. They feel shut out of decisions and they are getting agitated by it. They see you as one of their own remember, not their ruler, and the Companions were always meant to be a fraternity of equals. Even the king is just the first man amongst us."

"I know, but I still need to work out how things will be in the future, having each of them vying for position won't help that. They must understand that this is not Doldun, not anymore." Kelbal came back.

"I understand and I will do my best to reassure them." Kalu said,

Kelbal drained his cup again and said,

"Kalu don't tell the others about the reinforcements being sent yet. Having each of them competing for the command won't help."

He nodded and drained his cup, getting up to leave, expecting Kelbal to do the same. Instead, the regent motioned to the eunuch to refill his cup and pulled a serving girl on to his lap.

Kalu thought about saying something. Kelbal may have been the one bright light of leadership left in the darkness, but he had a dark and wild side to him which Tekolger's death had increasingly brought to the surface. There was a reason why men called him Two shades after all. Kalu paused, his mouth opened but he said nothing, instead turned on his heels to leave. One last check of the sentries and then he could feel his bed calling to him.

KALASYAR

17

The market in the Hunpil district seemed empty to her, despite still thronging with activity. Kalasyar guessed there must have been less than half the number who usually frequented the agora. Although the increase in the number of sellswords was going someway to make up for that. The place had been one of her favourite parts of the city as a child, full of vibrant and exotic wares and equally intriguing people. But now it made her nervous, like a tinderbox waiting to explode. It reminded her of the riots ten years ago. They had been sparked when the Nine released a decree that claimed the city's youth to be trained as what they called their guardians. The people, led by the city's smiths, had seized control of the market, and demanded the decree rescinded. The Nine had responded by unleashing their mercenaries, and fire and blood had followed. The scars of that time had disappeared from the market, but the memory remained, forge firmly into Kalasyar's mind. The atmosphere in the days since Dorthil Rusos assassination felt like those early years of the Nine's rule.

Her grandfather, as always, seemed oblivious to it all. He was happily going about his business and openly engaging with everyone in discussion on topics ranging from politics to art, nature, and philosophy, as the wandering philosophers were want to do before their teachings were banned by the Nine.

Koseun stopped at the stall of one merchant who was selling gold and silver wares and engaged him in conversation.

"These jewels are from beyond the Throat are they not? That stretch of ocean between Silsuw and the southern shores where the sea wails as if it were the song of Sem?" Koseun asked.

"They are indeed kind sir. Very rare indeed, the Putedun tightly control their supply. So only a few items make it this far each year. Would you like to see how they suit your companion?" The merchant asked,

"I would rather find out more about the far east. The League was never able to wrest control of the Throat from the Putedun and as you say, the Putedun guard it jealously, like it was their own vulnerable neck. How did a Xosu such as yourself come by these items?" Koseun asked as the merchant looked around nervously.

"I acquired them from a Putedun friend. He has left for home out of fear after the terrible killing of that kind young man. He allowed me to take the items off his hands to trade with."

"Well, it appears that you are a much bolder man than your friend, but not as bold as my flight of imagination allowed for." Koseun replied, "That is disappointing. For a moment I thought I had discovered another Rupoanos the Navigator. One more Xosu brave enough to slip past the blockade and journey to the further east. Oh, the things he claimed to have seen, something Dzotthisoni of old Kolbos could only have dreamed of despite his many expeditions." The merchant looked even more tense now.

"No, I am not bold or brave, just a merchant, sir. But I am Salxosu and this is my city."

Further down the street a patrol of sellswords was rifling their way through the wares of another merchant.

"We should not stay here any longer than needed grandfather. These sellswords are making me nervous." She said to Koseun. He looked at her and smiled,

"You worry too much child. They won't bother us; we have broken none of their rules."

"Have you not heard? Puskison has commanded his brother to seek out the killers of Dorthil. They are targeting those of the old blood." She responded. Puskison's brother, Kolpos Posuasthison, was a man who had always terrified Kalasyar. His narrow eyes seemed to have a venom behind them, and the words that left his black stained lips were always tinged with poison.

"Do not worry child. What reason do they have to arrest us here and now?" Koseun answered, interrupting his own musings with the merchant at the stall.

"No reason at all, and yet they had no reason to take the others that they have arrested. Many houses have been stormed in the dead of the night; the families taken to the fortress on Polriso's Hill for questioning. And they have only been seizing those of the old blood." Thinking about it only made her more nervous. "Even Buso Kolkisuasu and Polrinu Kinsol have been dragged off, questioned, and beaten by the Nine's thugs. Two men who only recently came to our home. The word amongst the other families is that the Nine know they are innocent but offered them as a perverse tribute to the Doldun. To show that the Nine are in control still." She told him everything she had heard from the Sipenkiso.

"But they have not come to us yet. Do not fret over a future that may yet not come to be. Live in this moment." Koseun turned and immediately began to question the confused looking merchant on that same cornel of thought. Kalasyar couldn't help but continue to worry though. Since Buso and Polrinu were taken, two of the younger sons of the Rososthup and Kisurusosi had also disappeared, and a man named Kinril Polriso had been seen being dragged off by a band of mercenaries from The Company of the Sacred Land. The rumour going around the city was that the assassin was one of the Polriso. Though few ever had a good word to say of that family. The common knowledge that Rinukiso Polriso had been summoned to the villa of Puskison did give Kalasyar pause for thought though. At least none of the other patriarchs had been arrested yet.

Few thought the men seized had anything to do with the assassination, it was merely the tyrants panicking, jumping at their own shadows. The sellswords patrolling the city had seemed to double in number, mercenaries from all over Xosupil, judging by their accents. Another two companies had apparently been hired, alongside The Company of the Sacred Land from Thelonigul, already in service to the Nine. And the Doldun. The Doldun were always there, never engaging directly, but never too far away either. Even now she could see several of the Doldun garrison lurking on the edge of the marketplace.

In the last few days, the Nine had escalated things further, fuelling her nervousness. Trials had started, held for the public to see, Kolpos presiding. There had already been executions, the heads of the accused lining the city walls. A few were even watching over the marketplace serving an audience of carrion birds. Kalasyar shuddered looking over at the slowly rotting heads and interrupted her grandfather as he was interrogating the merchant about his ideas of justice,

"Have all the men from Puteduntik gone home? They usually set up their stalls here."

The merchant looked to her, relief on his face as the opportunity to escape Koseun's questions arose. He spoke deliberately and formally this time,

"The Council of the Nine Philosophers has decreed that all the ships in the harbour are to be searched from top to bottom, since the murder of Dorthil Rusos. They are preventing any conspirators from escaping and preserving the peace in the city. No one gets in or out without their knowing." The man hesitated and looked around, one wary eye on the soldiers nearby. Leaning closer, he whispered, "Between you and me good lady, there are a few of the traders still in the city, but they have little left to sell, and little desire to be out in public for the moment. Many do not wish to be searched as they leave in fear that the Nine will tax them again for the goods and wealth they have acquired. A merchant does not survive long in business without thinking of such things." He stepped back and continued to talk in the formal manner he adopted before, "Even before the young noble was cut down, others were reluctant to come. Thasotun does not exert the same control it once did, and the seas have become treacherous. The war in Thelizum has caused much disruption of trade and everyone is wary of what will happen now that the king has been taken from us. The Doldun's history is well known and now they control the whole world…well, the prospect of war makes cowards of many a fine man."

The soldiers were coming closer, a bow and vine of Xosu on one shield, a gold eight-pointed star on a sky-blue background on the other. The merchant kept casting a wary eye toward them. Kalasyar took her grandfather by the arm and began to lead him away. Her handmaids slid behind them as they walked, carrying the few purchases they had made,

"Let us not let those sellswords overhear us talking about this." she said, "The Nine are already suspicious of everything you do."

She led Koseun away at a pace, careful not to walk too fast and attract the mercenary's attention, but she could still feel their eyes on her. Her feet felt heavy, and her footsteps seemed to ring in her ears, like hammers striking an anvil. The vision of the blue wraiths still haunted her, and she could not decide if it was a warning or not. Her grandfather carried on talking without concern,

"I don't think the Nine understand this city very well. For all their claim to be enlightened philosophers the real world eludes them, the port is Butophulo's lifeblood. They are panicking and looking out for their own safety instead of the bigger picture. No doubt Kunpit himself would not be pleased with his acolytes."

Kalasyar replied,

"I wish that you would look out for your own safety too sometimes grandfather. It is not good to linger and talk like that with so many soldiers around." She said as the mounted heads came into her view once more. Koseun laughed,

"You worry too much child. The politics of it all are difficult for the moment. With Tekolger gone, the Doldun are wary, but they will be more concerned with their own affairs. The Nine should not worry so much about what the Doldun think and be more concerned about the way they are perceived by their own people. At this moment, when leadership is needed most, they are like wraiths. It is something Kunpit never understood, and neither do his acolytes. The citizens of Butophulo have never taken well to poor governance. They threw out tyrants before and they will do it again. It is the same lesson which the last king of the city, Tebuthisonu, failed to learn. The people of the city cast him out and the kingship with him and the Polriso are still suffering under a miasma for it."

"Let the Nine do whatever they want. I am concerned about the Sisosi, about you." She replied, but Koseun was in full flow with one of his lessons.

"The legacy of their forbear, Polriso, destroyed. There would be no Butophulo if he had not gathered the survivors of the sack of old Kolbos and led them to the safety. That action gave his scions the legitimacy to rule as royalty for five hundred years. But all it took was one foolish boy and a period of bad governance for that all to be destroyed. We should be grateful I suppose. The ruining of the Polriso made our name. A revolution led by Yunsunos Sisosi. I would not have had such a prominent career without the legitimacy I gained from carrying his name. There is a profound lesson in that."

"I am more concerned with the lesson you are not learning, grandfather. If you will not stop, at least go home, and talk somewhere where there are not so many eyes on you. You said it yourself, the Nine are nervous and suspicious of you as it is. If they hear that you have been denouncing their actions in the street, they will be sure to act." Kalasyar answered in a firmer tone to hammer her point to him.

Koseun gave her that look he always did, the way only her grandfather could. She could tell that he thought she was overreacting, but eventually he said,

"Ok, if it gives you some comfort, I will head home. There is no one in this market to talk to anyhow. I'm sure I can find a more stimulating activity at the villa."

Relieved as her grandfather heeded her advice, she said,

"Good, I am glad. I will join you there shortly. First, I must attend the temple."

Her grandfather uncoiled a smile again, that knowing smile,

"You have been spending an awful lot of time there recently."

"And you have been hosting more symposiums. We all have a place to feel comfortable and able to express ourselves." Kalasyar answered, *and I must know more of what the Great God intends*, she thought.

He smiled again, a reflective one this time, as if he were remembering some far-off place,

"Off you go. I can make my own way home."

She left him there in the marketplace and headed to the gleaming temple whose statue of Buto she could see glimmering in the distance against the morning light, hammer in hand lifted as if it were reaching toward the heavens or crashing to the ground.

* * *

Buto's temple was quiet as well, an eerie feeling given the usual ceaseless activity. It was as if the veil to the world of the gods had been closed. As many of the temple's patrons were merchants and sailors themselves, it was not surprising that the place was quiet, she reflected. The small squad of soldiers outside was exactly what could be expected in these new days for the city though.

Kalasyar kept her head down and Tharoroz and Ralxuloz did the same. Their veils covering their eyes as they walked past. The mercenaries barely seemed to notice them, but she still found herself cowering behind the pile of silks she had purchased in the market ready for the fast-approaching festival of Buto.

The empty temple meant that Kalasyar did not need to be discreet. Leaving her maids in the main hall as only initiates could venture any further, she made straight for the door behind the altar, slipping past the drooping branches of the hulthul tree whose fruit was ready to harvest, and followed the stairs down to the sanctuary of Sem below.

In a strange contrast to the world above, the sanctuary seemed a hive of activity. She could see all nine of the priestesses, including the High Priestess of Sem, busily going about their daily routine moving like watery shadows through sanctuary. Many of the initiates were also in attendance, most having brought offerings and supplies as Kalasyar had herself. Two women were talking to Sipenkiso. They had been at the meal a few days before. Hisukol Posuausthison, the matronly woman who was always diligent in ministering to the god. In the years since the defeat to the Doldun, she had transformed herself into the foremost patron of the cult. Pusae Polriso stood next to her, the wife of the patriarch. Arrogant and haughty, she carried herself like royalty and told endless tales of the former glory of the Polriso. It was strange to see those two together. She hoped this meant that Sipenkiso would have news. She approached the High Priestess, waiting respectfully back just out of distance to not hear the detail of the conversation. Allowing the three women to finish.

Sipenkiso offered three blessings to the two women, her eyes found Kalasyar as she did. They were a mystical liquid blue, but had a warmth behind them, a maternal surety which she found comforting. With the crescent of a smile on her lips, the High Priestess left her two devotees and approached the patiently waiting Kalasyar,

"I see you have brought silks for us child. The god will be pleased."

Taking the silks from Kalasyar and handing them to a servant, she continued,

"You look troubled child. What weighs on your mind?"

"I was at the market today. Many of the traders did not attend and the Nine are searching anyone entering or leaving the harbour. I have also seen the increase in the soldiers on the streets, many people have been arrested, especially those left here who have links to the old League. My grandfather is very relaxed about it, but I am concerned that he will be next, and I will be powerless to stop it." She answered, the words gushing out of her mouth, it was a relief just to say them.

Sipenkiso held that warm look on her face. *She could almost be a maiden*, Kalasyar thought,

"It is a shame that the Council has decided to do that. The arrests have caused distress to many. I understand your concerns about your grandfather, he was a great servant to the city in its past, although the Council may not see that now. But you also must understand that to govern is difficult and sometimes those who were once respected in the past can become derided, even expendable, in the present."

"You speak to their wives." she blurted out, "Can you not get them to tell their husbands that my grandfather had nothing to do with the murder?"

"My child, the power we wield is much subtler than that. If their wives were to tell them that, then they would be even more suspicious of your grandfather and that suspicion would be turned on to us as well. What we can do, and what we try to do, is to ensure that these suspicions are never raised in the first place." Sipenkiso answered, with an aged wisdom.

"How do I do that?" Kalasyar said in an almost demanding manner.

"By being close to those who matter, shaping the conversations they have, the way they gather and view information and planting the seed of ideas in their mind. It is a long process that requires patience." Sipenkiso continued, in her maternal way.

"I don't have time for patience, for all I know the sellswords are already on their way to arrest my grandfather." She replied, unable to contain herself now.

"They may well be child and if this is the case then you need to gain power for yourself. A shield for when that time comes."

"How do I do that?" Kalasyar said bluntly.

"Find yourself a powerful protector who will come to your aide." She spoke firmly, as if invoking the power of the god. Her words crashed like a wave on Kalasyar. Sipenkiso had lost that warm smile. A serious look had descended onto her pale, round face, her lips forming a tight red crescent. Kalasyar knew what she meant immediately,

"How do I even know that he will protect me?"

"You don't. But without trying you will not have any protection, and neither will your grandfather." The High Priestess replied somewhat coldly.

"Why can't the followers of the Great God protect my grandfather?" She demanded.

"We can, through you. Go and think and look to Sem, you will know what to do when the time comes, the gate will open for you. But remember, greater things are afoot than you or I can understand, soon such concerns may seem trivial." With that Sipenkiso touched her gently on the shoulder, the warm smile had returned. The High Priestess left Kalasyar to ponder her fate.

SANAE

18

The moon had almost turned its full cycle since her first test, Sanae felt she had grown much and more since then. Grudgingly she had realised that Kolae was right, the tasks were not tests but ways of understanding the god, although she would never admit that epiphany to the High Priestess. But to her surprise it was not the testing that had caused the biggest change in the life since her first task, instead her chance encounter with the Zummosh had. Sanae had found herself drawn increasingly frequently south of the river, having a friend outside of the temple was somehow liberating. Lulpo often spent her mornings on the riverbank cleaning what possessions her tribe had in the flowing waters. Sanae had volunteered to do a similar task for the temple this morning, rising before the sun in her excitement, she tore through the city in a burning rush to the river. Leaving the care of the new cattle to the other uninitiated and, carrying a basket full of clothing, she found Lulpo exactly where she predicted.

"How is the water today?" Sanae shouted to the red haired Zummosh girl. Lulpo looked up and smiled wildly. Her hair was tied up in two bunches to keep it out of the river. It made her look as though she had two stubby horns on her head like some of the young bulls at the temple,

"Find out for yourself!" Lulpo shouted, splashing in the river, her hands like stones thrown from the sky, spraying the water toward Sanae. The water glistening in the morning light looking as if it had the power to change whoever bathed in its glow. Laughing, she nimbly dodged the water and made her way down the bank to join her friend.

"I have been given the temple's clothing to wash, I thought I would join you."

Lulpo replied,

"Well, plenty of room there is, and I am skilled enough to both wash and teach you how we do things at the same time. The Powouzo remember such things."

Sanae placed her basket on the bank and waded into the shallow waters to stand alongside Lulpo. She took out a tunic and dipped it into the clear waters, a contrast to the muddied churn found at the harbour. The tunic was white but looked to have been used during a sacrifice and the rust-coloured blood stain now seeped into the clear waters turning them a dark red wine colour. A shame to discolour the crystal-clear water, but the blood would nourish the soil.

"The broach my mother gave you. You do not wear." Lulpo said after a while.

She felt the embarrassment rise inside her. She had hoped that Lulpo would not notice or take offence,

"I am sorry, it was a valued gift. But the High Priestess at the temple took it from me. She says I am not to wear the symbols of your gods."

Lulpo nodded,

"I see. Do not worry about this, it is not your fault. This same High Priestess who demands all these chores of you, the one you call the white witch?"

Sanae nodded.

"Then she has clearly not learned much of the gods despite being a priestess. It is not the symbols that matter, not really. The Powouzo remember this."

"The symbols of Xosu are very important in understanding the aspects of the bright god." Sanae replied, "Through Xosu's symbols we can understand the light of civilisation he gave the Xosu, the protection he offered and the guidance he lent them, opening the doors to so many things."

"The symbols help us understand, this is true. But they are tools to teach us about what effect the gods have on our world and how we can influence them. It is a thing the Powouzo have remembered." Lulpo replied with the surety of a wise old teacher.

"So, The Paron is not three gods? The others are just symbols?" She inquired, a question which had been bothering her ever since Palon had given her the broach.

"Both. The Paron is one god and three. He has three forms, each divine, but also one form. Each form has a different influence on our world." she paused, "He may appear as one, or all, however he sees fit." Lulpo explained with the wisdom of a high priest.

"I am not sure I understand. Xosu is divine and so can take many forms, he ruled over the Xosu as a man, but this was because his divine form was taken by Tholo when she cast him from the heavens. She used it to raise her white hydra, a hydra that terrorised the world before the Dawn. But that form was destroyed when he ascended to the heavens. He also appeared to us as a panther to lead the Xosu to Thelonigul, his golden palace. Different forms, but he is always Xosu, the bringer of light, the giver of knowledge, the great guide and father of his people." Sanae said, bemused by the concept.

"The Paron, takes on each of his forms to affect the world differently. He is the lord of the sky, as The Chwur, the great sky sunderer, as The Pare he is the lord of the wild, prince of ecstasy, and as The Shaf he is the son of the sea, the guardian of the gateway to the otherworld. All are still The Paron, the radiant god who brings light to all. Different aspects, but distinct from one another as well. This is what the Powouzo remember." Lulpo said it in such an assured way that anyone would think it was obvious. But Sanae knew the world of the gods was more mysterious and maddening than humanity could ever imagine, even so she was determined to try to understand.

"I do not think the Xosu or Doldun have a way to describe this aspect of the gods." Was all she could think to say. *Helupelan might know more*, she thought.

"Is The Paron the only god you revere?" She asked, changing the subject slightly.

"No, there are many gods, in the rocks and the rivers, in the sky and the sea, some more benevolent than others, but all influence our world and so all need to be appeased. Even if their world is no longer quite as connected as it once was. The Hurrun, and many of the other tribes, have taken The Paron as our chief guardian." Lulpo said, just as assuredly as she talked before. "Wozpalar, who you met when you first came, is Hurrun as well."

Wozpalar, Xuxuxopolar and Zuwxoplar were the names of the three boys who had confronted her when she first ventured south of the river. She had been afraid to go near them even after Palon made them apologise to her, but Sanae was slowly realising that Palon was right. They were boys not men, aspiring to be great heroes, but lacking the maturity that comes with age. She was slowly warming to them after that epiphany.

"Are the Hurrun the only tribe to come to Tekolgertep?" Sanae inquired.

"Three tribes have people here. The Hurrun, the Poloarun and the Parerun, although mostly women and children and a few working men.

Xuxuxoplar is of the Poloarun and Zuwxoplar is of the Parerun. Many of the warriors are off fighting with the king and many of the other tribes have stayed in our homelands."

"Why did you come?" Sanae asked with the directness of an arrow, she did not know why.

Lulpo looked at her as if the question took her of guard, suddenly a young girl again rather than an enlightened elder.

"Zenidun is beautiful, but it is not our true homeland. Our people are used to moving if needs be, the Powouzo remember so we need not. Besides, Zenidun is not a rich place and not all our people are so intent on peace. We came here because we needed to, to survive, and to play our role as a part of Tekolger's new empire."

"And your mother is the leader of the tribes here? That is not something that would happen among the Doldun." Sanae asked, eager to learn. Lulpo laughed wildly,

"Mother is not leader, she is the Powouzo. A spiritual teacher. The women of our people spend many years with the Powouzo who live at Ruroxolnow in the land of Zenidun. It is a sacred pace where they learn the wisdom of the gods and the past, the poems of old. They are maidens dedicated to the maternal care of the old wisdom. When a woman has become a Powouzo she joins a tribe. Then she is judge, a bard and settles disputes amongst and between the tribes, because the Powouzo remember." Sanae nodded on intently. The Zummosh world was one she knew almost nothing about. She had so many questions.

"Why do you not live in the city?" She continued.

"We have never lived in cities, our people like the freedom of the countryside and do not want to be shackled to a city. We spread out over the land and only gather in one place for important occasions or to defend ourselves. It is a bargain we have struck ever since the last turn of the wheel, to not live beyond our means and upset the natural order. Man is not meant to live in the hives you call cities." Lulpo said, with a sense of pride in her voice. These people were so different to the Doldun and the Xosu, never mind the Xortogun. It was no wonder that they were not understood and were thought of as barbaric savages.

A rumble of horses interrupted their conversation. A small group of Rilrpitu men, carrying a royal standard, splashed into the river downstream. They rode a mix of small black and white ponies common to the horse lords of the steppe. Helupelan had told her that the Rilrpitu spent so much time a horse that they and the creatures were one. She had even heard some Xortogun say that the savage horse men lay with their horses. Though she did not believe that.

The hooves of the ponies smashed into the river like so many stones launched from a catapult, each landing with a thud and sending a small shockwave through the water. Emerging on the south bank without breaking stride they carried on toward the Zummosh village. The Rilrpitu were reputed to be even more savage and dangerous than the Zummosh, and even though the only horse lords in the city were those under the command of the governor, she had always kept well clear of them. They had a dark look and menacing demeanour which made her deeply wary of them.

Lulpo stopped talking and immediately gathered up her things and set off in a rush back to the village. Sanae did not know what was happening, but the dangerous look on Lulpo's faced gave her great concern. She collected the clothes and followed, not abandoning her friend.

* * *

Entering the village in a rush, the two girls did not see the large young Zummosh man, with a mane of shining blond hair that curled around his head like a vine, stepping out of his hut. They almost clattered into him. Lulpo stumbled almost drunkenly and then recognition and relief flashed over her face,

Lulpo said something in the Zummosh's guttural tongue, pausing and rummaging around in her basket and pulling out a mail shirt she had been cleaning the rust off. The interlinked rings of iron glistened in the sun, still damp from the river. Zummosh warriors were famous for their ring linked armour which sat on the body almost like a second impenetrable skin.

The tall man's expression turned from a startled but warm smile to a serious concern, but he pushed the armour away and said something in reply. His voice was deeper and more guttural than Lulpo's, but the lyrical rhythm of the tongue was still there. The man turned on his heels and headed into the centre of the village.

"What is going on?" Sanae finally managed to ask Lulpo.

"The horse daemons come." She replied, somewhat distantly.

"The Rilrpitu? They are the king's men; I saw the banner. What is the problem?" Sanae replied.

Lulpo let out a low and almost sinister laugh,

"King's men they may be, but they do not bring the king's peace. The Sarasen Saradaai they call themselves. Kings of Xortogun they used to be, but there is nothing kingly about them. They stole the throne of these lands whilst they were supposed to be protecting them, the Powouzo remember this too. The chief daemon is called Tabasa, named after some old hero, he claims. If so, it is not a name he lives up to."

Every Doldun and Xosu knew the tale of Yoruxoruni, how his empire rose so quickly, but after the League of all the Xosu defeated his invasion of Xosupil he was betrayed and murdered by his Rilrpitu bodyguard, and his empire burned out with him. Cut down on the night of a full moon whilst he slept. Before his blood had dried on the earth, the Rilrpitu took advantage of the chaos and seized the country, ruling and plundering it for two hundred years until Tekolger brought them down. Even in the act of casting down the tyrants Tekolger had sort to build an empire for everyone though, taking into his service those Rilrpitu who were willing to serve him. It was an act which Sanae imagined must have taken the force of will of a god to control the terrifying men of the steppe.

"Tekolger defeated them though. Now they serve the Doldun." Sanae replied. She knew the story of the conquest of Xortogun well. The king made an impossible crossing of the mountains and cut down the savage Rilrpitu king with his own hand at the battle of Gorzow.

"Some he defeated, the rest they joined him and now ride around as royal soldiers, but they are still horse daemons underneath. They have declared our village a part of the city and come to demand taxes." Lulpo replied.

"The city cannot function without taxes. Although it is the governor's job to collect them."

Lulpo laughed that deep, wild laugh again,

"Our governor doesn't care; he hardly knows we exist. The south bank of the river is not a part of the city. It is a part of the black land of Guntoga, ruled by Koluun of the Tholmash, but he is never seen in these lands. We pay him for living on the land once a year. So long as we pay, he does not care what we do. But now these horse daemons descend upon us, demanding we pay them instead. No doubt with the governor of the city's blessing. There are little fighting men here, so it is hard to defend ourselves. Come on, stay out of sight, but let us see what is happening."

Lulpo took Sanae by the arm and led her into the hut the man had emerged from to watch.

The riders had kicked up a lot of dust in the central square, creating a cloud which hung low over the village. As it began to settle, a group of at least fifteen horsemen emerged. With the dust cloud floating in the air around them it did look as though man and horse were one, like creatures from the old stories. The Zummosh were warily hovering around the edge of the village. The rider at the head of the column dismounted and stepped into the centre of the village square,

"That's him, Tabasa." Lulpo whispered,

Tall and lean with the wind burnt skin of the steppe people, but his face was as round as the moon, where most Rilrpitu had a long-tapered head. He did not look like the soldiers that Sanae was used to clad in riding leathers, painted trousers, and sleeveless scaled armour, with only tattoos to protect his arms. He carried a whip in one hand, a sword on his hip and a curved bow in his saddle. He shouted something, but he was so far away and, with his broken and accented Common Xosu, what she heard was unintelligible.

Evidently Palon understood. The matronly woman stepped forward out of the shadows with all the grace and baring of a maiden queen. A heated conversation between her and the Rilrpitu warrior followed.

"Mother, the Powouzo for all the Zummosh here, she is the closest to a leader and more formidable than any other, she will not back down to this aggression. The Powouzo remember." Lulpo said proudly, but Sanae did not like the look of what she was seeing. The argument was getting increasingly aggressive. Suddenly, Tabasa struck Palon with the back of his hand. She stumbled back and fell to her knees as the sun passed behind a cloud and the square suddenly seemed a whole lot darker. The blond Zummosh man then appeared, he rushed forward, swift as an arrow, emerging on the square before the sun reemerged.

He grabbed for the moon faced Rilrpitu warrior, striking him across his eye. A struggle followed as Tabasa smacked him back and the Zummosh warrior grabbed for the horse lord's throat. Then a pale sword flashed. The Zummosh hit the ground hard, a red rain flew off the end of the sword and a flood of thick wine dark blood oozed from the young Zummosh man's throat.

Calmly the Rilrpitu chief wiped away the blood which covered his round face and then cleaned his blade and remounted his horse, shouting something else she did not understand. Tabasa turned rode off, the mounted men with him followed.

Lulpo sat there in stunned silence, mouth open, staring out into the square. Sanae pulled her to her feet and took her outside as Palon was desperately trying to stop the follow of blood from the Zummosh man. The black earth drunk the blood eagerly. Sanae had seen enough sacrifices in the temple to know it was too late for him.

***

She left quickly after death took the man. She did not think it was sensible to stay as the Zummosh grieved for their kin.

The moon was rising in the sky, Tholo's great eye in all its glory gazed over the world. The time for her second task had almost arrived.

She entered the main chamber of Xosu's temple. It was empty, just torches for company. Taking one of the torches in hand, she stood and took a moment to take in the beauty of the statue of the god, thinking on what Lulpo had told her about The Paron.

Three gods and one, it was a strange idea. But there was plenty about her own gods that she did not yet understand, more to Xosu than she yet understood. The red kings in her dreams flashed before her eyes for a moment.

She heard a creak as a door was slowly opened. Helupelan emerged from the darkness carrying a torch in one hand and a sacrificial knife in the other. He was wearing his ceremonial robes which trailed to the floor and ringed his head like a halo. The glow of his torch lit up is face and gave him a warm glow. He was alone. The High Priest gestured for her to come to him, and the pair sat down by the still open temple door.

"Are you ready for your task tonight?" The old man asked her.

"I think so father. I feel I have learnt much from my first task, but the god will decide." Sanae answered.

"You have grown much over the last year, the tasks are a culmination of that." he paused, "I received a reply to the letter you had delivered to Thelonigul for me. The oracle was pleased to hear that the temple is complete." He paused again, but the look on his face made her think he wanted to say more. She had not realised the letter was meant for the oracle herself, Xosu's conduit between his people and the gods, who lived in the cave of Zilthil the great white hydra. She had always wanted to visit the oracle, to see such power and be so close to the god at the navel of the world. Helupelan had served at Thelonigul before he became the High Priest of the King of the Doldun and the tales he told of the place had sparked wonder in her mind as a child. Although just a common woman, the oracle was sort out by great kings and rich potentates from across the world, and not just the Xosu came as supplicants, but men of Thelizum and Gulonbel and even Xortogun. Each man who came made splendid offerings to the god for the chance to ask a question and receive a reply from the lips of the oracle herself.

It was just a dream though; she would never be rich enough to be a supplicant to the god and her attendants were all men of the priesthood. The only other way to see the spectacle was to be selected to be the oracle, but that was a choice for the god alone. It was said that those he chose to be his conduits would find themselves drawn inexplicably to the cave. Some claimed that Gelithul, Xosu's wild companion would lead them there, others that Xosu's arrow would guide them across the sky. Some believed the sweet odour from the cave itself drew the future oracle close. How ever it happened, once the maiden arrived, for it was always a maiden, they would have their true power revealed to them and the god himself would speak through them. But Xosu almost always chose common women from amongst those who dwelt in the shadow of Thelonigul, the sacred land where his power was strong.

Helupelan continued, "It pains me to see you grow. I still remember you as the small child who came with me to this new city, but you deserve your chance to prove yourself." His voice broke slightly, but he composed himself quickly and said, "Your parents would be proud to see your growth and the future the bright one has lit for you."

Sanae nodded, she had not heard Helupelan talk like this before. He never mentioned her parents and in truth she knew little about them, she always felt as though she could not ask.

"I know you do not always see eye to eye with Kolae but trust me she wants the best for you as well."

The suggestion maddened her. Sanae wanted to scream and shout and tell Helupelan of the contempt with which the High Priestess viewed her. She held her tongue.

"She told me about the incident after your last task. The broach you were wearing of some Zummosh god."

"It was a gift father." Sanae said,

"I know." he replied, pulling the broach out of his robes. "Take it, just do not wear it in front of Kolae."

She smiled and took the broach, brushing her fingers over the well-wrought metal. The three heads of the god staring at her.

"Lulpo says that The Paron, the god, is three gods but also one. How can that be?"

Helupelan smiled,

"The gods can be interpreted in different ways, and each have different aspects we mortals find hard to comprehend. What we know of the gods is like leaves rustling in the wind. We perceive what we can from the movement of those leaves, whether they fall to the ground or are swept away. But the true sense of the god lies in the wind which blows them and that we can only fleetingly feel against our skin.

All the gods come to us in different forms and emphasise different aspects of their power. Xosu took the form of a man when he ruled, but a part of him was in the white hydra whose blood nourished the world and birthed men. He also transformed into a panther and an eagle in his time among us. Dunsun interacts with mortals in the shape of many different animals and the sun is his great eye. The realm of the sea and Sem are one and the same, the sky and Bul as well and Tholo, the moon is her most obvious form.

Similarly, different peoples give the gods different names. We say Dunsun, but the Xortogun say Kurotor, or Gonphon or Xur depending on what time you are talking to them about. These are many different aspects and forms but all the same gods. The Zummosh may recognise these aspects as different divine forms, but it is all the one god."

Sanae nodded,

"I understand I think."

"Do not worry about this now, understanding will come with time. Focus on your tasks." Helupelan answered in a comforting tone.

"It is not that which I am worried about." she paused, "There was an incident today. I was down by the river, washing the clothes with Lulpo. Some Rilrpitu came to the Zummosh, claiming to be the king's men and demanding taxes. When the Zummosh refused they killed one of them and now I am afraid they will come back and kill more. Was it not king Tekolger's wish to build a city and an empire for all the people of east and west? Can you not speak to the governor, father? Lulpo says that the governor of their lands resides in Guntoga and does not care about them." Sanae pleaded. She knew that Helupelan was close to the governor. Keluaz of the Keluazi would often frequent the temple and talk with the High Priest in private.

Helupelan smiled, "It was Tekolger's wish, and I think your father would have said the same."

All she really knew of her father was that he was a nobleman at the king's court, but she had never felt that she could ask for any more knowledge of him. Of her mother she knew even less, just that she was of the oldest and noblest blood. Helupelan seemed so sad on the rare occasions when he talked of her parents. "Those events are concerning." he continued, "but if they acted with the king's authority and the Zummosh were refusing to pay what taxes they owe, the governor will not act." Helupelan said.

"They did not have the authority of king or governor. The Zummosh village lies beyond the river and the city limits, those are the domains of Koluun of the Tholmosh not Keluaz, and the Zummosh pay their taxes, but their governor has forgotten them. So, the Rilrpitu leader has seen his chance to exploit them, especially as most of the men are away and there is no king anymore." Sanae said.

Helupelan looked at her pensively, but with a slight smile, "If that is true then it will be of concern to Keluaz, and Koluun I am sure. I will see if I can raise the issue with Keluaz. For now, you must focus on your tasks though. Go and prepare, you do not have long. May the bright god light your way."

Sanae, feeling reassured, the High Priest was someone to rely on, headed to her quarters to prepare herself for the coming task.

**

The red hued dawn was nearing, Sanae headed back into the central hall of the temple, unsure what to expect.

Helupelan stood waiting for her, Kolae and some other priestesses alongside him. The priestesses were wearing the familiar masks of Gelithul, Xosu's wild friend and mentor, a tanned face surrounded by an auburn head of hair, pointed ears and antlers like a stag. She stopped in front of them and Helupelan began to speak,

"Xosu's heart had been cast down to the realm of the dead. In his grief after discovering what Tholo had done, Dunsun turned his back on the world and set out to search for what remained of Xosu. Without the Lord of the Cosmos to keep order, the world descended into chaos. Sem saw a chance and rose against the gods, his beasts and demons assaulted Dzottgelon, and the world was overrun and broken.

Dunsun discovered that Xosu's heart had been sent into the clutches of Phenmoph, the rich lord of the dead. He travelled to the underworld to bargain for his life, but the lord of the dead would not relinquish his prize.

Upon seeing the heart of his once bright son, Dunsun shed tears of sorrow and those amber tears fell on the heart, drying solid around it. Thinking quickly, the Lord of the Cosmos swallowed the heart whole, leaving the underworld before Phenmoph noticed his deceit.

Fearing Tholo's wrath, he went to Geli and cut the heart from his stomach. The queen of the underworld though she was, Geli would spend half the year tending to the fertility of the land at Mount Betgennon. Geli took the amber encrusted heart and swallowed it herself, letting Xosu grow in her belly. He would be born again alongside his friend and mentor Gelithul, the first Wildman. The god was raised by Geli to be wise and strong, teaching him about Gennon's great creation.

When Xosu was grown to near maturity, he set his eyes upon restoring the broken world to its former glory, because, although Dunsun had returned to drive off the hordes of daemons and cast Sem back to his domain, the world remained shattered and broken. The great dolthil tree, which had once been the centre of the world, lay poisoned, crippled, and ruined, and Tholo, still enraged by Dunsun's actions, had set her fierce white dragon, the nine headed hydra Zilthil, to guard it.

Xosu knew he must defeat the beast and slay it, letting its life blood flow into the tree to see the world flourish once again. However, in doing so, Gelithul told Xosu how he would be sacrificing a part of himself as Tholo had raised the hydra from the blood she spilled when she slaughtered Xosu as a child.

Unperturbed, together Xosu and Gelithul tracked and hunted the beast across the world. Though their sweet-smelling tricks could not draw the dragon out in to the open, finally they cornered it at the cave behind the great dead dolthil tree which it had made its lair.

The beast struggled fiercely, its nine heads breathing great rivers of fire, striking with its moon pale horns, and lashing with is ferocious tale. Xosu took the form of a panther, and an almighty clash broke out as he battled with the hydra.

Although he fought valiantly his flashing claws driving the leviathan back into the cave, the beast was a part of Xosu, and he could not subdue it alone. Forlorn and on the verge of defeat, Xosu cried out to his father, and Dunsun answered his call. Gifting Xosu his thunderbolt to wield against the hydra. A true test of his strength, for only those with the supreme power can control the fire of the heavens.

Thunderbolt in hand, Xosu and Gelithul subdued the great leviathan. Xosu sacrificed the beast to his father, cutting its throat and drinking the blood, letting what was left of the warm, wine dark blood seep into the soil around the great dolthil tree. The tree sprouted new life again, and the first vines grew out from the dark soil around it.

The world was remade, and a golden age would follow. Old kingdoms which rivalled the realms of the immortals would flourish. Some even say that the first of the Xosu people sprouted from the teeth of the defeated hydra as its blood sunk into the soil, those Xosu who would go on to be the most loyal and sacred followers of the god.

Xosu took the goat-like horns of the hydra for himself, from which would be fashioned his famous white-gold bow, sculpted to look like a writhing snake."

Helupelan produced a razor-sharp blade from his robes and handed it to Sanae. He continued,

"Today you will experience a similar struggle."

They wrapped a panther's skin round her shoulders and led her out of the temple into the adjacent grounds and handed her a flaming torch. There a beautiful white bull, shining in the waning moonlight waited.

She understood now why she had been asked to care for the new cattle, a part of her was in them, through her effort to nurse them. It was tied to the dolthil tree outside the temple. One look at the beast told her it was agitated. Helupelan pushed her forward gently as two of the priestesses untied the beast.

As the ropes dropped, the beast flung itself around the small, enclosed area in which it was kept, a fury in its eyes. Its horns thrashed, and its tail lashed liked a serpent. Sanae approached warily, creeping as she has seen the wild cats in the city do when they hunted.

Twice she attempted to get hold of the writhing beast and twice she was thrown backwards. The moon had finished its descent now, and the first rays of the sun were fighting their way over the horizon, driving the darkness back into the depths of the earth.

She put the knife away and began to talk to the bull in a sweet, calming manner, it was all she could think to do. Amazingly the animal responded to her message, becoming less agitated and allowing her to approach. She touched it, then moved closer, her arm wrapping around its neck. At the last minute, the beast realised and began to struggle, too late now though. In a swift motion as quick as lightning, as she had seen Helupelan do a thousand times before, she cut the magnificent white animal's throat.

A splutter and a squirt and blood poured out of the animal. The bull wailed, but the sound grew fainter as the acrid, metallic smell of life filled the air. She held its head over the base of the dolthil tree and gave to the plant the precious liquid of life, the weight of the beast was almost too much to bear. Kolae held a cup under the pouring blood and lifted it for Sanae to drink.

Through the blood sliding down the outside of the vessel, she could see the black figures of Xosu and Gelithul depicted, their own struggle with a much mightier beast fashioned around the outside of the cup. She drank deep as the sun's rays touched the grounds of the temple, it was warm and rich and sticky. She almost choked, but Kolae kept on pouring. She could feel the liquid running down her neck, but still she drank. It felt wrong, where was the reason in it? but she was overwhelmed by a sense of pleasure, delight even as the warm liquid choked down her throat, delight coursing through her, it tasted of honey at the end.

KALU

19

The night came on quick on the flat plains of Zenian. The evening sky burned with a murderous crimson red, like a wave of blood washing over the world and making it anew.

"You should go inside." Zonhol said. "Kelbal will be expecting you."

"It is not me Kelbal is concerned with." Kalu answered, "He tries to massage the fractured egos of our fellow Companions."

Already the torch light was dancing out of the citadel's open door to the sound of music, drinking and laughter. Kelbal had insisted on everyone attending, it had echoes of Tekolger, but it felt forced.

"Yes, but he will need your support to do that. Kelbal is..." Kalu interrupted Zonhol before he could finish,

"Kelbal is losing the battle with his second shade. I know. He has been in that spiral since Tekolger's death."

"All the more reason for you to go. You know better than any that Kelbal can give in to his temper when he is in his cups." Zonhol stated. Kalu took a long look at the open doorway of the palace and then turned to head towards the city gates.

"Later." he said with a sigh. "We have other duties calling us first."

The camp beyond the walls had been built in a hurry and, even though this was supposed to be friendly territory, good order needed to be maintained. The news from Thuson that the threat from the Rilrpitu was bigger than first thought was playing on Kalu's mind. The flat, open and desolate plains of Zowdel would let the noise of the camp drift across the land with nothing to stop it. With a poor defence, any would-be attacker would be gifted the element of surprise. Probably a foolish notion with the camp being placed so close to the defences of Yorixori, but Kalu still felt he needed to check.

"This is our last opportunity to ensure the army is well ordered." he said to Zonhol as they walked toward the camp. "Tomorrow, we ride to Dolzalo's aid, and I need to be certain all is well here before we go." Zonhol stayed silent. He knew that Kalu was speaking out loud to reassure himself. Kelbal had finally decided, and announced, that Kalu would be leading the reinforcements being sent to Dolzalo and the seers had approved of the plan. Kelbal needed to be able to rely on whoever he sent out and so Kalu was the natural choice. He would be leading his own White Shield cavalry squadron and Supo of the Dolozolaz and his guard would be joining him. The Togworwoh of the north was desperate to protect his province. Zenu had also assigned a squadron of his horse, they would be invaluable due to their knowledge of the land of Zowdel.

Kalu could not help but be looking forward to getting back out in the field again but leaving Kelbal alone to manage their comrades was worrying him. *At least he will have Zenu to lean on.* The reinforcements would be leaving the next day and so he would need to inspect the preparations for the expedition before attending Kelbal.

He sent Zonhol to inspect the walls of the camp and the ditch in front of it at the eastern section, anchored against the walls of the city, and the northern section pressed against the river. Kalu went to inspect the southern and western sections himself, they were the most exposed to attack. He had done the same every night since they arrived at the city.

Heading west from the city gates, the music slowly drifted off into the background as he walked further and further away. Beyond the walls and the camp there was nothing but a silent empty land, flooded with darkness. The light of the city behind him threw a dim streak of flickering, pale light across the floor to his front, transforming the small stretch of land it struck from dark to light. As he entered the camp, for a moment Kalu cast a long shadow through the heart of that arrow of pale radiance, overshadowing the illuminated valley forged by the shaft of light, the full moon floating above him.

The campfires of each squad lit the lanes of the temporary encampment, rows of tents laid out on a grid pattern. Kalu looked up and down these perfectly lined up rows with satisfaction. The army of the Doldun was the most experienced body of professional warriors in the world. They built a camp from scratch every single night almost as second nature whilst on campaign, always on the same pattern. In fact, it could be said that they built the same camp every night, to protect them from the dangers which lay in the land beyond its walls. It felt familiar, almost like home. Though this night Kalu could not help but sense a tension. The atmosphere in the camp was very subdued. It was strange given how agitated the men had been getting. However, he could not help but be pleased with the discipline shown in the camp's construction. There was something he always found pleasurable about good order in the army. Warfare was an art, and these were the basic elements which brought the form to perfection.

He took a moment to enjoy that sensation. The simplicity of a well-ordered camp was a world away from the politics of empire, and the tension building amongst the Companions was becoming too much for him.

He reached the western wall and strode up the earth bank on top of which the palisade was placed, then stared out into the darkness beyond. Below him was a ditch from which the earth for the bank had been dug. Placed in the ditch were smaller sharpened sticks which Kalu could just make out in the darkness.

Satisfied that the wall and ditch were placed correctly and still intact, he turned and began to walk along the perimeter, towards a torch in the distance held by a man on sentry duty. The warrior was leaning against his spear and staring out across the black empty plain, just as Kalu had been moments before. Kalu approached swiftly and was almost on top of the sentry, yet it appeared that he had not seen Kalu,

"Keeps your eyes open." he said, "You never know what is lurking in the darkness, even in apparently friendly territory."

The man turned about. Kalu recognised him, although he could not recall his name. He wore on his arm a golden armband, awarded by Tekolger himself for courage in the field. He had the eyes of a man who had seen the desperation and despair of a close fought battle, and the elation and ecstasy of a hard-fought victory. They were old, experienced eyes, yet the soldier could not have seen many more than twenty summers. He wondered whether his eyes looked the same.

"I saw you coming Companion." the sentry said, "It is what I can't see that worries me."

Kalu smiled at that,

"That is wise. It worries me too." he replied, "But our defences are sound and the Rilrpitu have been blown many leagues from here. If anyone is out there, I doubt they will risk an attack tonight."

"It is not them that worries me either." he answered to Kalu's surprise, "It is the future." he paused, "What do we do now? …Without the king I mean."

Kalu stayed silent, unsure what to say. Finally, he replied,

"Defend the empire, protect his legacy." The last words Tekolger had said to him. The veteran nodded,

"Does that mean Kelbal will rule?" He asked,

"Kelbal will be regent until Tekolger's heir comes of age, yes."

"I don't mean to speak out of turn, but…" he paused again with a pensive, sorrowful look, "Kelbal will not bring us glory like Tekolger did."

Unexpectedly, the remark took Kalu back to his education at the court of the king. Kenkathoaz had summoned the philosopher Yusukol Kosua from Butophulo to teach his son and the sons of the nobility. The wards the old king had gathered at his new royal palace of Thelanutep would attend classes every morning in the gardens of Zolsun the Golden to be taught by the great philosopher, and his apprentice Thuson Kosua, in the philosophy of Kunpit of Thelonigul. Yusukol was a demanding teacher but encouraged the children to be honest and inquisitive to the point of being intrusive. *'Never make assumptions, question everything you are told. This world is never as it appears.'* That was perhaps his most important lesson. Kalu answered the veteran with Yusukol's words echoing in his mind,

"He may not, but there is more than glory to be had now. The empire needs protecting, there is honour in that task, and reward for those who serve well."

The soldier smiled, but it was a smile full of melancholy and there was a look behind his eyes like he wanted to say more,

"Tekolger was more than respected, we worshipped him, and he made us feared and respected. The men marched to end of the world because he asked them to do it. Kelbal couldn't make them do that."

"Tekolger was like no other man, it is best not to try and compare. Be careful who you say things like that to." he placed his hand on the shoulder of the young man and continued, "I'm sure you know the story of Kolgophoas." the warrior nodded, "He was punished for his pursuit of his own glory and ignoring the will of the gods, Tekolger followed his path and Kelbal will take his own. There is honour in both." Kalu paused, hoping to see reassurance on the veteran's face, "Keep your eyes open. I know it is hard now with the king gone, we all feel like survivors of a great cataclysm struggling to find our way home. Especially with the Rilrpitu bellowing out of the north. But Kelbal will make sure the empire is stable, defended and protect Tekolger's legacy."

He turned on his heel and left, supposing it was about time he headed to the palace before he was missed. The distraction was welcome, but the defences were adequate, and he needed to show himself at the palace. He just had one more stop to make before he would feel relaxed enough to attend Kelbal.

He found his pace quickening the more he reflected on his exchange with the sentry, as if trying to escape the thoughts it provoked. But as he headed back up the main thoroughfare through the camp, the warm light of the city called him close, and he began to forget his concerns.

* * *

Halfway back to the palace, Kalu stopped at the stables attached to the citadel that held the Togworwoh's residence. The White Shield cavalry had been billeted in the city itself and so had the comfort of the Togworwoh's stables to prepare. Zonhol was waiting for him there, imposing even in just a tunic with his hair tied back and his beard oiled.

"I need to speak with you." The captain said.

"On the morrow whilst we ride, there will be plenty of time for talking then. Right now, I am needed at the palace. Let us do this quickly so I can take my leave." Kalu replied.

"But it is about the men, they are not happy."

Kalu cut him off,

"I know, I know, and I am doing my best to address their concerns. They will soon feel themselves again when we get back in the field."

He pushed open the door to the stable before the captain could answer.

Inside he found the men scattered around each making their meticulous preparations for a swift campaign chasing down the Rilrpitu raiders. Again, there was a subdued atmosphere that struck him as odd. They had been frustrated and bored by the lack of activity in Yorixori, the chance to strike out again with a target in mind he thought would have buoyed their spirits.

Kalu made his way up and down the vast stable complex. Lacking the time to check on each man individually, he marched around looking for any signs which concerned him and checking on the horses. The men were huddled in small groups sharpening swords, polishing armour to a pale white sheen, and brushing their mounts, but each seemed a shadow of themselves, spectres lurking in the depths of the stables.

Stopping every now and then to observe the preparations, Kalu was happy by what he saw and so quickly found himself making his way back toward the door of the stables. He had not been greeted quiet as warmly as usual, that seemed strange. Perhaps it was just some nerves setting in. The Rilrpitu had proved a dangerous and savage foe in the past, many of the men may not be relishing facing them again.

Two thousand men had been placed under his command for the mission. One hundred of his own White Shield cavalry, two regiments of Tekolger's veteran cavalry, the two hundred men of Supo's personal guard, a squadron of Zenu's guard, and the rest drawn from the new Xortogun recruits. Another few thousand Doldun and Xortogun would follow up behind, spreading over the country to root out any other

Rilrpitu. Kelbal had told him to bring the situation under control quickly so that Kalu could return to his side. To that end the men would be leaving early and travelling light. Tekolger had been renowned for the speed of his pursuits of foes. Now Kalu would push the men to their limits in his pursuit of the Rilrpitu. Once again Tekolger's veterans would be tested and the green boys from Xortogun would have to prove they had the resolve and metal needed to match the men of the Doldun. He left the stables and started making his way toward the palace.

As had become routine, he entered the palace to find Kelbal deep in his cups, but this time the rest of the Companions had joined him. They were sat on Xortogun couches, but none except Kelbal were reclining. A large fire was blazing opposite them. Kelbal was furthest from the entrance, bathing in the red glow of the fire and laying on a bench lined with silk which he had brought back from Zentheldel, Yare alongside him. Female servants were rushing back and fore, bringing food and wine to the new rulers of the empire. Each Companion had seized a woman to accompany them on their journey into the depths of intoxication, to glimpse the realm of the gods that lay beyond the mortal veil. Kelbal looked up as Kalu walked in and shouted,

"Kalu Pale arm! There you are! the army is still there I take it?" An amused grin graced his ruddy face, "Come and join us."

He is already drunk, Kalu thought with some concern, his second shade had taken over with its wild smirk. Kelbal ushered off a couple of the women to make way for his old friend.

Before Kalu had taken his seat, Kelbal had ordered a cup of wine to be filled by a eunuch stood next to him carrying a pile of scrolls, looking more like a secretary than a cup bearer. The regent in his flamboyant red royal robe, a gift from Talehalden the fallen king of Thentherzaw, took the cup of unmixed wine and thrust it into Kalu's hand, a wild smile on his face, saying,

"You will find all the knowledge you crave at the bottom of this cup Kalu, drink deep and see the world with clarity. Unmixed wine, it will give you a glimpse of the knowledge only the gods possess. The wine is good as well, a deep red vintage from Gelodun, some Putedun traders brought it here. All this way west we can still get a taste of home." He took a sip and allowed himself to relax into the evening, even though Kelbal's behaviour made him wary.

The last time all of them had properly sat together like this was the night Tekolger fell ill. O*r was poisoned*, that thought made him shudder, *surely no one in this room was responsible.* Zenukola's words about a traitor in their midst still echoed in his mind. Another problem for another day perhaps, right now all that mattered was keeping the Companions united and of one purpose.

Kalu took another sip from the cup. It was good wine, the Putedun certainly knew how to pick their drink to have the desired effect. But the nights with Tekolger still seemed like an eon ago, and now the endless days of marching and the nights filled with drink felt hollow.

Kelbal finished off his cup of wine and immediately called for another as he carried on the story he was telling before Kalu had entered,

"It was the first time all of us here fought together, and Tekolger's first battle as king. None of us knew what we were really doing then. It seems like a lifetime ago, but I remember the thrill of leading a charge into the mass ranks of the Rilrpitu. A marauding tribe of Rilrpitu, which had already ravaged the lands of the Zummosh and killed Tekolger's father in battle. We are fortunate that they are no longer able to range so far east on their raids. I brought Tekolger back to Doldun and saw him crowned. Then we led the army to battle."

This story seemed more directed at the servants and scattered nobles than the Companions. The battle of the Belzow river had been Kalu's first, only just a man grown at six and ten.

"The defiance of the clans had barely ended when a tribe of Rilrpitu burst into Doldun from the north, after ravaging the Zummosh of Zenidun. Kenkathoaz had rallied his army and marched to meet them. But he was overconfident and foolishly met them on an open plain with too few men, where their horse archers could rain a storm of death on his host from a far." Kelbal was almost telling the tale as a bard would to a packed drinking hall back in the hills of Doldun. "The old king fell on the field, cut to pieces when the Rilrpitu finally decided to put an end to the fight and closed in. Tekolger had not been there though, still in his self-imposed exile amongst the Thulchwal."

Kalu's memories of the battle were vivid. *Everyone's first stays with them*, he supposed.

"When Tekolger heard the news of his father's death, he raced back to Doldun, rallying the clans as he went. Zenukola, despite losing his arm in the first battle, had marched to aid Tekolger with the remnants of the king's army. We caught the Rilrpitu as they were crossing the Belzow river. Tekolger and I led the charge right into the heart of the enemy.

Weighed down by the treasures they had stolen, the Rilrpitu had no chance of escape. In the middle of the river Tekolger clashed with the Rilrpitu chieftain. A huge leviathan of a man who rode on a white stallion with ornate silver bull's horns on its head and wielded Dusk, the sword he stole from Kenkathoaz. The chieftain slew Parechwul, the brother of Tekolger's Thulchwal wife, with one mighty blow. Tekolger showed no fear that day though, only a mad rage when he saw Parechwul fall. He spilled the Rilrpitu chief's blood to drain into the river, then he drew Dusk from the chieftain's stone-dead hand and the Rilrpitu broke and ran." Kelbal finished his story, pausing as if waiting for applause, seemingly forgetting that all the Companions were at the battle with him.

Zela's laugh thrust through the air like a spear,

"You give yourself too much credit Kelbal, since when did you crown Tekolger? True enough you were in exile with him amongst the Thulchwal after that ugly business between him and the old king. But I do not remember you leading the charge, Tekolger was the point of that endeavour, like he was at every battle. You are spending too much time listening to the flattering's of that creature you keep with you."

Kelbal threw Zela an angry look, fire in his eyes, but his green eye had the edge over the amber,

"I don't seem to remember you fighting at all in that battle, Zela. No tales are told of your exploits."

"I was there, Kelbal. Right behind the king, the same place as you."

Kelbal drank deep again and snorted,

"And what about at Gorzow? Who held our flank while Tekolger cut his way through to the Rilrpitu king? Tekolger would not have killed him without my sacrifices. Xortogun wouldn't have been ours."

"I saved your life at Gorzow, Kelbal, don't forget that, and it was Dolzalo who drove through the mountain pass. Maybe I should have left you fall from your horse." Zela shot back.

Zela stood abruptly. Kelbal also sprung to his feet, a black smile on his lips. The atmosphere in the tent had suddenly become hostile, all was silent. Kalu slowly stood to try and talk Kelbal down. But Kelbal would have none of it,

"Do not threaten me, Zela!" he bellowed, "You will do well to remember who the regent is!" Kelbal said, thumbing the black ring in an irritated, anxious way. The look he gave Zela said that he would have happily cut out his heart then and there.

The tension was broken as a messenger nervously interrupted the exchange.

"General...it's the men General." He said, his eyes darting between the Companions still stood in confrontation with each other. "They sent me to tell you that they will not march with the Xortogun, they...they say that they do not trust them and will not fight alongside them."

The Companions were silent. Finally, Kalu spoke up,

"Who says this?"

"The men General. The whole army is refusing to obey orders unless the Xortogun are removed from their ranks."

Zela, still facing off against Kelbal said,

"For all your talk of unity Kelbal, look at what your decisions have caused. You sacrifice the loyalty of good men chasing the power Tekolger wielded. How do we rule an empire when our own army won't fight for us?"

Kelbal, fully in the grip of his cups now, his ruddy face crowned with a black fury and a white-hot rage, the prophecy of Kuso's cup ringing true once again, replied,

"Am I to take it you are one of the ring leaders of this rebellion then Zela? Is this treason?"

Everyone was stunned into silence, until Zela laughed and replied,

"You are even madder than we thought if you believe that to be true. It was your decision which caused this and now you seek to blame us? Remember, you are not yet regent, not officially, and the king's Xortogun bride is yet to give birth. Tekolger had other wives, other children, a son even, or had you forgotten that? A son of pure Doldun blood and almost a man grown. Or, if we wanted a king of age already, I am sure we can find other children. Tekolger was a man who liked to indulge. You are still just one of us and plenty can change in the coming months. Your closeness to Tekolger means nothing now and you will have to answer for these mistakes."

Zela turned to leave the room,

"Don't turn your back on me!" Kelbal continued, but Zela kept walking. Kalu grabbed Kelbal's arm and tried to pull him away. The regent reached out and took hold of Kalu's sheathed sword, Vigilance, drawing the leaf shaped blade so swiftly for someone so drunk that he took Kalu by surprise.

Before anyone could move, Kelbal turned and bolted toward Zela whose back was turned and blind to Kelbal's actions as he headed toward the exit. But his drunkenness took hold once more, his feet getting caught on the edge of his couch, he tumbled headfirst to the floor, the sword went spinning across the ground.

Zela turned and laughed,

"This man claims to be the Tekolger's chosen regent to lead the empire forward and yet he can't even make his way across a room."

Zela turned and left, followed by Deluan, Zonpeluthas, Thazan, Polazul and Zalmetaz.

* * *

Kalu followed the Companions out. Stepping into the darkness, his eyes adjusted quickly enough to see the group striding off into the night,

"Wait!" he shouted. "Zela let us talk about this." Zela was of the Zelkalkel, the clan was known for its poetry and love of language, Kalu hoped he would want to talk rather than fight. Although his kin were said to wield words like others did swords, there was a reason men called him Spear Tongue. Zela stopped and turned, a reluctant and impatient look on his face, his hand on the hilt of Rhapsode, his zilthum blade, the sword of poets. Kalu quickened his pace to catch up,

"Words were said in there that neither of you meant." he said, catching his breath, "Too much drink and the sadness that hangs over us all. Kelbal will realise his folly in the morning, don't take it personally. He is still in deep grief for the king."

Zela paused, his eyes were dark and blind to any hints of the man's inner thoughts,

"Drink was taken, emotions are running high, this is all true. But is this man that we want to be the regent of the empire? A decade or more before a new king takes power. How can we trust his judgement or ability to keep the empire together?"

"This was one night of drinking. I will speak to Kelbal. The worst thing we can do now though is show division."

Zela grudgingly nodded and answered, the smile had fallen from his lips,

"I trust you Kalu, that is why I will let this go. Make sure Kelbal pulls himself together or we will have to return to this issue."

Zela left, followed by the rest of the Companions. Kalu headed back to the palace and Kelbal, not knowing what he would say.

SONOSPHOSKUL

20

"The sea!"

The shout was faint and muffled at first, an echo from the front of the column, but as Sonosphoskul and his company crested the high mountain pass the cry went up again. This time it rippled its way through the ranks of the company as they scrambled over the top of the mountain, like a wave washing over a boulder on the shore.

"The sea!"

There was a relief in the cry, an ecstasy even, their trial was at an end. Sonos could not help but share in his men's joy, all the companies were shouting in their jubilance. But the men of Butophulo and the other Salxosu, sailors at heart, men of the sea itself, found the crystal blue water the most welcome sight. Buto had not abandoned them. Maybe now they could make good on abandoning the Salxosu of the White Islands, a new beginning for them all. The march into the heart of Thelizum had been done out of a sense of duty more than anything else. A band of mercenaries paid to conquer for a foreign king, spurred on by the words of the oracle and the danger which awaited them if they stayed serving Thasotun. The hectic dash which the retreat from the disaster at Gottoy had been was anything but that. Instead, they had banded together with a sense of purpose, Xosu and non-Xosu, united in the simple goal of escaping with their lives. They had done so by making decisions collectively, like the old League, a true republic on the march.

The crossing of this second set of mountains had been less perilous than the first. The mountains were not as high or treacherous, the native peoples less numerous and determined. Only twice had the column been ambushed and their attackers beaten back with ease. Even the supplies they had seized had held out, although they would need to be replenished soon. But for now, the vision before them was all that mattered. The sea had a sense of home in it to all Xosu. No Xosu city was far from it and the gentle crash of waves against the shore brought a sense of nostalgic relief that nothing else could, especially for the Salxosu.

Sonos looked to the sky, the sun burned bright, illuminating the changing world below. Dunsun's great eye watching over them and seeing them safely out of the heart of Thelizum. Ever since the foolish King of Gelodun had fallen on the field outside the walls of Gottoy, every day had been a fight for survival, but now the mountain path unfolded before them leading down onto a narrow plain, an easy walk and by the evening they would be out of danger. At the head of the plain, on a narrow peninsula assaulted on three sides by the sea, sat a city shining golden in the morning sun, a most welcome sight. The entire ordeal had lasted two cycles of the moon, with autumn now fully grasping the world.

"Rulrup." The voice was Pusokols'.

"You know it well?" Sonos asked him.

"Only by reputation, I've never ventured this far east. A Xosu city founded three hundred years ago by colonists out of Butophulo, with the philosopher Kunpit of Thelonigul as their leader. The city was said to be a chance for him to start a community afresh when the last of the kings of Butophulo banished him from the city." Puso replied.

"And the people. Do they still follow the ways of Kunpit?" Sonos inquired.

"Who knows. Kunpit eventually returned to Butophulo when the kings were gone, to establish his academy, the Panther's Den. But I believe the buildings and the society of Rulrup were constructed with his principles and philosophy as a guide. A new place from which to build a new society was the intention. I do know that it was never a particularly active member of the League, but as to how that means they will greet us, I have no inkling." Puso answered, still staring intently at the buildings glistening in the distance.

The thought of the city being devoted to Kunpi made Sonos uneasy. The nine tyrants who had seized power in Butophulo with the support of Tekolger had been raised and educated in the academy of Kunpit. *Would the leaders of this city be men like that as well?* It had been a League city once, if a distant member, hopefully that would still count for something. But for now, the golden city, caught in the light of the dawn sun, looked like a welcoming paradise, otherworldly almost, sat on its peninsula and surrounded by the sea on three sides. A precarious beauty about to be engulfed by the all-consuming ocean.

Sonos stopped at the crest of the mountain pass and watched as the men of his company filed passed him. Today was their turn to act as rear guard and Sonos was keen to make sure all his men were safely over the crest before he turned to descend himself.

With everyone accounted for, he faced the sea once more to take a final look. A deluge of people now descended the mountain side like a flood about to sweep its way onto the plain and into the city. The sight took Sonos aback for a moment, he could not quite believe they had made it. Perhaps ten thousand in total, fighting men and camp followers. They had marched through the most inhospitable terrain pursued by a victorious and relentless foe. Leaderless and disorganised hailing from at least a dozen different cities and lands. They had organised themselves, each man or woman taking the tasks which suited them best, much like the humble beehive. Working together, they had survived.

Stories will be told of this, he thought. When this was all over, he may even write an account of the expedition himself. For now, the sea beckoned to him, and Sonos could resist its call no longer. He touched the amulet at his neck and thought of home.

* * *

The sun was beginning its descent as the flood of people reached the city. Sonos was still at the rear and was able to watch as the men spilled onto the plain. The rich farmlands in front of Rulrup disappeared as men washed over them. The fields were empty though. *The farmers must have fled to the city when they saw the waves of warriors descending from the mountains.* Sonos couldn't blame them for that.

He pushed his way to the front of the army, to the gates of the city. Huge bronze doors barred their way and five disgruntled, half-starved men, who looked like shadows of their former selves, hammered on the gates demanding to be allowed in. He was quickly joined by his comrades, Pusukol and Kusoasu. Together they stepped forward to calm the men as Runukolkil made his way to the gate.

The commanders had developed a precarious balance to lead this ragged band of mercenaries, as much as anyone could with headstrong Xosu to command. A task made even harder when Rilrpitrol of Gelodun had succumbed to his injuries and his Gelodun were left leaderless. The mercenaries had taken to assembling to vote on important decisions of life and death. An action which seemed instinctive to the Xosu. But it had been the force of will of Runu, and some of the other commanders, which had kept the men pushing on rather than surrendering to a life of slavery in Gottoy. The stories of the republic forcing captives taken in war to kill each other in some grizzly sacrifice to a blood thirsty god had of course helped.

The city seemed quiet, but Runu shouted,

"We mean you no harm. We are Xosu. Mercenaries hired by the King of Gelodun to fight in Thelizum. We escaped when the king fell in battle at the walls of Gottoy. As one Xosu to another we ask for your city's protection and provisions so we may head for home."

His voice echoed like the ring of a smith's anvil. The sound hung in the air over the silence which gripped the city, just the soft crashing of the waves against the shore cut through the eerie vacuum. Finally, a voice came back,

"We know who you are. The whole of Xosudun will know soon, I should think.

Thildol, the High Kuson of Rulrup, has decreed that you will be given provisions and aid, but he will not allow thousands of men to swarm into the city. You have permission to establish a camp five stades from our walls. Once you have done this you will be sent provisions, and your leaders will be permitted to enter the city."

A groan of disapproval rippled through the ranks of the men and for a moment Sonos thought the discipline which had held so strong over their long march would finally crack. Runu was quick to react. Grasping hold of the situation he barked out orders to the company commanders. Despite an initial reluctance, soon the men were falling into their order of march ready to depart for an open patch of land between the mountains and the sea.

A camp sprung from the land rapidly as the routine of life on campaign once again took hold. A well-ordered space emerged as it had done every day of the march. The men dividing themselves based on their companies, so Sonos could see the diversity of the force that had marched through a hostile and unknown land.

The Daemons of the Deep, all Salxosu, mostly men from Butophulo and its hinterland, but also those from the White Islands still loyal to the League, had set themselves closest to the sea, six hundred strong. Next to them was The White Hydra's Teeth, a company of Silxosu from the sacred land around Thelonigul. Forbidden to carry arms and spill blood in the environs of the sacred palace, many of the Silxosu went abroad and had a fierce reputation as mercenaries. They counted five hundred men in their ranks. Further inland were the Tilxosu from the hinterland of Tusotik, formed into a company of horsemen called The Bulodon, named for the fierce sons of Bul. Two hundred men, but now only about fifty with mounts. There were even around a thousand Rinuxosu amongst their number, formed into a company known as The Exiles as their commanders had fled the Sacred Band of their king and chosen exile over submitting to Tekolger as he overran Xosupil. The Rinuxosu and the League of Butophulo had been the bitterest enemies only a dozen years ago, but now they were comrades in arms. That was still a strange thought. There were also about two thousand men from Gelodun who had fought their way through the ranks of the legions of Gottoy to escape with the Xosu mercenaries. They were Xosu as well Sonos reflected, if a little barbaric around the edges.

In a separate camp, the legion of the League of the Twelve Brothers settled. Although they had been through much and more with the Xosu, they kept themselves apart. Five thousand men had been raised, mostly by the city of Hotsujoi, to support Hunthisonu's campaign. The last fighting strength of the League of the Twelve Brothers. Only about fifteen hundred remained.

In amongst the well-ordered camp of the fighting men, a few thousand camp followers mixed. Those who had had the sense to flee when the battle with Gottoy had been lost and who had then survived the gruelling march to Rulrup.

As the sun dipped below the horizon, a line of torches emerged from the gates of Rulrup and wound its way toward the camp. A procession of carts filled with food rumbled in, followed by an abundance of cattle along with an invite for the leaders of the expedition to attend the theatre from the man named Thildol, calling himself the High Kuson of the city. *A strange title*, Sonos reflected, to name himself a huntsman when he ruled over a marble city, the influence of Kunpit of Thelonigul no doubt.

The provisions were divided amongst the men and each company took a beast to sacrifice as they had promised the gods they would if they would deliver them to salvation. The men of Butophulo made the appropriate sacrifice to Buto, the protector of the city and the giver of its wealth and abundance.

With the gods satisfied and the men rejuvenated, a vote was held, and it was decided that the commanders of the companies would be sent as representatives to Rulrup and that they would request provisions and aid to allow them to return to Thasotun. A prospect that Sonos and the men of Butophulo did not relish, sure that the Red and White Council ruling the city would either bar their gates to them, have them killed, or worse send them off to some bleak corner of the world to die in another senseless war. But they were outvoted by the other Xosu.

Sonos, Pusokol and Kusoasu removed their armour and dressed in the Xosu style togas which the representatives of the city had brought them and followed Runu and the other commanders to the city. The Hotizoz commanders came too, Dzotdoz looking awkward and ungainly in the garment he clearly had not worn before, but on Hozfotou the attire flowed like it was made for him.

* * *

Night had fully grasped the sky by the time the small party entered the city. Despite the illuminating torches fighting off the darkness and guiding their path through the well laid out streets, it remained quiet.

The people were likely wary of the small army which had suddenly emerged at the city gate, Sonos could not blame them for that.

They made their way through the streets rapidly thanks to the grid like pattern of the town and before long they were in what appeared to be a central square. At the heart of the square sat an enormous dolthil tree. The tree had two long branches which uncoiled towards the sky like majestic antlers. An unusual sight this far west. Dolthil trees were not known to grow wild further west than Thelonigul. The tree was more evidence of the influence of Kunpit who was known to have held them in high regard.

Hidden behind the tree was a large and ornate building set back from the rest, perched on a cliff overlooking the sea. The building was lit by so many torches it seemed to be a pool of daylight in amongst the darkness, and now Sonos could hear people and songs and revelry. *The rulers of the city are not perhaps as frightened as the ordinary citizens*, Sonos thought. Their guides led the small party up the brushed white marble steps.

At the rear of the building the group was met by a striking sight. A series of semi-circle marble benches carved into a cliff below them watched over a stage with the sea and sky as a backdrop. Even in the dark of the evening, the theatre was splendid, the immense stage at the heart of Butophulo seemed crude by comparison. Sure, Butophulo's theatre was bigger and its construction more elaborate and expensive, but the elegance of this theatre was something to behold. Positioned as it was, the moon illuminated the crescent shaped stage as it made its journey across the sky, giving the platform a silver glow and an otherworldly quality, as if the performances were a vision gifted by Tholo herself. The high culture here was quite the contrast to the weeks of empty rugged wilderness which the Xosu sellswords had just emerged from.

The marble benches were half filled with men and women dressed in fine clothing of silken togas and chitons, lined with cloth of silver and gold; the ruling elite of the city had turned out to greet their visitors. They were led to the front benches and their guide gestured for them to sit next to a dozen portly men, naming them as the grand council of Rulrup and announcing the fattest man to be Thildol, the High Kuson.

Runu, Thusokusoa, Possosous, Bospitu and Dzotdoz took the seats next to the councillors, whilst Sonos, Pusokol, Kusoasu, Dzulkoten and Hozfotou took a seat on the bench behind. As they sat, torches were lit on the stage, a silence fell amongst the onlookers and actors shuffled into view.

A chorus assembled off to one side, wearing their familiar masks showing the horned visage of the Wildmen, and a small group gathered at the centre of the stage to introduce their performance. Sonos could not remember how long it had been since he had last watched a play, but he recognised the masks of the actors. Xosu and Gelithul's story was a common play. *It will be interesting to see how it is interpreted in Rulrup,* he thought, allowing himself to finally relax. Pusokol would no doubt be captivated; he had always been more of an artist than a soldier.

The lead actor towered over the others, his larger-than-life mask of the bright god, complete with horns and beard, made him a hand taller than the other performers. Even the horns on the mask of Gelithul, Xosu's faithful teacher and companion, were dwarfed. Sonos smiled, the actor playing Gelithul was stumbling all over the stage, aptly already drunk. The actors bowed and the performance began.

The man named Thildol, dressed in a green Xosu style toga trimmed with vermillion that reminded Sonos of the priests of Xosu, was sat next to Runu. He leaned over to speak. As he did the stench of wine and his perfume overwhelmed Sonos, and the jewels which bedecked the fat man clinked together, the gold and amber of his necklace catching the flickering light as he moved. He had a Salxosu look to him, with pale skin and blue eyes, but the effort of leaning over saw a rouge flood over his face. The fringe of what was left of his dark hair crowned the top of his round head and bristled up in two horns, like the feathers of an eagle posturing.

"We thought we would welcome you with a performance. Rulrup may be on the edge of Xosudun, but we our famous for our theatre. I think you will find it intriguing with a depth you have not seen anywhere else, even in Butophulo. Kunpit of Thelonigul, our founder, believed that the whole universe could be explained and perfected by understanding numbers, they are the key to the rhythms of the cosmos. The whole city is built using those principals, and I think you will agree that the theatre has a rather pleasing aesthetic as a result." Thildol paused to take in the spectacle himself, before continuing. He had a jolly and welcoming tone to him, but there was something behind his eyes which made Sonos uneasy, a piercing arrow of a stare that accompanied the laughter,

"Stories of the death of Hunthisonu and the retreat of an army of Xosu from Gottoy reached us a moon past. Since then, we have expected your coming. We have much to discuss, but first please sit back and enjoy the performance."

Runu went to reply but he was interrupted. The performance had begun, and the narration of the chorus brought the audience to the shining palace of the gods, pearl white Dzottgelon. Dunsun, Lord of the Cosmos, placed the infant Xosu, his favoured son, on his throne before leaving the palace, descending to the underworld to continue his affair with Phenmoph's daughter and Xosu's mother, Bosithelon. Dunsun disappeared behind the stage and as he did the torches went out, letting darkness flood over the world.

A scream of terror, or ecstasy, or delight, echoed around the theatre and Sonos felt the hairs on the back of his neck stand on end as a fear rippled through the audience. The torches were lit once again, and the crowd was greeted with a scene of horror. Infant body parts were strewn about the stage. At the centre, on her knees and covered in deep red blood was Tholo, Dunsun's great queen and consort. In her jealous rage she had torn the boy, Xosu, Dunsun's heir, to pieces. Only his heart remained, clutched to her chest. Standing, she raised the heart aloft before casting it down to the depths of the halls of the dead, for Phenmoph to hide from the lord of the world.

Runu took the pause in the action on stage to answer Thildol,

"We are grateful for your aid, and we do not wish to place a burden upon your city for too long. With enough provisions we can return to the White Islands."

The fat ruler replied dismissively as he picked at a bunch of grapes,

"You do not want to go to the Islands. War is coming and nothing good will come of it. Enjoy the play, and we will talk afterwards."

Runu replied with some puzzlement,

"Why is war coming?"

The fat man chuckled,

"You do not know? The White Islands have been stained red with blood; many continue to reject the rule of the Thasotun."

"That was true before we left. Especially since the Doldun backed the coup that brought the Red and White Council to power. The Salxosu wish to rule themselves." Runu replied.

"Ah but now Tekolger is dead."

"He is gone...?"

Thildol chuckled again,

"The twilight lands took him it seems. Tholo's jealously still rages, and she caught up with Dunsun's new child. His generals will fight over the legacy he left them. The Doldun are half-barbarian and that violent side of them always rears its head when power is concerned. The panther cubs will fight over the territory of their sire. No doubt the Xosu will get drawn into any such fight now that the whole world is on offer to the victor. You would do best to stay here with us."

Tekolger is dead. Sonos could not quite believe the words. The King of the Doldun seemed divinely blessed, to the point that he hardly seemed mortal. Indeed, the stories about him whispered that he was the son of Dunsun himself, some semi-divine hero from a by gone age. A clatter on the stage brought their attention back to the performance, shaking Sonos out of his brief dream. Dunsun was stood centre stage having travelled to Mount Betgennon. Gelithul, the drunken Wildman staggered onto the stage alongside his mother, Geli. Dunsun tore from his stomach the heart of Xosu, where he had hidden it from Phenmoph and smuggled it out of the underworld. Entrusting the heart of his son to Geli to be raised and his body reconstituted, with Gelithul as his friend and tutor, Dunsun returned to Dzottgelon. He was needed to cast Sem back into the black depths of the ocean and banish Bul back to the heavens, restoring order back to a world plunged into chaos through his grief.

Thildol refused to answer any more questions until the performance had finished, and so Sonos sat back to watch the play unfold. He witnessed Xosu being raised on the sacred mountain, learning all he could of the wild and uncivilised world as it then was from Gelithul. When Xosu and Gelithul wrestled Zilthil, Tholo's white hydra, to the ground, the crowd cheered and groaned at every victory and set back, applauding as Xosu finally brought the beast low. None cheered louder than Bospitu, especially when the bright god sewed the teeth into the ground and up sprang the first of the Xosu. The audience openly wept as Xosu tore his hair out in madness and grief for his dying mentor, blaming himself for feeding him the fiery fruits of the tree which grew where the blood of the hydra watered the soil, whilst all around the Bulodon raged. The play came to an end as Xosu was cast out from the sacred lands by Kolsinos, the Bulodon's chieftain. Xosu travelled around the world, still half mad, teaching to a primitive and savage realm.

The performance was certainly a different interpretation of the Xosu story, relying more on the visual than the long philosophical dialogues of the plays in Butophulo. The ending had left Sonos wanting more, most plays finished on a high or some resolution, not the suspense of the bright god being cast out into the wilderness.

The audience as one stood and applauded, the captains joined them. Thildol laughed and slapped Runu on the back,

"Not what you expected I can see. The plays in Rulrup leave you asking more questions than the philosophical musing that passes for theatre in Butophulo."

**

Most of the theatre emptied quickly, but the councillors stayed in their seats and waited patiently, and so Sonos and his comrades waited with them. Not a word passed any lips. When the noise of people exiting had died down, Thildol spoke once again,

"I hope you feel welcome here in Rulrup. I will admit I was wary when we heard the news of a large mercenary army heading our way. And the offers of riches from Gottoy to not allow you to enter were very tempting.

But we are nothing if not honourable and practical men, and you are Xosu and kin. You and your men are guests of Rulrup now, my guest-friends no less. Although we will not allow the army into the city. You understand we are still cautious men. But we feel we have a proposition for you which you will find interesting."

Runu spoke cautiously in reply,

"Thank you once again for your generosity and your honourable actions. But I am afraid our men are only interested in returning to their homes. We will of course pay you for any provisions your city provides. With Tekolger dead, we need more than ever to return to the White Islands."

Thildol scoffed at the suggestion, barely even acknowledging it,

"Let me shine a light on the situation for you, my friend. The Doldun still hold Xosupil, a garrison sits on Polriso's high hill and Thasotun still has a grip on the islands, loose though it may be. War is coming, but it is not a war you can win. Returning means only death. And how many will follow you, one, two thousand? You are not all from Butophulo or even Xosupil after all. This would not be enough."

Kusoasu spoke before the others, chewing on the bitter hulthul leaves that he had found on the plain of Beligul,

"What would you suggest we do instead?"

Thildol smiled,

"This man asks the right questions. To the east of Rulrup lies the isthmus of Yil, I am sure you know it."

They all knew it; it had once been the site of a prosperous colony of Butophulo. The resources of the League poured into building the city barely a century ago.

"How could we forget it?" Runu answered, "The legacy of Rupoanos the Navigator. His family were close with mine own. I was raised alongside his grandchild. He spoke often of his grandsire, the only Xosu ever to have sailed beyond the Throat of Sem and travel the realms of the east. But I'd be surprised if there were any Salxosu who didn't know the name and the colony he drove us to build."

Thildol continued,

"Much heart ache and anguish lie in it for us all, I am sure. Rupoanos is not well remembered in Rulrup for many reasons, but there are some things he had the right of. He insisted the potential trade across the isthmus and to the east would have doubled the League's revenues and cut out the Putedun from the eastern trade altogether. In that I think he was right. The great vision of a haven of trade on the isthmus to gather the riches from the east, was a bold plan and should have been worth the risk. I'm sure you know that for a time it was. The colony even reported finding a deposit of zilthum in the area, valuable despite the art of working the ore being lost for centuries."

"Certainly, the League was thriving for that short period that Yil was growing. But we all know what happened next." Runu answered him.

"Do we know though?" Thildol replied.

"We know enough." Runu shot back.

"All we know is that in the year of the dark spring, the year in which Xosu's arrow was seen in the sky, red and angry, and the heavens blackened for weeks in a twilight hue, disaster struck. Just before the gods lifted the veil of twilight that the Arrow had brought, a great storm in the north cut off communications between the League cities for a time. You are too young to know, but I was a youth at the time, and I remember it vividly. Even as close as Rulrup is to Yil, we still could get no word to the city. There was much panic." Thildol's voice for once betrayed some concern as he remembered those days more than thirty summers past.

"In that tempest," he continued, "a fleet bound for Yil carrying newly forged arms from Pittuntik disappeared near the ruins of old Kolbos, and, even after the skies had calmed, Yil stayed silent. When the League dispatched ships to investigate, they found the city a flooded ruin, the land around it broken and reclaimed by the sea. There were no signs of the people, not even their corpses, but some of the sailors claimed that they could hear their shades howling from the depths of Sem's blue ocean.

So, as you say, we know enough to acknowledge it was a disaster, but no one can say exactly what happened there. Oh, there were some great arguments about it, there still are. Even some rather badly written plays have tackled it. Some blamed marauders from the east, others corsairs who they claimed had seized the Pittuntik fleet and used it to attack the city at the behest of the threatened Putedun. But an answer was never found, and few sailors are willing to return to the site. It was the spark that caused the war as well, the war that brought about the League's fall. The cities of the League were already unhappy with the resources being levied from them to build the colony so quickly. With the news of Yil's destruction, Pittuntik, always the most vocal of the League cities, and the most strained by the building of the colony, its famous forges being overworked in the effort, rebelled against Butophulo and the Rinuxosu were quick to lend their support. So, the great war started, the War for the Forge that would end with the destruction of the League and Xosupil ruled by the Doldun. But you know that part.

What I am trying to say is that we have a chance to turn that disastrous past into a bright future. Rupoanos was right, and still is right, a colony at Yil would be perfectly placed to grow rich on the trade with the east. He could not foresee the ruin that was wrought that year, only the gods could have seen that. But let me ask you, what are the chances of such a misfortune striking us a second time?"

"What if the gods were so displeased with us building the colony that they brought about its destruction? Why would we tempt that fate again?" Runu pondered.

Thildol smiled,

"Since the destruction of the colony bandits and brigands and worse have made the ruins their home. The gods have not struck them down. You are an educated man, I know. Are you telling me that you believe it was the gods that brought the colony low and not just some misfortune that not even the divinities had anticipated?" Runu only smiled and indicated Thildol to continue.

"Now these bandits, they regularly raid our ships and even our hinterland. We can patrol the waters constantly, but still some pirates will slip through, and bandits can disappear into the mountains all too easily. Our humble city lacks the manpower to drive the marauders away and occupy the ruins. You would think that the gods would feel that the plague which ravaged our land in the year of the dark spring would be misfortune enough, but the loss of many men from the sickness is still felt. At least until now."

Runu spoke, choosing his words carefully,

"And you are proposing that we do that task for you?"

"I am proposing an alliance. We can supply you with ships, horses, and provisions. Ten thousand men should be more than enough to drive the scum out of the ruins and reclaim them for the Xosu. But the great council of Rulrup is more ambitious than this. We wish to bring some light back to the land. With the settlement in your hands, and with our help, you can re-build the colony, do justice to the vision of Rupoanos and Butophulo. Besides, I would not be much a of a hunter if I could not dominate my own lands, and some of my fellow councillors have the predator's instinct. Competition is the more brutal side of Kunpit's gift to us. Success with this scheme would be of value to me, let's say."

Kusoasu went to speak, but Runu spoke first this time,

"It is a fine ambition and the pain of the loss of the colony is one which cuts us all deep, a tempting offer. But I will have to talk it through with our men, as you say we are not all from Butophulo and some may still wish to return to Xosupil. Besides the rumours that surround the ruins may dissuade the more superstitious in our ranks. So, I cannot make a decision without consulting them."

Thildol's face betrayed nothing of his thoughts. He merely smiled brightly and said,

"Of course, take the time to discuss our proposal with your men. It is this kind of leadership we would wish to see from our ally. As a token of our friendship and goodwill, I would like to present you with a gift, to show our intentions are honourable." The rotund councillor thrust his hand out like an arrow towards a nearby attendant. The slave placed a white-gold object in Thildol's palm. Embedded in a golden jewelled casing was an amulet much like the one Sonos wore, zilthum he knew.

"This amulet was gifted to Rulrup by the people of Yil before it fell, a gift to mark the finding of a deposit of the fabled ore. Apparently, this amulet was found alongside it, although who left it there none now remember, but I am sure you know this story. I present it now to you as a token of friendship." Thildol said, in a solemn way that surprised Sonos. A smile beamed across the councillor's face again as Runu took the amulet and he continued,

"The night is still young, stay a while and tell us of your extraordinary adventure through Thelizum. It must have been quite the journey, worthy of a poem or two I would say. We are all keen to hear how you escaped the armies of Gottoy."

Runu smiled, there was something likeable about the jovial magistrate,

"I am not a bard I am afraid I would not do the tale justice, but Sonosphoskul here my loyal captain is quite the storyteller. Sonos tell our new friends the tale of our adventure."

Sonos was taken by surprise and none too happy about having the attention thrust upon him but keeping the council of the city happy was certainly in the army's interest.

KALASYAR

21

The paranoia of the tyrants was growing everyday as they became more and more convinced a conspiracy against them was afoot. More arrests, more trials, and more exiles and executions. Koseun seemed to be enjoying speculating about what had really happened. He had concluded that far from a conspiracy it was a lone assassin, an idealist looking to restore the old League or a spurned lover out for revenge. *'A bee rejected by the Queen and thus the hive, turned its sting on that it loved best'* was how he put it. He had maddened her again as he explained that it was a more likely version of events but a fact that would yield little evidence and thus cause the tyrants paranoia to increase, not seeming to care about the danger that put him in. The Nine were still rounding up prisoners by the dozen and seizing wealth and property wherever they could, hoarding it all on Polriso's Hill, the only place in the city they felt secure.

Kalasyar tried to ignore the increasing presence of mercenaries in the city. The random searches were a nuisance, and the checkpoints slowed the pace of life down to a crawl, but the public trials and executions she could not push out of her mind. It reminded her of when the Nine first took control of the city and the people had resisted their reforms. She had been a terrified little girl then, maddened by the recent loss of her parents and not knowing what to expect. This time she was a woman grown and knew it would eventually pass. That knowledge was small comfort though, not with her grandfather being such an easy target for the Nine's paranoia. She knew that the tyrants would be watching the Sisosi manse, so she tried to carry on as normal. She was grateful that her grandfather seemed to be heeded her warnings too. He was staying mostly within the lavish villa of the Sisosi. She knew Koseun saw it all as an overreaction with nothing to worry about, but she was pleased that he had at least tried to show he was listening to her. The comings and goings from the villa had increased though. Old friends and new acquaintances came and went with growing frequency. Some were merely to hear the great old man speak and to tell their friends that they had attended one of his symposiums, others came for his advice or patronage. The activity made her nervous.

For a moon's cycle this pattern had continued, and the city began to relax into its new reality, the daily inspections by sellswords becoming an inconvenient part of a familiar routine.

The moon had become full once more, Kalasyar had watched it most of the previous night, praying to The Tulrinoi to keep her grandfather protected. Tholo to offer him her wisdom, Sem for the embrace of a father, and Buto for the energy of youth. As the night passed, the day of Buto's festival arrived, the people of the city would celebrate the sacrifice of the crippled god. The preparations for the festival had suffered from the turmoil, but even the Nine realised that banning the celebration outright would turn the haven of Buto against them completely.

As the sun began to rise that morning, but with the moon's wise gaze still present, Thororoz and Ralxuloz accompanied her to the seashore just beyond the city walls. Despite the early hour a crowd had already gathered, flooding over the fields just beyond the protective ring of the walls. The press was growing thick, even in the space closest to the shore reserved for those of the noblest blood. The sun edged its way above the horizon and lit the calm sea like a burning mirror of the sky above,

"It comes." Thororoz whispered in a voice which sounded worn by age, as she pointed to the city walls. A glint of bronze in the morning sun at the top of the towering walls gave the god away. From this distance looking to be nothing but a small child or even just a lump of red-gold rock, but she knew it to be the statue of the crippled god.

A gasp rippled through the crowd like a wave in the wake of a stone falling in a lake as the statue fell, plummeting into the sea and sending a plume of water towering into the air almost as high as the walls. It was the signal the runners were waiting for. Nine maidens in their first year of flowering set off sprinting to the sea. Naked but for the blue pigment that covered them and made them look like shadows set against the paler sea. It was a rite of passage older than the city itself, tracing its origins back to old Kolbos, but the random lots through which the girls were selected for the honour was perhaps the only hint of the egalitarian ideal of the League still left to the city. It was an honour for which Kalasyar herself had been chosen by the gods to perform. Many years ago, though she remained a maiden still. She could remember the day vividly.

The swimmers reached the eye of the storm, the swirling water where the bronze cast statue had crashed and disappeared into the open eye of the sea. One by one they dived and disappeared below as if venturing into a dark and dangerous cave. The sea grew calm again and an anxiety gripped the crowd. Kalasyar felt Ralxuloz' fingers coil around her arm tensely, like a mother protecting her child. The wait felt like an age, but finally the statue erupted from below the waves and the shining bronze emerged into the white light of the new dawn, the eyes of Buto burning red and fierce as his forge. The crowd erupted with cheer. The gods had deemed the daughters of the Salxosu worthy and gifted them with their quarry.

The maidens drew Buto from the water and raised him up to their shoulders, in imitation of the task the Kinsolsun carried out eons ago. The young girls would carry the statue, glinting red and gold, to the temple of Buto as the wizards of the sea once carried the god himself to safety at the Thelonbet on the site that would one day become old Kolbos. Those of the old blood followed on behind the maidens, carrying gifts for the god when he found his place of rest, as the people of the White Islands, the Salxosu, once did at the Thelonbet.

Crowds lined the way as they walked into the city and along the long straight road known as Xosu's Arrow. Flowers, garlands, and the bounty of the sea were thrown at their feet as offerings, and the crowds cheered as the music of lyre and pipe floated through the air. The sight stirred memories in her of her own time carrying the statue, the pride she felt and the joy, a time before the worries that troubled her now.

The Nine were nowhere to be seen, Kalasyar realised. Like wraiths or shapeshifters, they had all but disappeared from public view. Puskison Posausthison, who had taken it on himself to be minister to all the city's gods when he was lifted to leadership, had presided over the festival every year since the city fell, but this year he had become but a shadow. She at least expected to see Rusoson Rusos, who spoke so often of the need to weld the people of the city back into one. He was the only one of the Nine who had served the League in the war with the Rinuxosu and had taken a terrible wound which had never really healed for his efforts. He had also been the only one of their number who had tried to reconcile with the people. It was wise perhaps to stay away for their own safety, but their absence would be noted.

As Kalasyar made her way up the main thoroughfare, the crowd began to slow and thicken, and she could see the statue disappearing into the distance. A grumble rippled through the crowd. Muffled words of a new checkpoint at the top of the road reached her. She would have to wait. In the distance she could hear the parties that would carry on throughout the day. The wind carried on it the smell of clams and lobster, fish, and mussels roasting. In the past there would have been plays, performance and competitions of singing, dancing, and poetry, but now the Nine would not allow it. Every year the restrictions had grown.

After what felt like and age, the slow tide of people rolled over the checkpoint, each man, woman, and child checked and interrogated. *This is unusual, are they looking for something, or someone?* Kalasyar thought, *too late to turn back now though*. She was upon them.

The grizzled, ruddy faced, old captain at the front of the checkpoint looked her up and down as she approached. He looked less than pleased to be there. It was strange to see such a high-ranking man to be posted at a small checkpoint such as this. The captain motioned for her to come forward and said,

"What is your business here today?" His accent was thick with the sounds of the hill country to the north. At a guess she thought he was from the lands of the Tilxosu near Tusotik. Likely a captain of The Green Goddess's Men, one of the new mercenary companies.

"I am bringing fresh linen and incense as an offering to Buto." She replied, trying to sound as innocent as one of the maidens carrying the statue and not to catch his eye too much. The captain gave his response abruptly in his thick accent as he idly sipped from a cup of red, "You cannot pass without us searching your goods."

Without waiting for a reply, the captain signalled to the two men stood close behind him. Both were fitted in well made linen thorax and bronze grieves, one had a spear in hand as if ready for war, the other a bow slung at his side in the Rilrpitu style. The spearman even wore a Tilxosu style helmet, conical with horns sprouting from the top. The men stepped forward and took the linen and incense from her and began to rifle through it.

"Careful with that!" she said, "Any damage and the god will wish to be compensated."

The sellsword gave her a glance but nothing more. He finished his search and handed the goods back to her.

"May I continue now?" Kalasyar asked, not even attempting to conceal her frustration at being bound to this place, fixing them with a look to turn them to stone.

"Not yet." the captain replied. "I have a few more questions for you." He looked her up and down suspiciously,

"Where will you be heading after your visit to the temple? And more importantly have you seen anything or heard anything that you would consider suspicious or a threat to the Council and the safety of the city?"

"What is this?" Kalasyar replied, she was deeply suspicious now, "Have you questioned everyone who has passed through here so thoroughly?

If you are satisfied that I am not carrying any concealed weapons or whatever it is you are looking for then either let me through or let me head back home." She demanded, with a venom in her voice that hammered home her anger to them. Thororoz placed a hand on her shoulder as if to draw her away.

"I am afraid I cannot let you go until you answer our questions and if you will not answer then you will have to come with me to be questioned properly." The captain replied, taking her by the arm.

"How dare you touch me!" Kalasyar said with a crash, pushing the captain away. Her hand shot out as quick as a striking snake, catching him across his face. The strike echoed and the crowd stopped to watch the incident. The captain went red in the face, as if he were about to burst with rage. His fist clenched, but then a shout sounded from behind.

"Leave her!"

All three men turned abruptly.

Two other men approached, also clad in armour. These men were not Xosu though, not mercenaries. They wore bronze muscled cuirasses embossed with the eight-pointed star of Tholophos. The brilliant deep purple of their horsehair crested helms matched their purple cloaks to show their status as men of the royal household of the Doldun. The strange, accented way they spoke Common Xosu gave them away as men of the clans of the Doldun,

"Leave her be, the general has requested to speak to her personally seeing as you cannot do your job properly."

The captain said nothing, although it was clear that this imposition and subverting of his own authority angered him deeply.

One of the Doldun guardsmen stepped forward and took the linen and incense from Kalasyar, the other took her hand and ushered her through the checkpoint.

* * *

The two soldiers led Kalasyar to the huge bronze doors of the temple. As they approached the eyes of Buto's statue perched on the roof seemed to follow them. She said a prayer under her breath to the crippled god and to his father, the Great God who dwells below.

At the entrance to the temple stood a familiar, and strangely welcome figure. Doltopez, the commander of the Doldun garrison was dressed in much the same way as the two soldiers who accompanied her. A fine purple cloak slung over his shoulders, but in place of the cuirass he wore a simple navy tunic with a white star of Tholophos on its front. He greeted her with a smile. She had to admit to herself that he was not unpleasant to look upon,

"Please accept my apologies for that inconvenience. Had I realised you were there sooner I would have ordered them to let you through. We live through unfortunate times, and the ruling Council must take some hard measures to ensure that peace is maintained. I'm sure that you can understand."

She sarcastically threw back,

"I understand that the Nine are panicking, convinced one of them will be next." Doltopez laughed thunderously at the suggestion, a laugh which made Kalasyar think he would welcome the death of the whole lot of them. "I do not see how searching through the goods I carry will help the Nine find who or what they are looking for and disrupting the festival will serve them even less well."

The general smiled again,

"You are right, they are chasing their tails looking for conspirators everywhere. The checkpoints are more to reassure everyone that order will be maintained. The prisoners a folly perhaps and the property they have seized…well men are greedy creatures."

"There is no plot against them then. Grandfather was right?" The words leapt out uncontrolled, like the sparks from a smith's anvil. Doltopez fixed her with a more serious look and paused for a moment as if considering something intently, a dark cloud coming across his face,

"Sisuhul Polriso was his name. A spurned lover who Dorthil, foolish man that he was, had tired of or had outgrown. I am told that the Polriso family's standing is not high in the city, but their patriarch is an ambitious man. He encouraged the relationship as he thought it would be a way to win the favour of the Rusos family and a higher standing for himself. Especially as Dorthil was close to the king and had travelled with him for a time. Clearly the man was playing with a fire he did not understand." he paused, considering his words, "I find your customs quite strange and difficult to understand."

She tried to explain,

"An older man often takes a handsome youth under his wing to teach him the ways of the world. It is perfectly natural at a young age for a man to look up to his elders and an elder to desire to teach and nurture a youth." She stopped. From an outsider's view the custom did seem a little odd, "But it would be strange for it to continue beyond a certain age, it is a phase of life whilst a man is still learning. If a boy does not grow up and move passed this phase, then they may get jealous and lash out. It has been known even for the elder man to become jealous."

"Strange indeed. We Doldun have no need of this. There are things we all learn from our elders, how to be a warrior, how to rule and govern and how to treat with strangers. But there are things that only a woman can teach you." he paused again and then said dismissively, "This custom is what caused Dorthil's death anyhow. But I cannot rule out a wider plot against the Council. The politics of your city remain very cutthroat even with the fall of the League." Doltopez' voice was low and deep. Turning to the open doors of the temple, he continued, "I understand you were bringing gifts to the temple of Buto as a part of the festival when you were stopped."

She replied, cautiously,

"Yes, linen and incense to please the god."

"Another thing you can teach me about this city then. Buto is not widely worshiped among the Doldun. You can show me the path through these magnificent gates and tell me more about the god and his appeasement."

Doltopez took the supplies from the soldiers and gestured for Kalasyar to go inside. She told her handmaids to wait without. She thumbed the zilthum ring on her finger nervously as she went inside, the symbol of her devotion to the Great God, gifted to her by the oracle of Buto inside the Thelonbet of old Kolbos.

Beyond the bronze doors the temple opened out into a great hall. The dome above provided a spacious feeling to the whole building, even with the thick set, pale hulthul tree which sat in the earth below it, as light was allowed in through the numerous openings around the base of Buto's great dome. In front of the tree, the altar to the god was placed, shrouded by the smoke of burning incense. Above the altar had been placed the statue of the god the maidens had retrieved from the sea that morning, forged in bronze, a skill passed down to man by Buto himself.

The temple had still not returned to normal; the merchants of far-off lands had not yet reappeared in their usual numbers and so the attendants to the temple were reduced to those merchants still in the city and those few festival goers who had been allowed to enter.

Below the altar stood a man robed in fine blue linen, a golden sash around his waist. Kalasyar did not know the High Priest of Buto well but could recognise him by sight. His face carried a horrific scar taken as he led resistance to the Rinuxosu when his village was attacked in the darker days of the war. Despite his wounds, he had always seemed open and friendly to her. She approached the altar, followed closely by Doltopez, who in a hushed rumble of a voice said,

"This building is truly remarkable; Buto's good will must be very important to Butophulo."

"Buto is the protector of merchants and traders as well as the master of the forge. Being a trickster himself and the son of the sea, he is aware of its unpredictable nature. Butophulo has for centuries relied on the sea not only for its wealth and power, but also for its basic sustenance. The city could not have become the sprawling metropolis you see today with the food grown in its hinterland alone. Without the grain we import from Zenbel and Gelmophon we would starve. This means that Buto is the most important of all the Kolithelon for us, without his goodwill there would be no city. Without his aide the founders would not have made it to this place. Without the skills he taught us at the forge and at sea, the knots he invented, we could not trade." She replied.

Doltopez was listening intently,

"We are all Xosu, even the Doldun, but our societies rely on the gods in different ways. The sea has never been important to the Doldun. True the twin sons of Tholophos brought us to our land by sea, and they are still looked to, to protect sailors and fishermen, but the land is where our wealth and power lies. That is why to those in the countryside, Tulo, the green goddess, is important. Without her goodwill the land would not yield its produce to us. But we needs must court favour with Dolkoli for our lands and people are ever exposed to war. Dunsun of course protects all of us and Xosu keeps the flame of civilisation alive and guides us in what can be a wild land. For that he is very widely revered, by the kings most of all as they are the only true descendants of his line left to the world. But it is simpler in some ways to put all your reliance in one of the Kolithelon to ensure your people's survival."

"The Salxosu have always been different from our cousins elsewhere in Xosupil. But we are not immune from the whims of the other gods, and so we revere Buto most, but do not rely on him alone. That would leave the city exposed in ways others are not. Though our approach has brought us immense wealth and fame amongst the Xosu. For instance, the father must always be considered too and the wise mother." She replied beginning to relax in Doltopez's company. *These Doldun are not the savage conquerors from the barbarian north that the learned men of the city claimed them to be*, she thought.

The High Priest washed his hands in the golden bowl which always sat on top of the altar, whispering a prayer to Buto as he sprinkled some of the water at the feet of the bronze cast statue.

"Dear father, it is good to see you once again. I have brought to you offerings for the god on this day of celebration. The general was very gracious in offering to help me." Gesturing toward the nobleman from Doldun she continued, "May I present Doltopez of the Deltathelon, general of the Doldun and commander of the city garrison."

Doltopez stepped forward and presented the linen and incense to the priest, saying,

"I am honoured to be of service, and I must apologise for not attending this splendid temple before now, it was remiss of me."

The priest accepted the gifts,

"The god will be most pleased with your gift. I am Posuaus, tender to the temple and High Priest of Buto, but I am sure Kalasyar here has explained all that already."

Doltopez answered the holy man,

"Kalasyar has explained a great deal to me. I was aware of the importance Buto had to the people of this city, but its extent I had not quite appreciated. More so than anywhere else in Xosudun. A fact I should have known earlier, being the commander of the city's garrison and I am eager to learn more. You should expect to see more of me here Posuaus."

"You would be most welcome; the god is always happy to accommodate supplicants in his temple." Posuaus replied.

The same smile flashed again across Doltopez's face again,

"I will look forward to talking more. But if you would excuse us now, I am sure you are busy, and we do not wish to take up any more of your time."

The priest smiled and bowed his head, handing the linen and incense to an acolyte as he turned to leave. Doltopez faced Kalasyar,

"Your task is accomplished, and you have introduced me to an important aspect of the city. It seems we have both had a productive day, despite that unfortunate incident at the checkpoint."

She still found herself uncomfortable. Pleasant company as Doltopez was, the temple was a private place for her to reflect and she had no hope of attending to the Great God with the Doldun present. Appearing as aloof as possible, she said,

"Indeed, although I would hope not to encounter such a situation again. The day grows old, and I have many duties to attend to before the sun is on its way back down to its rest. I should head home to my grandfather."

"It is not so late in the day; I would invite you back to the Sanctuary on Polriso's Hill. I have an unopened amphora of the finest Gelodun red, mellow, sweet, and rich. I would share some with you and discuss more of the city's culture and history." Doltopez replied.

She was tempted to accept; she had always enjoyed the conversations with her grandfather about the history and culture of the Xosu. The way he lit up as he talked endlessly about the deeds of the heroes and the growth of civilisation as it triumphed over chaos and barbarism always brought a smile to her face. It also would be good to see the Sanctuary again, the view over the city was spectacular from up there, not that she had been able to go up since the garrison was installed. She had only been in her tenth year when that happened.

But what would people say, she thought. Butophulo's markets were terrible places for rumours and gossip to spread. She could not accept, the rumour alone would be humiliating, never mind being brandished a traitor by those who still longed for the old days. She could not do that to her grandfather. *Was this what the Great God was warning her of?* she wondered. The words of Sipenkiso were echoing in her head as well, this is your route to power, to protect your grandfather. *No, she could not do it,*

"Another time. I really must go to my grandfather; he will be worried that I have not returned when I usually do." Kalasyar finally replied. It felt like the right decision.

"Very well, at least allow me to give you an escort to your villa. My men will see to it that you do not get stopped at any more checkpoints." Doltopez insisted. She nodded in agreement, at least she would not have to suffer at the hands of some poorly mannered band of mercenaries again.

***

One of the two Doldun guardsmen Doltopez assigned to escort her, Kelanson of the Zelkalkel he named himself, offered his horse to Kalasyar. She mounted awkwardly with his help, not used to riding, and the man then took hold of the horse to guide it.

The second man, Kelankatha of the Zelrsaloz, as far as Kalasyar could tell, the younger and lower ranked of the two, rode alongside. Thororoz and Ralxuloz, were left to walk behind. They had always been wary of the Doldun, and she could tell they were uncomfortable walking with them, but the two soldiers were courteous enough.

Progress was slow through the city. The men took her by the southern route, around the market and Polriso's Hill. It was longer, but Kelanson assured her that it would be quicker as there were less people and checkpoints. He seemed to be proved right as they only encountered two groups of Xosu mercenaries. The first were Silxosu from The Company of the Sacred Land and the second from The Green Goddesses men. As they made their way through the winding streets of the city, the mercenaries waved the Doldun men passed but eyed them jealously as they did. Kelanson paid them no mind. The man liked to talk, and so she let him speak about his homeland, which he clearly missed more than he would let on.

"My father was the chief of our village up in the hills." The earnest guardsmen said. A fact Kalasyar could tell by his heavily accented and not quite fluent use of Common Xosu. The image of the mountain village and rolling plains of Doldun was a stark contrast to the winding streets of the crowded city, two very different worlds. Although closer to a barbarian than a Xosu, she had to admit that Kelanson had a certain sophistication to him that many city dwelling Xosu lacked.

"I am the youngest of his many sons and spent much of my youth tending to the village's herds, but there was little hope for me to become a village chief. Four strong and competitive brothers saw to that." Despite being the senior of the two, she guessed Kelanson had seen no more than twenty summers.

"So, I journeyed to the king's palace and joined the army, a year earlier than was required. I was seeking to join king Tekolger on his adventure. But the army was thousands of leagues away, deep in the mountains of Kelandel. I was posted to garrison Xosupil instead."

It seemed Kelanson was eager to tell her his whole life story. Kelankatha on the other hand stayed silent, casting a wary eye over the people. Whether they were mercenaries, citizens, or foreigners, he seemed to have no trust in any. Kalasyar could not blame him, the Doldun were hardly welcome in the city they occupied. Fear of the Nine and the retribution of a vengeful Doldun were the only things that kept many from tearing the garrison limb from limb.

Despite being able to pass the checkpoints easily, the journey seemed to take longer than she had hoped for. Kelanson insisted on walking her himself and so the slow pace along an unfamiliar route continued. Resigning herself to this, she decided to question Kelanson about Doltopez,

"Your commander seems eager to learn about our city." She suggested.

"Yes." he agreed, "The general is a very inquisitive man. He even asked about my clan when I was first posted to his personal guard."

"About your clan? But is he not of the Doldun too?"

"He is of the Deltathelon. I see you do not know my homeland."

"Please tell me more." Kalasyar was beginning to understand why her grandfather loved to play the questioner.

"The men of the coast, the Deltathelon we call them, are newcomers to our lands, and yet they treat the other clans as of lesser status, only slightly better than the Zummosh." Kelanson explained. His accent made his forming of the Common Xosu words sound laboured.

"Why do they treat you in that way?" She inquired. Kelanson started to explain enthusiastically,

"Doldun is a kingdom that Tholophos' twin sons and their descendants forged. The Deltathelon are the people who came with the twins, fleeing the Dusk that was falling, but the clans already inhabited the land. We are the older people; we settled the land during the time of the bright god. In fact, it was Xosu who gave us the land. The clans and the twin's people, we fought well together to hold back the Dusk. But since then, we have always squabbled. The Deltathelon are jealous of our pedigree and so like to pretend they are the more sophisticated people. We clansmen resent their attempts to lord it over us. Sometimes this means we fight each other."

"Ah, so you are another tribe of Xosu then, a fifth tribe perhaps. Not remembered since Xosu ascended and his sons split. My grandfather would enjoy learning this." Kalasyar exclaimed, joining Kelanson's enthusiasm.

"I suppose so, though we are the original Xosu. The other tribes have lost their way. Kelanson continued, sounding almost like her grandfather. "This is why the general surprised me. All I had heard of the Deltathelon was that they looked down on us clansmen, but Doltopez did not. He tried to understand me. You should answer his questions, he is an open man and will listen to what you say."

Kalasyar nodded thoughtfully as Kelanson continued to recount to her the story of how the twins and Phalazkon the Unifier created the kingdom of the Doldun.

Eventually they snaked their way into the Kobon. The sky was just beginning to turn from blue to navy, a lone star had risen on the horizon before the moon.

Something is wrong, why are there sellswords lining the street?

"They are supposed to be done already." Kelankatha said frustratedly.

In that moment she knew what was happening. Kalasyar kicked the horse on before Kelanson could stop her. She galloped up to the house just as her grandfather was being led outside by a group of Xosu mercenaries. She dismounted, shouting,

"Stop! He has done nothing!"

She dismounted and tried to run to her grandfather, but an arm grabbed her. Kelankatha appeared and held her back. She screamed and fought but could not get out of his grasp. Her handmaids rushed forward in her defence, but Kelanson blocked their path. Koseun looked up, realising the distress of his granddaughter he shouted back,

"Do not worry my child, they have done me no harm and I will be back before you know it. I just have to clear up this misunderstanding."

With that the group of soldiers marched off, taking Koseun and Rolmit toward Polriso's Hill. Kelanson caught up to her and tried to speak, but Kalasyar, unable to contain herself, pushed him away and fled into the house.

ZENUKOLA

22

Supo of the Dolozolaz was a decade or more younger than Zenukola. The two old comrades had fought many times together, their partnership first formed decades ago during the civil war which plagued the kingdom under Kenkathoaz. The Dolozolaz were one of the few clans to have stayed loyal to the king throughout his reign. The Dolozolaz and the Zelrsaloz had provided the horsemen to add mobility to the formidable infantry force Kenkathoaz created. Supo had played an important role in that, leading the men of his kin from the outset. After those times, the pair had vowed never to let the kingdom fall so far again. With the stakes higher than ever, Zenukola was feeling the pressure to fulfil that vow.

Supo was in his fifth decade but fitter than many men half his age. Zenu had seen more than sixty summers and no longer had the strength of a warrior. His mind was still sharp though and he was determined to wield it to keep the empire whole. *It is a partnership that reflects the kingdom as it should be,* Zenu thought to himself. *The clans providing the muscle and the manpower and the Deltathelon the leadership.*

The two men strode through the governor's palace in Yorixori. Zenu in a Xosu style toga as befitted an old and wise councillor, despite the difficulty he had wearing the garment with one arm, and Supo in his riding leathers, ready for the road and the battle with the Rilrpitu which lay ahead.

Although Kelbal and the other Companions had proved more stubborn than Zenu had hoped for, he had managed to convince Kelbal of the need to send Supo and Kalu with reinforcements to Dolzalo. Better still, the introduction of the Xortogun had been as effective as Supo had claimed it would be. The army was refusing to obey orders and that meant Kelbal had no choice but agree to send Kalu with Supo and Zenu's guards alone. The White Shields would stay behind. Persuading Kalu and Kelbal of the importance of sending the column despite the munity had been the easy bit of that manoeuvring.

Kalu's dispatch north would mean Kelbal would be isolated and Zenu would have the space he needed to initiate the actions to save the empire. With the army in revolt, the Companions would soon begin to feel the need to choose which loyalty mattered more, to Kelbal or to each other and the empire. The time to act had come.

Breaking the silence, Zenu said to his old comrade,

"Leave Dolzalo and Palmash to deal with the Rilrpitu. They are no more than a band of savages and should not be too much trouble once cornered. You must focus on Kalu, make sure he is not able to return and aid Kelbal."

Supo nodded and replied. He had been quieter than usual, but Zenu put that down to an anxiousness towards the tasks he would soon face, an anxiety that Zenu himself was not immune to.

"The battlefield is a dangerous place, our fate there is in the hands of the gods." Supo paused, "It will be unfortunate to lose a leader of Kalu's quality, we will need such men to help control this empire." Supo stopped again, there was a restlessness to him, like the sea before an oncoming storm. "It is here that the trickier task lies though. No matter how isolated, Kelbal will not be overthrown easily."

Zenu knew this to be true, even with the army refusing to obey orders. Supo always had an incisive insight. But Kelbal was still behaving like an absolute monarch, issuing orders from his secluded palace rooms. Not to mention the frequent arguments he was having with the rest of the Companions. He was vulnerable. Zenu answered,

"I don't mean to overthrow Kelbal, not yet. With Kalu out the way, I can convince the others that Kelbal is acting the western tyrant and not in the spirit of the Doldun. The last king to act this way was murdered by his noblemen and the Companion system established to hold the monarch in check. One man from each of the twelve clans to advise and check the worst instincts of the king, it was about the most civilised thing the clans have ever done. I will remind them and Kelbal of that. The feeling amongst the Companions of unease is already there I just need to stoke it. With them at my back we can force Kelbal to listen. We will usurp the power not the man. I will take his place as regent and ensure things are done properly. Sooner or later Kelbal will become an isolated figurehead that we can quietly remove with no protests. In time we may even be able to find proof of his guilt once we put the Xortogun to the question."

Supo was listening intently,

"We cannot spill blood. That would only cause a rift which could never be healed. But that means we will require a longer transition than we had hoped for, maybe even several years. With Kelbal still around, he will always be a rallying point for future challenges for the throne. Perhaps there is another way to do this?"

"I know, but we are left with little choice." Zenu answered swiftly, his phantom fingers grasping. He had thought the same himself but could see no other way to prevent Kelbal's worst instincts coming to the fore, and he was more convinced than ever now of the man's complicity in Tekolger's death. There could be no other explanation. "The bonds between the men are too great and it is blinding them to the danger to the empire. A few difficult years is still better than over a decade of Kelbal as regent and the Xortogun child inheriting the throne."

Both men grew silent as they left Zenu's residence, keenly aware that anyone overhearing their conversation put them at risk. Supo looked away and stared pensively into the distance, as if contemplating the new beginning that lay in front of him. It was an awkward silence, understandable though, neither of the men were acting out of desire but out of duty.

In the square that the entrance to the governor's palace opened out on to was gathered the cavalry force that was to be sent to aid Dolzalo. Five hundred horse drawn entirely from Zenu and Supo's guards with no loyalty to their new commander. At their head Kalu was already sat upon his charger, ready and eager to get on the road. Zenu embraced his old friend and said,

"Gods be with you."

A horse was brought to Supo by one of his guardsmen. Supo mounted the animal and rode to the front of the column. Exchanging a word with Kalu, he raised his arm and the column sprung into life.

***

Zonpeluthas had turned out to see the reinforcements off. He had been agitating for the command ever since the messengers from Thuson had first arrived. The young Companion had wished Kalu luck for the campaign, but Zenu knew it was done behind gritted teeth. Zonpeluthas was the youngest and least experienced of the Companions, of great noble stock and desperate to prove his valour.

Zenukola approached the boy who, despite his age, having seen no more than twenty-three summers, was still an experienced veteran having fought in Zenian and then as a Companion in Kelandel and Zentheldel. Although the fine robes he wore now made him seem more court musician than seasoned warrior. The tortoise shell lyre, crowned with arms of oak, he habitually carried, a gift from Tekolger, did nothing to dissuade the image. Zenu said in the most paternal manner he could muster,

"I would imagine you wish you were going with them, Zonpeluthas. A man such as yourself should be itching for chances at glory."

The young Companion took the bait and replied,

"Unfortunately, Kelbal felt the command needed someone with the experience of Kalu, but I will not lie I am eager to test myself in the field once again."

He continued with the paternalistic approach. The boy was keen and ambitious but seemed to crave the guidance of a father figure. Zenu put his hand on the young man's shoulder and said,

"There will be plenty of opportunities for you to test yourself in the coming years, I am sure. You must accept the thread laid before you by Yulthelon rather than pull against it, otherwise a divine retribution will await you, punished like Kolgophoas. You still have long years ahead of you to prove yourself, and from what I hear you have already forged a reputation from your actions on the field in Zentheldel. No doubt your clan has seen nothing like you before, forging a reputation to make them proud."

The young man looked pleased to gain some recognition. A smile sung its way over his face as he brushed his long hair aside. He had the look of the clans about him, but his hair was a shade darker than was typical, closer to black than bronze. He answered,

"I am glad that my efforts have been noticed, it is an honour to hear such words from you. But I am eager to do more. Unfortunately, Kelbal doesn't seem to have the same confidence in me."

There was a sad melody to the boy's voice. Zenu flashed a smile in a way that tried to look sympathetic toward the androgynous youth,

"Kelbal has a hard task governing this vast empire. But he is foolish not to use someone with your talents, a gift for song that could charm even the rocks is a useful skill for a statesman. The problem is that he is anxious to keep the power close to himself, understandable but it has annoyed the other Companions as well."

A cloud of words that concealed the truth. Zonpeluthas nodded,

"It is not how the kings of the Doldun are expected to behave, even Tekolger treated us as equals and Kelbal isn't even a king. Is it not the role of the Companions to advise the king and share in his decision making?"

Zenu laughed like thunder,

"I'm glad we are all of one mind on this issue. You are correct, it is our duty to the kingdom to remind Kelbal of his obligations to the Companions. You know what happened to king Kenthelonu the second don't you?" Zonpeluthas nodded but did not look completely sure. *Maybe the Kelawath only teach their children music and not history.* Zenu continued,

"Black Tongue the clans called him, maybe you know him by this name. He was king when Yoruxoruni invaded Xosupil. He played a duplicitous game, siding with the great king of Xortogun, but secretly sending aide to the Xosu. It was an action which gained him great support and power the kings of the Doldun had not experienced before. For perhaps a year or more it seemed that he would rise to lead all the Xosu. But then the power and success went to his head, he thought himself a god. As Yoruxoruni's forces retreated, he tried to assert his control over the whole region claiming the credit for the victory and began to govern with an iron fist.

As his behaviour became more and more tyrannical, his nobles banded together in secret and killed him, placing his infant son on the throne, and appointing a man from each of the twelve clans as his advisers. These where the first Companions of the king and ever since their role has been to advise, but also to check the power of our monarch.

I will not have the kingdom descend back into the weakness it was gripped by when I was your age, the clans defiant, the royal court weak and ignored. It took great strength, energy, and blood on behalf of myself and Kenkathoaz to bring order back to the Doldun. With your support, I could ensure we do not head down that path again, bring the power that Kelbal has taken for himself back to the Companions again."

For a moment Zonpeluthas looked at Zenu with suspicion, but the naivety of youth sung through,

"You would have my support in that Zenukola. We would all like to see the empire governed properly."

"Good, and no doubt when the power is divided again there will be some important appointments to be made. I am sure Kelbal will want to keep Kalu close by, as an advisor. So, the White Shields will need a new, young, and vigorous commander." Zenu said in a low rumble. With that suggestion the light behind Zonpeluthas eyes reached a fiery crescendo. The youth tried to hide his ambition.

"I am sure whoever was gifted that honour would be very grateful and would give their full support to whoever it was that honoured them so." Zonpeluthas said attempting to be tactful. Zenu smiled,

"What can you tell me of the events around Tekolger's death? It is important we discover exactly what happened, for the sake of the empire."

Zonpeluthas looked taken aback by that question, as Zenu had hoped. *The surprise should make him more honest,*

"Very little if truth be told. I am a Companion, but not as trusted as the others yet. All I know is that he fell ill after our victory celebration and never recovered. Dolzalo claimed that Talehalden had poisoned him, but how he would know that I cannot say."

Zenu did not suspect the boy of complicity in the king's death. He had little to gain and probably lacked the tact and gall to carry it out,

"And what can you tell me of the events of that evening. I am told there was a cup?"

Zonpleuthas nodded,

"Yes, some Putedun traders arrived at our camp with gifts and wine. We purchased it all and drunk it that night. The cup was a gift and a jest brought by one of the men, a Companion I should think. It was passed to Tekolger by Talehalden if I remember correctly, but it came along a line through a busy hall. It was Thuson Kosua I believe who handed the cup to Talehalden, but it was a crowded room, and I did not see where the cup came from."

Zenu nodded and gave the Companion a final pat on the shoulder as he left. It would seem the key to Tekolger's death lay in the cup, but none of the king's Companions were observant enough to identify who brought the object. It would have to be someone who knew the Sinasa well and knew how Tekolger would react. It would be of great use if Zenukola could locate the cup itself, but he had so far failed to do so. In the confusion after the king fell ill, the cup seemed to have disappeared, or the murderer took it.

* * *

He found Zela as expected amongst his men. The Companion was well liked amongst Tekolger's infantry and could become indistinguishable from them when he chose to. The men even talked to him as one of their own. *Typical of the clansmen, no conception of nobility.*

His clan, the Zelkalkel, was famous for its pride in its poets and its reputation for charm and diplomacy, *although that had not stopped them taking arms against Kenkathoaz*. But Zela had always been loyal to Tekolger and had shown himself to be somewhat open to overtures on the march to Yorixori. *Any approach to Zela must be done carefully though. Zela is as sharp as a spear and blind to little.* If there is a conspiracy reaching beyond Kelbal and the Xortogun, then Zela was almost certainly involved, although his quarrel with Kelbal would seem to suggest otherwise. *Zela also knows about the accusations against Dalzenu now.* He may not prove to be so open if he suspected Zenu's hand in that affair. Another dirty game which Zenu had taken no pleasure in. His phantom fingers clenched as he approached the Companion.

The quarrel with Kelbal was still fresh in everyone's memory and so Zela would likely be the most open to persuasion in this moment, he reasoned. The backing of the infantry that Zela could bring would be useful in any power struggle, and if the Companion had any hand in Tekolger's death, getting close to him would be the only way to discover the truth.

Zela was sat amongst the men taking their morning meal. Laughing and joking with his comrades. He did not seem to be traumatised by his dispute with Kelbal and it appeared that the mutiny of the men only went so far.

As he often was, Zela was telling a bawdy tale to the soldiers, a roar of laughter went up as Zenu got closer. *A good sign,* he thought. If Zela was still close to his men despite the mutiny, distancing him from Kelbal would be easier.

The soldiers, always respectful of their elders, quickly cleared a space for Zenukola to sit and offered him food, another good sign, the men still held him in high regard. Zenu took a piece of the bread he was handed and a small bowl of olives dripping with oil, and spoke,

"I heard what happened between you and Kelbal."

Zela looked at him. The summery grin still crowned his face, but the smile behind his eyes was replaced with melancholy. After a pause, he answered,

"Kelbal was out of line, but he was drunk."

"So, he didn't insult you then? You do not blame him for all that has happened? All is forgiven?" Zenu came back quick, keen to pressure Zela into a response, aware of his clan's reputation and not willing to allow him time to think in this duel of words. There was a reason the men called him Spear Tongue. The young Companion replied,

"No, I have not forgiven him, but it was an argument over the past and a disagreement over Tekolger's legacy, nothing more. We both want what is best for the empire."

Zenu carried on eating and nodded his head,

"You have no complaints then about Kelbal's actions as regent?"

Zela laughed and a smile lanced its way over his face. He was intelligent so Zenu figured there was no point being indirect with him,

"I have been blind to some of his more extreme behaviours perhaps." he replied cautiously, "Where are you going with this Zenu?"

"Some of the others are concerned with Kelbal's performance as regent. They say he is not a king and yet he acts as an absolute monarch, like the tyrants of Xortogun, parading around in that robe and indulging like the god-kings before their fall. He even keeps that pet of his from Zentheldel too close. The kings of the Doldun are the first among equals not god

-kings." Zenu replied bluntly, hearing a ripple of agreement from the nearby men.

"And you think this as well Zenu?" Zela inquired, skewering his way to the heart of the issue.

"I am concerned that the power is too much for Kelbal. I think we may need to step in and remind him of his duties. You know the history of the Companions and what your role is of course." Zenukola replied.

"Say I was to agree with you. How would we go about reminding Kelbal?" Zela answered. Happy that he was getting to the man, Zenu said,

"I feel it has reached a point where the Companions would have to take the power that Kelbal has usurped from them back. Kelbal is regent, that seems to have been Tekolger's wish, but the power should be exercised with the agreement of the foremost men of the Doldun, as it always has been. That way we can ensure that the blunders that have happened are not repeated, and we can reverse some of the damage. Even make sure all Tekolger's loyal Companions are properly rewarded, there are governorships which need to be distributed."

The smile briefly crept up Zela's face again before he hid it from Zenu. *He will go far,* Zenu thought to himself. Finishing off the heel of bread and the olives he had been given, Zenu stood and said,

"Think on it, but not too long, we will need to act soon before more damage is done. Tekolger's legacy is something that needs to be protected and nurtured." Zela nodded in agreement and Zenu continued, "What do you know of Kuso's cup?" An abrupt question, but if Zela were as intelligent as he liked to pretend, he would understand,

"I am blessed Kuso's cup, rich wine good for drinking, take gulps long and deep. My knowledge is what you seek, beware madness that will creep." Zela replied. Zenu looked at him quizzically. "It is what was written on the side of the cup given to Tekolger on the night he fell ill. A quote from Riso of the Tilxosu's poem. I assume that is what you are inquiring about, Zenu?" Zela continued, hitting the mark with his javelin. Zenu was almost impressed.

"Then you know what happened that night? Who may have been responsible for Tekolger's death?" Zenu asked, his phantom fingers grasping at the prospect.

"It is a puzzle I have been trying to solve myself, truth be told.

Talehalden handed him the cup, but Dolzalo is hot headed and wrong. Talehalden was merely the pawn. I believe it was Thuson who handed Talehalden the cup, but I do not see what he had to gain by the king's death. His position was entirely down to the king's patronage." Zela replied thoughtfully.

"Revenge for the destruction of the League of Butophulo? He is a man of that great city." Zenu suggested, not quite believing that himself.

"I do not think so. Why would he have waited for almost twelve years to take revenge, plenty of other opportunities had presented themselves. Besides, Thuson is not a typical man of Butophulo. He is a follower of Kunpit and a man with a vision of what he thought Tekolger could achieve. The cup was given to Thuson by someone else, I am sure of that and whoever that was is likely the poisoner. There were plenty of servants handing out drinks who had the opportunity, but they were all men of Zentheldel. The Putedun traders who brought the wine were there, filling cups. It could have been any of them. But it is the cup that bothers me. I do not see how men of Zentheldel or the Putedun would know the story of Kuso's cup and have had the opportunity to have such a device made. The complicated mechanism in the cup, it was able to appear as if it refilled itself, makes me think this was a well-conceived assassination long in the planning and execution." Zela explained. Zenu was listening intently. *If Zela was involved then he is a convincing liar*, he thought, *and what he says makes sense.* Zenu said,

"I fear we have both come to the same conclusion then. I only hope the perpetrator was not someone in our midst now. Think on what I have said here Zela."

With that Zenukola left, satisfied that he had done his work well.

* * *

Heading back to the palace, Zenu found Thazan consulting with several of his commanders, as always diligent in his labours. Not wanting to cut in, Zenu hung back, waiting for the Companion to finish so that he could talk to the man in private.

Thazan is a tricky prospect, stern and solemn as he is with a fearsome reputation for his sense of justice, but his clan had its pride and its need to feel listened to. There is leverage in that. As the captains shuffled off toward the exit, Zenu gestured for Thazan to follow him, saying,

"How are the soldiers? They seem in surprisingly good spirits."

The priestly man smiled, displaying the white crowns of his teeth,

"They are on the surface. The integration of the Xortogun was tough on them and they feel guilty about refusing to obey orders, but their resolve is strong. I can't talk them down. I don't wholly disagree with them if I am to be honest."

"I will talk to Kelbal. He seems to have locked himself away, but he will have to address the men sooner or later. The longer this goes on the weaker we become. News has not leaked out beyond Yorixori yet, but no doubt we will face rebellions if the lords of Zowdel learn of the army's refusal to obey orders. Thorgon of Yorotog is ambitious and duplicitous even if he calls himself Oathmaker. He would jump at the first chance to cast off the Doldun." Zenu replied, "And how are you feeling about the Xortogun? You had some reservations." He continued.

Thazan took his serious look now, standing like a stout staff and grinding his white teeth,

"It was Tekolger's will, but to speak frankly, it was not Kelbal's decision to make. He is right we will need the manpower and in the long run it may be the only way to pacify the whole empire. But Kelbal overstepped his authority, he is not the king, and we all know why the Companions exist. Surely now we should be exercising our judgement more than ever."

"I feared as much. The others are of a mind with you, they feel that the institution of the Companions is being ignored. Kelbal is pushing the boundaries of his authority too far, and he walks around dressed as a Xortogun king. It is unsettling and I fear belies his ambition." Zenu said, feeling free to speak his mind.

"The others will look to your lead Zenu, they all respect your opinion, even Kelbal does. What can we do?" Thazan answered solemnly.

"We must stand united and make Kelbal remember he is not a western tyrant or even king of the Doldun. The king of the Doldun is always the first man among equals. We must take back the power that Kelbal has taken for himself." Zenu answered assuredly.

With some suspicion Thazan said,

"The Companions will not stand for a coup Zenu."

Zenu rumbled a laugh to ease the tension. That remark alone answered Zenu's next question for him. He found it hard to believe that Thazan would be involved in a plot to murder Tekolger. *Perhaps he was looking in the wrong places for more culprits? He had his man in Kelbal no doubt.* He replied,

"No one is talking of a coup. I lived through too many coups and civil wars to want to return to that. We stand together in front of Kelbal and tell him he cannot exercise power absolutely. He must consult us on his decisions."

Thazan stopped walking and thought for a second,

"If the others agree with you, then you have my support. These are difficult times, and we must stay united." He turned to leave, but as he passed by the old general, he said, "I will have no part in any coup Zenu, be careful."

SANAE

23

A flash of red rippled over her, then a burst of light sent rivers of flame now white, now black, now red covering the entire sky. A horn sounded and the rumble of a thousand thousand hooves echoed as the wild scene unfolded. At the centre of the burst of flame, the red king emerged enthroned, descending from his heavenly realm, swooping like an eagle. Three times he raised his arms; three times the flames went forth. At his feet there lay an iron black rock slick with streams of blood or the wine dark waters which the world floated upon, scattered around him were the fallen corpses of horned men. He stood again and raised his arms. At his feet knelt another, of red and azure, who placed nine bloody horned skulls, bone pale, but alive like the ocean, with fangs protruding like swords, on the iron black rock and in return received a crown of black and gold. But the red and azure hero roared when he sighted the fallen corpses of the horned men. He stood in a mad rage and struck down the red king with one swift arrow from a bow flashing of white and gold. Then he led his people to wander in the west as clouds closed in all around them.

The red king's body fell, sweet and bloody, onto the black rock and from it burst a dolthil tree. It grew and grew, and she knew. Soon the tree covered the whole of the sky, its branches stretching their long grasping arms across the world, celestial light shining through the leaves as they blew in the warm wind and Sanae felt their power. Then she saw the face again, the red face. Eyes aflame and the black tongue. The power of the celestial light had a wild and dangerous edge she knew. Closer and closer it came but never seeming to move, the mouth closing as if to speak…

Awooo!

A horn bellowed and the image before her shattered and the sea came rushing in to carry her to another place. She found herself on an open plain, the wind rushing over her.

Awooo!

The horn bellowed again and out of a huge dolthil tree to her front danced a troupe of creatures, half man, half goat, all with flowing mains and antlers on their heads. Each one carried a horn or pan pipes as they stumbled forward. In their midst was a creature towering over the rest, tall with pointed ears. Although bald on top of his head, he still had the remains of a flowing auburn mane now running to grey, his stag like antlers even bigger than the rest. With a pot belly, thick lips, and a squashed nose, he carried a horn in one hand and a wine skin in the other, eyes as green as the wood. Gelithul, she knew.

As he drew closer to her, she could see rings of amber around his arm and neck, and a scar that arrowed along his cheek. The procession stopped and Gelithul stepped out from the crowd to approach her. The others forming a chorus like in a theatre,

"Oh! Oh! Oh!" They chanted as Gelithul theatrically bowed before her, swaying slightly as he did.

"Sweet child, we bring you gifts of wine and song." His voice was rasping like the wind and the wild, but it had a certain lyrical quality to it.

"Sweet gifts they are indeed, but at what price? Such things come from a cruel bargain, cruel indeed. No more can we run and feast and frolic in a free and untouched paradise, not once touched by the celestial light. Oh! civilised life is a poisoned bargain indeed. Far better not to pass such a burden on, but to live and die and let memory of us scatter like leaves in the wind. Or perhaps not?"

He drunk deep of his wine skin, the rich red liquid dripping down his throat. "Drink with me, sweet child, the rich wine of the dolthil fruit." He offered her the skin. Sanae stood, open mouthed, she could feel the blood pumping around her face. The sense in her told her not to drink and she shook her head.

"You dream the dreams of old I am told! You see glimpses of the celestial realm come to our own. The blood of the god flows in your veins, the blood of the heavens, find your blood and you will find your home. Imagine the delight. No! the ecstasy you will feel with the epiphany which comes from the power of the god. Drink the drink and taste the wisdom of Gelithul!"

This time she accepted and drank deep.

Visions flashed fast and furious before her eyes. A great white hydra lay on the poisoned ground, broken, toppled from its glory. A crippled woman in its midst maddened by the world, nine blue shadows at her back and a wanderer at her side. In a tower touching the heavens, twelve godlike men sat and argued over the sweetest portions of a pale white bull. Each received a choice serving but coveted what the others had. They fought tooth and nail and then the tower crumbled. Far away she then flew, far to the north. The drums of war beating as a cloud gathered around a lord of horses who gazed hungrily south. A young maiden in a robe pulled down over her eyes, sat at top a golden throne, flanked by an androgenous warrior carrying a vicious looking blade, a wise old man with a fiery torch whose tendrils grasped towards the heavens like so many arrows and a young king who prowled behind her. Three times the girl threw her head back in a cry of ecstasy, three times her eyes blazed. The heat of them felt like piercing arrows against Sanae's face. A sweet smell accompanied her and drew men and women and beasts towards her. At her feet, the ground was slick with blood or wine, kings and generals, queens, and common people, all came to seek her advice.

Now, so close to her that she could feel the heat begin to blister her skin, she saw a raging fire, a great tree loomed over her all ablaze. Wildmen surged about in a panic and a fury whilst a terror of a horse galloped off into the distance lit only by moonlight.

Sanae woke in a cold sweat, for a moment unsure where she was, or even who she was. Slowly she came to her senses, but, although she knew she was safe in Xosu's temple, the sense of fear and imminent danger still lingered. She could still feel the heat of the flames, as if they were brushing against her face. Three times she blinked and shook herself before the feeling started to ease.

Dawn's rosy fingers were creeping into the temple, or at least that was what she thought at first. Still coming to her senses. She got up and went to the window, it was then that she realised that the light was coming from the south. She leant out and looked east, dawn's fingers were still dipped in the calm, wine dark sea. Only a single star lit up the otherwise empty, red sky. She looked south again; the light flickered just in front of the southern horizon. *Fire,* she thought. Sanae rushed back to her bed and scrambled to get dressed.

She darted through the great hall, passed the altar with the blood of last night's sacrifice being scrubbed off the polished black stone. The city was basking in the morning light as she made it to the river. She found a man to aid her crossing over to the south bank. She could smell the sweet smell of burning wood. She rushed into the central square of the Zummosh village to find chaos flooding through it. People darting about wildly left, right and centre, some just sat on the floor in despair. In the square there was nothing but destruction, a cataclysm transforming the once tranquil village.

At the top of the hill, the Zummosh great hall had smoke pouring out of its roof, more smoke than the great hearth at its centre could produce. As she got closer, she could see that it was not just smoke pouring out, the building was ablaze and the tree behind was basking in the fire.

The flames roared with an intensity which Sanae had never seen, for a moment she felt like she was dreaming again, her mind galloping over the open plains of the void between worlds. Some men were running back and fore, from the building to the riverbank, gathering water in buckets and attempting to quash the flames. She did not know how they could bear to get so close.

Her eyes darted back and fore, following the figures charging about. *Please no*, she thought, *please not them*. A few desperate moments passed as she looked for Lulpo and Palon her eyes scanning the village, back and fore, back, and fore, back, and fore. Through the thick smoke she saw a silhouette of a small-framed girl. *That must be her,* she thought. Sanae ran over to find her friend covered in soot and dust, but alive, her mother too was close by.

"Thank the god." She said, feeling the relief a mother must feel having found a lost child. "I had a dream; I saw the flames and just ran over. I didn't know what to do, thank the gods you are ok." Sanae said without drawing a breath. Lulpo, in a much calmer manner than she could muster, replied,

"We are ok. The building was empty fortunately. I think they knew that. This was meant as a warning."

"Who knew it?" Sanae answered, still in a daze.

"The horse daemons. This will ruin the village; the heart has been ripped out. We will end destitute, fleeing to live amongst the dregs of the city." Palon answered her, a tone of despair in her voice, her maiden like looks pained.

"No, it can't. The High Priest says he will talk to the governor who will order the Rilrpitu to leave you alone." Sanae blurted out, "You will be fine, you'll see. The bright one will guide you."

Both mother and daughter looked at her in despair. Palon eventually said,

"First we put this fire out, go and help fetch water from the river."

* * *

She had never worked so hard and desperately in her life, but by the middle of the day the fire was extinguished. All that was left was a smouldering pile of burnt wood and ash, a steaming crater at its centre. The epicentre of the blaze and the point at which the Zummosh's simple life was transformed.

She returned to the temple, exhausted, and covered in dust, ash and sweat, still feeling the heat of the flame against her skin. Her robes were sodden, faded and torn. Inside she found Xosu's acolytes hard at work cleaning the temple, seeing to the wellbeing of the god, and preparing the altar. Helupelan, wearing his great red robe and golden crown of office, with pale faced Kolae next to him, in the centre of the hall, observing the preparation. Konthelae was stood to Helupelan's right, Zenthelae in between the High Priest and Priestess, one image of a pristine morning, the other of a beautiful sunset. She felt a pang of jealously in that moment.

Sanae hoped that she would be able to sneak past without being seen, with a little luck her absence would not have been noticed. She kept her head down and made her way toward the back of the temple. A voice echoed over her shoulder just as she thought she had made it through,

"Where have you been?" Kolae's voice reverberated. *Why did she have to see me?* Sanae thought. She turned slowly, trying to keep her face covered to hide the soot and ash,

"South of the river, there was a fire. I went to see if the Lulpo was ok."

The High Priestess walked over to her,

"Look at the state of her." One of the High Priestesses' attendants said, although she did not see which.

"You were needed here, there are others to see to the safety of the city." As she came closer Sanae could see Kolae's face change as she realised that Sanae was covered in ash and dirt and her robes were torn, a red of anger flashing over her,

"What exactly were you doing on the south bank? You are covered in filth."

No point trying to hide it now, she thought,

"I was helping. Unlike most people in this city, I care about the Zummosh. I am sure king Tekolger would have done the same, he wanted this city to be for all the people of the empire. They are not savages, just people and nobody is helping them." she shouted, "It was the Rilrpitu who set the fire. Men who are supposed to serve the king and the empire and nobody cares."

The commotion had drawn the attention of everyone in the temple. Sanae could feel their eyes on her. Konthelae laughed with a look of disbelief on her face, Zenthelae had a much darker image on hers.

"That is quite the accusation, and not your place to say. I do not doubt that you care, but they are not people you want to associate with. They already have had you risk your life and walk across the city dressed in filthy rags like a common beggar. Soon they will have you practicing some savage ritual to honour their blood thirsty gods.

Why can you not behave like the twins? They came to us as babes just like you, and worse they were given to the temple for their safety when the Zelrsaloz were threatened by the other clans. Yet they are a model of what a priestess of the bright god should be." Kolae shot back in a stern manner. Calm, but Sanae could feel the rage behind the words.

Helupelan had by now approached, the heated nature of the discussion drawing his attention. Sanae ignored Kolae and appealed straight to him,

"Father, did you see the fire? You must help like Tekolger would have; he was a father to this city just like you. I know the governor will be coming to the temple today, please you must speak to him." She pleaded.

Helupelan had his usual calm, consoling, bright eyed look, as if all were ok. He replied,

"I saw the fire, and it is commendable that you went to help. But you really should have let us know where you were and not risk your life like that. As Kolae says, there are soldiers who will handle the situation."

"You must speak to the governor. It is the soldiers who are causing the fires and the deaths, I saw it." She continued.

"If it will put your mind at rest, I will speak to him." Helupelan relented, a warm smile falling over his disc of a face, "Now go and change and then help your fellows with their chores."

Reluctantly Sanae nodded and headed to her chambers.

Helupelan had agreed to speak to the governor, that was important, but she was determined to be there when he did. She put on her best robe and returned to the great hall of the temple. With the king gone, it was important that all is subjects helped to see his vision come to fruition.

She spent the rest of the morning sweeping and clearing the entrance to the temple, waiting for the governor to arrive. What seemed like a whole year passed and the sun beat down hard on the entrance despite the time of year, but eventually her patience paid off. The quiet streets were suddenly a throng of activity as a slow procession made its way to the steps of the temple. A black Xortogun style palanquin carried by half a dozen slaves in flame red tunics and tailed by soldiers wearing the distinctive purple cloaks and breastplates embossed with the white star of Tholophos approached. A contrast to the star of Xosu which hung on banners on the side of the temple with their bright yellow stars and sky-blue background. Inside the palanquin she knew would be Keluaz of the Keluazi, the man king Tekolger had personally appointed to build and govern his new city, a task he had set about with relish for over a decade from his residence within the great lighthouse.

The governor made regular visits to each of the public buildings in the city, and as the temple of Xosu contained the city's hearth fire, the governor was a frequent attendee. Sanae knew that the High Priest considered him a friend, this was surely the only way to see the Rilrpitu brought into line.

She grasped the basket of flowers she had placed behind one of the columns holding up the portico and rushed to the bottom of the stairs to greet the governor.

The palanquin was placed on the ground at the foot of the staircase and two of the slaves hurried to open the curtain which protected the governor from the blazing heat of Dunsun. A white cane was placed onto the floor by a shaking hand, the slaves stepped forward to help the tall man of middle years to his feet.

The Meanderer the Doldun called him, as Keluaz began his slow ascent of the steps she could see why. The story she had heard was that he had fallen off the top of the palace of Thelanutep when he was a child. His father had been instructed by the old king to build him a great palace and even at that young age Keluaz had shown a flair and enthusiasm for the craft. The fall had shattered the left side of his body though, leaving his leg and arm almost useless and his jaw broken.

Keluaz did not have the bearing of a typical Doldun, even without his injuries he appeared more Xosu, but his tan-coloured hair streaked with grey, and his olive skin showed him to be a man of the clans. Even if his experiences had left him gaunt and paler than most clansmen.

Behind him came Rososmosh, his Salxosu adviser. A shorter and rounder man, with the crescent of a smile always dripping off his lips, clearly fond of the riches and abundance of the great valley. His pale complexion was the only thing about him which struck Sanae as Salxosu. His flamboyant robes and jewel covered hands and nose spoke more of Xortogun than Xosupil.

As the fat man struggled out of the palanquin behind the governor, Sanae could see why some of the Xortogun called him The Great Baboon. She approached through the ring of guardsmen and said,

"Governor, the High Priest sent me to greet you, please accept these gifts to honour your visit."

She bowed down as she presented the flowers to him, red flowers which grew wild beyond the limits of the city. The governor took the flowers, which she had fashioned into a garland, in his good hand and placed them over his head,

"Thank you…schild. Such a lovely gift and off a schild with such a royal air about you." He said in a long slobbering drawl, before turning to Rososmosh and saying "What ish it that Helupelan craves I wonder? I appreciate the gift, the flowersh are very beautiful this time of year, but I attend Helupelan regular enough and never hash he shent giftsh before."

She lifted her head and replied eager to make her point,

"That is a question you will have to ask the High Priest, governor."

"Show me to him then schild." He gestured toward the steps as he said it and Sanae bowed again and turned to lead the governor to the temple.

She found Helupelan waiting under the portico, a quizzical look on his face greeted Sanae. Lurking in the shadows behind him was Kolae, fury in her eyes.

"Thank you for the welcome, Helupelan. It was mosht unexpected. What ish the reashon for it?" The governor said, slurring as he regained his breath.

"It is good to see you again, Keluaz. There is no reason we just wished to share the bounty of a fruitful year with the city." Helupelan said. Hopefully, he had understood Sanae's purpose. He gestured for the governor to enter the temple. She caught the High Priest's eye as he did, staring at him and willing him to ask the question.

"I trust all is well governor?"

"The city goesh from shtrength to shtrength, new buildingsh are completed every day and the population shwells, we will be needing more shpace to expand shoon. More of my clan intend to come and shettle and trade will need to exshpand to cope with the new citishens. I hope Tekolger would be proud of what we have achieved, if only he could shee it." The governor responded, the pride in his work clear in his voice despite the slurring. Sanae was further understanding why Keluaz was known as The Meanderer.

"To create a united city and empire we will need all the varied people who have come under the rule of the Doldun. Much like the different bees that make up the hive." Rososmosh said as his flamboyant Xosu style toga, unusually streaked with many colours, flowed behind him like a peacock's tail, "Hopefully the new king and his regents will see the sense in our plans."

"And what of the king's remains and the royal army?" Helupelan asked,

"The lasht I heard the army had crossed the mountains back from Kelandel and ish on the road to Torfub. Shome rumblingsh of Rilrpitu raiding in the north, apparently a shmall group have managed to bypassh the fort and sholdiers at Tekolgerdeloan shomehow. Zenukola should have been more vigilant. But there are plenty of sholdiers in the area and the royal army to the shouth, they should not be too much trouble. I will be shending a delegation to the royal court shoon, there are many thingsh

I wish to do which will need royal approval." Keluaz slurred as the group made their way into the private chambers at the rear of the temple.

Sanae forced a cough and caught Helupelan's eye again as they entered the great hall and the governor stopped to look at the statue of the god. She could feel Kolae's eyes on her, staring at the back of her head. Even though she could not see the High Priestess, she could feel the fury in those eyes.

Helupelan spoke again, a slight splutter in his voice as he started,

"Talking of Rilrpitu, the fire on the south bank of the river this morning, in the Zummosh settlement. I have heard rumour from the people that the Rilrpitu in the city's garrison are to blame, something about the Zummosh not paying taxes. I know the governance of the city is nothing to do with me, but the people come to me to seek reassurance."

Keluaz stopped, his cane echoing off the walls as he planted it. Looking at Helupelan intently through his round grey eyes, he replied,

"My remit is just the city and her boundariesh do not shtretch over the south bank. Thoshe landsh fall into the province of Guntoga where Koluun of the Tholmash governsh. But if my garrishon was involved, I will inveshtigate it, we can't have them shetting firesh so closhe to the city." he shrugged nonchalantly, "The Rilrpitu shtill do not understand the concept of law and order. They are good warriorsh but awful at keeping the peace. I would have rid of them if I could afford it, but the Zummosh shavages have no real right to build there."

The governor looked off into the distance as if remembering something, "It ish good land south of the river, a thriving shuburb of our city could be built there if the king had permitted me to expand that way. It is a shame that Koluun ish of the Tholmash and sho fond of trees, if not he would shee the potential to build there rather than jusht collecting the poultry taxes he raishes from the Zummosh." he paused, his eyes meeting Helupelan's again. "I am afraid that with the abshence of the royal court for sho long things beyond the city of gotten a little out of hand. Zenukola has a sholid grip on Zowdel, these Rilrpitu raiders ashide, and Dotmazo holds the easht tightly, Doldun, Xoshupil and Zenidun all in his grashp. There is a shtability in the lands not sheen shince the time of the old kingdoms. But Tekolger shaw fit not to appoint a shtrong hand in Xortogun as well."

Rososmosh was nodding along with his superior. Tittering, he added, "The king was wise to do so. Rolmit taught that unity can only come from multiplicity. A man cannot have a head of hair with only three strands of hair," the bald man said, "a beehive cannot function without workers, foragers, drones as well as the queen. Similarly, the Doldun cannot have a kingdom without their many clans coming together and an empire cannot stay strong if divided amongst a few strong men. Far better to share the bounty out, unity will flow from there." His arms doing as much of the talking as his mouth.

Keluaz smiled, "Rososomosh, you advishe me well, but such idealishm ish not what I expect from you." The short, plump man dipped his head theatrically, and with a sly smile said, "Idealistic, yes and Rolmit had the right of it. But the king was pragmatic as well."

The smile returned to Keluaz' face, "No doubt it wash good politicsh on the part of the king. Away sho long in the wesht a divided Xortogun was probably for the besht. We all know how ambition and hubrish can overcome my fellow Doldun, not to mention healthy clan rivalry shpiralling out of control. But this empire ish young and shtill not shettled, a shtrong leader in itsh centre ish needed to guide it on the right path. Eshpecially with the accushations now being made againsht Dalzenu of the Balkalkel. With his poshition in doubt at Torfub our rule over Xortogun ish much weakened." Keluaz stopped and looked at Helupelan, "With the royal court returning I mean to shee that many of these problemsh are addreshed, your people need not be concerned."

"Thank you, governor. The people will be comforted to know that you are looking out for them. No doubt you are correct, with a royal presence at the heart of the empire once more peace and prosperity are assured." Helupelan replied, looking over to Sanae as he did.

By now Sanae could feel that Kolae was about to explode with rage. Satisfied that the governor was made aware, she felt it best to head back to her quarters. She paid her respects to the High Priest, the governor and the god and left hurriedly, trying to stay ahead of a furious Kolae.

* * *

Kolae soon caught up with her and she spent the rest of the day scrubbing the floor as punishment. She did not care though, the governor knew about the Rilrpitu, a day of punishment was only a small price to pay. Besides, her next task was due to take place, so she agreed to scrub the floor without complaint, best not to annoy Kolae too much before then.

By the time the sun had set, her knees were raw and her hands throbbing but looking at the shine off the floor of the great hall where the water had washed over it. Sanae was pleased with her work. She was starting to feel relaxed for the first time in days. Even her dream and the fire that morning did not seem so much of a burden anymore.

The door to the side chamber creaked open and Kolae came back into the room, no doubt to check up on her. The High Priestess glided over to Sanae; her moon shaped faced peeking out from her robe. She stopped for a moment to inspect the floor. Sanae expected to be ordered to clean it all again, but the High Priestess instead just nodded and said,

"Good, the god will be pleased that his abode is clean. You should go and rest before your next task, but first we have a guest here. The High Priest would like you to take him some food and keep him entertained until he is free to speak to him."

Kolae handed her a plate of the small fruit of the dolthil tree, the guest must have been of the upmost importance. The fruit of the dolthil tree looked like figs but were golden and much richer, a rare delicacy and a much sort after commodity. Freshly picked from the tree in the temple's garden she knew, the tree which she had watered with the bull's blood during her last task. Plump, fat, and juicy the fruit looked. No wonder if the tree was being fed with such a rich diet. *At least it has not all gone to waste*, she thought.

She made her way into the High Priest's chambers, finding a man sat at Helupelan's table, waiting. He was not what she expected, usually guests for the High Priest were city officials or high-ranking men visiting from Doldun. This man on the other hand had a dishevelled look to his greying auburn mane and there was something wild in his green eyes. His scarred face only made her feel more uneasy. She walked over and placed the plate in front of him and said,

"Please accept our apologies, the High Priest is caught up in an engagement, but he will be here to see you soon. Whilst you wait, I thought you may enjoy some fruit from our garden."

The man smiled, a look which made him seem even wilder,

"I can wait a little longer."

He pulled the plate toward him and inspected the fruit. The wildness in him seemed to subside as he rolled one of the juicy crop in his hand. He seemed almost pensive now.

"How old are you?" He asked her.

"I have just passed my fourteenth summer." Sanae replied cautiously.

The wild smile returned to his lips,

"Many years ahead of you then. Use them wisely, it is cruel world you grow into."

The man took a large bite. The fruit exploded and juice streamed down his chin. She answered him warily as he did so,

"I intend on doing just that, I will become a priestess of Xosu and someday his high priestess."

"Good." the man croaked, "that is a noble path, to bring the light of the god and civilisation to people. This bargain we call civilised life needs someone to guide us."

The last words were barely audible as he started choking and coughing wildly and uncontrollably. A sudden panic came over Sanae, what was she to do?

"Help!" She cried out, but no answer came. She rushed over to the man, who was now grasping at his throat as his face turned a bright red. Grabbing him, she threw the fruit away and tried to scoop the rest of it out of his mouth, his tongue had turned black from the juice. His choking only got worse, his face turned a crimson red and he collapsed onto the floor.

Her heart was pounding in her chest, her vision darkening with every beat, even when the choking stopped and the man went silent, the sound of her heart pounding in her ears drowned out everything else.

His eyes looked wilder now than ever before, anguish, fury and dread all rolled into one. She shut his eyes as she felt tears trickling out from hers. She knew there was nothing else she could do.

The door to the High Priest's chamber swung open and Kolae came in with Helupelan a few steps behind her. Still kneeling next to the dead man, Sanae turned with tears in her eyes and said,

"I didn't...I don't know." It was all that would come out. Helupelan just looked at her, no emotion marked his face,

"Xosu's tutor, mentor, and great friend Gelithul ate the fruit of the dolthil tree which sprang from the blood of Tholo's white hydra. The Lunar goddess struck him down with a terrible illness for daring to challenge the gods and eat of the fire of the heavens. He died in Xosu's arms.

The sight of his old friend dying in his arms, because of the actions of the bright god, drove Xosu mad, a curse sent by the white armed goddess. He set off in a frenzy across the world which had been reborn by his actions, bringing his torment and anguish with him, but also all that he had learnt from Gelithul and the slaying of the hydra. He would teach the people of the world how to build anew after the cataclysm of the war in the heavens had broken their once peaceful realm, he brought them a new dawn."

The tears dried on Sanae's face, confused she asked,

"Was this the task?"

Helupelan nodded,

"But what about this man, he died. Did you poison him?"

Kolae answered her this time,

"He chose to die like this. A condemned man who wished to give his life to the bright god and a taste of the dolthil fruit."

Sanae's heart was still pounding, but less so now. She was beginning to understand what had just happened, but words would not come to her. The suddenness and brutality of it was a shock. Helupelan helped to her feet and said,

"Your task is complete, go now and rest. We can talk more in the morning."

Sanae just nodded and started to leave, Kolae added,

"Think about all that happened today, the unintended consequences of your actions." There was spite in that comment, Sanae knew, but she did not care.

ZENUKOLA

24

The mutiny had rolled on for days now. The army was refusing to follow commands and demanding that Kelbal rescind his order that the men from Xortogun be integrated into the ranks of the Doldun. Surprisingly, the soldiers had remained jovial and friendly toward the other Companions. But Zenu was worried which way they would turn if this stasis continued and, more importantly, how the provinces would react if news of the mutiny began to spread. Most of his own men had ridden north with Kalu, and so he no longer had as many eyes and ears amongst Tekolger's veterans to feed him information and the lack of knowledge gnawed at him.

Kelbal had at first ignored the demands. Instead, he had descended into one of his darker moods and locked himself away in the palace. That was until this day. Kelbal's gregarious second shade had remerged, and he had suddenly announced in good spirits that he would address the men and put an end to the mutiny himself. Kelbal seemed increasingly prone to such whimsical notions, lurching from inactivity to being the centre of attention in a moment. Behaviour of a man plagued by guilt no doubt. Nonetheless, it was a bold but risky decision to address the men himself. One wrong move from Kelbal and the mutiny may turn into a full-blown revolt. Zenu had determined that that outcome would be a step too far. If word spread to the provinces the rumblings of rebellion may turn into an earthquake and in trying to save the empire from Kelbal, Zenukola's own machinations may destroy it. But he knew there was more value to be squeezed from this mutiny before he sought to end it. The balance required to prevent chaos engulfing them was a difficult act to get right. *One more push to widen the rift between Kelbal and the others is all I need.*

He found Kelbal in the governor's quarters. A flurry of activity surrounded the young man as eunuchs hurried back and fore bringing various garments and jewellery to the Companion. Kelbal had always had a strange and bold style of dressing and he had embraced the Xortogun ways to a fault, even oiling and braiding his beard as they did. Kelbal was stood in the centre of the room, being dressed by two of his servants and Yare, his favourite from Zentheldel. That slave was another problem Zenu would have to deal with. He may have looked an innocent youth, with long hair of beaten bronze and skin rouged to an almost crimson hue. But with his face drawn back like a bird of prey, the androgenous boy had an air about which Zenu disliked, he did not trust him. If Kelbal had an accomplice in his treachery, then it was almost certainly this creature in a man's skin.

An intricately woven red silk robe of the Xortogun style, the golden trim flowing like feathers, had been draped over Kelbal and now the two eunuchs were fitting him with the finest jewellery. A three-tiered studded tiara of jet, ruby and moonstone had been placed upon the crown of his head, framing it like the disc of the sun. An unnecessary flamboyance.

Zenu stood in the entrance to the chamber watching this spectacle unfold. His phantom fingers flexed and his silver eye itched. Kelbal looked every bit the western king, the absolute ruler of a vast kingdom. Impressive but not right. If they carried on like this, the leaders of the Doldun would lose themselves in these barbarous lands, be devoured by them and lose their connection with the old country. With that the empire would be lost, and no doubt chaos would return. Zenu entered the room and spoke,

"What is your intention here, Kelbal? What do you mean to tell the men?"

Kelbal answered without turning to face him. "I mean to lead as Tekolger would and show the men that the empire will be one of both east and west."

"What does that mean? You will not give in to their demands?"

The Companion turned to face Zenu, smiling in that way he did when his gregarious shade had hold of him,

"The order will not be rescinded; however, I will be magnanimous. Perhaps a compromise can be found to reassure the men. But they will listen to me. Who could refuse the command of a man dressed as such?"

Zenu knew the question was rhetorical, but he still had to resist the urge to boom an answer anyway. *The Doldun!* he felt the urge to shout as his phantom fingers clenched. *No, I must let him fail.* Kelbal continued, oblivious to the storm that raged inside Zenukola.

"This is Tekolger's wish. For an empire that embraced the traditions of all the peoples within it. I am protecting his legacy."

"And how do you suppose the men will react when they see beyond this peacocking? See through to a man who compromised when they began to protest?" He answered more sternly than intended, but he could stay silent no longer. The smile fell from Kelbal's face, and his mismatched eyes focused on Zenukola intently. After a pause, Kelbal answered,

"How would I do that, Zenu? Your actions are a mystery to me I must say. One moment you urge caution and compromise and a return to the ways of the clans, the next I am to be firm and unbending."

With Kelbal softened to his advice, Zenu sort to press his advantage,

"True, I would have urged caution before taking this action, but you have chosen your route now. The goddess does not let you retrace steps down the path of fate. So now you cannot let the army dictate what you do. Some in our ranks are already doubting your actions, giving in would only embolden them and make strife amongst us more likely when we least need it. Tekolger's killer may be lurking in the shadows, looking for division and the opportunity to strike, and the conquered peoples will jump to rebellion from any sign of weakness."

Clearly agitated, his second shade rising to the surface, Kelbal demanded,

"Then what do I do Zenu?"

"You lead, Kelbal." Zenu said firmly. Truth be told, he did not like to see Kelbal fall in this way, sacrificed on the altar of power, he was one of the Deltathelon after all. But he had made his choice and the Doldun came first.

"Go out there and tell the soldiers that you are sorry that it has come to this, but you will not back down and that you will be integrating the Xortogun into their ranks. Confirm their fear and take away their bargaining power."

Kelbal was nodding and already standing taller. A fiery determination on his ruddy face. Zenu's phantom fingers flexed again, he could almost feel the dirt he was having to cover them in. The whole affair was conflicting. A harder line may finally drive the veterans over the edge, a rebellion amongst the army would make his task easier. But division among the Companions could drive the provinces into revolt. He closed his eyes and settled his mind. His phantom fingers clenched. *We can hold off rebellion in the provinces a little longer.* Zenu continued,

"Then you start making some decisive decisions."

"What decisions?" Kelbal inquired.

"Begin the march to Torfub or appoint some more governors. The title of Togworwoh would calm many a rebellious mind. Or even lead the least mutinous of the soldiers on an expedition. We know there are more Rilrpitu bands to the north. The men watched Kalu ride off with my guards. If they see others head off to defend the empire with you, they will be shamed."

"I can't lead an expedition myself Zenu. I need to be here, especially with tensions running so high."

Zenu nodded in agreement,

"That is wise. I was probably a little hasty. You could send what men you can north though, hunt down the Rilrpitu as quickly as possible. With someone you can trust in command." he paused as if pondering the issue, "Put the twins in charge of a couple of columns, they can fan out and sweep up any Rilrpitu they come across."

Kelbal stopped dressing and thought,

"Yes, we can reduce the rebel's numbers and shame them at the same time, and deal with the Rilrpitu. It could work Zenu. Your wise council is welcome in these trying times."

His phantom fingers grasped, pleased that he had achieved his goal. He contained his delight and said,

"First let us address the men and strip them of their feeling of moral superiority."

By now Kelbal was in his full ceremonial attire. He made his way out of the room, striding passed Zenu with an undeserved confidence and out into the courtyard beyond.

**

The camp outside the walls of Yorixori was still as well kept as it had been before the army had mutinied. Zenu took this as a good sign, discipline in the camp had clearly not broken down and the army was still behaving rationally, they could be reasoned with. He relaxed a little with that realisation. If rebellion did grip the provinces, then the army may still be of use, they may not be lost.

The Companions had each filed in behind Kelbal as he marched down to the camp. The group flanked by guards drawn from the ranks of the Xortogun at Zenu's insistence. If nothing else that would maintain the feeling of distance even if Kelbal was able to reconcile with the men.

Despite their own disagreements, the Companions had agreed on a show of unity in front of the men. It was something else that Zenu had insisted on. All the Companions being in concert was a pleasing sign, even better that each of them was beginning to defer to Zenu's authority, that would be important for the future.

Kelbal steadily paced to the centre of the camp, the men beginning to gather, a trickle at first and then a flood as word spread of his arrival. Zenu positioned himself some way back, with the city gates not too far behind him. He had ordered Kolothutalaz to wait near the bronze doors with a troop of his personal guard in case things went badly.

Pausing until the centre of the camp was filled to the brim, Kelbal stood tall his tiara making him tower over the men. He began to speak,

"We have all sacrificed much and more together over the last few years and through that I consider every one of you, my brother. It is because of this that I do you all the respect of talking to you today." He paused and looked around at the faces of the men he had come to call brothers. He took off his tiara carefully and paused. Looking intently and the jewels inlaid into the metal bands,

"Tekolger may have had the vision to build this empire, but it is off the back of the blood, sweat and tears of all of you that the empire was forged. It was your sacrifice that brought the Xosu cities to our side, it was you who smashed the fierce horse lords on the field in Xortogun and it was you who scaled the walls of the world and flooded into the twilight lands. Your blood was spilled onto the hard-black earth that gave power to the Doldun. For these deeds, your names will echo down the ages. Tekolger may stand tall, but it is only because he stands on your shoulders." He paused again, the emotion clear in his voice,

"Tekolger knew this too. Often, he would speak of his great affection for his vicious but valiant Doldun. It was always to your care he would look to first, and your honour and glory that he would talk of to his closest friends. He would be the first to acknowledge that without you his vision could not have come true. The vision of an empire spreading across all the inhabited lands, east to west. An empire which shared the knowledge of the world and an empire in which civilised life would flourish and hold the forces of chaos at bay. That is what you built and that is the legacy that Tekolger left to you." Stopping, Kelbal look around at the men again, a tear in his eye,

"It is for the maintenance and growth of this vision, this message, the legacy that you forged, but a legacy that is yet to take its final shape, that I made the decision I did. Tekolger's vision was never for an empire just for the Doldun, but for all the peoples under his rule. He decreed that the men of Xortogun be trained so that they could join us in our great endeavour, not to compete with us. Stamping his foot on the black, blood-stained soil to raise men as loyal as you or I. All those loyal to Tekolger and his vision should be working hard to make this happen, it is but the next challenge in a long line, and I know you have overcome greater odds. It is a sacrifice I know, we ask much for you to give your hearts to this cause, to maintain the power and the glory of the Doldun." He paused as some emotion gathered in his throat,

"It is for these reasons that I cannot now agree to your demands. To do so would be a betrayal of Tekolger's vision and would put his legacy in jeopardy." Sighing, his body appearing to shrink, Kelbal took a deep breath and puffed up his chest,

"Therefore, as Tekolger's old comrades in arms will no longer support his cause, his heirs will have to. The soldiers from Xortogun will form the core of a new force to see Tekolger's vision fulfilled. A new royal guard unit will be formed, Yoruxoruni's Tears of Xura will rise again, and a royal squadron raised from the Xortogun cavalry. For your years of loyal and exemplary service, none of you will be punished for this disagreement. Those of you who wish to carry on serving are welcome to, those who aren't will be led back to Doldun by Zenukola of the Deltathelon and given a plot of land to farm and a lifetime exemption from taxation as a reward for your many years of service."

A ripple of emotion echoed across the assembled soldiers. The noise was one of agony but also anger and confusion. For a moment Zenu thought the meeting was about to take a dark turn, the fabled discipline of Tekolger's soldiers about to break. He took a few steps back. But the feeling of confusion and fear of rejection is what prevailed amongst the majority of the men. He could see a few soldiers walking away, unable to accept the situation offered by Kelbal, but the majority stayed and protested. That was a not a good signal, they were open to persuasion from Kelbal still.

The few Xortogun guards which had accompanied Kelbal into the midst of the mutinous troops nervously closed ranks around him as the crowd pressed closer, but Kelbal waved them away. He had the flash of Tekolger about him once again, a light on a dark horizon.

When the men reached him, they prostrated themselves at his feet. Soldiers grabbed at Kelbal's ankles and begged him to reconsider. Kelbal picked each one back to his feet and consoled the grief-stricken men.

Zenu realised in that moment that he had made a mistake. This was perhaps the emotional relief the army needed. They had loved their king dearly, following him without question to the ends of the earth, and had never really had the time to grieve for Tekolger. This great outpouring of emotion was perhaps the result of that.

Whatever the reason for it, the reaction took Zenu back. Despite the dispute, it was clear that the connection between Kelbal and the army was strong, even with Tekolger gone. Any attempt to remove Kelbal would clearly be met with resistance from these soldiers.

At least he had planted the seed of sending the twins north. The loss of two more allies would weaken Kelbal and many of the Companions were still distanced from him. The time to act would come soon.

KALASYAR

25

The days since Rolmit and her grandfather's arrest had been a blur. She had spent the first night shut up within her family's villa, not wanting to see anyone. After all, how could she trust any of them. Only her handmaids were left to attend her, but try as they might, even they could not raise her spirits.

After a few days, a new morning had approached. A gentle light had crept into her bed chamber and Kalasyar had awoken slowly. It had still felt like a dream, but on that new day she realised there was somewhere and someone she could trust. Since then, Kalasyar had not left the temple of Buto. In the sanctuary, the world above need not exist, she need not observe the ongoing trials, she need not see the flesh sloughing off the skulls of the mounted heads above the city gates.

It had been hard to leave Thororoz and Ralxuloz behind, they had barely left her side since they were given to her, but Sipenkiso had taken her in without any questions. 'The Great God looks after his own.' she had said when Kalasyar had arrived in the sanctuary early that morning. She had spent the days since working for the priestesses of Sem, the nine virgin women selected from the old blood by the oracle at old Kolbos when they were children to give their lives in service to the Great God.

On the morning of the thirteenth day since her grandfather's arrest Sipenkiso had told her that Koseun had been charged with conspiracy to overthrow the government, corrupting the youth of the city, and impiety, there was to be a trial the next day. Thankfully, her cousin had been released.

They were false charges, much like those Dunsun had levelled against Buto when he led the gods in rebellion against their over mighty lord. At first Kalasyar had expressed relief that her grandfather would be given a trial, a chance for him to argue and clear his name. Her grandfather had always been adamant that such institutions underpinned civilisation and gave men freedom, but Sipenkiso had given her a pitiful look,

'You show the folly of your youth my child', she had said, *'Why do you put so much hope in these systems of control to give you justice? They are merely the tools of the powerful to cement their rule. These are the same systems which have placed in power the people who now accuse your grandfather and seek to make a sacrifice of him to enhance their own standing. The only way to achieve true justice is for you to find power yourself.'*

The foolish moment of hope the news of a trial had given Kalasyar was shattered in that instant. Of course she was right, the other trials had been for show, why would her grandfather's be any different. Desperately she had asked Sipenkiso for help. The priestess had replied,

'We will do what we can, but I fear it may be too late. The Nine are intent on sacrificing your grandfather to secure their power. We can use our connections to push for a lesser sentence, exile perhaps, maybe the Doldun will agree to keep him safe at their Royal Court.'

That had been some comfort. If her grandfather would accept it and live out the rest of his days in some foreign land. Sipenkiso had continued,

'You have the tools of persuasion yourself though. You know where power in this city resides, find a way to wield that power and you will get what you desire.'

It was with these words echoing in her head that Kalasyar now found herself leaving the temple, taking her first steps beyond its huge bronze gates in what seemed like an age. Back to her grandfather's villa, his friends would surely be there and together they could find a way to stop this injustice.

The Sisosi villa was busy, busier than it had been for a long time. The last time this many people had attended was at the height of the League, when Kalasyar was a small child.

Taking a deep breath, she confidently strode inside, passed faces both strange and familiar, feeling buoyed and encouraged by the number of people who seemed to be there to help her grandfather, at least twenty she thought. She saw faces she knew from the Kinsol, the Rososthup, Kisurusosi, the Kolkisuasu and her own Sisosi. Rolmit, her cousin, came to her when she entered,

"We were all worried about you." He said as he brought her in for an embrace. Her cousin was of an age with her, lean and tall with jet black hair and the pale skin of the Salxosu. He was of a slight build and scholarly demeanour. He had only returned to the city recently, spending most of the last decade in the city of Rulkison with its famous honeycomb cliffs, receiving an education no longer available to him in Butophulo.

"I worried for you as well cousin. I am pleased to see you were released unharmed."

In the central room, where her grandfather held his famous gatherings, Dunobos and Kolkobuas reclined in their usual positions, surrounded by younger men discussing the situation. Polrinu and Buso she recognised, even with the bruises on Polrinu's face, but many of the other faces she did not. Her grandfather's couch was left empty.

Kalasyar walked to the centre of the room, a silence descended as she did, only her handmaids rushed to her and coiled their hands into hers. She drew strength from that. Looking Dunobos straight in the eye, she drew a breath and let the words flood out,

"Dunobos, I know we have our differences and you do not think I should involve myself in matters of politics and philosophy, but right now I do not care. We all want to see my grandfather released and justice done, and I am staying to help no matter what you say."

The old man looked at her, pausing for a moment before slowly nodding. Kalasyar let go of her breath and relaxed, sitting down on her grandfather's couch. Kolkobuas continued what he had been saying before she entered the room,

"My friends close to the council tell me that all the Nine are concerned about is the succession of the next king of the Doldun. They are eager to show that Butophulo can be stable and loyal to the new king and to try and win his favour. Removing a known figure and champion of the old League they think is a good way to show that loyalty. Sacrificing this city's soul for the power our new godly rulers can grant, the Nine would make the Kinsolsun jealous. Ironically, they are bringing back the old open-air court to do it."

"So, there will be a jury of citizens then?" Dunobos asked. Kolkobuas laughed,

"Yes and no. It will be more than the show trials we have seen up until now. There will be a jury of citizens, hand-picked by the Nine. In their positions as the Tukis of the city, the Nine will reside as judges and have the final decision."

"He doesn't stand a chance then." Came a voice from the gathered group.

"In the trial? No. They are using the system Koseun championed all his life to condemn him. The most we can hope for is that they decide to show clemency, maybe exile or imprisonment and a fine." Kolkobuas replied.

"There is more. With Foson Rusos too frail to maintain his position and Dorthil dead, Rinukiso Polriso will be taking the vacant seat on the Council." Kolkobuas continued. The announcement brought only silence from the room, until Dunobos said,

"So Polriso scheming is really what is behind all of this then."

Kolkobuas nodded,

"Polriso scheming and the rivalry between the Posuausthison and the Rusos. Even in Puskison's perfect city run by philosophers it seems family politics is paramount." he sighed, "Koseun is insisting that he will go through the proper institution and show them for the tyrants that they are. Stubborn as he is, there may be an opportunity. They have made a mistake in giving Koseun a platform to speak, it is what he is best at after all. We need to make sure he has a sympathetic audience, that way the Nine may feel compelled into being lenient."

Dunobos interposed,

"That seems a sensible plan given the circumstances. It is settled then; we will each gather as many attendees as possible to create a supportive crowd. The Nine will not dare be too draconian in front of so many. We will also petition to the Nine to show clemency. All in agreement."

A murmur of accord went around the room, but Kalasyar felt compelled to speak,

"Is that all we will do, gather a crowd, and beg the tyrants to show mercy? I may be a young maiden, unaware of such things, but this seems a weak response."

"At this point it is all we can do. We do not have the strength to oppose the Nine, especially with their Doldun allies, and I do not think Koseun would try to escape even if he could. He seems set on a confrontation, the chance to put his arguments to the people and win the day, one last grasp at glory." Kolkobuas replied.

"You've seen him?" Kalasyar asked,

"Yes, they finally allowed me to, earlier today. He was asking after you, but I did not know where you were. I would suggest you visit him this evening before it is too late."

* * *

The villa of the Posuausthison sprawled over the northern side of Polriso's Hill and was large and lavish, much more so than the Sisosi's rather modest quarters in comparison. Before the fall of old Kolbos the Posuausthison had been the stewards to the gods and the family had kept their prominence and wealth after the flight and founding of Butophulo.

Before the Doldun came, Puskison was a philosopher and head of the Academy of Kunpit, who had shown little interest in the reality of governing the city, although he was fond of producing great tracts on how a perfect city should be governed. *'A haven of glowing white, burning in the minds of all its citizens'* was how he had termed it she recalled. The followers of Kunpit had never made their disdain for the League a secret and their admiration for the kings was well known. Many had wanted them expelled from the city, some had tried and failed. No doubt those who did not lend their support to those efforts regretted it now.

Puskison and his acolytes from Kunpit's academy had benefitted immensely from siding with king Tekolger after the League was defeated on the field of the Bulodon's wail and the Xosu world transformed in the aftermath. The king had raised them up from obscure outcasts and placed them in charge of the city. Finally giving Puskison the chance to put his ideas into practice. But the strict hierarchy and division into classes which the Nine had tried to implement had only been partially successful. Many of the children of the old blood, those with gold in their hearts as Puskison had said, had been taken to Kunpit's academy to be trained as philosophers and the future rulers of the city. Children of lesser families had also been taken to receive a soldier's education to become the city's guardians. Their other reforms had failed, or only been grudgingly accepted by a city which resented their rule.

Kalasyar looked up at Polriso's Hill looming over the villa. The white, rocky outcrop in the middle of the city was a shadow in the evening light. On top sat a palace of light set high in the heavens. It seemed otherworldly, almost peaceful. She looked back down the hill to the great mansion, built on the side of the ridge which overshadowed the city and now illuminated by the setting sun glowing crimson and filling her with dread. She put her foot on the first step and began to ascend the steep marble staircase.

At the top, three guardsmen waited. Sellswords again, except these men were not Xosu. They wore the distinctive mail shirts and long curved blades of the savage Zummosh tribes of the land of Zenidun. *It seems that Puskison does not trust Xosu to guard him,* she thought.

The first guard barked in a guttural language at the others. In broken Common Xosu, the second told her to halt, the third paid her no mind,

"I am here to visit my grandfather before the trial tomorrow. I was told that I would be allowed to see him." Kalasyar said politely, deliberately avoiding eye contact. Again, they barked at each other in their guttural tongue before the second man said in heavily accented Common Xosu,

"Come with me." And turned to head into the mansion.

The building was more a palace than a mansion it seemed as they descended into the lavish quarters that she guessed was dug into the side of Polriso's Hill. Great works of sculpture lined the corridor down which Kalasyar was led depicting scenes from the history of the Xosu. From the Dawn and Xosu's defeat of the white hydra to the destruction of old Kolbos, the Dusk and everything in between.

A second corridor continued the history, after the Dusk. The kings of Butophulo were especially prominent alongside the scions of the Posuausthison, Puskison was not a subtle man. More sellswords were resting, drinking, and gaming in the few rooms they passed, but eventually her guide halted and gestured for her to enter a room at the end of the large corridor.

Inside she found more art and sculpture. At the far end of the room sat a huge marble piece depicting the death of Xosu, his mortal body burning as it hung on the great dolthil tree, the god reaching up to the heavens with his dying breath. But Tholo, the night wanderer, refused to allow him to enter Dzottgelon. In the background of the piece lurked Phenmoph, the rich lord of the dead, ready to accept the shade of the fallen god.

Opposite was a work showing the mighty Lord of the Cosmos casting Buto from Dzottgelon after his failed rebellion. A look of disdain on Dunsun's face and one of anguish on Tholo's who stood behind her husband beaten and bloody, reaching out to try and save her discarded son. Below, the Great God and his attendants waited to save the crippled god.

Reclined on a white marble couch in the corner of the room was Koseun picking at a pomegranate as he poured over a pile of scrolls. The old man was lit by a small fire burning in a hearth. The open roof allowing in the moon light contrasted against the flickering flames, giving her grandfather a strange complexion and the couch a deep fiery glow. Now red, now white, Koseun appeared a beacon of light as the darkness of night crept through the corridor and into the room. Kalasyar could not stop herself, she ran to her grandfather and embraced him. The foolish man was taken by surprise and laughed,

"Have they treated you well grandfather?" She inquired.

"Yes…yes, do not worry about me. I have been allowed free reign of Puskison's villa and treated as more a guest than a prisoner. The man's library is very impressive, if only I could stay here." Koseun replied, he seemed in as good a spirit as he always was. He uncoiled his arms and wrapped them tightly around her.

"We will find a way to get you out of here." Kalasyar rushed to tell him, "Even now your friends sit to formulate a plan to win the trial."

Koseun smiled and touched her face,

"You don't even fool yourself child. I will not be getting out of this predicament. I could be as innocent as a newborn child and still be convicted by this court. The Nine require a monster, a dread serpent to hold up to their people and blame for their own failings. They also need a blood sacrifice to prove their loyalty to the new king of the Doldun. They will find me guilty of all the charges."

She shot back quick,

"Kolkobuas believes that with enough support we can get them to show clemency, maybe exile or house arrest and a fine. He says that this is all to do with the Polriso scheming and the rivalry between Rusos and Posuausthison."

"Kolkobuas is a good friend, the gods bless him for his concern, and I am afraid he is right. The men guarding this villa do not realise that prisoners can hear, even if their Common Xosu is poor. It seems that Rinukiso was offered the place on the council by Puskison himself. I understand that he was not pleased with the way Dorthil was conducting himself and seized on the chance to weaken his rival family." he paused, and took a more serious look, "I am afraid that Kolkobuas plan would not do. The Nine would relish the chance to appear merciful. It would vindicate them to find the chief conspirator and then be graceful enough to demonstrate their capacity to forgive. It would only strengthen their position." Koseun said, with some conviction in his voice which scared Kalasyar. Koseun continued, calm as the sea on a tranquil summer day,

"No, I am afraid that now is the time for these tyrants to be confronted, it is a knowledge that as lurked in the depths of my mind for a while, but only with my arrest did I see fit to pluck it from that well. They have given me one final platform it is only right that I use it to make the people of this city see the truth. Yunsunos Sisosi did the same for the people of this city the last time the tyrants ruled. He was called the Hammer for his prowess on the field, that is a skill I have never possessed, a tongue as cunning as a snake is the only talent the gods saw fit to bestow upon me. I will use that gift as a trident to skewer the tyrants and expose the Nine for what they are."

"Then you would martyr yourself for nothing." Kalasyar said, more aggressively now, like a smith hammering at a blade, to shake her grandfather from his delusion.

"Not for nothing." he said softly, "For an ideal, which you can see come to fruition. Help return this city to the glory that it once was." he spoke with a calm conviction. "My time has come, I have lived a good and long life, but I miss the glory of my past. Old age has seen me shrink in stature. Long ago I shed the skin of a noble statesman, now I am just a tired old man." he paused and smiled in a melancholy way. "A man should not have to witness the demise of his own position and reputation. I have the chance to use my death for a greater purpose. My star waxed as high as any, but it has been on the wane for some time, I would see it go out with one final flourish."

"And what about those you leave behind? What about me?" Kalasyar asked, anguished.

"You will be fine. You are far stronger than you know. You remind me so much of your mother. She faced down Hulsen the mad prophetess, and you will find the same courage to stand up to these tyrants. You do not need me anymore." He grasped her hand in his, "Just remember to be smarter than I ever was. If I am right, then people will begin to take sides after I am gone, they may even look to you as my flesh and blood. Help their cause but be cautious. Do not let these tyrants catch you as they have me." Koseun advised, stroking her cheek, and brushing her hair out of her face. She wanted to argue with him, make him see sense, but his mind was made up. There was never any point arguing once her grandfather had decided on a course of action, he stuck with it for better or worse. Instead, she spent the night talking with her grandfather, forgetting about the problems of the world.

THUSON

26

The dawn light was encroaching through the open door of the shack of a building Thuson had been given as his quarters. As the creeping fingers of light turned into a grasping hand, their touch pulled Thuson from his sleep. He wearily turned to wash his face in a bowl of murky water by the straw mat where he slept. Then he slowly stood and stepped through the ramshackle doorway. His eyes were flooded with a cascade of light that blinded him for a moment. As his vision adjusted to the brightness, he was pleased to see his men about their tasks for the day. Hur the Hunter, true to his name, was stripping the corpse of a stag. Next to him sat Puro the Hornblower, polishing his carnyx and Llalon sat amongst them tending to his falx. A thunder of hooves rumbled by as a group of horsemen streamed out of the camp.

The further north they had pushed, the more warbands of Rilrpitu the army had encountered and the more burnt husks of villages and columns of smoke they witnessed, without any signs of life. Who held responsibility for the devastation Thuson did not care to think about.

He had finally caught up with Dolzalo and Palmash a few days previously and the reunited force had made camp in a small valley a few stades south of the Zolkelonzow river. This northern area of Zowdel had been ravaged for years by the Rilrpitu and so hardly any settlements existed on the north bank of the river, and very few even dared settle this close to its southern bank. Only the city of Yorotog remained as the last bastion of civilised life in northern Zowdel, its kings implacable foes of the tribes. Although since Tekolger's conquest, the peace he brought had seen settled life slowly returning to the region.

He had been worried that a few days of rest would let boredom and idleness creep into a force he still did not feel fully in control of. The command of men, and veterans at that, was a much more difficult and fluid task than the overseeing of logistics and running the king's court. But the men had quickly settled back into the familiar routine of campaign and alleviated his fears somewhat.

The scouts had reported that the main Rilrpitu band had set up their own camp at a bend in the Zolkelonzow river on the reverse side of the wooded hills the loomed over their own camp. Other warbands were apparently joining them every day. Dolzalo, impatient as ever, was keen to attack before they moved again. However, Thuson's demands for reinforcements had finally been heard and messages had reached them that Kalu of the Zelrsaloz was leading mounted aid to the army. Hearing that news, Thuson had insisted that they wait for the extra horse. Dolzalo had ignored his advice at first, determined to press on with the few horsemen he had. Only a rider carrying a message directly from Kalu had seen him relent, at least for a few days.

The presence of a calm and competent Companion would be welcome. Kalu had been one of the first to join Yusukol's class along with Tekolger and Kelbal. He was a good student and over the years of campaigning, Thuson had come to see him as a friend. He looked at the horizon to the south, hoping to see the oncoming reinforcements. Instead, he saw nothing but a wide-open plain basking in the light of the dawn. The sight left him in dismay. He doubted he could hold Dolzalo back for another day, and in part he even agreed with the impetuous Companion, the Rilrpitu would not stay put forever.

There are other means of gaining an advantage though, he thought, looking around to see the captured Rilrpitu from their previous engagements chained amid the Thulchwal. He had claimed one for his own, the defiant amazon captured during his encounter with this savage foe as they surprised and tried to overwhelm his flank. She spoke no Common Xosu and his own Rilrpitu amounted to a few words he thought he understood. But he was certain that she could offer useful intelligence about the enemy they faced and so had sought out a camp follower who spoke a little Common Xosu and a little Rilrpitu to act as a translator.

It had not been easy to communicate, and his prisoner had been less than willing to cooperate, but he had discovered that her name was Yersada, and her comrades were called Yadatardar and Taran. They were members of the Tardarden, an all-female tribe from the vast plains of Belon beyond the borders of the empire. The thought of tribes of female warriors streaming across the open plains invoked in Thuson the tales he was told as a child. The amazons who rode to the aid of Semontek and swirled like a cloud under the walls of old Kolbos as they came to blows with Tildun and his Xosu. Useful information, but he needed to know more. The confirmation that there were all-female tribes was one thing, but the scholars who had studied the Rilrpitu had made some even more fanciful claims about cannibalism and mating with daemons amongst other things. He needed to separate fact, fiction, and speculation if he were to learn how to better contend with these fierce people.

He found Yersada, Yadatardar and Taran, along with his translator, down by a small stream which ran alongside the camp, one of the many that fed into the Zelkelonzow. Hurlar the Green, another of the Zummosh who liked to paint himself green from head to toe for battle, stood over them. He was making the women wash his armour whilst he attempted to cut the gilded horns from a head piece of bronze made for one of the Rilrpitu horses.

A pang of sorrow echoed through Thuson as he approached the women. The men had seen them as no more than servants, fit to wash their panoplies, but the little he understood of the Rilrpitu told Thuson that Yersada and her kin were as proud and skilful warriors as any of the men in this camp, making the same sacrifices as they had. The battered pale bronze scale armour Yersada wore like a second skin and the golden girdle which hid the scared remains of her right bosom were more than enough physical proof of this. The translator had told him that the burning of the right breast as a child was common among the women of the Tardarden, a mark of their status as a warrior and allowing them to draw a bow like any man. His own research had uncovered a garbled account of this practice, but that was a claim that the women were cursed with this affliction as the first Rilrpitu was born of a woman who lay with one of the Bulodon and the suckling of the child at the breast caused it to shrivel, an affliction which the writer claimed was passed on to all the women of the Rilrpitu.

Drawing closer to the stream and the gaggle of slaves who were cleaning their new master's equipment, Thuson caught the eye of the women and signalled for them to approach. Once they were within earshot, he said to the wizened old woman of Zowdel who was serving as translator,

"The battle with the Rilrpitu draws nearer. I want to try and find out more from Yersada. One more attempt to garner some useful information."

The woman nodded and shouted something in the guttural tongue of the Rilrpitu to Yersada. The proud warrior, as always wearing a scowl as if it were the last piece of armour left to her, spat something back, but began to walk toward Thuson's quarters. She gave him a lingering glare with her fierce pale eyes.

Back inside the tired hut, the light of the morning withdrew toward the doorway like the sea retreating with the tide. The first exchanges in his quest for information had been sharp and aggressive. Yersada had been as likely to try and kill him as answer his questions. This time Thuson would opt for a more tactful approach.

Pouring a cup of hot water which had been left on the heat of the open fire for him, he added the dried gold leaves of the dolthil tree to make the drink the people of Xortogun called thori. A priest of Kurotor had taught him how in Kurotormub, the man had claimed it was used by learned men to investigate the world beyond. The liquid quickly turned gold and had a strong honey-like taste to it and gave a man an uplifting feeling. Thuson had become quite taken with the drink during the conquest.

He offered the cup to Yersada, who reluctantly accepted, but only tentatively sipping it after she had watched Thuson do the same. Asking for his words to be translated, Thuson took a moment to taste his beverage, and began,

"Let us go back to the start. When did you cross the river into Zowdel?"

A guttural exchange occurred, and the translator answered,

"Three moons back warriors of the Tardarden crossed the great river and the old wall, but warbands from many tribes had gone before."

"And what about the garrison in Tekolgerdeloan?" He replied,

Another guttural exchange,

"She says that most of the metal men left a few moons ago. The rest are still inside their stone camp, but none came out to stop their crossing. The Rilrpitu are too fast and too many."

"How many crossed the river?" Thuson asked pleased his new approach seemed to be getting somewhere,

"She doesn't know, at least three warbands."

"And the tribe we face now?"

A guttural exchanged happened, followed by a laugh that cut like an arrow from Yersada,

"You do not face a tribe yet, just a warband of excitable young men looking for plunder. If you want to face the tribes, you must go north. They gather at Yarrtar, in the shadow of the great mountain, a new Saradi calls them there. The holy men saw the great charger ride across the sky, your king was the Outrider, we know what happens next."

Thuson did not understand, "A new host gathers? The raiding parties are just the scouts for an invasion then, is that it? Will they stay and fight us? Young men eager for war."

"At first, they will. But they are easily distracted and will see you as a nuisance to the real fun of raiding. You will only catch them if they want to be caught."

"Why do your people gather?"

A furious exchange happened, longer than he expected. Finally, the reply came,

"The tribes have been moving south for many years, some tribes even ruled these lands before your Doldun came. In that time, we had the freedom to come south, but your king stopped us, turned us back to the steppe. But the land of the steppe is changing, each year the snows fall further, and further south and the winds of Ger are coming closer."

Thuson replied somewhat confused,

"The winds of Ger? Are these other tribes?"

Yersada laughed again, there was a sinister tone to that laugh,

"Tribes maybe, but not like men. Ger is the great lord of the blue sky; the winds are his children, sweeping across the open plains. The tribes flee from them, pushing the others further south."

He stopped, thought, and replied,

"Ger is what the Rilrpitu call Bul, am I correct? She is saying the children of Bul are pushing the tribes south and have been for many years? She must think me a fool to believe this nonsense."

"I believe she is sincere. No one makes light about these things." The woman's voice took on a serious and melancholic tone.

"She expects me to believe that the Bulodon are sweeping over the plains of Belon? This is the stuff of myths, not reality." Thuson said dismissively.

"Who are the Bulodon?" Came the reply, although he was not sure who from. The answer came too quick for the old woman to have translated what he had just said.

"A creature like a man, but who gallops on four legs, at least that is how some tales describe them. Others claim they are more like a menacing cloud that howls. We were told stories of them as children, the children of Bul who enslaved the Xosu before the Dawn of the old kingdoms. Xosu himself defeated them in battle and freed his people from them, leading us to start a fresh in the lands of Xosupil. Other tales tell of the Bulodon terrorising the old kingdoms. Tholophos slayed a band of them to win the high kingship of the Xosu. The later tales tell of the Bulodon returning after the fall of old Kolbos and the collapse of Tholophos' kingdom. But they are just stories to scare children and no doubt memories of the ancestors of the Rilrpitu raiding deep into the civilised lands." This was at least the opinion of learned men in Butophulo. Yusukol certainly held this view, and he was the wisest man Thuson knew, and the most learned in the philosophy of Kunpit.

The guttural tongue of the Rilrpitu once again flooded the room,

"She says she doesn't know these stories, but what you say sounds like the winds of Ger, but they are more creature than man. Born of a cloud impregnated by Ger as he tried to force himself on Tari, mother earth. They spilled on to the plains of Belon and spread death and terror. The clouds have always hung over the plains, but now they move ever closer and attack the tribes every year. The plains are no longer safe. It is as the great charger in the sky presages, the outrider brings the message to the people."

The exchange was interrupted as the sound of a trumpet suddenly flooded the room. Frantic shouting could be heard from the camp. Thuson sprang to his feet and rushed outside. To the south side of the palisade ringing the encampment a rumble of hooves could be heard, and over the horizon a mass of cavalry, above their heads the royal standards of the Doldun. Kalu had arrived.

***

Kalu's cavalry thundered into the camp, streaming passed Thuson and towards the centre where Dolzalo's own royal standard stood.

It will be good to see Kalu again. Thuson followed close behind the deluge of horse and dust toward Dolzalo's quarters. He reached the wooden shack which Dolzalo had been using just as Kalu and another general were dismounting and heading inside. He broke into a run and caught up.

Dolzalo's quarters were almost luxurious compared to what Thuson had received, but now was not the time to feel aggrieved. The generals were wasting no time in gathering for a council of war and Thuson needed to be a part of it. A series of short courtesies happened as Kalu, and the other man, entered and then the talk of war began. Kalu acknowledged him with a smile and a nod of the head, before he spoke,

"What do we know of the enemy?" A broad question but directed at Dolzalo,

"There are about two thousand, camped next to the river in a flat open plain, all a horse. Between us and them is a thickly wooded hill, which is probably the only reason they have not yet fled." The slight annoyance in Dolzalo's voice of having to explain the situation to the younger man was evident. The proud Companion had always found deference hard, especially to younger men.

"And they know we are close by?" Kalu replied, ignoring or oblivious to the annoyance in Dolzalo's voice.

"I have been harassing them for a few weeks now, so yes they know we are here." Dolzalo answered.

"And they know your numbers?" Kalu continued still ignoring the Companion's frustration. Dolzalo replied,

"They know of my numbers yes; I have been breathing down their neck."

"Then a swift assault before they realise our numbers have increased. We have the advantage now." Kalu said, almost the image of Tekolger. He had grown even in the few short months since Thuson had seen him last in Kelantep. Dolzalo came back,

"Exactly my plan. We strike them hard this coming night, no chance for them to scatter or flee, they will not know what hit them before it is too late."

The other general now spoke. Supo of the Dolozolaz, Thuson had not recognised him at first, after all he had only met the grizzled veteran a handful of times, the last almost ten years ago now. Supo had not accompanied the army into Xortogun but had arrived from Doldun with reinforcements during Tekolger's drive north. Indeed, Tekolger had left him as the Togworwoh to govern the northern border, trusting in his skill and wit to hold such a difficult position. But the absence of his forces, that Yersada had just confirmed, was strange to say the least. *There are some questions Supo needs to answer.* The older general said,

"Agreed a swift assault with mine and Kalu's horse in the van, we have done the least of the fighting. A swift strike at dawn and we can put an end to this nonsense. Tekolger would not have stolen his victories at night, and neither will we, best to have the whole empire see us defeat these marauders in the full light of day."

Thuson took his chance and intervened,

"They won't stand. We have more horse yes, but theirs are smaller and swifter. They did not come here to fight but to plunder and as a scouting force. As soon as they see the fight is lost, they will scatter and flee, and we will be chasing them all over the country. That is not an outcome you want, the tribes are gathering to the north, I fear they mean to invade. You need to offer this warband a reason to stand and fight and we need prisoners to put to the question."

Kalu was listening intently, but Supo spoke up, the words crashing into Thuson like a violent wave,

"You want us to offer them something?"

"Yes, some of our baggage train as bait. They will be drawn to it and an ambush can be set; the battle will be over before they can flee. Send to Thorgon as well, Yorotog can block the crossings of the river further downstream, force them to fight on our ground." Thuson answered.

Supo looked unimpressed,

"It wouldn't be an honourable way to win a battle, a brawl over some food in a wagon. Much better to storm into the camp and drive them into the river, hit them like a flood before they know what is happening." he turned to Kalu, "It is what Tekolger would have done. Gods, Tekolger would have been at the head of it all, the first man to wet his spear with the blood of the enemy. That is your role here Kalu."

The young Companion nodded along and said,

"We will strike them at dawn tomorrow. The cavalry will march through the night and engage them early in the morning. I will lead our horse to pin them in place until the infantry can form up and crush them. We will have to take the direct route through the woods that lies between us, it will be difficult, but it gives the best chance of surprise.

I will command Zenu's guard in the van, Supo's men will follow on behind. Dolzalo you will command your contingents on our flanks. Thuson, as it seems you have acquitted yourself well with the reserve, I will rely on you for that role now.

The orders were met by silence, but no one protested, and Kalu was not in the mood to wait to hear if there were any disagreements. Supo and the young Companion both turned on their heels and headed out the door to prepare for the coming battle.

* * *

Thuson left the shack in a hurry, aggrieved that his insights were dismissed and ignored by the Doldun. He knew their attitude to him, a scholar from Butophulo, was unlikely to be welcoming but the indifference to his suggestion was what really hurt, he was not even worthy of rebuke in their eyes. *At least Kalu had listened.* Yet Thuson was sure that he was correct, the Rilrpitu would not stand and fight in an honourable battle, as these Doldun would see it.

They had never taken the time to understand the cultures of the people they were conquering, only Tekolger had seen the value in such things. These men, by contrast, still had one foot in the past, looking to engage in a dual on an open field, an encounter which poems could be written about. Yes, there would be a fight, and some Rilrpitu would be killed, and the rest would scatter and the whole chase would happen all over again. Worse, others would flee north and bring a full-scale invasion down upon them.

Returning to his men, he sought out the commander of his Thulchwal. He could at least do something more than just command the reserve.

Finding Llalon sat amongst his men, slowly grinding his fearsome falx with a whetstone. Over the past weeks the two men, complete opposites of each other, had developed a strange rapport. Thuson still felt in no way in control of his men, but he had a growing respect for the Zummosh chieftain who had proved himself as reliable and trustworthy as he was fearsome. Thuson took a seat next to him and said,

"It seems we will be in the reserve tomorrow, but I do not want to sit idly by."

The huge blonde-haired man had tattoos over his arms and chest, swirling blue patterns which made him seem otherworldly. He said in broken Common Xosu,

"The Thulchwal will not sit out the fight."

Thuson smiled,

"Good, then you will need to gather our supplies together on carts. Your men are fond of an ambush, aren't they?"

Llalon's laughter had a certain poetry to it,

"What will you have us do sage man?"

SANAE

27

A burnt husk still sat where the great hall of the Zummosh once stood. Blackened, burnt, and mangled pieces of wood piled on a scorched patch of ground that was once the centre of the Zummosh's life in Xortogun. Over it loomed a blood red dolthil tree, its golden leaves glistening in the morning sun as if sucking up the energy of the burnt shell below. *Destruction in the name of order,* Sanae thought. That is what she saw, what the Doldun, the Xosu and the Xortogun would see, but the Rilrpitu only seemed to see power, the power of the strong to dominate the weak. She walked on by. *No matter, out of the ashes will rise something new.* To quell the fears of the citizens the governor had made it known in the city that he intended to petition to have the limits of Tekolgertep extended over the south bank so that he could offer his protection to the Zummosh who lived there and ensure that such a thing could not happen again.

The news had buoyed Sanae after much time spent questioning herself. The image of the man choking to death had not left her. Days afterward she was still seeing his image every time she shut her eyes. His blood red face and that black and bruised tongue. It was a hard lesson for sure, shattering her innocence perhaps, a painful experience, a sacrifice to re-forge her view of the world. She could not say what it meant yet, but she was determined to draw the right conclusions from it, as Xosu had. At least her efforts on behalf of the Zummosh seemed to have changed things for the better.

She found Lulpo and Palon in the centre of the village as usual. Palon sat enthroned in a seat of twisted wood. She wore the full ceremonial dress of her priesthood, a Powouzo. On her head an antlered headdress, with feathers that spiralled down her back. Her face was red and blue with the paints the Zummosh claimed were sacred, and her eyes darkened with charcoal. She wore a woven green robe which exposed her stomach and barely covered her chest, revealing the swirling and snaking tattoos that covered her body. Her exposed arms were embraced by many bands of gold.

Two men had been brought before Palon; both had their heads facing to the ground as if they were naughty children reticent in the presence of the formidable matriarch. Sanae did not know what was being said. The guttural sounds of the Zummosh language, strange and lyrical as it was, had no meaning to her. But it was clear that Palon, as the Powouzo, was passing judgement over a dispute. A bronze cauldron sat between the men, Sanae guessed this was the cause of their disagreement. She was bursting to tell Lulpo the good news and so approached straight as an arrow, without regard to the proceedings,

"Have you heard?" She announced before any of them saw her, with the pride of a mother watching her child take its first steps in her voice. "The governor, he is to make the south bank a part of the city."

Lulpo looked up and acknowledged her with a smile. It had a knowing sadness behind it though, one she had not seen in Lulpo before. She was usually so strong and positive.

"The Rilrpitu will not be able to harass you if you are under the protection of the governor and the king."

Lulpo looked up again and said,

"The king is dead; the horse daemons are Keluaz' men. He may look clean and innocent in his white robe, but he has blood on his hands, the Powouzo remember these people. We already have a governor, for all the protection that has offered. It is too late, even if he could protect us, the horse daemons have a taste now, they come every day. Some of our people have started paying them, others leave. Some back to Zenidun, some have fled to the city, now they live on its streets. Those that are still here are much changed, they argue amongst themselves. Look." she pointed at the ongoing trial, "Chaos, the governors' rivalry has brought. My mother will restore order, she is the real governor here, the mistress of our people and the Powouzo will remember this."

"But the with king's law extended over you, you will be able to petition the governor for his help. The Rilrpitu were exploiting you because there was no protection. The High Priest spoke to Keluaz himself and asked him to intervene. It will bring law and governance here and the Rilrpitu will be powerless to stop it." Sanae protested. She thought the Zummosh would at least see the positives of the governor's intervention.

"The law you talk of is just a mirage, power dressed up in fancy clothes, the Powouzo remember this too. All that will change is we will now come under a different governor's control, one with a heavier hand. He would have no need to send the horse daemons to harass us then. He spills our blood to increase his power, that is all." Palon answered this time having dismissed the two supplicants in front of her.

"The Rilrpitu were acting alone. I don't think the governor would allow such violence in his city, let alone order it." Sanae replied. "He loves the city. He oversaw its construction after all."

"The horse daemons lack the mind for such schemes." Palon replied in a rather oblivious manner, emphasised by the dark black circles around her eyes.

Sanae felt the despair rise in her. The shock of the man choking to death flashed before her once again, the red face burning crimson, the fire in his eyes. The positive news from the governor had given her something else to focus on, but Lulpo and Palon had torn that to shreds.

"What will you do?" She asked after a long moment of reflection,

"Of that we have no knowledge. There is no desire to return to Zenidun, but there is little left for us in the city." Palon answered with a sweet and innocent smile. The despondent feeling coursing through Sanae must have become evident as Palon stopped, and touched her face, "So depressed child? We will be ok."

Sanae forced a smile back,

"I know, but I tried hard to get the High Priest to speak to the governor. With everything else going on I thought this news would be something positive, for everyone."

Palon's lips parted,

"I see." she paused, "Your efforts are very much appreciated. That is a noble thing which you have done, but it was always too late, I fear." The graceful priestess paused again and looked Sanae deep in the eye, "There is more than that though child, this Powouzo can see. What else is troubling you?"

Sanae had hoped she would not ask, but she could not hide her emotions. She felt the tears well up in her eyes,

"The tasks." she said, "My tasks to become an initiate of Xosu, they are very taxing on me. The lessons are hard to learn…" She shuddered and stuttered over the words. Three times she tried to speak but nothing would come out. "He died." She eventually said.

Palon pulled her close,

"Who died?"

"A man, he was a condemned criminal, but I didn't know. In my task I gave him dolthil fruit. It was poisoned, and he choked in front of me. I didn't know what to do and I don't know what lessons I am supposed to learn." Sanae answered, it all came out in a rush.

Palon was silent, but the comfort of the embrace and a gentle hand on Sanae's head was enough to calm her. Lulpo, however, spoke,

"This is what you call civilisation? You cannot try to sell us the virtues of this life under the rules of your city when it does this to you."

Sanae was taken aback,

"He was a condemned man; a criminal and it was done to learn the secrets of the bright god. Nothing against the rule of law. I am told that the Zummosh carry out some horrific practices without the law to prevent anything."

Lulpo nodded,

"Indeed, some of the rituals may be cruel, but as you say, they are done in times of need to gain the favour and protection of the gods. The Powouzo remember that the god's protection is a bargain, it requires a great sacrifice on our part, for the greater good. But we do it all out in the open, no secrets. How are we any less civilised than you?"

She had no answer, it was all too overwhelming, and she did not know what to think of any of it anymore. She knew that the tasks would be hard and challenge her, but she had never imagined that they would push her to the boundaries of what she felt able to do and what felt right. All she could think was that the bright one must have a purpose to test his followers in such a way.

* * *

She spent the rest of the day with the Zummosh, helping in any way she could, but the spectre of recent events haunted her. The walk back to the temple of Xosu had felt long and lonely and the contrast between the rough, broken village set amongst the wilderness and the city of shining marble could not have been starker. But her next task was approaching and the one thing she was still sure of was that she had to see her initiation through to the end. Having all the mysteries of Xosu revealed to her was the only way she felt she could begin to learn from her experiences. By the time she reached the stairs to the temple and began to ascend, the sun had fallen from the sky and the moon had not yet risen.

She found Helupelan in his chambers. High Priest or not, he was the closest thing Sanae had to a father, and he had always been willing to listen to her. She joined the High Priest at the table in the centre of his chambers. It was a place she had many fond memories of, and it had a homely sense of comfort for her. Helupelan was washing down with wine the last of a plate of fruit, including some from the dolthil tree, from the same batch which was picked for her tasks no doubt.

"What is wrong?" He asked, without looking at her. He raised his eyes from his plate to meet hers,

"You only come to me like this when there is something wrong, ever since you were little. In fact, it reminds me of Tekolger, he would do the same when he was a boy. What has upset you?"

At first, she could not find the words, but eventually she said,

"The governor will protect the Zummosh won't he?"

"If they move into the city, or the boundaries are extended to cover the south bank then they come under the laws of the city and the governor embodies that. If they do not break that covenant, they will be protected." Helupelan answered with a warm smile, it was not really the answer Sanae wanted to hear.

"Lulpo says that it has all been a trick to extend the power of Keluaz and that the Rilrpitu wouldn't have acted without his say so. Many of the Zummosh will leave instead." She told him, hoping for the High Priest to say something to make it all better.

"There is no trick, but there is no way to make the problem vanish either. But the Rilrpitu have never had to live under law, power is all they know. Expanding Keluaz's reach will allow him to exercise control over them more thoroughly, especially as it seems that Koluun was unable to protect the Zummosh from Guntoga. The expansion of the city will be a good thing in the long run, for everyone, not just the Zummosh." Helupelan said with such assuredness that she could do nothing but believe him. Sanae nodded and said,

"Xosu brought civilisation to man to allow us to thrive and prosper, but it seems that civilisation is condemning the Zummosh. Palon provides them with guidance and judgement in disputes, I witnessed such a thing just this morning. Perhaps they do not need the governor's guardianship? Perhaps their civilisation is different?"

"Xosu taught us the knowledge of civilisation, a wisdom previously the reserve of the gods alone, when we were unable to live the primitive lifestyle which man did before the Dawn of the old kingdoms, for the world had changed. It had become closer to the realm of the gods, more aligned. Bringing freedom, fire, farming, and the vine saw us prosper but, as what happened to the bright god himself shows, there is a cost to such knowledge. It is like grasping a sword which is only a blade. It has power in it, the potential to make people strong and prosperous, but it can also hurt us as well. It is our job to use that knowledge to strive for the best, for ourselves and society, but we must be aware of the dangers which come with it." Helupelan replied.

The door creaked open and Kolae entered. Her two shadows in toe as always and the usual dissatisfied look cracking a crescent across her round face.

"There you are. You know your next task is tonight. Where have you been?" She demanded of Sanae, a hint of angry red creeping over her face.

"Helping Lulpo and Palon, they need all the aid they can get." Sanae defiantly answered,

"So, whilst we have been working for the good of the temple all day, you have been playing with your savage friend, no doubt discussing things which should not pass these walls as well. Maybe you should consider your commitment to the bright god if that is how you wish to spend your days." Kolae's reply was scornful and cut deep.

"Leave the girl be Kolae. You are right, perhaps she should not be spending so much time with the Zummosh, but do not be so harsh." Helupelan interjected, "Please would you fetch a plate for Sanae. There are things I would like to discuss with her."

Kolae was clearly unhappy with this suggestion, Sanae felt a smile creep over her lips. The High Priestess nodded her head to the High Priest and left the room, Zenthelae leading the way and Konthelae trailing behind. Turning back to Sanae, Helupelan said,

"The High Priestess is hard and firm in her views, but there is truth in what she says. Being a devotee of Xosu takes time and commitment. You should be spending your days at the temple, and you know you cannot tell those outside of the mysteries of Xosu."

"I have told no one of Xosu's mysteries, not that I know enough of them myself, and I am committed to the temple, but I am also fearful for those outside of these walls. Xosu found and helped his people, it feels right that we should seek to do the same." She defended herself, she felt justified in her decisions and would not let anyone tell her otherwise.

Kolae came back into the room and placed a plate of olives, chickpeas and bread and a cup of dark red unmixed wine in front of her. Sanae looked down at the plate, a golden dolthil fruit sat in the middle. Grown from the blood of the bull she sacrificed, it was plump and juicy, rich even, but it was from the same batch of sweet fruit that the man she killed was poisoned. The thought of eating it made her feel sick. She picked up the fruit first. *Best to get it over with,* she thought. Taking a big bite out of the fruit, she felt the honey within trickle down her chin as Helupelan answered her,

"What you did for the Zummosh was good and noble. Although your behaviour was beyond what is proper, I was proud of the way you took a stand."

Sanae suddenly felt lightheaded, the fruit was sweet, but the memories it brought were unpleasant, a dizziness took over her, her head felt light, as if it were floating to the sky. She grasped for the red wine, dark as blood, it flooded down her throat, burning as it went. Unmixed, the wine filled her head, the divine knowledge it contained undiluted by the waters of the earth. Helupelan continued,

"The governor is aware of the problem now, perhaps it is best if you leave it in the hands of the proper authorities…" Sanae's vision went blurry, the High Priest was just a blobbed outline of a shape shining brightly as rays of light jumped off his robe, around him all was black. "Besides your next task is about to begin and the bright god requires all of your attention, focus on his path."

Everything went black.

**

She ascended to the river valley again; it was beginning to feel like home. She looked to the trees, the forest with a mighty dolthil rising from its centre, and listened for the horn, but no sound came. She waited for an age, but nothing happened. She had drunk Gelithul's wisdom before and had a taste for it now. She pressed the fruit herself, after she scaled the dolthil tree which loomed overhead.

The wine dark liquid tasted bitter and sweet as honey as it passed her lips and burnt with an intensity only the gods would know as it drained down her throat, lifting her up and up. She took three long gulps, it was almost more than she could bear, was it agony or delight? It was exquisite nonetheless and she realised so many things now, things she had not known before.

In front of her she saw horned men flee from falling trees as cities rose all around them and a bright gaping hole formed in the sky. The wind picked up and clouds swept across the heavens and lightning branched across the sky's canopy. Hooves rumbled in her ears as riders stormed across the night, only the protective light of the moon shielded her even though it glowed red with vicious intent.

She turned to run, but her steps took her nowhere. Finally, she reached the sea, a young white serpent crawled out and stretched itself across an open plain to gorge on the fruits of the earth. It grew rich and fat from the succulent earth and the gifts brought across the sea.

Then it came in a burning red arrow across the sky, two heads it had and two births, from the shining sky the bright god descended and beneath the earth the other rose. Together they met and clashed for a third and final birth. A red-faced god with a crown of white and red and black. A fierce, single-minded logic to his purpose and a message for all the peoples of Kolgennon. He drove a wild ecstasy in Sanae, a madness that she had never experienced before, as if some god was trying to speak to her, but the power of his voice was too great for her to bear.

Then nine shifting wraiths rose from the waters as again branches of lightning crackled across the canvass of the sky. The white leviathan resting on the plain was caught in a flood, drowned, and slaughtered, carried off by the blue shadows. The power in its blood theirs to use. For a moment she was terrified, but in a flash of bright light, the world came together, and the realms of gods and men were settled as one.

A sweet smell roused her from her sleep, rosy coloured fingers crept towards her, but the world was still a blur and her head thick with fog. She looked around but did not know where she was. A voice called out to her, and she felt compelled to follow it. Stumbling to her feet, Sanae slowly began to follow the lyrical tones of whoever was calling.

Her feet felt awkward as if they were the wrong way around. The light dancing through her window pranced with colour and dawn's blood red fingers clawed at her. She tumbled away, towards the door, more falling than walking, the madness of the night before still upon her. Down the corridor which twisted and turned and spiralled, she bounced off the walls but eventually found her way to the end, dawn's dancing fingers still chased her, bright with light. Falling through the doorway, the great hall stretched before her, the reflecting pool alive with light.

In the distance she heard the pounding of hooves, and then she saw it. A cloud and a creature, galloping, with a terrifying menace in its eyes. The creature raised itself on to its hind legs and let out a deafening cry as it crashed down, kicking, and trampling a man and a woman beneath its feet. Sanae's heart broke to see the anguish and defeat on their faces, she knew then she had to do something.

She felt a hand on her shoulder and another on her back, lifting her to her feet. A beautiful maiden, pale, and dark, with cascading navy locks. Her figure sculpted from flowing, rushing water, translucent but glowing as if lit by moonlight. A shadow of a figure had arisen from the ground. The wraith smiled at her and placed something in her hands. Sanae looked down, it was a weapon. Flashing white, now gold, now red, the colour glistened like a serpent up the curving bow. She knew the arrow was sharp and deadly, it felt as hard and vicious as a hydra's fang, as if it could just as easily kill its wielder as its target. She knew what she must do.

Her legs moved before she had time to think, her feet splashed through the shallow water that surrounded them and with a scream she drew the bow to her cheek and loosed the arrow. The vicious yet beautiful white-gold shaft drove into the heart of the beast. It let out an almighty scream as its crimson red blood washed like a tide over the arrow and then collapsed on the floor. Sanae helped the oppressed people to their feet.

Suddenly, she felt queasy and weak, collapsing to her knees. The colour of the world seemed to crumble around her, and she was transported back to the great hall of the temple, kneeling in the reflecting pool before the statue of the bright god and his altar.

A hand touched her shoulder, she looked around. Kolae handed her a cup which Sanae eagerly drained. Others came and helped her to her feet, guiding her back to her chamber and her bed. Helupelan was waiting for her there. After a few moments he spoke,

"Relax, the effects will wear off soon enough."

She tried to reply, but she was too weak.

"You have now experienced madness, like the madness which Tholo struck Xosu with after he slew her scaled white, many headed, dragon. For years Xosu wandered in the west, overcome by the madness and the grief he felt for the loss of his dear friend and mentor. When he came across men, who had been broken by the onslaught of the daemons of the hidden realms, he taught them the ways of civilisation and the way to harness the fire of the gods, but his madness and grief only grew when he saw how men, scattered and weak in the broken world, had been enslaved by the vicious Bulodon, the cruel children of Bul. But not all the gods were happy to see Xosu fail.

Sem, although defeated and banished by Dunsun, still has power in the world, he sent his children to aid Xosu as he had his son Buto. The children of Sem, the Kinsolsun, took the maddened Xosu in, housed him in their Thelonbet, cured him of his affliction and used their famous skill to forge a white-gold bow from the horns of the hydra for Xosu to fight the hordes of Bulodon who had overrun the land and enslaved men. A hard-fought battle saw Xosu succeeded in driving away the cruel Bulodon, those savage sons of Bul, freeing the people who would later take his name for their own. Those same people who had sprung from the hydra's teeth so some claim. Rest now and think on what I have told you."

Helupelan got up to leave and soon darkness descended on the world once more.

* * *

Gelithul came to her again, though wilder than before. His antlers more horns than branches, his auburn mane ablaze with colour, the music of his pipes and his followers deeper and darker than before, the whimsical sounds and dancing now gone. He bowed before her, stumbling drunkenly forward, the wineskin gripped tightly in his hand, his green eyes shot through with blood,

"Sweet child." his voice was long and drawn and he slurred his words, "You tasted the wine of Gelithul and saw my wisdom."

Sanae nodded slowly, "The fire, how did you know?"

Gelithul let out a shrill laugh, deep, low, and sinister, the chorus behind him echoed it, *Oh! Oh! Oh!*

"I did not know, you saw."

"And what of the other things I saw? Will they come to pass as well?"

"Some will, others have already happened, some are a glimpse of what may be." The crooked smile on his face was unnerving.

"How do I know which?"

"You don't sweet child, but you could. Find your blood, and you will find your home."

"How?"

"You know sweet child." The voice echoed as he disappeared.

Sanae found herself lying on her back, a familiar hand on her shoulder. The water maiden had returned to aid her, the moonlight glistening on her and through her, her shape ever changing. The maiden whispered something in her ear,

"Zummosh...Lulpo...Xura" were all the words Sanae thought she understood. Her world was engulfed by shadow.

Gentle warmth of dawn crept into her chambers, and she awoke, not knowing how much time had passed. Her head was still cloudy, but she found herself getting up with a compulsion to head into the city. The first few steps she took were more a stumble toward the door, but soon she regained control of her legs and found herself descending the steps of Xosu's Temple.

The world seemed alive with colour, even before Dunsun's great eye had fully emerged. Her head was still foggy, her thinking not clear, apart from knowing that the solution to the Zummosh's problems lay with the temple of Xura, although she did not know why. *Find my blood, find my home*, the words did not make sense to her.

The clouds seemed almost alive, and the sounds of the waking city jumped out to her. Before long she knew she was in the Xortogun district, although she could not remember how she got there. She only knew where she was as the dress of the people changed. The distinct tunics and hairstyles of the Xortogun unmistakable. She did not recall them being so outlandish though, or the strength of the scent of perfume and incense, almost jumping out and dancing before her eyes.

She turned suddenly. The eyes of a great menacing bird came baring down upon her. She whirled to run, but her legs would not allow her. She stumbled again grasping a wall, looking up, the long beaked bird was on her again, the floor came on fast in her panic.

A hand encrusted with jewels touched her shoulder and a kind voice reached out. She turned and opened her eyes expecting the worst. *The priest, Kurmush,* she thought, *at least it might be.* His hair was styled, but wild in its own way, flowing like water, his bright eyes glowing like two full moons and fire in his eyes, but he seemed translucent, more wraith than man. The priest opened one of her eyes wide, his hands firm on her face, his fingers felt like claws. He did the same with the other eye and said with a tongue that was long like a rasping snake,

"What daemon has possessed you? This servant has seen this before, this way."

He helped her to her feet and led Sanae inside the temple. Kurmush sat her on a stone bench and handed her a cup.

"Drink this, it will help."

She sipped at the strange, maroon liquid. It was and thick like honey, almost too much to swallow.

"Don't sip, you must drink it all. It tastes acrid, but it will help. The sap of the sacred trees is difficult to stomach, but it will taper those who seek wisdom in its branches." The priest insisted. Sanae drained the cup slowly. She struggled to swallow it all, the liquid was warm like fire and had hard lumps of something in it. Kurmush continued, the perfume on him was thick and burnt like fire,

"Now tell this servant why he found you wandering outside the temple having consumed so potent a concoction of dolthil fruit?"

Sanae was coming back to her senses slowly, but when she tried to speak the words did not come out how she wanted,

"The water maiden made of moonlight…to help the Zummosh…she said to come here."

Kurmush paused for a moment before a wry smile crept over his lips, his mouth forming a crescent from ear to ear,

"This servant knows of no water maiden, but she is a blessing no doubt. Xura's light is a source of protection after all. This servant presumes you mean the way the governor is using his Rilrpitu to seize control of the Zummosh on the south bank. A pitiful situation, but apt work for those savages."

"Can you help…? the Zummosh will be ruined." Her ability to speak was slowly returning.

Kurmush was stood by what appeared to be a small shrine, with his back to her. After a long pause, he replied,

"The goddess may have a solution for you. If the Zummosh were to come under her temple's protection, they would not be subject to either of the governors. The king, Tekolger, restored all the ancient privileges of the goddess, crushed under the foot of the savage Rilrpitu kings. The protection of Xura extends over the whole of Xortogun. They would have to submit to the will of the goddess though, working for her priesthood."

He took something from the shrine and slid back round to face her,

"Take this, it is the seal of Xura. All who bear this are under her protection, the governor and the guards will be unable to touch the Zummosh if they produce this."

Sanae took the elaborately crafted seal. The avian head of the foreign goddess staring back at her looked both menacing and somehow comforting, with two great disks for eyes, each like the moon at her fullest, there was a warmth to the figure.

"Thank you, I can't say if the Zummosh will agree, they value their freedom and independence more than most. But I will ask."

KALASYAR

28

The morning came too quickly. Dunsun took his seat on his mighty throne to preside over a new day. A Zummosh sellsword, a different one from the night before, entered the room and signalled to Kalasyar that she had to leave. Reluctantly she bid her grandfather an emotional farewell and headed straight to the theatre.

The Nine had announced that the public theatre, a crescent cut into the side of the dome that was Tholo's Tear, would host the show trial of Koseun Sisosi. The theatre had witnessed many spectacles performed for the crowds of citizens to impart wisdom to those who ruled the city, from *Xosu and Gelithul* to the *Legacy of Tholophos* and *The Hubris of the King of Kings*. It had also played host to the most important trials of the old League, held for all the public to see, but this was a mockery of what once was.

When she arrived a crowd was gathering, the Salxosu coming together as they had done for centuries to show their appreciation to the artists and playwrights or to bring tribute like in the days of old Kolbos or the Kinsolsun before then. Dunobos, Kolkobuas and a small entourage were already there along with her handmaids.

"Kalasyar, how is he?" Dunobos asked her with some sympathy in his voice.

"As foolish as always. He would not listen to reason; he is determined to fight this losing battle."

"Koseun has found his old spirit again. I would be lying if I did not say it gladdens my heart a little to see once more the man I remember, who stood up to the Rinuxosu all those years ago. Do not be so dismissive, he follows reason still, but it is a reason driven towards a greater goal than self-preservation."

She sighed,

"I know. But there are younger men who could be leading this fight. My grandfather should be allowed to live out his final years in peace."

"The world is not always a just place. The gods can be fickle. But this may not be the end, I have managed to rouse many to come to Koseun's support. Who knows, maybe the old snake is right, and his example will shake the people from their stupor. He has friends in this audience, if we can make enough of a ruckus then perhaps the Nine will think again before continuing down this path."

"Well then let us hope the gods take notice. Bosguli most of all so that justice will win out."

They allowed themselves to be swept into the theatre by the tide of people and took their seats on the carved benches. The benches had been lined with marble shipped to the city from Xortogun. Purple in colour and unique to the great valley, the ability to acquire this marble once symbolised the wealth and reach of Butophulo.

On the stage had been constructed a platform with nine chairs facing the audience. An old statue of Buto, tail curling and hammer raised ready to strike, sat behind them, said to have been a relic from old Kolbos, rescued from the ruins. The shadow of the old circular harbour sprawled in the distance, the writhing sea as a backdrop to it all. The Nine would sit on this raised platform and preside over the trial. To one side on another set of benches slightly out of the way, the Doldun officers would watch.

Doltopez had already taken his place, wearing a white Xosu style toga trimmed with a blood red he looked on as the stage was prepared. About a dozen Doldun officers sat around him, gathered like clouds around a mountain top. Opposite them was another row of seats where the jury would sit. Here the Nine clearly had felt they could not take a risk and had broken with tradition. Instead of the whole citizen body having their say on the matter, as would have been done of old, a handpicked jury, which the tyrants claimed represented all citizens, would pass their verdict.

The growing crowd fell silent as first the jury walked on to the stage, then the Nine appeared like shadows behind them to take their seats.

"Look at them all." Dunobos whispered, "Koseun has reopened my eyes to the injustice of their rule. Turning against their city to side with the Doldun. So much for their principals and philosophies. No, they are shapeshifters, changing so that they could discard the old traditions and behave as gods amongst men. The seats they take now are perhaps the worst example of that. The position of Tukis is our oldest tradition, going back to old Kolbos itself yet they distort it for their own ends."

Dunobos voice was growing louder as he spoke.

"Careful" she whispered to him as faces in the crowd turned to look at Dunobos, "You will get us removed before the trial even begins."

Dunobos scoffed but nodded.

"Even that would be a mockery. The Tukis' most important role was to preside over debates and trials. To let the people of the city speak."

"I know, they were also chosen by lot and only meant to serve three months. My grandfather ensured I learnt how our League functioned. But now is not the time, focus on the trial."

"My apologies, I had not realised the depth of fury that has grown inside me."

Dunobos finally grew silent as the Nine took their seats. Puskison and his kin took to the stage first, followed by what was left of the Rusos. Then came the Kosua, led by their patriarch Kera. He was a strange man, sighted even less in public than the others, with a hooked nose and pointed features. It was whispered around the city that his manse had become the haunt of mystics and sorcerers, where blood rites were performed and attempts to fulfil strange prophesies went unhindered. In contrast, his son, Kisonsun, was almost never out of the public eye. A young man with the body of a dancer, he spent most of his time in pursuit of the maidens of the city. Indeed, he maintained an entourage that many western potentates would be jealous of. Kalasyar had never been sure which, the father or son, she found most unnerving.

Rinukiso Polriso was the last onto the stage. The Polriso patriarch was in the prime middle years. He had a typical Polriso look to him, the dark, almost navy, hair, and the deep, royal blue colour in his eyes. His dress was lavish and aimed at accentuating these features. He was well known for his feeling that the Polriso's fall from grace was an injustice, speaking often in public of the great Polriso kings of the past. The sight of him hurt the most, it was his schemes which had caused this trial to happen.

Finally, Koseun was led in and placed at the centre of the stage. Puskison Posuausthison, sat in middle of the nine wraiths, stood. The wizened old man looked like a philosopher should, but the way he spoke, sniffling and yelping, made him seem more tired old hound than the panther he claimed to be. The sweet-smelling perfumes he wore could not hide the stench of deceit on him which drew likeminded people to his side. The bronze statue behind him seemed to glow as he made to speak,

"Koseun Sisosi, you stand accused of impiety, corrupting the youth of the city, and conspiring to overthrow the Council of the Nine Philosophers. This trial will seek to find the truth of these accusations and so I ask those who accuse you to come forward and speak."

What followed was a grotesque scene. A host of the Nine's sycophants were led on to the stage to present their supposed evidence. Some who had attended symposiums in the Sisosi villa others Kalasyar did not know. A Kolkisuasu son who she recognised despite his bruises, was first to be led on,

"I frequented the symposiums hosted by Koseun Sisosi for many months, naïve as I was in my youth. At first, they seemed innocent, a place to gather and discuss interesting but harmless questions, but slowly I was drawn further into the inner circles. As I was trusted more, I was allowed closer and closer to Koseun's own discussion groups. What I found being debated there chilled me to my very core. Our generous and benevolent patrons, these nine men who have brought peace to the city were denounced and degraded and worse." He lied and did not even seem to be convincing himself of the truth of his words.

Even a Kinsol and a Rososthup appeared. The claims they made about the symposiums were worse.

"They are a place for those hostile to the rule of the Council to gather and plot. But more than that, lewd acts are carried out, the old coercing the young and leading them astray in worship to their horrific serpent of a god, in mockery of the proper traditions." The Rososthup proclaimed.

"They spoke openly of overthrowing the Council of the Nine Philosophers. 'Slaying the many headed hydra, bleeding them white to bring about a new dawn', is how they described it. These poisonous words were poured into our ears." The Kinsol added.

A Polriso, who Kalasyar recognised as a friend of Koseun from before the fall of the city to the Doldun, was led out next,

"This man was a champion of the corrupt regime which ran the League in mockery of liberty. How many times did you see him stand at the foot of Polriso's Hill and give speeches whose twisted words concealed the truth of the corruption of the League from the people of the city? In front of the Hill which my ancestor led our people to escape the chaos which the League brought back. Let me refresh your memories.

'We must not faulter, fail or flounder, one more push, one more effort, one more sacrifice of blood and treasure and the Rinuxosu will fall.'

Words this man spoke to keep the people of this fine city committed to a war from which only the corrupt men like Koseun Sisosi benefited. Now there is peace and prosperity, the Rinuxosu and the Doldun are our allies, all brought about by the benevolent rule of the Nine Philosophers. Is it any wonder that men such as Koseun Sisosi were planning to commit vile murder? The only question is why it has taken them so long in the attempt."

His old speeches made to keep the city united and free during the height of the war with the Rinuxosu. Words that had been lorded and praised by these very people, copied, and acted upon, were now being used to condemn her grandfather.

Throughout it all, Koseun just stood and watched, indifferent. He seemed settled, relaxed even. A contrast to the crowd who made their displeasure known and felt. They shouted down the so-called witnesses to a point where the mercenaries lining the front of the dais were forced to step in and restore order. The most farcical display was left until last. A final witness, Kinril Polriso, was brought before the court and proclaimed with a jester-like smile,

"Far from being a lone assailant, the man who viciously attacked and murdered Dorthil Rusos on the streets of our proud city, Sisuhul Polriso was his name, was a regular attendant of Koseun's symposium. A young man lured in by the charisma of a dangerous demagogue whose only desire was to bring back the chaos of the League for his own benefit. I know this as he was my kin, and I attended these sessions as well, and for a time was almost seduced myself. The promise of changing the city and bringing our once prominent family back to the station our ancient blood demands was a tempting reason for sedition, but it was a promise based on lies. Koseun took particular interest in Sisuhul, often taking him off to talk privately. Who knows what cruel deeds and poisonous words were exchanged, but it had the desired effect. No doubt this was the first step in a much wider conspiracy to sow chaos amongst the Council of the Nine Philosophers which has brought stability and prosperity. I am ashamed for my attendance at these events now. Folly and naivety drew me there. Thankfully, mine own, Rinukiso has more sense and set me back on the right path." His smile turned sinister.

A ripple of shock went through the crowd. Kalasyar felt the fury rising inside her, her face reddening and her tongue felt thick with fury. She had no idea who this man was, but he had never attended any symposium of her grandfather. She remembered every face that came into her home.

Puskison rose again from his seat below the god and said,

"The evidence would appear damning, but we believe in a fair hearing and the rule of law, so the accused will have the chance to defend himself. Koseun, do you deny the charges brought against you?"

Koseun took a moment to look each of his judges in the eye, like a snake eyeing up its prey. *He looks more composed than I have ever seen him,* she thought. He then turned to view the jury and then the Doldun, all the while remaining silent. Finally, he turned back to the Nine and spoke,

"I do not address any of you Nine tyrants, or your Doldun masters, the king who put you in place, the old general who rules from his palace to the north, or the man who sits here today occupying our city. Instead, I talk to you." He said pointing at the jury and continuing around to the crowd, "The people of Butophulo, this once glorious metropolis of the Xosu. As for these charges, I do not protest my innocence, as I will not condone your mockery. But there was no corruption, no conspiracy, and no killing on my part. For anyone else I cannot speak." He said these words as he fixed his gaze upon Puskison, "I do not speak to defend myself, but to defend Butophulo and the glorious citizens of this fine haven. I do not blame those of you who have spoken against me, it is the cruelties of the system that has been imposed upon us that drove you to do it." He paused; his old speaking skills had not grown rusty in all the years since the fall of the League. He let what he had said sink into the crowd,

"It may be true that the oligarchy in which we now reside has brought peace and stability to our once troubled city. The streets are safe, and we do not go to sleep every night with a fear that the next day may bring an army to our walls with all the brutality that would ensure. This is all true. But at what cost?" It was a rhetorical question, but Koseun still paused as if to allow an answer,

"In a word, our freedom. These nine men sit enthroned as gods amongst you, the sovereignty which once rested with the citizens of this city is horded with them alongside the riches they have seized. They attack the old League, saying it brought us nothing but chaos, war, and defeat." He stopped, looked around and then continued, his voice raised, and the intensity of his speech increased,

"They are wrong! It brought us the freedom to choose, to govern our own lives and to strive for greatness in a way we could not do before or since. It allowed us to pursue trade and look to the open seas, each man a king on his own ship and an equal in the assemblies. The history of our League was not a story of fated heroes or benevolent kings, but of ordinary men working together for a greater good. We were a realm free of the burning tyranny of haughty kings ruling from on high or the writhing oppression of cruel oligarchs rising from beneath our feet.

Look at how we were viewed with envy. Some chose to throw off the shackles of their tyrants, learning from our example, and joined us in the greatest League of cities since old Kolbos was offered the paternal care of Sem, the wisdom of Tholo, and the enterprise of Buto.

When our League became rich and powerful, the old kings feared that their time would end and turned on us in their jealously. It took two of those kings, and treachery from within to bring us down. That is the strength our League gave us." He stopped again and surveyed his work; he had the crowd in the palm of his hand. Kalasyar could not remember the last time she heard her grandfather speak in public like this, but he had lost none of his ability and was clearly revelling in the task, even with the danger looming over him,

"They may sit here enthroned as gods among us, allied to a divine king who has subdued the world, looking down their noses at us as barbarous and chaotic, but they sit there in fear. Fear of our freedom, fear of our ability to stand alongside them as equals and face down their tyranny. Most of all it is a fear that deep down they know we are equal to them as men, and civilised men at that." Turning back to the silent Nine watching on, Koseun continued,

"My ancestor, Yunsunos Sisosi once led the people of this great city to overthrow the last tyrants who ruled us unjustly, I now take up that mantle. Punish me how you like, use that power you have stolen from your fellow citizens. I do not care what you do to me. I have lived a long and good life, and I will enter the realm of Sem with a smile and greet the great serpent as I would an old friend. But be wary of your actions, you can only push the good people of this city so far. Other tyrants were too slow to learn that lesson and all that remains of their legacy is akin to fallen leaves scattered by the wind."

A ripple of agreement went through the crowd, some of the mercenaries warily gripped their spears. Kalasyar even thought, or hoped, it resonated in the jury. The silence was broken by Rinukiso Polriso, standing, and proclaiming,

"He does not deny the charges, his guilt is therefore clear. The only thing left to do is decide his punishment." the crowd was getting restless, "Clearly execution is the only suitable punishment for someone so treasonous and disrespecting of our city and our Council."

The crowd reacted poorly to the suggestion, shouts and jeers filled the theatre. The mercenary soldiers who lined the front of the stage lowered their spears, fearful of the crowd surging toward them. Koseun went to speak again, an act which silenced the crowd,

"I have been nothing but honest with everyone here. I think a ruling that I be allowed free meals at the sacred hearth would be suitable for someone who does such honest and honourable service to their city."

Some in the crowd laughed at the suggestion, Rinukiso looked on horrified. Puskison stood again,

"The admission of guilt is clear to us. Does the jury agree?"

Slowly the jury indicated their assent. Kalasyar felt like she had been punched in the stomach.

"Very well, the judges will retire to consider their verdict."

With that the Nine stood to leave. Everyone else stayed in place but the crowd was restless and ready to explode in fury. She looked to Doltopez, perhaps he might intervene, one word from him would stun all into silence. He was sat relaxed, drinking a cup of wine seemingly enjoying the storm his puppets had unleashed. He motioned to an attendant and whispered in their ear. The man ran off after the Nine. She hoped it was an intervention but knew in her heart that was unlikely.

The crowd eventually settled down and began to filter out of the theatre as the mercenaries nervously stood their ground.

* * *

She did not know what she was doing after it all had ended, she found herself walking alone, but she was not sure where she was going. Following the line of the road that circled around the Kobon heading to the carved staircase that led to the summit of Polriso's Hill.

The shadow of the immense walls of the Sanctuary loomed down over her. The natural rock formation, and the walls above stood like a sheer cliff where the sea abruptly meets the land and strife follows as wave crashes against rock. On top of the walls the temple complex loomed over her like a great tree, casting a shadow around her that seemed to stretch forever. The stairs themselves had a wooden palisade on their front, one of the first acts of the Doldun garrison when they were placed in the city was to construct the barrier. Turning the beating heart of the city, open to all comers, into a fortified citadel from which the Doldun could dominate the metropolis.

She approached the two guards who had been left at the entrance, the purple of their cloaks matching the sky.

"My name is Kalasyar Sisosi, I am here to see your commander." She said in a confident and commanding tone hoping that they would listen. To her surprise they seemed to be expecting her. No questions asked, one of the men merely motioned for her to follow him inside.

She had not been inside the Sanctuary since she was a small child, she wondered what had changed since then. Her memories where of a wondrous realm where the gods and men seemed to meet. She was not to be too disappointed. Although the Doldun had turned the site into a barracks, the visible signs of which made her shudder, one civilisation smothering another it seemed, underneath that layer it was clear that the heart of the city was still beating.

Nine small shrines dotted the landscape in a circle around the temple of Buto which sat directly in the centre, fully exposed to the gaze of the mother, and hiding the father who dwelt below. The shrines and temple had been raised during the height of the League, lavish now but underneath were older structures, less spectacular but more sacred. Stone pillars held up the central temple and a pattern chiselled into it which appeared to wrap itself around the building like a snake coiling around its prey. Atop a red and bronze statue of the crippled god, only depicted from the waist up, the building itself where his legs should have been, forming a writhing tail instead. It brought back memories of her journey to the oracle of Buto in the ruins of old Kolbos. The great temple of Buto at the centre of the Thelonbet bore the same image, although ten times as large.

Legend said that the Sanctuary was the place the survivors of old Kolbos gathered, led by Polriso under the guidance of the oracle, a gift given to the faithful by the great smith. A safe harbour and a hill to fortify, a haven for those ejected from their city to shelter from the storm of the aftermath of its fall. In the central shrine there was a spring, said to have burst out of the ground when Sem blew his horn for the survivors to quench their thirst, although it only flowed with saltwater now. Atop the spring had sprouted an enormous hulthul tree, nurtured from the seeds of the one which grew within the Thelonbet of old Kolbos. Her grandfather had always said that the hulthul trees of the White Islands were a gift from the gods, grown from seeds buried deep in the ground, watered by the blood of the crippled god. Unlike the dolthil trees of the west they shone like the moon rather than the sun.

The guard led her to the huge building in the centre, it sat on a promontory of its own, watching over both the city and the sea beyond and once served as both temple and treasury for the old League. The huge bronze door at its front was open. She was taken inside, right to the centre of the building, what appeared to be the old quarters of the high priest. Below the dome which now sheltered the hulthul tree that sprouted from the earth spring.

There Doltopez stood over a white gold table in the heart of the room. Doltopez was still in his blood red trimmed robe. He stood staring out across the city illuminated as it was by the stars which appeared before the moon rose in the sky. He spun round quickly when he heard her enter the room. A smile flashed like lightning across his lips,

"I did not expect the pleasure of your company this evening." He said as he glided towards her and poured a cup of a fine red wine, gesturing for her to take a seat. He poured another and handed it to Kalasyar. She said nothing and drank deep. The liquid was rich and mellow, its tendrils reaching through her and telling her what she needed to do.

Absent mindedly he pointed towards the strange table in the centre of the room.

"Do you recognise it?"

The white gold table was round and smooth, with a flat top. But the closer she looked the less like a table it appeared.

"It looks more like an anvil than a table." she replied, "like one you may find in the smith's quarter, though much more polished and elegant. If I were to guess I would say it is the Anvil of Buto, but I know that not to be the case. Tekolger took it as part of his price of peace."

Doltopez smiled,

"It was offered as a gift when Tekolger invited Butophulo to join the League of Thelonigul. That doesn't mean all the relics were taken from here though." Doltopez said as he produced a hammer from a fine wooden box. The hammer was smooth and striking, a thing of beauty. Two serpents were carved out of the handle that twisted their way to the top.

"The hammer of Buto, it is a partner to the Anvil. Your city painstakingly sought these objects in the centuries since the Dusk. The Doldun know the value of tradition and those links to the past, so we did not undo that hard work."

"There were once weapons and armour lining these walls too. Relics from old Kolbos and the work of the Kinsolsun before that. Yet I don't see them now."

Doltopez's smile grew,

"Tekolger found another way to honour them and put them to use in the way their creators intended. That shows respect to those ancestors wouldn't you say?"

Kalasyar did not answer. Doltopez put the hammer away and faced her.

"I am pleased you have come to see me here and can only apologise for the spectacle put on this afternoon. I can assure you it was nothing to do with me." he paused as if to weigh up his words, "Such a needless public display, though I am assured that it is a long tradition of the city to hold trials for all the citizens to see. It was not a sensible way to handle this delicate issue. In Doldun this would have been a matter for the king and his court alone."

She smiled at him. She needed to remain courteous,

"It is a long tradition for justice to be seen to be done yes, but more than that, the citizens must also participate. When each citizen is sovereign and all contribute to the running of the state, it is a duty to attend and contribute. If we are all to be equal under the law, then we must see and contribute to its functioning."

"The law?" a low rumble of a laugh gripped him, "This is why you must teach me more of the city. Butophulo has its institutions and the rule of law. So many hard rules that all must obey."

"All citizens participate in making the rules which govern them. The institutions are there to ensure no one holds too much power and abuses it. Having power without the need to resort to force is a lesson all the followers of the crippled god Buto should understand. It is why his city pursued that end so vigorously. Instead of violence and tyranny, all citizens hold a small amount of power that we pool together for our own freedom." She interjected. She sounded like her grandfather, she thought.

"How can it be freedom to live under so many hard rules and with no power?" Doltopez inquired. *Grandfather would enjoy spending an evening with him.*

"It is autonomy citizens give up not freedom. Which is why a free citizen must be able to participate in creating and enforcing laws, to ensure the sacrifice in autonomy does not compromise their freedom." Kalasyar put to him, *grandfather would be proud to see me now*, she thought. A liquid smile came to her lips as she talked,

"We Doldun think of ourselves as Xosu, but we are so different. It is convention and the power of lords and kings which rule over us. We do not write our laws down but behave as our ancestors and the gods would expect us to behave towards one another. If you come to my home, I will treat you as a guest and a friend and in return I would expect the same. If you do not, then all society will know that you are not to be trusted. It gives us our freedom as we are not constrained by a need to participate in rule making or obeying written rules but acting as we see fit." Doltopez replied.

"But what happens when one of you violates your conventions? If there is no consequence the violator has the ability to limit others freedom and behave as a tyrant." She put to him as she had seen her grandfather do on countless occasions.

"Then the king would move against them, execute them, or imprison them or banish them, depending upon how gross the violation is." He replied.

"Is that not a sort of tyranny then? All that power in the hands of a king. With no written rules, what constrains the king? Can he not decide what is convention and what is not and what should be punished and how harshly?" Kalasyar was enjoying this conversation now, she had almost forgotten the events of the day.

"That is why the king has his Companions. Twelve men selected from the clans to be close advisers to the king, much like Dunsun did when he distributed the domains of the cosmos to his children. He is still master of all, but he heeds their advice. The King of the Doldun therefore is not an absolute tyrant, like the god-kings of Xortogun, but a first among equals. If they dislike the king's actions, together they have the power to oppose him." Doltopez shot back, with a triumphant grin.

"How do they oppose him in a way that does not end in violence? Buto led his rebellion against Dunsun for this very reason. And even if we concede that this means the men of Doldun are free, it is freedom for a select few nobles who are just as open to a corruption of power as the king." She answered.

"They are meant to be the best men in the land, and so able to make decisions that are the best for all. But I will concede, maybe writing a set of rules to follow would make things clearer. Although spectacles like today would be hard to avoid. Our worlds are very different Kalasyar. Yours one of wandering philosophers mine of roaming rhapsodes." Doltopez replied.

"Today was a mockery of the rule of law and the ideals of the Salxosu. The Nine have degraded our institutions to merely the tool of their own power." She stopped. Maybe she had gone too far, there was too much venom in her voice, but Doltopez was still looking at her intently. Sighing she continued,

"I know you have said before that you do not wish to intervene in the governing of the city, but a word from you would sway the Nine. You saw how popular my grandfather is amongst the people. If you intervene to have mercy shown the people will view you just as well and your grip over the Nine will be stronger." Her plea was blunt and to the point, but she felt comfortable enough in Doltopez's company to be so straight.

"I wish it were that simple." The Doldun commander replied, with what sounded like genuine remorse in his voice, "The Doldun have no king, which means I have no orders. My only imperative is to keep the government here functioning for when the new king is crowned, that means ensuring the Nine stay loyal and in charge. They are set on the course they have taken, and as you have said, all was done in public… But I do have some influence over them." Doltopez finished his sentence looking off into the distance at the clouds gathering out to sea as if considering things more deeply. He did not look bad in this light, she thought.

The words of Sipenkiso came to mind once more,

'You know where power lies, find a way to use it.'

Kalasyar took a deep breath and removed her veil completely. The Doldun general turned to look at her as she did, his eyes fixed on hers and his face frozen as if stone. She leant forward and placing her cup down and taking Doltopez's as well. Then she leaned towards him.

KALU

29

Between the branches of the trees the first trickle of light began to seep into the woods. Slowly the grey black world in front of Kalu filled with colour. The army of the Doldun may not steal their victories with a night attack, but a march through the darkness to catch their enemy unaware at dawn was a tactic of which they were masters.

The distance from the camp of the Doldun to that of the Rilrpitu was short, but the thick woods which lay between them had meant a long and clumsy march in the dead of night. Each man on foot leading his horse on so as not to tire the animals or fall in the dark forest. As Dunsun raised the sun above the horizon, the edge of the woods came into view, and beyond that lay the camp of the Rilrpitu. The seers had declared this new day to be auspicious and sacrifices to win the favour of the gods had been made the night before. All possible preparations had been made, nothing else but battle waited.

Kalu raised his hand and the men around him halted. He could hear the ripple down the line as the rest of his force followed suit, not a word was uttered. Turning to Supo of the Dolozolaz, who had been marching at his side, he said,

"Here we are, beyond that line of trees lies battle. I will lead Zenu's guards in the first wave, you follow me into the camp with your men in the second. Forget about the flanks, Dolzalo will take care of that. We capture the camp and slaughter the marauders, don't let them escape."

Supo nodded his agreement and withdrew to the second line of men.

Supo had been restless on the march north which had surprised Kalu. He had been asking questions of Kelbal, Tekolger's death and the campaign in Zentheldel as if Kalu was hiding something, but he had seemed to settle as battle approached.

Kalu stroked his horse's mane and mounted, another ripple went down the line as the men followed his lead. Then his thoughts went to Tekolger. This would be his first battle without his king, it made him feel a nervousness he had not felt since that day at the Belzow river. Then as now he was facing an unsuspecting tribe of Rilrpitu, except this time the weight of victory or defeat lay on his shoulders. Even as one of Tekolger's veterans that felt like a heavy burden. He could not imagine how Tekolger must have felt at the Belzow, a young and untested boy of barely twenty summers. But Tekolger had never shown any weakness, never any doubt. His vision and belief in himself and his men had been unshakable, the confidence only a god had any right to.

Kalu whispered to Xosu to give him some of that confidence now. He looked at Zonhol, the imposing captain's dark wild eyes and thick beard all that was visible under his horned Rinuxosu style helm, crested with the great stallion of the Zelrsaloz. Kalu nodded and turned to face Zenukola's guardsmen. Zonhol had been the only one of his White Shields to come with him, the betrayal he felt over their actions had cut deep. His bond with those men was as brothers, fighting together for so long and through unknown and hostile lands had made it so. Zonhol had tried to warn him, but he had been too caught up in his own thoughts and worries to listen.

Placing his own great horsehair crested, zilthum lined helm on his head, the brilliant flame red of the crest now illuminated in the light of the dawn. He raised his voice so that all Zenu's guards could hear, no need to worry about the noise anymore, it was too late for the Rilrpitu,

"None of you have fought with me before. My men laughed when they heard it would be you who were assigned this task." Kalu paused and looked at the mounted men staring back at him, "Who are they but jumped-up palace guards? They said. They look pretty stood in their gilded halls, but they would be no match on the field of battle for the veterans of Tekolger. I scolded them for their hubris."

He paused and started to trot down the line, his zilthum lined armour glinting palely in the morning light,

"When circumstances became difficult, those men refused to obey orders. Tekolger's veterans refused to continue to build his vision, but you stood strong. You knew your duty. When I asked you to ride with me to face this savage foe, despite not knowing me, none of you flinched from the task. When I pushed you to the limit of endurance to catch our swift foe, none of you faltered. When I asked you to march all night through rough and unforgiving terrain, none of you questioned me, and now your prize awaits you. Just beyond those trees lies the camp of our barbarous foe. An enemy who has come bellowing in from the north to rape and pillage and plunder. Senselessly destroying all that you have worked hard to build over the last few years. Whilst Tekolger was winning glory in the west, it was you who built and maintained his empire, there is honour and glory in that. And now these barbarians from beyond the limits of civilisation, these children of Bul, come to destroy your legacy. Will you let them?"

A wave of approval washed over the ranks. Kalu turned his white charger, "Let fly Tekolger's ferocious banner!" He bellowed as the standards of the Doldun were raised, "Drive fear into them as if the white hydra itself has come for their shades!" He raised his lance, and advanced. *'Protect my legacy'*, the words echoed in his head.

Bursting through the trees as the full light of the dawn flooded onto the plain in front of them. In the wide-open expanse before him, Kalu could see the camp of the enemy braced against a bend in the river. Not the well-ordered marching camp of the Doldun, but a sprawling, chaotic web of tents, like some god had just discarded them and dropped the Rilrpitu into the plain below. A commotion was taking hold in the midst of the enemy as they realised that the Doldun were upon them. Warriors scrambling to mount their horses and meet the charge, but others were heading for the river, fleeing as soon as they realised the merciless fury that was bearing down on them.

Kalu halted to give his men a chance to regain formation as they left the safety of the tree line. Some of the Rilrpitu horse were being marshalled into a defensive line ready to meet the charge. As the last of his men emerged from the woods, they startled a group of deer close by. The creatures bolted stampeding between Kalu's line and the enemy. To his surprise the Rilrpitu at the far end of their chaotic line broke away to chase the fleeing animals, letting out a shrill scream of delight as they went.

He shook off this confusing incident and raised his spear once more, holding it aloft like the tongue of some great serpent ready to spit its venom. The men struck up their paean and charged.

***

The Doldun hit the ramshackle line of Rilrpitu like a torrent. What arrows the enemy did loose from their bows took none of the momentum out of the charge. The lightly armed raiders scattered immediately, fleeing in all directions. The force of the charge carried Kalu through the line, skewering the first man he came to with his spear. The blade ripped through the warrior like a hydra's talon, blood splattering across his armour. The momentum carried him through, and he found himself in the middle of camp. Men and women fleeing in all directions, Zenu's men chasing them down.

In the tight quarters, Kalu dismounted, out of the corner of his eye he saw a flash, the glint of a sword. Instinctively, he dodged and drew his leaf shaped blade in one motion. The white gold zilthum glistened in the morning sun and felt as though it pulsated, hungry for blood.

Another flash, another dodge and a sword flew passed Kalu's face, a shout came forth from his assailant. Calmly, he kicked the front foot of his attacker, a spit of fire to his enemy's leg that sent the man spinning to the ground. A blazing downward thrust from Vigilance and death came spinning down across the warrior's eyes as the blade eagerly drank his shade.

Looking around, the Rilrpitu were fleeing in all directions, Zenu's men hunting them. Others had dismounted with Kalu and were scouring the camp, slaughtering men, and women alike. A fire was gripping the tents closest to the river. Then a war horn sounded, Supo's men spilled out of the trees. The battle, if you could call it that, was now surely over.

A flash of flame burst out of a tent close to Kalu. He spun around to witness a screaming amazon come charging out of it ablaze, an axe held over her head. He stood his ground, calm descended on him, there was a clarity and purpose in battle that he found somehow peaceful despite the chaos around him and in his hand Vigilance felt powerful.

He waited, time seemed to slow, but still the woman came on, fire in her hair and fire in her eyes, swinging the axe over her head. Kalu waited until she was almost on top of him, a perfectly timed thrust and his sword slid into her throat, biting deep, the fire in her eyes extinguished. Her shade slipping away as her blood ran down the blade. He could feel the intense heat of the flame that was engulfing her against his face. He withdrew his sword and let his foe fall to the floor, her shade sent tumbling into the lap of Phenmoph. The king of the dead would have his due as always.

Supo's men came thundering into the camp. Zenu's men had begun to pillage, the world around them burning and broken. Three men emerged from a nearby tent, the lead man with a magnificent blue and white horsehair crest on his helm front to back. In his hands he carried a chest. Horses were thundering passed Kalu now, a great charger swept by, the man a top wearing a helm with a crest of a deep, sea green colour.

The horse continued at full speed, toward the men exiting the tent. The spear was lowered, it smashed hard into the blue and white crested helm. All at once the blue and white turned red, blood and gore spraying across the white fur of the tent. The chest thudded to the floor, gold coins spilling across the ground. Another horseman appeared, a curved heavy blade came whipping down twice and death fell on the other two men.

Zonhol appeared next to him, wild eyed and covered in blood. Another horse swept past them, in between Kalu and his loyal captain. It passed by, and Zonhol still stood next to him, only now a lance lay buried deep in his chest. He turned and tried to talk, only thick red blood spilled out from his lips, and he collapsed.

Confused, Kalu spun round as he felt the thunder of more hooves. A flash of blue and white crossed his eyes, instinctively he weaved as a sword rushed past his head. Kalu's warrior's instinct took hold completely, not really aware of his own actions. He thrust his sword into the exposed side of his opponent, blood gushed out of him, and death came swirling down as his shade darkened Kalu's blade.

A cry rang out as another soldier stepped forward. A giant of a man clad in bronze, a blue cloak slung over his shoulders and a leaf shaped blade in his hand, there was a frenzy in the man's eyes. A clang of swords rang out as Kalu met him blow for blow, Vigilance cutting chunks from the well-wrought metal. The hooves where thundering closer, streaking towards him, an arrow loosed in his direction. A quick sidestep and Kalu was inside the frenzied man's reach, bring his own blade down hard upon his neck. Sinews severed, blood spilled, and the king of the dead had another shade to greet.

The rumble of the hooves felt like it was almost on top of him now, like a thunderbolt cast by Dunsun himself. Three times he turned and looked; he saw nothing but chaos all around him. A soldier in a green cloak, sword in one hand and burning torch in the other, dealt a death blow to another man, a blue cloak covering the dying guardsman's face.

Fire flared up bringing a new light to the battle, a bright and furious intensity. He felt a knot in his neck as he realised the betrayal at hand. It felt as though his throat had been cut, like a sacrifice to some god. He stood rooted to the floor unable to move, like his feet were caught in a vine that had sprung from nowhere.

Kalu did not see where the blow came from, the bright light of the fires and the dawn sun blinding him. He heard the thud before he felt anything, an arrow hard blow to the top of his head and it exploded in agony, another thud felt as though a panther had clawed at him, dragging him down. He hit the floor like thunder. Everything went black.

THUSON

30

The horizon was stained a blood red, as if some great beast's throat had been cut in a dispute in the heavens, or perhaps the gods were making their own sacrifices. The crimson sky loomed ominously above as if it were about to flood the plains and transform the world, but Thuson could not decide if that would be a good or a bad thing. A single star streaked across the sky proudly showing itself to all before it fell below the horizon and out of sight.

With a loud clunk the wheel of the wagon was dislodged, the Thulchwal holding it let the supply cart crash to the floor. With the final cart in place the carefully crafted scene was complete. Thuson took a step back to admire his work. The image reminded him of the complex preparations for the great dramatic plays staged in the theatre of Butophulo, except in this play there would be no chorus to narrate events to the crowd and the blood would be real. The last play he saw in Butophulo was *The Rebellion of the Smith,* he recalled. Many years ago, before the end of the war with the Rinuxosu, before he made the journey north to Doldun, so much had changed since then.

The men were tired after a hard night's march and setting up the site of his tableau. Dolzalo's horse had made the swiftness of the march possible, pulling the wagons behind them, but the men had still marched far at pace and then worked hard to set the deception. He ordered them to get as much rest as they could before the dawn brought battle upon them. There was nothing left to do but sit and wait, the Rilrpitu would be needed to complete the scene. He only hoped that his messaged had reached Yorotog and that Thorgon would act as asked.

He was left with his thoughts. It was strange to think how he had ended up on this wind swept plain on the edge of the civilised world. Almost twenty years had passed since Yusukol had taken him north to Doldun, convinced that the opportunity offered by Kenkathoaz would allow him to mould the heir to the Doldun's throne into a philosopher king not seen since the fall of the old kingdoms. He was barely more than a child then, with his fourteenth summer approaching.

Kunpit of Thelonigul had believed that with the right upbringing and education a man could be perfected. He had taught that the heroes of the past only seemed godlike because they had come close to this perfection, Tholophos most of all. He even believed that the god-kings of the old kingdoms, when those realms were strong, appeared divine because the kings had reached a state of enlightenment. Kunpit had therefore determined that a king, taught from youth by the best teachers, could be raised to such heights again and that one day, when man perfected the upbringing and education needed to reach such prowess, a philosopher king would come to usher in a new golden age. Kunpit had claimed this new man would be a panther, strong and fierce. He would claim his domain and protect it like a predator, whilst also spreading the sweet message of civilisation that would draw all to his side. In so doing he would allow peace and prosperity to flourish, in the same way animals who are not the prey of such beasts, flourish in the realms they create for themselves.

Yusukol had attempted to fulfil this vision among the Doldun. Neither Yusukol nor Thuson had anticipated what happened though. Tekolger had been so much more than they imagined. In fact, he had worried they had gone too far at first. In his eighteenth year the king had returned from a visit to the oracle of Xosu, frantic and restless. *'It appears that the gods expect me to usher in a new dawn'* he had said. Thuson feared the pressure placed on the young man was too much. His actions in the following year even pushed Kenkathoaz to send the young prince into exile. But in time, Tekolger had become calmer and more focused, with a new vision. His second visit to the oracle after his conquest of Xosupil was a very different affair. The oracle bowed down to him and proclaimed Tekolger *Xosu's Arrow*, his instrument, gifting him a vision of the world he would bring into being.

It was the king's vision which had seen Thuson travel over half the world, and it was that vision which drove him to this wind swept plain and the danger of battle. Something for which he was ill suited and unprepared. Thuson had always thought Doldun would be as far as he would ever travel. He was not a man meant for adventure and leadership. But now he found himself on this empty, windswept plain far to the east, wondering which god had possessed him to take this path.

His orders from Kalu had been to bring the infantry up behind his cavalry as a reserve force to occupy the enemy camp after Kalu's attack. Kalu was an experienced general and more than capable, his plan was a good one, but the headstrong Companion had failed to understand the culture of his enemy. The Rilrpitu would not stand and fight in the way he expected, they were not here to conquer empires or win glory on the field of battle, plunder was their goal.

Thuson had left the command of the bulk of the infantry to one of the Xosu commanders and taken his Thulchwal off to the right flank, stopping someway west of the Rilrpitu camp on the road to Yorotog. It had been easy to convince Dolzalo and Palmash to join him once he had pointed out how his plan would allow them to claim credit for the victory ahead of Kalu. The scattering groups of Rilrpitu from the camp would not be able to resist attacking a poorly defended and stuck supply column, then their cavalry would descend on them as the horse lords dropped their guard to plunder.

He sat against the wagon nervously waiting for the dawn, he could not sleep. He was certain his plan would lure the Rilrpitu in and a bigger victory than the one Kalu could claim awaited him. With Companions in Dolzalo and Palmash to witness his triumph, this was the best chance he had to prove his value to the Doldun, perhaps even be given a command himself, or a province. But it was a risk. He had defied Kalu's orders to be here, Dolzalo was rash and difficult to trust, and Palmash was Palmash. He knew Kalu would be less than pleased with him, and he had no desire to upstage his friend, and yet he had still found himself here and could not really say why.

Time seemed to pass slowly, Thuson felt as though he had been sat there for days. Most of the Thulchwal around him were asleep, but Thuson just sat and stared up into the starry sky trying to remember the names of all the constellations. He had been taught them all as a child, every citizen of Butophulo learnt them. Sailing was the lifeblood of the city, and any self-respecting citizen should be able to navigate by the stars. The panther was above him now, poised as if about to strike as the serpent floated over the horizon. The thought took him back to his days in the city. Butophulo and the League seemed like a lifetime ago. Yulthelon, the shining goddess in her wisdom, had sent Thuson Kosua on a different path. His family had been out of favour in the city for centuries, ever since the fall of the kings. Whilst the Kosua, Posausthison and Rusos families had plotted and schemed and charmed to try and regain their position, with the guidance of Xosu's oracle, Yusukol had seen another way, beyond the frivolous politics of Butophulo.

For years he had reached out to kings and petty tyrants with an offer to take residence at their court and train their sons in the ways of Kunpit of Thelonigul. Some had even taken him in for a time, only to die or be overthrown, and with the change in regime Yusukol would be expelled. Finally, Kenkathoaz, King of the Doldun, had sent for him and given him the opportunity he needed to mould a new champion for their cause. A philosopher king sculpted by the teachings of Kunpit. They had succeeded more spectacularly than they could ever have imagined, proving Kunpit to have been correct all along. But there was a personal cost. Thuson had been the secretary to the king of a semi-barbarous land to the north, to a king who had conquered the Xosu and Butophulo. No longer was he able to claim his place as an upstanding citizen, sailor, and statesman of Butophulo. It had been a big sacrifice to make, even if he could never have hoped to gain high office in Butophulo.

But both those worlds were gone now, it suddenly dawned on him. Thuson sat somewhere in between. He could not see how he would be able to return to Butophulo. The old League was gone, smashed by Tekolger. The ruling council Tekolger put in place may have been drawn from the families who still followed Kunpit, but they were seen as tyrannical by most. Besides, he wanted no part in their political schemes. But where was he now with the Doldun? He was not one of them, and his sole benefactor was gone. Although some of the Companions saw him as a comrade, that would not be enough. The only option which seemed left to him was to carve out a new role for himself in the new regime and to try to see the teachings of Yusukol, the vision of Tekolger and the philosophy of Kunpit, that final Sage of the Xosu, come to fruition. This battle then seemed the only way, for the Doldun were still a people with one foot in the mythical past. To win the Companions approval he would need a victory on the field, if that meant defying their orders to do so then so be it. He would be bold like Tekolger always was.

The amphorae of wine stacked on the wagons caught his eye as he thought of Tekolger. The two images combined, and a deep sadness washed over him and a regret at not being more vigilant. *It could not have been poison in the cup, I would have known, I would not have been that blind*, he thought or hoped. The memory of that night was blurry, he had definitely passed the cup to Talehalden who then handed it to Tekolger, but he could not remember who had handed the vessel to him. The amphorae were surrounded by people, Dolzalo was there for certain and Palmash of course, as were a couple of the Putedun merchants. Palmash had been talking to them, the Companion had become quite friendly with the merchant princes. Thuson remembered Palmash telling him to see the cup reaches Tekolger, but someone else had handed it to him. Of course, there were servants everywhere as well, it could easily have been any of them, or someone else entirely or maybe he was just paranoid, and the cup contained no poison at all.

Finally, the crimson blot on the horizon changed and dawn's fingers crept over the land, but even that seemed slow. Dunsun took his time taking his seat upon his throne, but eventually the light flooded the plain, bringing colour back to the world. The colour was accompanied by echoes of trumpets far off beyond the western horizon. *It has begun* he thought, getting to his feet, and waking the man next to him.

In an instant the sleepy calm around the supply wagons had gone, men were rushing to their stations and preparing their weapons. No one was panicking though, the Thulchwal were as much Tekolger's veterans as his Doldun, and it showed. Thuson's heart was thumping in his chest, the calm of his men reassured him, but he was even more nervous about this battle than his first two.

He drew his leaf shaped blade and took his position on the middle wagon of the carefully arranged position. He stood surrounded by large amphorae filled with rich Xosu wine. From a distance it would appear to be a stalled supply convoy, but the wagons had been arranged to give the Thulchwal the best defensive position they could have on the open plain. The men prepared their javelins. Each wagon would be a bastion able to cover each other with a rain of javelins, but they would still be very exposed to the swift mounted archers of the Rilrpitu.

Thuson glanced over toward the east, hidden in a defile unseen from the road the rest of the Thulchwal waited. Several hundred men tasked with blocking the Rilrpitu's route to the east. He glanced over to the tree line to his southwest, Dolzalo and Palmash with the cavalry lay just beyond, hidden amongst the branches. Exposed as he was on the plain, their timely intervention would be the difference between life and death for Thuson.

A pang of doubt rippled through him. *How did it come down to relying on the judgement of Dolzalo and Palmash*, he wondered, *maybe this was a mistake.* A pillar of smoke was rising on the western horizon, more trumpet blasts came thundering down the road and a cloud of dust, closer than the smoke, it was too late to have doubts now.

* * *

Another age seemed to pass, but the nerve-wracking wait was broken when the cloud of dust on the horizon turned into mass of men and horse. Thuson's instinctive gamble was correct, the Rilrpitu were scattering in front of Kalu's assault. Despite the imminence of battle, the realisation that his instinct was correct calmed him. His heart was still pounding, but a clarity fell over him, all he had to do now was stay alive until the cavalry ended the fight, there was a simplicity in that.

Several hundred Rilrpitu thundered onto the plain, a shrill cry and a whooping filled the air. *They have taken the bait,* he thought. In an instant the rampaging horses had encircled the wagons, the whooping stopped, and an even more ominous noise filled the air as arrows began to fall amongst the wagons. The men kept their heads down, the arrows rained hard and fast, but few casualties were taken. Another shrill cry went up and the horsemen began to close at a pace.

"Now!" Thuson cried out, with the Rilrpitu almost on top of them.

The Thulchwal rose from behind their wagons and unleashed a storm of javelins on their assailants, men and horse were showered and the impetus was taken from the charge. The Thulchwal wasted no time in taking advantage of this opportunity and soon they were amongst their enemy, their long-curved blades hacking and slashing indiscriminately at horse and man.

The Thulchwal counterattack was vicious and took the sting out of the Rilrpitu, they were bogged down in hand-to-hand fighting, the perfect time to strike. Rilrpitu and Zummosh were hacking mercilessly at each other. Two horselords charged Thuson, only to be pulled from their mounts and slain before him. Hurlar the Green jumped passed him, looking like a Wildman from the stories of old, until the green paint was washed with blood as a Rilrpitu arrow struck him in the neck.

Thuson looked to the trees, searching for a sign of the cavalry, for Dolzalo's red beard and thunderous cry or Palmash's mocking grin. He was not given the time to think, two men leapt from their horses onto his wagon. The first one he instinctively swung his sword at. It was a clumsy blow, but the blade was sharp and bit into the man's shoulder. Thuson tried to wrench it free. Too late, the second man was upon him. He let go of the hilt and caught the man's arm as his downward stroke came hurtling towards his head. A desperate struggle ensued, the amphorae around them clattering to the ground and smashing, spilling the rich Xosu wine on the earth below.

Thuson reached out, grabbing at the man, he had a knife hooked on his hip. His fingers grasped the hilt. He pulled it loose and stabbed violently and without control into his attacker's gut, blood gushed out and joined the pooling wine. The man slumped forward onto Thuson, causing him to stumble. A great crash rebounded, and the wagon slumped to one side sending him, his assailant and all the amphorae tumbling to the ground. He hit the floor with a thud, face down, his attacker on top of him and pile of amphorae all around them. He was gifted with a mouthful of wine and gore.

He tried to get up, but he could not move, he could not breathe, *the wine would consume him*, he thought, *where is Dolzalo?* A blast of trumpets echoed in the distance. The world was black and silent, the din of battle faded, all he could hear was an echo of hooves the gush of the wind calling out to him, he thought he heard his name being whispered as a breeze brushed passed his ears.

***

Thuson coughed and spluttered, somehow, he was lying on his back. Acid wine filled his throat, choking him, he coughed again and rolled over spitting out the wine, warm and rich, almost sickeningly so. *Is this what Tekolger's last moments were like?* he thought. That image shook him back to his senses.

The full light of the day was now flooding the battlefield, blinding him. One of the Thulchwal laughed as he coughed up the last of the wine but helped him to his feet.

"Where is Dolzalo?" Thuson croaked, but the man did not need to answer, a shout came from behind,

"So, he is alive!

I thought that you had become so confident in my victory you were already celebrating in the midst of battle." Dolzalo was there. Thuson stumbled and sat against a wagon. Dolzalo's *victory?* he thought, *how was this his victory?*

"Where were you?" he managed to splutter, "You were supposed to take them as soon as they engaged with us."

"And I did, waiting until they were all engaged before I sprung the trap and won a great victory. Kalu is lucky that I was on his flank ready to destroy those raiders he let escape." Dolzalo replied triumphantly.

Thuson had just about managed to gather his wits,

"Your victory? It was my plan and insight which led us here, it was me and the Thulchwal who risked death to draw them in."

"And all under my command and I led the charge which vanquished the enemy. Just as they were Tekolger's victories when his armies won and when he led all those charges into the jaws of the enemy."

He looked at Dolzalo and then swept his eyes over the field, a victory it certainly was. The plain was strewn with the dead and the dying. The once proud Rilrpitu horse lords had indeed been vanquished, those who had not been killed or fled were being rounded up by Dolzalo's men. But it was not Dolzalo's victory. Thuson had anticipated their actions, baited the trap, and fought the deadliest action. It was in that moment that he realised that Dolzalo, maybe all the Doldun, would never give him the credit he deserved. In this competitive world of theirs you take what you can and claim what you must. His merit would not be recognised like Tekolger had recognised him; he would have to force them to see it.

SONOSPHOSKUL

31

The fire was raging in the distance, the wrath of the gods spreading its way through the already ruined streets and gutted buildings. But the cries and clamour of war were beginning to fade. Now as the sun reached the midpoint of its journey across the sky, the last resistance was being crushed.

Sonos waded through knee deep water in what must have once been a wide street running toward the centre of the town. The water was dark as wine and rich like the blood of a sacrifice. Although ruined and half submerged, it was clear that Yil would once have been an impressive place. Small as it may have been, no more than a thousand citizens and the same number of women and slaves, the rich white marble buildings in the sheer Salxosu style showed the splendour of what the League of Butophulo had been, building an ornate haven even in this remote corner of its domain. However, now the city was being reclaimed by nature. Trees and plants had sprung up from the ground where the merchants had once gathered as the lifeblood of the city, the only signs of life the occasional lizard which seemed ubiquitous in the east.

Gods know what must have happened here, Sonos reflected. Large parts of the city were still intact, but many of the buildings had begun to crumble after more than thirty years of being abandoned and neglected. Traces of the scorch of fire crept over the walls of many of the alabaster white structures, and the city was half submerged. The pale stone which the builders had used to construct the city made the broken husk seem like the bones of some great beast left to rot after a hunter had stripped the corpse for all that was useful.

The assault on the city had been a rather one-sided affair, the Xosu companies had appeared like wraiths and stormed into the ruin like a flood with the sky still black and a sudden downpour to cover their approach. The intruding sea had allowed the men to row themselves through the collapsed harbour and onto the streets in the dead of night and they caught the bandits and raiders who had sort shelter in the dead corpse of the city by surprise. The Hotizoz Legion and the Gelodun, who had marched up the coast, had then swung into the city from its landward side, catching its occupants in a pincer.

The enemy were numerous, and many had shown the courage to stand and fight, but they lacked the training, discipline, and equipment to make it a real contest. More like a grand sacrifice to thirsty gods than a battle. Sonos had barely bloodied his spear in truth. The men's minds had quickly turned to search for plunder and riches.

Much like the vote on whether the army would take part at all, the prospect seemed more daunting than it turned out to be. They had all thought that persuading the army to venture into the supposedly cursed ruins would be an impossible task. Especially when, upon hearing the news of the tyrant's death, many the Salxosu would want to return to the White Islands. But the other Xosu had argued that there was nothing for them in the islands and the opportunity offered by the leaders of Rulrup was too good to turn down, a chance to start afresh. Sonos could not blame them for that. The Xosu mercenaries were a mixed band of exiles, forgotten sons and criminals with little reason to return home, and Xosupil itself held no pull for the Hotizoz. Even many of his own Salxosu had thought twice about returning. Only the Gelodun had argued fiercely to reject the offer and head west, they after all had homes to return to. But many of them had soften to the idea once Thusokosoa had pointed out that there would be a succession crisis in Gelodun, and many may call them craven for having abandoned their king.

Although his heart told him to argue fiercely for a return to the islands, to finish what Kolmosoi had started, Sonos knew that chance of success in that venture would be limited. He had kept quiet and the vote to attack Yil had been overwhelming.

Rulrup had provided ships for the endeavour. Enough to carry all the Xosu companies, but the Gelodun contingents and the Hotizoz Legion had had to march up the coast. A fleet the size needed for ten thousand men had not been seen since the height of the League, or maybe even the expedition against old Kolbos, and they could not have expected one small Xosu city to provide it.

The seas had been calm and clear and it had felt good to get a deck under his feet again. Sonos had missed the waves and the roll of the ship on top of the sea, even when the waters became rough and unrelenting as they approach the broken city. The feeling had brought back memories of the time when the fleets of the League had swept all before them and the sea was their realm. Bittersweet thoughts that they were, the memories were ones that he savoured.

The march along the coast had been more eventful. It was rough terrain with rolling, thickly wooded hills, and high mountains with little in the way of paths along the narrow but flat coastal plain. Closer to Yil, the column had had to deal with raiders and ambushers attempting to prey on the baggage train as it made its slow progress through the wooded hills. Even so it was only a little over a week after leaving Rulrup that the army was storming into the lost colony.

***

Sonos continued wading through the sea water which had turned many of the streets of the city into wine dark veins. The road soon opened into a central square, the marketplace which had been the focus of all life in the port. Around the square stood the most magnificent buildings. Most prominent was a white marble temple to Xosu, where the hearth fire, taken from the mother flame at Thelonigul, once burned. The temple was overgrown and had started to sink into the sodden, swampy ground, but it still had a grandeur to it which could rival any other in the Xosu world.

Opposite the temple of Xosu and facing out to sea was an ornate temple to Buto. The tell-tale sign of the League of Butophulo, for it was Buto who had gifted the Salxosu the secrets of the sea, the trade and commerce and the riches it could bring. The grandeur of what was once clearly an awe-inspiring building was long gone though, the temple had sunk almost completely into the swampy ground and the patter of incessant rain threatened to sink it further still. The tops of its columns and the carved front of its portico was all that remained above the surface. That and the thick, white arms of the hulthul tree grasping from below, wrapping around the remains of the dome which once protected it, its inky black leaves and their white underside almost hiding the remains.

Hardy things those trees, he thought. Even though the dome had collapsed onto it, the branches had snaked through and around the cracks from beneath showing that the tree still lived in the earth below. The statue of the god, once resplendent on the domed roof of the temple surveying the activity in the market, had now sunk so low that a man could look Buto straight in the eye and see the red fire in their depths. His broken and twisted leg depicted in the finest bronze a reminder that even the gods could be brought low. It was apt perhaps for the crippled, fallen god to be level with man.

Sonos continued into the square. Here the water slackened and instead of wading through knee deep sea water, he found himself struggling through a muddy swamp as the sky cracked like a broken branch overhead. Beyond the square he could see there was no water at all and just beyond the sunken temple of Buto his comrades waited for him.

The men of Butophulo had been voted to command the Xosu companies in the assault. Even the proud Rinuxosu recognised the superiority of the Salxosu in commanding an attack from the waves as they had sea water running through their veins. Runu had delivered the initial hammer blow himself, leading The Daemons of the Deep in the first wave of the assault, coming in with the rising morning tide. A blood red dawn sky had lit their way and mist and rain had shielded them from the sight of their enemies. There had been an acrid taste in the air that morning, like blood and iron, the gods anticipating the fight.

Kusoasu and Pusokol followed Runu into the city, like shadows out of the sea, bringing The Exiles in the second wave. Sonos had been posted with The White Hydra's Teeth to bring in the reserves. They had expected a tougher fight due to the way the men of Rulrup had talked about the wild brigands, their numbers and strength in arms. They were certain that the reserves would be needed to punch their way through the enemy. As it turned out, the men of Rulrup were exaggerating, probably to justify their own failure to deal with the problem.

Even so it had felt good to be on the winning side again and not in some desperate fight for survival. It had hit him that the last time he felt that way was fifteen years ago after the battle of the Griffin's Rock, when the League fleet had lured the Sacred Band of the Rinuxosu into the jaws of a trap. The first time that fabled force had been defeated on the field. Koseun Sisosi had planned the whole thing. The Rinuxosu had been led to think that the League meant to besiege the town of Dzulkoyusos, deep in the heart of Rinuxosu territory, to use as a base to raid the rich farmland of the Rul Valley, exactly as Koseun had planned.

The Sacred Band had bared its teeth and was lured onto the Griffin's Rock, a huge stoney outcrop which projected into the sea, that was shaped like a resting griffin and overlooked Dzulkoyusos. At the top of the rock was a ruined fortress from the days of the old kingdoms, which the men of the Sacred Band reoccupied thinking a new fortress could spring from the earth. Then the fleet of the League had swept in from the sea, like a wraith emerging from another world. The defenders were trapped and besieged into submission.

The victory had almost broken the Rinuxosu, a sweet and splendid feeling at the time, but with hindsight it had led to disaster. The Rinuxosu king had died at the Rock and the Grand Assembly of the Rinuxosu cities ignored their new young king and sent to Tekolger for aid. Sonos could only hope that that was not an omen for the future. The thought reminded him of a marching song of the Sacred Band, sung to remind others of their famous stand against the hordes of Yoruxoruni at the Jaws of Zilthil, when five hundred men faced down five hundred thousand. *Into the Jaws of Zilthil* it was called. The Salxosu had taken to singing the song to taunt the Sacred Band during the siege of the Griffin's Rock.

To arms! To arms!
Forward, arrow like, King of Kings, fire has no sheath!
But fierce Xosu bite, time to feel the hydra's teeth!
Our spears silver flash, come and face the Sacred Band!
We fall on this field, blood to free the Sacred Land!

To arms! To arms!
Thrice loosed his fierce horde, arrows shade all beneath!
Spears crack and swords may shatter, flee the hydra's teeth!
Fume, fury, foolish great king, firm footed we stand!
We fall on this field, blood to free the Sacred Land!

With the song in his mind, Sonos moved to reunite with his comrades, who were in a deep discussion. The ease of the victory no doubt had moved minds towards what to do next.

"This city is a sunken and broken leviathan on the edge of the world with little prospect of rebirth, and how many of these so-called bandits are plague ridden outcasts? Just look at their weak and wizened corpses, no wonder this was such an easy fight. We've been tricked by Rulrup to deal with their diseased problem."

Kusoasu was saying as Sonos arrived. A blue shadow had fallen over his lips, stained by the bitter leaves he was chewing, they gave him quite a haunting look. There was truth in his words, the partnership with Rulrup did not feel quite the way it had been sold to them.

Pusokol, looking toward the dryer areas inland as they sheltered under the marble ruins from the hammering rain, answered. His hair and beard once again styled, braided, and oiled. The short stay in Rulrup had allowed him to transform back into the artist he liked to portray.

"There is good land further away from the coast. Yes, we would have to start from scratch, but the potential of the city is still the same as it was a century ago, fire will deal with the plague. Besides, what do we gain from leaving? Death more than likely."

In his brightly coloured armour, Pusokol had a slightly androgynous, even effeminate look to him, never growing out of the litheness that most men did in their youth, and his gregarious style only emphasised it.

"I'd rather die fighting for a reborn League than slave away rebuilding a cursed city for the benefit of Rulrup." Kusoasu retorted bluntly.

"How would we get back to the White Islands anyway? Even if only the

Salxosu came with us we would need a fleet. Or are you proposing just the four of us return to take on Thasotun and the Doldun?" Pusokol replied. Continuing, he said, "Besides the army voted for this course of action and we swore an oath to see it through, would you renege on that?"

"Rulrup has left plenty of ships just offshore and the sailors come to dry land every evening to eat and sleep. We could slip on board and be off with them before anyone knew what was happening." he paused, "We only swore an oath to retake the city, which you may have notice we did this morning." Kusoasu replied, in his usual sarcastic manner which emerged when he was sure of himself.

Pusokol opened his mouth, but Runu, who had been sitting on the marble base of what was once a column, towering over the other captains as they argued, stood, and interrupted him. The white of the column matched his arsenic pale skin, making him seem like one of the many statues that littered the square.

"Puso, you are right. It would be hard work here, but there is still a lot of promise on this site, we could become rich and grow old here and leave the cares of Xosupil behind. But Kuso also makes a good point." he paused before taking a different course, "The city of Rulrup will dominate us, we would have traded one master for another and before long we would yearn to be free as the Xosu always do. And with Tekolger's death we have a chance that may not present itself again. The Doldun will be concentrating on the succession and governing their new empire and it seems Thasotun still struggles to maintain its hegemony. The White Islands are ripe for the taking and Kolmosoi's schemes may yet work."

Pusokol turned to Sonos,

"What do you think?"

Sonos thought for a moment before replying. Staying would be the sensible thing, the city may be a ruin, but the land beyond was good and full of potential. But the shadow of guilt for abandoning the islands loomed overhead like the canopy of clouds which branched out above them, and the call of home sang to him. They may never have another chance,

"We could become rich merchants here, lay down our spears and put our energies into taking on the Putedun at their own game. The beehive we could build would please Rolmit himself. The domineering of Rulrup may not be as bad as you think. Yil may even surpass that city one day. We would have the better position and at least as many fighting men." Stopping, he pondered his own thoughts for a second, what did his heart say? He took a deep breath and his fingers reached for the amulet which hung around his neck,

"But we have wandered to the ends of the earth, fought half a hundred battles all with the goal of one day returning to rebuild the League. We all feel guilty for fleeing after Kolmosoi's death. Yil will never be home, but the people of the White Islands are our own. I say we go back."

Runu turned to Pusokol,

"Looks like you are out voted Puso. Are you coming with us?"

"You know I am Runu. What of the men?" He replied without hesitation.

"We will ask them, but only the Salxosu. We will have to move fast to slip passed Rulrup and take advantage of the chaos that is engulfing the islands. We can't move quickly with all these men." Runu replied. Sonos found himself answering,

"The other Xosu and the Gelodun, have no reason to come with us, and we have little reason to trust their word with this. The Hotizoz are a different matter. They will want to return home, and if we offer them the chance to return with the support of the Islands at their back, then they may support us."

Runu stopped for a moment, before saying,

"There are five triremes in the harbour here, and several smaller vessels. It will be a tight fit, but the manpower of the legion would make our task easier. You are confident that the Hotizoz would agree to such as scheme Sonos?"

He stopped and thought for a moment, touching the amulet at is neck and hearing the words of the song in his mind. *I want to return, but not to die foolishly.*

"I am." He replied assuredly. Runu looked off into the distance and then back to him,

Very well, Sonos you talk to the Hotizoz, they seem to trust you. A few days to prepare and allow routine and complacency to overtake the sailors, then we seize the ships and head north toward Tikusu, strike across the open sea toward Xosupil and then return to Pittuntik from the west. We will have vanished before they know what has happened. Go to your men, spread the word, but do not let the other Xosu know, and no bloodshed. Let us try not to cause too many problems for those we are leaving behind."

The four men dispersed to find their companies.

* * *

The army was billeted in the ruins of the city after the fighting had ended. Runukolkil ensured that the Salxosu were placed closest to the shore. The men had grumbled and resisted at first, not wanting to be placed in the half-submerged ruins that had been claimed by the realm of the sea. But the grumbling had soon stopped once the plan to return to the Islands had been passed around and preparations had begun.

Sonos stood on the ruins of an old stone tower on the edge of the sea front, looking inland toward the rest of the army. Numerous fires lay sparkling among the ruins, against the black night they looked like the tears of Tholo which rained from the sky when her son Buto was cast from Dzottgelon. Drunken song came floating on the air. Night had finally fallen and the hour to move would soon be on them.

He looked up at the sky, a bright moon, and a clear night over the sea. Not the best cover to move toward the ships, but the light would be useful to sail out with the rest of the world blanketed in darkness. Glancing toward the shore, Sonos could see yet more fires glistening, less this time, but bunched closer together to try and avoid the rain over the city which never seemed to cease. The sailors from Rulrup had left their ships anchored in the bay and were enjoying a night on the shore, the time was right.

Sonos climbed down the tower to the hand-picked men of his company preparing to seize the ships. They had spent much of the last few days secretly turning their calf skin tents and wine flasks into floats to carry them across the water, enough for a hundred men to slip like shadows across the bay. Even though every man of the Salxosu learnt to swim before they could walk, they would need the support of the floats to make it to the ships ready to fight if needed.

Sonos took the float that was handed to him as he waded toward the open sea, the patter of rain against the water the only noise to be heard. Turning, he looked toward his men and nodded, nothing else needed to be said. Putting the float under him, he pushed himself into the deep water and began to paddle toward the nearest trireme. The words of the Rinuxosu marching song came into his head again, but they seemed more serious than the last time he had sung them,

To arms! To arms!

Forward, arrow like, King of Kings, fire has no sheath!
But fierce Xosu bite, time to feel the hydra's teeth!
Our spears silver flash, come and face the Sacred Band!
We fall on this field, blood to free the Sacred land!

The water was cold and choppy. Sonos had exchanged his heavy bronze cuirass for a lighter lamellar one, but the water soaked into it quickly as the restless waves grasped for him, it weighed him down and his sword dragged in the sea. No matter, he carried on paddling, edging closer to the ship. The sea was the natural environment for the Salxosu, they were sailors and marines before they were soldiers and each man danced silently and elegantly through the water. They had made swims such as this countless times before, all they had to do was stay focused, keep paddling, and rely on the float to keep them above the water.

Time seemed to slow, and an age went by, but Sonos crept slowly toward the trireme. Soon the great ship, which had looked small enough to pick up in one hand from the shore, loomed over him, darkening the sky just as the rain eased off. He headed toward the front and the huge bronze ram. Reaching up, he grasped the lump of metal used to tear the heart out of ships and pulled himself up out of the water. Discarding his float, he climbed up toward the deck, others followed on behind.

The ship was quiet, a single light flickered at the far end revealing two shadowy figures. Sonos crept along the deck, silent as a wraith. He could see the ghostly silhouettes of the other men climbing aboard the nearby ships. Silently but swiftly, he reached the far end of the deck, the first shadowy figure turned as Sonos got close enough for colour to flood over him. The man went to shout but it was too late, Sonos bundled him over and the other men seized his companion.

With the ship secured, he ordered a lantern to be hoisted up the mast, a signal to the others waiting ashore on crudely built rafts ready to paddle out to the ships. This was the most dangerous part of the escape. Surely the sailors would see so many men making for the ships, but all the Salxosu would need is a head start.

The lantern was raised, a single light rising in the night sky to challenge the darkness. Sonos' eye was drawn to movement along the shoreline; it was difficult to make out the men in the darkness, but a shadowy mass seemed to move all at once, they were coming.

Moments passed, but it felt like years, the shadows crept closer, and still no reaction from the sailors. Movement again caught Sonos' eye, then shouting, the sailors of Rulrup knew something was amiss. Scrambling and chaos gripped the sailors, the flickering of their fires illuminating them as they scrambled toward their small row boats which had been pulled onto the rocky beach. *Where are they?* He thought. The shadows had abandoned them, now was the time for speed. Sonos shouted to his men,

"Make the ships ready! I want to leave as soon as the men reach us!"

The ships erupted in a flurry of activity as the few men on board each did what they could to prepare for departure. The men paddling came ever closer. The sailors from Rulrup launched their rowing boats quicker than Sonos expected. They were soon bearing down on the triremes as the Salxosu began to scramble on board. *Where are they?* Sonos grabbed two of the prisoners,

"Can you swim?"

Both men nodded,

"Tell your comrades if they come any closer our archers will loose their arrows." He said to the men and then pushed them into the water, sacrifices to the cause. He prayed to Buto that releasing them to the deep would give him the power to escape. They resurfaced and gasped for air and began to swim toward the rowing boats. Sonos shouted to the men swarming on to the ships,

"Rowers take up your positions. Any archers to me, bows strung."

The prisoners made good progress toward the boats, but the sailors were getting uncomfortably close. There was no way now that those sailors could retake the ships, but there would be plenty of blood spilled if they tried.

A stream of men passed him, heading below deck and to the oars. Half a dozen more stopped next to him, bows ready. It was not many, but it would have to do. His freed prisoners had almost reached the boats. He shouted, loudly, hoping the sailors would hear,

"Nock, draw!"

The archers obeyed; arrows poised to rain death on the Xosu of Rulrup. Sonos paused; he could see the shadows of the prisoners being pulled on to the boats. The boats stopped, he waited a few moments more, the boats did not move. He looked to the shore again. *They should be here by now.*

"Lower your bows." He said in a hushed tone.

The boats stayed in the bay, watching the men of Butophulo silently. Sonos stood still, tense, the danger had not passed yet. Time seemed to stop as both sides weighed each other up, and then they moved again, still coming on, the warning not heeded.

A shout echoed from the shoreline. More men appeared, shadows illuminated only by the moon's glow, but there must have been hundreds of them, swarming into the camp of the Rulrup sailors. *Finally.* He thought.

"Ship ready!" Someone shouted.

A chant went up as the rowers strained sinew and the hundred legs of the great beast of the sea groaned into life, the ship lurched forward out toward the open sea.

SANAE

32

Her knees stung. Barefoot and crawling, the heat pounded on her back and the dirt rubbed against her bare hands and knees, cutting deep and leaving her skin red and raw. The smell of the incense she carried, sweet and overwhelming, the weight of the panther skin on her back dragging her down.

A just a little further now, she thought. Around a third and final corner and she could see the pool of water which was her aim, her target, and the place of transformation. Just like the panther which Xosu transformed into to guide his followers to the cave of the hydra, where his oracle now resides. The place where he would found the golden city of Thelonigul. Sanae would crawl into the sacred pool and be transformed.

She reached the edge of the water. The cool and refreshing liquid lapped against her fingers. She took three long, deep breaths and crawled in, plunging under the water like an arrow striking the surface, leaving the panther skin behind, a weight from her shoulders suddenly lifted. It was deep, deeper than she had realised, but somehow comforting, like she had entered a different world, the sounds of the city muffled, and the gentle touch of the water against her skin helped her relax.

She allowed herself to drift and be taken in by the sacred waters and time seemed to slip away, like none of the worries and stresses of the world above mattered anymore, a supreme ecstasy washed over her and with it came clarity. Just like a gentle hand, it seemed to take her in its embrace, the water wrapping around her. Sanae began to drift into a serene nothing.

An arm hooked under her own, and then another. With one heave they lifted her out of the water and held her aloft, like the star that rises before the dawn. The lamp of the sun loomed over her and in its light she was reborn. Sanae felt powerful in that moment, like she was flying, soaring above the world like the eagle which Xosu would transform into. A sword of a shadow over her made her look up. Looming large was the great dolthil tree, long and tall, its thin, red branches grasping for the celestial light, golden leaves, sweet and fragrant in the morning sun. The tree leaned over the pool, entwined around it was a vine of grapes ready to harvest.

They placed her on the dry ground below the tree. She felt a loss and a sadness of having to return to the world where time and stress could affect her once more, but as the water of the pool still glistened on her skin, she felt like some of its serenity still clung to her as well. Although the feeling would, no doubt, drain away like the water now streaming down her legs. Helupelan was there to greet her in his blazing red robe,

"Congratulations child, you have attained something few people will ever achieve. Your path to understanding the true mysteries of Xosu is almost complete. Having received a divine vision from his father, Dunsun, Xosu transformed into a panther whose sweet smell his people would follow back to the cave in which Xosu had slain Zilthil, the great white hydra.

Where the blood of the hydra had spilled in front of the cave, a sacred pool had formed, from which, some say, the first of the Xosu had emerged. Looming in the sky above, its red branches reaching for the heavens, stood the dolthil tree which had been watered by the blood of Zilthil, entwined and inseparable from the tree was a grape vine.

The panther walked the sacred boundary of the new city three times and then descended into the pool and remerged as an eagle, soaring up to the heavens and coming to rest on the tree. This was the place where Xosu would found his great palace, golden Thelonigul, the sacred home of all the Xosu people."

There had been something cathartic about this task for Sanae, the trials and trauma of the past few weeks and months seemed to ebb away, a clarity and serenity gripping her. She spent the rest of the day at the temple, basking in this splendour.

***

A renewed vigour gripped Sanae in the following days. The fight which had been so thoroughly beaten out of her was returning, so much so that she found herself rising before Dunsun had mounted his golden throne. Just a single star in the sky to light the peaceful city and a single light in Sanae's chamber from where she watched Tekolgertep stir.

She got dressed, putting on her finest green robe, pinned with the broach of The Paron. She took the seal of Xura which Kurmush had given her and left the temple heading for the south bank of the river. Xura's offer was yet another bargain, but it was the only option left.

Dawn's rosy fingers were spreading themselves over the city as she crossed the river, the water glistening at dawn's light caress. The blackened and scarred remains of the long hall which the Rilrpitu had burnt down remained untouched in the Zummosh village. A dark crater to remind them of the power which was held over them.

The number of people in the village had fallen and many more of the buildings had been pulled down. The Rilrpitu had clearly been back, even after the governor had claimed he would take control of the situation. Even this sight did not dampen her spirit though, it only made her doubly determined. Her renewed sense of vigour would not countenance defeat.

Sanae wound her way through the muddle of huts and wooden halls of what was left of the village, searching for people. The place seemed deserted, until she heard the noise and commotion coming from one of the large halls on top of a small hill at the northern edge of the village. She creaked the door open. The room was filled to bursting with the Zummosh, in the centre a fire roared. Stood next to the dancing flames was a man in a Xosu style toga, flanked by two guards wearing the purple cloaks and white star of the Doldun, the governor's men she knew.

Sanae stepped inside, spying Lulpo and her mother sat near the front of the group, she quickly moved up next to them. The flickering flames caused the men's shadows to move with a rhythm, like grass in the wind. The man in the toga was speaking to all the Zummosh. They stood silent, listening intently.

"The governor has heard of your plight, how your own governor forgets about you. It pains him to see you brought so low. When the great king Tekolger conceived of this city, his city, on the mouth of the greatest river in the world, he saw it as a place for not just the Doldun and the Xosu, but for all the people of his empire, the Zummosh included. It is with this spirit of openness that the governor wishes to treat you now. To have you all included in the embrace of the city and the peace and prosperity of civilised life. But all who benefit must also contribute. Pay your taxes to the governor and join your village to our glorious city, under the protection of Keluaz of the Keluazi."

A murmur went around the room, some seemed to approve, others did not. The murmur soon turned into heated debate.

"Don't listen to him!" Sanae shouted. She did not know why. The madness of some god had gripped her, but she felt she must offer guidance to these people. Lulpo looked over her shoulder, surprised to see the young Doldun girl there.

"Don't listen!" Sanae proclaimed it louder now, over the rancour of the debating tribesmen. Only those nearest to her heard her cry, but it must have been forceful as they all stopped and looked at her. Nervously, she stepped forward and began to speak,

"Don't listen, his words are filled with deceit. The Rilrpitu are the governor's men, who do you think sent them here to terrorise you in the first place? Pay the governor what he demands, and he will have won. The south bank is not a part of the city, he has no right to claim taxes from you."

All in the room were quiet now. A shout came from the crowd in very broken and barely intelligible Common Xosu,

"Victory is already his. We do not pay, and the horse daemons will be unleashed upon the Zummosh and slaughter us all. Koluun is invisible. There is no other choice, the Powouzo remember such things."

"There is another path that has been lit for you." Sanae said proudly, holding the seal of Xura aloft. "This is the seal of the temple of Xura. The great king Tekolger was recognised by the priests of the goddess who protects this valley as the son of Kurotor and appointed ruler, the Thoruri of Xortogun. In return Tekolger in his wisdom conferred all the ancient rights and privileges on the temple. Those who accept the temple's protection cannot be placed under the thumb of the governor. Kurmush Xura Ya Kuria, the priest of Xura, gave me this seal and told me to come here to offer the temple's protection to all the Zummosh. If you choose to accept it. Neither the governor or the Rilrpitu would dare to defy the commands of Tekolger or the goddess of this sacred valley."

She did not know where the words came from, a moment of inspiration no doubt. A gift from the bright god or Tholophos the protector, or perhaps the shade of the fallen king. This was Tekolger's city after all, he was the father of this empire.

The room went silent. Sanae realised that only few Zummosh could understand her and the murmurs and mumbled voices in the rhythmic tones of the Zummosh language were her words being translated. The delay cause by the translation had the odd effect of a silence cut only by a lyrical murmur which was almost musical to her ears. Then the voice shouted out again,

"How can we trust this Kurmush if we cannot trust the governor or his sage man pleading to us." The Common Xosu was broken but made the point well. Those who understood seemed to nod in agreement. The governor's man spoke again,

"You have your choice then. Uncertainty under the yoke of some foreign god, or inclusion in the great project of building the new capital of the empire. I will leave you to decide."

He turned to leave with his two guards hot on his heels. Some of the

Zummosh also began to file out. Sanae felt dejected once more, she was sure that given the choice the Zummosh would choose the protection of the temple and the freedom from oppression it offered. Someone grabbed her hand. She turned to see Lulpo slide up next to her,

"We trust you, child." Palon, stood behind her, said. The matriarch spoke loudly in the Zummosh tongue, the rhythm of the words dancing across the hall. A few of the Zummosh came to join them, but not many.

"Give it time." Lulpo said confidently, "We are not a people who trust quickly, but they will see eventually that you are trying to help. They know the Powouzo remember."

***

For several days, the Zummosh argued amongst themselves. Lulpo had advised her to stay away and be patient. The Zummosh may seem chaotic, but they do things in their own way she had said, "G*ive them time and they will see that the option you offer is the lesser of two evils.*"

Sanae could do nothing but focus on her duties in the temple, her final two tasks where approaching and soon she would be one of the initiated into the mysteries of Xosu. It was something she had hoped for all her life, but recent events had really made her question her commitment. She had consoled herself that this was all a part of the learning process along the way to the higher mysteries, but deep down she knew she was questioning everything she understood to be right and true. *Find your blood, find your home*, Gelithul's words haunted her every moment.

Even sticking to her chores, she could not escape the attention of Kolae. The High Priestess had come to her the day after she made the Zummosh the offer of Xura's protection,

'You have been with those savages again haven't you!' she had shouted, 'The governor is furious with the Xortogun priests meddling in the affairs of the empire, and he said a priestess of Xosu was seen there with them. Helupelan now risks losing the trust of the governor and worse, the temple may lose its privileges to pay for your folly.'

Sanae had wanted to scream and shout and hit her, but Helupelan had intervened before she could reply. Kolae had stayed away after that, although Sanae could feel her piercing liquid eyes following her around everywhere she went.

A new day came, the gentle touch of dawn's fingers roused her from her slumber. As had become routine now, she donned her working garments and set out to fetch water for the priest's breakfast. She stepped out into the freshly lit city, slowly descending the steps of the temple with a pail in each hand, unaware of the world around her. At the bottom of the steps, she took a right turn and started to make her way to the nearby well. To her surprise, Lulpo blocked her way, several other

Zummosh were with her, all looked bedraggled and covered in dirt and soot.

"We are ready to accept the offer from the redmen." Lulpo said to her. "The horse daemons came again in the night; the governor is impatient for his taxes."

She did not need to say anything else, Sanae nodded and said,

"Come with me, we will go and see Kurmush immediately."

* * *

The small group of Zummosh walked along the riverbank, following her lead. They walked in silence, but beaten and broken as they were, Sanae could sense they still had spirit and fight left to give. This was not a submission to the will of another, it was an agreement from which all could benefit, that had to be made clear to Kurmush.

She let herself daydream as they walked, sure that Xosu would approve of her actions, after all he had sacrificed much and more to save the Xosu people. This had to be the right thing to do. She was also sure that Tekolger would have wished for the people to be protected, why else would he have granted the power to the temple of Xura. She found herself thinking of her parents too, wondering who they were and if they would be proud of her actions. It was not something she had thought of much before, being raised by Helupelan meant that her own parents were only ever an idea, a thought, a whisper on the wind.

The city was beginning to stir as they approached the temple, the air already thick with the sweet smell of incense. A black cat, common all over the city due to the Xortogun's reverence for them, broke the tense silence as it scrambled out of a window chasing some bird or other. It ran in a circle around the group and then bounded up the steps of the temple, passed the imposing statue of Xura, with her lapis halo seated on her throne. Sanae led the Zummosh inside.

The pale stone temple was a hive of activity. The Xortogun's entire community revolved around the temple, dealing with both spiritual and corporeal matters. It was said that after the fall of the old kingdom of Xortogun the priests took up the rule of the valley as there was no longer a god-king to sit upon the Amber Throne. Yoruxoruni himself was a priest before the people of the valley rose and threw off the yoke of the dynasty of the desert, nomads from the southern deserts of Felwohan who had conquered the shattered valley in the centuries following the Dusk of the old kingdoms.

She found Kurmush as usual at the back of the complex, near to the enclosed space in which only the priests could venture. In front of the enclosure, blocking access to the public, was a white marble wall with water running down it. Fed by the river she knew, although Kurmush had claimed it was through the will of the goddess. The water looked pure, like moonlight frozen in time. Only the gentle splash it made as it pooled below revealed it to be water.

Kurmush was deep in conversation with another priest, both wearing their beards twisted in the distinctive fashion of the Xortogun elite. The other priest was tall and willowy. Kurmush shorter, but with a snake of a neck which made him seem almost of a height. As he saw her approach, he ended his discussion and headed toward her, his fish shaped cloak billowing behind him like a serpent's tail.

"You can't bring them all in here." he said fervently, "Follow this servant." In one fluid motion, he breezed past the group and led them through an opening into a wide courtyard with a stable at the far end.

"The Zummosh have come to accept your offer." Sanae said,

"Excellent, the goddess will be most pleased. This servant will begin making the arrangements immediately." The smiling priest replied, his mood transformed in an instant.

"But it comes with some conditions" Sanae continued, "The Zummosh are a proud and independent people. They will accept the protection of the temple and work the land on behalf of your goddess, but they must be allowed their independence to rule over themselves and conduct their affairs as they see fit."

The grin on Kurmush's face suddenly became serious, a dark shadow falling on his cheerful smirk,

"That is an understandable request." he paused, "Perhaps this servant should tell you the end of the story of the first time the serpent king Yob tried to overthrow the natural order." he paused and shut his eyes as if remembering, "When the world was young, before what you call the Dawn of the old kingdoms, before this valley existed, Xur and Xura ruled the realm of the sky and guarded the gateway to our world. Each shined as bright as the other and men lived free and without fear or the need for civilised life. This was the first age, the time of the first sun, before the realms of gods and men collided.

The plumed serpent king, who lurked in the hidden realm, was jealous of the gods and hated men. When all seemed calm and tranquil, Yob launched a vicious and surprise attack on Xur and Xura, streaking across the sky like a furious arrow whilst sending his shadowy demons to roll over our world and drive men into the abyss. Xur, he killed and Xura he wounded so badly that she bled and bled and bled and the world was plunged into darkness.

Gonphon and Tora, the son and daughter of Xur and Xura had come to live amongst man in our realm at that time. The two children united the wild people, teaching them the crafts and skills of war. They fought to defeat the demons of the serpent king and drove them back to their hidden realms. When that fight was done, they took their father's body to rest in the realm of the dead, where he now oversees the passage of the shades of men. Then Gonphon, shining red and amber in triumph, ascended to the heavens to take his father's place and Tora dedicated herself to creating the sacred valley that would protect the people.

Together, Gonphon, Tora, and Xura drove off the serpent king, casting him out of the heavens and back into the hidden realm. This ushered in the second age when Gonphon ruled the sky and guarded the gateway. The sons he produced with the daughters of men took up the Amber Throne crafted from the golden blood of the fallen Xur. The blood of Gonphon ruled over Xortogun and made her prosper. Xura, her light diminished but her desire to protect fiercer than ever, still defends the valley from the demons of Yob at night.

Now, Gonphon shines no more on the sacred valley, his light faded too when the Dusk fell, and the serpent king returned. The last of his sons, Kurotor, rose to take his place at the beginning of this third age, but that is a sad tale that I will not tell.

Gonphon left his sons to rule over the old kingdoms of men, to make their laws and sit in judgment and defend them, because the world was a different place after the great war at the Dawn. Closer to the realms of the gods with all the brilliance and danger that brings. Yob and his demons had twisted it and fear of the wild things which lay just beyond their horizon gripped the souls of men. It was a bargain to be sure, men gave up their freedom for peace and law and order and all the things which civilised life brings, and most all for the protection of the gods and their divine sons.

For their part of the bargain, Gonphon, Tora, and Xura offered their protection, light, and nourishing earth but they do not presume to dominate, this is left to the rulers on the earth." Again, he paused and smiled, "You see? The goddess will offer her protection and take control of the property. The people, your Zummosh, will then be subject to the goddess and not the governor or even the king. In return they must provide a proportion of what they produce to maintain the temple. As long as we stick to this arrangement then whatever else you do is your business." he turned to the group of Zummosh, "Is this an acceptable offer to you all?"

Although all the gathered Zummosh spoke Common Xosu, they seemed to be struggling to understand his guttural accent. Lulpo turned and translated, despite being the youngest in the group, she seemed to be in charge. A signal of approval rippled through the ranks.

"Excellent, this servant will let the governor know that the land has been taken under the protection of the goddess. The Rilrpitu will have no choice but to leave you alone. A delegation will be sent to the regent and the king's court to have the new arrangement formally recognised."

KALASYAR

33

Sipenkiso stood at the head of the pale white stone table, arms covered in blood and sodden to the elbow. She chanted and ululated three times in thanks to the Great God, the eight other priestesses joined her in the chant and the sound flowed around the room as the worshippers took it up. Kalasyar found herself absorbed by the magic of the sound, despite the worries and anxieties that had plagued and maddened her since her grandfather's trial. It had been days since those events in the theatre and still no verdict had been announced. She kept telling herself this was a good sign, if the Nine wished to execute him the decision would have been swift. Maybe her actions with Doltopez had worked, maybe he had intervened. The mixed feelings of shame, ecstasy and freedom had dogged her ever since, but it would be worth it if her grandfather were to be saved.

The chanting ended; the sacrificed beast was taken by the acolytes to be carved up. The fat, sinews and bones wrapped and burnt in the fire before the statue of the Great God. The flames rose and illuminated the chamber, flickering against the white-gold, pale copper colour of the god's writhing image, almost alive in the flicker of the flames. The arsenic white of the roots of the hulthul tree which sprouted from the earth around them, seemed to wriggle and squirm in the light.

The food was then brought out, the meat of the sacrificed joined by fish and seaweed, clams, and mussels, Sem's rich bounty laid out in front of the worshippers. The acolytes mixed wine in a huge bronze cauldron, a sweet red vintage from Gelodun. They poured a libation to the gods before taking a sip themselves and beginning their meal. Sipenkiso rose once more and lifted her cup,

"I would like to congratulate everyone here, thanks to your hard work and dedication," the High Priestess caught Kalasyar's eye with her own moon shaped, sea blue eyes in a knowing way. *Or was that just her imagination,*

"The Great God's order is being restored. A few hard sacrifices on our part, these have been difficult and testing times. Outsiders have come, with their strange ways of doing things and their difficulty understanding our customs, but despite some ups and downs, we have succeeded and look to be on a true and righteous path, united."

The group stood once more and raised their cups to the Great God, pouring out a further libation. Kalasyar stood with them, confused. *Why and what were they celebrating? and who do they think they have come to an understanding with?* The look Sipenkiso had given her made her feel more uncomfortable now. *She cannot believe that I did this for them. How does she even know?* Kalasyar thought. The vision the Great God granted to her came again, the wraiths on their thrones. *Had they told the High Priestess?*

The end of the ceremony came and went in a blur, she found herself leaving the temple even more confused by the whole experience. She had done nothing to help the cult, other than her usual duties, but Sipenkiso's words implied there was some grand design afoot. The whole thing made her feel even more uneasy about the events of the past few days.

Dunsun had just taken his seat on his mighty throne as she left, the rosy fingers of the dawn crept up the quiet streets. At least the city had calmed somewhat since the trial and the protests which had followed. The patrols of sellswords had lessened. The port was almost back to normal as well, the usual throng of ships coming in and out had returned, despite the pirates which now seemed to be dominating the seas around the White Islands as Thasotun struggled to maintain its grip. The clarity of the day did nothing for her mind though. Baffled, Kalasyar wound her veil back around her face and began her walk home as her handmaids drew alongside her. She was churning over events in her head and barely heard when Thororoz said,

"One of the household slaves brought a message for you whilst you were inside. You are to return to the villa as quickly as possible, there is some important news about your grandfather."

She only really heard the word grandfather. She was heading home anyhow, but her heart skipped a beat when she heard the word and her pace quickened.

* * *

Mercenaries stood watch outside, Zummosh men not Xosu. The villa was a hive of activity, household slaves coming and going, familiar and some unfamiliar faces rushed past her. Without stopping, she strode into the central hall. The room was filled with her grandfather's friends and admirers, but even in the dense swarm she knew what was going on.

Pushing her way through to the centre of the room, she found her grandfather sat on his couch, surrounded by his closest friends. She levered them aside and wrapped her arms around Koseun, tears flooding down her face. Koseun laughed with a crash, like a wave against a cliff, but there was a melancholy in his voice,

"I am home now, don't worry child." he said as he coiled his arms around her and gathered her in a warm embrace. The same words he had said to her the day he had returned to the villa after going out alone to treat with king Tekolger and the occupying Doldun when they first entered the city. The king had seemed a semi-divine figure unmoved by pity, and the same worries which plagued her now had haunted her then.

"Have they released you grandfather? Is it all over?" They were the only words she could manage. He looked at her with a kind smile snaking over his face. He liked to appear jovial in the face of any threat, but Kalasyar knew him too well and could see the sadness in his eyes.

"You have to be strong and do not worry." He spoke. He did not need to say anymore, she knew what he meant, and the realisation hit her like she had fallen from Dzottgelon all the way to the earth below. Her grandfather left her grasp, uncoiling her arms from his neck. He stood in the middle of the room to address the crowd,

"My friends, thank you for coming here today and thank you for the support you have lent to me over the last few days." Koseun took a moment, the emotion clear on his face, but the followers of Rolmit were never fearful to show their emotion,

"Today a judgement has been passed and it is one I am afraid none of you will like. But I have come to realise it is a necessary step to ensure that our city does not remain in the grip of these tyrants and their barbarous backers any longer. The Nine have decided that I am guilty of the crimes of which they accuse me and that for that I must die. They thought themselves gracious in allowing me to choose the method of my own death and that is why you are all gathered here now, like bees returning to their hive, for I would see and speak to all of you. A final gathering before I drink my poison, not only to thank you but to tell you what must happen after I am gone."

A groan rippled around the room. Kalasyar just sat in disbelief. Dunobos spoke up,

"The Nine won't listen to reason, but there is no need for you to accept their verdict, many in the city are sympathetic and still remember you as a hero of the League. I have already made approaches to the guards outside; a small bribe and they will let you slip away unseen. We can have you halfway to Rulkison before the Nine have realised what is happening. The city will welcome you, Rolmit's followers still rule there, and they have fond memories of the League."

Koseun smiled and slid a hand on to Dunobos' shoulder,

"You have also been a true and loyal friend Dunobos, but no. I am afraid I must take this action. Not for the tyrant's sake but for the city, to shake it out of its stupor.

Twelve years ago, we lost a war to an all-conquering king. There is no shame in that, just look what Tekolger went on to achieve after he conquered the Xosu. But that also does not mean that the people of this city must sit down and accept occupation and tyranny.

What government there is here is weak. The Doldun have lost their king and are divided and more concerned with their own affairs. The Rinuxosu are proud and have no love for the Doldun, even if their Assembly did invite Tekolger into Xosupil. The other Xosu value their freedom too much to tolerate occupation and submission for too long. The time is right to take back what we once had, you will use my death as the catalyst to make that happen, to make the people see. From all the people gathered here, and those multitude in this city who loath the tyranny imposed upon us, one clear purpose can emerge. More still, all the Xosu can gather to one purpose again, like a hive of many parts working toward one goal. In so doing I will not really die, I will transcend and become a symbol, an image of what Butophulo can be once more. Yunsunos Sisosi showed us the path to a better way to govern ourselves and lost his life to achieve it. Like him I will reach an immortality as the memory of my sacrifice drives the people of this city to take back their liberty. That will be my legacy."

The anguish was evident in the air, the atmosphere was so thick with it that Kalasyar felt she could almost see it, but everyone knew Koseun well and knew his mind could not be changed. She had come to accept this outcome as inevitable as soon as her grandfather was arrested, although she did not want to admit it to herself. Only hearing the words from Koseun made her realise it was true.

An acceptance and determination settled in the room and Koseun motioned for a cup to be passed to him. Pito Kinsol had brought an ornate vessel for the occasion, of an intricate Putedun design. He had rushed back to the city when he heard of Koseun's arrest although he missed the trial, he had done all he could to help.

Pito was rich and a merchant to his core, thinking mostly in terms of profit and loss. But Koseun had found a great delight in a man who was such a contrast to him, and they had been fast friends for years. Kalasyar had always liked Pito too, he often brought her gifts as a child when he returned from some great voyage. He was now rarely seen in the city, preferring to regularly sail the trader's route. Some said he resided more often in Puteduntik, fearing the Nine would seize him on false charges to lay their hands on his wealth.

Pito had also brought poisons, acquired in Puteduntik, where all the best poisons were found.

"Choose which Koseun." he said, "I cannot say any will give you comfort in your final moments, they are all too cruel." Koseun lay a hand on Kalasyar's shoulder,

"Help me child." He said softly. She froze, crippled with dread. *I cannot,* she wanted to say, but the words would not grace her lips.

"The golden liquid is called *the red kiss.* A nasty concoction truth be told, the priests of Xortogun make it, do not ask why. It chokes a man quickly after consumption, leaving you red faced and swollen upon death. This white one is *the gift of the moon,* and the plant is called *Wildman's Horn.* But I would recommend these." he held out his hand in which were three crystal like stones. "*Sleeping Stones.* When dissolved in wine they make a man's body go numb like a stone and then send him to an endless sleep. They are the choice of The Ushers of the Tribute, assassins who reside in Puteduntik."

"Will he suffer?" Kalasyar found herself asking. Pito smiled, sadly. "I cannot say it will be peaceful child." She struggled to take him seriously today, dressed as he was in an extravagant robe which reached over his head, a sorry attempt to hide his baldness. But Koseun nodded. Pito poured a deep red wine into the cup and then a slave with a nervous yet jester-like grin tipped in the stones. They handed the cup to Tilmosh, Koseun's faithful housekeeper and secretary. The cup was slowly processed towards Koseun. A scene depicting a band of heroes battling a panther, ringed the outside of the cup, some Putedun legend. The figures coloured a soft white against the black background. But the cup seemed more like the cup of Kuso to Kalasyar, bringing an awful and unwanted knowledge.

As Tilmosh brought the vessel ever closer to her grandfather, the wine mixing with the poison that would take Koseun's life, she could barely bring herself to watch. She felt sick, but she knew she had to be involved in her grandfather's final actions. A morbid assuredness took her, the way a wise king must feel when making decisions of life and death. She stood up and took the cup from Tilmosh, approached her grandfather, and handed it over to him, making sure to look him directly in the eye. No words came to her, but she was glad she could at least hand him his final drink.

Koseun took the cup in both hands and raised it high, draining it swiftly. Nothing happened. Koseun placed the cup down and said,

"The poison will take its time to seep through me. I would bid that my granddaughter and friends stay with me until it does."

The room soon emptied until only a few remained. Her grandfather insisted on pacing around the room to aid the poison on its path and soon enough the deadly substance began to take hold. The old man's legs started to numb, and he was forced to lie on his couch. Eventually sleep overtook him, but death did not come, and his shade was not taken to Sem. Instead, he contorted in pain. Kalasyar laid her veil over his face to offer what dignity to him she could. A deathly silence fell over the room as those gathered stood and watched on as a great man was slowly taken from them. Kolkobuas finally cut through the quiet,

"There lies the best man of all of us, true to his principles right to the end. As a young man he spoke eloquently on the protection of our city and our constitution and put those words into action, working hard to expand the reach and influence of the League, through diplomacy and war. He faced down the armies of the Rinuxosu, his master stroke at the Griffin's Rock saw even their far famed and feared Sacred Band thrown down in defeat. He would have put an end to the war and brought victory to the League of Butophulo if it were not for the King of the Doldun, but even in defeat he was instrumental in securing peace and saving the city from destruction. In his later years he sought knowledge for knowledge's sake, ensuring the flame of learning was kept alive within the city. Even after the academy of Rolmit was closed by the Nine he carried on teaching. He was not afraid to speak out when a tyrannical government made every abuse against the city. It was the fear of him which made those tyrants act, cowardice of nine weak men which has seen this great man brought low.

But his last act needs not be one we remember with sadness; he was right to the end. Let this be a moment where we agree to throw off the shackles of an oppressive and cowardly regime, in the memory of the greatest among us."

Kolkobuas lifted his cup of wine, poured a libation to the gods, and drank. A cheer went around the room and the others did the same. Kalasyar just sat there looking at her grandfather. She left before the cheering finished.

***

As the sun reached the mid-point of its journey across the sky, the city was awash with people, but Kalasyar did not see them. Their faces were just a blur. She could not really remember leaving the house, she just knew that she needed to leave.

The sanctuary stood tall and splendid on top of Polriso's Hill, the few clouds in the sky almost touching its peak, tranquil and brilliant, a realm secluded from the chaos of the busy streets below. She found herself approaching the entrance, there were twice as many guards as before and the door was shut. It seemed only Doldun were allowed on the heights this day, but she approached anyway.

One of the guards stepped forward as she neared. The man wore a bronze breastplate embossed with the white star of Tholophos, a purple cloak thrown over his shoulders. He raised his hand and said,

"Hold it there, the Sanctuary is closed to everyone but the garrison."

"I need to speak with your commander." she replied softly as a shy maiden.

"The commander is not seeing anyone. Please leave." The soldier replied in a stern voice.

"You tell him that Kalasyar Sisosi is here to see him. You will regret it if you don't." She did not know where the threatening venomous tone in her voice came from. The soldier laughed,

"I have my orders directly from the general. No one is to be allowed up."

She understood now, the realisation hit her like a wave against a cliff. She laughed, it was all she could do,

"It seems the Doldun do see themselves as above us all then, gods amongst men. Your general is a coward and a fool hiding up there in the heavens, and he will get what is coming to him."

The soldier took a more serious tone,

"Threats will get you nowhere, now leave before I am forced to arrest you."

"Fine arrest me if it will get me an audience with your duplicitous commander." She bellowed back, offering her hands to be bound. Before she could continue, she felt a hand grasp her arm tightly and drag her backwards. She whirled around to see the face of Kolkobuas. He must have followed her. Thororoz and Ralxuloz stood behind him. *They led him here.*

"What are you doing?!" she hissed, "Leave me go."

"I know you are upset about your grandfather, we all are, and believe me vengeance is highest on my mind right now, but we must be rational. Getting yourself arrested or worse by the Doldun will achieve nothing." He said firmly, almost like her grandfather might have done.

"I need to see Doltopez, he lied to me." She exclaimed as she fixed him with a stare and tried to break free of his grasp. But his hand was like stone. He was too strong for her and continued to drag her down the street.

"There will be time for all that in due course. First, we must honour your grandfather and then we will make plans to honour his final wishes. You can be a part of that if you wish, but not like this." Kolkobuas said with a grim determination that made Kalasyar stop. They were away from the soldiers now anyway and the seething anger in her was not so immediate.

"Fine, I will come with you, but Doltopez must answer for what he has done."

"They all will." He answered.

* * *

The Sisosi villa was still alive with activity when they returned, she could only hope the same could be said of her grandfather. She stopped when they reached the threshold of the door,

"Is he…" the words would not come out.

"He lives still, he is stronger than he looks. But he rests between the realms for now." Kolkobuas replied. "Tonight, we will hold a feast to celebrate his life. After that we make our plans."

They went inside, preparations for a lavish celebration were already well under way.

The evening came quickly, her grandfather stilled lived but could not be roused from his sleep. The contortion on his face and body made him curl like a snake on his couch. The sweat streaming off him made it difficult for her to look upon him, but she made herself sit by his side and tend to his needs. Soon she was called to greet the guests. She would host them, but Kolkobuas had agreed to oversee proceedings.

The old man stood at the head of the table and raised a cup of wine. Next to him sat Pito Kinsol and his kin Polrinu, on his other side sat Dunobos and Buso. Rolmit sat further down alongside the other Sisosi. Some Rusosthup and Kisurusosi had also dared to attend. The Nine had succeeded in reducing them to a sorry rump. At the height of the League a feast to celebrate the life of Koseun Sisosi would have drawn half the city.

"We gather here tonight to honour a great man and remember his contributions to our city and our people."

A chant of agreement rippled around the table as the others joined in, but Kalasyar's attention was still fixed on her grandfather. The poison had not yet killed him, maybe that was a good sign, perhaps he will fight it off and recover, return to the realm of the living. Perhaps that would even be the end of the matter, his sentence had been carried out after all.

The silence that greeted the end of the chants of approval shook her out of her dream, as they did so the meat was brought out. A sacrifice to Bosguli in the hope that Koseun would be treated fairly by the gods and the judges of the dead. Perhaps they would see fit to grant Koseun a place of honour in the hidden realm. Kolkobuas rose and raised his cup once more,

"I would like to thank you all for attending, you take great risk to openly show your affection for Koseun and I would hope that it is because you were inspired by his message. The path ahead of us will not be an easy one, but we must use his death as a symbol to free this city."

A ripple of approval went through the gathering once more and Dunobos spoke,

"Then we must act swiftly whilst the shock is still new and the feeling still raw, show the people leadership and they will follow us."

Another indication of approval came, at least from some of the gathered supporters.

"A bold move Dunobos, but a folly. You have seen how many mercenaries patrol the streets, and what of the Doldun garrison?" Kolkobuas replied, with agreement from the rest.

"There are many more people in this city, and they have faced down tyrants in the past, once they realise that the city has turned against them, they will flee." Dunobos confidently replied.

"I admire your boldness Dunobos, but we must be cleverer than that. Otherwise, the streets will run red with blood, and we will be left with nothing but ruins." Kolkobuas answered.

"And what would you propose we do, sit on our hands and lose this opportunity?" Dunobos said, with more voicing their support.

"No, I propose we work to undermine the Nine, gain support within their ranks and work to ease their suspicions so there are less mercenaries on the streets. We should even look abroad for support, there is much sympathy among the White Islands and the old cities of the League. Pito has seen it for himself." Kolkobuas shot back, his supporters became much more animated now. Kalasyar looked on in a confused bewilderment.

"How long would that take, years? The islands have their own problems, Thasotun is likely to side with the Doldun and the Nine, and Thasotun has its thumb over most of the old territories of the League. But those cities may rise if Butophulo gives them an example to follow. Thasotun itself may even come back to us." Dunobos replied, angrily this time. She could not take it anymore. She stood and exclaimed with the force of a hammer on an anvil,

"Look at yourselves. My grandfather has not yet passed, and you are already arguing with each other. You are both right. We cannot let this moment pass, but neither can we risk the lives of the citizens of the city in such a reckless way."

Her intervention brought a hush to the room, until Kolkobuas cut through it,

"She is right, fighting like this won't solve anything. We have drunk much tonight and the anger over Koseun is still raw. Let us meet again tomorrow with clearer heads and work out our way forward."

A subdued agreement rippled through the room, but it was clear that disagreement and indecision had already set in. Kalasyar left to tend to her grandfather.

ZENUKOLA

34

The messenger had arrived early in the morning, just as dawn had come. The writhing light on the horizon snaked red across the sky as if escaping from the clutches of the dark world below. It brought with it good news. The savage Rilrpitu had been defeated on the field and Supo had dealt with Kalu. Zenu took no pleasure in that news, he had been fond of the young Companion, but the stability of the empire had to be put above personal feelings. Better still Dalzenu of the Balkakel, Torfub's former governor, had arrived under guard. He would get a trial soon, but it would be best to wait until after the business with Kelbal though, Dalzenu had kin amongst the Companions. But trial or not, another of Kelbal's allies in a strategic position had been removed. Zenukola had also successfully persuaded Kelabl to dispatch the twins, Pelapakal and Doluzelru, north with what forces Kelbal felt he could trust to pursue the rest of the Rilrpitu a few days before. Kelbal's closest allies were gone now, the Companions that were left were all suspicious of him and Zenu's overtures were bearing fruit. The veterans left with the army had had their loyalty to Kelbal rocked to its core. With the news of Kalu's death the plan was ripe for execution, the future security of the empire within his grasp.

Zenu found getting old did have some benefits, he rose earlier than the rest of the city and so was able to receive the news before the rumours spread through the army. He had chosen his finest chiton for this day, sky blue trimmed with silver white which matched the blue of his one good eye and the silver shard that had replaced the other. He felt his phantom fingers twitch with nerves and excitement, everything would turn on the next few hours, an empire won or lost.

He left his chambers stroking his long grey beard and ordered

Koloathutalaz to summon the Companions to attend a meeting of the regency council, everyone except Kelbal. Those who were with him were already primed, they merely had to stick to their role. That was the one element he was not confident in, Thazan did not seem to be paying attention the last they spoke. The other Companions he hoped would be caught off guard and would be too slow to respond.

He also ordered Koloathutalaz to rouse the rest of his personal guard and have them occupy the palace, barring the gate. Zenu made his way to the old throne room of Yorixori and sat in the great black seat at the head of the table. The old throne of Zowdel, crowned with what he believed was a carved spear that the god-kings of old used to proclaim their might. *This is spear won land, and spear won power,* he thought as he settled into the chair. There he waited and thought on the new beginning he would bring about this day as the dawn light flooded in through the open windows. The pleasure he found in that thought struck him like a thunderbolt. The seat was more comfortable than he had expected, it was a position he could get used to. Although the presence of the king's coffin behind him was unnerving. *I am doing this for the Doldun,* he thought, *your ambition always did need to be tempered Tekolger, you were too much for us.*

One by one the Companions that where still left in the city filed in, some looking half asleep, yawning, and only clothed in their fine robes. That was a good sign. Zenu waited for them all to sit before speaking. His phantom fingers twitched again as his voiced boomed and echoed around the great hall.

"News just arrived of a battle. Our men, led by Kalu, defeated, and destroyed the Rilrpitu savages." he paused, "…but the gods saw fit to take Kalu from us, when his glory was at its height. No doubt his shade is now being guided by the bright god to the hidden realm and he will be judged well by Tholophos and join Tekolger on the plain of Zulbeli, under the protection of Xosu, the bright god."

There was silence around the table. Zenu continued,

"There will be plenty of time to mourn for Kalu and celebrate his glory as we will Tekolger's, but the empire is still at risk. We must stay committed to maintain Tekolger's legacy. Kelbal's decision making has been questionable at best. We all agree that he has overstepped his authority, and you have all seen how hard the death of the king has struck him. Kalu's death will be just as hard for him to take. We, as the protectors of Tekolger's legacy and the leading men of the Doldun and you as the King's Companions, must act now and take control of the empire, to save Kelbal from himself. Remember as Companions it is your duty to advise the king and ensure he does not act as the tyrant. Without a king to advise, we must instead rule together."

There was silence still. Zenu took that as approval,

"I will inform Kelbal of the news privately and then we will hold a council meeting in which we shall tell him of our collective decision to take the power he has usurped back. A new regency council will be established. Initially headed by me to ensure the empire remains stable as power is transitioned to the new king. Are we all agreed?"

A murmur of agreement and the nodding of heads at the table was all that Zenu needed. He got up and left, a sense of purpose which Zenu had not felt in years was swelling up inside him. The subdued feeling around the table buoyed him, the Companions knew not to resist and to look to the Deltathelon for guidance. Although silence from some figures, such as Zela, was concerning, he would surely not stay so quiet for long.

Zenu had spoken to him several times but had not felt confident enough to confide the full plan to Zela. Although the Companion was displeased with Kelbal, he was also wary of taking any action against him. Zenu knew a man of torn loyalties when he saw one.

He strode into his old chambers where Kelbal had taken up residence. A burley eunuch at the door tried to protest his entry, but Zenu was having none of it. His phantom fist clenched angrily as his guards pushed the man aside.

Zenu's old sleeping chamber was barely recognisable, the modest set of rooms he kept had been decked in luxury from all over the empire. Several empty jugs of wine were strewn on an ornate table alongside half a dozen cups. One had tumbled to the floor and was lying in a thousand pieces. Two women and a boy, barely clothed, pushed themselves passed Zenu and ran off giggling under their breaths. Kelbal's new toy, Yare, was also there. He strode out confidently rather than running, flashing Zenu a smile that maddened him.

Kelbal was in the corner of the room by the balcony that allowed the ruler of the city to look out across their domain. He was once again wearing a robe of the Xortogun style, but he looked dishevelled as if he had dressed in a hurry. His beard unkempt and hair matted into a many tiered crown. The morning sun cast an amber light upon him and split his shadow across the floor.

"News from Supo arrived early this morning. I thought I should let you know before the council meeting." Zenu said.

Kelbal did not answer but turned to acknowledge Zenu's presence. His face was flush as if from drink and his lips stained black by the unmixed wine he was swilling. Zenu continued,

"Kalu and Dolzalo's combined army engaged the main Rilrpitu force four days ago. It was a short but bloody affair and the Rilrpitu were defeated and scattered. The army is now spreading out to root out what is left of the Rilrpitu in the region and drive them back north. They will regroup with us at Torfub once it is over."

Kelbal replied happily,

"Good, those Rilrpitu were a mere distraction to the bigger issues at hand. We should begin preparing to move to Torfub as soon as possible…"

Before Kelbal could continue. Zenu cut him off,

"There is more. Kalu led the assault on the Rilrpitu camp and was cut down in the thickest of the fighting. Supo informs me that it was a death worthy of Tholophos himself and stories will be told about it for many years to come."

The words struck like thunder. Kelbal opened his mouth, but nothing came out, his tongue just hung there, thick with grief, his heart caught in his throat. His face barely reacted, but the pain behind his eyes was evident, his gregarious spirit quashed. His green eye seemed to dim, although there was still fire in the amber one. When the Companion stumbled forward and reached for the edge of the dolthil wood table next to him for support, Zenu knew he had succeeded.

"I know he was like a brother to you and this news must be almost as hard to hear as the death of Tekolger. He will be a big loss and all the Doldun will weep for him, indeed the whole world will, such was his fame. He was killed in the thick of the action, winning glory and renown. No doubt his shade will be allowed to enter Zulbeli, and we will do him honour in time. But now, we must continue as we were, the empire needs us to stay strong."

Kelbal nodded. His stature had visibly shrunk. Reflecting on the silence for a moment, Zenu realised that he would miss Kalu as well. He was a good man and a more than competent general, undoubtedly one of the greatest Doldun of his generation, even if he was a son of the barbarous clans. But saving the empire from ruin had to come first, and the business of running and maintaining the empire was much less glorious than conquering one. As wise as Tekolger was, he never understood that. His phantom fingers flexed.

Having allowed Kelbal a quiet moment of contemplation, Zenu continued,

"You must not show weakness now, the Companions are gathering for our council meeting."

Kelbal looked at him quizzically,

"There was no meeting today." He said.

"Yes, there is one this morning, or had you forgotten?" Zenu shot back, his eyes glancing at the empty jugs of wine as if to portray concern. *Another dirty trick,* he thought, but Kelbal needed to be pushed off balance this morning, *he brought all this on himself*. Clearly shaken, Kelbal replied,

"No…no I hadn't forgotten. Very well allow me to dress properly and I will attend our comrades."

The uncertainty in him was obvious. Zenu placed a hand on his shoulder and then turned to leave.

* * *

None of the Companions had moved from their seats when Zenu returned. He noted that none of them was eager to make eye contact with him either. These godlike men who had wrested control of the world from the mightiest of foes were uncomfortable with taking power from across a table from their comrade. *Good,* he thought, the less resistance from them the better. Even solemn and serious Thazan looked a little insecure. Zenu said a silent prayer to Dunsun hoping that Thazan would play his part well.

He sat back down on the old throne. It was more comfortable than the seat at the far end of the table he had been using. The king's presence felt less judgmental this time.

After a long wait Kelbal finally entered the room, looking much more together than when Zenu left him. A new and finer Xortogun style robe, royal red in colour, trimmed with eagle feathers dyed saffron, was draped over him and his hair brushed and held in place like a disc circling his head, his beard oiled, which brought out the red, and tied. He had sacrificed almost everything that made him Doldun for a taste of the power of the kings of Xortogun, he probably would even have given his very blood if he could.

Kelbal gave Zenu another quizzical look with his green and amber eyes as he realised where Zenukola was seated, but he raised no objection. He took his seat to the right of the throne. The silence in the room was deafening. Zenukola sat calmly and watched. Eventually Kelbal spoke,

"I am sure you are all aware of the news. Kalu won a great victory over the vicious Rilrpitu, but the gods saw fit to take him from us in the process. He was a brother to us all and will be sorely missed." Kelbal's voice sounded strong, but there was a hint of it cracking as he said Kalu's name, the power it once held dissipating. He paused for a moment and then continued,

"Dolzalo, Palmash and Supo will use their forces to secure the northern border and then regroup with us at Torfub. We will prepare to march immediately; the priority now is to return to Xortogun and crown Tekolger's heir."

As Zenu had instructed him to, Thazan was the first to speak,

"Will the green boys from Xortogun be marching with us? Would it not be better to send them north to secure the defences?" Zenu was pleased to hear the north mentioned, Thazan listened more closely than he let on,

"We have already settled this issue Thazan. The Xortogun will march with us integrated into the army." Kelbal replied, giving Thazan a look like daggers to his heart.

"You decided on this settlement Kelbal, not us." Came an angry response, almost emotional for Thazan, the daggers turned on Kelbal. A murmur of agreement went around the table, which seemed to take Kelbal by surprise. Zenu decided that this was the moment to intervene, Thazan had done his job well. Leaning forward and raising his hand to prevent the others from speaking, he said in a commanding voice,

"Kelbal, the other Companions and I have been talking. We feel that the burden and sacrifices needed to rule have placed too much strain on you. You have not been yourself, indeed it has transformed you. As there is no king for the moment, you are not regent. The decisions of rule should be taken as a group, as the Companions have done for two hundred years. Even the King of the Doldun is never an absolute ruler."

Kelbal had that quizzical look on his face again, but it soon dropped away as he realised what was happening. He looked around the room, desperate for any signs of support. The other Companions shied away from his gaze. Despite the warrior he was at heart, the fight had been knocked out of Kelbal and he looked back to Zenu and meekly nodded his head. Zenu continued,

"You will still sit and make decisions with us, but we will do so as a collective. A newly constituted council with myself as its head will lead the empire until the new king comes of age."

Kelbal was desperately thumbing the black ring of the Doldun. Zenu looked at it and said,

"I think it best you hand over the ring for it to be kept with the other royal regalia. Until a regent or Tekolger's successor is appointed."

Now thoroughly and visibly broken, Kelbal reluctantly handed over the ring and slumped back in his chair.

Zenu turned to the assembled group and said in a loud and thundering voice,

"To business. The Xortogun will be ordered north to garrison the border defences. Yoruxoruni's crumbling wall is no barrier without a garrison. It will be fitting for men from Xortogun to man the wall their old king built. The rest of the army will depart for Torfub. All in agreement?"

They signalled their consent.

"A new Companion will need to be appointed to take Kalu's place. As the new military commander of Torfub and a long-time servant of the Doldun, I propose Pelu of the Deltathelon, any objections?"

A few puzzled looks went around the room, but no objections were raised.

"Good, as he is now a Companion of good Doldun stock I also propose we make Pelu Governor of Torfub."

Again, there was no disagreement.

"Very good. If there is nothing else, we should end it there, I want the army ready to move to Torfub as soon as possible."

SANAE

35

She was handed a worn looking broom from a dour faced acolyte. Sanae may have been on the verge of having all the secrets of Xosu revealed to her, but she still had her chores to complete. The temple would not look after itself after all and the dwelling place of the bright god needed to be kept in a suitable condition.

She took the broom to the high altar and began to sweep. Despite the city's location in the rich, fertile land of the river delta, the dust from the desert to the north that the Xortogun called the Broken Land still provided a thin layer of sand to blanket the city and constant vigilance was needed to keep it from the temple. A quiet and humdrum day loomed for Sanae before her penultimate task, but given the excitement of the last few weeks, she welcomed the thought of forgetting the world and focusing on putting the temple in order. She began sweeping the area in front of the statue of the god, feeling tranquil as she passed under its shadow.

It had been several days now since the Zummosh had accepted the protection of the temple of Xura, she had visited Lulpo once since then and things seemed better. Priests of Xura had started to frequent the Zummosh village, compiling an inventory and assessment of the land to calculate how much they could expect in offerings to their goddess. The first but only signs that the Zummosh had given up some of their freedom, but much less intrusive than the Rilrpitu. The priests slipped in and out of the village like shadows and they conducted their business so quietly they could have been wraiths quietly entering from another realm. The mere presence of the priests also seemed to be dissuading the savage horsemen from returning for now. All in all, she was feeling pleased about her intervention.

Sanae's pleasant daydream was broken by the sound of the High Priestess entering the chamber. As usual she was followed by a gaggle of young acolytes eager to serve and please. She made her way around the chamber, dispatching each of her followers on various tasks and errands as she did. Even in this simple undertaking, Kolae had a way of drawing the eye. Sanae found herself watching the High Priestess intently as she went, a feeling of some resentment building in her. *If I were the High Priestess*, she thought, *things would be very different around here.*

Almost as if Kolae could hear the young priestesses' thoughts, she turned and looked directly at Sanae, their gaze locking. The two watched each other closely for only a few moments, although it felt like days. She could see the flash of disapproval in the High Priestesses' eyes. No doubt she would find some issue with Sanae's sweeping. But Kolae turned away and carried on walking.

The clang of an opening door drew her attention back to the rest of the room. Helupelan came in, alone, drawing no attention from the rest of the servants of the temple. He solemnly made his way toward the altar, not stopping to acknowledge anyone before he had made a small offering to the god. Paying Sanae no mind, he stood at the foot of the statue and muttered a prayer under his breath.

Having paid his dues to the god, he finally turned to Sanae and smiled. Saying nothing he beckoned her over and gestured for her to sit on the chair usually reserved for the High Priest at the foot of the statue of the bright god. She walked over, catching Kolae looking at her again through the corner of her eye.

"I hear that the Zummosh have accepted the protection of the temple of Xura." Helupelan said in an enquiring way. "Am I to assume you had something to do with this?"

She hesitated, eventually replying,

"There was nothing else left for them. It was clear the governor could do nothing for them. I merely introduced them to Kurmush Xura Ya Kuria, the priest at the temple." She thought it best not to mention that she was now certain the governor had been encouraging the Rilrpitu.

"I am told you did more than introduce them." he paused for a moment. "You should not really have been interfering in the way you did. There is a delicate balance in this city, upsetting it may have unforeseen consequences."

"I only did what I thought was right. What I thought Xosu, and king Tekolger would have done, lighting a path for them to follow." Sanae said in an apologetic way.

"I know. You have a kind, generous heart, and a nurturing spirit; you get that from your mother, and that bright spark and lofty ideals from your father. He would have done the same." Helupelan replied, the mention of her parents made her heart flutter. Feeling as if a vine had suddenly wrapped its way around her tongue. Three times she tried to speak, but the words would not come.

"You acted on impulse, but your intentions were honest and good, I am proud of you for that." Helupelan continued, shining a smile at her, "Although some of the others are concerned that you are too close to the Zummosh and the Xortogun, that you will share the secrets of the god with them or embarrass the temple."

Sanae's eyes darted toward Kolae who seemed to be lurking in the background of their conversation,

"You know that was not my intention though father." She said, her ability to speak suddenly being reborn.

"I know, I am just telling you to be careful. Perhaps with the issues of the Zummosh resolved you should stay away from them for a while. Concentrate on your duties here." Helupelan said with a conciliatory tone.

She nodded,

"Will you tell me more of my parents?" She did not know why she asked, a sudden madness had gripped her. Helupelan sighed, a long and regretful sigh. Looking off into the distance as if he were watching another life unfold before his eyes. Finally, he replied,

"You have two tasks left, focus on those, complete them, and concentrate on your duties here at the temple. When you are settled as a priestess of the bright god, I will tell you about your mother and father. Know that they would have been proud of you though and the bright future ahead of you." he paused and with a smile changed the subject, "Keluaz will be attending me here at the temple this evening. The governor was not best pleased when he heard what had happened, he had announced his intentions to all and has now seen them undermined. There may be consequences for all of us as a result." the High Priest paused again, "I want you to attend me as our cupbearer for the evening. Say nothing, only listen. There is a lesson in this for all of us."

He stood up to leave, lovingly squeezing her shoulder as he did.

* * *

The rich, dark wine, a vintage from Gelodun, cascaded into the shallow cup washing over the image of the great dolthil tree on the bottom. She placed the cups, with the image of the bright god in red on black along the side, in front of Helupelan and his guests.

Keluaz of the Keluazi, the governor of Tekolgertep, reclined awkwardly on a couch in the High Priest's chambers in a fine white Xosu style toga, trimmed with red, and picked at a plate of olives from Butophulo with his good hand. A second couch had almost disappeared completely under the hulking figure of Rososmosh, the governor's adviser, the Great Baboon as the Xortogun liked to call him. Sanae stepped back and stood near the fire as Keluaz spoke in his slurred and meandering way,

"Those accursed prieshts are now crawling all over the land on the south bank. Rivalry between my fellow governorsh is bad enough, but theshe Xortogun prieshts are something elshe. They sheek to interfere in the affairsh of the empire." Helupelan was listening intently and nodding along, the disc of his face bobbing up and down in a way that Sanae had to try and contain a laugh, "and then I was told that a priesshtessh of Xosu was involved." as he said it, the governor's pale eyes lingered on Sanae, "What ish your game Helupelan? Why ashk me to intervene and then go behind my back in thish way?"

Helupelan placed his cup down and in a voice, which barely sounded like his own, replied,

"That was not my intent and I apologise for any damage done to your reputation. We merely meant to involve every community of the city in an important decision. How can we build an empire and a city for all when we do not include them in crucial choices like this? The temple of Xosu would be happy to make any gesture or compensation you desire to make amends."

Keluaz eyed him warily for what seemed like too long. It was Rososmosh who replied,

"Your intent was noble, but Keluaz sits atop the multitude of the city. We cannot have the priests undermine the unity of Tekolgertep, especially without the king. The land is like a hive without a queen right now. You must remember that, unlike your good self, the priests of Xortogun have much more corporeal ambitions. They ruled this land out right for many centuries and do not doubt they would wish to do so again." He finished and plunged an oil covered hand into the bowl of olives, a ring on every finger and even one on one of his thumbs, each encrusted with jewels, except the plain ring which went through his nose. Finally, Keluaz slowly spoke,

"Very well, I believe that you did not intend theshe conshequences. I will forgive you for thish folly. The matter ish before the royal court now, they will make their decishion. I may ashk for that compenshation if they rule againsht me."

Helupelan bowed his head curtly and asked,

"What news of the royal court?"

"They make their way to Torfub as we shpeak. Although I undershtand that shome of the Companions have been detached from the army to deal with theshe Rilrpitu raiding in the north. A few minor battlesh have been fought.

It ish fortunate for you that my own delegation wash deshpatched before the prieshts could shend theirsh. Dam Xortogun think that they can go directly to the king and ush governorsh hold no shway, ash if we shtill lived at the height of the old kingdoms." he paused, a flush of anger clear on his face, "Konguz, the man the Putedun shent to treat with ush, hash gone ash well, to ashk for permishsion to trade in the city. Tekolger wash dead againsht it. *'Not until we have eshtablished ourshelves in thish land'* he shaid, but new tradersh would bring much needed wealth and food to the city. I wish to shee the population grow and would welcome it." the anger gone now, he shrugged in his nonchalant and awkward way, "We shall shee, I shuspect the new court will be much more open to the idea. Dotmazo would like to shee it happen, and no doubt the new king will follow his advice." the governor paused as if in thought and sipped at his wine, "Yesh, more Doldun in the city would be a good thing, and more of the Keluazi even better. I intend to shee mine own clan provide an honour guard to bring the king's shon here from Doldun to be crowned. Dotmazo assures me all ish in place for him to make the crossing."

"Keluunsen's son will be crowned king then? Tekolger had other wives and other children and Surson Tora Ya Kuria must surely have given birth by now." Helupelan's eyes caught Sanae's as he said it, a look that made her feel suddenly awkward. He placed his cup down and she moved forward to refill it. The governor paid her no mind and answered,

"Keluunsen's shon, Koliathelanu the boy ish called. He ish the only child who ish closhe to manhood, and a boy of pure Doldun blood, the blood of Tholophos and Xosu no lessh. Why would we crown any of the othersh? As for Shurson, I have had no word, Torfub hash gone quiet. With theshe accushations againsht Dalzenu there ish little leadership in the city for the moment."

"I believe the noble lady has born a son, we all pray that she and the boy are doing well." Rososmosh said uninterested, "And there has been some heavy fighting in the northern regions near Yorotog. The news of the king's passing has shaken the western regions hard, rumblings of rebellion among the old lords of Zenian and clan rivalries no doubt will resurface amongst the King's Companions." he stuffed another handful of olives in his mouth, "But Zenukola has taken charge, they need an old and experienced had to guide them onto the right path. As for the crowning of Koliathelanu, I fear that is not so simple. There is much division on the issue of the succession and Dotmazo is yet to stir, as is his way. But in the long run this may be a good thing, Tekolger's teachers taught him how to conquer, but the teachings of Rolmit are much better suited to governance. Perhaps the new king will be given a wider education."

Helupelan nodded again and asked,

"How does the east fair with the news of Tekolger's passing?"

"Ash well ash could be expected. Dotmazo hash Doldun and Zenidun in hand, the Zummosh are too divided amongsht themshelves to care either way. No doubt the Xosu cities will be reshtless. Butophulo shtill chafes under the rule of thoshe nine shadowy foolsh Tekolger placed over the city and the king of the Rinuxosu shees himself ash Xosu come again.

If I were Dotmazo, I would march an army into Xosupil and have the boy elected the new Hegemon of the League of Thelonigul before bringing him here. Otherwise shomeone elshe will try to claim the allegiance of the Xosu cities. The pan-Xosu games would be the perfect opportunity to do sho. Shwift action to maintain order ish needed now, I fear. Tekolger won thish empire with decishive and bold action, but a different kind of ruler will be needed to shecure it." Keluaz answered.

After the governor and his aide had had their fill of wine and olives, they bid their farewells as they said they must move on to other important business. Afterwards, Helupelan pulled Sanae aside and said, "You see how complicated and delicately balanced the politics of empire are. Even what seems like a small and insignificant action can have unknown consequences."

* * *

The wall flashed white, now gold, now red. It was only a small wall no more than twice her height, but she knew that its surface was sheer, the prospect in front of her was not an easy one.

The light of the midday sun glinted off the surface. *Zilthum*, she thought, although she knew it was just an imitation, a sheet of polished bronze covering a brick wall, but the impression it gave was real. The almost mythical material which the Kinsolsun, the wizards of the sea, built with and forged their weapons, was mined in the White Islands by the men they took as slaves, serving the great smith Buto. As hard as it was light and as sharp as it was flexible. The impenetrable walls which ringed the Thelonbet, the inner ring of old Kolbos, was constructed by the Kinsolsun from solid blocks of the mineral, once abundant among the White Islands, to provide a sanctuary where they could nurse Buto back to health after he was cast from Dzottgelon. The walls had stood the test of time. More than eight hundred years had passed since the sacking of the once great city of old Kolbos, and it was said the only part of the crumbling ruin still standing was the great wall which encircled the inner sanctum.

But before the great city rose to rule the seas and before the sons of Tholophos brought all the heroes of the world to do battle outside its walls, the Thelonbet stood. The home of the wizards of the sea, the children of Sem who ruled like tyrant king's over the White Islands. They had aided Xosu once, and he considered them his friends and allies, it was all a trick. When he discovered their foul deeds that poisoned the land, how they horded the wealth of the people they enslaved, and their nefarious plans for his people, he scaled the walls of their impregnable citadel, battled amidst the fires of the forge, and cast the Kinsolsun out.

Sanae took a deep breath and stepped forward. She reached up, finding a place on the metal sheets where one joined the other, it looked less like zilthum up close. She had only seen the moon pale material once, the time she met king Tekolger, his armour glistened with it.

Helupelan had told her that Tekolger's armour and weapons and that of his Companions and White Shields had been given to him as a symbol of submission by the League of Butophulo. From treasury of Butophulo itself. The swords were of pure zilthum, said to have been forged with arcane magic by the Kinsolsun, a skill which had been lost like so much else. The other relics were forged at old Kolbos' height. The smiths of that great city of the Salxosu could rework zilthum, but only in small amounts, even they could not rival the skill of the Kinsolsun.

Her finger's straining, she pulled herself upward, scraping her foot against the wall to find a grip. Her fingers ached, another strain and she pulled herself further up. The top was close, she could see it, almost reach it, but her hands were giving way and her feet slipping against the smooth metal sheets. *One more heave,* she thought.

With all her strength she threw herself upward, grasping at the top, her feet slipped, her shoulders jarred as she slid down the wall, but her hands were left planted on the top. Giving herself a moment to recover, she pulled herself upward, her shoulders straining and her feet scrambling against the side. Rolling over onto the top of the wall, she lay on her back exhausted and was greeted by a putrid smell, like rotting eggs.

Rolling on to her chest and scrambling to her feet. The floor felt sticky, as she pulled her hands off the ground, they came slick with gore. *Blood,* she thought. There were pools of water around, but it smelt wrong, poisoned, the poison the Kinsolsun were said to spread.

She could see lumps of yellow rock arranged neatly on pedestals in front of her, nine she counted, behind them a great white rock, she knew what she must do. Covering her mouth and nose with her robe, she approached the rocks, lifting them one by one and launching them over the side of the wall toward the river. Each one hurtled toward the ground, making a satisfying splash as they landed, sending a small wave to wash over the banks. The final and biggest rock she threw with all her might, it made a deep splosh as it hit the water, sending a big wave to sweep over the river and burst the banks, scattering all before it.

A door creaked open as the last rock caused havoc in the water below. Sanae looked around to see Helupelan walking towards her, his ceremonial robe wrapped around him, he raised his arms and said,

"Xosu scaled the walls of the Thelonbet and cast out the wicked and duplicitous Kinsolsun, who foolishly denied him their recognition as a god and son of Dunsun. The crippled god Buto, he bound to his forge under the earth. It was only then he knew the true horrors of the wizard's crimes, the blood-soaked rooms of their palace a testament to their hubris. He would purify the place."

Another priest appeared behind Helupelan, carrying a bucket filled with scented water. He handed it to Sanae, and both turned to leave.

Placing the bucket on the ground, she began to scrub the blood stained and putrid floor, to remove any trace and smell of the rocks she had discarded. The gory, sticky mess that was plastered everywhere and proved stubborn to remove. Even where Sanae managed to scrub it off, it had dyed the surface red, the taint still very much there. All the while the putrid smell still lingered.

It felt like hours passed as her knees grew sore as the sky turned from light to dark. Her back ached and her hands became raw and red, but still she scrubbed, the ground had to be purified. Slowly but surely the battle was being won.

The door creaked open again, but Sanae paid it no mind, she was too focused on her task. Besides, it was probably only one of the priests come to check on her progress. She could hear footsteps coming towards her and then feet appearing before her eyes as she continued to scrub. She knew who it was before she looked up. Kolae, the High Priestess stood looming over her.

"You are taking your time with this task." she said in her usual condescending tone. "No matter, I am glad I caught you here, we need to have a discussion if you are to become and initiate to the mysteries of Xosu."

Sanae acknowledged her but carried on scrubbing. She could tell Kolae was annoyed by this, but the High Priestess carried on regardless,

"I heard those Zummosh have taken up with the temple of Xura." Sanae nodded, "One group of barbarians with another I suppose. As long as they do not become a menace for us." Kolae paused for a moment.

"What did you think you were doing with them?"

Sanae looked up at her,

"They needed help. I thought it was the right thing to do."

"And what do you think gives you the right to decide such things?" Kolae shot back.

Sanae looked her square in the face now.

"No one does, they needed help, I did what I thought was right."

"I know the High Priest is soft on you and allows you to get away with more than most, he is soft on you because you remind him of his past. He was a different man back then, more concerned with worldly wants and desires, but do not think that gives you the right to ignore the rules. I know you have been revealing our secrets to those barbarians." Kolae's voice had turned to venom now.

Sanae stopped scrubbing,

"I have revealed nothing. I helped people who were in need, like Xosu himself did."

"Do you think you can take my place? Is that your game? I've seen the way you show off in front of Helupelan, do you think you can make him replace me?" There was a real anger in Kolae's eyes now.

She carried on scrubbing, saying,

"You are absurd, leave me alone."

Kolae's blood was up,

"I know your game and I know that you have revealed our secrets, the High Priest will hear of this, and he will see through your little charade."

She turned and left in a hurry, her robe flowing behind her. Sanae carried on scrubbing, fearful of what the High Priestess would do.

SONOSPHOSKUL

36

The harbour was a welcome sight, the small, battered fleet limped its way toward the open mouth and the marble city beyond. Pilsipon had been the northern most of the founding cities of the League of Butophulo, and one of its most loyal bastions.

"Do you think they will welcome us, Captain?" The voice was Dinon the Fisherman's. One of the senior men in Sonos' company.

"They welcomed Zolmos. Why not us?" Answered Dinon the Shipwright, a younger man but still experienced and respected by the rest. Sonos sighed and turned to them.

"Who knows. Zolmos was an unpredictable rogue and could talk his way into anywhere. But Pilsipon will be more cautious now since Thasotun ordered his expulsion. The ruling council is supposedly an ally of Thasotun and the Doldun, we should know, we helped install them. But we can hope there is enough sympathy for us exiles from Butophulo to allow us to pull into the harbour and make repairs."

The five triremes crept toward the mouth of the port. Sonos' ship, which the men had dubbed Tale Teller, was at the rear. He watched on as the other four, which the men had begun to call Buto's Hammer, Sea Sculptor, Poisoned Kiss, and Wave Wanderer, entered the calm waters of the harbour entrance. Unsure what kind of reception they would receive at Pilsipon and the other former League cities, especially those now under the sway of Thasotun. They had initially elected to avoid approaching the White Islands directly and to keep as far away from Thasotun as possible. Instead sailing around the coast to the northwest from Yil and then south toward Xosupil before cutting back across the islands from the west towards Pittuntik.

"The skies have cleared now. Maybe the gods are looking kindly on us again." Dinon the Shipwright said.

"Do not tempt fate or the gods my friend. Events appeared favourable when we left Yil, but appearances can be deceptive." The Fisherman answered, with all the wisdom of those who spend their lives at sea.

"The gods sent the Hotizoz to aid us there. Stopping those sailors from doing anything foolish. Why would they let us get this far if only to see us fail here?" The Shipwright retorted.

"The captain, played no small part in that." The Fisherman answered quickly.

The Legion had seized the men of Rulrup's camp and stopped their attempt to retake the ships on the night they had fled Yil. The Hotizoz had then marched up the coast and met the small fleet at an inlet the following evening.

"No small amount of luck in all of it I am afraid. But that is something the gods may have sent our way. Something moved the other Xosu to act how they did." Sonos replied absent mindedly, his eyes still fixed on the harbour. To Sonos' surprise, the other Xosu had not intervened in their escape. Allowing the ships to leave and the Hotizoz to march without complaint. It was about as clean an escape as they could have hoped for. Though the nature of their leaving had meant abandoning most of the plunder that was left to them. Sonos had managed to save the zilthum amulet Thildol had given them, but little else of value had been brought to the ships.

Despite the apparent ease the other Xosu showed to their leaving, abandoning them amid hostile territory, no doubt drawing the ire of Rulrup upon them, had left a bitter taste in Sonos' mouth. *Another betrayal to add to the ever-growing list.* He could only hope that the gods would sympathise with their cause but found little reason for the confidence the Shipwright seemed to have.

"And how many times did we almost come unstuck Dinon? Driven off with little food at Tikisu and then a storm blowing us across the sea. And what about in Gelodun?" The Fisherman argued back.

"I did not say the gods would make our path easy. Besides, Tikisu was never a member of the League. Why would they have any sympathy for us? And do you blame them in Gelodun, their king dead and then we turn up as raiders along the coast. That militia captain did nothing that we wouldn't have done in his position. Though he did get an arrow in the eye for his trouble." The Shipwright sounded almost gleeful.

Dawn's light flooded across the horizon. Pilsipon seemed to glow and change as it was bathed in the morning light, the sea had brought them to a realm secluded and beyond the tumult of the war they left behind. The city was a tranquil, peaceful place, a contrast to the journey that brought them here.

"And we spent a night trapped in those caves. The gods seem to enjoy testing us that way."

"If we had not been trapped then none of us would have got to see a company of men chasing sheep. That trick with the torches tied to the sheep's tails, making them think we fled in the middle of the night so that we could slip back to the ships, don't tell me that was not inspired by the gods."

Sonos observed as several small skiffs glided out from the harbour of Pilsipon, across the pale mirror of the sea to greet the ships and guide them into the port. He had missed the organised and civilised city life more than he knew. Home was close, he could feel it, even see it in the sea. He touched the amulet at his neck.

"Maybe, but our raiding was punished by the storm, forcing us to test Pilsipon's loyalties. Even if they allow us to enter Thasotun will still know of our return." The Fisherman shot back.

"Quiet you two." Sonos said, "The gods had a hand in this, but our survival rests with our own wits. No more talk of this, I don't want you to unnerve the others."

The skiffs had reached the other ships, Sonos could see figures clambering aboard. One of the skiffs had peeled off and was approaching Tale Teller. Shouts echoed from the other ships, Sonos could see a man grappling with a shadow on Puso's ship, Sea Sculptor, before they were pulled apart. The skiff approaching Sonos' ship was now close enough to hear. A man stood at the front, cupped his hands like a horn, and bellowed toward Sonos,

"The city of Pilsipon will not allow ships of war to enter its harbour. Turn back and leave now!"

Sonos could already see the lead ship, Buto's Hammer, which carried Runukolkil, was beginning to turn away from the harbour and the men from Pilsipon were disembarking from the other ships. Cowardice or a change of heart, clearly Pilsipon was no longer a friend of Butophulo. No doubt they were fearful of the wrath of the Red and White Council. Thasotun aspired to rise to the mantle that Butophulo once held, and she was jealous of those who threatened her ascent.

"The gods are fickle." The Fisherman said.

A wave of disappointment overcame Sonos. Ships of Butophulo would once have had a warm welcome here, now they were met with fear and suspicion. He did not bother to answer the man on the skiff, instead ordering his men to follow Runukolkil's lead.

***

Being refused entry to Pilsipon was a blow. The surety that the former members of the League were still loyal to its memory was what had given them the confidence to return to the White Islands. With Pilsipon this was especially so as it had been more loyal to the League than most. Even after the expulsion of Zolmos, Kolmosoi had had allies in the city ready to rise in his support against Thasotun. A lot had changed in two years. The hope of a return home, which had gladdened all their hearts when they saw Pilsipon from afar had been shattered, that gateway now closed to them.

Fortunately, Runu was not so easily defeated. He immediately set a course for the southern tip of the island of Zilkusup on which Pilsipon sat. A relative of his, a man named Kuso Rusosthup, lived on a large estate there, in retirement, or exile depending how you looked at it. Runu was sure that Kuso would give them shelter for a few days and at the very least some information on what they could expect on the path ahead.

Another half a day's sail saw the southern tip of the island come into view. It was a much less welcoming sight than the harbour at Pilsipon, the rugged coast offered little in the way of safe anchorage. Sonos found himself hoping that the contrast would continue and the welcome they received would be much more pleasant. He was wrong, there was no welcome at all. Just the silent white cliffs looming over them ominously.

After much searching, they finally found a cove to anchor the ships, sheltered by wild hulthul trees which were bursting from inside the cliffs, another sign of home. Here the men could make what repairs were possible. Leaving the company to their labours, the commanders of the Daemons of the Deep and the Hotizoz Legion went ashore to find the estate of Kuso Rusosthup.

The estate lay atop the white cliffs, overlooking the calm and tranquil sea. Having discovered a small path which wound its way up to the top, the party found themselves suddenly in a vineyard with slaves toiling in the fields. Still no greeting awaited them, but nevertheless it was a sight which evoked much. The grapes on the vine warmed Sonos heart. *Civilisation at last,* he thought, this was the kind of exile he could have tolerated. Vineyards sprawled as far as the eye could see, tended by slaves, tied to the land like working animals. *Civilisation was always a bargain for man.* Amid it all sat a large house built of black rock, not very common in these lands, atop the crest of a hill. The party made its way there.

The strange silence lingered as they reached the building, but Runu led them inside. Runukolkil headed upstairs to the private quarters to seek out his old kinsman. Sonos and the others set about searching the lower levels for any signs of the property's masters.

They entered a room with a table set, cheese and wine laid out and a suckling pig roasting over an open fire, the white fat glistening and popping in the heat. It was enough to distract them. The door slammed shut. Kusoasu rushed over and shoved it hard,

"Barred from the other side." he said in frustration. A voice echoed from behind the door, a woman's voice,

"I knew you would come for me sooner or later. Which of them sent you?"

Perplexed, Sonos answered,

"Which of who sent us? We came here of our own free will to seek your help. Open the door and let us talk, we mean you no harm."

An almost hysterical laugh followed,

"You think me foolish enough to believe that. Which of the councillors sent you? Hulkophoas? Or Xusuthil? Rilpisu is the boldest of them, was it him? Or was it all of them?"

"What council?" Sonos replied, "The councillors of Pilsipon? We were denied entry to the city by the council."

"Pilsipon?" the voice replied, "Why would I be fearful of what those cowards thought. The Red and White Council of Thasotun are who should be feared. Do not try and feign ignorance. Tell me why I shouldn't just have you all killed?"

As she said it another voice echoed, a man's voice this time. Runu, Sonos knew,

"Sunpos? Gods it has been years."

There was a clunk as the bar was removed from the door and opened.

* * *

Day rolled into night, Sunpos Rososthup proved to be much more pleasant host than first impressions suggested. It was good to see that kin and guests were still afforded a warm welcome in at least some parts of the White Islands. The red wine flowed, and the marbled suckling pig was the tastiest thing Sonos could remember, the mix of herbs and potions Sunpos applied to the meat had transformed it. The food lifted his spirits like nothing else could have.

Sunpos was matronly woman, but with a softer face than her first angry words suggested. With her flowing dark hair cascading around her shoulders, the sunburst in her pale eyes and delicate white skin, she must have been a great beauty in her youth, Sonos thought. Now time had taken that from her, but in exchange she seemed to have been gifted with wisdom.

She explained what had happened since they had left for Gottoy. An outbreak of rebellions amongst many of the garrisons that Thasotun had installed on the White Islands. Many of the men in the garrisons owed their loyalty to Kolmosoi and the other captains from Butophulo not the new rulers of Thasotun. It had meant much fighting, a rise in piracy and strange stories of empty ships haunted the seas. A sad tale made sadder when she revealed that Pitae, Kunae, Thil, Kivuun and Puso, friends who had elected to stay in Pittuntik after Kolmosoi's death, had disappeared. One of their ships had been found adrift without a soul on board and no clues as to what had happened to them.

"Any news of Dinon Rusos?" Runu asked, it was hard to tell whether he hoped to hear that The Wanderer was still at large or not.

"Who knows with that one. I have not heard tell of his death. He was terrorising the southern islands the last I heard, drawing out ships from Thasotun and putting any and everyone he could get his hands on to the sword. But where is he now? Hiding in the islands? Among the Putedun? Maybe he has disappeared beyond the Throat? Only the gods know for now." Sunpos exclaimed. Dinon The Wanderer had always evoked such passions.

"What about Sol?" Sonos found himself asking. Kolmosoi had been fond of Sol he recalled, uncoiling the hand of friendship to the man who had always seemed a little broken. In truth Kolmosoi had treated him almost like a son. He had never been fully accepted by the others though. He was not of Butophulo, not of the old blood, and some instincts died hard amongst those who were. He had disappeared after Kolmosoi's murder. Where and why he had gone though no one had known or really cared at the time.

"Hard to say, he disappeared after Kolmosoi's murder, but you know that. Rumours abound that he has turned to piracy, others say he is dead. Some are even saying that he is in thrall to that wife of his, that she is Hulsen the Mad Prophetess returned. A daemon witch who has dominated his mind and sends him out to capture men to sacrifice in some blood ritual. I do not know what Kolmosoi was thinking when he suggested the match. Some convoluted scheme I would imagine, my cousin was as cunning as a snake, but sometimes his plots were too twisted to work. But they are fanciful tales, Sol probably fled at the first sign of trouble and is now at the bottom of the sea with the rest of them."

Sonos could do nothing but nod as Sunpos continued, a feeling of melancholy washing over him,

"The reaction by the tyrants of Thasotun has been brutal. They fear that the islands are more loyal to the memory of Butophulo than they ever will be to Thasotun and do not wish to displease their Doldun masters. Especially with the rumours of a new oracle from Buto which swept the islands after you left and again when rumour spread of a Xosu army marching for the coast from Gottoy."

"So, you heard of our coming then?" Kusoasu asked,

"After a fashion, some said it was an army of Gottoy, coming to seek vengeance on all the Xosu, others said the King of Gelodun was returning a conqueror to lay claim to Thasotun and the White Islands. When news of the king's death reached us and that the mercenaries in his hire had fled, that gladden some hearts and put fear into the rulers of Thasotun. They were expecting you to arrive any moment at the head of an army."

Kusoasu laughed,

"At least we managed to put the fear of the gods in them. Alas we marched north and then got waylaid at Rulrup and Yil."

"What did the oracle reveal?" Puso asked her.

"I have heard a few different versions of what was said, but most agree that the oracle confirmed that only the scions of old Kolbos could rule the White Islands. It was enough to light the fire of rebellion against Thasotun. The people of that city may be largely of the Salxosu, but the rulers certainly are not, they are Silxosu wine merchants to a man. Such distinctions matter to our people."

"Ever since the days of Sal, the bright god's son, the Salxosu have ruled the islands, even the fall of old Kolbos didn't change that although our people were scattered. Such an ancient lineage is hard to overcome in less than a generation." Runukolkil said solemnly.

"The tyrants know this. It is why they sent to the oracle of Xosu at Thelonigul for their own pronouncement." Sunpos replied.

"And what did the bright god have to say?" Kusuasu asked in his sarcastic way.

"Oh, as you would expect, Xosu told us that the blood of his line should rule all the Xosu and that we should all unite once more to meet the coming threats. Convenient for the Silxosu rulers of Thasotun, what better pedigree for that than hailing from the sacred land itself." Sunpos replied with a wry smile. "But you all know how prophecy can be. *The wheel turns and the wanderers will find their way*. We are still waiting for its fulfilment and more than eight hundred years have passed." she continued, a melancholy overwhelming her smile. "Anyway, the rebellions have largely been crushed, but the islands are still chaotic, and the cities fearful to provoke the tyrant's wrath any further." she stopped as if to gather her thoughts, "You should have stayed after Kolmosoi's death, his plan to topple the tyrants would have worked, you could have taken his place Runu. What is that rubbish you lot from the Academy always say? You could have been the queen of the bees by now, Runu." It was said in jest, but there was a hint of desperation in her voice.

"We couldn't stay, the knives of the tyrants were everywhere. They got to Kolmosoi, that was a calamity, but only the eye of the storm it would seem. As you tell it the aftermath claimed Kunae, Pitae, Puso, Thil and Kivuun, and chaos in the islands. We could not have won without Butophulo, Thasotun is too strong for the other cities to contend with. Maybe if Zolmos hadn't have been so reckless." Runu replied, but Sunpos cut him off,

"Kolmosoi should not have driven Zolmos away."

"Kolmosoi had no choice, we weren't ready. We had to prevent open war with Thasotun, Zolmos should have waited."

"Zolmos was brash yes, but that was because he believed in his cause and listened to what the oracle said after the fall of the League."

"It was too much too soon. We had no choice when Thasotun ordered his removal, it was a test of our loyalty. We did all we could to ensure his survival, but we had to be seen to move against him. I know you were kin, and I am sorry for his death."

"That part was not your fault. As I said, Zolmos was always reckless and Kolmosoi was my kin as much as Zolmos was. Tell me what happened when you tried to enter Pilsipon?" Sunpos asked. When Runu explained what had happened at Pilsipon and the disappointment of the men, Sunpos laughed,

"It is because you are from Butophulo that they didn't attack you on site. Thasotun would have any ship of war not under their control destroyed or taken. The leaders of Pilsipon may be cowardly, but they still remember the League, that is why they let you go."

"So, there is still some memory of the League left here then. How fair the other islands? And Butophulo itself?" Runu asked of her.

"Butophulo still suffers under the thumb of those nine fools. One of their number was assassinated in the street though. Some lovers quarrel if the rumours can be believed and…" the feeling in the room changed with that pause, "I am sorry to say that Koseun Sisosi has been arrested. I had word of it through Pito Kinsol. He stopped here before making the traders loop of the northern sea, but returned to Butophulo when news of the arrest reached him. I have heard nothing of a trial yet, but I think we all know how much the Nine fear him. I know how close you all were with him."

There was a brief silence in the room.

"Koseun was my mentor and I loved him like a father, but truth be told I am surprised he has survived this long. He never was one to hold back and he would have found the regime of the Nine intolerable. It is yet another reason for us to return to put an end to this madness. What of the other islands?" Runu replied in his considered way.

"They still remember the League well enough. Pilsipon still remembers Kuso as well, many of the city's fighting men went with him to Dzulkoyusos, it was their victory as much as Butophulo's. When the League was in the ascendancy. The oracle was proved correct then, when Buto encouraged us to take the fight to the Rinuxosu. We should have pressed our advantage instead of trying to negotiate, we lost the favour of the god when the assembly offered terms." she paused and sighed with a heavy heart, "but Koseun always was able to sway the crowd to his own will." Sunpos said reflectively.

"Perhaps you are right, but both sides were exhausted. Twenty years of war had shattered us. A firm victory and peace on our terms seemed like a good outcome at the time. It would have worked as well if not for Tekolger. What happened to Kuso?" Runu asked.

Sunpos explained that Kuso had died last autumn of a sickness and left his estate to be run by his wife. Ever since the tyrants of Thasotun had been trying to get their hands on the land. First, they tried to buy it, but recently force and intimidation had become their preferred option. Sonos could not help but admire the resilience Sunpos had shown, she was determined not to leave.

Towards the end of the night as Runukolkil explained their intention to return to Pittuntik and take Kolmosoi's place. Sunpos became more serious again,

"The White Islands are ripe for revolt still; all they need is someone to lead them. Take Kolmosoi's place Runu, but do not make the same mistakes Zolmos and Kolmosoi did. Thasotun is too strong, and the islands are exhausted. Please promise me that you will go and visit the oracle at old Kolbos first. There is ancient power there, beyond that of any king or tyrant. Thasotun cannot compete with the word of Buto himself. The god will guide you to the right path. Put your plan to the god and follow his advice."

The conversation reminded Sonos of the marching song of the Rinuxosu Sacred Band again, although the words were feeling increasingly apt to him now,

To arms! To arms!
Forward, arrow like, King of Kings, fire has no sheath!
But fierce Xosu bite, time to feel the hydra's teeth!
Our spears silver flash, come and face the Sacred Band!
We fall on this field, blood to free the Sacred land!

To arms! To arms!
Thrice loosed his fierce horde, arrows shade all beneath!

Spears crack and swords may shatter, flee the hydra's teeth!
Fume, fury, foolish great king, firm footed we stand!
We fall on this field, blood to free the Sacred Land!

The party stayed the night. In the morning Sunpos gifted them as much supplies as she could spare. The ships departed early that morning with a new sense of purpose and a new heading.

ZENUKOLA

37

A gust of wind swept over the plain and blew Zenukola's cloak over his head, covering his one good eye, the world went black. He pushed the cloak back down to his shoulder and colour flooded into the world again, a changed world, one which was on the right path once more. Surveying the open plain to their front he smiled as the sun, Dunsun's all seeing eye, warmed him.

A flat wide road, paved with black stone and rutted for the use of chariots, lay in front of him. One of the legacies of the old kingdom of Xortogun which still remained. The Kelonzow river, flowing alongside the road, had begun to turn into a torrent, but its fast-flowing rapids would guide them back to the heart of the empire, back to a new beginning. Zenu would be entering the great valley at the head of an army. It had been decades since he had held and independent command like this, and the exhilaration of having thousands of men under his control was a rush he had missed.

Behind Zenu marched his own personal guard, the blue and white of their horsehair crests standing resplendent, alongside them rode the Companions. Zenu had been courteous in his victory and allowed Kelbal to ride alongside him. Flush and filled with regret and embarrassment, the removal of the source of his power had seen the Companion's spirit flee to some dark realm. Broken, he had barely spoken to anyone in the days since. An act of generosity could be afforded in the circumstances Zenu thought. No need to be too harsh, a year or two to cement his control and Kelbal could be quietly made to disappear. Exile would probably suffice unless evidence of a hand in Tekolger's death did emerge when the Xortogun were put to the question.

Dalzenu had also been given a trial. It had been swift, there was no need for it to be otherwise. Although Zenu had not yet passed sentence on him as the leverage may prove to be useful to maintain control over the Companions.

In the days after Kelbal's fall, he had given the army what it wanted. He had rescinded the order to integrate the Xortogun and sent the men of the great valley to be the new garrison on the northern border. He had also let it be known to the Doldun that it was Zenukola who had given the command. He was sure that would be enough to win the troops support, at least for the moment. The force he marched with was less than ten thousand strong now anyway, the rest had been sent north with the twins to root out the Rilrpitu. With his guard and the army waiting at Torfub, Zenu would have Tekolger's veterans outnumbered if they were foolish enough to try to oppose him.

Tekolger's fierce champions had also been rather subdued since the day that Zenu had reclaimed the empire. A few promises of future governorships and time to adjust to the change in circumstances and Zenu was confident none would pose a serious threat. They were still boys really, and none had experienced the vicious civil strife of the past, they lacked the ruthlessness for it. It was a different game to conquering far off exotic lands, but it was a game Zenukola knew far too well.

The only possible obstacle to the fruition of his plans were the White Shields, Tekolger's guards. They were like a clan unto themselves and would bare their teeth if threatened. The elimination of their commander was a step toward neutralising them, but the men themselves were fiercely loyal to Tekolger still and would not take his stated heir being deposed lightly. Even if that heir were of Xortogun blood. Zenu had noted the way they had taken Kelbal into their ranks since his fall, allowing him to sleep alongside them and dragging him back to his bed when he appeared drunk amongst the other soldiers.

He would keep the White Shields close for now, granting them all the privileges he could muster. But he had also placed his guards to march alongside the rich baggage train which represented the accumulated wealth of more than a decade of unbroken conquest for the White Shields. For many of the men it was all they owned in this world and Zenu knew the threat he was making would be recognised. It gave him a certain power over them at least.

Perhaps Pelu would make a good new commander for the White Shields he mused, and in time their numbers could be whittled down through fighting rebellions, forced retirement, and distributing them amongst the garrisons. Divided they would pose little threat.

Zenukola was shaken from his daydream by the chatter of the men riding next to him. Some of the Companions were more naïve than the others, still expecting big things from the future. Zonpleuthas, young and inexperienced as he was, had not seemed to have fully grasped the gravity of the situation, instead he was singing his usual song to the others,

"Soon Torfub and then Xortogun, an empire for us to enjoy. But we should not get soft and complacent, this empire was won by hard work and hard men, we must remember that. We should take some time to recover and consolidate the empire and then look to other conquests."

A few of the men riding with him were nodding in agreement, but with no enthusiasm. Obliviously he continued,

"We could explore the south, see what lays beyond the great desert. Or go east, I hear that the armies of Gottoy are no easy challenge to overcome." he looked over to Zenu, brushing his long hair from his eyes, "With a command of my own I would bring them to heel, another conquest to add to the glory of the Doldun."

Zenu ignored him, but Zonpeluthas was expecting to be rewarded for his loyalty, a fact he was making clearer every day. He had assumed that the White Shields would be his if he gave Zenu his support. *The tactless fool,* Zenu thought, *at least the others had the sense to keep their mouths shut.* He would get his own command, maybe even the White Shields, but on some forsaken frontier where his song would fade into obscurity.

* * *

The night came on quick on the open plains of Zenian, but a hard day's march had seen the army cover good ground. When Zenu ordered a halt, a marching camp was thrown up quickly by the disciplined soldiers. He took satisfaction in seeing the army respond to his orders in such a manner. The square grid of the camp felt familiar, like returning home after having spent years away. The speed in which the city of tents sprung up made it feel as though a god had simply stamped his foot and seen the tents spring from the resulting crater. He felt his phantom fingers grasping as he paced through the rows of tents.

In a matter of days, he would arrive in Torfub and from there the empire would lay at Zenukola's feet. Dotmazo would bring Tekolger's wives and son of Doldun blood to meet the army in Tekolgertep and Zenu would crown the boy with the black and white crown of the Doldun and the red crown of Xortogun himself. A swift succession and stability would return to the empire and, with Zenu at the new king's side as chief adviser, the Doldun would flourish.

He had ordered the royal tent to be erected at the centre of the camp, the heart of power for the whole empire in one place. Kelbal had been too grief stricken or guilt ridden over Tekolger's loss to raise it when he was in command, but this was the royal army after all, even if there was no king with them. The huge structure, twice the size of a usual commander's tent and resplendent in rich purple, the colour of royalty, the white star of Tholophos emblazoned on the side, still filled Zenu with a sense of awe. The image had always resonated with power to him. It took him back to his youth, the days on campaign at the side of Kenkathoaz riding up and down the country trying to keep order, fighting off rebellions and invasions. They were hard days, but even though he feared a return to civil strife he had always looked back on them with a sense of nostalgia. What man does not look back on his youth in that way?

In contrast to the darkness quickly engulfing the plains around the army, the tent was filled with colour, noise, and life, like the sole star in the black canvass of the sky. Zenu entered to find food being served. A gazelle brought down by Polazul and his hound, was roasting over an open fire surrounded by several of the long-necked birds that nested near the river. The wine was already beginning to flow. Though Kelbal was no longer attending the nightly drinking sessions, the Companions had found their appetite for such events once more.

The tent was erupting in laughter and the sounds where reverberating around the camp. Couches had been laid out for each of the army's commanders. A golden one inlaid with jet, which Zenu had brought from Yorixori, sat in the centre, its light overshadowing the golden coffin of the fallen king which lurked in the background. Next to the coffin, Tekolger's throne still had pride of place within the royal tent, his crown placed where the king should have been sat. Next to the crown rested Dusk, the zilthum blade of the kings of the Doldun, that sword of Tholophos which filled so many with fear and dread as it felled the children of men like leaves that drop at the wind's breath. For all the talk of power and the future, the simple act of laying a place for Tekolger at every one of these sessions betrayed the fact that Tekolger's Companions still mourned the loss of the king and had not a clue of what the reality of a future without him would be like. *At least their fawning over him probably confirms their innocence,* he thought.

Zenukola took his place on the couch and motioned for a cup of wine to be filled for him as Zonpeluthas sat in a fine robe of dark silk and a cap worn by the poets of Yorixori, playing his lyre and singing a sweet song full of melancholy,

"Mix it." Zenu said to the slave who had made to pour for him a cup from the jug of pure red that the other Companions were drinking. He had not taken to the barbarian habit like the others and was not about to start. Such things invited the ire of the gods for only they should seek the knowledge which lay in the world beyond.

Zenu motioned towards the mixing bowl he had had placed in between the couches. A favourite of his, it had followed him here all the way from Doldun. The round beaten bronze bowl depicted the life of Tholophos in freezes around the edge. Wine was poured into the vessel which was glistening with a pale light reflecting from the fire at the heart of the tent. The wine flowed like the blood of sacrifices at the altar, water followed it in, a cleansing flood of the clear liquid. The slave then mixed the two substances together, blood red wine turning a soft pink. The clear, untainted water obscured, two extremes, mixing to find a balance in the middle. Zenu motioned to another slave to bring him his scrolls. He could relax tonight, but the work of running the empire never dried up.

The Companions sat around the central fire to drink, talk, and listen to Zonpeluthas play, unaware and uncaring of the true business of governing the vast realm that Tekolger had left them. Zela was the last to arrive. He seemed in high spirits, loudly making his presence known. Zonpeluthas stopped playing at the sound of his voice,

"Comrades!" he proclaimed, "As we stand on the verge of entering Xortogun once again, I say we raise our cups, pour a libation to the gods, and celebrate our return. It is what our king would have done." A chorus of agreement echoed around the room and the men poured their libation. Zela continued, blind to Zenu's gaze, his voice flowing like a bard,

"The great valley is a shadow of its former self. In the days of old, great civilisations dominated from Zowdel to Xosupil, but Xortogun was the greatest of them all. The place where civilisation began. If you can believe the tales. Tekolger has left it for us to see these lands climb to those heights once again, but do you know why those civilisations fell?" he paused dramatically and looked around the room, allowing his gaze to linger on Zenu. The Companion was fond of telling stories. Quick of wit, the laughter behind his eyes showed his teasing intent,

"No? Then I will tell you. We all know the tales of famine and disease, invasions by men and daemons after the gods turned their back on the old kingdoms and Dusk fell on their golden civilisations. But singers and poets never tell you why."

"And I suppose you know why Zela?" Thazan asked as if his piety had been affronted.

"Indeed, I do. Many years ago, whilst we sojourned in Kurotormub after the conquest. As Tekolger, Kelbal and his new bride made their journey to the Oracle of Kurotor deep in the Broken Lands, I made some inquiries of mine own. A poet I found told me the tale. The time of tears they call it. When the god-kings of Xortogun were usurped and cast from their Amber Throne. The last of the god-kings, they say, lost the favour of the gods and the Dusk fell when they turned away from the world, but the real culprits were a man of his court and a concubine of the god-king.

No one really knows who the man was. Some say a traveller, some a priest, others a scribe, some say he was not a man at all, just a wraith taken on a man's form, and his name is forgotten, as the Xortogun wish to forget his deeds. All that is remembered is that he was wise and rose high in the god-king's favour, eventually being elevated to the position of Vizier. Indeed, it is said he shone almost as bright as the god-king himself. But he was a deceiver, for he fell madly in love with the god-king's favourite concubine. A girl of platinum hair, haunting white skin and piercing blue eyes, the Gift of the Moon's Grace as she was known.

Maddened by love, the Vizier made a pact with the plumed serpent king to win the concubine's affection, becoming the serpent's instrument, his tongue to spread poison in the world of men.

For many years, the god-king had wished to sire an heir, but the Moon's Grace had failed to produce a living child. Fearing that with him the dynasty of Gonphon would end, the god-king discarded his favourite for another. A dusky maiden whose sultry tones spoke of the soil, with cascading dark hair of jet and black eyes deep as the pits of the earth. Jealous of this rival and fearful of her fall from grace, the serpent's dark magic turned the first concubine against the god-king.

Within a year a son was born to the god-king, and this was the cause of the events that brought the Dusk. With the Moon's Grace's aid, the Vizier seized his chance, convincing the god-king that the child, named Kurotor, was not of his blood, but that of one of his courtiers. The god-king ordered the child and the dusky maiden to be seized and sacrificed to the serpent god on the advice of his Vizier, but he was deceived.

With the god-king increasingly isolated and paranoid, trusting only in his Vizier, the kingdom was drawn into ever more depravity and all the while the power of the serpent grew with each new sacrifice. Every time a life was given more of the serpent's daemons would pour forth into the world to assail the old kingdoms. Panicked the god-king would turn to his Vizier who in turn would advise more sacrifices to appease the gods.

Eventually, in the depths of madness from the poison poured into his ear by the Vizier, the god-king was persuaded that a sacrifice of his own blood could see him open the gateway to the shining realm and ascend to complete godhood to drive back the hordes of daemons. It was a lie. The blood of the last god-king poured over the altar as the Vizier performed the rite himself. The blood of the king was sacrifice enough to open the path to the hidden realm and for the serpent king to return to the world. With the god-king dead and the kingdom in chaos, the Vizier usurped the throne. He did not take the title king for himself, instead he wore the moniker of the Lord of Wisdom and Defender of the Valley, but the people merely called him the Pale Lord and they came to fear his wrath.

When, on rare occasions, he was seen in public he would wear white robes, light as a feather, and a pale stone mask to cover his face, with the horns of a bull and a vicious serpent's tongue. In private he was an artificer of dark magics and played minister to the cult of the serpent. He taught others the art of his worship and the whole kingdom danced to his tune as he bestrode the great valley like a colossal leviathan.

But there were other whispers, tales that the Pale Lord was a shapeshifter, it was why he hid his face. At night it was said, he would venture out into the city of Gonphonmub with his cultists in toe, each time in a different form. Like a shadow he would sculk and seize unsuspecting victims to sacrifice to the serpent on an altar made from the tooth of that daemon. In this way he fulfilled his bargain with the serpent king, whose own power grew in this world until he was able to challenge and defeat the old sun, who the Xortogun call Gonphon, by passing into the realm of the gods.

The sun's death shook the world and caused more daemons to erupt from their prisons in the hidden realms, plunging darkness and the Dusk upon the world. Death and destruction, famine and flight followed in their wake and one by one the god-kings were toppled from their thrones. But not all was lost.

Kurotor, the son of the last god-king, had not been sacrificed as the Vizier thought. Instead, the child had been spirited away from the Pale Lord's wrath, an orphan babe slaughtered in his place. The boy had been found exposed in the wild desert and raised by nomads, not knowing his true lineage. The gods came to the young man in a dream vision, for although the people of the valley had turned their back on the gods, the gods had not abandoned all hope. They told Kurotor where he could find the last flame of Gonphon. With the blood of the sun in his veins, only he could wield its power.

With flame in hand, he confronted the Pale Lord and slew him, freeing the kingdom from his grasp. Using the flame of Gonphon, he forged the serpent's tooth into a mighty sword of white and gold that glowed red as twilight with the power of the bloody shades contained within. Kurotor rose like an eagle to the heavens to confront the serpent. Their battle raged across the sky, and the deserts to the north now called the Broken Lands were shattered as they clashed. But, with flame in one hand and sword in the other, Kurotor cut down the serpent king, the black blood of the daemon washed over the world and saw it reborn.

Kolgennon was saved, but it was never the same place. The rule of the serpent and the Pale Lord had seen to that. Kurotor could not sit the Amber Throne, instead the heavens called, and he took his place as the new sun. However, he left his people with a prophecy.

> *The tainted tears fall, they will come to rest in the wild land of sun's spawn. Blood to sit the Amber Throne and herald the coming dawn."*

A rumble of hooves, enough to shake the ground, interrupted the still of the evening. One of the guards stood on duty outside the tent entered, making his way without hesitation to Zenu,

"Hegemon, a party of horsemen has just arrived. They come from Tekolgertep with a message from the governor."

Zenu took another sip from his cup, savouring the moment,

"Show them in."

The flap of the tent opened again, a man in a Xosu style chiton, one of the army's secretaries, stepped in, two men in the distinctive purple cloaks of the royal guards alongside him. The dark purple horsehair crested helms and the bronzed cuirasses embossed with an eight-pointed star further gave them away. Governors of the second rank, and all the important garrison commanders who had not been afforded the honour of raising their own guard units were gifted men from the royal bodyguards. The Governor of Tekolgertep was a special case. As the intended seat of the king, its governor was gifted with a double strength unit of guardsmen.

Behind them, more men entered the tent. At first, they seemed to be a part of the royal guard, but as they came in further and separated from the guardsmen, it was clear they were not. Zenu did not recognise them, they certainly were not Xosu or Doldun. Instead, they wore the distinctive sea blue robes and gilded turbans of the men from the Putedun Confederacy. Merchant princes no doubt looking to make a profit from something. He had dealt with the Putedun before. Profit driven as they were, their envoys were pleasant company, and their council was often insightful and illuminating. No doubt these men would prove of some use. More men entered separately, local magnates of Xortogun judging by their dress and complexion.

The Companions rose to greet the Doldun as comrades, taking the arm of each as if they were brothers, a fraternity which can only have grown amongst soldiers. Zenu stayed reclined on his couch.

With the greetings out the way, the two Doldun soldiers approached Zenu. *News travels fast,* Zenu thought. The elder of the two began to speak,

"Hegemon, thank you for agreeing to see us so late. Keluaz sent us from Tekolgertep to petition the royal court.

Tekolger's great city has grown quickly under the governor's stewardship, he laments the fact that the king is not able to see his vision come to fruition. The city's growth is the reason for our visit. Tekolger originally mapped out the city into twelve districts on the northern arm of the Kelonzow river. Keluaz has seen the city grow to fill those districts and now the population is exploding beyond them. Therefore, the governor has sent us here to petition the court to create a thirteenth district on the south bank of the river to better accommodate this growth and add to the glory of Tekolger's city."

Zenu smiled,

"I can see why Keluaz sent you on this task, you put the case very elegantly. I am sure the growth and development of the city has been very impressive and no doubt Tekolger would have been pleased to see his vision coming to fruition." he paused for a moment, savouring the taste of power, "I am sure the governor would be grateful if the court saw fit to extend his power. You will ride with us as we march to Torfub. The court will consider the governor's appeal and send you back to him when we have decided. Sit and have a drink with us."

The two soldiers bowed their heads in respect and took a step back, turning to join in with the night's frivolities, a slave handing each a cup of wine as they did.

Zenu turned his eye to the Putedun princes lurking in the background. A strange people he reflected. Polite to the point of being infuriating, but he had enough dealings with them as Governor of Zowdel to know it was a mask. He gestured towards them,

"Come forward friends, your journey must have been long and hard, the least we can do is hear what you have to say."

The men shuffled forward, theatrically bowing. Their round white turbans descending as they threw back their sea blue robes. One of them, more flamboyant than the others with a ring on every finger and thumbs, one with a large white jewel, in a thick accent which spoke of the sea, said,

"My lord, my name is Prince Konguz the admirable, the bringer of gifts. We have come to you to make our entreaties on behalf of the princes of the Confederacy. I am here to serve in the king's court as the emissary of the princes.

In the time of the dynasty of the sand, when men of the deserts to the south ruled Xortogun, the ships of the Confederacy would dock in their hundreds in the port of Guntoga, trading the riches of the east with the produce of the west. It was an arrangement which benefited all, the kings grew rich and so did the princes and the people. Even when Xortogun fell to the savage Rilrpitu they recognised the value of this trade."

The Putedun always made their point in a convoluted way. A way of speaking that suited the image they liked to portray as princes when most were merely merchants with a high opinion of themselves. Zenu interrupted the man,

"You spin a good tale. No doubt you are about to ask for the same privileges to be extended to the Putedun with regard to Tekolgertep." Zenu knew this to be the case, it was not the first time he had been asked to grant this request. He was even sympathetic to the idea. The merchant princes knew trade better than anyone and would turn the city into a thriving port, but, as he had explained numerous times before, the decision had been out of his hands. It was Tekolger's wish for the Doldun and Xosu to establish themselves in the city before others would have the same rights granted to them.

Konguz smiled, a sinister smile in which the polite mask dropped for a moment and his fair appearance disappeared. His sea green eyes fixing on Zenu, he replied with his salt-stained voice,

"The great general has discerned my purpose. The new city grows fast, and the traders now prefer it over Guntoga, but the great king did not extend the right for us to trade in his grand new city. We have brought gifts for you to thank you for taking our audience and to demonstrate what riches could be brought to your great kingdom through trade with the princes. Precious metals from the east, beyond the Throat of Sem, rich wines from Gelodun, grain from the valley of Thelizum and a special gift for the great general. A statue inhabited by the spirit of the gods."

The slaves following in the train of the princes brought in the goods, the final two dragging in a bronze statue of a foreign god, some powerful being worshiped by the Putedun no doubt. It was polished up to a sheen so that it shone like pale gold reflecting the red flame of the fire roaring in the centre of the tent, its bejewelled eyes like piercing arrows. Konguz took a cup over to the statue and placed it in the palm. What he said was not a lie, as the spirit of some god inhabited the bronze sculpture, it moved and poured wine into the cup. Konguz took the drink and handed it over to the slave who had been handling Zenu's scrolls. The man struggled with the cup and the scrolls, almost spilling the drink, and dropping the cup, an embarrassment in front of Zenu's guests. Zela was quick to stand and take the cup, wisely handing it to Zenu.

Zenukola smiled again as he took a sip of the rich wine. Konguz continued revelling in his role,

"Just like your Kuso's cup, the god pours his wine for you and brings you the knowledge of the gods." A smile crept over the prince's lips as he said it. That sinister undertone, which was hiding below the surface, remerged once more. The Putedun were famous for their love of such contraptions, but Zenu had never seen one himself. Konguz would have made a good priest in Doldun he reflected,

"The king was careful when he founded the city, he was keen for it to grow in a controlled manner." he paused, "but maybe it is time for that to change, the city has grown beyond its original bounds after all. You will ride with us as well I hope, whilst the court considers your proposal."

Konguz and his associates bowed theatrically once more and faded into the background. The final delegation was from a local town, Fonfub, requesting leave to build a temple to honour Tekolger. Zenukola had little interest in their entreaties at this point, they could do whatever they wished as far as he was concerned.

The evening's festivities carried on as if they had not been interrupted at all. Zenu presided over it all, keeping his head clear as the others descended into their cups drinking their unmixed wine.

* * *

The next few days on the road seemed to pass quicker than the previous. Zenu had to admit the company of men who had not spent years on campaign was a welcome change. The Putedun, and even the Doldun guardsmen, provided more stimulating conversation and were less prone to bouts of drinking deep into the night. They were also a much welcome source of information on the state of the empire. He had not received a report from Pelu at Torfub for some days now which had worried him, but the guardsmen had assured Zenu that the city was peaceful when they passed through. Pelu had hosted them himself and Surson was in residence, although they had not seen her as she had confined herself to her chambers. He could only hope that Supo's northern army had arrived too.

Zenu found himself riding with the Putedun often on the days that followed, such men were useful to keep close. On the fifth day he made his decision, the Putedun could have their trading rights in Tekolgertep, it would be good for the city and the empire. The governor could have his land as well, the city would need more space with all the increased trade.

The morning of the sixth day saw the army set off bright and early. Torfub was now only a few more days march at a normal pace and there awaited Surson and the key to the empire, what Zenu needed to be sure in his control. He found himself full of hope, like he had once been as a bright young man eager to earn a position amongst the King's Companions. The only pangs of nerves he felt were over the status of the Xortogun witch. Hopefully Pelu had acted quickly and had her under control. His phantom fingers flexed at the thought.

The old royal road, which tracked the course of the river, became easier to follow as the army got nearer to the great valley, the old heart of empire. The roads here were still relatively well maintained, even though the Xortogun favoured travelling via boat along their great river. As the torrent grew wider and deeper, the volume of shipping along it increased and the wild thickets of dolthil trees turned to well-tended groves surrounded by heavily cultivated farmland in the rich but narrow alluvial plain that flanked the river. All signs that the army was nearing a more sophisticated and civilised land.

Zenu was riding with the Putedun along the bank of the river, the men telling him of their history in these lands. A rumble of hooves gave away the small group of Companions approaching. He felt his phantom fingers twitch. Four by Zenu's reckoning. He turned to greet them already certain what they might say. The clans always resisted being led by their betters sooner or later.

Zela was at the head of the group. Of the Companions who remained with the army, he was the one who most worried Zenu, intelligent and quick witted as he was. He had still been subtly voicing disapproval with Zenu's actions spinning stories as he was want to do. Zenu's men reported that he had made several visits to Kelbal alone. The silver-tongued man pulled his horse up alongside Zenukola and spoke,

"Hegemon, might we be permitted to speak with you in private. It is a matter concerning the empire."

Zenu had to admit he was almost impressed, finally some resistance from these conquerors of the world and done in a controlled manner as well. He nodded and turned to the Putedun,

"Might you excuse me gentlemen, we will have to finish our conversation later today."

The men bowed their heads theatrically and rode on ahead. Zela waited for them to be out of earshot before continuing,

"Thank you, but we have just been informed that you granted both the governor's request and the request from the Putedun."

He smiled. *Formal but direct* he thought. Zenu boomed back forcefully,

"Yes, I have. Growth and trade will be good for Tekolgertep, it will see Tekolger's vision of a new world city come to life."

"This may well be true, but it is not the reason why I and the rest of the Companions are concerned. In absence of a king, the council must make decisions collectively, as equals. Like you said yourself when pointing to Kelbal's transgressions. You were right about that, and this decision should have been taken as a group." Zela said in a composed and assured manner which unnerved Zenu slightly. It must mean he was confident in the support of the others. In a considered and conciliatory tone, he replied,

"Of course, although this was a decision to do with the day to day governing of one city. It did not seem something worth troubling the council with. The council has much bigger issues to burden it."

"Whilst I am sure we all appreciate your concern for us, the decision should have at least been put to a vote Zenu." Zela came back. Zenukola, paused for a moment, gathering his thoughts the way a storm does before it breaks,

"Perhaps you are right Zela. I fear I am too used to ruling as the

Hegemon over a restless conquered land. I will stop to consider the Companions in the future." He replied in as friendly manner as he could muster. His phantom fingers clenching into a fist and his silver eye itching.

Before Zela could reply, an order echoed from the front of the snaking column, like the rumble of distant thunder. The men halted, the action rippling down the line like flooding water, causing the sunlight to glimmer off their weapons like the sun rising over an empty plain. The action caught the attention of Zenu and the Companions, all kicked their horses and rode for the head of the column.

A large and ornate barge glistening like the moon when it reaches its fullest extent in the sky, gilded images of some bird headed goddess patterned across its exterior, its front shaped like the same flying terror, mouth opened as if to swallow its prey, sat moored against the shoreline. A symbol crashed as a ramp was lowered by a mass of eunuch slaves. A procession of priestly figures made a slow and steady progress onto the riverbank, like the creeping shadow retreating from the morning sun. A group of mounted guardsmen had also approached the column.

The shadowy priests moved on to the road in front of the column. The nine figures stood solemnly, Zenu could not see their faces, the robes they wore covered their heads and made them appear as fish grown legs, come to bow down before the Doldun.

Zenu trotted forward to greet them. One fish man, stood in front of the others, bowed down in a fluid style which rivalled the Putedun for its theatricality. In a Common Xosu that was thick and dripping with the tones of the people of the great valley, he said,

"Your most gracious lord, these servants have been sent here on an errand on behalf of the goddess Xura, protector of the great valley. The Thoruri, when he liberated the valley from the oppression of the Rilrpitu restored the ancient privileges of the goddess and we servants seek to invoke those rights now. The land on the south bank of the river, opposite the city of Tekolgertep, its people have called upon the goddess for their protection, a protection which her servants have sort fit to extend. These servants come here now for the royal court to confirm this."

Zenu felt his phantom hand clench into an angry fist.

* * *

That evening the encampment rose like it had every night, it would be one of the last times though, a few more days march and they would reach Torfub. The barge of priests had come via the city of towers and to Zenu's delight had informed him that a royal host sat outside the walls of the city. Supo's northern army had arrived just in time.

That had been the only good news of the day though, the priests had come to claim the land which he had granted to Keluaz and seemed to think that they need not petition, only inform the court, due to some ancient privilege. To make matters worse the Doldun guardsmen who had arrived with the priests were from Guntoga. Koluun of the Tholmash was the governor there and his men had been sent to voice his displeasure of the seizing of the land which he claimed fell within his province. It was a problem which could have been handled swiftly if the petitions had not been made in front of the entire army with the Companions already complaining that they had not been included. Now he had no choice but to allow all the assembled Companions to hear the competing claims and decide. It was to this end that he had summoned all the parties involved to the royal tent that evening. But first there would be entertainment.

If Zela could voice disapproval through old stories and poems, so could Zenukola and his warnings would carry more bite. With the Companions and the petitioners assembled in the tent, wine flowing, the fire roaring and Zonpeluthas strumming his lyre, Zenu ordered his blind bard to be led in. The tent fell silent as the old man was led to stand in front of the fire.

His blind eyes surveyed the silent tent, with just the crackle of the fire to break through the noise. Then a noise began to emanate from him, his mouth still closed, just the hum of a song beginning to form reverberated from his throat. Then he began to sing and strum his lyre,

"Oh, goddess I beseech you now, sing through me, tell us of the old tales and of the heroes who battled valiantly for fame and glory. Tell us the tales of the kingdoms before Dusk fell so that we may learn the lessons of those doomed to disappear behind the veil."

The ululating song gripped the attention of the tent as the blind bard began to sing the tale of Rinu and the fall of the high kingship after Xosu ascended to the heavens. *The Zelkalkel are not the only people who could use words as weapons.* Zenu thought, a subtle message before the discussion should be enough to quelle any thoughts of resistance. He carefully watched Zela's face as the bard's voice flooded out the words, each one washing over the bold tongued Companion.

He watched for a long time as the details of the folly that was the brother's war for Xosu's kingdom smashed the unity of the Xosu. Zela's confident expression did not change. *Enough with subtlety.* Zenu rose to speak,

"My friends, we have serious matters to consider this evening, but before then, one last poem to remind us of the glory of the Doldun." he turned to the bard and said, "Recite for us The Broken Spear".

The bard paused and looked at him with confusion.

"Hegemon, I am afraid I cannot. I am not of Doldun, and I only tell the ancient epics to impart their wisdom. This poem you ask for is a song for a different man."

"Of course you can tell us this tale. Have you not heard it?" He felt his anger rising and the eyes of the Companions on him. His phantom fingers balled their way into a tight fist.

"My lord I do not know it, nor do I wish to tell it. It is not a tale inspired by the goddess of old, an ancient epic that is a part of my craft…" Zenu interrupted,

"Yes, you can, you know the tale, *Ashen branch with leafy blade, rising in a new spring glade.* I believe that is how it opens. Invoke the goddess and she will send you the right words."

"Perhaps the bard has had enough for today." Zela's voice cut through, "he is an old man and must surely need to rest his voice. Besides you are right, Zenu. We should be spending this time discussing the important decisions that have been pressed upon us."

A murmur rippled around as Zenu's phantom fingers squeezed the fist they had made even harder. He sighed,

"Very well! Bard you are dismissed, as is everyone else! Out!"

The tent was filled with subdued activity as people shuffled towards the exit. The guards led the bard out and the pipe players took up their tune again as the supplicants were invited to state their cases for the land in question.

Keluaz' men first restated their case for expanding the city. An appeal for the Companions to think about the future of the empire and the vision that Tekolger had when he ordered the building of the city.

Zenu invited Prince Konguz to sit next to him in the tent, a better companion than those boys seated in front of him. After Keluaz men had finished their appeal, the prince lent over to Zenu and said,

"Keluaz is a wise man and is well advised. You should see the city that he has built for your king. It is enough even to impress this prince who has travelled far to the east beyond the Throat of Sem and far to the west to the rich land of the dying flame."

"You believe it would be best to allow Keluaz to expand the city?" Zenu asked the emissary.

"I do Hegemon. These priests will sing to you about ancient rights and privileges, but they merely wish to enrich themselves through the work of those who live on the land. The governor, Koluun, he is not as well advised, and has no vision for the future. What has he done with this land that your king gifted to him? Only now he complains when he fears that he will lose his pot of gold."

Prince Konguz' words were proved to be sage council as the priest of Xura, the bird headed goddess of the Xortogun, stood to address the room dressed in an absurd robe which made him look like a fish.

"Great lords, this servant has come as a representative of the goddess to inform you that the people of the land in question have submitted themselves to the service of the goddess. By decree going back to the first kings of this land in the dawn of days when civilisation first took root, it is a sacred right of the goddess to take possession of any land whose people would submit. The king knew this, it is why he restored her rights as he did other ancient privileges when he cast down the wicked horse lords. This servant's only wish is that today you acknowledge these rights as Tekolger did."

Finally, the envoys from Koluun of the Tholmash, the Governor of Guntoga, rose to speak.

"The Togworwoh is pleased that the royal court has returned to the heart of the empire. Too long have issues such as this not been addressed. Too long have governors behaved as if they were still clan chieftains fighting over scraps of land in Doldun itself. Tekolger, in his generosity and wisdom, elevated Koluun to the governorship of Guntoga, a province which includes the land now in question. This is the situation to this day, Tekolger did not change his mind. It is just that in his absence Keluaz has seen fit to seize the land with force, unleashing his Rilrpitu on the people who lived there. Are we not here to civilise? To restore the order that the Rilrpitu smashed to pieces? What of fairness and law and the stability that the empire now so desperately needs? By royal decree, the land is controlled by the Togworwoh of Guntoga and so it should remain."

The envoy took his seat and now the first test of Zenukola's regency was about to begin. He rose to address the room,

"Thank you for those words. You have all given us a lot to consider, if you would be so kind to leave us to our deliberations. Entertainment, food, and drink will be provided for you." Zenu motioned and his guards escorted the envoys out, followed by the pipe players and the eunuchs carrying the wine.

Zenu was left in the tent with the six Companions who remained with the army. He knew he count on the loyalty of Thazan and Zalmetaz, but Zela had made his displeasure known and may not have been cowed by the bard. Polazul was of the Kolbun a clan close as any to the Tholmash, he would lean towards Koluun, that left Deluan, who was kin to Dalzenu, and Zonpeluthas who was agitating for an appointment. He would only need to win over one more to have a majority as Kelbal had not joined them.

"You all know what my view on this matter is. Tekolger envisioned a city larger than any seen before, made up of all the peoples of his empire. The only way to achieve that is to see the city grow. Besides, a growing city will mean more tax revenues, to finance new wars of expansion. Those wars will need generals to command the armies." he looked over at Zonpeluthas, "Or new building projects, new provinces to civilise, those provinces will need energetic and capable governors."

Zonpeluthas' face lit up at the suggestion, politics would never be his game it seemed. Zenu was pleased to note that the rest of the Companions offered no resistance. Then Zela spoke,

"We cannot allow such a change. Tekolger put things as he did for a reason, we would need the approval of a king to overrule the orders of another, especially when the king's own city is of concern. Besides, who are we to deny a millennia old tradition? Or perhaps more importantly to disrupt the stability of the heart of the empire at such a delicate time. Far better to keep things as they are, leave the land in the hands of Koluun. It is not our place to make such drastic changes, we are the stewards of the empire until the new king comes of age to lead us."

Watching the faces of the Companions closely, Zenu could tell that his was about to become a long sleepless night.

SONOSPHOSKUL

38

With the days and weeks sailing on the cramped and overcrowded ships, the patience of many of the men was running low. The Hotizoz could not understand why the fleet did not make straight for Pittuntik and take the city by surprise after they had left Pilsipon. Instead, they had turned their prows south and west. Avoiding the busiest sea lanes made sense as ships from Thasotun would no doubt be patrolling the trade routes, but Sonos was sure that the Salxosu would have worked out their destination immediately, they were all sailors who had spent much of their life crisscrossing these waters. Today the Hotizoz would learn as well.

Sonos stood on the prow of Tale Teller as the sun rose off to the east, throwing a stream of light across the glistening mirror of the sea and its hidden realm below. The land to starboard of the ship went from darkness to light as if a god had breathed fire upon the earth. The island it illuminated had once been densely populated, even on this, its northern side, there would have been farms and villages teaming with life, the open plain where old Kolbos' famous horse breeders once grazed their herds. But now there was nothing, nature had seized back what man had taken and tamed. With eight hundred years undisturbed, dense woodland now flooded over the land, wild hulthul trees sprouted from the dark earth and turned the plains into a deep wood. Ruins could still be found amongst the trees, but they had become the haunts of pirates, outlaws, and brigands.

Not long after the island came into view, the calm mirror that was the sea was shattered, revealing the hidden perils of the world below. The seas were always dangerous around old Kolbos, as if the waters were still angry at the sacrilege that was committed there. The sky had darkened now as well, and the men struggled to keep the ships under control. Most sailors avoided the area for that reason and the choppy waters saw many of the Hotizoz, and even some Salxosu, running to the side of the ships as sickness took them. The chaos lasted for all the hours of the morning, but ended just as suddenly when old Kolbos came in to view and Mount Zilgulon threw a shadow over them. The men just stopped and stared at the ancient ruins.

"I had heard stories of this place but seeing it for myself, it is nothing I could have imagined." The voice was Hozfotou's. The commander of the Hotizoz legion looked gaunt from sea sickness, but the wonder in his eyes was clear.

"At its height maybe." Sonos answered him, "Old Kolbos was the largest and mightiest city in the world, Butophulo could fit into the metropolis nine times over and there would still be space to spare. Now though, nature has spread its chaos through the order that old Kolbos brought. I fear it is a symbol of what awaits us. The mantle of the past that we all strive towards, and yet we refuse to see the destruction."

The ruined buildings still stood, in stone, in marble, the colour now faded and fled, like the bones of a once magnificent beast left to be bleached by the sun, but the streets were flooded and overgrown. The buildings covered with moss and vines, hulthul trees sprouted from windows and doors.

Hozfotou smiled with melancholy,

"I fear the same my friend, but does the ruin come because we strive to hold the mantle or because we lay it down on the ground?"

The fleet ploughed on and soon the black silhouette of the ruins began to take on a more discernible form, the broken, half sunk structures of what was once a city to rival Dzottgelon itself. The ruins curled like a broken tail around one untouched spot. Down the throat of a channel known as the Funnel, the gleaming walls of the Thelonbet stood on their island within a lake at the heart of the city. Untouched, unbroken, strong. Sonos felt like the walls met his gaze, the glare of the morning sun and the shadow of Mount Zilgulon that loomed over the city, made it seem as if they were turning to follow the fleet. The Kinsolsun had forged that edifice from pure zilthum, that white-gold ore which gave the White Islands their name. They had been built before the Dawn of the old kingdoms to protect the fallen god. Nature could not reclaim them, and they seemed to pulsate with a strange and fierce power still. There was a dangerous edge to the place, as if at any moment it may erupt in flame.

After a long time stood in silence, Sonos finally gave an answer to the question, even though he did not think Hozfotou expected one.

"There in the centre, the temple of Buto. That was Sal's doing, the son of Xosu. When the Xosu split for the first time and the sons of the bright god went their separate ways, Sal led his followers here. He picked up the mantle. Brought Buto's Anvil back to the Thelonbet and raised the temple around it." The temple's partially collapsed dome still loomed in the distance. The colossal statue of Buto visible even this far out, his hammer raised ominously as if about to strike the ground in rage. "Thelonigul may shine brighter in the memories of the other tribes of the Xosu and the words of the poets, but for the Salxosu, old Kolbos is where our hearts lie. Where that mantle was lost when Tildun's army sacked this city. The other tribes of Xosu seemed to have forgotten where the nobility of Butophulo came from originally, the survivors of old Kolbos fleeing the wrath of Tildun's army. But the old blood of the Salxosu remembers. You are right, maybe it is time we picked up the mantle that was dropped."

He did not say any more and Hozfotou soon tapped him on the shoulder before leaving him to his thoughts. Thoughts that drifted to the ancient traditions of the Salxosu. The one and only time he had travelled to the ruins of the city. When he came of age to partake in the initiation ceremonies and indulge in the mysteries of the gods, the old divinities of the sea. He was a Polriso after all and the blood of kings ran in his veins. He had been a child on the verge of manhood then and the League had still stood strong. For better and for worse, his innocence had been stripped away that day, his first day as a man of the Salxosu. The League of Butophulo had risen because of the favour of those old divinities, its fall came when the hubris of the city saw the gods turn their back on the League. Maybe now these humbled men of Butophulo could win that favour back.

A storm raged over the Thelonbet, lightning flashing in thick white branches as distant thunder rumbled like thousands of hooves stampeding across the sky, though the sea and sky beyond old Kolbos were a calm blue. The fleet sailed as close as it dared to the stormy coast, finding a suitable beach to drop anchor. The men were told to go ashore, forage for supplies and make further repairs to the ships. The patrols from Thasotun were unlikely to come and search the ruins.

**

The small party of the commanders and their attendants, a dozen men, headed into the ruins as the rest of the company and the legion sat down to their midday meal. Dunsun was well on his way through his journey across the sky and so they would not reach the Thelonbet until the evening even if they made good progress.

They entered through what remained of the Gate of the Hydra, two huge white carved eyes staring down at them. The destruction wrought by the Xosu army of Tildun had turned the entire city into a blackened broken wasteland. The walls had been torn down and the sea had flooded in, half sinking the city, but the gates still stood. The whole company was quiet as they moved, until Hozfotou spoke again in a whispered voice,

"What happened here? My people did not come to reside in Thelizum until after this place had been destroyed. We know very little about its fall."

It was Sonos turn for a melancholy smile,

"The gods abandoned Semontek, son of Tholophos and the last King of old Kolbos. He fell to the hand of his brother, Tildun, and Dusk, the zilthum blade of their father, outside old Kolbos' mighty walls. His blood left to soak into the ground as the shade of the final lord and protector of the city left his pale corpse. The greatest heroes of the age then burst into the city, as the gods tore at the walls, and gutted the haven." He answered, remembering the old tales he was told as child. Tales that filled him with wonder and a desire for adventure as a young boy. "According to the poets, Tildun died during the sack. Some claimed that he was killed by his own brothers who had become tired of his tyrannical behaviour, others that the Kinsolsun themselves reemerged to deal the fatal blow, but what really happened none can say. The glory of the Xosu died with him though, that is certain. As the population of the city was slaughtered a great cry went out, a shockwave that would engulf the world. Like a hammer striking an anvil it resonated and the rains have cried over the ruins ever since." He stopped and reflected once more. "I am afraid that is all I really know my friend. We seem to have forgotten too and instead tell ourselves stories of tragic heroes, foolish wars and the vengeance of the gods."

Beyond the Gate of the Hydra lay the first of the three rings of the city that coiled around the eye of Sem and the Thelonbet. Each had housed a different part of the conurbation's population. This first ring was known as the Tulkob, it was home to the labourers from the fields, the horse breeders, the soldiers, and their families. It was the largest ring and would take the most time to cross as the sea had wrought its destruction and claimed most of the land here.

They began the long journey through the city in silence, the incessant sound of the rain, the water as they waded through it and the distant stampede of thunder the only noise that could be heard. The experience made Sonos feel small, like a shadow creeping over something greater than himself. He touched the amulet around his neck, it suddenly felt heavy.

It was said that when Sal first came to see the Thelonbet, he ventured alone into the depths of the forges after finding and squeezing through the only entrance left on the surface. As he walked, Sonos was beginning to wonder at what the son of Xosu may have felt as he first ventured into this place, did he feel as small as Sonos did? Could a divine hero feel such a way? What Sal found deep in the fires no one could say for certain. The crippled god himself it was rumoured, still bound to the forge where Xosu had left him defeated. Others whispered that it was not the son, but the great serpent. Sonos gripped the amulet tightly as he pondered those old stories. Sal, so the legends claimed, returned the Anvil to the god, and made a pact with Buto to serve him as the Kinsolsun had once done. In return Buto gifted Sal's daughter with prophetic visions and the ability to hear the voice of the god. She would become the first oracle of the crippled smith and from that day on a woman of the royal blood would serve as minister and oracle to the god. A tradition which carried on beyond the fall of the city. Although how an oracle was found now that the Salxosu lay scattered, and the royal blood spilled was a mystery known only to the secretive seers themselves. But that was not important now, winning the favour of the god was all that mattered, pleasing his oracle to be gifted a message that would fuel their struggle to free the Salxosu from the thumb of the Doldun.

The conduit to the god and the favour which it brought the Salxosu kings had seen old Kolbos thrive and the Salxosu survive the Dusk of the old kingdoms, weathering the storm of chaos which followed. The city of Butophulo was founded through the guidance of the god and his oracle who directed the survivors to the haven where the city would be built even as old Kolbos was ravaged. In the times of the League, the oracle had proved its worth time and time again and it was her guidance which had almost seen Kolmosoi succeed. Sonos hoped that the god would see to it that the sorry band which came to him as supplicants now, survivors of a cataclysm of their own at the gates of Gottoy and shadows of their former selves, transformed by their numerous trials, would be saved by his mercy. He touched the amulet again and felt for the other gifted by Rulrup. They both felt more like a burden now, almost burning to the touch.

Progress was slow through the Tulkob, slower than they had hoped. The rain lashed down hard within the limits of the city making wading through the knee-deep water which veined the ruins, even more difficult to navigate. Eventually they found themselves at the edge of the first of the inner waterways which surrounded each section of the city. They had hoped to use the Bridge of the Minister to the God to cross. One of six which linked the Tulkob to the Dunkob, the second ring, but they found the stone arched bridge a ruin. The carvings which once lined the crossing had crumbled and the bridge itself fallen into the restless sea. Elegant shapes darted through the water and seemed to point them north toward the Bridge of the Sorcerer.

The day was almost over when they reached that span. Thankfully, the gods were good, and the bridge was still intact. They crossed into the Dunkob as the sun began its descent and lightning flashed overhead.

The Dunkob was filled with marketplaces, harbours, and shipwrights. The arrow straight channel from the sea called the Funnel would bring ships into the heart of the city where the merchants of the world would flock to sell their wares. Only the wind whistled down the Funnel now, but at its height, old Kolbos' fleets sailed from here to dominate the waves, building a far-flung empire of the seas and all the wealth that came with it. An empire which made the Salxosu the richest of all the Xosu, perhaps the richest people in the world.

Sonos could not help but reflect on the war for the city as they marched and the reasons it came about. When Tholophos seized the throne of Thelonigul and declared himself the High King of all the Xosu, the Salxosu and old Kolbos had defied him. It was a defiance for which they would pay dearly. Tholophos put king Dzotthisoni, to death and installed his own son by Dzotthisoni's daughter, Semontek, as King of old Kolbos. Tholophos would pay eventually for his betrayal of the man who had taken him in his time of greatest need, and he miscalculated placing his son on the throne of the city. Semontek's mother was Salxosu after all. Her son found himself seduced by the sea.

When Tholophos passed from the world, he bequeathed his kingdom to the worthiest. As his other sons competed in elaborate games to win the crown, Semontek eloped with Tholophos' last wife and sought to rule independently from old Kolbos. Defying the demands of his half-brother Tildun, who won the right to call himself High King, to submit to his authority when he assumed the throne of their father. Tildun denounced Semontek and the Salxosu as barbarous and called all the heroes of the world to a great war. A war that lasted for twelve long years and would see the utter destruction of the great metropolis and with it the fall of the Xosu. Some even said that it unleashed the forces which brought about the Dusk of the old kingdoms themselves as the gods turned their back on the world. An age of darkness followed, but the survivors, now scattered, remembered, and rebuilt. The League of Butophulo was old Kolbos come again, although only a few could see it.

The sun, Dunsun's great eye, had disappeared, slowly being replaced by the moon. The small group of ghostly figures reached the Bridge of the Smith, one of the three which linked the Dunkob to the eye of Sem and the bridge over which the Kinsolsun were said to have carried Buto to safety. The white-gold walls of the Thelonbet, straight as a tree trunk, loomed over them and the storm raged overhead covering the city like a canopy, rain lashing down everywhere except inside the walls. Behind those walls the temple of Buto waited.

On the island the old nobility and the priesthood once lived, it was a sacred place and so they left their weapons at the edge of the bridge. All Sonos carried was the two zilthum amulets, but they felt like burden enough.

**

They passed through the Serpent Gate which still guarded the entrance to the Thelonbet, the white-gold walls still glistened as if glowing in moonlight, despite the storm raging all around them and the ravages of time. Beyond the walls a strange and tranquil atmosphere awaited, a contrast to the raging tempest, as if they had passed through a gateway into another world.

Ahead loomed the temple of Buto, once the greatest structure in Kolgennon. Even larger than the great temple of Gonphon in Gonphonmub and taller than the towers of the gods at Torfub. The temple rose straight from the ground. The figure of Buto overshadowed them, his torso a part of the dome of the temple, appearing almost like Buto possessed a merman's tail. Indeed, other than his hammer, which was raised as if about to strike his anvil, unleashing the power to change the world in an instant, the men of old Kolbos had depicted Buto in a form more serpent than man, a style almost completely fallen out of favour now. A great hulthul tree, which was sheltered beneath the dome, was the only sign of life beyond the walls. Bursting through the dome, its thick, white branches had wrapped themselves around the statue of Buto as if tying him to the earth. Despite the relative calm, the temple had not escaped the ravages of the sea and the sacking of the city. The foundations had sunk so that the dome and statue leant forward. It felt like Buto was watching their small band with an intense burning gaze as they passed into the Thelonbet.

Here, in eons passed as the old kingdoms were dawning, the peoples of the world brought their bounties as offerings to Buto, as the Kinsolsun played minister to the god. In return Buto and his servants offered protection to the people of the islands after their world had been shattered and made anew and they could no longer roam and hunt like the beasts on the plain. When Buto struck his Anvil, it was said, the daemons of the Dusk were driven away by the resonating shock.

Pusokol and Kusoasu strode forward and pushed open one of the bronze doors. It screeched as it strained backwards, and the groan of its hinges echoed through the empty hall behind. The inside of the temple was as ruined as the rest of the city, the sea had even found its way into the sacred space. Parts of the floor were covered in sea water not quite knee deep. *Perhaps Buto approved of the sea coming to his temple,* Sonos thought. Despite it all, it was clear what a magnificent building this abode of Buto once was. Sonos remembered his childhood trip to this place, the fear and wonder it evoked. The temples of Butophulo were rich and grand, but none of them had awed him in quite the same way as this splendid ruin. It was a feeling which had stuck with Sonos ever since.

Suddenly he felt the weight of the two amulets he carried pulling him down.

They slipped quietly through to the rear of the temple, passing by the thick, pale trunk of the hulthul tree. Retracing the steps that they had all made as children on the verge of manhood, much changed from the people they had been then. Behind the altar was a wall which separated the main chamber from a small antechamber, a hidden doorway lay inside. Runu felt across the wall, clasping the hidden handle, and pulling the door aside, they entered the darkness.

The corridor was pitch black except for a flickering light in the distance. They moved toward it and Sonos remembered the fear, apprehension, and dread of his first visit. They reached the flickering torch and those feelings dissipated, as they had before. The room opened into a huge sanctuary, the abode of the crippled god. Fires flickered against the wall, the roaring of flames echoing in the chamber, hinting that the forges of the Thelonbet still burned. The flame danced along the wall and made the carved image of Sem which ringed the chamber look alive as it writhed in the firelight. The white roots of the hulthul tree above had burst through the ceiling and were snaking their way towards the centre of the chamber. In the middle of the room a tall tripod stood. Enthroned upon it he saw the shadowy figure of a woman. Below the tripod there was a hole and a warm glow that suggested a fire below them. To the front of this throne, a large white-gold rock sat like an altar or an anvil.

Immediately upon entering the sanctuary, they were approached by a young girl, no more than one and three. She greeted all four men, who displayed the tattoos and zilthum rings which marked them as initiates. Runu spoke,

"We wish to consult the oracle."

The girl nodded,

"What gifts do you bring to pay for the service of the Great God and his dutiful son?"

"The riches of the east." Sonos helped carry forward what plunder they had left from their expedition, little as it was, "and the blood in our veins, the ancient blood of old Kolbos." Runu replied. The girl said nothing, she turned and looked toward the blue shadow sat upon the throne. The woman looked up and said something Sonos could not understand, it sounded more like the crash of the ocean than a word. The fires beneath seemed to burn intensely as she said it and the white-gold altar glowed.

"This is not all you have to offer. The god says it is so." The girl said, turning her gaze to Sonos. He felt a sudden relief as he found himself wearily lifting the amulet, the gift from Rulrup. The girl smiled,

"It feels the power of this place. It is a wonder you can carry such a thing; the blood of the kings runs through your veins does it not?" Sonos looked at her in surprise as the girl took the amulet from him. Suddenly the world seemed a much brighter place.

"The Amulet of the Traveller will please the god; he will allow you to keep the other. The Amulet of Record will mark events for posterity." she continued, "Such things are important." She turned away and gestured for the men to follow.

The girl led them to the centre of the sanctuary and stood them before the rock and the throne. The robed woman, older but not yet middle aged with the classical Salxosu looks of pale skin and a deep dark colour to her hair, raised her head and smiled. It was said that all the oracles of Buto went mad eventually. No mortal could take the whisperings of the god in their ear long and maintain a mortal's sanity, the burden crippled them.

"The great smith will accept your gift." The girl said, gesturing to a bowl that was sat on the rock altar. Inside was a thick oil, dark, black, and blue. The pressings of the fruit of the hulthul tree. Runu drew the knife which lay across the altar and the four men stood around the bowl. Each cut his hand and passed the knife on, allowing the thick black blood to drip into the bowl. Runu said,

"We wish to ask the god what we must do to regain his favour and freedom for the Salxosu?"

They stepped back.

The girl handed the bowl to the Oracle, who had been motionless on her throne. She raised the bowl high, pouring some of the thick liquid over her head. The gory fluid trickled down her face and her neck before touching the amulet which sat between her breasts. Sonos had not noticed it until then, but as the blood touched it the zilthum shone and resonated, as did his own. It burned and he had to resist the urge with all his strength to tear it from round his neck.

The rest of the blood and oil she drank, and then the great smith took her in his grasp. Writhing around uncontrollably, a mad ecstasy grabbed her, and she laughed. A laugh so deep and strong that it could only have come from the mouth of a god, it shook Sonos to his core.

The Oracle collapsed in pain and ecstasy; the young girl struck the altar with a hammer that seemed to appear in her hand from nowhere. The sound was deafening, as if the gateway to the hidden realm was screeching open. The amulet at Sonos neck felt as if it would burn a hole in his chest. The older woman grabbed the girl and whispered in her ear. The girl spoke,

"The great god's son speaks to you Sons of Sem,

Buto has not been lost, but his city is a bound slave in bondage,
Glory awaits the Salxosu, when unchained the Smith's white haven".

The girl then produced a white-gold helmet in the Rinuxosu style with a moon white horsehair crest running horizontal across the top and two great bronze bull's horns protruding from it. It shone white gold in the flames. None needed to say it, but they knew it was made from pure zilthum, the like of which not seen since before the fall of the Kinsolsun.

"The god wishes you to have his helmet. You will be his protectors, his ministers and will see his people rise to greatness once again."

Runu took the helmet and thanked the girl. "There is more." the older woman croaked and again whispered to the child,

"You will find her forlorn and broken, fear not for the path she will open,

When the white wanderer wakes and hydra finds its token"

They left in silence. They would need to overnight in the city, but outside of the sacred place and then it would be another half day walk back to their ships on the morrow. They had much and more to consider, but their purpose was now clear.

Huddled for warmth lacking a fire that evening, in one of the few ruined buildings which still had a roof, the lyrics of a song danced around Sonos' head,

To arms! To arms!
Forward, arrow like, King of Kings, fire has no sheath!
But fierce Xosu bite, time to feel the hydra's teeth!
Our spears silver flash, come and face the Sacred Band!
We fall on this field, blood to free the Sacred land!

To arms! To arms!
Thrice loosed his fierce horde, arrows shade all beneath!
Spears crack and swords may shatter, flee the hydra's teeth!
Fume, fury, foolish great king, firm footed we stand!
We fall on this field, blood to free the Sacred Land!

KALU

39

The black became light, hazy, and blurred, but light, nonetheless. He could not say where he was or how long he had been there, only that his head was throbbing as if some mighty giant were trying to force its way from inside. The black was descending again and again, he knew he was moving, the nausea caused by the motion told him that much. How long he had been moving for he could not say, where he was going, he could not say. Was this death? Was his shade being carried to the hidden realm? Several times the sky went from blue and clear to navy and star speckled, days must have passed.

Finally, it stopped. Kalu was lifted and placed on the ground, the nausea disappearing almost as soon as he was on the firm earth, he had stopped losing consciousness as well. Feeling strong enough to lift his head, he surveyed his surroundings. He had been placed on a small hill rising out of the plains of Zenian. A scattering of wet looking iron-coloured stones lay strewn across the summit, as if some god had carelessly tossed them there, a clutch of red and gold dolthil trees keeping them in place. If Kalu had not known they could have been dismissed as nothing, but it was a habit of the people of the old kingdom of Zowdel to build temples in places like this that they deemed close to the gods. Who knows what the place looked like when it was standing, but now it was just a ruin and the haunt of the wild cats that roamed the plains. Destroyed during the fall of the kingdom, or maybe sacked in the centuries after by marauding Rilrpitu who had flown down from the north.

Kalu had been propped up against one of the stones, it was the perfect place to watch the stream of horsemen filing their way on to the hill. The men around him were already setting camp and building a fire. *No infantry,* he thought, *just the cavalry, we must be moving quickly in pursuit of someone, perhaps some of the Rilrpitu escaped in the confusion of the battle.* But he could hear the river, wide and fast flowing. Painfully he rolled over, his head spinning again, he could see the river off in the distance on the army's right flank, they had to be heading south and east.

"You're awake!" The shout came from behind him. Kalu recognised the voice, but his head was still foggy, and he could not say who it was. A shadow swept over him like the flooding sea engulfing the earth. He carefully craned his head upward and was met by a liquid smile,

"Supo?" He said unsure and uneasily using his hoarse voice.

"Well, you remember my name at least. That is a good sign."

The well-built clansman knelt next to him, still smiling, and biting into a juicy fruit,

"How do you feel?" He asked.

"Like Dunsun struck my head with his thunderbolt." Kalu croaked.

Supo laughed, nostrils flaring as he did,

"Good, at least you still feel alive. You hit the ground hard enough to shatter the earth, but you did at least pull a fair few of the screaming chargers with you. Rest now, the men will build a fire. I will come and see you once the camp is up and running."

Kalu nodded and Supo disappeared, blasting out orders as he did. The fire was almost built and some of the men had begun preparing food. Kalu could hear the bellowing of sheep, others were busy constructing a makeshift palisade at the foot of the hill. Trying to ignore the pounding in his head, he rolled over to watch the sun drop below the horizon, as Dunsun took another trip to the underworld to visit his mistress.

He must have dozed off again, but he was shaken back to his senses as he felt the presence of someone sitting down next to him. Supo was still wearing his armour, undoing its fastenings as he sat, and placing it next to him on the ground, his riding leathers next to them. Although well into his middle years, Supo clearly had the strength and physique of a young man and the energy to match. It was only the weary lines, like waves on the sea, which rippled across his brow and the tridents they formed aside his eyes, which gave away his age. Supo uncoiled his hands and warmed them against the now roaring fire. Pouring himself a cup of sweet wine, he said,

"I suppose you will be wanting to know what happened." There was a melancholy in his voice, as if he did not wish to talk on the subject himself.

"You may have to fill me in on a few details Supo. The last thing I remember was charging into the Rilrpitu camp." Kalu replied, his senses almost restored to him now.

"Savour those moments of ignorance then my friend, the rest of the story is not a pleasant one."

Zenupal of the Tholmash, the army's physician and seer, was knelt the other side of Kalu, vigorously checking him over. The man was as experienced as any, he had been with the army since the days of Tekolger's father and even went into exile with Tekolger amongst the Thulchwal. Like all the forest dwelling Tholmash, he was skilled in healing and the knowledge of herbs, but Zenupal also had a strong connection with the gods. He took a few moments and then handed Kalu a cup,

"Drink this." he said, "It will ease your head. You will be fine in a few days."

Kalu took the cup and sipped at the white liquid. A sweet milk, mare's milk more than likely, it was abundant on the plains. Laced with honey, it was not unpleasant, but the sweetness made him feel a little sick again. He turned back to Supo,

"How did the battle end?"

Supo smiled,

"A victory. Dolzalo and the king's secretary caught the rest of the Rilrpitu fleeing on the road to Yorotog. The few survivors have fled north."

"I take it we are in pursuit of them now, that is why there is just the cavalry here. What about Zonhol?" Kalu paused after he asked the question, sipping the sweet milk again. The memory of that at least came back to him now, but he hoped Tholo was playing a trick on him. Supo shook his head,

"This is where the tale becomes unpleasant. It was not the Rilrpitu who dealt you that blow, it was Zenukola's guards. You were fortunate that my men arrived when they did. As the battle began one of Zenu's men revealed to me that they had been ordered to see you fall on the field to remove you as a supporter of Kelbal. I fear for what Zenukola may have done in our absence, so now we race for Torfub to stop Zenu before it is too late." he paused, "Zonhol did not make it, I am sorry. Silver eye's men got to him before my own."

Kalu did not want to believe what he had just heard, but something told him it was the truth. Zonhol had been a loyal man and a good friend, a pillar of support when he needed him and a strong right hand. Wild and fierce in battle as he was, Zonhol had a kind spirit. He had been looking forward to returning to Doldun, only his bones would return now. Kalu muttered a prayer to Xosu and beseeched Tholophos to judge him well and permit him to enter the plains of Zulbeli, his shade deserved that.

"Why Torfub? We should head straight back to the army now that we have the element of surprise."

Supo was staring into the fire, deep in thought. The light flickered and reflected like fiery tridents in his eyes.

"The rest of the army of the northern frontier is near there, my army; it is why the Rilrpitu were able to make it this far south so easily. Zenu ordered me to march them south and camp just north of Torfub. At the time the order was given, I was told it was to help to quell a rumoured rebellion by one of the Xortogun lords of Zowdel who had planned to surprise the city. With hindsight, I fear his plan was to strip the northern border of its defences and allow the Rilrpitu in, knowing it would force Kelbal to send his forces to contain them. He would then be able to ambush Kelbal's reduced force when it reached Torfub and seize control of the empire." he paused again and looked Kalu directly in the eye. The liquid blue of Supo's eyes glowed in the light of the fire. "Zenu has been making statements about grand plans and how the Deltathelon will lead the clans to civilisation. I had hoped all of that had been left in the past where it belongs. But looking back, his disparaging remarks about crowning the child of Tekolger and Surson were what gave him away. He is still not reconciled with Tekolger's vision of an empire of both east and west and fears we will be lost if we allow the Xortogun nobility a say in the kingship."

Kalu lost his appetite, the sweet milk was sickening him once more and he felt the colour drain from his cheeks again. He placed the cup on the floor where it wobbled and spilled out near the fire, but he did not care. He went to speak, but no words came out, just a burning in the pit of his stomach. Supo looked at him and poured another cup of sweet wine out. Handing the cup to Kalu he said,

"Have something stronger."

The two men poured a libation to the gods and Supo continued,

"I feared Zenu might be planning something drastic. I knew he worried for the future of the empire, but I did not think he would turn against his own. Our own comradeship goes back decades, so I suspect he thought I would merely follow his lead. But I am my own man. Although I share his view that the Doldun can never fall back into the civil war which plagued my youth, I fear his actions are driving us towards that very outcome. His words and deeds only confirm that, I think. I only wish I had seen his intentions sooner. I should have told Kelbal about the moving of my men to Torfub, although it did not seem important at the time." Supo paused, contemplating something, "The more I think on it the more I fear that Zenu had something to do with the king's death. His failure to embrace the king's vision and his concerns about the future of the empire are motivation. He has been endlessly questioning everyone about it ever since, perhaps from guilt. He has even been suggesting that Kelbal wielded the poison. All could be co-incidence I know, but the timing seems to fit, and the fact that the army would have to return home through the lands he controls, it all fits too well. But maybe the days of riding with nothing to do but think are making me paranoid."

Kalu nodded, who knew if it was true or not? Zenu had certainly betrayed them, it would not be too much of a leap to think he had betrayed the king as well. Other generals had done so before, and to blame Kelbal? The only reason could be a guilty conscious and a desire for power.

The difficulty in what Supo was saying was clear in the emotion in his voice, Zenu was like an older brother to him, much like Kelbal was to Kalu. He found it hard to comprehend what he would do or how he would feel if he had come to similar conclusions about Kelbal's leadership. He sipped the sweet wine, it was just as sickening, but the hit of the alcohol did much more to dull the throbbing in his head,

"How do you know that the northern army won't merely turn us over to Zenu?"

Supo laughed like a horse,

"I don't, but they are my soldiers, and they were not privy to his schemes. An offer was made to double their pay for the year, and they were told that they would be needed in ensuring the succession and the stability of the empire. But we all thought that this was to quell a threat from the conquered. I am gambling that if we get to them first, we can turn that promise against Zenu. They are Tekolger's veterans after all, and they will listen to you."

"We had better beseech the gods that you are right Supo." Kalu replied hoping for Tholo's protection.

The conversation was interrupted by the distressed cries of a sheep being slaughtered. The noise and commotion ceased as its throat was slit and the blood ran over the black rocks and into the ground, mixing in a ditch by the fire with Kalu's spilled milk and honey and the libation of sweet wine the two men had poured.

As he rolled over to sleep that night, he muttered a prayer under his breath to the gods wishing to see Tekolger again. The king would know what to do.

A deep dark sleep took Kalu. As soon as the darkness took him, he felt as though he was falling, hurtling down into the halls of the dead, perhaps Phenmoph had come to take his shade. He found himself on the edge of a river, murky water slowly sliding past him. On the far bank there were figures, old warriors, young boys, men and women and children, all shuffling passed. Something deep in his core told him that they were dead, the shades of half-forgotten friends and enemies and those he had not known at all. Then a familiar figure pushed his way through the crowd,

"Father?" Kalu said, but that man did not move, did not speak, no flicker of recognition crossed his face. His father had died when he was a boy, slain in a Kolabon raid during the height of the civil war, the same day he had met Kelbal and Tekolger. His father's shade disappeared back into the throng on its slow march to receive the judgement of the court of the dead. Another familiar face emerged, "Yusukol?" Kalu shouted, this time the man answered,

"It is I, my son."

"I did not know you had passed. When? How?" Kalu asked the man who he had come to view as kin, a father when his had been ripped from him.

"A winter fever two years passed. You look well son; your kin are proud of you. Protect them." Yusukol shouted across the river. It was all Kalu could do not to charge out across the flowing water, but in an instant his mentor was gone, melting back into the throng. A final figure emerged and Kalu felt all the emotion of the past months well up all at once.

"Tekolger." He said softly.

"Kalu, my loyal friend. It is good to see your face once more." The king replied.

"What is this place? Why am I here?" Kalu asked.

"There is something you need to see." Tekolger answered, "Follow me." He began to walk along the riverbank and Kalu shadowed his every move.

"Look along this line Kalu, every single shade which ever existed waits to be judged by the lords of the dead. Phenmoph will take those not worthy into his hidden realm before they are reborn anew." They had neared the front of the queue now. Kalu recognised heroes of old queuing to have a taste of the sweet waters of memory. The Rinukol was the river's name, he knew that now. Those judged worthy by the gods could rise to enter the plains of Zulbeli within the shining realm, ruled over by Xosu and near to Dunsun himself, departing the cycle of existence. Only the greatest heroes found their place there, those who had lived the best life they could, men like Rinu, Sal, Dzotthisoni and Phalazkon. The other shades would be sent to taste the waters of memory, to forget their previous lives and be born again, a new path placed at their feet.

"I may be gone from the world, but my legacy remains. Great heroes from the days of the old kingdoms, when man was close to the gods and their realms touched, will soon have their times again. The cycle repeats as it always has. The old kingdoms came close to building societies to rival the realms of the gods, their dawn was signalled by the coming of the most powerful of shades, when the realms of men and gods were at their closest and one could pass between them. But the Dusk also came when the cycle turned, and those shades returned to the world. Prosperity is not a given.

Now the circle has turned again. Xosu's red arrow at my birth signalled a new age when the worlds of gods and men would reconnect. I was its herald, and with it the chance to rebuild what was lost. The gods made the world for us, it is up to man to tame it. We tried before and came so close to succeeding. But we made one mistake, the united realm I leave you will succeed where others failed, one unending empire for man to rival the gods in their heavens. Protect my legacy or we are doomed."

Protect his legacy. It sounded easy, but Kalu feared he had already failed. He asked his old friend,

"What is death like? Are the plains of Zulbeli really as magnificent as they say, a place of comfort and delight?"

A melancholy smile lit up Tekolger's face,

"Nothing compares to life itself, complete my task. The challenges you will face are greater than those I tackled."

Tekolger faded into the darkness.

* * *

After a few more days Kalu was fit enough to ride alongside his comrades. His recovery could not have come soon enough, the encampment of the northern army was close now, and Torfub itself only a day's march beyond.

The column set off before first light, when only the stars which rise before the dawn were visible. Kalu rode alongside Supo at the head of the column, joined by Dolzalo and Palmash, who wore a sun hat he seemed to have acquired from one of the peasants of Zowdel, a thousand cavalrymen at their back.

The column had already crossed several leagues before Dunsun's great eye peaked over the horizon. They turned away from the river now, heading inland over rolling hills to the north of the glittering, towered city of Torfub.

"What do we do when we have Silver eye in our hands?" Dolzalo asked, cracking the silence of the morning.

"I would not want to spill blood. Arresting Zenukola will be hard enough for me to do, but the empire comes first, and we may have no choice, this is treason after all." Supo replied.

Kalu sighed and said somewhat protectively,

"Zenu has been like a father to me and is a giant amongst the Doldun, bloodshed now could only make the situation worse. It will unleashed forces we cannot control or understand and may sweep away everything we have built. Exile and retirement may be the sensible choice."

Dolzalo scoffed at that notion,

"Treason is treason, the punishment is clear. I will do the deed myself if you do not have the stomach for it. What do you think Tekolger would have done in this situation Kalu? He was ruthless as any, more so. He was not Kenkathoaz first born son if you remember that far back."

"His brothers all died as babes, or in battle before Tekolger was of age, Dolzalo." Kalu exclaimed angrily.

"Not all Kalu. What happened to Helupal?" Dolzalo spat back,

"He was not of sound mind, and you know it." Kalu answered defensively, his head throbbing.

"May be so, but what happened to him?" Dolzalo retorted, a smile flashing over his face. Kalu did not answer. As ever, Palmash agreed with Dolzalo, a menacing jester-like smile changing his face from a scowl which sent arrows coursing through Kalu,

"We are all dancing around the issue. Zenu started this, he has brought his execution on himself. I will do it kindly if you wish, a drop of poison in his wine and our problem is solved."

"There is no king to issue that sentence. It would be dangerous for us to assume that power for ourselves, and Zenu has many friends back in Doldun. Executing him may lead to the civil war we are trying to prevent. Do we know what Dotmazo's position is?" Kalu answered, irritated with the ease at which his comrades concluded that execution was the best course. He could still remember the burning white ruin of Thentherzaw. If he had been there when Dolzalo sacked the city, he was unsure if he would have been able to control himself and now Dolzalo was suggesting such violence once again.

"I fear that Zenu would not act alone. Dotmazo likes to keep his distance, but his hands are all over this. The rumour is that he has taken the king's wives and son under his protection back in Doldun." Supo paused and gave Kalu a knowing look. "He also keeps Tekolger's mother close too. This may reveal his intentions to us." Supo finished.

"All the more reason to act decisively then, remove the threat from Zenu and isolate Dotmazo." Dolzalo said, forcefully intervening again, "Need I remind you of the blood moon conspiracy."

Kalu did not need reminding of that affair. Kenkathoaz' old generals had tried to overthrow Tekolger after he had married Surson, unhappy with the Xortogun practices being introduced by Tekolger and his encouragement of other Doldun and Xosu to take Xortogun brides.

The king and Surson had married in Torfub, then Tekolger had struck south into the desert to re-found the outpost now called Tekolgerzel, leaving his new bride in Torfub. On the night of a full moon, a blood moon, five of Kenkathoaz old generals had tried to murder Tekolger as he slept. Fortunately, Kalu's White Shields had been vigilant and under question the traitors had revealed that four more of their number were rallying men in Torfub to seize Surson, they were prevented from succeeding only with the blessing of the gods. Dolzalo continued,

"Tekolger did not worry about the consequences then, he acted and eliminated the threat to him and the empire."

'Protect my legacy' Tekolger's words in his vision came back to Kalu in that moment. Supo, Zenukola and Dotmazo were the only generals of Kenkathoaz old guard who survived the purge that followed the attempt on Tekolger's life.

"The old generals conspired once and failed. Who is to say that Dotmazo and Zenu were not involved the last time and escaped Tekolger's wrath? All of this would make sense then, and Tekolger's death would be on them as well."

An uneasy silence hung in the air upon hearing Dolzalo's words, like the calm in the sky before the first crack of thunder. None of them wanted to hear it, none of them wanted it to be true.

They set their final camp that night, the next morning they would arrive at the encampment of the northern army and their fate would be left in the hands of Yulthelon.

* * *

The familiar grid pattern of a marching camp of the Doldun emerged on the horizon in the shadow of the thrusting sheer peaks which marked the northern edge of Xortogun. Kalu could not help feeling his heart gladdened by the sight. The northern army may have been garrisoned on the frontier guarding against the Rilrpitu for years, but they were still Tekolger's veterans, the most formidable fighting men in the world.

The horses thundered through the camp's entrance, along the wide avenue which led to the command tent at the centre, kicking up a cloud of dust as they went. Soldiers were gathering to meet them, intrigued by the arrival of a large force of men and no doubt eager to break the humdrum of weeks spent encamped.

Kalu dismounted at the central square in front of the command tent, his head still pounded and getting off the horse was a welcome relief. Every step the horse took felt like another thunder strike from Dunsun inside his head and the thought of Zenu's betrayal and what may have become of Kelbal was making him feel even worse. Waiting for the veterans to gather, Supo stepped forward to address them, uncoiling his arms to greet the men,

"It is unfortunate that I come to speak to you with bad news, as if the news of the king's recent passing and the threat of rebellion were not bad enough. But it is to you as Tekolger's loyal soldiers I must appeal once more." he paused mid flow and looked around at his men, "I am ashamed to admit that we have been deceived. You served with the king through the highs and the lows of his rule. The desperate struggles to retain the kingdom in the face of invasion, the triumph of uniting the Xosu once more and the glory of the conquest of Xortogun and with it the lordship of Zenian. None of that could have been achieved without your labour, sweat and blood.

Even when the king asked that you garrison the northern frontier, that desolate place disconnected from civilisation, and face off against the savage tribesmen of the north, you did not waver. I know you did so because you believed in Tekolger, you believed in the empire he was creating and the civilisation he strived to see cover the lands of east and west. And you did your duty with honour.

Now the peace and stability your efforts have created are under threat, and it saddens me to say it is from one of our own. Zenukola of the Deltathelon, has betrayed the memory of his king, he has seized the royal court and tried to have one of the king's most loyal Companions killed." Supo swept a hand towards Kalu, "What is more he plans on placing his own claimant on the throne, disregarding Tekolger's stated heir. Worse, he lied to me to march you here, he believed he could fool you in to supporting his claims." Supo stopped again, his fist clenched as if enraged, "And so, it is in desperation that we come to you now. You hold the power in your hands, the power to rescue Tekolger's legacy from the edge of destruction. You, Tekolger's loyal soldiers, can ensure his line lives on.

I understand promises were made to you by me and Zenukola, they were made on false premises, but march with us now to Torfub, help us bring this traitor to justice and you will receive what was promised to you and more."

A cheer of approval cascaded through the ranks of the assembled army. Within hours, the entire force was marching south.

SONOSPHOSKUL

40

The mist had descended quickly, Sonos could barely see the other ships. The two lead triremes and the merchant hulk had completely disappeared and the fourth, another trireme, was just a faint outline in the distance. The further south they sailed from old Kolbos the thicker the mist had become. But south and west was their heading now, the Oracle had been clear.

No doubt their presence had been noted at Pilsipon and Thasotun was aware of their return, but the Red and White Council would likely be expecting them at Pittuntik. None would foresee so bold a move as against Butophulo itself. But that is exactly what they intended, the oracle was clear, the Salxosu would never be free if their city were not. Even Dzotdoz and Hozfotou had agreed, how could they not? They dreamed of a similar assault on their homes once Thasotun was toppled and the Salxosu free to aid them.

However, their new heading was dangerous, the fleet had to negotiate its way through a series of rocky outcrops and small islands. The sea in this region south of old Kolbos was also plagued by pirates attacking ships and taking the entire crew for slaves, not doubt to be sold in the market at Rulkusup. Sol was leading the raiders if the rumours could be believed, taking the crews as thralls and blood sacrifices for his daemon witch of a wife who claimed to speak with the voice of some old forgotten god.

A day's sail south of old Kolbos, the stories where at least partly confirmed when the lookouts sighted a single black mark on the otherwise blue horizon. The small fleet closed in to find a merchant craft, bearing the standard of Thasotun, adrift and in danger of colliding with anything that dared to come too close, the crew nowhere to be seen.

They had boarded the ship half expecting an ambush, Runu had even set three of the triremes to circle around to guard against a surprise attack, but none had come. Eerie as the empty ship was, it was otherwise in good condition with an expensive cargo of wine, olives, and grain. Runu assigned a crew to man it and alleviate the cramped conditions on the overloaded triremes. Dzotdoz took it as his own command and the men dubbed it The Smith's Attendant.

That was the last clear day, the sky bright and blue and the sea tranquil. Within an hour of finding the merchant hulk the mist had flooded all around them, blocking out the sun and transforming their world. For four days since the ships had crawled along, resorting to their oars rather than sails. In the dense fog the ships had looked like many legged beasts of burden struggling to find their way through a blizzard, desperately trying to see into the open sea beyond. At times they had thought they had heard other ships nearby, but none ever emerged from the fog. Some of the men had even claimed they had glimpsed shadows in the water, following them. Sonos put that down to fatigue, nerves, and the strange way the mist seemed to twist the light and amplify or muffle sound. When he could see the other ships, Sonos had noted Runu had taken to standing on the prow of Buto's Hammer, wearing the zilthum helmet gifted by the oracle and staring into the distance, as if the helmet would give him the power to see beyond the dense grey mist.

Storms were all too common in this area at this time of year, but Sonos had never seen a mist quite like this. It had engulfed the fleet quite suddenly, it was dense and seemed to just sit on top of the ships, moving with them. In amongst it all the mist had left a fine film of water all over the ship and on the crew. The men had grown increasingly nervous, some claiming that the gods were displeased and had shrouded their path, blinding them to what was to come. Sonos replied that they would have to use their ears instead. He had even gone so far as to claim that the mist had been sent by Buto to cover their approach to the city when the men had become particularly restless.

The complaints made him think of the amulet he wore. The Amulet of Record the oracle had called it, all he had known as a child was that it was a family heirloom, a relic of old Kolbos, but maybe there was more truth to the stories which surrounded it than he knew, the god was maybe even watching him. Either way, it would not be able to make a record in this mist.

He had ordered that the men stick to their posts and do their jobs to the best of their ability, placing himself in front of the mast in middle of the ship. There he had an all-round view of the craft, keeping his watchful eye on the crew, the ships to their front and the rocks either side of them, although it felt like a hopeless task to steer the unwieldy beast. It reminded him of how he always felt when riding.

"Keep it steady." He ordered, just as the ships to their front disappeared into the mist again. *All alone now,* he thought. A moment of doubt crept in. There were islands, he knew, just a short distance to one side or the other. A tempting destination, they almost sang to him. An enchanting siren's call to sail to an island and wait for the mist to pass. Sonos felt himself walking to edge of the ship and staring hard into the dense cloud. He felt as though he could reach out and touch the land. *I should have tied myself to that mast,* he thought, *these tempting notions will see us ruined.*

Something moved in the water, he only caught a glimpse of it and then it was gone. It moved swift and elegantly whatever it was. The distraction shook him out of his daydream, *no we must continue our course forward, we will hit open sea soon enough and this mist will clear.* To change course in either direction would almost certainly see the ship smashed against some rocky outcrop. The vessel creaked slowly onward.

Half a day passed and still the mist sat on top of the ships, as if their world had been reduced to this tiny space, the sea, the ship and the mist, nothing else. No wind, even sound seemed unable to penetrate it, except the call of the rocks. Then, a sudden crash shock him from his stupor, a crash of waves? it had to be, a rumble echoed in the distance, and the mist evaporated revealing a world full of noise and colour and vibrancy once more.

To their front, water crashed against a small island, the sea battering it into submission. Five ships were waiting just off its coast, the others had made it through. Butophulo was no more than a day's sail away.

* * *

The fleet regrouped and Runukolkil called the commanders to a meeting aboard Buto's Hammer. They were close to their destination now but could not simply walk into the city. The Doldun garrison on Polriso's Hill and the tyrants they supported would have them killed immediately, even with the support of the thousand men of the Hotizoz Legion. The oracle may have told them what they needed to do, but they would need to work out the how themselves.

When Sonos boarded the ship, he found Runu stood at the prow staring at the silhouette of the mainland resting on the horizon, the zilthum helmet under his arm. It was the first time any of them had seen Xosupil for more than a decade. The last time they had been sailing away towards Thasotun and into exile, exhausted by the long war with the Rinuxosu and their defeat at the hands of the Doldun. Before that, the fleet of Butophulo had dominated these seas, bringing wealth and riches beyond imagining to the city. It was a story Sonos would have to put to page one day. He approached Runu and said,

"It is a beautiful sight isn't it, and we have been away from it for far too long."

"It is and we have, but the closer we get the more fearful I am that we will never make it back. The city is well defended, and we have not set foot there for twelve years. Things may not be as we expect. If it were not for the words of the oracle, I would counsel against this action, it may be too bold by half." Runu replied, pensively looking at the helmet the way a smith may inspect his finest work. "I can hear the oracle's words echoing to me when I wear this fine craft, a mirage no doubt, but it is like the god himself is whispering in my ear."

"Many things may have changed, but the people of Butophulo will remember the League and the freedom that was so cruelly wrenched from their grasp. We can win their support by showing them that we can bring that back. We just need to get inside the city, and they will rally to us." Sonos replied confidently. He was certain he was right, once a man had a taste of liberty it was hard to give it up, the memory of that sweet drink will be in the minds of everyone in Butophulo.

"I hope you are right." Runu replied, turning toward the gathering commanders, "But first a more immediate problem. I have already sent a small patrol across the island to see if anything is waiting for us. Unfortunately, there is. A squadron of ships flying the red bull of Thasotun is anchored on the other side of the straight. Whether they were sent to find us or not I am unsure. But they lie between us and Butophulo. We have a choice, we can either try to slip past them at night along the coast, but it is rocky and dangerous to shipping on the best days, likely we will lose one of the ships. The other choice is that we fight our way through."

Silence hung in the air for just a moment, before Kusoasu spoke,

"I sailed these waters a lot growing up. I think it likely we lose more than one ship if we try to slip past at night. The waters are filled with hidden outcrops below the surface, and they are not small, more like tower shaped blocks than rocks, the sunken city my father used to call it. They are hard to see even in the best light and it would be slow progress. If we get stuck and dawn comes, we will lose everything."

Runu nodded,

"Pusokol, what do you think?"

"Our ships are overladen with men, can't see us doing any sneaking past them, but it may work to our advantage in a fight. If we take them at dawn, with the sun at our backs, forget about the usual ramming tactics, use our numbers to swarm them. It will be worth the sacrifice if are able to seize a few more ships and increase our power ready for the next fight."

"Sonos?"

"A victory before we reach Butophulo will be good for morale." Sonos replied.

"Dzotdoz, Hozfotou? It is your men who will make up the boarding parties if we fight. What do you say?" Runu asked their allies.

"My men are not sailors; we would be of no use if you attempt to sneak around, and they sicken from spending so long at sea. But get us on to their decks and we will make short work of them." Dzotdoz answered.

"We fight then. Rest your men, make any repairs you can. We will make sacrifices and hit them at first light."

* * *

Night came and went, dawn emerged, and the men prepared themselves for battle. Sonos donned his armour. The bronze muscled cuirass glinting white in the morning sun, bronze grieves to match, and a blue horizontal horsehair crested helm which marked him out amongst his men. Where it went, they would follow. He took up his round shield and tested the weight, then gripped the ashen shaft of his spear and pointed the sharp iron tip toward the horizon, it glowed in the light of the morning sun. So used to his panoply, Sonos felt at home in the armour, like the embrace of an old friend, but it transformed him from ordinary man to a spectre of war. He touched the amulet around his neck to invoke the god's protection.

The pine wood oars of the ship splashed into the water, the smooth blades cutting into the sea. Sonos stood at the prow, riding the beast of war to battle, watching their opponents rushing to assemble a battle line, surprised by the sudden dawn assault. The red bull of Thasotun flashed brightly on their banners, against a black background and crowned with vines.

He turned to see his men assembled on the deck, the sight took him back to the war with the Rinuxosu and his first battle. At the height of the War for the Forge, when Sonos was barely eight and ten, the Rinuxosu had become bold and reckless, thinking they could challenge the League on the sea, it was a foolish thought.

The fleet of the League had emerged from the sea like twisting shadows, catching the poorly led Rinuxosu ships in a trap in the gulf off Peskusukul as they tried to blockade the city of the same name which had recently defected to the League. The battle of the Bloody Gulf it became known as the corpses reddened the water so thick did the blood flow. It had been more of a ritual slaughter than a real battle; the gulf was still known by that name now, the Bloody Gulf. This was a small skirmish by comparison to that great clash where much of the work was done by the rams of the sleek galleys of the League fleet. Today Sonos would have to bloody his spear. Across the deck of the ship, all those who were not rowing would form boarding parties, they would close with the nearest ship and swarm on board. Most triremes only carried twenty marines to defend themselves, relying instead on their rams in battle. Each of their five triremes had at least fifty men in the boarding parties and the merchant hulk would bring in a reserve to finish the battle.

Sonos paced down the deck, his shadow shifting and growing as the sun rose higher,

"My friends!" he shouted as if about to tell them a tale of great deeds from the past, "We are men who have met all kinds of trouble before. Today will be no harder than the odds we have already beat. Through our skill, intelligence, and the favour of the gods, we escaped the clutches of Gottoy, soon this day will be just another story like that journey from the gates of the underworld. We need only rely on your skill and listen to my orders. Oarsmen, stay at your oars, row hard, and lay us alongside those ships. The rest of you, fight hard, show no mercy, Sem will have his due today, make sure it is not our shades he takes. Buto is with us."

The men let out a roar, and the oars began to beat a rhythm against the sea, the ship's speed picked up. Sonos turned once again to stare down the foe and the words of a song whispered to him as he touched the amulet at his neck.

Thrice loosed his fierce horde, arrows shade all beneath!
Spears crack and swords may shatter, flee the hydra's teeth!
Fume, fury, foolish great king, firm footed we stand!
We fall on this field, blood to free the Sacred Land!

The triremes closed the distance quickly, galloping wildly over the green sea. In the lead was Buto's Hammer, Runu stood on the prow wearing the bull horned, zilthum helmet, his eyes focused on a single goal, like a hunter riding a great stallion, chasing down his prey. Arrows began to fall, raining on the deck, bouncing off the hard wood and skidding along the surface. A few cries went out as one or two men were struck, the rest ducked and raised their shields. Sonos stood motionless, showing no fear in the face of the rain of death. Onward the ships glided through the water. Despite his armour and his helmet, his fate was in the hands of the gods, an arrow could easily find a gap. *Show no fear,* he thought, *I must seem more than a man, a shadowy spectre the enemy will fear, the men will follow your lead.* The enemy had their battle line forged, but had no time to begin to manoeuvre,

"Brace!"

The cry went up, but Sonos could not tell if it came from their side or his. He ducked down all the same. Tale Teller slammed into the side of one of the enemy triremes, skidding down its flank and sheering off any oars which had been put out, leaving the beast shattered and helpless in the rolling sea.

In an instant Sonos was on his feet, he leapt the short distance between the two ships. Faced with two foes he barged the first with his shield, then drove his ashen spear deep into the guts of the second. Blood burst out around the buried spearhead, flooding like a wave over the unfortunate man, more still poured from his mouth as death whirled down upon him. The man collapsed a lifeless corpse. Sonos stepped over him and pressed on, sending two more shades down to the halls of the dead. Sonos' men swarmed over the ship, barely any resistance was found, many of the defenders had not even time to don their armour.

He drove his way across the deck, a man in a full panoply stood between him and the end of the ship and the open sea beyond. A thrusting spear flashed at him. he parried and stepped inside its reach, barging his opponent with his round, domed shield. The man stumbled and fell off the edge into the sea below. Sonos peered over the side, but the man was gone, pulled beneath into the realm of the waves. The sea was littered with corpses as the fighting raged on ships all around, some floating on the surface, the shadows of others lifeless beneath the waves. Yet others still were alive, struggling to stay afloat, some struggled and writhed as they sank below the waves, but some seemed to move as elegant shadows beneath the surface.

The fighting did not last long. Once it was obvious which way the fight would go, the last ship of the enemy squadron broke and tried to run. Kusoasu aboard Poisoned Kiss chased them down. All the companies had taken casualties, it was unavoidable in the close packed grind of a naval battle, but two more ships had been seized and a further sunk.

The small fleet of now seven ships, moved into a cove on the nearby island to take stock, make repairs and treat the wounded. They would rest here and move on to Butophulo the next day, but the way was now clear. Sonos could not help the feeling of guilt creeping back. *Were they abandoning the White Islands once again to their fate?*

***

Sonosphoskul slept deeply that night, the deepest he had slept in many years.

The city sprawled before him, Butophulo in all its glory. It looked exactly as it had on that fateful day that he had departed, but somehow different. Bright, shining white, almost ablaze. He stood at the foot of Polriso's Hill, on the stage of the Kolmob, where all the great statesmen of the city had stood before him, using the platform to give voice to the city. The eyes of the statues of the city's greatest men staring down at him, as if trying to see into his very soul.

The sea glistened off in the distance, the morning light creeping over its mirror-like surface and into the city, inundating its streets with a gleaming white light. People, were flooding onto the seats now, streaming past the statues and Sonos. People he knew, people he had lost, some he had not seen for many a year. The last of them chilled him to his core.

Zolmos Kisurusosi, the Conjurer, his body bloody and bleeding from the thousand cuts that brought him low. Behind him Kolmosoi, his face still a deep red, his throat taught where the poison had strangled him, and black snaking tendrils writhed across his neck. Following on and soaked to the bone, Pitae, Kunae, Thil, Kivuun, Puso and even Sol walked past him, broken, and dragging himself as if he weighed as much as an anvil.

"Speak!" The crowd demanded, and so he spoke,

"We must return to the city!" he declared "The White Islands cannot stand alone; the god has decreed that the city must be freed from the Doldun."

Zolmos stood, he opened his mouth and only a dark black water poured out, a haunting voice underneath the surface,

"You abandon them now as you abandoned me."

"We didn't, we won't!" Sonos protested, but was he right, the feeling of guilt told him otherwise.

Kolmosoi rose, his tongue uncoiled, it was thick and black and his voice rasping and hissing,

"You fled when I died, and now when the time is ripe you flee again, towards this folly."

"We fled to survive, to return and fight. The god told us what we need to do." Sonos felt the conviction flee from his voice, he was on his knees now, salty tears rolling down his face. Then he felt a hand on his shoulder, a strong hand and a firm grip pulling him to his feet. The weathered face with aged lines that snaked across it greeting him was a welcome sight,

"Rise boy, you return because you must. To free the Salxosu the haven of the god must be liberated, even if that means your own death." Koseun Sisosi had a fatherly voice, soft and encouraging but with steel behind it, he turned to the accusing dead,

"The city will rise again; your deaths will not be in vain. Through your sacrifice we will become whole once more."

When the brightest star in the sky rose, the one which ushers in the dawn, Sonos awoke, dazed, and confused, but with a strange calm conviction. The ship was already moving by then drawing near to the land. Rolling hills and steep cliff sides greeted him as he awoke from his slumber. In the distance the distinct outline of a city was illuminated by the sun rising over the horizon. Still dazed from sleep, the thought crossed his mind, *what foreign country have we sailed to now? Did some storm strike us in the night and blow us across the sea once again whilst I slept so deeply? What battles lay ahead in this foreign land that we, who have endured so much, will have to endure once more?*

Sonos got to his feet and made his way to the prow of the ship as the fleet turned towards a small cove.

"Who gave the orders to sail?" He asked Dinon the Fisherman, who had the watch.

"Runukolkil sent the order, just before the last watch." Came the reply,

"Where are we?" Sonos said, still half asleep, his shoulders aching from the previous days battle.

"Xosupil. That is Butophulo in the distance. We are home."

Sonos took a step forward. *What a fool he had been, of course this was home.* He could not quite believe it, the silhouette of the city still looked alien to him, it had changed tremendously in the last decade. But the harder he stared the clearer it became. The sanctuary stood tall and indomitable, the great long walls running down to the harbour, the bustling merchant's port, were all lit up by the sun now streaming its way into the sky's blue realm.

He tried to answer Dinon, but his words caught in his throat. Instead, he patted him warmly on the shoulder and turned again to watch the city. It had been a long and hard journey back to his homeland, and hard fighting lay ahead, but for the moment none of that mattered. Butophulo may have stood for many things to many people. Freedom, liberty, the rule of law and good governance away from tyranny, all ideas which the men had carried with them wherever they went. But in truth nothing could replace the sight of Butophulo itself, the gleaming white metropolis, Sonosphoskul was home.

Thrice loosed his fierce horde, arrows shade all beneath!
Spears crack and swords may shatter, flee the hydra's teeth!
Fume, fury, foolish great king, firm footed we stand!
We fall on this field, blood to free the Sacred Land!

KALASYAR

41

Days, maybe even weeks, Kalasyar had lost track time, had passed and still these old men could not agree on a way forward. More used to the symposium or the academy and the hypothetical questions posed by philosophers than real action. She had come to despair that her grandfather's memory would be honoured in the way he had wished. The people of the city had done more than any of these men. As soon as the word spread that Koseun was to be executed, protests had flared up all over the city. A blacksmith had even led an angry mob to the gates of Puskison's villa and the Doldun garrison had been needed to restore order on the streets. But the promise of revolution had proved nothing more than that, a flicker of light, that was all.

Koseun had awoken three days after the poison took its grip and a moment of hope had grasped Kalasyar. Her grandfather had used the time to admonish his followers with some venom for their squabbling, but it was a false hope, a jest by some meddling god. In time Koseun had slid into sleep once more. His shade was finally taken by Sem, Koseun ushered to join his fraternity.

Now Kalasyar was numb and already weary of the future. She sat yet again in her grandfather's central hall, the room in which he hosted his many symposiums and intellectual pursuits, but now she was listening to Kolkobuas talking up his elaborate scheme to bring down the Nine, when all that was on her mind was vengeance.

"The allies we need are gathering to our cause. Friends in Pittuntik, Supokul and Riltuntik have written to me expressing their support. I am even hearing encouraging news from Pilsipon and Rulkison. With these allies on our side, the old League could even be reformed, like Buto's hammer forging these disparate elements back into one."

Kalasyar was looking at the gathered followers of her grandfather as Kolkobuas spoke. Old men, many too old for war, although they had seen their fair share, friends from her grandfather's time as the head of the Academy of Rolmit, but too many of the best had died during the last war or fled into exile. The others were too young and inexperienced to offer any real help, drawn to the cause by Koseun's reputation. All old and noble blood, Sisosi and Kolkisuasu were in the room, as well as Kisurusosi and Kinsol, but the Rososthup and Polriso were absent as well as the tyrant's kin. But none of those present were the leading members of their families, other than Kolkobuas and Pito Kinsol. Kolkobuas continued,

"The games at Thelonigul will take place in the summer. This offers the perfect opportunity to reach out to the other Xosu, beyond the boundaries of the old League. The Tilxosu and Silxosu chafe under the rule of the Doldun and the Rinuxosu may have invited Tekolger to invade, but they must surely regret those actions now. Huluthisn is a proud man and ambitious king, even if the Assembly of the Rinuxosu is wary of the Doldun. We can turn all the Xosu against the Doldun. A new war for our freedom, drive out the Doldun as we did Yoruxoruni."

A noise of approval echoed around the room as Kolkobuas finished, but Kalasyar could not help but feel that this was all a nonsense. A speech to show off to the mob, like a wandering philosopher or a demagogue boasting to the crowd for attention. She spoke up, cutting through the noise,

"With respect Kolkobuas, it is a fine plan in theory, unite the Xosu with a common purpose. Our people have been unstoppable in the past when someone has achieved that aim. You will be like Tholophos, or even Xosu, come again." She paused to let the sarcasm in her voice sink in, "But this all sounds like mere words. Letters of sympathy from friends in old League cities do not show that we have popular support. Indeed, even warm words of encouragement for our plans do not mean those who utter them will act."

The room fell silent. She knew many of the men there were not happy that she was included in their plans, but she did not care. Kolkobuas, for all his flaws, was slowly beginning to accept her thought and council. After a moment of consideration, he replied,

"There is truth in what you say Kalasyar. But we must build a foundation of support first, these words are an important first step, small as they may be. Further assistance will flood to us once we have created a solid base of support. Trying to act now would be foolish and rash and only serve to destroy us before we have the chance to build any base of power."

She knew that there was truth in that, but there must be something more that could be done,

"What of Dunobos? He wished to take some action, maybe we could find a middle ground between the two of you."

Kolkobuas sighed,

"Dunobos is a danger to himself and us I am afraid. He and his band of followers have decided that immediate and direct action against anyone who supports the Nine and the Doldun is the way forward. I fear he will do something brash, and he has taken with him all the Rusosthup."

The foolishness of both groups was only serving to frustrate Kalasyar further,

"He will only unite the Doldun and those Xosu who would rather an easy peace if he acts indiscriminately. If there is one thing people will loath and fear it is chaos on these streets."

"I know, but Dunobos did not take the death of your grandfather well. The desire for vengeance is consuming him." Kolkobuas said with a melancholy in his voice which betrayed his fear for his old friend.

She sat silent whilst the rest of Kolkobuas' followers talked of grand schemes to bring others to their cause. She knew Kolkobuas was correct, the only way to rid themselves of the Doldun was to unite all the Xosu against them, but such a thing was not an easy feat. Many had tried, and few had succeeded. Unless a strong hand was put over them, the Xosu had a tendency to scatter like leaves in the wind. The Rinuxosu kings still claimed the title High King of the Xosu, but it was a hollow claim at best, the kings of the Rinuxosu did not even hold unrivalled power in their own lands. Not since the days of Tildun more than eight hundred years ago, before the sack of old Kolbos and the fall of the old kingdoms, had one man ruled all the Xosu, and only Tholophos and Xosu himself had managed to do so with any skill or longevity. She laughed to herself as she realised that it took a god to give the Xosu any sense of unity.

Kalasyar could not help but feel that all this talk of grand alliances was folly anyway. They lacked the men and resources to seize control of Butophulo never mind the whole of Xosupil. For that they would need a tool, a weapon to beat the Nine and drive off the Doldun. A hammer, like that wielded by the crippled god, to descend from the sky and smash the cruel tyrants and forge the world anew. But where or how they could find such a thing alluded her and her only real concern now was vengeance. On the Nine if she could get it, but more importantly on the man pulling their strings, the man who had deceived her and taken advantage of her.

* * *

The temple of Buto had always been a place of solace for her, and even though she did not feel as comfortable there as she used to, it still offered a sanctuary to reflect. Sipenkiso had always been willing to listen to Kalasyar and she was a wise woman with a direct conduit to the Great God and had become a maternal figure for her in the years since her mother passed. Whatever the differences between her and Sipenkiso, surely the Great God would wish to see those who would see his city restored to prominence succeed.

Inside the temple of Buto, she paused and did something she had not done before. She approached the altar to the crippled god, who had been nursed back to health by the Kinsolsun after being cast from Dzottgelon by Dunsun. Kalasyar whispered to Sem's son.

"You, who knows the pain of loss, and what it is to struggle in a world who sees you as weak, show me the way to succeed. To free your city from the grip of tyranny. Give me a weapon to drive them out."

The blood and gore of a recent sacrifice to Buto was still thick on the altar. She ran her fingers across the top and anointed herself with the lifeblood given to the god. She then took the flask of wine left there by the priests and poured herself a cup. Approaching the white gold statue of Buto placed to oversee his altar, she poured a libation to the god and then drank deep. The liquid was rich and dark and almost burned as it washed down her throat. It felt good, as if the god would hear her prayer and look favourably on his loyal servant.

As ever, the sanctuary of the Great God, below his son's temple, was alive with activity, the nine priestesses busy about their work maintaining his domain. The noise of the flowing water from the natural springs which fed the city the only thing cutting through the silence. The springs were hidden under ground now, the only place they could be seen on the surface was on Polriso's Hill or flowing out of the city's numerous fountains.

The priestesses Kalasyar passed acknowledged her with a look, but no words were passed between them, they moved like shapeless shadows in their long flowing blue robes. She did not care; she was here to find the quiet and solace of the Great God. She took a seat before the statue of Sem and began to think.

The city could be freed with the right tools, she knew this to be true. The Nine were weak and unpopular, the Doldun garrison small and the attention of the Doldun's rulers was elsewhere. If a strong hand were shown she was sure that the people would side with her, and the Nine tyrants could be overthrown without much bloodshed. Where such tools were to be found alluded her though. Sellswords would fight for the highest bidder, and she could not hope to match the Nine for funding whilst they controlled the city. What fighting men the city once had were either in exile or had been taken west with Tekolger to be left in garrisons scattered across his vast new realm. What men there were left in the city were young green boys, the best of which had been taken to be educated as the guardians of the Nine. Even if they would fight against their masters, they likely would not stand a chance against the seasoned mercenaries in the Nine's employ, especially with the Doldun garrison in the fight too.

Any foreign power willing to send soldiers would just replace one tyranny with another and the only country capable of doing so was Gelodun. With the talk of that country's king lying dead at the gates of Gottoy, and crisis brewing in Gelodun over the succession, if the rumours coming from the docks were to be believed, it seemed an unlikely prospect. Further talk of an army marching from Gottoy to take revenge on the Xosu had also come to nothing. Besides, she did not think Gottoy would be interested in provoking the wrath of the Doldun.

"What troubles you child?" The flowing voice was unmistakable. Kalasyar looked up to see Sipenkiso stood over her, a maternal smile on her maiden-like lips with the wisdom of age passing between,

"I find myself at an impasse. I wish to see the Great God restored and to carry out my grandfather's final wishes but lack the tools to do so." She found herself relaying, Sipenkiso had a kind face and a soft voice, tranquil like a gently flowing waterfall over a small cliff.

"Do not despair. We despair when we run into a wall and can see no way through. You must be like water, water which flows around anything which would block its path. Your grandfather's death, that was…not what we wanted, exile to Doldun would have served us all better. But there are some among us who prefer struggle. That is not the way of the sea…but the Nine are weak men who believe that violence shows their strength. Look to the Great God, he will guide you."

Sipenkiso squeezed her shoulder and left Kalasyar to her contemplation.

She stood and approached the pool, gazing at the statue of the Great God beyond it. As she reached the edge, she grasped the raised side of the pool tightly in her hand, looking intently toward the god for inspiration. The blood of the sacrifice to Buto was still sticky on her fingers, as she lifted her hand from the edge of the pool, she left several bloody fingerprints. A fresher bead of blood trickled down the side and plunged into the water, leaving a red trail in its wake.

In that moment, the Great God's statue seemed to glint, as if it caught in the first rays of the sun on a crisp winter's day. The gentle flow of the water turned to a rush as it began to spin and a hole in its centre opened. *The god is speaking to me,* she thought. He had heard her prayers and was answering. Kalasyar knew what to do, she plunged her head into the swirling pool, the salty water washing into her mouth and stinging her eyes as she entered the watery realm.

She was in the shadowy chamber again. Familiar yet strange, the serpent writhed, restless around the honeycombed walls and the white gold rock glowed in front of her. The nine shapeless figures sat enthroned before her once more, watery shadows she could barely see. One of their number rose and filled the cup again. This time she was ready and drank willingly, she felt a power well up inside her, like the glowing forge of the smith brought to life.

The wraith motioned for her to come to the edge of the crater in which the white gold rock sat, and her feet carried her forward with no hesitation. The rock looked lost in the centre, the crater dwarfing it in size. The shadow signalled again.

Two other blue spectres appeared, dragging a man in full panoply to the edge of the crater, on his cuirass there was a garlanded bull, blood red. The first shadow turned to Kalasyar, as if from nowhere, a pale sickle shaped knife appeared in its hand, offered to her hilt first. In that moment she learnt her lesson and knew what she must do. A poisoned, sickening feeling washed over her, but then she felt the heat of the wine grow inside her again, forging her spirit anew.

She took the blade in hand; it was impossibly sharp. In one swift movement, elegant as a dancer, she drew the knife across the warrior's throat. The blood flowed like a torrent, flooding over the white gold altar, which willingly drank the sacrifice and glowed with delight. Then there was an almighty crash, one of the shadows raising a flashing gold hammer to the sky and bringing it down on the white gold rock with a furious roar. The sound shook her to the core and resonated around the chamber as if a key had been turned and a great bronze door was rumbling open. The spectres stood and chanted in a language she did not know, like the rushing torrent of the sea it sounded. From the glowing rock a strange mist poured forth and engulfed her. She heard the creak of wood and the wash of waves against a shore. Through the dense mist and a rolling sea, the hint of the sun rising behind them, she saw blue, and sea green shadows appear. All wielded Buto's hammers with a poisonous fury, casting down her enemies as they advanced towards her, emerging from the sea to save her. Lurking in the shadowed background, away from the others who seemed not to see him, there was one wanderer who stood out to her most prominently of all.

***

She stumbled out into the street in something of a daze, the saltwater burning her mouth and stinging her eyes, her head spinning and delirious, but for all that she had found a new sense of purpose. Kalasyar did not know where or how she would succeed, but the Great God had shown her something, he had given her his blessing. It was enough to give her hope.

As her eyes adjusted to the light of the day and the rawness of the saltwater subsided, the street flooded with colour. Something was wrong, people were running, swiftly moving away from the centre of the city, shouts and screams echoing like hammers in the distance. She looked toward the centre of the city, in the shadow of Polriso's Hill, a plume of smoke was rising, a ripple of flame peaking over the rooves.

Instinctively, Kalasyar moved toward the flames, walking against the crowd which rushed away from the danger in a great wave. Eager to see what was happening she slid her way through the press, but in the pit of her stomach she feared the worst.

Fighting through the crowd, she made slow progress down the street, the pillar of smoke was still way off in the distance when she felt a hand grab her.

"We need to leave!" She heard, turning to see Kolkobuas, her handmaids behind him,

"What is going on?" She asked, dreading the answer she feared. Before she could get a reply, a scream rang through the crowd and sellswords appeared at the end of the street. Kolkobuas pulled on her arm harder,

"We need to leave the city now! I'll tell you everything later." Kolkobuas said forcefully.

Kalasyar would usually have argued and been given her answer eventually, but the mercenaries were advancing swiftly, arresting people who got in their way. *They are looking for someone*, she thought.

She turned and pulled her veil over her face, moving with the crowd toward the Gate of the God.

* * *

The Academy of Rolmit was exactly as she remembered it, the Apiary as many called it, although it was in a somewhat sorry state of disrepair. It had been a famous place once, almost sacred. The site where the wandering philosopher Rolmit of Rulkison had settled to teach his philosophies, his gathered followers building the Academy for him as a place to rest and spread his teachings. But now the olive trees had grown wild and unkept, but worse, the bees, whose music she loved as a child, were gone, their hives ruined husks. Only the whitewashed walls of the Academy looked untouched by decay and neglect. She had spent every summer of her childhood playing on the grounds of the Academy, the rich olive plantation against the side of the hills and the numerous coves, caves, and hulthul trees which dotted the cliffs and overlooked the sea.

Rolmit of Rulkison had come to Butophulo after travelling the whole of the Xosu world. Famous for his hedonistic love of pleasure. A misunderstanding of his teachings her grandfather had insisted, he had advocated delving deep into one's emotions to seek the truth of those feelings. The Academy had quickly grown to rival that of Kunpit of Thelonigul, which could be found to the north of the city. Rolmit's reputation had soon come to rival the older mans. So much so that Dinon Kosua, Kunpit's greatest pupil, had felt the need to write a dialogue of a conversation between the two, called *On the Greatness of old Kolbos*, which Dinon insisted took place in the grounds of Rolmit's academy and proved Kunpit the superior philosopher. Koseun had always said that interpretation depended on who the reader was.

'From the great multiplicity of thoughts and feelings we will find one purpose' he was supposed to have said. *'From many comes one'* was all the average man new of his teachings.

Kalasyar was only young when her grandfather was head of the Academy, but the memories she had of that time where dear to her. However, like with so many other things that she remembered fondly from her childhood, the Nine had put a stop to it. Along with music, poetry and art which did not meet their approval, they had closed the academies and banished the wandering philosophers. The Academy had lain abandoned ever since.

However, with Dunobos' folly days before, the Academy had once again come to serve a useful purpose. Dunobos' band of followers had attempted an attack on Puskison and Doltopez as they had walked through the agora. The attack had ended as badly as might be expected and the Nine's response swift, unleashing their mercenaries into the city, with lists of prescribed names to hunt down. Kalasyar, Kolkobuas and his followers had fled the city, unsure if their names were on the lists. Some had fled for the White Islands, abandoning the city entirely. Pito and his Kinsol had gone that way, easy when they had the ships and money needed to disappear. The others who could not reach the port in time, or lacked the resources, sat in the Academy, impotent and debating whether to follow their companions into exile, desperately searching for a ship to take them away. What had become of the others, including her kin, she could not say. No word from the city had reached them since they fled, and they dare not make their presence in the Academy too well known. Although she supposed that the tyrant's men would come searching the old place soon enough.

With waiting for the appearance of the mercenaries and the indecision of Kolkobuas' followers, Kalasyar's patience had all but run out. People who could not even come to a firm decision whether to flee for their lives or not were clearly not of the substance needed to free a city from tyranny and avenge her grandfather. Only the Great God was left to her now and she would follow his signs and look for the shadows from the mist.

The morning was crisp and clear, a single star hung in the sky before the sun had risen above the horizon. She found the crashing of the sea against the cliffs calling to her. Before her fellow conspirators had risen from their slumber, she headed out of the estate toward the caves carved into the cliff face by the sea, where she spent her summers playing as a child.

She reached the top of the cliffs, slightly breathless. The climb had seemed effortless as a child, but not now. The morning light was crawling across the sea, slowly bringing light back to the world, the dawn mist retreating in the light of the sun. The sky was clear, a brilliant blue, seemingly merging with the sea on the horizon. The world was quiet, save for the sound of the sea lapping against the foot of the cliff.

The rhythm of the sea drew her eye to the south. Her eyes following the line of the cliffs reminded her of the hidden cove around the headland where she would play when she was a young girl, ruling her own city as an enlightened philosopher king. Her friends would serve as the soldiers and merchants and workers. The memory made her shudder as she thought of Puskison and his council of philosophers. Nonetheless she found herself walking along the edge of the cliff, following its contours. She scanned as she walked, looking for a small indent hidden by a smattering of hulthul trees. Only those who knew where to look would see it. She walked to the edge of the cliffs, scrambling down the face, a few loose rocks slipping over the edge as she did. Composing herself, she turned and looked west, where the cliffs turned inward, revealing what she sought. In the otherwise straight line of cliffs was concealed a small sandy cove lined with caves. But what she saw within the cove hit her like a hammer. The shadow of a ship's mast. *No, it could not be? no ships ever put in here, the waters are too treacherous.*

She walked further along the cliffs to see more of the small bay, another mast appeared, then another. As the whole of the cove came into view, Kalasyar could see at least five triremes beached on the small sandy cove, men swarming around them like so many bees, others still emerging from the caves. They were too far away to make out in any detail. They were not Doldun, perhaps more Xosu mercenaries hired by the Nine. If so, the Academy was in danger. *But why would they be beached here? No, maybe, they are hiding from the Nine?*

Footsteps behind her drew Kalasyar's attention back to the cliffs. She turned quickly, two men in full Xosu panoply stood before her. Her heart beat out a heavy rhythm. The men approached her, she felt the bind of deaths hands coil around her neck, and she once again felt powerless in this world of men.

She did not know what happened next. Her legs took her, she broke free of the bounds constricting her and fled. Over the rise of the cliffs and back towards the Academy. *I must warn the others* she thought. She heard a cry and a muffled shout behind her.

She bounded over the hills and down through the terraced rows of olive trees, passed the dry-stone walls and through the long dead beehives.

More cries went up, in front of her now. As she passed through the whitewashed walls of the Academy she saw why. Mercenaries of the Nine, this time she knew for sure, swarming the grounds. She froze on the spot as if struck by Dunsun's thunderbolt. Two of the mercenaries in fully panoply broke off from the group entering the building and began to advance towards her. Their shouts shook her from her stupor and her legs took her once again back towards the white walls.

She burst through the gateway and out into the olive groves, but then Dunsun hit her with a second strike. Her legs tangled and she tumbled to the floor. Her heart was pounding now, the blood thudding and thumbing in her ears. She rolled over and tried to scramble to her feet. Up to her knees, but then a third blow hit her, and she collapsed to the floor as the mercenary loomed over her.

A grinning face behind the terror of a helmet as the man pushed her onto her back and grabbed her dress. She tried to scream, but her voice caught in her throat. She shut her eyes tight. A laugh rumbled, she raised her arms and tried to fight, but to no avail. Then a shout echoed, and the world seemed to stop.

"Leave her!"

The weight of the man on top of her suddenly eased. She opened her eyes. The mercenary was standing now, head down like a scolded child.

"One noble born woman we are looking for, you were told. The Doldun want her, untouched." The voice said with some anger.

"It is just a household slave sir, fair game."

"Look at her clothes, look at her baring! That navy black hair and piercing blue eyes, she may as well be the blood of the crippled god himself, unmistakably the blood of old Kolbos you fool. You are lucky I do not hand you over to the Doldun and be done with it. Get out of my sight!"

The mercenary shuffled off quickly and a second man appeared in her sight. A horizontal crest across his flashing bronze helmet to mark him out as an officer. The man offered his hand and helped her to her feet.

"Please accept my apologies my lady."

Kalasyar shot him as scornful and petrifying look as she could muster, but to little effect.

"If you would come with me, please. The Doldun have requested your presence on Polriso's Hill."

KALU

42

The moon was full, the only light in the dark canvas above to illuminate their way. Kalu whispered an invocation to Tholo, the white goddess, to offer them her protection. The old ferry bobbed up and down in the water and felt as if it may fall apart at any moment, despite the calm river. The ferryman looked as though he may fall apart himself. Old and dishevelled as he was with an unkempt beard and a dirty cloak hung over his shoulders, but his eyes had lit up when he saw the gold they offered him to make the crossing in the middle of the night.

Kalu pulled his own cloak around himself to cover the hilt of Vigilance. He wore the cloak in the reverse, the cream colour marking him as one of the king's White Shields now on the underneath and the black lining on top. He did not trust the ferryman, or anyone else in the village who may have seen them.

They were only a small party, Kalu, the two burley eunuchs and Surson, but any visitors to one of the small villages that dotted the banks of the Kelonzow river would be noticed. The whole thing was making him anxious. Surson had insisted that they needed to see Kelbal in person. Kalu could not refuse her. *'Protect my legacy'* Tekolger's words still rung in his ears, yet here he was walking Surson into the camp of a traitor.

Even dressed in the clothes of a common merchant's wife, Tekolger's Xortogun bride was as mesmerising as he remembered. Surson Tora Ya Kuria a daughter of an old and respected priestly family of Kurotormub and a direct descendent of Yoruxoruni. She embodied the beauty of the fabled land of Xortogun, delicate skin almost red in its hue with dark bronze hair and dark eyes to match, but with a hint of red behind them which spoke of a sharp and fertile mind. Yet despite her nobility and otherworldly beauty, she had an earthiness to her and a fierce spirit.

She had been a controversial pick for a wife of the King of the Doldun, even more so than the Zummosh bride Tekolger had taken years before. Tekolger had married her after he liberated the great valley and was crowned its king despite the misgivings of some of his generals. What better way to add legitimacy to his rule than to marry the direct heir of the last native king of Xortogun. With her Tekolger believed he could produce a worthy heir, a king to unite all the peoples of the world. She had proved ever formidable and equal to the task presented to her. More than that, she had brought the loyalty of her people to Tekolger, a people as old and respected as any. Despite what some of the Doldun thought, Tekolger had known that the Xortogun would be needed to fulfil his vision, their knowledge of the world invaluable.

When he had seen her and her new-born son, the heir to the empire, after their arrival at Torfub the grief over Tekolger's death had come flooding back to Kalu. The reality of the threat to Tekolger's legacy had never felt more real, and Zenu's betrayal had shown him that danger could come from anywhere, more so from those he trusted most.

The northern army had arrived at the city of Torfub seven days previously. A fear had gripped him as they advanced on the city, knowing that Pelu of the Deltathelon had been raised to the command there. Kalu had imagined the worst for Surson and the child. Even so Torfub had still struck him like it did the first time he had come to the city for Tekolger's crowning as king of the great valley. Torfub was a strange city, not large in comparison to the other cites of Xortogun, but, in its maze of streets and monumental nature, dwarfing anything seen among the Doldun or even in Xosupil.

The city was circular in shape, dissected by the three rivers which entered from the west, they merged into a single river in the city's heart, which flowed east into the great valley. Looming over the walls was a forest of towers built from the strange iron coloured ore which marked the great valley and decorated with gold. They were like huge fingers striking up towards the sky as if grasping for the heavens. In the centre another tower stood, taller than all the others and built of the white stone common in the area, with a great palace at its heart, the Floating Palace as it was known around the world.

When they had come to the city for Tekogler's coronation, they had been told by the priests that each of the towers had been built at the height of the old kingdom by priestly families competing for the favour of the gods. Then one of the god-kings of the great valley had taken up residence in the city to be closer to his southern frontier to fight off raiders from the deserts. He had raised the central tower and seized all the others, linking them with a series of bridges to form a palace in the sky.

Once inside the walls, the trunks of the glistening towers overshadowed everything. The servants of the various temples and the palace lived in the space between the towers, forever in their shadow, but the bridges which linked the dwellings of the gods meant that the priests and royalty rarely had to set foot in the lower town. It was the position of the city that made it so valuable though. At the point the rivers merged into one and where the mountains rose in the north and the sea in the south, it acted as the gateway between Zowdel and Xortogun, a door from one realm to another.

The ferry lurched forward as the ferryman pushed on his oar again, the whole craft swayed and for a moment Kalu thought they would fall into the water and death would take them there. The ferry soon steadied though, and the far bank of the river came into view, an earthy realm previously hidden from them, and a firm footing. Surson had been adamant that she would meet with Kelbal and look the traitorous Companion's in the eye. Kalu had been wary, and he had only agreed once he had learnt more of what had happened to Kelbal.

He had taken her a few leagues down river when the royal army arrived, insisting that they approach the army from the opposite direction to the city. They had sent trusted men to the army when it had pitched camp, to contact the White Shields and find answers as to what had happened to Kelbal and the other Companions.

To his great relief, the men reported that Kelbal lived, and they had found the soldiers who had been protecting him. They had also reported rumours of tension between the Companions and Zenukola. It was those reports which had seen Kalu relent and agree to take the risk, perhaps the sight of him alive and in the flesh, and the knowledge that Surson had given birth to a worthy heir, would remind the Companions of their loyalty and help them see through Zenu's treachery.

The arrangements had been made for Kalu and Surson to meet Kelbal at the camp and allow the small group to slip in unseen. The whole affair was making him fearful though, it may have been too much of a risk for Surson to descend into the realm of their foe. He should have gone alone.

It was the same fear he had when they had entered the city. Supo had left the army to set up camp outside Torfub, on the north bank of the Kelonzow river. Then he had taken his bodyguard and entered the city in force. Kalu had worn the cloak and armour of one of Supo's men so as not to alert Pelu to what was happening.

In the end that had not mattered, Supo had marched into the throne room of the Floating Palace at a pace, barely pausing to take a breath. Pelu had only the time to turn and greet Supo before the general had drawn his sword and thrust it into Pelu's gut. In his last moments, Pelu's eyes had caught Kalu's as death swallowed him. The flash of recognition was a sight which would never leave him, the visage of confusion, betrayal and failure was something he never hoped to experience himself. Supo's actions had made him uncomfortable as well, it was too rash, too reckless. Something he had expected from Dolzalo and Palmash, but not the veteran general.

He looked toward the far bank of the river and the camp beyond, if such discord and lust for war took over him as it had Supo then only disaster would follow. The ferry bumped into the far bank and Surson's two eunuch bodyguards leapt onto the shore. Kalu stood and followed them, helping Surson to step onto the colourless earth and thanking Xosu for their safe passage.

***

The camp of the royal army was a black mark on the horizon. From the rows of tents behind the earthwork ramparts and wooden palisade the sounds of song and drinking floated towards them. That was a good sign, the men's guard would be down.

As Kalu had arranged with the agents inside the camp, they approached the eastern gate at the start of the third watch, with the moon at its highest point. Men he trusted from his White Shields would have the gate at that time. Nonetheless they approached with caution. Kalu led the way, ordering the eunuchs to hang back out of sight with Surson.

He pulled his cloak over his head, his hand drifted to the hilt of Vigilance. He moved as close as he dared to the wooden walls and stopped and waited, crouching in a thicket of coarse bushes. Three men were at the entrance, alert, looking out into the black of the night. Their faces obscured by the dark; they could easily have been menacing hell hounds for all he could see. Kalu froze, *were they his men? Had he been betrayed again?*

One of the men strode over to the others, they paused to talk and then looked back into the camp. The first man then lowered his spear and hung a white cloth on the point raising it up above his head. The material glittered a silvery white in the moonlight, that was the signal.

He got to his feet and whistled like a hawk. The three men looked over and Kalu swiftly moved towards them. As the faces became clearer to him in the darkness, recognition of his loyal White Shields eased his anxiety. Tepo of the Dolozaloz, Dazkeltel of the Zelkalkel and Kensunazu of the Zelrsaloz. As he walked, the men looked upon him as if they had seen the shade of a man long dead and gone. He wanted to say something, but no words would pass his lips, a single tear rolled down his cheek as his men crowded him. The look of confusion on their faces turning to delight, like a hungry hound greeting a master who had just returned from a long voyage. They closed in to clasp their commander by the hand and confirm that he really was alive and well. Kalu knew in that moment that he need not say anything. He turned to signal Surson to come forward.

The men took them to a tent near the eastern gate. All four of them slipped inside and sat waiting in the dark. Four other White Shields arrived and set a fire by the entrance, sitting to drink and talk as if this were a tent like any other.

They sat patiently for what seemed like an age, Kalu was determined to keep an outward façade of stoicism despite the turmoil he felt within. Even seeing old loyal friends, he could not shake the fear of betrayal, it was something he had never experienced before. He was thankful that the usually headstrong Surson was quiet, she must have felt the tension as well.

Soon enough though the tent flap opened again, and three others stepped inside. Dressed in common soldier's uniforms, but when they raised their heads Kalu recognised them immediately. Zela of the Zelkalkel, Deluan of the Balkakel and Polazul of the Kolbun.

Zela smiled in that way he always did. Outwardly pleased to see him, but the man was too clever by half and would have immediately understood what it meant for Kalu to be alive, even if his eyes gave nothing away. Polazul and Deluan, drew an intriguing look on their faces, a combination of shock, delight and disappointment displayed all at once. Reflecting, Kalu saw it clearly now, the Companions were brothers in arms, childhood friends and deadly rivals all at the same time. Zenukola had in many ways been the only thing keeping them from tearing themselves and the empire apart now that Tekolger was gone.

Zela stepped forward and grasped his hand,

"Gods it is good to see you Kalu. We were all devastated, shocked even, when Zenukola told us you had been slain." Zela said, "I think that is exactly what he intended, shock us, weaken us, and divide us so he could take power."

Kalu greeted them all warmly, Zela had just confirmed all he needed to know. There was enough regret in these three, and they knew now that Zenukola was doomed. Kelbal would have their support again.

"It is good to see your faces too. I feared for the worst when Supo told me what had happened." He turned and motioned for Surson to come forward.

"I am sure you all remember Surson Tora Ya Kuria. She has come here in person to urge you to stand strong against the threats from Zenukola."

The three men greeted Surson with great courtesy, as would be expected.

"Thank you for meeting us here." she said in a low voice that shook with the tones of the land of Xortogun, "I know you take great risks to do so. But I wanted to come to tell you that a son was born to your king. He has the blood of Xosu, Tholophos, Yoruxoruni and Tekolger coursing through his veins. Kalu here and Supo saved him from Pelu, and I hope now that you and your comrades will do the same, save the legacy that was left by your king."

Her words were met with approval from all three men, now more eager than ever to show their loyalty to the heir they were questioning only days before. The affirmation of loyalty out the way, Kalu asked,

"What can you tell me of the army and the other Companions?"

Zela spoke on behalf of the others,

"The army is content for now, although they know little of what has actually happened. Zenu has been careful to placate them. As for the other Companions, Zenu's hold over them is weak at best. Thazan follows him as he believes he can acquire power for himself and his clan. I doubt that loyalty would last for long if the situation changed. Zalmetaz has decided to take what Zenu says at face value, you know what he is like, he will change his mind when he learns the truth. Zonpeluthas believes that Zenu will ensure he has a command, he even has his eye on your White Shields, again his loyalty only runs that deep. As for the others, I believe Dolzalo and Palmash are with you and the twins were dispatched north with the veterans most loyal to Kelbal."

"Good, I will send riders to bring them back here as soon as I can. What about Zenu?"

"I think Silver Eye has his mind on other matters. He believes you dead and Kelbal broken, he also found Dalzenu guilty of the crimes he was accused of and holds him captive still. But he knows his power is not absolute yet. I was able to challenge him and extract a compromise on some issues. This is why Zenu raced to Torfub. If Silver Eye had arrived with Pelu in charge, Tekolger's heir in his hands and that army of yours under his command, he would be unchallengeable." Zela replied.

"Yes, he came within a breath of succeeding, it is only through the favour of the gods that he failed, although it has come at some cost. He still believes his plans are intact?" Kalu inquired.

"I believe so, although he is concerned that he has had no word from Pelu for a number of days."

"He won't have any word from Pelu again." Kalu answered with a deliberate satisfaction the others were sure to note.

"He intends on arriving at the city tomorrow. We have only camped here for the night so that Zenu can arrive fresh in the morning, with an honour guard of Companion's and White Shields at his back." Zela finished.

"And that will be his undoing. See if you can speak to the other Companions, and make sure that my White Shields are ready to support us in Torfub. It will all be over before Zenu realises his plans have shattered." Kalu answered, this was the part of the game he understood best, it was almost like any other military operation. Zela nodded, "Your men will be ready, and I will speak to the other Companions. But for now, we must leave you. Zenu is hosting a banquet in the royal tent, our absence will be noted."

Kalu nodded and the Companions made another affirmation of loyalty to Surson and Tekolger's son before they slipped back out into the night.

* * *

Before long they could hear the music from the royal tent echoing around the camp. The tent flap opened once again, a flash of light from the fire illuminating them, another man was led inside.

Once his eyes adjusted to the light of the dimly lit tent again, Kalu could hardly believe the man he saw in front of him. Dishevelled and bearded, wild in his complexion and appearance, the Xortogun robe he wore, and his mismatched eyes, were all that gave him away.

Kelbal looked up and blinked,

"Do my eyes deceive me or is this some god playing a cruel trick upon me. Kalu?"

Kalu said nothing, words did not come, as if Tholo had taken his tongue. Instead, he just nodded and smiled. Kelbal embraced him warmly as the sun,

"My old friend, I cannot tell you how it gladdens me to see you. When Zenu told me of your death, I...I must admit the shock almost broke me, my shade cast out in madness. The loss of Tekolger was a blow like a thunderbolt, the loss of you a second strike."

"Zenu lied Kelbal. He tried to have me killed, if it were not for Supo I would not be stood here now." Kalu answered.

"He turned the Companions against me, I fear he plans to seize the kingship." Kelbal said with trepidation in his voice.

"It seems he was the traitor in our midst all along." Kalu answered, "Tekolger's death may even have been by his hand, circumstances would fit that explanation. But my own brush with mortality and seeing the threat to Tekolger's legacy close has given me a new clarity. I feel like I have been reborn, Yulthelon spinning a new thread for me. Together we must do all we can to ensure the fruition of Tekolger's legacy. An empire of all the peoples of east and west, and we must protect it from enemies from without and within." he paused, "I saw him Kelbal, he came to me in a vision and told me to protect his legacy."

Kelbal looked straight at him, he seemed to stand taller as Kalu spoke, his old flamboyant gregarious shade returning, the fire returning to his amber eye,

"Then you have done more than I have yet achieved to keep that legacy secure. Tekolger would have been proud of your efforts and has sent you back to me to avenge him. What of the other Companions?"

"Dolzalo and Palmash are with me they knew nothing of Zenu's plans. The twins match north as you know, Silver Eye likely wanted them out of the way. The others I think were manipulated by Zenu's lies like the rest of us. But that doesn't excuse the fact that they went along with the plan to dispose of you." Kalu was sure of what he was saying, what needed to happen. "But let us not be hasty. This brush with disaster has shown that we cannot continue with things the way they are, but neither can we let vengeance consume us. If we begin to fight amongst ourselves then all will be lost.

We need a new settlement, give the Companions some small power of their own, something else to focus on. We can divide them, make them Togworwohs of the provinces, whilst we build a strong royal court at the centre. It will strengthen the empire." Kalu replied assuredly. Then he turned to the waiting Surson,

"Surson has come to see you as well."

"I cannot tell you how much it gladdens my heart to see you well my lady." Kelbal said as the Xortogun woman approached him, "And the child?"

"Tekolger's son is well, he is strong and bold like his father." Surson replied with a smile. "I will put my faith in you to see him sat upon the Amber Throne." She continued as she embraced the Companion.

"It will be done." Kalu answered, "Tomorrow you must ride with Zenu to Torfub, behave as if nothing has changed, but Zenukola rides into a trap. Pelu is already slain at Supo's hand, the northern army is ours. Zela will bring the other Companions back to us and my White Shields stand ready."

Kelbal nodded and replied,

"Very well, now you must take Surson back to the palace before you are spotted here. It is too dangerous to linger much longer."

They left as the moon began its descent. Kalu thanked Tholo for her protection.

ZENUKOLA

43

He had chosen to wear his full panoply for his entrance into the city. It was a decision Zenukola had taken a long time to ponder, but the armour of a warrior of the Doldun made the most sense. It was how the people of Xortogun understood their new rulers and the soldiers of the Doldun would expect their new supreme commander to be dressed as one of them.

It had been long years since Zenu had worn a full battle dress, not since he lost his arm and his king in battle. When the slaves set the breast plate on him, it felt heavy, much more so than he remembered. No matter though, it was only a burden he need carry a short while, by the end of the day he would regain the crown, if not the king and the arm. The Deltathelon would be able to lead the other clans towards civilisation once again.

He had ordered the army to halt and build its camp just out of sight of Torfub, so that he could approach the city fresh with the dawn, making an impressive display of the return of the royal host. One more short uncomfortable march and the supreme power would be in his hands, he would not have to compromise again.

The memory of that night of debate was bitter. Zela had led the mutiny against him, arguing fiercely against his decision to give Keluaz land to expand Tekolgertep, instead pushing for the status quo to be maintained. *Zela will need to be dealt with before long, elsewise he will become a focal point for resistance.* The Companions had argued the decision into the depths of the night, unable to decide. In the end Zenu had won a small victory of sorts, getting them to agree to uphold ancient privileges whilst maintaining the status quo. Which meant that the Temple of Xura would take the land, but, with the Temple under the authority of Tekolgertep, the city would still expand as a result.

It was the last time that Zenu would be forced into such a position. Supo and Pelu waited for him at Torfub, with the northern army and Surson and her child secured. Once he entered the Floating Palace, Zenu's power would become almost unassailable, and he would no longer have to deal with these petty squabbling men. His phantom hand twitched.

With his armour fitted, Zenu picked up his Rinuxosu style helmet with the blue and white horsehair crest running horizontally across the top and tucked it under his arm. One of his guardsmen lifted the flap of his tent and Zenu stepped out into the morning sunlight to see the camp frantic with activity as the men took it apart in preparation for their march to Torfub. A column of horse was already prepared to leave, waiting just beyond the entrance to the camp.

Zenu's own guardsmen would lead the column led by the golden coffin of the king, with Zenu and the Companions in the centre and a tail of White Shields behind. All wearing their ceremonial armour, to put on a show for the people of Torfub.

Zenu mounted his horse with aide from a slave, the weight of the armour too much for him to lift himself up with one hand. He rode out to his waiting column. The Companions were already assembled, their scarlet cloaks and zilthum lined armour flashing in the morning sun. Behind them a guard of White Shields wearing their pale masks which made them seem spectres rather than men. Even Kelbal was there, and for once he looked sober and had even braided and oiled his beard.

Zenu said nothing as he approached, he just took his place at the head of the Companions and nodded to his captains to march on. A trumpet blasted and the column sprung into life.

* * *

Zenu kept his eye fixed on the horizon for the entire ride from the camp. As Dunsun took his seat on his golden throne and the sun emerged, the towers of the city were revealed glittering in the distance, like Dzottgelon itself, appearing to rise directly out of the river.

The towered city stood at the gateway to the great valley of Xortogun, holding the key to the fabled fertile valley. Whoever controlled Torfub could also impose their will on Xortogun beyond. As the old kingdoms dawned, the towered city had even been the seat of kings itself. Priestly men, independent and implacably opposed to the god-kings who ruled from the mouth of the great river. In the time before the sun set on that rich kingdom, the god-kings had moved their seat to Torfub after seizing control of it, best placed as it was to defend against incursions from Zenian and the deserts of the south. An even more pressing task after

Zowdel fell to the Dusk.

As the column streaked closer to the city, Zenu realised that this was the farthest east and closest he had been to Doldun in years. The thought filled him with a sense of joy and nostalgia, but he could not help the fear creeping in as well. His silver eye itched at the thought as his phantom hand grasped for the reins. He muttered an invocation to Yulthelon, hoping that his return east would be one in triumph.

Supo's northern forces would be waiting near the city. With their support he could sure up the position he had tenuously secured and set about building a stable and prosperous empire for the Doldun under the stewardship of the Deltathelon. Without that he dreaded what may happen. The Doldun were a fierce people. It had taken the great, semi divine, efforts of Kenkathoaz to tame that ferocity and direct it toward a singular goal. Without a firm hand to guide them, Zenu knew that his countrymen would descend back into civil war and the infighting which plagued their past. He would not let that happen. The memories of the defiance of the clans still haunted him. Kenkathoaz was a brilliant man and a formidable king, but it had taken all his strength and endurance to keep the kingdom from fracturing into a thousand pieces. That effort laid the foundations for everything the Doldun had achieved since then.

If only Kenkathoaz could see it all now, if he could see Zenukola now, he would not believe what his people had accomplished or the power they held.

This would also be the last time he would have to clean up the mess Tekolger left in his wake. As indomitable as the king had been, he was also prone to creating problems and leaving loose ends to be tied up, a task which usually fell to Zenu. Although this one was more of Kelbal and the Xortogun's making. *I warned Tekolger about trusting them.*

He found himself thinking back to Tekolger's youth and the burden of the oath he had sworn to Kenkathoaz to watch over his son. Zenu had always tried his best to contain the young man, but the Salxosu woman, Kisuunsinu, who travelled back with him to Doldun after his victory in the games, had unleashed him. Zenu had never discovered what she said to Tekolger to drive him forward, or what the oracle of Xosu had told him when she took the young prince there. The opportunity to discover those truths was shattered when Kenkathoaz took another bride, a moon eyed woman of the Kolabon. The clash between the women was fierce and caused a rift between Kenkathoaz and his son. It took the intervention of Zenu and the High Priest of Xosu to broker a peace between the two men, and then only through Tekolger announcing that he was to go to the northern border to treat with the Thulchwal. With Tekolger's first marriage to the daughter of their chieftain, a woman named Zolzan, he secured a peace with that tribe. But the rift with his father had never been healed and the treating and marriage turned into a yearlong exile. Kisuunsinu had vanished as abruptly as she had appeared in that time and Tekolger was not to return until Kenkathoaz fell in battle.

You were a gift and a burden Tekolger, but this last act will see my oath to your father fulfilled.

The city was coming into full view, no longer just a blur on the horizon, like his dreams for the future, it was becoming solid, so close he could almost reach out and touch it. Torfub was rooted at a point where three great rivers merged into one. From the distance it looked like a great tree that straddled the river, covering the three channels and the point where they merged. Each of the great priestly families which ruled the city in the past had built towers to rival the other, all competing to reach for the gods. The competition to build the highest towers had seen some of the most impressive buildings ever constructed by man. Twelve in total, a wonder of the world they were called by Kisonkenril of Supokul, reaching so high as to disturb the gods in the heavens and covering the city in a canopy of shadow.

When the old god-kings had taken the city for their seat, they had cast down the over mighty priests and seized the towers for themselves. In the centre of the city, they had constructed an even larger structure, linking all the towers with a branching series of bridges so that now it formed one great glistening palace floating in the sky. With the flat plains of Zenian all around, it was said a man could see the edge of the world from the top, the place where the outer ocean drained into nothing and all the realms beyond.

When Tekolger first arrived at the city, the priestly families had flung open its doors and handed over the Floating Palace to a man they viewed as a divine liberator from the savage Rilrpitu. An act not seen since the days of Yoruxoruni. It was said that the doors to the palace had been locked and barred since the fall of the last king of Xortogun and even the plundering Rilrpitu had not found a way to enter.

The priests treated Tekolger as the son of their chief god, strange as their barbarous culture was. They thought he was the fulfilment of some ancient prophecy; it was just an excuse for their own weakness though.

Closer still they drew, each stade they covered gave Zenu more confidence, feeling more assured as he went. As the tents and palisade of a military camp came into view, Zenu felt a flitter of excitement and relief course through him, his phantom hand reaching out toward the encampment. In truth it was the safest and most relieved he had felt since the army had returned from Zentheldel. He had had no word from Pelu or Supo for many days now, causing him to fear for their fate, but the army was here, there was surely a good explanation as to why no messages had been sent.

His need for the support of Pelu and Supo was only growing. The Companions were cowed for now, but they were becoming more restless by the day. Zonpeluthas was pushing for a command, his eyes on the White Shields, as he felt he had been promised. The others, Zenu sensed, were increasingly regretting the action to remove Kelbal. He had tried to keep Tekolger's favourite hidden from them, to banish thoughts of him from their minds, but Kelbal had taken evermore to drink and, drunk, he would wander the camp and disturb the men.

Reunited with Supo and Pelu, and with an army which now outnumbered the returning soldiers at his back, Zenu would be in a position of strength once more. The Companions could be divided and sent off to govern distant provinces, their power slowly waning as their glory faded. These men may have helped forge Tekolger's legacy, but their childish lusts for power and glory would see it undone. Zenukola would ensure that such a thing could not happen. He was protecting them from themselves as much as anything else.

*　*　*

The gates of the city rumbled open so that the column of horse could ride through without breaking their stride. Torfub was not a large city, especially in comparison to the other metropolises of the great valley, but its streets were a maze, none of which led directly to the royal tower at the centre of the city, the place where the three rivers met. Instead, they coiled around the base like the roots of a great tree.

The welcome was not quite as Zenu had expected, the streets were largely empty, not many of the Xortogun had gathered to see the return of the royal army. That struck Zenu as odd, the Xortogun always showed great respect to their royalty, and they had taken Tekolger to heart.

The snaking column thundered down the winding roads, the shadows of the towers blanketed the city in shade despite the sun which was now beating down hard on the land. Torfub held a certain melancholy and dread for Zenukola. The last time he had been in the city was more than five years past, not long after Tekolger had married the Xortogun sorceress. That action was what had set them down this path, and Kelbal was at the heart of it. The Companions had been reluctant to integrate with the Xortogun so closely, but they had all followed Tekolger's lead. However, it was Kelbal who had sort out the woman and whispered in Tekolger's ear about marriage and an heir, all the while assuring the old generals of the need for stability and the connection to home. The more experienced men, those who had served with Kenkathoaz, had seen the danger such a match posed to the future of the Doldun.

Surson's family was of the old priestly class of Xortogun, they were the true power of the old kingdom and had survived this long for a reason. Surson's own clan, the Tora Ya Kuria, hailed from Kurotormub, they were priests of the Xortogun goddess called Tora. When the burned men of the southern desert ruled Xortogun, the priestly caste had conspired to overthrow them and place their own scion on the Amber Throne and now they threatened to do the same to the Doldun.

Tekolger had married the witch for Yoruxoruni's blood and there was no doubt the family had their eyes on the throne of Tekolger's empire. But Tekolger would not listen, blinded by Kelbal's word and Surson's beauty. His actions had pushed the old generals to act. The blood moon conspiracy it was now called, the executions had taken place in Torfub. Tekolger's wrath had been terrible, Zenu had feared for his own life that day. The old generals were his friends and comrades and he had known something of their plans, he urged them only to act against the woman, not the king, but they would not listen. Fortunately, the gods had seen fit to spare Zenu from that ordeal, no doubt in anticipation of this day.

The column halted before the royal tower, the carriage carrying the king crashing to a halt first. The Floating Palace, high above the city, waited for them. The gates opened and three men came out to meet the column. It was a sight which gladdened Zenu's heart as Supo was one of them. His old comrade stood tall, looking very assured of himself, the way only a man surrounded by loyal soldiers could, his ocean green eyes alive with success.

The sight of his comrade in arms filled Zenu's already soaring confidence to the brim. Surely the hard actions of the succession were now over. Zenu dismounted and gripped Supo in an embrace, waving his guards away as he wished to talk in private,

"It is good to see you again old friend, everything is well I trust?" Zenu inquired as they began to walk toward the tower.

"All is well. The battle went as expected, the Rilrpitu scattered and are retreating to the north. Thuson Kosua, Tekolger's secretary, has proved useful. I left him to bring up the infantry, but it should all be over by the time they arrive here. They need not concern us for now. I have reaffirmed the northern army's commitment to securing the succession, they will do what is necessary. What about on your side?" Supo answered in his considered but free flowing way, but he seemed more agitated that usual.

"Kelbal is broken, the man has descended thoroughly into his cups and has gone wild in the process. The other Companions are cowed and leaderless but are starting to regain their composure and push for their share of power. I have managed to keep them divided. The twins I dispatched with some of the men most loyal to Kelbal to chase after your Rilrpitu, but we need to act quickly to end their pretentions. Are Dolzalo and Palmash with us?" Zenu said as they entered the tower. The greeting he received from the men they passed was subdued he thought, and there was no sign of the men he dispatched with Supo.

"Dolzalo and Palmash are here, although I fear they do not know the gravity of the situation about to confront them. Dolzalo is the one we need to win over, but I suspect it will not be easy. Power is what the man understands, overawe him with a demonstration and he will know which side to take."

Supo's council was always wise and considered, and Zenu knew he had the measure of Dolzalo, there could be no holding back with a man like that. *Now was the decisive moment,* he thought, either this battle of wills was won, or the wolf of power that he was riding would turn and swallow him whole and the world the Doldun had built would fall into ruin.

The Companions had followed them inside as they began to make their ascent to the floating palace and the throne room at its heart.

After a long and tiring climb, they entered a vast open room, a grand hall to hold court. The room glistened with gold and gems. Along its walls were the usual friezes with the pictograms of the old kingdom and the sequences depicting the realm of the gods.

On the far side, below a portal opening in the wall where the sun streamed in, were placed two thrones. On one of the thrones sat a woman dressed in a fine silken dress in the Xortogun style, shining black, lined with gold, both shoulders bare, and her earthy coloured neck decorated with golden necklaces. Surson, Zenu knew from the thick hair of dark beaten bronze that framed her head, although he could not see her face. But even if he could, she would be hard to distinguish given the thick pigments the women of the valley wore.

Lurking in the shadows behind was a man, probably a protector assigned by Pelu. Three of Zenu's guardsmen filed in behind him.

Dolzalo and Palmash were sat at a table, sipping from cups of unmixed wine as Palmash played on a pan pipe. It seemed that all the Companions had adopted the habits of the barbarians whilst on campaign.

It had been at least three years since Zenu had seen either of them, but unlike the other Companions, neither had seemed to change one bit. Dolzalo still had the arrogant self-satisfied grin which he could never justify with his actions, and Palmash a disinterested face which hid the cruelty which could only be glimpsed through his piercing eyes. Dolzalo rose to greet them,

"Zenukola of the Deltathelon! Silver Eye! There is a sight for sore eyes, the years running the empire in the king's absence have been hard on you."

Zenu hated the name Silver Eye, but the clansmen would insist on such labels, it showed that they still had one foot in the barbarous world from which the Deltathelon were constantly trying to pull them. He felt his phantom fingers twitch.

"Dolzalo of the Zowo, Mountain Strider. In contrast, the time in the west seems to have done you good and Palmash of the Tholmash, Weaver, you have grown into a formidable man these past years." he knew they would take the use of their absurd monikers as a compliment, "I am afraid we do not have time to remake our acquaintance. I am sure you realise by now the delicate nature of the situation we find ourselves in and the risk to the empire's future."

"Supo has told us something of the situation. But I would wish to hear it from your own mouth." Dolzalo replied. The hot-headed Companion would not be so easy to crack after all it seemed,

"Very well." Zenu said, "The Companions feared for the future of the empire. Although Kelbal was once a formidable man, the devastation of the loss of the king, his closest companion and oldest friend, has broken him. His decisions were becoming increasingly erratic and his rule tyrannical. The news of the death of Kalu was what finally pushed him over the edge though. With the blessing of your comrades, I stepped in and removed Kelbal from his temporary position as regent. For now, I have taken up the role and intend to oversee a succession to a safe and stable ruler, to ensure the success of the empire. I need your help to see that through."

"Who will be the king's successor?" Dolzalo asked, his tone was almost mocking.

"We cannot afford a long minority; the conquered people would see it as an invitation to rebel. I have a candidate in mind, the king's own son no less. He is secure with Dotmazo in Doldun." Zenu answered, keeping his tone sure and confident. Dolzalo to be shown that Zenu was in complete control.

"It seems as though you have thought of everything Zenu, ever the schemer that you are. It all sounds rather treasonous though, how could you betray Tekolger's memory in this way?" Dolzalo was jesting, something was wrong.

"Treason is often a matter of perspective, what I do is for the good of the empire, you know that to be true." Zenu felt the urge to back out of the room or call for his guards. He looked around, the Companions had entered now, followed by several White Shields, faceless pale shadows. His phantom fingers grasped frantically for his sword.

"What about ordering the death of Kalu? That would certainly seem to be an act of treason. Or worse, the death of the king?" Palmash said, that jester-like smile back on his face.

Zenu clasped the hilt of his sword in his good hand, taking two steps back, glancing at Supo who stood there impassive.

"What nonsense is this? You were there, you know the Rilrpitu cut him down as he led the charge. And I was half a world away when Tekolger was murdered. Perhaps you should ask Kelbal…"

Palmash placed a basket on the table, a cruel look now flashing across his face. Zenu peered inside, he felt the confidence drain from him as he saw its gory contents. The head of Pelu, red and dripping with blood, a pained expression permanently scarred across his face, his tongue bruised and hanging out of his mouth. In that moment Zenukola knew he had failed, only death awaited him now and these men, the conquerors of the world, would tear themselves apart fighting over the scraps of Tekolger's legacy. In a panic Zenu drew his sword clumsily with his good hand, as his phantom hand grasped helplessly for the blade,

"What is the meaning of this?" He demanded, unsure what else to say. A different, but familiar, voice answered him.

"This is the result of treason Zenu." The voice sounded determined, set on a purpose, but there was an emotion in it, a pain. He spun around; the man behind the throne now stood next to him.

"Kalu? Thank the gods, Supo told me you were dead."

"You can't hide behind that now, your treachery to Tekolger and his legacy is clear to us all."

Zenu glanced back to Supo, he understood now, his old friend had betrayed him. He looked his old companion in the eye,

"Why?" He asked.

No answer came. He turned to Kalu,

"Have you asked Supo how he knows about all…"

He had no time to finish, Supo gave a signal and his two guards advanced. A madness gripped Zenu, he would not go down without a fight, the old warrior in him remerging. At the very least he would die an honourable death and hope to join Tekolger on the plains of Zulbeli.

The first guard advanced, Zenu slashed at him awkwardly, cursing that his sword hand had been left on the field where his king fell. Blood spurted, dashing across his face, the man dropped, his spear falling from his grasp back toward Kalu, Zenu turned to face the second. Then there was a thud, it felt like the strike of Dunsun's thunderbolt, an angry god casting a rock into the sea, and it was just as devastating.

He dropped his sword and clutched his stomach, despite his armour, the point of the sword had driven deep, so that just the hilt remained to grasp. He heard someone say,

"But now the spear lies broken, fallen like an autumn leaf."

The blood, thick and black, flooded from the wound. He looked Kelbal in the face, the tears in the young man's eyes glinting like the morning star against the dark canvass of the sky, but a fire burned in both the amber and the green. Then all went black and the growling jaws of death swallowed Zenukola whole.

SONOSPHOSKUL

"What news of the city?"

Runukolkil asked, his voice betraying a hint of hope and emotion which could only have come from the return home after a long exile. Runukolkil had been as focussed as ever in the days since they had made landfall, approaching their task as any other military operation, but the emotion running through the camp had been hard even for him to ignore. Even the Hotizoz seemed to have felt it.

"The patrols have all returned now, none dared get too close to the city in case we were discovered, but it seems the Nine are getting nervous. The city and countryside are crawling with sellswords and there are rumours of harsh crackdowns and prescriptions from within the walls itself."

Sonosphoskul answered as he would any other report, but he had to admit the sense of destiny and fate of their return to Butophulo was making him nervous. He touched the amulet around his neck.

"What about the people? What is their mood?" Runu turned to interrogate his other captains.

"We have not been able to speak to anyone inside the city yet, the Nine have the gates well-guarded. Getting in and out without being seen is almost impossible. What people we have spoken to in the countryside have been supportive. The League is remembered fondly, and they have offered us food and shelter." Kusuasu answered.

"Well, that is a good foundation for our efforts. We cannot afford to sit here too long though. A force this size will not be able to stay hidden for ever and we are too few to face the combined strength of sellswords and the Doldun in the field. We need to get inside the city." Runukolkil said in his considered manner. He paused and placed his hand on the zilthum helmet the oracle had presented him with in a way a priest might touch an altar, "Buto has trusted me with this task, I will see this helmet rest within his sanctuary on top of Polriso's Hill as a gift to show the god his faith was not misplaced."

Calmly as the prospect may have been presented, they knew that it would be difficult, impossible even. The chance of discovery was high, the chances of getting inside the city low and even if they did, the question of whether they could take and hold Butophulo with just two thousand men hung over all of them. Deep down everyone knew this expedition was likely a folly. Heroic, but almost certainly doomed to failure.

"A frontal assault will never work, the defences are too strong, even a few hundred men could hold us off for weeks, long enough for a relief force to arrive. We need a way to get inside unseen and for that we will need information on the garrison, their numbers, habits, where they are strongest and weakest. Which gate we could seize if we could slip a few men inside the city." Sonos added to the conversation, he had known this would be the only way to succeed from the beginning, the information he needed was proving elusive though.

"Don't forget Polriso's Hill." Kuso added, "That is where the Doldun are. Even if we take the city, all will be lost if they can entrench themselves atop and hold out for a relief force from Doldun."

"You are both right, but I will not send men inside the city blind. What do you propose Sonos?" Runu asked, the commander knew Sonos too well.

"Let me take a patrol out, strong enough to stand and fight. We can set up a position in the hills south of the city. Ambush one of the sellsword patrols, take some prisoners, they will tell us what we want to know." Sonos replied straight away, already having decided on the tale he would tell before he entered the tent. He knew the place he would set his ambush, a small, wooded hill south of the city, just out of sight of its gates. Any patrol heading south would have to pass through there.

Before Runu could give his answer a commotion on the edge of the camp drew the attention of the commanders. A runner from one of the outlying sentry positions dashed across the sand coming to a halt at the feet of Runukolkil. The man tried to speak, but breathless he could only gasp for air,

"Mercenaries…moving through the olive groves…at least fifty."

"Catch your breath soldier." Runu said. Composing himself the runner continued,

"About fifty men entered the grounds of the Academy, they are burning it and look to be taking prisoners. Two sentry posts have fallen back to avoid discovery, they are very close to the ships. A girl was also spotted on the cliffs, she fled back towards the Academy before we could seize her."

Runu smiled in the way he always did as a plan formed in his head,

"Sonos, looks like you have your chance. Our hand has been forced, it was inevitable we would be discovered at some point, so let us throw caution to the wind. Take a company beyond the Academy and catch these mercenaries on their way back to the city."

***

The column of smoke rising over the hill and the warm red glow, like the early morning light, marked the position of the Academy of Rolmit. Sonos took his hundred-man strong patrol in a wide sweep of the estate, skirting round to his chosen ambush point. He pushed his men hard, marching at the double to get ahead of the enemy before they left the estate. The pace of the march was hard dressed in the full panoply of a Xosu warrior, but the hardened men under his command were used to such rigours, their bodies accustomed to being hard pressed. Sonos led the way, determined that he would always lead by example, body and soul he would push himself harder and further, asking nothing of his men that he would not do himself.

Before the sun had made it halfway across the sky, the place he had chosen for his ambush had come into view, just as he remembered it, there was something about that fact which gave him hope. In contrast to the fire and chaos of the estate to the south and the hustle and bustle of the city less than a few hundred stades to the north, the small, wooded valley was a secluded and tranquil place.

Sonos stopped and surveyed the position. It would be the perfect spot to take the enemy unaware, especially if they had prisoners to guard and were overconfident in their control of the region. He ordered twenty men to take position at the head of the valley, blocking the way to the city, another twenty would be hidden at the entrance to the pass ready to cut off any retreat, the rest in the centre ready to charge into an exposed flank. Satisfied that all was set and selecting five men to accompany him, Sonos set off toward the column of smoke in the distance to get a good view of his enemy.

His small band crested the nearest hill, careful to stay inside the tree line out of view and keeping their cloaks wrapped around them to prevent the sun from glinting off their flashing bronze armour.

Crouched near the thick trunk of a hulthul tree and following the pillar of smoke with his eyes, Sonos could see the buildings which dotted the Academy's grounds ablaze, though the sellswords had left the olive groves largely untouched. It was an image which told a clear story. *Men with one goal in mind,* he thought, *no doubt one of the Nine has their eye on these lands and saw to it that they were not too badly damaged.* A band of men were gathering on the edge of the grounds. It was hard to make out how many at this distance, but a sizeable group, in glinting bronze, were herding together a smaller group of prisoners wearing pale white chitons.

Sonos sat and watched them for a while, getting the measure of his opponents. They were well armed and forceful in their treatment of the prisoners, but he noted a lack of discipline amongst their ranks and a lack of urgency with no sense of danger. No sentries had been posted to guard against surprise, and the men seemed more concerned with what they had looted from the burnt buildings.

Eventually, with the prisoners corralled and the sellswords gathered, the men began to march back toward the city, towards the jaws of his trap. He turned and headed back into the trees and down the hill toward his company.

They lay in wait amongst the woods for what seemed like an age, no sounds except the wind rustling through the leaves and the occasional crash of a wave echoing the distance. The men lay silent as shadows, each contemplating the short and sharp brush with death that was to come. Sonos gripped the ashen shaft of his spear tightly, when the enemy marched into the killing ground in the valley below, his spear throw would be the signal to spring the trap.

The gentle sounds of nature were suddenly and abruptly broken by the chattering and chanting of men coming closer and closer. Tension gripped Sonos and he sensed it in the men around him as well. The final moments before the beginning of a battle were always the hardest, the waiting almost unbearable, the urge to forget tactics and strategy and just charge headlong forward was almost overwhelming. The temptation was there, but Sonos stayed his hand, he must stay calm, a battle could be lost on the turn of a rash decision.

The marching footsteps drew closer and closer. Through the trees he could see the brightly coloured horsehair crests, the flashing bronze and the shields emblazoned with the symbols of the gods, vines and bows and a red face, Silxosu symbols he knew. Still, he waited. *Let them march deeper into the trap,* he thought. Sonos could see the prisoners now. Mostly old men dressed in fine Xosu togas. Hardly a band of dangerous rebels, but he knew now that the centre of the column was below him, the time was right.

Standing, he picked out an earthy looking man with a red horizontal crest of bristling terror upon his helm marking him out as an officer. With all his might, Sonos threw his spear, its long shadow cast its way across the crowd, its polished iron point flashing as if aflame. It thudded into the bronze cuirass of its target, ripping through metal, linen, flesh, and bone, sending death hurtling down upon the man.

The officer's cry of agony was met by a cheer of ecstasy as Sonos' men rose as one and charged, letting out all the tension which had been building and transforming the peaceful valley. They flooded down the side of the wooded hill, no longer men, but vicious daemons risen from the depths, crashing hard into the surprised and unprepared enemy ranks. Sonos was the first to hit the enemy line, smashing the rim of his shield into the face of a surprised man who had no time to raise his own. A slash to the throat with his leaf bladed sword and Sonos left the man to be taken to Sem.

A wild hacking sword flew passed Sonos' face, brushing against his armour, the flash of an iron sword against gleaming bronze. Shifting his feet quickly as a wraith, Sonos stepped aside the wild cut, thrusting with his own blade, and sending death whirling down upon his opponent. A final man stepped forward, a final cut and thrust from Sonos' blade and it was all over. Those who were not dead were surrendering, realising they were surrounded and outnumbered, a mercenary always knew when it was best not to fight and throw their life away. A good sign for when the inevitable battle for the city took place.

Throughout the whole encounter, the prisoners had stood motionless, fear fixing them to the spot. Some did not even move despite being splattered with their captor's blood. One man at the front of their group had stood strong however, even grasping for a sword from one of the dead mercenaries. Sonos approached him and took the leaf shaped blade from his hand. Looking him up and down, a flash of recognition crossed his mind,

"Kolkobuas Kisurusosi?" Sonos said, removing his helmet. The stern expression on the man's face turned to a smile as Sonos transformed from furious shadow to man of the Salxosu once again,

"Sonosphoskul Polriso? Gods be good, I never thought I would see your face again. The last I heard all of those who had been exiled had signed up for an expedition with the King of Gelodun, a war against Gottoy?"

Sonos laughed,

"Yes, we marched all the way to the walls of Gottoy itself and then that foolish king threw his life away. We were lucky to escape with our own."

"Well, I am glad the gods saw fit to spare you, otherwise I fear I would have shared a similar fate. What brought you back to Butophulo?" Kolkobuas replied.

"The death of Tekolger and the oracle. We took it as a sign from the gods and we have come to free the city or die trying. Come back to our ships, Runukolkil will be pleased to see you."

***

The sun was at its highest point in the sky by the time they arrived back at the hidden cove. The beach was alive with activity. Patrols returning with more information on the city and the countryside, sentries retreating and others making their way out for their stint, the rest of the men where relaxing cooking their midday meals. Sonos and his men were greeted warmly as they returned.

As expected, Sonos found Runu, the other captains and the Hotizoz commanders right at the centre of things. Ensuring the smooth running of the camp whilst receiving the reports of the incoming patrols to paint a picture of the challenge they faced in seizing control of the city.

Leaving his men to rest and eat, Sonos took Kolkobuas to meet with the other captains, they would all be pleased to see their old friend he knew. Runu said nothing as they approached, a quizzical look on his face turned to a smile as he realised who Sonos had brought with him. The general stood and embraced his old friend, followed by Kusuasu and Pusukol.

"That is a face I did not expect to see here." Kusuasu said, "Have they not retired you yet or packed you off to some school of philosophy?"

Kolkobuas laughed,

"They had, I had all but given up on the real world of politics, but the death of a friend and mentor is more than enough to bring me out of retirement."

Runu nodded thoughtfully, "We heard that news too. Koseun will be avenged, but right now, we have little time to reminisce. I fear we need to move fast; our position was spotted by a girl, she fled back towards the Academy. A spy for the Nine perhaps?"

"What did she look like?" Kolkobuas asked with some concern on his face.

"Salxosu I am told. Possibly of the old blood."

"Kalasyar." The old man whispered fearfully. "She is no spy, but I am afeared if she was taken by those mercenaries. She is Koseun's granddaughter."

Runu put a hand on Kolkobuas' shoulder,

"Then the urgency to act just became more acute. But we need information, we are too few to take the city by storm and I would not go into the dragon's mouth completely blind. Anything you can tell us about the defences of the city would be helpful. Sonos, were you able to take any prisoners of use?"

"A few, they will be able to tell us something of their numbers and dispositions in the city. The captured equipment may be useful as well." Sonos replied.

"I can give you all the information you need on the city's defences and now you have a way in as well." Kolkobuas.

"How so?" Runu asked, always keen to hear ideas.

"It would be a risk, but the Nine nor the Doldun know you are here and will not be expecting an attack, at least not yet. Strike now whilst the element of surprise is with you." he stopped, with some pangs of doubt etched on his face, "What they will be expecting is the return of a large group of their hired mercenaries, with prisoners. You have their equipment, if you head into the city at dusk, disguised and bringing the prisoners. The men they have hired are from such a wide range of places, they would not question one group among many. You could certainly stay hidden long enough for night to fall and a gate, the Gate of the Teacher I would suggest, could be seized. Your whole force could be inside the city before they knew what was going on."

Runu smiled, and Sonos knew exactly what he was going to say before he spoke,

"It is a bold and risky plan indeed, but it may be our best chance to get inside the city. They will certainly notice if the patrol does not return and begin a search. Which one of you would volunteer to lead this endeavour?"

The words of a song came to him again,

To arms! To arms!
Forward, arrow like, King of Kings, fire has no sheath!
But fierce Xosu bite, time to feel the hydra's teeth!
Our spears silver flash, come and face the Sacred Band!
We fall on this field, blood to free the Sacred land!

To arms! To arms!
Thrice loosed his fierce horde, arrows shade all beneath!
Spears crack and swords may shatter, flee the hydra's teeth!
Fume, fury, foolish great king, firm footed we stand!
We fall on this field, blood to free the Sacred Land!

Sonos stepped forward.

THUSON

45

Trumpets blared as the end of the column snaked its way into the sprawling encampment surrounding the city of Torfub. Thuson Kosua looked on as the men trudged through the wooden palisade, the final regiments recalled from chasing the Rilrpitu in the north and with them Doluzelru of the Keluazi. All Tekolger's Companions were now together once again.

Half a moon's cycle had passed since Thuson had led his own soldiers into the city. He had to admit it had felt good to have finally returned to what felt like civilisation. The life of a general on campaign had been hard on him, he lacked the strong constitution needed for it. A fact he only realised with his brief stay in Yorotog as a guest of Thorgon, the city's careful king. Unlike the Doldun, Thuson's upbringing had been inside the Academy of Kunpit, surrounded by scrolls and wearing Xosu style togas, such things did not prepare one for the hard life of a soldier.

After he arrived in Torfub, Kalu had set him the task of taking stock of the army, counting their numbers, ensuring there was enough supplies coming in. Demoted from general back to secretary, it was the only rebuke he had received for his actions in the north, and it felt as though the last year had never happened. He would not have been surprised to see Tekolger once again leading the army, as if nothing had changed. The comfort of his old role was welcome in many ways, but he was frustrated at the lack of recognition for his efforts in the field.

He stood with his logistics officers at the edge of the column, directing each regiment to the billets which had been allocated to them as they came in. As the final batch of soldiers marched passed, kicking up dust as they did so, he turned to his chief adjutant, a scholarly looking man of the

Deltathelon named Dazzel,

"That is all of them, how many came through?"

"Four thousand eight hundred and seventy-two. Those last detachments will be billeted on the southern bank." Dazzel replied. *It is good to be working with him again*, Thuson thought. Tekolger may have been famed for his decisiveness in battle, but the army would have gotten nowhere without its efficient logistics system.

"And what of our supply situation?" Thuson inquired.

"The army itself was carrying sufficient supplies for a moon's cycle. We can requisition another moon's cycle worth from the city granary with no problems and I have ordered a contribution from the outlying villages. We will be fine to spend the rest of the winter in the region if that is required."

Thuson nodded and clasped the man on the shoulder as he walked past. *There was a simple satisfaction to be drawn from this work*, he thought, *and a glory in it as well, not every man could organise an army on such a scale*. No poems would be written of his efforts for Tekolger it was true, but Tekolger's glory stood on the shoulders of the hard work of men such as himself, he could take satisfaction in that. He laughed at himself. Maybe he had let the culture of the Doldun grow on him too much. As he strode towards the gates of the walled off inner city, he could not help but laugh at himself, his pace quickening. Trying to comfort himself with such thoughts was foolish, the speed at which he eagerly made his way to the palace told him everything, he wanted to be at the heart of the action.

Having arrived days after the death of Zenukola and its fall out, Thuson felt he had missed his chance to win acclaim, instead he had been used as a tool by the others to allow them to win the glory. He was determined that would not happen anymore. He was their equal in command if not in the heat of battle. In his short time as a general he had already won several engagements and defeated the fearsome Rilrpitu. He deserved recognition for that, even if he was not a world conquering Doldun. Tekolger's vision saw beyond those differences, he hoped his Companions would as well.

The inner city of Torfub created an almost overwhelming atmosphere, more so than he remembered. Dominated by the great towers, it made a man feel small and insignificant in the face of the power of the gods as they stared down on you from above. The distant tops of the towers looked to be a shining paradise amongst the clouds. It was a feeling only enhanced by the claustrophobic, winding maze of the city's streets. He felt as though he had passed through a portal and was trapped in one of the dense forests of Zentheldel.

Eventually finding his way to the base of the great tower at the centre of the city, Thuson made his way through the White Shields who had been garrisoned there. The gleaming white, zilthum lined armour of the two guards stood at the entrance impressed as it always did, and the faces frozen on their shining masks made them seem like the shades of long dead heroes defending the realm of the gods. When the zilthum armour was removed from the treasury of Buto on Polriso's Hill he had been upset, even disgusted by the action. Supporter of Tekolger or not, he was still a man of the Salxosu. But he had come to realise that the armour was forged by his ancestors for a purpose and what better reason than serving the vision of Tekolger to unite the lands of Kolgennon.

He entered the tower and slowly made his way to the Floating Palace. The height of the towers, and the numerous bridges which connected them, made the palace even more of a labyrinth than the streets below. He would have become lost and disorientated inside if he had not been shown the thread of red paint which lined the walls and pointed the way to the centre.

Inside the Floating Palace, the Companions were already starting to gather. Kelbal had ordered the royal council to convene as soon as possible in the great temple to Kurotor which stood at the heart of the tower complex. There the Companions would swear their oaths to Tekolger's newborn son and heir, and the child would be crowned. Thuson had been surprised and pleased to be invited to the ceremony as well. Over his shoulder, he heard by now a familiar shout, his name echoing off the walls,

"Here he is, the fearsome slayer of the Rilrpitu! Thuson the wine warrior."

The sarcasm in Dolzalo's voice was palpable, but at least there was some admission of Thuson's role in the fighting. Dolzalo wrapped and arm around his shoulder and crowned himself with a smile,

"Come on, the others will want to hear your stories of valour and war."

Thuson smiled at him. It was always best to humour Dolzalo, keep him in a good mood. The pair walked into the chamber which had been set up for council meetings, nine of the Companions sat ready waiting for the gathering to begin.

"Dolzalo tells us you drove off the Rilrpitu by yourself Thuson." Zalmetaz exclaimed over the table, in an equally sarcastic manner. The eyes of the fox head which wrapped around the shoulders of the Companion's cloak stared at him mockingly.

"I can't take all the credit, but yes I commanded the infantry, and it was my plan which drew them into an ambush." Thuson replied, humbly, wanting his contribution to be recognised, but not to overstep the mark.

"Fearsome as a lion he was." Dolzalo continued, "So undaunted he even stopped for a drink halfway through the battle."

A laugh rippled around the room.

"You mock Dolzalo, but we all know you would have still been charging around the northern provinces chasing your tail if it wasn't for Thuson here. Give the man some credit, Tekolger always did." The words came from Zela. Brash and confident as he was, he was more intelligent the rest, Thuson had always liked him.

"The Rilrpitu would have fled from me and be licking their wounds back on their windblown steppe. I will admit though that Thuson made sure that we caught more of them than we might otherwise have done." Dolzalo reluctantly said.

"Any one of us given the chance of an independent command would have done the same or had you forgotten that we conquered the world." Young Zonpeluthas remarked, ever eager to prove himself and win his glory. He had always struggled to hide his feelings of inferiority in front of his older peers.

"Whatever the case it matters little now. The future of the empire will be decided today, let us all hope that Kelbal gives us the opportunity we all want." Deluan cut in ponderously.

"Do you mean Kelbal or Surson?" Thazan asked in his solemn way, his priestly demeanour making him seem at home in this tower of the gods. Doluzelru cut him off,

"Kelbal is the regent, we would all do well to remember that now. Zenukola's treachery should be a fresh reminder. We will all get opportunities to win ever more glory, but the king and the empire come first."

Silence fell over the room at that point. *The future of the empire*, Thuson thought, *and what place will they have found for me within it?*

* * *

Surson Tora Ya Kuria, a vision of beauty, her hair flowing like the water of the river of memory, so mesmerising that a man could lose his mind in its locks of dark honey, and her amber eyes glistening with a red fire hidden in their depths, like deep pits that conceal the fires of the earth, sat enthroned at the end of the inner chamber of the temple. Behind her two eunuch guardsmen carried the baby king.

Kalu and Supo were close behind. Kelbal sat enthroned in the centre of the temple of Kurotor on a magnificent golden throne with wings which unfolded toward the open roof. Through the opening a dolthil tree sprouted, red and gold and resplendent, the Xortogun had somehow managed to entice it to grow inside the temple, reaching desperately for the heavens. Kelbal wore a blood red Xortogun style robe with long, golden, glistening arms. His beard had been trimmed and oiled in the Xortogun style so that it shone like the rays of the sun. His eyes burned bright as if they had swallowed the fire at the heart of the temple.

The Companions silently took their places at the back of the temple as a door rumbled open and a resounding pattern of booms echoed. The priests of Kurotor entered and Thuson's eyes were drawn around the walls, covered in the ancient hieroglyphs of Xortogun and the statues of the animal headed gods, to the entrance. As the lead priest paced solemnly into the chamber, he pounded the floor with a long staff of dolthil wood topped with a pommel of black stone. The sound did not seem to match the staff, as Thuson felt a shudder to his core every time the staff struck home, his heart quickening, and beads of sweat forming on his brow.

The procession of priests made their progress towards the iron black altar in front of Kelbal. Their fire red robes flowed behind them like great swirling tails as they strode. Each wore a false, jewel encrusted, golden beard which resembled an eagle's beak, and each was crowned with collars fashioned as lion's manes. The High Priest stood in the centre, holding a many tiered gold crown of red-amber from Kurotormub, jade from Guntoga and white sapphires from Torfub. Behind the priestly procession, a magnificent black bull was brought forward toward the altar.

Without a word being uttered, the eunuchs brought forward the baby king and placed him on the altar. The priests took up a chant in the tongue of the old kingdom that even few of the Xortogun themselves now understood. In a swift and violent movement, the High Priest drew a sickle shaped knife and dragged it across the throat of the black bull. Blood sprayed the child king, who, in silence watched on. Then the High Priest raised the crown aloft and proclaimed in heavily accented Common Xosu,

"The gods show their approval and name the child the beloved son of Kurotor and protector of Xortogun. I now crown him in the sight of men, King of Kings, Thoruri of the Great Valley, King of the Doldun, King of Zowdel, King of Zenidun, and Lord of Zenian and name him Phalazkon in the tradition of the Doldun and Ponthorsuruf in the tongue of Xortogun for he will be a unifier of his people and bring a new dawn to the world."

He placed the crown on the altar next to the baby king as the string of titles placed the weight of the world upon the boy's shoulders.

The Companions then stepped forward to show their respects to Surson and affirm their loyalty to the new king. Thazan and Deluan stepped up first, followed by Zonpeluthas and Zela, Polazul and Zalmetaz came next. The twins came forward eagerly, even Palmash and Dolzalo showed some humility and did the same, but those who had remained with the army when Zenu had moved against Kelbal were most eager to show their support. *Maybe a little too eager* Thuson thought.

Taking a knee in front of the altar and Kelbal seated on his golden throne, they said as one,

"We swear by the bright god, by the twins and by Phalazkon's mighty shade to be loyal and trusted Companions of the heir to Xosu's throne. To give him good and honest council, to serve as his faithful bodyguards and protectors and to do whatsoever is required. We also pledge to tell the king the wishes of his clans, so that harmony and kinship may be remembered and strengthened within the kingdom."

The men were anointed with the blood of the sacrifice.

Thuson did not swear the oath, as he was not of the Doldun or a Companion, but Surson knew him well from the long years he had spent at Tekolger's side and embraced him as an old friend. He could only hope that she would be vocal in her support for him. As a fellow outsider within this close-knit group of Doldun, Surson and Thuson had been drawn to each other and formed an alliance of sorts to survive. The succession of her son to the kingship could only be a good thing for Thuson, he hoped.

All seated, Kalu rose to speak, the light of the day shining into the chamber through the open roof and illuminating the Companions. Although regent, Kelbal was increasingly leaving Kalu to take a leading role, preferring to sit back, listen and watch, a caution which was not unfounded. He had been quieter and more reserved since his return to power, but despite that and his well-oiled, braided beard and Xortogun robe made from the finest silk, he still had a fury in his eyes and a wildness to his ruddy bronze hair, the cerulean streaks untamed throughout.

"Tekolger left us all with a great legacy, an empire stretching from east to west, the greatest conquests since Tholophos himself. But it is a delicate legacy, one that needs a firm hand, a guiding vision to see it come to fruition. We will be challenged, even now threats exist, rumblings of rebellion of those who saw Tekolger as half a god and were kept in check by his sheer force of will. The Rilrpitu are raiding over the northern frontier, the situation in the far west remains precarious, the Zummosh may have been conquered but they are still fierce warriors on the fringes of civilisation. The Putedun are not warlike but are devious and duplicitous and will pounce on any weakness and there are many amongst the Xosu who would see us overthrown. The last thing we need now is division amongst ourselves. If Zenukola's treachery has taught us anything, it is that we must not allow our own disagreements lead to infighting." The Companion paused as if to contain his emotion, "We understand that you wish to be given opportunities to enhance your glory, we wish for that as well. Tekolger's legacy is not just his own, but all of ours and a platform from which to build. It is clear therefore that we need a new division of power to ensure the empire works for all of us and that it is well governed, and its integrity assured. This way Tekolger's legacy can be nurtured and grown and be passed on to his heir when he comes of age. You will all be given those opportunities, whilst a new regency council is established to oversee the governance of the empire and the raising of the king to his throne." He looked around the room, as if seeking approval, "As were Tekolger's wishes, Kelbal will be named Regent of the empire, and he will take his seat next to the king in Tekolgertep. I will serve as Vizier and the army's supreme commander alongside him.

Supo will be named Hegemon in the west with Zalmetaz and Polazul as his subordinates. They will march with the retiring veterans to Doldun and Dotmazo will in turn bring replacements to the capital. Tekolger's young son Koliathelanu will also be brought to Tekolgertep, and he will be found a place in the king's court.

Dolzalo, you will be named the Togworwoh of Zenidun, Palmash Gulonbel is yours to govern. Zela you will take up residence in Yorixori as the new Togworwoh of Zowdel with Zonpeluthas taking responsibility for the northern frontier. Thazan will remain here in Torfub. Deluan will head to Tekolgerzel and govern the southern provinces. Doluzelru and Pelapakal you are to oversee the construction of the new royal fleet in Tekolgertep.

Finally, Thuson, we want you to take a place on the new regency council as an adviser to the regent and tutor to the king. Your efforts on the field were noted, but your skill lies in more scholarly pursuits."

Kalu finished speaking, a ripple of discussion went around the room. It was a fair settlement for most, Thuson reflected. For himself he did not know what to feel. A place at the royal court to educate the inheritor of an empire that reached across the whole world was more than Yusukol had ever dreamed of. It would be the opportunity to truly bring about a new world and the enlightened kingship of which Kunpit spoke. But he knew in his heart he had wished for a command, a romantic dream perhaps, he had spent too long amongst the Doldun and absorbed too much of their notions of glory.

*　*　*

He found Llalon and the rest of the Thulchwal in the outer city, camped in the shadow of the Tower of Xur.

"All is well sage man? The new king?" Llalon asked, his thick accent rippling across the wind.

"The boy king is well, and the empire is in safe hands." he replied with a sigh.

"Then what is the thing that is troubling to you?"

"I have been appointed to the king's new council, to advise the regent and help raise the king to his throne." Thuson told him, saying the words made the proposal sound ever grander and more pregnant with opportunity, but his heart sank at their sound.

"This does not please you though? Your heart wishes for recognition to be yours yes. The chance to prove yourself to these clansmen, you have had a taste of glory and want more. It is always the same my friend, the Powouzo know this to be true." Llalon said in his incisive way.

"This is an opportunity, to fulfil the dream of my cousin and our school. But I must admit my heart yearns for the opportunity to prove myself as the Doldun would, with a sword in hand." Thuson replied, his gaze now fixed north across the river to the rolling plains of Zenian and the steppe beyond where the savage Rilrpitu roam. But that was a fool's dream, in Tekoglertep he could see Tekolger and Yusukol's vision come to be.

Llalon had paused a moment before he spoke again,

"It will be a difficult task, this is true. But this is your opportunity to escape the pull that had seen so many dragged into the depths of depravity by the allure of glory. It was a fate that even Tekolger could not escape from, but that was the tragedy of his shade. It happened with Chwor ZoShaf as well, the curse afflicted so many of the incarnations of The Paron. We Thulchwal are guardians ourselves, reluctant though that task is, we watch the Gateway Isle so that the world may prosper." he paused and smiled, "But you will have people from all over the empire under your authority, a chance to mould the young mind of the king. With your help he could be even greater than Tekolger ever was. Is this not the vision you had when you first went to the land of the clansmen? And you can see to it that Tekolger's vision comes to pass."

Tekolger had often spoken of a vision. The oracle of Xosu at Thelonigul had set him on that path, a prophecy to unite the people of east and west, it had inspired the men to feats to rival the heroes of old. Thuson had to admit the Thulchwal warrior had a point,

"Tekolger always dreamed of such things, and Yusukol proved Kunpit's proposition with Tekolger. I would be foolish to throw away such an opportunity. Besides glory is not only to be found on the field of battle."

"It will be difficult you are right, but whilst the others play their games and pursue the narrow glory to be found in great battles, you can build something which Tekolger himself would have been proud of." Llalon's thick accent made his advice seem like ancient wisdom, perhaps he was right,

"Llalon, you were born in the wrong place, you have the mind of a philosopher, the people of my city would have loved you. They would have made you rich and famous." He said with a newfound optimism coming to him. With a smile Llalon replied,

"Rich and famous yes, but Tekolger gave me something they never could have done."

With that he left to see to his men and Thuson found himself wandering to his own quarters looking for the Rilrpitu woman he had grown fond of. He found her tending to the horses,

"You had best prepare them to ride. We are heading to Tekolgertep."

She turned and faced him, her Common Xosu was still very poor, but she had learnt a lot in a short space of time,

"You learn much in the valley, like my Rilripitu did. More I think than you would like." Through the thick guttural tones of her accent, Thuson could not decide if that was meant as threat or not. No matter, he knew the path ahead of him would be long and winding and may even lead nowhere, but Yulthelon had laid a road in front of him, it was up to Thuson to explore it.

SONOSPHOSKUL

46

Evening had set in by the time the city came into view. It was not the way Sonos had imagined seeing his home, the place of his birth, after almost thirteen years of exile, but somehow it felt fitting. He gripped the shaft of his spear tightly, his armour felt uncomfortable and heavy suddenly, the unfamiliar shield of one of the fallen mercenaries awkward on his arm.

At the point where the sun had dipped below the horizon, but before the stars started to shine in the sky, they reached the southern gate of Butophulo, the Teacher's Gate as it was known. The sky was calm and clear, a gentle breeze blowing across the plain before the city. Sonos, fifty of his best men, and the old men from the Academy approached the gate, the carved faces over the portico staring down at them ominously. The gate was shut, Sonos raised his hand and the column halted. *Too disciplined,* he thought, *the men we are replacing were not.* A voice came over the top of the wall,

"You are late. A few old men and green boys give you trouble?" Sonos looked up. A pair of hollow eyes were peering over the top of the wall.

"They were hiding among the olive groves, took us all day to track them down. There was more in that estate than we thought too. Open the gate and we will share some of the spoils with you." Sonos shouted back in as jovial a tone as he could muster, hoping that the guard did not know the man he was expecting.

The eyes disappeared and there was a deadly silence. The worry and anxiety started to creep in again, worse than the prelude to any battle. *They know who we are,* he thought. His hand tightening on his spear again, lifting his shield up to his shoulder. The gate creaked and then shuddered into life, the bronze slowly swinging open.

We fall on this field, blood to free the Sacred Land!
To arms! To arms!

The last time he had set foot inside the city was almost thirteen years ago. Koseun had urged them all to flee into exile after the defeat at the hands of the Doldun. *'Stay free and live to fight another day'* he had said. Koseun had insisted on meeting Tekolger on neutral ground to negotiate the city's surrender. Delaying the approach of the victorious Doldun had given them their chance to flee, taking as many ships of the League fleet that they could crew and running to Thasotun. Now here he was returning as promised.

Sonos waited until both gates were open wide and then signalled his men to march through. The man on the wall was waiting for them on the other side. Sonos approached him as the men streamed passed,

"I thought Kusoasu had the command of the first watch this evening?" Sonos asked to try and throw the man off the scent of a ruse, amused at the idea of Kuso guarding a gate. The mercenary shook his head,

"No, never was, I don't know him. Perhaps he is on the next. What spoils do you have to share?"

A mercenary through and through, Sonos thought. *At least his mind is focused on what he can gain and not who we are,*

"Plenty, I must take these prisoners to be secured, but please take one of the amphorae of wine. It is a deep red vintage from Gelodun, very good, it will certainly make the night pass quicker. Pour some to the god to show our gratitude."

The sellsword eyed him for a worryingly long time. His eyes fixed on Sonos' shield, an image of a red face staring back at the greedy mercenary.

"Aye Xosu will get a taste as well." He finally replied.

Sonos signalled to his men, and they offloaded an amphora from the wagon they had been pulling behind the column. The man grunted his approval and went over to check on the wine. Taking the opportunity to avoid any more scrutiny, Sonos motioned for his men to carry on marching.

The city was growing dark and eerily quiet, although Kolkobuas insisted this was normal now in the days of the tyrants. During the days of the League, the city's streets would be awash with activity day and night, the people would be out drinking, and socialising, plays would be performed until the depths of the night and wandering philosophers would be pinned on every street corner arguing until the dawn. A sadness washed over him to see the city fallen to this low, its freedom crushed and its spirit along with it.

The column wound its way round the streets entering the edge of the Kobon, passing under the shadow of Polriso's Hill. Sonos noted the Doldun men stood guard at the entrance to the winding path to the top. *Only two, the entrance should not be hard to secure by surprise. But what lies behind that palisade?*

Further on, he could see the villas of the noble families clinging to the bottom of the hill. The Polriso villa was lit by torches, his own kin would be inside he knew. Rinukiso, the family patriarch, had betrayed his own kind for a seat amongst the Nine according to Kolkobuas, that revelation had cut deep. Family names had come to mean little during their long years of exile, and Rinukiso was only a distant cousin, but the news had hurt all the same. He touched the amulet around his throat, the family heirloom always gave him comfort.

There were more sellswords in this district, so many it seemed that the area had become a barracks. Kolkobuas had assured him that there were a little over a thousand mercenaries in the city itself. Four companies of Tilxosu and Silxosu mostly, The Company of the Sacred Land the only one of any size or note. Combined with the Doldun garrison, they were of more or less an equal number with the combined strength of the Daemons of the Deep and the Hotizoz Legion. The Nine had also pressed many of the young men of the city into their new guardian units, but Kolkobuas was sure that they were poorly trained, led, and motivated, more hostages than loyal soldiers, and they would not stand and fight. Sonos only hoped that he was right. It was the Doldun garrison that worried him most. Five hundred disciplined and motivated soldiers encamped on top of Polriso's Hill.

Careful to avoid any checkpoints as best they could, the column, guided by Kolkobuas, slid through the city silent as a shadow, heading towards a mansion on the edge of the Kobon. A place seized from a rich merchant named Yilthuprol, whose gold the Nine had coveted in the early days of their rule. The building had been converted into a barracks and armoury for the mercenaries garrisoned in the city so that they could be close to the Nine. Kolkobuas had picked the place as a bastion in the heart of the city to strike rapidly at the villas of the Nine when the time came. Sonos halted his men in front of the building, another bored looking mercenary stood on the gate.

"Good evening?" Sonos asked,

"Dull and long, these the prisoners from the Academy?" He replied,

Sonos nodded,

"We were told to bring them here, only place left to keep them locked up."

The man shrugged and gave the men a cursory glance,

"They will have to go in the empty armoury."

He stood aside to let them pass. Sonos signalled for some of the men to take them through.

"How much longer are you on guard here?" Sonos asked the guard.

"Until the second watch."

"Long night, you look tired. Some of my boys can take over, they were slow in their duties today, I need to teach them a lesson." Sonos answered.

The sellsword looked at him slightly confused,

"I shouldn't, my captain…"

"He does not need to know, and if he does find out, send him to me. Take one of the amphorae of wine we seized today, a gift from the god, and enjoy the rest of the night with your comrades."

Hesitantly the sellsword nodded his head.

Inside the armoury, two mercenaries lay dead on the floor, the blood pooling in the corner of the room. The men had already seized the entrance, arming Kolkobuas and his followers. Nothing for it but to wait until the moon reached its height.

* * *

A long and tense wait followed as Tholo's great eye rose in the sky. After what seemed like an age, the full moon sat at its highest point, illuminating the haven of Buto in a magnificent silver glow. *Time to stand and die,* he thought as the images of Zolmos, Kolmosoi and the others came suddenly to mind.

Leaving twenty men and Kolkobuas to guard the armoury, Sonos slipped back into the shadows of the city. The streets were still unnervingly quiet, the occasional light flickering from some of the buildings and the odd shout or song floating over from the garrisoned soldiers. Those noises at least gave Sonos some comfort. As long as the sellswords were singing and shouting, they were not aware of what was about to happen.

Clouds had quite suddenly covered the sky and a dense mist was descending, the moon was just about still visible, but it still felt as though Tholo was watching them. The White Goddess was a jealous guardian of her own home and children, he hoped she was guiding them now.

The men moved swiftly and silently like ghosts, the clink of armour and weapons the only noise giving them away. They quickly made their way through the winding streets, Polriso's Hill once again looming over them.

Pausing before the open space in front of the winding entrance to the Sanctuary, Sonos dispatched fifteen of his most trusted men to seize the entryway, quickly and silently. Without a way onto Polriso's Hill the swift assault on the city may rapidly turn to a siege which they could not afford.

Taking his remaining men, Sonos headed for the southern gate. His nerves were almost getting the better of him, this was perhaps the most dangerous part of the night. If they were caught now, out in the open streets and unable to escape, they would be slaughtered. *Give me a battle on an open field any day,* he thought, *at least then everything was clear, kill the man in front of you or be killed yourself.* The uncertainty of sneaking into a city was a very different prospect.

They reached the Teacher's Gate in good time. Everything was still quiet. Sonos was beginning to find that comforting now, at least it meant his men had not been seen yet. The thickening mist was helping in that regard, maybe the gods were watching over them.

Two mercenaries stood behind the gate, one resting on his spear, the other slumped against a wall. The sight pleased him, they had drunk the wine, there would be no fight here, just a sacrifice to the god. He stopped and crouched by the side of a wall; his men bunched up against him. Turning, he placed his shield and spear on the ground and drew his sword. Pointing to the first three men, they did the same and followed him.

Moving swiftly but silently toward the gate, slightly crouched amongst the shadows, Sonos could hear nothing but his own breath and his heart pounding in his head. The short stretch of open ground between him and the gate disappeared quickly, and before he knew it, Sonos was on the first man slumped against the wall.

The mercenary's eyes opened, but it was too late, Sonos covered his mouth and slit his throat with his razor-sharp blade. Turning quickly, he saw two of his men seize the mercenary leaning against his spear, pulling him to the ground and plunging their swords into his chest. Sonos' eyes darted over to his men crouched amongst the buildings, already they were streaming forward and into the gatehouse.

Inside a scene of slaughter had unfolded, like a grand sacrifice to a hungry god. The men had made swift and silent work of the small garrison, blood pooled on the ground and mixed with spilled wine, a gory spectacle. Sonos stepped over the bodies and made his way up the stairs.

Four of the men stood around the winch which served to prize open the heavy bronze doors,

"Open it up." he said, "Let us retake this city from these tyrants."

A creak and a groan, the loudest noise of the night, echoed as Sonos made his way onto the wall. *Someone probably heard that, but it matters little now.*

On top of the wall, the countryside around seemed calm and tranquil, the rolling hills were pitch black, blanketed by a soft layer of silver light emanating from the moon. Sonos paused for a moment to take in the view and brace himself for the trials and dangers he was about to face. Thunder rumbled overhead and lightning cracked almost as violently as it had in old Kolbos. Then the heavens opened, and rain began to hammer down.

One of his men handed him a burning torch. He took the wooden handle, and the flames flickered, a glint shining off his bronze cuirass. He felt the fire against his face, the heat warm and welcoming, like home. He raised the torch above his head, waved it back and fore three times and then threw it over the wall into the dark night. In the black draped hills beyond, a single light appeared and mirrored his signal, all was well. The blackness in front of him seemed to rise and begin to roll relentlessly toward the city. A tidal wave to reap the vengeance of the gods upon those in the city who had taken power for themselves, against the will of Buto.

Noise could not be avoided now as streams of heavily armed men flooded into the city. Runukolkil led the first five hundred through the gate himself, the helmet of Buto sitting proudly on his head. They did not stop. Their first and most important goal was to seize Polriso's Hill, the heart of the city and the place where the hated Doldun had lorded over the people like self-appointed gods.

A break in the waves of men flooding in told Sonos that the Daemons of the Deep were all inside. Shouting and screaming could be heard echoing throughout the city. No more need for stealth, speed and ferocity would win the day now.

The second wave of five hundred men of the Hotizoz Legion Sonos would take command of himself, leading them into the city to hunt down the mercenary companies before they could organise. Kusoasu and Pusokol would lead the other two groups of Hotizoz with some picked men of their own, to guide them around the city and because, reliable allies as they may have been, they were still foreign soldiers and could not be trusted not to loot and rape once their blood was up.

He joined the Hotizoz captains at the front of the column as it entered to lead the men into the heart of the city.

KALASYAR

47

The night was calm, quiet, and tranquil, the sky clear but for the distant light of a thousand thousand stars. The moon was full this night as well, it had bathed the city in a warm slivery glow giving Butophulo a peaceful almost serene feeling, a haven like it was intended to be. It was all a contrast to the storm which was raging inside Kalasyar. The tension of knowing what was to come but feeling helpless to control it had frayed her nerves and the waiting was almost unbearable. If this was what the wait for a battle was like, no wonder men always seemed so keen for the fighting to begin.

She had been escorted back to the city by the mercenary captain who had saved her from his own men. With each step she had taken back toward the city she had felt more power draining from her. She was just a pawn in this game now, a prize for the men of power. Sipenkiso was wrong, she was completely powerless in this world bound by those who did control it. The only solace she had was knowing that she was on her way to Polriso's Hill. A chance to confront the man who betrayed her, she hoped. She found herself eagerly eyeing the hilt of the sword secured to the saddle of the Doldun man's horse. *All in good time*, she thought, *you are not there yet*.

"I am glad we got this chance to talk again my lady." the voice cut through the air like a knife, slicing open the silence, "So I could apologise for the way your grandfather's arrest was conducted, that was not…not the way we wanted it." Kelanson of the Zelkalkel said. Choosing his words carefully with what sounded like genuine regret in his voice. She had been met at the Gate of the Teacher by the two Doldun guardsmen who had escorted her, tricked her, on that fateful day that her grandfather had been taken. The sight of the purple cloaks and enamelled bronze armour which had once held such terror for her now only filled her with hate. Kelanson continued,

"Koseun was a great man, many of the men in the garrison were sad to see him treated in that way." he paused as if he expected a reply. She had liked Kelanson when first she met him, courteous and eager as he was, in truth she still felt no ill will towards the man. But that first impression was gone now, coloured by the actions taken against her grandfather, actions the Doldun could have stopped.

"We were all sad to see him treated that way, he deserved more." she paused, her words poised to be delivered like a hammer blow, then she sighed, "It was not your fault though, you were only following your orders."

Kelanson nodded knowingly, before saying,

"I know that the general was sad as well. He admired and respected Koseun, as the king had done. It seems this year has taken two great men from us."

Kalasyar had no doubt Doltopez admired and respected her grandfather, but it had not stopped him from allowing his death, or exploiting her, taking her dignity. He had the power to stop the Nine and yet he did nothing, or worse he encouraged them. She felt a rage building inside her, she felt an overwhelming urge to reach for the hilt of the sword again, but she held her composure and instead simply replied,

"I am sure the general had his reasons for what he did."

Soon Polriso's Hill loomed overhead, throwing its shadow over them, hiding them from the gaze of the moon. Up above the walls glistened in the moonlight, glinting off the pale bronze of its upper levels. The walls had been raised in imitation of those of the Thelonbet at old Kolbos and covered with bronze and polished to glimmer like zilthum. *Soon they will be washed with blood,* she thought, although she did not know how.

The survivors of old Kolbos had come this way before Butophulo had existed she pondered. Led here and gifted this site by the god and the word of his Oracle as a haven from the fury of Tildun's army. The broken men, women and children who had washed up here as refugees had been saved by one of their own. He had been named Polriso, the man from which the family took its name. Those refugees had raised the first Polriso up to be a king, and now his descendant had betrayed them.

They continued down Xosu's Arrow toward the fortified entrance. Two Doldun guards stood ready at the gate and raised a hand to greet Kelanson and Kelankatha. Kalasyar's heart began to hammer in her chest. Once beyond that gate there was no turning back, this tranquil night would be shattered, and she would have to confront the man who may well have ordered her grandfather's death. It was then that she remembered that three hundred years ago another man had led his broken people down this road to confront a tyrant and save his people, re-founding the city as a haven where people ruled themselves, and that man was a Sisosi. She looked at the hilt of the sword again and took solace in that thought.

"How goes the night?" Kelanson asked one of the men on the gate.

"Quiet, just how I like it. The Nine fear their own shadows, so the people all stick to their homes once Dunsun steps off his throne to visit that mistress of his." the man laughed, "If it keeps my life quiet and easy, they are welcome to their fear and the lord his lust."

"And the general?"

"He is here, that one never sleeps."

The second man knocked the wooden door, and it creaked open. Two more Doldun on the other side looked her up and down before ushering them through.

* * *

The Sanctuary looked much as it had done that fateful night she visited after her grandfather's trial. Only now it was alive with activity, the full strength of the garrison on display.

Despite turning the sacred heart of the city into a barracks, the Doldun at least seemed to have kept away from the shrines. The nine which rung the upper walls were untouched and the temple at the centre had no armed men inside, for that she was grateful. Kelanson led her inside the temple of Buto, and she silently invoked the god as they passed under the gaze of his statue. She was led once again to the central room.

"The general wishes for you to be treated as his guest not a prisoner. You have nothing to fear under this roof, my lady. Please make yourself at home, there is wine in the jug, a fine red from Gelodun, and olives in the bowl from your city's own groves. I will let the general know that you are here." With that Kelanson took his leave.

Left all alone, she suddenly felt like a small girl again, as she was when she first visited this place. The thick white arms of the hulthul tree which grew under the dome seemed to be writhing like serpents in the moon light. The inky blue leaves almost hidden in the falling twilight.

The challenge which lay before her was not one she felt she could handle, the enormity of it, but she must, for the city and for her grandfather, for him most of all. She may have no power to change events, but she could at least show her fury to the man who had manipulated her.

She picked up a knife that lay on the table next to the food and felt the blade against her hand. She took strange comfort from that, even if it proved how lowly Doltopez held her, not even fearful enough to remove a weapon from her presence. She went to pour herself a cup of wine to calm her nerves. The cup had an image of Buto on the bottom, confronting Dunsun in forlorn hope with his hammer raised, the Lord of the Cosmos about to strike him down. *Is that the fate that awaits me?*

She poured the wine, drained the cup, and poured another. Then wandered over to the white marble Anvil that Doltopez claimed was the god's own, in the centre of the room. Placed on the Anvil was the Hammer of Buto, a relic of old Kolbos made of pure zilthum. Said to have been forged by the Kinsolsun for Buto himself and used by the great smith to craft the weapons he would later gift to the rulers of the Salxosu, the weapons Tekolger had stolen when he imposed his peace.

The twilight streamed through the window and settled in the sword thin groove cut from the heart of the marble block. The Anvil was the most precious relic that had been rescued from old Kolbos the most sacred object of the Salxosu, said to sing when struck due to the hollowed-out heart. Kalasyar picked up the hammer. It glinted white-gold, slender and elegant. It was beautifully crafted, with intricate carvings down its side which writhed, twisted, and coiled like a snake. The head was small, but imposing, looking as though it could crush bone and muscle and sinew just as easily as it did metal. She drained her cup again and walked to the window to get some air.

The window looked out over the sanctuary, the hill and across the city to Tholo's Tear, she whispered to the mother to find some of her wisdom. A mist had descended now, blanketing the city in a fog so that it appeared that Polriso's Hill was a mystical island, the dwelling place of the gods high up in the sky. Somewhere out in that mist Kolkobuas and the others were being taken to a prison to await trail. She wondered if their whole band had been caught, or if some had escaped. Then her thoughts turned back to her own predicament, what would she do? Her eyes flicked toward the knife again, vengeance could be close at hand, if she could swing the blade, once she had that she did not care what they did with her.

Troubled by her thoughts she lowered her gaze. A plinth in the courtyard below caught her eye. She had not noticed it before but now the memories of it came flooding back. There was a statue there once, Yunsunos Sisosi, the Hammer of Kings as he was known by the Salxosu, had stood there defiant, a symbol to all who would attempt to impose their tyranny on the city of Buto. No wonder the Doldun had removed it. Yunsunos had rallied the other noble families around him, Sisosi, Kinsol, Rososthup, Kisurusosi and Kolkisuasu and the people of the city to oppose the tyranny of the last of the Polriso kings, Tebuthisonu. Yunsunos had stormed the sanctuary and expelled the king and then presided over the city as its new government was established. Even though he was wounded and crippled during the assault, he still led an army of Butophulo to victory over a coalition of other Xosu kings attempting to re-establish Tebuthisonu on his throne, succumbing to his wounds as the victory was won.

Yunsunos was said to have been generous and open handed to his friends but cunning and unrelenting when his fury was aroused. His eyes burned with a passion that other men were captivated by. Even today the people revered him as a second founder of the city. Yunsunos was her most illustrious ancestor, she would take inspiration from him to do what needed to be done tonight, to see the city and the League born again and her grandfather remembered as fondly as Yunsunos was.

A flash of lightning branched across the sky, and she heard a door open and footsteps behind her.

* * *

Doltopez of the Deltathelon entered the room. He had not shaved since she last saw him, a red beard was beginning to form on his chin. He paid her no mind initially, walking to the table in the centre of the room and pouring a cup of wine. She stood there, motionless at the window, unsure what to do. Her eyes flitted to the knife on the table, but she did not know if she had the strength to use it.

The Doldun general took a sip of the wine and then seemed to notice her.

"Kalasyar Sisosi, you are a most welcome sight. Please come here, I wish to talk with you."

She did not know what else to do or what to say, so she found herself sliding cautiously towards the general, as he continued talking,

"I hope you are well?" she nodded, "An unpleasant business, all of this, I did not want it, advised against it. But the Nine are nothing if not single minded."

Kalasyar was stood at the table with him now. He refilled her cup and continued,

"Your grandfather." he said, in his deep rumbling voice, "I am sorry about that, I did not wish things to run as they did. He was a great man who had my utmost respect and admiration, as he did the king's."

She felt a pang of anger, tasted venom on her lips, finally some emotion. A flash of lightning illuminated the room as rain began to hammer down from the canopy of clouds.

"I have been told many times how much you and your king admired my grandfather. But if that was the case, why did you allow the Nine to pass that judgement?" she asked. Doltopez made an expression which could have been pain, or frustration,

"Your grandfather was a great man, but he was a man of a different time and a different place. When a master sculptor comes to create his greatest work, he selects the best block of marble. But when the time comes to chip away at the stone to reveal the masterpiece beneath, he does not hesitate to chip off even those pieces which are perfect. They may be the right colour, the right consistency, smooth and beautiful to look upon, but if they are not chipped away the statue will remain merely a block of marble and not a great work of art. It is much the same with building a new civilisation, the one which Tekolger envisioned."

Thunder rumbled in the distance as if to end Doltopez's sentence. Kalasyar felt a pang of rage inside grow and grow. She reached for the knife. A soldier rushed through the door,

"General, there is some kind of disturbance in the city again. We are not sure what, there are reports of fighting and it looks of though the Hunpil district is on fire."

"Summon the officers and have a squadron assembled to go out and patrol in force. Thirty men should do it. I will be with you presently."

The soldier left and Doltopez turned back to Kalasyar,

"It seems your people have not learned…"

The knife was in her hand, hammering down as he turned. It slammed into his neck like striking an anvil, blood welled up around the hilt. The look in Doltopez's eyes was a mix of surprise and fury, he stumbled backwards, as she looked on in shock, frozen to the spot. He stopped at the marble anvil, grasping and then swung his body with all his might. Something hit Kalasyar in the leg with the force of a thunderbolt, sending pain shuddering through her like lightning. She screamed, a primal scream, it did not sound like her own voice, more like that of a monstrous serpent, then she collapsed.

She lay on the floor, darkness closing in around her, lightning flashing and the rain thumping down outside. She watched as Doltopez stumbled away, his hand unclenched, and the hammer fell to the ground, the clang of its fall echoing inside her head. He only took a few steps and then fell.

Kalasyar Sisosi lay motionless on the ground as waves of pain washed over her and she sunk into the depths of agony as a thunderous roar echoed from the city below.

SANAE

48

The priestess approached Sanae, her long flowing robe trailing behind her. She carried a cup in a solemn way, as if its contents were sacred, but Sanae knew they were anything but. Sat at the head of the table, as if at a feast in celebration of some great victory, she accepted the cup when it was offered, graciously. Raising it aloft, her arms straight as an arrow, to the cheers of the assembled priesthood of the bright god. She was about to join their number and all of them had assembled to witness her final task.

She drained the cup, the sweet, but not unpleasant, liquid flowed like honey down her throat with nothing more than a slight burning sensation as it coursed through her. Suddenly the world seemed a bit brighter, the colours of the robes seemed to dance off the priests, she could almost see the smell emanating from the food. Helupelan came forward, his white beard flashing red, his smile extending from ear to ear, gentle but sinister all in the same image. He took her hand and led her round to the tree. A pile of wood sat in the front of the dolthil tree, piled high, stacked like a funeral pyre. Sanae could see the rough splinters peeling off the freshly cut wood, behind it, on the tree, hung a navy-blue coloured drape, almost touching the floor. The grasping branches above them allowed in just enough light from the evening stars to illuminate the whole assembly. It glistened and twinkled to her eye, almost leaping back to the heavens. Helupelan spoke,

"Xosu and his people celebrated his great victory over the duplicitous Kinsolsun, freeing the world from their tyranny and sickening practices. But the wizards poison had been sunk deep into the land. The world was breaking once more as it had done during the time of the great white hydra.

Xosu although victorious, knew what he must do. The hydra was a part of him and its blood, its death had brought life back to the world and so would the bright god's. He would drink of the poison of the Kinsolsun he declared. Having proved his skill and power amongst mortal men and ruled over the Xosu for two hundred and sixty-three years, he wished for his mortal body to be destroyed so that his divine shade could take its rightful place amongst the Kolithelon in shining Dzottgelon and Kolgennon could be born anew by his sacrifice."

Helupelan handed Sanae a burning torch, the flaming dancing like a panther bounding across the plain in front of her eyes, lost her in a trance.

"Xosu felt the poison grip his mortal coil, with the last of his strength he climbed the great dolthil tree which sat outside the cave of the hydra. In its branches he hung himself and put it to flame."

On that signal, Sanae put the torch to the pyre in front of her. The flames caught quickly as the wood had been soaked in oil, it spread wild and almost out of control. The flames shot up high, dancing toward the sky, like Xosu grasping for the heavens as the flames consumed him. She felt like she was being lifted with them, her body feeling lighter and the world suddenly becoming filled with a white and striking light. She was almost overcome, consumed by the ecstasy and searing pain of gazing upon the divine, but it only lasted a moment.

Just as swiftly as they rose, the flames fell back to the earth, crashing back into the pyre. Darkness seemed to descend once more and Sanae felt sick as she was cast back to the ground, a descent from the gloried halls of the gods to the depths of Phenmoph's dark hidden world where the shades of men meet their judgement. Just for a moment though, she felt she glimpsed the light which lies in the shining realm, the glory which awaits the greatest heroes of men, the fabled plains of Zulbeli.

The flames licked up again, this time jumping elegantly toward the navy-blue drape which hung behind the pyre. With a roar, they ripped their way up the hanging cloth, tearing it apart, bits of burning drape rained down on Sanae, like falling snowflakes. With the draped burned away, a statue was revealed. An androgynous youth, strong yet lean and supple, wrapped in the skin of the Dolsunpil Panther, hair of azure and amber, skin of crimson, the mark of the heroes. In his hand an elegant blade and on his face, he wore an anguished look. She knew the image immediately,

"Tholophos." she whispered.

"Now the final mystery of Xosu is revealed to you. A secret only a select few are privy to know and even fewer will come to understand." Helupelan announced. "Tholo's jealously of Dunsun's bright son had not abated, she would not allow Xosu to enter the glorious palace of the gods.

With honeyed words she convinced Dunsun that the other gods would not allow Xosu to enter Dzottgelon and sit among them. Dunsun could see no way around this argument and so Xosu's shade was cast down to the hidden realm, to reside with his mother. But Xosu was not content, he determined to return to the world of the living to rule as he had once done. His shade inhabiting the mortal body that came to be known as Tholophos, he would rule the Xosu once more. A final light in the darkness as Dusk fell on the old world."

* * *

She stayed rooted to the spot, staring at the statue of the sullen youth who defied convention, kings, and even the gods, to unite the Xosu once more. She had understood him, as most Xosu and Doldun did, as the last and greatest hero of a by gone age when demi-gods roamed the earth and man stood close to the gods who had raised him up. A final light shining as the darkness came and the Dusk fell on the old kingdoms.

If Tholophos was Xosu come again to walk amongst men, it changed everything. The Paron came to mind, the Zummosh god who was three and one at the same time, *maybe it was possible for Xosu to do the same.*

Initiated members of the priesthood were coming over to congratulate her. Sanae acknowledged them but was still lost in a world of her own. Others set to performing a final sacrifice to the bright god. Then Helupelan came over again, Kolae, *the White Witch*, lurking ominously behind him,

"Can we talk in private?" he said, motioning towards the door to his chambers. She said nothing, she just headed toward the door. Helupelan passed her as he went in, taking his place on the high seat reserved for Xosu's chief priest. Kolae and Sanae stood in front of him as supplicant, the light of the torches illuminating Helupelan like Dunsun sat on his mighty throne.

"What is the matter you wish to discuss Kolae?" Helupelan said with a wearisome look on his face.

"I fear that the sacred mysteries of our order are at risk. Sanae has shown herself not ready to be allowed to become a member of our ranks. I fear she has shared many of the secrets of Xosu with the uninitiated already, those Zummosh of which she is so fond." Kolae answered him.

"Is this true?" Helupelan turned his gaze to Sanae,

"It is true I am fond of the Zummosh; they are good people, and it is true we talked of Xosu and The Paron, the god who they raise above the others. But I have not shared any secrets." She said, feeling the anger and madness rising in her.

"Do not trust the girl Helupelan." Kolae interrupted, "She seems sweet and innocent, whispering honeyed words in your ear. I know she reminds you of times past, but she risks the future of the temple. Whether she understands that or not."

Those words were the last straw for Sanae. She turned on Kolae, with a fire in her voice,

"I have had enough of your jealousy and paranoia. It is clear that you crave the attention and affection of the High Priest just for yourself and the fact that he shows the same respect to all the members of this temple that he does to you is clearly a source of deep loathing for you. So, you turn your hate towards me. I am but a young girl trying to do what I feel is best, and yes, I have made mistakes, but we all must do so to learn. Even Xosu, the bright god himself, made many mistakes. I am not trying to usurp your position."

Silence gripped the room, even Sanae was surprised by her outburst. Kolae's expression flittered between anger and exasperation, red creeping over her round, pale face. For a moment She thought the High Priestess was about to hit her, but Helupelan spoke before anything could happen,

"Kolae, I have heard everything I need to from you. Please let me speak to Sanae in private. I will sort this issue out and allay both of your concerns. May the bright god light your way."

Reluctantly the High Priestess bowed her head and left the room, even she knew better than to challenge the High Priest's authority in that way. Helupelan stepped down from his chair, drawing near to Sanae,

"As we are alone now, please tell me. Is any of this true?"

The anger drained almost immediately from her, she could never stay in such a state with the man she viewed as a father,

"I have not given any secrets away father. I have tried to help people, my friends. I spoke long with Lulpo about the gods. About our relationship with our gods and about the Zummosh's relationship with theirs. You always taught me to question and learn as much as I could."

Helupelan put an arm around her and smiled,

"Are you sure you have not revealed anything by accident?"

Maybe she had, she could not remember everything that had passed between her and Lulpo. They had talked long and hard over many weeks and Sanae had always been more focused on what Lulpo had to say about her own people.

"I don't know, I have spoken about Xosu, but I had not completed the tasks, so I could not have revealed all his secrets. Certainly, not such revelations have you have shown me tonight."

Helupelan's face softened,

"The bright god has great plans for you, for the future. One day I hope you will rise to the leadership of this temple, in a city which has grown from strength to strength. Indeed, once the new king takes up residence in his capital, I would hope the followers of Xosu would become key advisers at his court. You will be a big part of that."

As he thought of the future, Helupelan's face portrayed a sense of hope and a dream of utopia which Sanae could not help but be sucked in to. It felt as though she could feel the brightness and optimism jumping off him. But then his face grew more serious once more,

"But Kolae will not be satisfied unless I do something to discipline you. You will be confined to the temple and tasked with its upkeep until I decide that you have learnt to be more controlled in your efforts."

Sanae could feel the anger rising once more,

"I have done nothing wrong. You would reduce me back to the duties of one of the uninitiated to satisfy Kolae's paranoia."

Helupelan tried to speak to calm her once more, but she had had enough. Her anger was so intense she could see it bouncing from the walls, the sounds of Kolae's laughter at her punishment echoing in her head. She turned and stormed off toward her own chamber.

* * *

She dreamed of a blinding celestial light, bursting forth onto the world, so bright it scorched the land. Through it she saw a face she knew to be the bright god's himself, but it all seemed to be over in an instant and the world collapsed into darkness again. Just as she began to feel despondent and lost, another light flickered in the darkness and she saw the face of Tholophos rise from the ground, an ecstasy of relief gripped her, so much so she almost cried, but his face faded too. A third light was there now, but whose she did not know. She drank the dolthil wine for strength and reached out to take the light in her grasp and reveal it to the world, reaching, reaching. If only she could grasp it, she knew all its secrets would be revealed, an epiphany the world needed.

Awooo!

The horn bellowed,

"No!" she cried out, she was almost there, but the image shattered into dust. Gelithul drunkenly bowed before her again, she collapsed to the floor,

"Why did you sound the horn? I almost had it, I almost knew."

Gelithul smiled a whimsical smile, took a long drink from his wineskin, and blew into his pan pipes, his chorus took up the chant, *Oh! Oh! Oh!*

"And almost it will always be, unless..."

"Unless what?" she demanded, "There was a third, what was it?! I must know!"

"...drink the wine of Gelithul, find your blood, find your home and you will know."

"How do I do that?"

"Tonight, you tasted but a tiny morsel of the knowledge of the bright god, seek those who know all of his secrets and you will know."

She awoke suddenly in a daze, the shudder as she did so almost threw her out of her bed. Unable to get back to sleep and fearful of what she would see if she did, Sanae got up to walk the temple grounds. Throwing the cloak which Palon had given her round her shoulders and pinning it with the broach of The Paron.

The temple seemed dark, even serene in the dead of the night, with only the moonlight bursting through the open ceiling to illuminate the place. It felt almost a world away from the bustle of activity during the hours of daylight.

Sanae approached the statue of the bright god, his face was an image of calm serenity, but behind the ruby eyes the sculptor had grasped the anguish and pain Xosu must have felt as he was tested over and over. The moonlight glistening against his beard made it seem alive, a deep, dark, red colour hidden within the amber, as if blood were pouring out of the god.

She stood and stared at the divine figure who had been the centre of her whole life, but she found herself looking at him anew, the youthful image of Tholophos in her mind's eye. *How could the two be the same?* she thought. It changed everything; she had lived in the shadow of the bright god all her life but felt now like she knew nothing about him. Far from having the mysteries of Xosu revealed to her, she felt as though she had more questions than answers. Questions a lifetime of contemplation may never reveal the answer to. *There were three,* a voice said to her.

A noise echoed behind her, like footsteps. Sanae started to turn, too late. Something was thrown over her head, the world went dark and then the blows started to fall.

Someone, two maybe three, she could not tell how many, blow after blow struck her and her head began to spin.

She did not remember falling, just the thud as she hit the floor, her heart pounding in her head, her eyes flashing colours. The world descended into increasingly incomprehensible noise and pain, she could feel the blood flowing from her nose, her arm felt wet as well.

The jerk of being lifted by her arms and legs sent searing pain coursing through her body, like her limbs where being ripped apart, momentarily the shock of it brought her back to her senses. The world was black, but she knew she was being carried, it felt as though they were descending some steps. The shock of being lifted faded quickly, and the world went completely dark and silent.

"Find your blood, find your home and you will know."

ABOUT THE AUTHOR

Lewis A. D'ambra

Lewis is an award winning author from South Wales and comes from a mixed Welsh and Italian background.

Studying History at university, he went on to join the British army, whilst also studying for a Master's degree in International Security and Development.

Moving on from the army, Lewis moved into the political world working in the UK Parliament. In this role he honed his skills as a writer having to produce everything from reports, policy documents, through to political speeches.

Lewis then went to work for various Government bodies in senior communications roles, work that included writing newsparer articles, hosting roundtables and giving presentations to large and diverse audiences.

He created the world of Kolgennon as a way to explore his love of history and mythology and to exercise creativity in a way that cant be found anywhere else.

BOOKS BY THIS AUTHOR

The Year Of The Dark Spring

Eight hundred and thirty-two years after the fall of the great city of old Kolbos and the civilisation ending event known as the Dusk, a burning red streak appears in the sky above the world of Kolgennon. The flaming tail causes the sky to darken for weeks, turning spring from a time of new life and renewal to a time of desperation and turmoil. Old myths and old gods re-emerge as the magic and knowledge that was lost to the world during the Dusk begins to return. The comet pushes societies to their limits as they struggle to contend with an unending darkness. As tensions grow, the rumble of war comes closer and each of the cultures and peoples of Kolgennon interpret and react to the omens in the sky in different ways.

This collection of short stories is a Literary Titan Book Award winner. Set in the world of Kolgennon, in a time akin to our own classical world. Each of the nine stories places the comet as the key event of the narrative and each follows a new protagonist, seeing the events of the dark spring through the eyes of a variety of characters and settings. The narrative is framed by a short prologue and epilogue from a historian reflecting back on this time and speculating on what went through the minds of the people that these events effected.

www.theworldofkolgennon.com

Printed in Great Britain
by Amazon